PHANTOMS

by

Sam Accardi

Copyright Information

This is a work of fiction. Names, characters, places, and incidents are the product of the author's imagination and are used fictitiously. Any resemblance to actual persons, living or dead, events, or locales is entirely coincidental.

Copyright © 2023 by Sam Accardi

All rights reserved. No part of this book may be reproduced or used in any manner without written permission of the copyright owner except for the use of quotations in a book review.

The cover was designed by me, using elements from Freepik.com and Vecteezy.com

ISBN: 978-1-7390746-5-4 *(Paperback)*
ISBN: 978-1-7390746-4-7 *(eBook)*

For inquiries, check out my website:
samaccardi.ca

Or contact me at:
samuel.a.accardi@gmail.com

Dedication

To my father, who chose to make my book
his first foray into fantasy and whose support
and feedback has been my favourite so far.

To Catherine Swartz, who planted the seed
that grew into my love and passion for history.
A passion that has helped greatly as I write this series.

To Julio, whose unyielding support
and friendship has been a source of
inspiration throughout the writing process.

Other Books by Sam Accardi

<u>The Chronicles of Enayra</u>
Dragonkin
Phantoms

All books are available via Amazon, in Paperback and eBook format on Kindle.

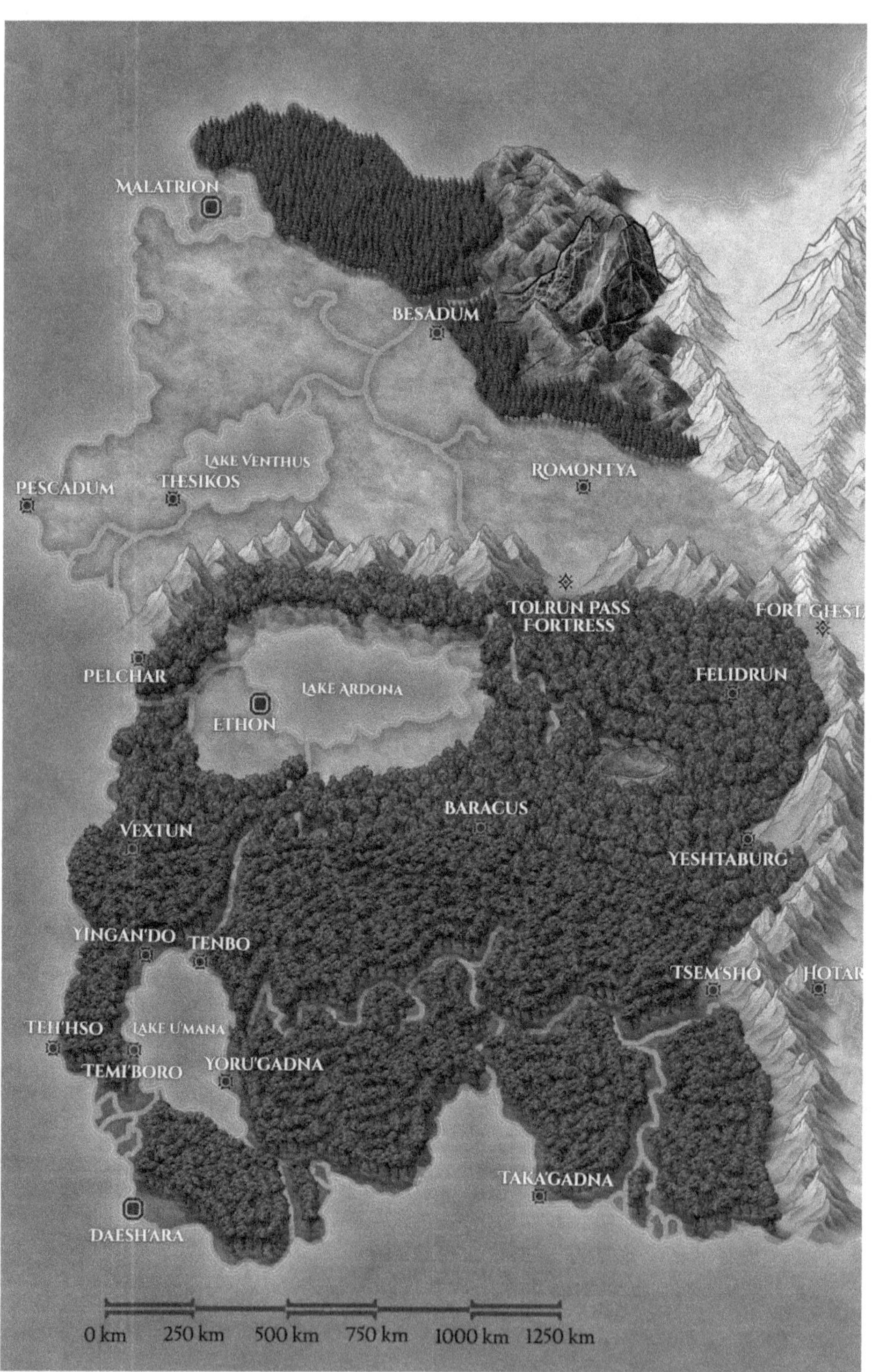

MALATRION
BESADUM
LAKE VENTHUS
THESIKOS
PESCADUM
ROMONTYA
TOLRUN PASS FORTRESS
FORT GHESTA
PELCHAR
FELIDRUN
LAKE ARDONA
ETHON
BARACUS
VEXTUN
YESHTABURG
YINGAN'DO
TENBO
TSEM'SHO
HOTAR
TEH'HSO
LAKE U'MANA
TEMI'BORO
YORU'GADNA
TAKA'GADNA
DAESH'ARA
0 km   250 km   500 km   750 km   1000 km   1250 km

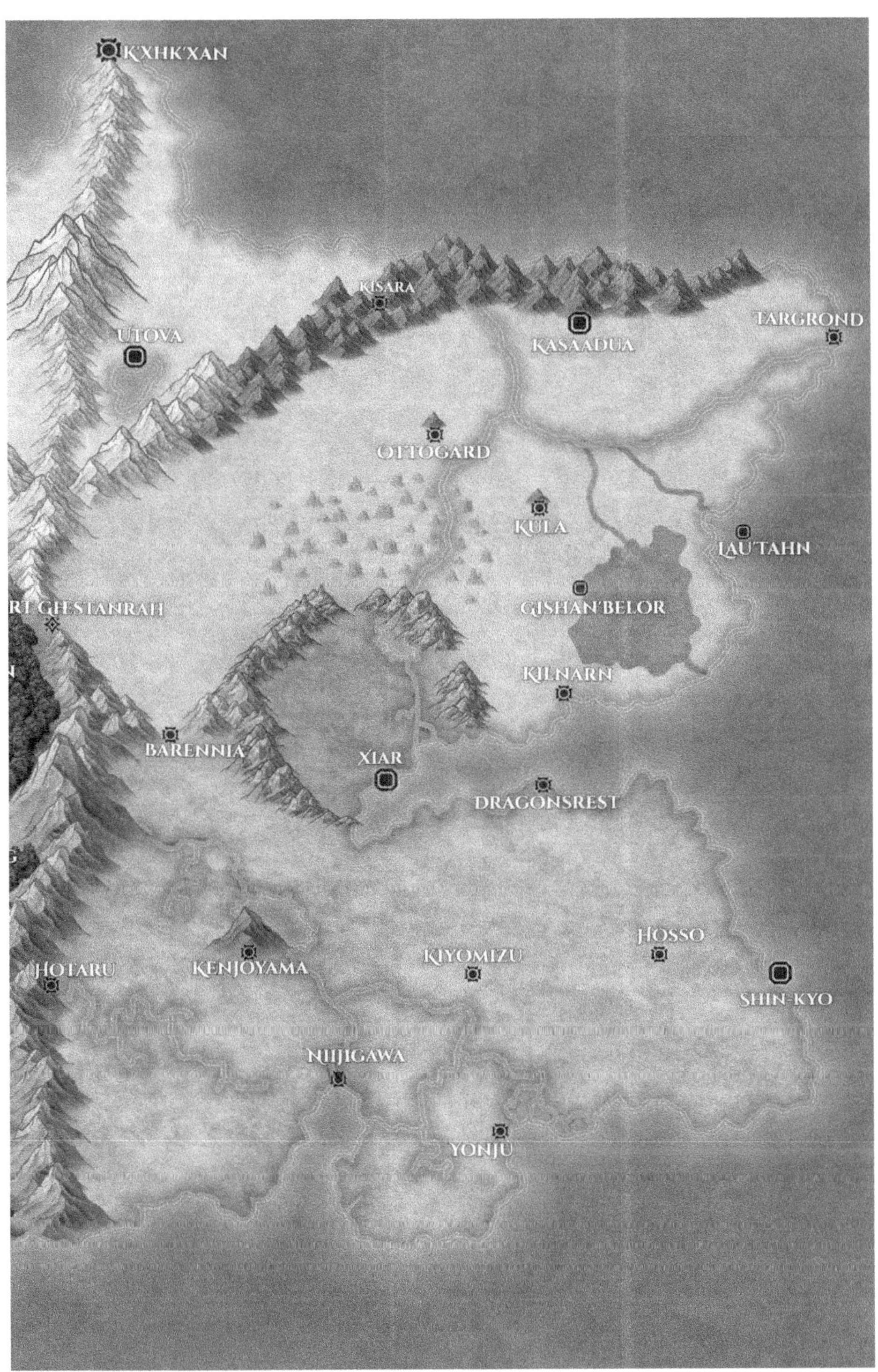

K'XHK'XAN
UTOVA
KISARA
KASAADUA
TARGROND
OTTOGARD
KULA
LAU'TAHN
RT GHESTANRAH
GISHAN'BELOR
KILNARN
BARENNIA
XIAR
DRAGONSREST
HOSSO
HOTARU
KENJOYAMA
KIYOMIZU
SHIN-KYO
NIIJIGAWA
YONJU

Table of Contents

Chapter I

"The nobles are arriving," announced Elandyr'ni. She stepped from the spiral staircase out onto the balcony where Drakhart had perched himself.

The tall, dark-haired Khaleesh leaned against the black, stone railing and watched the procession of nobles and their retinues enter the city. The city's inhabitants lined the streets to greet the nobles as they arrived from their manors and castles in faraway cities.

It had been three weeks since the "death" of King Meland'ar, Last of the House of Thraendaron. Three weeks since Drakhart and the Regency Council, by order of Tenebrae, had called for the Royal Conclave to meet. The Kingsmoot would start soon now that the nobles had arrived. Every duke, count, and baron in the Kingdom of Altimara had arrived in Kasaadua to fulfil their political duty. They would choose a new King of Altimara since King Meland'ar had "died" without an heir. Several nobles no doubt coveted the throne for themselves—no less than thirteen if Altimaran intelligence was to be believed—but only two nobles had the respect, blood relations, and prestige to claim it.

"I've seen," Drakhart replied. He did not look away from the procession. He dabbed at his sweat with a kerchief and tugged at his collar.

The one thing Drakhart had never grown accustomed to in the capital was how hot the city was during the day. The whole city had been constructed from a hardy, black rock mined from the mountains that guarded the city's northern flank, earning it the name of the Black City. The Black Citadel—the palace and compound of the royal family—was just as bad. The heat was sweltering, and it was like living in an oven.

"Calandor is greeting them at the Shrine of the Aspects. Tenebrae has recommended we greet them as they arrive at the palace," continued Elandyr'ni.

Drakhart playfully scratched the neck of the large dragon that stood beside him. His fingers grazed the growing scales on the dragon's head. The large beast nudged Drakhart for more, but Drakhart had a duty to Tenebrae, and could not indulge his new partner much longer. This new dragon was the size Ölüm had been at his death, and Drakhart was amazed the balcony could still hold him.

Drakhart still mourned the loss of Ölüm. He had considered naming his new dragon, a hatchling of Tenebrae, Ölüm as well, but decided it was not right. Instead, Drakhart named him Isunath, after the ancient human Aspect of the Night, from the time before the worship of dragons began. Before the Altimaran kings had brought back the Old Religion. Though as Elandyr'ni had stated, it had been less of a return, and more of an uncoupling of the dragons from the original Aspects.

Drakhart took one last look at the column of nobles. He noticed all of them had stopped at the Shrine of the Aspects to pay homage to their ancestors and their patron Aspects. He and Elandyr'ni had ample time before the nobility would arrive.

"Let's be off then. We'll meet Calandor and the nobles in the courtyard. He's no doubt frantic enough as it is." Drakhart turned to his dragon, giving a soft smile. "Back to your keep; and do not go down to the stables when the nobles arrive. If you're hungry, go hunt."

The dragon lowered his head. "But horse meat is much more tender than anything I can find in this desert."

Despite his protest, Drakhart knew he would not have to warn Isunath a second time, and the massive dragon flew off towards the lower chambers of the tower where he and Drakhart lived. Tenebrae had ordered a dragon roost be built within the tower's bowels and unsurprisingly the work had been carried out quite quickly. More surprising was that the tower was large enough to hold Isunath and would likely do so for at least a few years.

"He's grown fast," Elandyr'ni said. She and Drakhart left the balcony and made their way over to the spiralling stairs.

"He has," Drakhart agreed. He grabbed a torch from its sconce and began the long, dark descent down the staircase. "Tenebrae has seen to that, of course. Isunath must grow fast if I am to battle the other Khaleeshir again soon."

Elandyr'ni frowned, and even in the dark Drakhart's heightened senses allowed him to see it. Drakhart could already tell he wasn't going to like whatever it was she had to say.

"You will not have to worry about that," Elandyr'ni started. "You'll be too busy training for the next while to battle anyone."

Drakhart stopped and turned to face Elandyr'ni. Whatever he had expected, it had not been this. He looked at Elandyr'ni. He was not angry but displeased with the news. Drakhart wanted revenge on Kanaahn, and he was going to have it.

"You can't be serious!" Drakhart demanded.

"Unfortunately, I am," Elandyr'ni replied calmly. She grabbed the torch from Drakhart's hand and continued to lead the trek down the long, spiral steps of black stone. She expected Drakhart to complain and walk. "Aside from having to forge a new Blood Covenant between you and Isunath, Lord Tenebrae demands you train more in the ways of blood magic. You must learn to master the skill, as well as your powers as Khaleeshir. Regardless of what side you choose, you are still Khaleesh, and so you must train like one. Besides, the stronger you are, the more thorough your victory will be against Kanaahn."

Drakhart grumbled but did not argue. Elandyr'ni had crafted her argument well. She knew well that Drakhart wanted revenge on Djall and Kanaahn for the life of Ölüm. By putting forth his training as an avenue to greater power, she had made it hard for Drakhart to disagree. He admired and resented her for it but said no more.

The remainder of the trip—down the tower steps, across a vast courtyard and through half a palace wing—was passed quietly and quickly. Elandyr'ni and Drakhart had finally arrived at the entrance plaza. This grand, cobbled courtyard was walled in on all sides by high edifices and overlooked by skilled archers. It was a massive space that seemed to become the size of a garderobe as all these nobles, their retinues, retainers, carriages, and detachments of Altimaran soldiers swarmed across it like an army of ants.

Drakhart had arrived not a moment too soon.

Calandor, flustered, red-faced and frantic, limped partway up the grand staircase to where the Grand Enchantress and the Dragonkin were. Sweat beaded his brow, from a combination of the stress, the heat, his heavy robes, and his fancy hat. In the time it had taken Elandyr'ni and Drakhart to travel across the palace, most of the nobles had already started to clog the main courtyard.

"Where in the Hells have you been?" Calandor demanded in a harsh whisper.

"I had to get Drakhart. He is to lead the Conclave, by orders of our Great Lord." Elandyr'ni replied. Her tone was both soft and cold, like silk made of ice that hid a blade aimed at your throat.

It was no secret that she and Calandor did not see eye to eye and that they only worked together for the sake of their master Tenebrae. Their devotion to his plans was greater than their disagreement.

Calandor sneered. "But of course. Come now. No more delaying, the conclave is about to begin!"

Drakhart quickly checked his armour. Everything had to be immaculate. Nothing could be out of place. Everything had to be perfect for this conclave. Not a strap left unhooked, not a button missing, not a speck of dirt or dust on anything he wore. Drakhart's armour was polished to a sheen, and black as night. It almost seemed to glow since it had been imbued with powerful protective magic. Drakhart's custom armour had finally been finished since Xiar. Not only was this armour stronger—and enchanted—it was decorated with beautiful silver filigree. His cape was of woven black wool, trimmed with the fur of a silver wolf and lined with red silk.

Drakhart readjusted his heavy iron gloves and tightened the straps of his greaves one last time.

Elandyr'ni handed him his helm, which Drakhart tucked beneath his arm while the Altimaran soldiers lined the stairs to welcome the nobles.

The trio turned and greeted the many nobles who began to walk up the staircase towards the palace. The nobles arrived in order of rank, starting with the more prominent dukes, followed by the counts, and then finally the barons. All in full armour, with their attendants and pages not far behind them. Many of the nobility were wary of Drakhart, but many others were respectful and welcoming. Several of the nobles saw Drakhart as an upstart who had uprooted the old, anti-dragon ways, and this much Drakhart knew for a fact thanks to Altimaran intelligence. As a newly created noble, and as a Khaleeshir, who was already so close to the royal court, Drakhart was under intense scrutiny by the other lords of Altimara. Rumours circulated that it had been Drakhart who had killed King Meland'ar, while others hailed him as a hero of the Battle of Xiar. Yet for all the rumours and whispers, none would dare speak a word of it within the halls of the Black Citadel, let alone to Drakhart's face.

Drakhart had always been somewhat disgusted with how quickly most of the nobility seemed to forget the fact that dragons were the most wanted creatures in Altimara. None had raised open objection with their king when Drakhart and Ölüm had come to serve the Crown. Nor did they seem to complain when the Black Dragon Clan, under the leadership of Balgorax, had descended upon Xiar on the side of the Altimarans. They didn't question it; they didn't openly dispute how this spat in the face of centuries of propaganda. Whether these nobles held reservations or objections, they did not make it known publicly. It was different when the dragons served the Crown, apparently. Drakhart knew that the nobles who opposed him because of their anti-dragon views were a threat to him, but he respected that they at least held to their beliefs and had not simply abandoned them out of convenience and self-preservation.

One eternity later, the nobles had been welcomed, led through the palace, and seated within the massive chamber where the nobility of Altimara held court.

Drakhart had been thoroughly briefed by Calandor on the workings of the Altimaran government. He had made sure Drakhart could recite the hierarchy of power forwards and backwards, in his sleep and in High Altimaran, High Xiaran, and Common. Dukes or duchesses were required to attend the Council of Lords at each meeting, once per month to bring forth any petitions or concerns to the royal court. While counts or countesses were only expected to attend every four months and barons or baronesses only twice per year. The nobility could, of course, attend more often should they choose, but as barons could petition the counts that they were beholden to, and the counts could do the same to their dukes, there was no need to appear more than required. Their voices would be heard one way or another in the Council of Lords, and then they would not need to worry about bogging down the meetings with bloated attendance and countless speeches and petitions.

Many nobles, male or female, had had their chance to ogle Elandyr'ni unsuccessfully as they entered the chamber, though none would have admitted to doing so.

Drakhart entered the room last. He and his cohorts' presence was announced by blaring trumpets and a puffed-up courtier. Calandor and Elandyr'ni flanked Drakhart on either side as they walked down the silver carpet toward the high table that faced the conclave of nobles.

The nobles sat on several tiered benches that curved around the central walkway and faced the high table. On the lowest, smallest ring, sat nine of the twelve Altimaran dukes or duchesses, known as the Sacred Twelve. These twelve noble houses were some of the oldest noble lines in Altimara. They were tasked by the Crown to watch over the twelve provinces of Altimara. Two dukes were missing from the conclave: the Duke of Qintarth, a title that once belonged to the recently extinct House of Zinlari, and the Duke of Virith, which was a position normally reserved for the Crown Prince of Altimara. The third of the twelve dukes was Drakhart himself, but he was heading the conclave with Elandyr'ni and Calandor and thus was not required to be seated with his cohorts.

On the ring above the dukes, sat the fifty-seven counts or countesses, who watched over the counties that made up the provinces—these counts owed their feudal fealty to their provincial dukes.

Finally, on the two highest rings were one hundred and fifty-two barons or baronesses, who watched over the larger towns and cities of Altimara—excluding Waystations and smaller settlements only large enough for mayors. These barons and baronesses owed fealty to both the counts and the dukes.

While only the Sacred Twelve and the royal house had their banners hanging from the rafters of the throne room, the minor nobles each had a standard bearer holding their colours and emblems in neat rows along the walls.

Drakhart could recognize and recite the names, colours, designs, and histories of all the banners and to whom they belonged. Another instructive lesson from Calandor. He also noticed that two ducal banners were missing from the grand display. The first banner was that of the House of Davenpourte; Lord Krystor had been executed and disavowed during his failed rebellion. The second was the banner of the House of Zinlari, which had been dissolved by the Crown Lord Rudolphus' death at Xiar—the duke had left no living heirs. Instead, in the place of Lord Davenpourte's rampant red lion, holding golden lilies on a field of green, hung the banner of the House of Ghast: a crimson banner emblazoned with a passant black dragon baring his green fangs; its tongue lolling from its mouth, with green claws sharp as knives. It would not do well for Drakhart to lead the conclave while appearing lesser than his peers, so his heraldry was decided on quickly, tactfully, and added to the roster with all haste before the Conclave. If he was to be one of them, Drakhart would need to look the part, and not just act it. Everything had to be perfect, or there would be talk—more so than usual anyway.

The Royal Conclave and the Council of Lords were a crucial part of Altimaran politics after all. All the nobles here would be looking to jump up to the prestigious role of Duke of Qintarth, as well as High General of the Army. Tenebrae had already planned to elevate a trustworthy baron to replace Lord Zinlari, unbeknownst to any, while Drakhart—after the Conclave had concluded—would assume the first double dukedom in Altimara for four hundred years, being appointed the Duke of Virith; Drakhart was already Duke of K'nar, having replaced Lord Davenpourte after his death and deposal.

Drakhart buried a smirk as he passed by the greedy nobles. If only they knew.

He, Elandyr'ni and Calandor arrived at the curved high table and took their seats, situated just before the throne where the Altimaran monarch would address and lead the court. Drakhart was seated at the centre of the table, facing the Royal Conclave before him. Elandyr'ni remained on his right, with Calandor sweating up a storm to his left. The Major-domo nervously culled flakes of skin from his thumbs using his index fingers. The room was dead silent. Drakhart could hear his heartbeat, and not just because of his enhanced hearing. He had to make the speech that would change the course of Altimara's future, the war, and a thousand years of monarchical rule.

Drakhart took a deep breath and began. "Welcome, noble houses of the Kingdom of Altimara, to the first Royal Conclave in over three centuries."

Drakhart's voice boomed across the hall. It was a combination of Elandyr'ni's magic and the way the hall had been built to carry a voice. He looked to the left, and the right, pausing for dramatic effect, then continued. "We come here today, under the most grievous of terms. Our beloved King, Meland'ar I Thraendaron has passed on. Age has taken him after his glorious campaign against Xiar."

Drakhart took another pause. Memories flashed black to him. The war, the screaming, the blood, the violence, but most of all, the horrible death rattle of Ölüm as his head was removed from his body, and his neck snapped beneath the force of Djall's crushing grip. Drakhart's fist clenched as he remembered the black blood that spilt across the desert when the dragon's body shattered against the ground.

"The King's victory at Xiar was absolute! Nothing remains of the city but an empty crater! Nothing of those traitors remains within Altimaran borders!" continued Drakhart. His rage turned to passion.

There was a raucous cheer from the nobles, whose support for their king and their hatred of Altimara's enemies united them, however briefly. In truth, very few knew about the failure at Xiar. Even the soldiers who had been there had had their memories modified by Elandyr'ni under the guise of a post-battle sleeping draught for fatigue and trauma. The official report was that Xiar had been a victory, especially since, only a week after the battle, Altimaran spies reported that the city had merely vanished.

Reports stated that there had been a bright flash of light that filled the Antigorus valley, and when it ceased, the ancient city was gone. All that remained of Xiar was an empty crater that crackled with the last vestiges of ancient arcane energy. Not even the fabled Mana Well, from which the city drew all its wondrous power and prestige, remained. Elandyr'ni had proposed that the city's mages had attempted to cast a protective spell that went wrong, but changed her theories when reports came in that no rubble or bodies were discovered at all near the crater. It was a mystery, but until answers could be given, Calandor and Tenebrae agreed that it would be used to further war propaganda and strengthen the reputation of the monarchy.

"But, now that he is no longer with us and as His Majesty passed without an heir, we have called this Royal Conclave to decide on who would be best suited to take the throne in his stead."

Two of the nobles stood up. The first was a large, muscled man with ancient and battle-worn armour. His cape was imperious and wrapped around his body like a jealous lover. He sported a full beard and long silver hair. His eyes were hardened by age and war alike. A massive scar ran from his left jaw, up his cheek, across his eye and to his scalp.

The other noble was a slender man. He was very young and incredibly handsome. His armour was newly polished, newly forged and he was not at all scarred. His hair was the colour of the night sky, his eyes the colour of a lush forest and his skin the colour of the sands of Altimara. He was in stark contrast to his counterpart.

Yet for all their differences, both nobles held an equal claim to the throne. The first claimant, the aged warrior, was Lord Hellabore Drungvist, of an ancient noble house. He was the Duke of Orogreth, ruling from the massive port city of Kilnarn. It was from Kilnarn that Lord Drungvist commanded Altimara's navy as its Grand Admiral. It was because of Lord Drungvist's ancestors that Altimara had a navy at all. He was well-loved by his men, but not as popular amongst the nobles, who found him boorish and uncouth. Lord Drungvist did not care for politics, or niceties, and often spoke his mind—often to his detriment. There was too much sailor in him, as Calandor had put it. The lord's perennial military service was long and well documented, but his blood ties to the monarchy were slightly outdated. He was the late King Meland'ar's second cousin through marriage. King Meland'ar's grandfather, King Kairnador III, had married his niece to the current Lord Drungvist's father, tying the House of Drungvist to the Royal House of Thraendaron.

Lord Drungvist also had the unknowing honour of being the only noble that Drakhart had known anything about before he studied for the Conclave. Drakhart had grown up in Kilnarn, where his father had once served as a navigator in the navy until his untimely death. After losing his father, Drakhart's mother Kinraea had taken them both to her hometown of Kula, for she could no longer bear to look at the sea that had claimed her husband.

Lord Drungvist's competition was the younger duke, Lord Sylvio Marneron. The newly inherited Duke of Verthoro. He ruled from Kisara, a modest northern city located within the frigid mountain ranges northwest of the capital.

In truth, Kisara was more a military outpost than a town; in the words of Calandor, it was a fortress that happened to house civilians as well. Lord Marneron's military service was short, if extant at all, and his noble house was but a century and a half old, but their devotion to the Crown was respected. They battled constantly against the Kingdom's Utovan enemies in Anglum, leading raids into the snowy country to the west and defending against enemy raids in turn. Lord Marneron's father had died in battle a few months ago, struck down by the Anglish Grand Duchess of Utova herself on the battlefield. Lord Marneron was not as popular amongst the common man or foot soldier as Lord Drungvist, but he knew how to play politics, and seemed to enjoy it very much. He had mastered the art of talking with two tongues and weaselling his way through Altimaran social circles. He was a clever wordsmith when he needed to be, and incredibly charming. Despite his lack of military service, he was equally as bright as Lord Drungvist, with just as much potential given the opportunity to prove himself, but he would need to be tested and tempered. While Lord Marneron was not as experienced in war or battle as his opponent, his blood ties to the Crown were closer. He was King Meland'ar's nephew, as his mother was the late King's youngest sister.

Both Dukes laid bare their claim to the empty throne that stood but a few short steps behind Drakhart and his council. They were the only two permitted to step forward by the Regency Council, who did not wish to bog down the proceedings with endless claims and claimants.

"Our first claimant is Lord Hellabore Drungvist, Duke of Orogreth and High Admiral of the Altimaran Navy. Second cousin to King Meland'ar through his paternal first cousin, once removed, Her Royal Highness the Princess Eglantine Thraendaron."

Several nobles on either side stood up and cheered on Lord Drungvist. It took several moments for Calandor to calm the court down again before Drakhart could continue.

"The second Claimant is Lord Sylvio Marneron, Duke of Verthoro. Eldest and only remaining nephew of the late King Meland'ar through his youngest sister, Her Royal Highness the Princess Sylvania Thraendaron."

Another cheer, equal to the first, from the remaining members of the conclave. It seemed to Drakhart that the court was evenly divided between the two claimants. Not that it mattered though.

"As you all know, both claimants meet not only the blood requirement but are both equally notable in their loyalty and service to the Crown and country! Both claimants will soon have the chance to petition the Royal Conclave and the High Council with their case before a vote takes place. But first...our gracious host would like to say a few words."

Confused looks abounded. Murmurs and whispers erupted throughout the nobility. King Meland'ar was dead, and those who had called the meeting were sitting at the head table. If Drakhart and those at the head table were not the hosts then...who was?

There was a rumble beneath the palace. A minor quake, but it still shook dust from the ceiling and toppled glasses and decanters from where they sat before the nobles. The nobles gazed around with concern, but Calandor, Elandyr'ni and Drakhart knew better. They knew the truth. Tenebrae shifted beneath the surface of the earth, from within the massive cavern beneath the city. And then he spoke, picking up where Drakhart had left off.

"Welcome, venerable nobility of Altimara. You have served the Crown loyally over these many millennia, and for this, I am eternally grateful. For now...there is some very important business to take care of," rumbled the massive black behemoth. His voice echoed through the minds of all above. Several shouted out in terror, while others blanched with fear, but remained silent; all were scared.

The doors slammed shut, and two hooded, black-robed figures hovered near the doors, putting a stop to any exit attempt.

Drakhart had recently noted that Tenebrae spoke with a slight accent. It was incredibly faint and happened only when he spoke in Common. Tenebrae spoke Common well, and it took Drakhart being incredibly observant to even realize that there was an accent at all, but it was there, and it intrigued the young Dragonkin. If he had to guess, Common had been much different when Tenebrae had last spoken in it frequently, as well as Common not being his mother tongue, and something he learned later in life.

Tenebrae resumed speaking. The nobles fell about the place, collapsing as they clutched their skulls, screaming in pain. Tenebrae had begun his "delicate" work. The rumbling voice echoed throughout the minds of all in attendance again as Elandyr'ni and Drakhart watched the proceedings without batting an eye. Calandor, however, seemed more perturbed by it all.

"I would very much appreciate it if you would continue your diligent service...under a new cause. And so, before we proceed, we must deal with the small matter of your loyalty. Your undying, unyielding loyalty."

Chapter II

The green dragon veered left, then right. The others were close behind him. He could hear the ragged breath of the red dragon draw ever closer. The heat from his breath radiated off the green dragon's tail. The green dragon flicked it and caught his pursuer on the snout. A roar reverberated across the sky.

The green dragon tucked in his wings and dipped down like a dart. He fell below the cloud line, cloaking himself with the fog and moisture. For now, he was safe. He checked left and right—spoke too soon.

A silver behemoth came from the left, silent as an owl on the hunt, but as subtle as an avalanche—with all the power of one behind her strike. The green dragon extended his wings and raised them. The wind filled his wings like sails, and he caught the updraft fast enough to rise out of the way of the silver dragon's attack. His foe roared in frustration as she passed him by.

He had to keep moving—no, not up!

A white and a blue blur descended upon him from above, like eagles diving for a fish. The white dragon was smaller than he, and the blue dragon was close in size. Despite this, they didn't provide much space for him to glide between them. He'd need to go on the offensive; part them by force. The green dragon inhaled sharply, closed his third eyelid, and let loose a noxious cloud of green-brown toxic gas. The gas streamed from his mouth but did not go far from his body. Instead, it pooled around him, trailing beside and behind him like someone had disturbed the silt bottom of a streambed. He was immune to its effects, but his opponents were not. They were quick to dodge out of the way, hoping to avoid having their insides dissolved by the toxic exhaust.

The green dragon was above the clouds once more, but he was still being pursued. A brass dragon circled him from far above. She was not going to strike yet, but she saw him, and she was preparing to move. Perhaps she wanted to wait for him to wear down first. Perhaps she was just hoping to scare him with her presence. Or perhaps she was only meant to serve as a distraction for the red dragon, who had returned to claim his prize.

There was nowhere to run for the green dragon. Three foes below, one circling above, and one coming at him head-on. Should he fight? Perhaps it was necessary.

He gave a defiant—if half-hearted—roar as the red male trumpeted his war cry. The two drew nearer and nearer, closer, and closer. The green dragon could smell the brimstone on his enemy's breath. The brass dragon began to dive as the red dragon closed in. Claws ready, fangs bared. He could see the shapes of his three foes below moving in closer from below. He was surrounded. No choice but to fight then.

He gave a louder, but still shaky roar—

"Kanaahn!"

Cecil's voice cut through Kanaahn's mind like a bolt of lightning. He was no longer the green dragon flying through the sky. He was no longer seeing the world through Djall's eyes. No, he was back on the ground, sitting in the driver's seat of the camel wagon, stopped in the middle of their path for no explicable reason. He gave an embarrassed look to his passenger and his friends who drove the other wagons behind him.

"Were you daydreaming again?" Cecil scolded.

"It's not daydreaming!" Kanaahn retorted. "It's...it's more like slipping into Djall's head. Ever since we left Xiar it's been happening more and more."

"*They are becoming one,*" Valence interjected. Her voice rang out as an echo through the minds of the group. She was somewhere high above them, teaching the dragons important lessons in flight and aerial combat along with the brass dragon Kinokaze.

"*It's only to be expected,*" added Kinokaze. "*That was the point of the Blood Covenant. Two souls in two bodies becoming bonded, eternally. They change and melt together until they are one soul in two bodies. Drazhanii and human. Their fates ever intertwined, as are the fates of our two species. Each learning, taking, and growing from the other.*"

"It's poetic when you put it like that," Kyeit said. She pulled her wagon up beside Kanaahn's, her face somewhere between bemused and annoyed. "But that does not make it any less inconvenient when we're in a hurry. This is the third time it's happened today. Shooter, can you take over for him?"

"Yes, ma'am!" exclaimed Shooter. He gave Kyeit a goofy salute and clambered from the back of Kyeit's wagon over to the driver's seat of Kanaahn's.

Kanaahn didn't bother arguing. They had a tight schedule to keep, and the sooner they left Altimara the better. He crawled into the back of his wagon with Cecil and leaned his head against the canvas of the wagon. He turned his head skyward as if trying to see Djall through the canvas and clouds above.

Cecil smiled at Kanaahn sympathetically. "It's an amazing feeling, being up there."

"It is," agreed Kanaahn. "It's even more amazing to experience it as if *you're* the one flying. The weightlessness, the rush of adrenaline, the *speed*!"

It made Kanaahn's heart ache for the sky again.

"I'm truly jealous," said Cecil. "You Khaleeshir are lucky. You get to experience things about each other's species that most humans will never even know of."

"It's bittersweet, really," replied Kanaahn. He let out a sigh and closed his eyes, but he couldn't get back in the mindset to meld with Djall again. It wasn't voluntary just yet, though Kinokaze and Valence assured him it would be eventually, as was to be expected of the Khaleeshir.

One soul, two bodies. What would that even be like? Kanaahn knew he had to clear his head of such thoughts, or he would only miss the feeling of flight more. Instead, he chose to preoccupy himself with how much had changed in the few short months he and his friends had become Khaleeshir. They had left the only town they knew. They had trained in magic and weaponry. They had become best friends with dragons, joined a rebellion, and they had fought in their first battle against the King and army they once claimed allegiance to. Perhaps the biggest change was Kanaahn getting used to wearing a shirt regularly—it had been harder in the deserts of Altimara, but while in Xiar and the Antigorus Valley, it had been...enjoyable.

Yet for all they had experienced the same thing, Kanaahn did not know if they felt the same things he did: confusion, excitement, and even a little bit of guilt.

Drakhart had attacked Kula several weeks ago, striking against the former duke, Lord Krystor Davenpourte, and liberating the town from the corrupt rule of the Town Watch. It was something that the group had always dreamed of doing together, for the sake of their home and the people they loved. Yet Drakhart had done it alone, and he had done it in the service of the wicked Tenebrae. It did not help that since the attack on Kula, Arial's mother had gone missing, as had Arkas's father and siblings, and Drakhart's mother. Shooter's parents did not survive the attack. Kanaahn refused to believe that everyone was dead. There was just no evidence of their death, and Kanaahn could not bring himself to believe that Drakhart had killed them. Kanaahn held genuine hatred towards Drakhart, but even he could admit that Drakhart had not fallen that far...yet.

"Information will come soon, Kanaahn," spoke the ever-deepening voice of Djall in his head.

"I cannot wait any longer," replied Kanaahn anxiously. *"It's been weeks and there hasn't been a single hawk or missive, or any information as to the whereabouts of Menalaea or our families. Any news, even bad news, would be something...but the silence is agonizing."*

Kanaahn felt Djall's pleasure at the mention of the hawks. The dragon chuckled and let out a low rumble, which Kanaahn had come to understand as satisfaction.

"Quite a tasty snack, those hawks," quipped Djall. *"A shame they were not to be eaten."*

Kanaahn couldn't help but laugh as well. Djall had devoured a week's worth of the messenger hawks before being told they were not a snack. It was hard to tell a dragon no, Kanaahn had learned, but it was possible.

There was a lull in the conversation before Kanaahn spoke again. *"Go back to your flying. If you fall from the sky I'm not cleaning up the mess."*

"Dragons do not fall from the sky. We are too graceful!" Djall protested before withdrawing to a small corner of Kanaahn's mind.

Kanaahn shook his head. He turned his attention back towards the path they were taking. According to Kyeit and Cecil, they were to avoid the main roads as much as possible until they reached the Kingdom of Estion. They had been safe in Xiar, but every Altimaran Waystation from Targrond to Fort Ghestanrah would be on the lookout for their group of travellers. They also didn't know if they had to worry about pursuers. The Altimaran Army, though still large, was reeling from their failed siege, and would likely need time to regroup and mount another attack, but that wouldn't stop the dogged pursuit of a few dedicated Altimaran agents. Xiar did not need to worry about retaliation, but the Khaleeshir could not be so relaxed.

It had helped Altimara's case that King Meland'ar had died since the siege. Altimara would likely in be disarray for at least a few more weeks as their nobility met at Kasaadua to decide who would succeed Meland'ar as Tenebrae's puppet—though the nobility did not know that part. The hope was that in the confusion, the Kingsmoot would eat up valuable time and allow the Khaleeshir the chance to slip past the border and into a friendly kingdom. It was a slim chance, everyone knew, but still a chance.

Kyeit and Cecil would have preferred to remain in Xiar longer, where there was an army, and high walls, and safety in numbers, or at the very least they would have preferred to depart by sea, but the High Council had insisted that the Khaleeshir needed to be moved for their safety, and so the plan was to go to Estion, or more specifically, to the capital Ethon, to continue their training.

Kanaahn could see their destination on the horizon: a line of sharp razor-like mountains that pierced the clouds like the teeth of some great beast. These steel grey mountains were the southern range of the Rishi Mountains, part of the larger mountain group known as Enayra's Spine. The group planned to meet a set of Darond agents at the foot of the mountain. These agents would take the camels and wagons, and the Khaleeshir, their dragons, and their guardians would cross the mountains on foot into Estion. They would be given enough supplies to get them over the mountain, but otherwise, they would take with them only what they needed to make the trek over the mountains—the lighter the load, the better. On the other side, they would travel to a safe house located in a city called Felidrun. The Khaleeshir would check in with the High Council at this safe house, receive any news or new orders, and then depart again immediately for the capital of Estion, Ethon. It was the longer, more dangerous route, but it was still a better idea than attempting to pass through Fort Ghestanrah.

The massive fortress complex sat nestled in the only gap in the mountain range. It was garrisoned by one of the largest garrisons in Altimara, and they were guaranteed to be recognized and captured within minutes of coming in sight of the fortress's walls if they went that way.

"It'll be sad to see them go," said Shooter suddenly, cutting through the silence like a blade through fabric.

"Pardon?" Kanaahn asked.

"The camels," Shooter clarified. "It'll be sad to leave them behind. I know they'll be cared for and housed by the Darond at one of their bases, but they've been on this journey just as long as we have. They've travelled every step of the way with us. From Kula to Xiar and now to the Rishi Mountains."

There was a pause. Kanaahn thought over Shooter's words. It had been easy to forget the camels had been around about as long as the dragons had and travelled just as far from where they had been purchased. These fine Kulan camels had seen more adventure and excitement than most Kulan camels ever would.

"We'll be sure to come back for them," Kanaahn finally responded. "Once we've finished up with our travels, or whenever we need them next." Kanaahn had never thought he'd get emotional over a camel. He smirked and changed the subject.

"What can we expect once we reach Ethon?" he asked Cecil.

She poked her nose up from the book she had been reading: *Wisteria in the Wind*. It was a popular romance novel in Asardaea, according to Cecil's prior explanation. It was something she brought with her on long journeys and one of her favourite books that she read—or rather reread—when she had downtime. It was one of three books that Cecil currently had on her person.

"More training," said Cecil flatly. "You'll be training under Dragon Master Anducaerleonis and Aurichalcum the Brass. They haven't told me what they intend to teach you; every Dragon Master is allowed to tailor their teachings however they see fit. At this early stage, it will likely be much of the basics and continuing what you've already been learning until you've mastered it."

"Will they be training us until we're ready to fight Tenebrae?" asked Shooter.

"No. Only until they deem you fit to proceed to the next Dragon Master…or until the war catches up to us." Cecil frowned. "I don't know when that will be. No official declaration of war has been made by Altimara against the other nations, and the other nations aren't expected to declare war against Altimara at this time."

"What do you mean?" Kanaahn asked. He was suddenly even more confused by Enayran politics than he had been back at Xiar.

"The nations settled on the proper conduct of war and diplomacy back at the Peace of Gerovia in four-o-seven Conflict. It was signed as a way of trying to calm the lawless war and discord that consumed the continent after the collapse of the Enayran Empire," explained Cecil. "It didn't stop all wars, but it at least applied a certain code of conduct that made wars somewhat less barbaric. There are rules for conducting a war, the proper protocol for declaring it, and much more. If Tenebrae wanted to chase you to Ethon, he'd need Altimara to declare war. But for Altimara to do that, they'd require what's known as a 'just cause.' Without a proper reason to declare war, it would be an unjust and unprovoked attack, and the other nations would be treaty-bound to side with Estion in her defence. Altimara is mighty, but even she cannot defeat a coalition of the other nations."

"What's stopping the other nations from just declaring war on Altimara then?" asked Shooter. "The Darond *know* Tenebrae is pulling the strings in Altimara, and the other nations have Darond advisors and the Metallic Dragons behind them, so surely they know this as well."

"It is not a question as to whether they know it," Cecil answered. Her frown deepened as she explained. "It's whether they actually believe it. We've only been privy to this knowledge for two decades. Some of these nations and their rulers have had previously amicable relations with Altimara for a thousand years before that. Tenebrae may have been hunting dragons in Altimaran borders, but he's never violated the Peace of Gerovia, nor has he taken his Glorious Hunt past his borders. He's free to do as he pleases in Altimara.

"What's more, he's played a wonderful political game over the centuries. He's kept the nations from ever fully aligning against Altimara in a grand alliance by using clever statecraft and political dealings. He's allied Altimara with Danaen, for example, and they've had amicable relations that continue until now. He's played Asardaea and Espias against one another; ever trying to stoke discord between two already hostile nations. Utova, though not a friend of Altimara, is isolated in the frigid wastes of Anglum, and their nation is small and ill-supplied. They could not fight Altimara without major support from the other nations. Minds are not so easily changed, and unfortunately, rulers and monarchs are. Parents are not like their children, and children are not like their parents. The nations deal with us, but their leaders do not always like or trust us, or the harsh truths we bring. There are truly only two nations that the Darond has ever been able to rely on dependably: Asardaea and Espias. That says a lot since Espias and the Darond have only had normalized relations for the last century or so, before that our relationship was...contentious to say the least. Even Estion's loyalty has waxed and waned over the years.

"The truth is Enayra does not *want* to go to war and to deal with Tenebrae, that is exactly what is needed. The Darond represents that harsh truth. Despite the decline the dragons have experienced, Enayra has been largely at peace for a thousand years. There has been conflict between one nation or another, but nothing that has spanned the continent. Nothing like the last war with Tenebrae, the Dragon War. Nobody wants that again. Not when everything seems so...stable by comparison."

Kanaahn had grown to appreciate Cecil as a guide a bit more than Kyeit. He liked Kyeit, and his friendship with her—and his feelings—were not something he'd ever wish to trade for anything. But Cecil was much more forthcoming with the truth and information that the Darond High Council was keen to keep away from the Khaleeshir. Cecil still had her secrets, but she would tell what she could. Kyeit, on the other hand, was a dutiful and loyal soldier. She was conflicted by her duty and her friendship. While she was coming around, it was easy to tell she could hold back the information and follow orders more naturally than Cecil.

"And what's a powerful dragon-like Tenebrae need with the rules and conduct of war?" asked Shooter sardonically.

"Resources," Cecil replied flatly. "War costs resources, and just because he is an ancient and powerful dragon, does not exclude him from that. Tenebrae has spent a thousand years amassing resources and rebuilding his allies and armies. If he pounces too early, he'll be forced to expend much of his resources to hold off an Enayran coalition; resources he could conserve and spend more wisely by picking off the nations one by one. Whenever war consumes our world for long periods, it always descends into a long war of attrition. The side that can outlast, out-bleed, and out-supply their enemy will be the victor. Unfortunately, righteousness, justice, and the moral good have nothing to do with winning wars."

An awkward silence filled the pause after Cecil's words.

Kanaahn could see the slight worry and regret on Cecil's face. He could only imagine the thoughts that flitted behind her eyes. Had she said too much? Had she made things look too bleak? On the contrary. Kanaahn preferred the honest appraisal of Enayra's situation, and why things had been allowed to go on like this for so long.

Before Kanaahn could reassure Cecil, Shooter charged through the silence as subtly as a charging vurk. "Has there been an update on that thing I asked you about?"

Cecil shook her head. "No word, yet. I'm sorry. It's been hard to get information from there without our agent."

Shooter didn't respond.

Kanaahn didn't ask for clarification or get himself involved. Whatever it was Cecil was looking into wasn't Kanaahn's business. Shooter would've respected the same of him. Perhaps that's why Shooter was willing to ask Cecil so boldly in front of him.

"Speaking of information," added Kanaahn, "We haven't heard from the Darond in a while, and I know it's not because Djall has been eating the messengers again."

Cecil shrugged. "It could be the flight routes for our hawks have been compromised, or it could be that there has been no news. It's normal enough."

The conversation was left there. Cecil went back to her book, Shooter sat with his private thoughts and worries as he drove the wagon forward, and Kanaahn closed his eyes and leaned his head back against the canvas. He let his mind disappear into the warmth of Djall's thoughts. The dragon's eyes became his once more, and Kanaahn's spirit left his body behind. Once more he returned to the sky. He had the time now. The night would fall before they reached the secret Darond outpost, and Kanaahn no longer had to focus on driving the wagon. Nothing would disturb him.

* * *

"You're late!" called a tall, dark-skinned man. He poked at the campfire a few times and checked the small pot nestled over the flames.

"Well tell me when you'd like me to arrive in your note next time," responded Kyeit, a smirk spreading across her face. She stepped from the wagon and hugged the man. "I haven't seen you since I last visited headquarters. How've you been Kaltar?"

The man shrugged and scratched his bald head. "I've been better. Living in a cave in the side of a mountain in the desert isn't exactly the lap of luxury. I miss my wife and kids back home, but this is where I've been posted for now, so this is where I go until I get my leave."

"I'll pass along a message if you want?" asked Kyeit.

"If you're heading that way, I'd appreciate it," Kaltar said. He pulled a thick letter from a small pouch on his hip and pressed it into Kyeit's hand. "I'd feel bad sending this by hawk. The poor thing would collapse just carrying it."

Kyeit chuckled and carefully packed the letter away in her pouch.

A tall, stocky woman with a bow and quiver of arrows slung across her back stepped out from the shadows.

"You usually have an arrow trained on anyone who approaches, Edva," said Cecil. "I'm surprised we got through unseen."

"Saw you coming," Edva replied curtly.

Kanaahn, Cecil, Arial and Arkas stepped forward awkwardly from the wagons.

"Is this them?" asked Kaltar. He stepped forward, beaming brightly. "Khaleeshir. It's an honour!" He placed his fist over his heart in a formal salute.

"There's no need for that," Kanaahn said sheepishly. He still couldn't get used to all this reverence.

"Are your dragons nearby?" asked Kaltar. He brimmed with excitement; like a child on the last day of Unthyr.

"They're out hunting, but they'll be meeting us on the other side of the mountains. A large group of dragons in Altimara isn't exactly subtle, but, if we need them, they will come," explained Kyeit.

Kaltar seemed a bit deflated that he could not meet the other half of the Khaleeshir, but he did his best to hide it.

15

The Khaleeshir shifted uncomfortably, just as uneasy with the show of deference as Kanaahn was. Cecil caught on quickly and interceded, changing the subject, and pressing forward with why they had come here. "Do you need help with the camels?"

Kaltar turned, oblivious to the fact his excitement had caused the Khaleeshir discomfort and waved his hand dismissively. "No, we've got it from here. Do you have everything you need?"

Everyone checked their bags, and belongings, and made sure they had everything that they needed to continue the trek over the mountain. Once everyone was certain, Edva snapped her gloved fingers and pointed to the wagons and camels. Several people emerged from the cave and began unhooking the camels from the wagons and bringing them all into the cave. Everyone had said their goodbyes to their camels before entering the camp. It was less embarrassing that way.

"Will you be needing some food or a place to rest?" asked Kaltar. "I've got some stew on the fire, and I'm sure we could find a couple extra loaves of bread for you." He sounded as if he was trying to be more enticing and convincing than genuinely wondering. Something told Kanaahn that he was familiar with how Kyeit worked.

Kyeit shook her head. "No thank you. We need to keep moving."

Kaltar frowned. Worry creased his brow. "Are you sure you want to make the climb in the dark?"

"Better that way," responded Kyeit. She checked the straps on her gear and pack and tightened them as she saw fit. "Less likely to be spotted. We have no idea who or what might be chasing after us or spying on us. We can rest once the day hits and we're higher up. We'll descend the mountain in the dark."

"Will you have enough light?" Kaltar pressed. His concern was not abated by Kyeit's reasoning.

"We'll be fine, Kaltar. I promise." Kyeit hugged the man.

While it seemed to calm him down, it didn't fully assuage his fears. Regardless, he didn't press the issue further. Yes, he was *very* familiar with how Kyeit worked.

Kaltar returned the hug, then saluted Kyeit, Cecil and the Khaleeshir. He ran a hand over his bald pate. "Be safe. I'd hate to have to pass the message on to your father that you'd been hurt or worse."

Everything in the camp seemed to stop. Kanaahn could hear his heartbeat in his ears. He didn't know. The Khaleeshir and Cecil looked over at Kyeit, and then to Kaltar. Their eyes drifted between the two for a long, painful moment. The tension was palpable; almost crushing.

"You weren't told?" Kyeit asked finally. If there was any sadness in her heart, she did not betray it.

"About what?" puzzled Kaltar.

"My father was killed during the defence of Xiar," replied Kyeit, stalwart as ever. "His soul has joined the ancestors and returned to the Mother."

"Inor's beard..." muttered Kaltar. He finally realized the error of his words. "I'm so sorry, I had no idea. May Astalos guide his soul to the Mother."

"When we see him, we shall ask," Kyeit answered. Her face bore the semblance of a half-smile. Her attempt at a joke was half-hearted. She was suffering inside, and this was the first time her façade had cracked since Xiar.

"We must be going," Cecil interceded. She hoped to end this awkward confrontation—for everyone's sake.

It didn't take Kaltar long to pick up on what Cecil was trying to do, and he seemed to thoroughly agree and threw himself behind the cause. "Yes. You must keep to your schedule," he added. "It was nice to see you again. It was a pleasure to meet you Khaleeshir. Please be safe and look out for one another."

"Take care of yourself," Shooter responded.

The other Khaleeshir echoed the sentiment.

Kyeit turned to her charges. "Cecil, take up the rear. I'll take the lead. The rest of you stay between us and follow closely."

"Are you going to be able to see?" asked Arial. She was just as concerned with this plan as Kaltar was. The Khaleeshir would be able to see at night better than Kyeit and Cecil due to the Blood Covenant, but their Darond guides would be near blind in the darkness.

Kyeit opened her hand and began to mutter in Draconic. "Vit wiluthyr vat ja thanir."

A small ball of light erupted from her palm, floated around her head twice, and set itself a few paces ahead of Kyeit, illuminating a small area in front of her. The wisp of light seemed to have a mind of its own, for with each step Kyeit took, the light would move at a similar pace, occasionally bobbing around near rocks or other things to beware of.

Kyeit stopped just shy of the steep path cut into the mountain by the cave. "See? Like my own portable moon."

Arial was impressed and would be asking Kyeit for instruction on that spell later.

Kyeit pointed towards the narrow path to the left of the cave entrance. She led the group towards it, and they began their climb up the mountain. It wasn't steep to start, but Kyeit assured everyone that would soon change.

Kanaahn looked back as they began to climb. He caught the sad eyes of Kaltar, who watched the group as they ascended. It was visible how he worried for the Khaleeshir, and for Kyeit most of all. For how she was coping with her father's death, and how she was throwing herself headlong into her duty with a moment to rest, or a moment to think—a moment to feel. Kaltar nodded, and Kanaahn returned the gesture. For a moment, a silent understanding passed between the two, but as soon as it started, it was over. The two returned to their tasks at hand; Kaltar to his pottage, and Kanaahn to his climb.

Chapter III

The group sat huddled in a small cavern on the side of the mountain. They had just had a quick meal from their rations and were settling in for a nap. Sunlight crested over the mountain tops and reached through the clouds, painting the skies copper, bronze, and yellow. Traces of blue and purple ran through a sky still dotted with silver stars that clung jealously to the horizon, trying, and failing to maintain their grip on the world.

Kyeit had decreed they would travel up and down the mountain by nightfall, to avoid detection. Cecil thought it was unnecessary, but Kyeit won out. The group didn't know what means of wicked beasts Tenebrae had at his disposal. He would surely throw them all out into the world to discover and hunt down the Khaleeshir before they could reach the protection of a Metallic Dragon. Tenebrae could not risk his enemies growing stronger and defeating him. Surely he was having them followed. The High Council believed as much, and so did Kyeit. Cecil was not so sure, but even she couldn't discount the possibility. Tenebrae was still far too mysterious a being—even to those who had known him a thousand years ago. He had been plotting for ten centuries; gathering resources, and allies, and buying himself time. This would not be an easy victory. The Khaleeshir would have to pry victory from the cooling corpse of the mad dragon himself.

Kyeit had taken the first watch—she had insisted on it. No one could convince her otherwise. She had declared her intention to take the first watch and charged from the cave with her blade drawn before anyone could try. Everyone stared blankly at her when she departed. She had left before anyone could even process and respond to what she said. So there Kyeit stood, not far from the mouth of the cave, eyeing the sky uneasily as if it would soon collapse on her.

"What should we be looking out for, anyway?" demanded Shooter. He rubbed his eyes as he settled into his bedroll.

"What do you mean?" asked Cecil.

"What kind of creatures are we hiding from?" Shooter clarified. "What does Tenebrae have at his disposal that's got Kyeit so scared to travel at a normal time of day?"

"You noticed," stated Cecil, sarcastically.

Arkas snorted. "We've got eyes."

Cecil couldn't help but chuckle, but she didn't answer Shooter's question. So, he pressed again.

Cecil sat up and sighed heavily. Her breath rattled through her teeth, escaping her throat like a spectre. If it was a spectre of anything it was the ghost of a decent day's rest she had planned to have. "We can't be certain—"

"Kyeit seems pretty certain," Kanaahn said. He tried to keep his voice low so that Kyeit couldn't' hear them discussing her.

"Let me finish," hissed Cecil. She gathered her thoughts before she continued. "We can't be *completely* certain. Tenebrae, even two decades ago, had several servants at his disposal. These terrible creatures were known as Kotharii, in the Common tongue, or Kotharii as an Asardaean loan word. It roughly translates to Wicked Ones. The dragons know them as Tulkaz: abominations."

"What makes them so scary?" wondered Arial.

Cecil paused and looked over at Kyeit. "They seem to appear as if from nowhere. No one was ever certain how. They descend on their black dragons and murder anyone their master commands. He points the finger, and they draw their blades."

"I knew killers for hire like that in Kula," said Shooter. "They weren't that scary."

"These Kotharii are half man, half dragon if the stories are to be believed. No one has ever seen them without their hoods," Cecil admitted. "They are terribly strong and fast. Few can match them. Some say they were supposed to be Tenebrae's answer to the Khaleeshir. His own perverse version of that."

"How is that even possible?" asked Kanaahn.

"Blood magic, most likely," answered Cecil. "Tenebrae created blood magic after all. I'm not surprised he tried something so depraved. If anyone could figure it out, it would be him."

Arkas shifted into an upright position. "Has anyone seen these Kotharii recently?"

Cecil shook her head. "They come and go, like the night. They disappeared for a thousand years and popped up again suddenly two decades ago. Then they disappeared again until a few years ago."

"Surely they can be killed?" asked Kanaahn.

Cecil shook her head. "Not even the original Khaleeshir could kill these Kotharii. It was said that it was the Kotharii that had killed the Khaleeshir Nayondel Darond. They teamed up to defeat him and took his head as a trophy. When the fight was over, he was dead, and the Kotharii had disappeared into the shadows, never to be seen again—or so we thought. What's worse is that we don't even know how many Tenebrae has under his command. They will only ever appear in pairs of two, but they appear so quickly and disappear just as fast. Some think Tenebrae has a small army of them, others think it's just the two. We don't even know where they choose to make their home."

Kanaahn had not known much of his predecessors, but he knew that Nayondel Darond had been the leader of the original Khaleeshir, bonded to the red dragon Veryll. He had been a skilled swordsman and one of the strongest of the original five humans. Kanaahn also knew that he was the namesake for the knightly order that Cecil and Kyeit served.

A pregnant pause filled the cave. Cecil took this opportunity to peak over at Kyeit; she was still none the wiser.

Shooter broke the silence with another question. "What else do we have to worry about? What other things is Tenebrae hiding in the wings?" Shooter's face made it clear the pun was intended.

"What isn't he hiding," answered Cecil. "Tenebrae was a wicked, cruel beast, and his tongue was made of silver. Whatever creatures he didn't make, joined him of their own accord."

Djall brushed against the back of Kanaahn's mind. Even when at great distances he was always there, though the farther he was the more dimmed the presence. The deeper and longer their bond grew, the farther Djall could go without becoming just a gentle tug on Kanaahn's consciousness, but now he was back within a decent range.

"*Where are you?*" asked Kanaahn.

"*Not far—other side of this mountain. You should see the trees. It is* unbelievable" replied Djall.

Kanaahn noticed something odd in the way that Djall said that and Kanaahn made a note to ask him about it later.

The dragon continued. "*I've never seen so many trees, except in the memories of my ancestors. We lived here, once.*"

"*What's it like to be home?*" asked Kanaahn.

"*It is...it is not home,*" admitted Djall. "*Home is elsewhere in this land, though the exact location is...fuzzy. But this...this is close to home, and I am happy.*"

Kanaahn was flooded with feelings of joy, flashes of what Djall was seeing. There was so much green, that Kanaahn didn't know if Djall was looking at himself or the trees.

The others had felt the presence of their partners return because Cecil had stopped talking. She waited for everyone to finish up with their dragons before continuing.

"Sorry," Arial apologized. "How is Kinokaze?"

Cecil shrugged. "I don't know. I can't communicate with her at the same distances as you can."

"Do you want me to ask?" Arial asked.

Cecil shook her head. "No, that's okay. I know she's fine. We've been apart for longer, a few more hours won't hurt. I want to finish talking about this before Kyeit returns."

"Are we not supposed to know?" asked Kanaahn.

"No, that's not it. She's...sensitive about the topic of the Kotharii, that's all," explained Cecil, "I can't say more. Don't ask me. It's not my story to tell."

No one pressed the subject, though their minds went wild with imagination.

"Tenebrae had many other well-known allies, besides his own clan and the Kotharii," continued Cecil. "There was the Brown Dragon Clan, the Bizhak Harzok, the Qiri'ar; he even managed to turn Venu'shael against his mate and clan."

A hiss emanated through Kanaahn's mind. Visceral hatred coursed through him from Djall.

"What's wrong?" asked Kanaahn.

"The brown dragons are not dragons!" Djall spat. *"Those abominations never knew what it meant to be drazhani. Those flightless, blind wretches turned upon their kin so readily. Harzok! They were no different than Khin'shala!"*

"Khin'shala?" asked Kanaahn. His confusion had not been abated.

"They live in this mountain range; look like snakes with white feathery wings. You call them Rishi beasts, I believe?" Djall explained.

Yes, Kanaahn knew of them. Everyone had heard of Rishi beasts in Altimara. The name was misleading because they did not just keep to the Rishi Mountains. They had become invasive in many parts of Enayra in recent years, and they now spanned out across several hundred kilometres east and west of the spine, spreading into all other nations of Enayra except the frozen lands of Anglum. In Altimara, the creatures had spread from the Rishi Mountains as far as Kula. Some had even been seen as far as the bluffs of Targrond, making their homes in the ocean cliffs outside the city.

Cecil noticed Kanaahn had zoned out. "Everything okay, Kanaahn?"

Kanaahn zoned back in. "It's Djall. He...explained his distaste for the brown dragons."

Risasi used Shooter's mind as an anchor point for his own and boomed through the heads of all present. *"The Brown Dragon Clan are traitors to their race!"* he snarled.

Everyone paused to make sure Risasi hadn't accidentally looped Kyeit into his declaration.

"Why do you hate them so much?" asked Arial.

"The brown dragons are not like other dragons," explained Adalinda. Her distaste for the brown dragons was present in her words, but she was not as vehement about it as Risasi or Djall. *"They do not fly. They are wingless, armoured, and live beneath the ground in tunnels away from the light."*

"How can they call themselves drazhani if they cannot even fly!" scoffed Fyete.

"Maybe this treatment is why they joined Tenebrae?" suggested Shooter.

An uproar erupted amongst the dragons. They did not take kindly to the suggestion that they had ostracized their brethren and pushed them into the arms of the enemy.

"Tenebrae's silver tongue sounded pretty to them, compared to how the other dragons spoke about them," confirmed Cecil. "He had been a well-respected member of Draconic society before he turned his back on it. The brown dragons felt abandoned by their surface-dwelling brothers and sisters…but Tenebrae offered them a chance at dominance and supremacy. The chance to get back at those who flew high above and mocked them.”

“What happened to the brown dragons after the last war? Were they imprisoned like the black dragons?” asked Arial.

Cecil shook her head. “No. They disappeared from Enayra completely. Likely they burrowed too deep underground for anyone but a gnar to find them. No one’s willing to go look for them. They have the advantage down there. It would be tantamount to literally walking into the belly of the beast. It’s unknown if they still serve Tenebrae at this time, but we can’t be too careful.”

“*Traitors!*” roared Risasi.

Cecil deemed it time to change the subject. “They weren’t the only ones who joined Tenebrae. I assume you know about the Qiri’ar?”

Everyone nodded. They were very familiar with the travelling tribe of nomadic traders. They spent most of the year travelling the land and trading goods and wares, only to return to their capital for winter with their traded treasure trove. Some of the best goods came from the Qiri’ar. For example, Qiri’aran earthenware. In Kula, it was both a symbol of status and an everyday essential. They came in both fancy, expensive designs, and basic, hardy models meant for practical daily use. Everyone owned at least a single piece—some had owned them for generations.

“They followed Tenebrae?” asked Arkas. “They didn’t seem so evil.”

“They’re not inherently evil. No, they’re not even close,” warned Cecil. “It would be better to call them misguided or blinded by loyalty. The Qiri’ar were bound to Tenebrae by one of their chieftains a thousand years ago. His name was Eshgalon the Mad, and he declared that the Qiri’ar could only worship the dual Aspect Isunath-Kistharoth as their people’s prime Aspect. I don’t know what they teach you in Altimara, but for most of Enayra, Isunath-Kistharoth is embodied in their familiars of Ten’ebraex and Kyna’braxa, Tenebrae and his former mate. They are…not often worshipped anymore.

“In exchange for learning the intricacies of blood magic, and the promise of power over all of Altimara, Eshgalon the Mad pledged his peoples in a blood oath to Tenebrae for all time. It never occurred to Eshgalon that they could lose. The Qiri’ar are now forever bound to Tenebrae. If he calls for their support, they will have to pledge it.”

“Wasn’t the Altimaran army aided by a Qiri’aran woman at Xiar?” asked Kanaahn.

“I remember seeing her,” said Arial. “She was strong. It was…amazing and terrifying at the same time.”

“That woman is Elandyr’ni Vigor’iath. Intelligence tells us that she’s Altimara’s new Grand Enchantress. Before that, she was a Qiri’aran priestess at the Great Temple of Isunath-Kistharoth in Gishan’belor. She showed a lot of promise and an aptitude for magic,” explained Cecil. “She came into Tenebrae’s direct service in Kasaadua about six months ago. She is an incredibly powerful warlock and is very skilled in blood magic.”

“If she’s serving Tenebrae in Kasaadua, then it’s safe to say the Qiri’ar are likely in the service of Tenebrae,” concluded Kanaahn.

Cecil nodded. “It’s likely, but if so, they’ve been kept in reserve for now. We don’t know and can’t begin to guess when or where Tenebrae plans to deploy them.”

“What about the other two you mentioned?” asked Kanaahn. He couldn’t remember how to pronounce them, nor entirely what they sounded like. His Draconic was improving, but it still sounded so foreign to him some days.

“Venu’shael was the Patriarch of the Red Dragon Clan,” explained Cecil. “He and Tenebrae had always been close. When it came to the war...he chose Tenebrae. His clan tried to rise against him, led by his mate, Kara’imla, but...while he was defeated, the cost was terrible. The red dragons never fully recovered.”

Shooter staggered. He could feel intense emotions emanating from Risasi. Some odd, bleeding mixture of crushing sadness and all-consuming rage engulfed the normally gruff and stalwart dragon. Red dragons were passionate and felt emotion easily and freely. Often that emotion was anger, and so Shooter forgot that red dragons were as easily susceptible to feeling sadness, joy, jealousy, and a of myriad other feelings. Shooter prompted Risasi for a response, but the red dragon dimmed their connection.

The look of discomfort was clear on Shooter’s face and Cecil quickly changed the subject. “Then finally there’s Bizhak Harzok; it’s Draconic for Bloodless Mountain. This was perhaps one of Tenebrae’s most vile experiments.”

“What do you mean?” asked Arial.

“Tenebrae wanted to combine a dragon of every colour into a single being,” explained Cecil. Her face contorted into a look of disgust. “The blood that was spilt to perfect the creation of this abomination was...prolific.

“Nulgo’riaz, Patriarch of the Orange Dragon Clan, and Vernix’iol, Patriarch of the Blue Dragon Clan were but two of the victims of Tenebrae’s mad experiments. They were murdered by his ilk, Balgorax, and their remains were returned to Tenebrae for experimentation. It is said their bodies were cobbled together to form the wicked base for this creature to stand on...but many more drazhani were murdered for the creature’s eleven heads.”

“Eleven heads...” murmured Kanaahn. He tried to wrap his head around how something like this could even exist. It must have been a depraved, pained existence; not much of an existence at all—just a burden.

“Why would Tenebrae do something like that?” asked Arkas, aghast.

“He needed powerful allies,” explained Cecil. “How else could he compete with the Khaleeshir, all of the dragon clans, the Metallics, and the nations of Enayra?”

“Except Altimara,” snarked Shooter.

“Except Altimara,” Cecil echoed.

There was nothing but silence as everyone tried to wrap their head around what they had just learned. Kanaahn and Shooter kept looking back out to Kyeit. She remained on guard, ever vigilant. Her attention was turned to the sky as if she expected Tenebrae himself to descend upon the mountain to destroy them all.

Cecil looked as if she was having some great internal struggle. Kanaahn surmised that it had something to do with how much more she could get away with telling the Khaleeshir. She had likely risked much saying as much as she already had. Kanaahn greatly appreciated how far Cecil was willing to push her luck to ensure the Khaleeshir weren't entirely blind.

"I wish I could say you don't have to worry about those last two former allies," Cecil said finally, "But they killed Kanothir. She was an ancient dragon and a Metallic one at that. Her blood would have been a veritable treasure trove for Tenebrae and his enchantress. Even without it, Tenebrae is powerful. He was able to claw himself back from the brink of death as a spirit without a body. He clung to life for a thousand years, and now he's strong enough to be a serious threat to our cause again."

"How much blood do you think they have?" asked Kanaahn. He tried to be as delicate with his questions as possible. "Kanothir was...well she was a large and old dragon. I mean, what could they do with that much blood? How long would it last?"

"Unknown," replied Cecil. "It would depend on the type of spells they were performing, and what they were trying to do. We believe they may have used some to free the Black Dragon Clan from their imprisonment. It's possible that flashy retreat at Xiar required some of Kanothir's blood to pull off; no mage or warlock is that powerful on their own."

"So, they could have a little left, a lot left, or none left," concluded Shooter.

Cecil nodded. "Unfortunately."

This time the silence lasted longer. It was more permanent, and it permeated the entire cave. Kyeit had wandered off somewhere; likely to sweep the perimeter of their camp for any signs that they were being followed.

A minute passed in silence.

Two minutes.

Five minutes.

Finally, when no one said anything for ten minutes, Cecil spoke again. "Let's get some rest. We've got a long climb down tonight and we'll need all the energy we can muster. There's no sense worrying about what we *might* face until we actually see it."

Shooter yawned. "Besides, once this war is done, I'm sure we'll have seen things far worse than anything you've just described."

No one responded to Shooter's quip, but it was clear that no one disagreed with the sentiment. Least of all Cecil. No one knew exactly what she had seen in her few years as a Knight Commander, but even the Khaleeshir could tell she had seen much for her age.

Kanaahn had made it a point to ask Kyeit and Cecil how they had climbed so high in an organization as ancient and traditional as the Darond. They were both relatively young, with only six years of service and training under their belts. Shooter had suggested that the Darond had been that desperate. Admittedly, from everything they had seen so far of the order, it didn't seem so far off from the truth. Yet Kanaahn had a feeling there were good reasons for each of their promotions to such high positions. Whatever that reason was, though, Kyeit and Cecil would keep it to themselves for now.

Chapter IV

Drakhart, Elandyr'ni, and Calandor. Tenebrae's three lieutenants stood before the kneeling procession of Altimaran nobility. Some now lay slaughtered in their seats in the most horrible of ways. They were the unlucky, unfortunate few who resisted Tenebrae's dark beckoning. Heads blown apart by Tenebrae's dark magic. Hearts exploded from chests. Entire people popped like an old, overflowing water skin. Blood, gore, and intestinal tracts littered the raised daises and seats where they sat. Splattered across even the faces of those who remained loyal.

In the end, one duke, one duchess, seven counts, five countesses, fifteen barons, and twelve baronesses had openly refused Tenebrae's "offer." They had rejected their long-held beliefs for the sake of their king, for the future he promised them if Drakhart led the way, but in the face of Tenebrae himself they had found their spines. It had not ended well for them, and perhaps they knew it wouldn't, and that was why they chose to resist. Drakhart was disappointed it had taken them so long to find their morals again, and yet a part of him admired how willing they were to face certain death.

The two hooded guards near the door almost appeared to vibrate with glee as they smelled the blood wafting from the stands. They watched eagerly from beneath their dark cowls as Tenebrae brought the nobles to heel.

Haggard and exhausted, the remaining, loyal nobles now knelt before the empty throne. There were no more secrets between them and their new masters. Tenebrae controlled Altimara, and he was going to lead Altimara to ascendancy, and supremacy above the dragons and the other nations. Altimara would be all-powerful, and they would be rewarded for their loyalty. They would rule it all once Tenebrae had what he wanted: the destruction of the Darond, and the death of Aurum and the other Metallic Dragons.

Lord Marneron and Lord Drungvist remained behind as the nobles quickly—but not too quickly—filed from the throne room to their chambers. They had been released for the day. Tenebrae had made the two claimants to the throne new members of his trusted Regency Council. Lord Marneron would take over as High General of Altimara, and Lord Drungvist would retain his position as Grand Admiral. Elandyr'ni would remain as the Grand Enchantress and Calandor as Major-domo. All would answer to Drakhart in time, though Drakhart would require more training before he would be allowed to lead Tenebrae's generals unassisted. For now, Tenebrae would oversee Drakhart's command closely.

The people would be told that the now-dead nobles had staged a coup, attempting to take the throne for themselves. In response, the ruling council, Lord Marneron, and Lord Drungvist put aside their differences and worked together to quell the rebellion and kill those who were responsible. The Kingsmoot would be delayed for now, and the two claimants to the throne would work with the Regency Council to ensure Altimara remained stable, and the government didn't collapse in the meantime. Once the stability of the country was restored, and new nobility appointed, then—and only then—would a new Kingsmoot be held to choose the new king of Altimara.

The newly created councillors joined the other three upon the dais as they began to talk of plans going forward.

"We should gather the navy," suggested Drungvist. "Use it to guard the southern and northern shores of Altimara. In case Espias or Asardaea try to push their luck near our waters."

"Not a bad idea," noted Calandor, "Lord Tenebrae?"

"Not a waste," rumbled the Black Dragon, ***"We cannot begin to take chances anymore. We were routed at Xiar...we cannot allow another defeat like that to occur again."***

Elandyr'ni and Drakhart glanced at each other at the mention of Xiar. A sore spot for the latter, more so than the former.

"Patrol the Altimaran sea and the Bay of Milon," ordered Tenebrae. ***"I would rather be on alert than caught off guard. Perhaps, if the opportunity presents itself to disrupt trade and shipping between our enemies..."***

Drungvist gave a knowing smile. "Of course, my Lord Tenebrae."

"As the new High General," Lord Marneron said. "We should take the opportunity to claim the land now left unoccupied by the disappearance of Xiar. The Antigorus Valley is prime farmland that has been left vacant and untended. We should set up farming communes and secure the land with our soldiers. We will need that Xiaran grain to feed our soldiers in the coming campaigns."

Tenebrae grunted. ***"I had almost forgotten. We shall send the Duke of Xiar to head the mission. You will be responsible for drawing up the plans. Work with Calandor regarding the logistics. Duke Folberen shall follow your orders for the occupation."***

"Also, I would request more armaments, a full legion, and a handful of Black Blades. I would like to start leading raiding parties deeper into Utova to destroy key resource points and sabotage as much infrastructure as possible. We cannot afford a large-scale invasion or a prolonged siege of Utova at this time and diverting that many legions to the frozen wastes with poor supply lines would be foolish at the best of times. We need to keep the Grand Duchy from allying with our enemies against us, and if we can at the least keep them on the back foot, and always on the defence against us, we can hope to remove another player from the game."

"That would be a fruitful effort, I think," mused the black dragon within the heads of his current wards. ***"Give Calandor the logistical details for what you had in mind, and it shall be done. If we are lucky, it will also be beneficial***

towards another purpose. Our spies have long whispered that the Darond headquarters lies secreted away somewhere in Anglum. I have long had an idea where, but it would be good to have confirmation. Perhaps, while our forces are disrupting the Grand Duchy, we may happen upon a way to disrupt our enemies as well. I have no doubt the city-state serves as a stopping point for supplies, it is one of the few settlements in Anglum, and large enough that a few errant supplies may get lost in the shuffle before they're smuggled elsewhere."

Lord Drungvist let out a sharp cackle. "The Sacred Order of the Knights of Darond? They're but a myth nowadays. They died out centuries ago during the Fall of Dragonsrest."

"I can assure you," hissed Tenebrae. *"They are very active."*

"I can vouch for this," interjected Drakhart, his hand resting on his belt. "When I was in Ottogard I was trained by a man named Osamu. He called himself a Dragon Master, and he was bonded to a silver dragon named Kanothir, the mate of Argentum. He had an apprentice who travelled with us as well, Kyeit Karaglen, who was bonded to a silver dragon named Valence, daughter of Kanothir and Argentum. Kyeit was a Knight Commander of the Darond. The Darond are currently aiding and training the other Dragonkin as we speak. They seek to rally the other nations against us; it was them who helped organize Xiar against our forces."

Lord Drungvist's face went red with embarrassment or anger. No one was ever sure which.

"This matches intelligence from Ottogard," added Elandyr'ni. She pulled a report from the table in front of her and handed it to Lord Drungvist. "The search for the Darond outpost that Drakhart mentioned turned up fruitful. I killed Osamu and his dragon Kanothir myself. Their blood was vital for the revival of the Black Dragon Clan and for our retreat from Xiar."

"I'll be damned," muttered Lord Drungvist in disbelief. He scanned over the document carefully, turning it over several times in case he had missed anything.

"Two decades ago, their spies infiltrated the very heart of the Black Citadel and discovered proof of my existence. From what we've been able to ascertain, I was not what they had originally hoped to find. Regardless, their discovery of me has proved troublesome for us ever since." Tenebrae explained. *"We struck down many of their members in return for their impudence. But once more they have grown emboldened enough to stand against us. We shall make them regret their bravery."*

"No wonder, with the arrival of new Dragonkin," added Lord Marneron. "If what Lord Ghast says is true, they've likely already been snuck past our borders into one of the other nations. They'll only get stronger and inspire more people against us."

Drakhart turned to Calandor and pointed to the small map on the table before the major-domo. "Where does intelligence place them?"

Calandor frowned. "Our spies last noted them travelling west towards Estion. We lost track of them as they neared the border. A sandstorm caught our agents off guard and prevented them from following any further. By the time it cleared, they were gone."

"Have any of you seen anything?" Tenebrae asked no one in particular. No, not no one. To the guards. The silence watchers that stood along the walls, hooded, and wreathed in shadows.

The two guards seemed to glide forward. They did not make a sound as they floated across the cobblestones. Then, suddenly, a hiss vibrated from somewhere beneath their blackened hoods, and Drakhart saw something that almost made his eyes go wide. A tail swished back and forth across the carpet, like a cat's; only it wasn't a cat's tail. It was black, and scaly, with spines and ridges running down the centre. Were the tail larger, Drakhart have thought that the tail belonged to—no, no he *had* to be seeing things. Yet he wasn't. He blinked several times as if to reset his vision, but the tail remained, swiftly flicking back and forth from beneath the guards' robes.

Elandyr'ni didn't seem disturbed by this at all. Calandor looked like he might vomit though, but otherwise attempted to keep his composure. Lord Drungvist kept a straight face but was likely panicking internally—he hid it well. Lord Marneron not so much. His face showed discomfort, despite his best efforts.

The guard on the left spoke with a voice that seemed to Drakhart like wind howling in a sandstorm. It hissed and wailed, and the world seemed to melt away before it. It made Drakhart feel cold. The creature spoke, or at least, seemed to convey its words across a mental link. There was no voice, just emotions, memories, and intent. These hooded guards confirmed the reports from the human scouts. The Khaleeshir were indeed crossing into Estion. Drakhart wished he could see the mouth of whatever creature was beneath the hood, but every time he tried to catch a glimpse he could see only darkness.

"They're likely looking to avoid Fort Ghestanrah," Calandor intuited. "At this point, they may already be beyond our borders, and thus our reach. To pursue them with an army or any of our scouts would be considered grounds for war."

"But to send **them…"** replied Tenebrae. He implied the two hooded guards with his words. ***"We have sent them against the Darond and their agents before. They have experience."***

Drakhart began to connect the political dots. "They would not be agents of Altimara. It would not be a cause for war."

"Would that not be dangerous?" asked Drungvist. "The Darond could prove our existence to the other nations and unite them against us."

"It will depend on if the other nations believe what the Darond says about Tenebrae controlling the Altimaran Crown," added Elandyr'ni, "But it is the safest way to proceed."

"It is likely the lines have already been drawn, and the alliances made. Whatever happens now, has already been set in motion. It would be worse to send an Altimaran agent and violate the Peace of Gerovia than it is to send them. *We cannot fight a coalition made up of all other nations of Enayru we can fight the nations individually. If we can divide and conquer, and control the when and where of each confrontation, we can tear our enemies asunder."*

Calandor seemed to be of similar mind to Tenebrae. "The kings of Estion have ever been clever. They've never openly pledged their loyalty one way or another. Moreover, the real power in Estion lies with the barons, and *they* have been willing to do business with Altimara if it is profitable, and with war looming, they will continue to do so until the final moment possible. Truthfully, if I had to wager a guess as to Estion's loyalty, they will likely join our enemies. There is no doubt that Asardaea is wholly against us. They have always been wrapped around the Darond's finger."

"And if Asardaea is supporting the Darond, then it is certain so are the Espians," Lord Drungvist spat. "The same would be true if it were the other way around. They're like starving wolves at each other's throats, fighting for a scrap of the other's glory. If Asardaea stands to gain, Espias wants a piece, and vice versa."

Lord Marneron chimed in next. "Whether Grand Duchess Vylsa believes the Darond or not, she would not openly join them against us. She, like her mother, grandfather, and great-grandmother before her, is too stubborn and proud. The Utovans pride their independence, and to join the Darond would mean to submit, in one way or another, to their will. She would trade, supply, and be cordial—at absolute most—but she would never throw in her lot with them unless forced to."

"Besides, doing so would incur the wrath of Altimara, and they have enough to deal with from us already," said Elandyr'ni. "A fully dedicated and supplied invasion force would be the last thing they want at their doorstep."

"A desperate hatchling will still devour its nestmate," warned Tenebrae. *"It is why I am allowing Lord Marneron to keep them occupied. Proceed with your infiltration as soon as you are supplied. Once the Falcon's wings are broken, we shall swoop in to deliver the killing stroke."*

Lord Marneron bowed towards the empty throne. "At once, my lord." The handsome young noble dipped his head towards the others, carefully making sure to avoid eye contact with the guards as he sidestepped them and disappeared from the hall with Calandor in tow as the two went off to discuss logistics and deployment.

"You," boomed Tenebrae, indicating the guards, *"Follow those Khaleeshir. Keep us apprised of their doings and whereabouts. Follow them for as long as possible; return if it is no longer safe."*

The two hooded figures bowed low and disappeared, floating away like spectres, their tails flicking back and forth behind them. Drakhart could feel the tension in the room dissipate as they disappeared. Everyone's breathing seemed to return to normal.

"Lord Drungvist, patrol our waters with your navy, as we discussed. We cannot appear weak or idle to our enemies," Tenebrae commanded. *"Furthermore, I have considered the request you had submitted to His Majesty a few months prior, and I have concluded that your logic is sound. I am granting your request. Contact the shipwrights in Targrond and Kilnarn and tell them to get all hands to the workbenches. We'll be needing many more ships soon enough. I am keenly interested in these plans of yours."*

Lord Drungvist gave a quick "my lord." He had always been a man of few words according to Calandor. But unlike his counterpart, Lord Marneron, Lord Drungvist did not flit off towards his assigned task immediately. He merely stared intently at Drakhart, as if he was trying to read the boy's mind. It made Drakhart slightly uncomfortable.

Tenebrae seemed to pay no heed to the remaining noble. Whether this was because he trusted Lord Drungvist's new loyalty, or because he never saw him as a threat to begin with wasn't clear to Drakhart.

"Drakhart, call my k'zir and meet me at my lair. Elandyr'ni, you shall come as well. We will discuss your training; we should be expedient with it, I have a feeling you will be needed on the battlefield soon enough, and we cannot have a repeat of Xiar."

Drakhart's eyes went downcast. "No, my lord."

With that, Tenebrae withdrew himself from their heads and returned to the murky darkness of his caverns. Drakhart's head felt somewhat emptier afterwards.

Elandyr'ni looked at Drakhart, then Lord Drungvist. The noble's face was still screwed up, and it occurred to Drakhart he might be thinking very hard. His deformities and stern demeanour made it hard to tell what face he was really trying to make. "I need to grab something from my chambers before I meet with our lord," she whispered. "I'll return shortly. In the meantime, perhaps see what Lord Drungvist wants."

Drakhart nodded as Elandyr'ni slipped away. She gave a polite bow to Lord Drungvist, who merely nodded as she passed. He was still fixated on Drakhart.

Drakhart approached the old nobleman. Not many things made him nervous anymore—facing down an ancient dragon that predated humanity seemed to have sapped most of the fear from him—but Lord Drungvist made him nervous.

"Drakhart Ghast, eh?" the noble growled. "Ghast. Hm. Aha! I've got it!"

"Yes, sir?" asked Drakhart. He could feel sweat bead on his forehead.

"We've met before, Drakhart," Lord Drungvist declared. "Your father was Vurkhart Ghast, your mother's Kinraea."

Drakhart was dumbfounded. "You...you remembered?"

"Not at first," admitted Lord Drungvist, "It took me a bit, but the name sounded familiar. Your father was one of my best navigators. Went down with the *Predestiny*. It was a real shame; too many good men were lost in that storm. I never forget a sailor—and I've seen a lot of sailors in my day. Last time I saw you was when I came to pay my respects, you left Kilnarn after that."

"We went to stay with my mother's family in Kula, yes," answered Drakhart. "My mother couldn't stand to look at the sea after my father passed, so she took us somewhere far away from it."

Lord Drungvist nodded and scratched his chin. "How is your mother?"

"I...don't know, my lord," said Drakhart. "After I liberated Kula from the former Lord Davenpourte, I went to see her, and she wasn't home. No one knew where she was, or when she left, but it looked like she had been gone for a few weeks. I don't know where she went."

"I hope you find her soon," Lord Drungvist said supportively. "I know I couldn't sleep a wink if my own family went missing."

Drakhart gave Lord Drungvist a small bow in thanks for his kind words.

Lord Drungvist simply burst out laughing. He slapped Drakhart hard on the back and wiped a tear from his eye. "No need to bow to me, my boy—and none of that my lord crap either! You're one of us now." Lord Drungvist held Drakhart by the shoulders and examined him with his one good eye. "Look at you. The son of a navigator grew up to become the Duke of K'nar. I look forward to working with you!"

Elandyr'ni reappeared through the hall's man doors. Her rings and bracelets jangled as she walked, creating a chorus of chimes that echoed throughout the large room.

Lord Drungvist nodded acknowledgement at Elandyr'ni, saluted Drakhart, and then laughed again before turning towards the door. He limped from the hall, off to his assigned duties.

Elandyr'ni said nothing as she approached the throne, and yet Drakhart felt the need to explain.

"I met him once, long ago." Drakhart's explanation came out more frantic than he had hoped. "My father was a navigator in the Altimaran navy and served Lord Drungvist when we lived in Kilnarn. I met him when my father died at sea—his ship went down and—"

Elandyr'ni placed a long-nailed finger on Drakhart's lips. She smiled kindly at him. "Drakhart, you are rambling."

Drakhart mumbled an apology.

"You don't need to explain anything to me," said Elandyr'ni. She opened the secret passage that led to Tenebrae's cavern. "I left to give you privacy because the business was not mine."

Drakhart was thankful for his master and colleague. She never judged him, never made him feel lesser or an outsider. Not like Calandor. The major-domo tried, as best he could, not to look down on the former commoner—at least for someone as old and traditional as he—but every so often Drakhart could feel the displeasure and disdain that emanated from the old, wizened aristocrat.

"Come," called Elandyr'ni.

Drakhart hadn't even noticed that she was far ahead of him, already down the tunnel. A blue flame sat cradled in the palm of her hand, floating just a hair's breadth above her skin, flickering in the draft. She guarded it close as she turned back to beckon Drakhart. Drakhart jogged to catch up with Elandyr'ni. He sent a mental call for Isunath to join him down in the caverns below Kasaadua. There were other entrances to the cavern system, ones that could accommodate a dragon as large as Isunath was, and some that accommodate dragons even larger. It made Drakhart wonder if Tenebrae ever left the safety of the cavern himself.

Drakhart could hear the stones that formed the entrance of the tunnel grind against each other as they slowly closed behind the duo, leaving them alone in the darkness.

* * *

Elandyr'ni led Drakhart out of the dark winding tunnels and out into the luminescent light of the cave.

Their master, Tenebrae was already waiting, as was Isunath. The dragon's massive head crept out from the deepest, darkest pit she had ever seen. He truly was a massive dragon. She wondered if she'd ever be able to see the dragon in his entirety...likely not until all their work was done.

Tenebrae had not left his cave in...a very long time—at least as far as Elandyr'ni knew. Altimarans would've noticed a dragon as large as him flying about, to say nothing of their enemies. She had always wondered how he ate or drank, or drew any sustenance if he did not leave his cavern. He must have left...but how, and when? These were not her questions to ponder. She was but the apprentice and did not question her master.

Elandyr'ni and Drakhart stopped before the dragon's head and bowed before him. Isunath sidled up beside the two humans and nuzzled Drakhart with his snout.

"I have summoned you here to discuss the manner in which we shall proceed with your training, Drakhart."

Tenebrae's voice echoed through their heads. He did not speak out loud. His voice in this cavern would've been deafening. Instead, he spoke "like a proper dragon", using his mind while also forcing through words, images, and senses. It had taken Elandyr'ni a few years to adjust to this. But to Drakhart it came easy—being bonded to a dragon had helped ease his mind into the assault on one's senses that was communicating with a dragon.

Tenebrae continued. *"If you are to lead our forces, I need you to have the same training as your Khaleeshir counterparts. They will not be sitting idle as they flee Altimara. They will be learning to inspire, lead armies, and cast spells beyond most human comprehension. I require you to learn the same."*

"How would you have me do so, my lord?' asked Drakhart.

"Calandor will oversee your political training, as he already has been. I will have Elandyr'ni train you in the ways of blood magic. It is a much more powerful alternative to the arcane magic the Darond will be teaching. I want Lord Drungvist to oversee your military training. He has experience leading and inspiring men to fight to their bitter deaths. Once he has seen to his appointed duties, I will see about getting him relocated to Altimara; he can command the navy as easily from here as from Kilnarn."

"I feel Lord Drungvist would prefer the deck of a ship," retorted Drakhart.

Tenebrae chuckled. *"Perhaps you are a right, but preference has no meaning when bitter work must be done. Elandyr'ni, have you put together a training regimen for Drakhart?"* Tenebrae turned his head to face Elandyr'ni, training his massive, glowing eye on her. She could smell acid and flame on his breath.

"I have spent much of my spare time since returning from Xiar doing so," she explained. "I'll have him start with the basics immediately."

Tenebrae blinked, though whether out of necessity or acknowledgement Elandyr'ni wasn't sure. *"You intend to start once you have finished here?"*

Elandyr'ni nodded. "What of the binding ritual, my lord?"

"The Blood Covenant between Isunath and Drakhart will soon be forged. I am making the preparations. The artefact you brought me from Ottogard will assist me greatly. I am surprised he did not try to hide or destroy it."

"An oversight on Osamu's part," chided Elandyr'ni. "One he did not live long enough to regret, it seems."

Tenebrae grunted.

Elandyr'ni knew how the murder of the silver dragon, Kanothir, had pained Tenebrae. He had known her personally many millennia ago. They had been friends, family even, at one time. Elandyr'ni had been surprised to find just how large Kanothir truly was, once she had been dismembered in death. The pieces grew to a ridiculous size. She was only slightly smaller than Tenebrae now. Tenebrae had explained that Metallic Dragons, in exchange for not having a secondary breath power, could control their size and form at will. They could transform into anything they so wished, and even shrink and grow themselves at will, though they could not grow larger than their actual size.

"Dalgorax and the rest of my brood will continue instructing Isunath while you are training," continued Tenebrae, training his eye back on Drakhart. *"You will be flying together more often. I want you comfortable in the saddle, both in terms of casting spells, fighting with weapons, and just riding for long*

periods. I've also summoned a sword master from Targrond to help you better master your weapon."

Drakhart placed a hand on the hilt of his great sword. It peaked from over his shoulder like a small lamb from behind its mother.

"Is there anything I'm forgetting?" Tenebrae asked.

Elandyr'ni gave a sideways glance to Drakhart. "There is that matter you asked me to investigate my lord. Our spies have turned up something. Shall I return after my training with Drakhart to discuss it?"

Tenebrae nodded his head slowly. *"Yes, do so. We will be needing it very soon, if the Khaleeshir are heading to Estion, that means they will likely be going to Ethon. If so, I think it shall serve our needs well."*

"Then with that, we shall be taking our leave, my lord." Elandyr'ni bowed.

Drakhart did the same. If her student had any issue with being kept out of the loop, he did not show it. He knew he would be told all in time.

"Go then. There is much work to be done."

Tenebrae kept many secrets, even from Elandyr'ni, and shared them with very few people. When the great dragon planned, he would often only involve the smallest number of people most necessary to his plan's success. It was his assurance that all information would be strictly controlled. He had worked for so long in secret; the key to his success was how few people had been able to fully grasp the scope of his plans. The fewer people he involved in his plans, the fewer risks there were of them leaking. It also limited any potential spies or double agents to just a handful of people who could easily be disposed of, and it also ensured that everyone only understood a small, minute piece in a much larger machine. The information they held alone was virtually useless without greater context.

Elandyr'ni and Drakhart took their leave of Tenebrae, while Isunath departed for the cave entrance he had entered from. Drakhart resisted the urge to look back, as Tenebrae lowered his head and disappeared into the blackest depths of the earth, to continue his plotting and planning.

Chapter V

The moon hung high in the sky. It was about midnight, by Kyeit's estimation. She had been leading the group down the mountain since nightfall. Cecil was taking up the rear-guard, while the Khaleeshir were situated between them both. They just needed to get to the treeline.

Everyone had their weapons close at hand, but Kyeit kept hers drawn. She wasn't risking an ambush, and as far as she was concerned they were vulnerable until they hit the tree line. She didn't know if they were being followed by Tenebrae's spies, but she assumed that much was likely. With her luck, it was likely to be Kotharii.

It was just a bit further to the treeline.

She gripped her sword hilt tighter. Kyeit breathed deeply, trying to calm her suddenly rising heart rate. It was a mixture of fear and excitement, but she couldn't risk it poisoning her vigilance.

They just needed to get to the tree line.

They were currently stuck in a narrow gorge. The rock walls were high, the ground was a constantly shifting mix of scree. In terrain like this, it was easy to trip, lose your footing, and slide the rest of the way down on your face while making a terrible racket. It was also the ideal place for an ambush. Kyeit scanned the rocks that surrounded them for any sign of a trap. While she found no traces of an ambush, it did not help her relax, and Kyeit's grip tightened around her hilt, turning her knuckles white.

Just a bit further and they would be able to see the trees.

The massive Estian trees that towered high above all creation. As ancient as Enayra itself, some say. They would be safe there, in friendly territory, with the trees for cover. No flying enemy could see them, and they'd stay off the roads, following the winding forest paths. Nothing could follow them—she hoped.

The rock walls began to slope back down toward the ground as the gorge began to give way to the bare mountainside. They were almost there. Just a bit longer and they'd be at the—

Kyeit froze. She stared in disbelief. Everyone stopped behind her, confused, shocked, and expecting an ambush.

"Why didn't you tell me?" she asked Valence, whose consciousness she could feel brushing against the edges of her own now.

The dragon tiptoed to the edge of her mind. *"I...did not know how."*

"Dammit Valence, after all these years you didn't know how to tell me that it's spreading?" Kyeit snapped.

Valence's mind grumbled like a thundercloud, and Kyeit quickly apologized.

"Do the Khaleeshir know?" she asked.

"No. We did not think it right to tell them just yet," Valence replied.

Kyeit shook her head and turned to her confused column.

"Are we under attack?" asked Arkas.

Lightning crackled across Arial's fingertips; she held her mage staff at the ready.

Kyeit gave a heavy sigh, then pointed down towards the valley below.

Cecil gasped from the back of the column, but the Khaleeshir were still visibly confused. They looked down at the treeline Kyeit was leading them to, trying to understand what the concern was...and then it seemed to dawn on their faces. The tree line did not end at the bottom of, or on, the mountain, as Kyeit had told them. No, in fact, it seemed to have receded at least a kilometre from the mountain's base. Dry, brown earth and crumbled, desiccated husks replaced what should have been the trees. They saw details on the former forest floor that only the eyes of a Khaleeshir or dragon could see. It was not yet a full desert, but it was barren, dying, and strangled. At the edge of the carnage stood bare trees, feeble grasses, cracked earth and chalky soil.

Cecil scanned the valley and could see that this decay and desertification spread along the entire length of Enayra's Spine. "The rot of Altimara is spreading."

"Rot?" asked Arkas.

Kyeit pursed her lips and glared in displeasure at the valley below. "Altimara was not always a desert. Originally, the desert only included the western portion of the country, but ever since Tenebrae was defeated a millennium ago, the whole kingdom began to turn into the barren desert that you now know. No one could ever explain why everything suddenly started to die...but now it seems to be spreading past the mountains and into Estion."

"How long has it been since it crossed the border?" asked Kanaahn.

Kyeit shook her head. "I don't know. I was here a year ago and the tree line still overlapped the mountain base. The trees should've been visible from here. I never thought the rot would pass over the mountains, let alone so quickly."

"Is Tenebrae doing this?" asked Arial.

Cecil shrugged. "Aurum isn't sure, but many of us in the Darond have suspicions that he might be. We just don't know how."

"Or why," added Kyeit. "I'll send a message to headquarters when we reach Felidrun. They may not be aware."

"We should tell them to check the border with Espias and see if the rot is spreading there," added Cecil.

Kyeit nodded.

Somewhere nearby, but out of sight, an unknown creature let loose a piercing cry into the night. It sounded like a Rishi beast, but Kyeit couldn't be too sure.

"Shit," Kyeit hissed. She readjusted her grip on her blade and pointed to the tree line. "We need to keep moving. We've stopped for too long."

No one needed a second urging. Rishi beasts were invasive to their part of Altimara, and many had seen what a pack of Rishi beasts could do to a winged-wolf for fun—not even for food. The large, vicious, bat-like winged-wolves were wicked enough on their own. They hunted by flying their prey up into the sky in packs and dropping them, then feeding on the broken remains. Even they feared Rishi beasts.

Kyeit broke into a brisk jog, careful not to lose her footing on the crumbling mountainside. The desertification that had occurred had destabilized the ground around her. Rocks and dirt sifted away, flowing downhill toward the base of the mountain. Dust blew easily in the wind, and it was easy to trip. She leapt over a large patch of sand. If she had missed she would be expedited to the bottom of the mountain in a painful and deadly way.

Kyeit paused to ensure the others saw where they should jump as well and only continued running once Cecil was over. They were almost to the base of the mountain. Another Rishi beast cry cut through the night, louder and closer than the first. Truthfully, Kyeit didn't know if the Rishi beasts were after them—or if the cry had even come from a Rishi beast—but she wasn't going to take any chances. You didn't tarry when a Rishi beast was chasing you—even if it was but a small possibility. It was a risk you didn't take in Enayra.

They ran until sweat beaded down their backs and stained their clothes. Until their breaths began to draw sharply and stung like daggers in their lungs.

Kyeit skidded to a halt at the bottom of the mountain. She stopped by a massive fallen tree—the width of the trunk itself was almost three times her height—and tried to catch her breath. They panted like dogs as Kyeit did a head count; everyone was safe.

"Not," she started as she began to catch her breath, "Much further to the tree line. We'll start moving once we've caught our breath. Drink some water."

Shooter didn't wait for her to ask twice and the bottom of his waterskin became well acquainted with the moon until he had half drained it. Arial sipped slower, water dribbling down her chin. Arkas and Kanaahn nearly choked on their water, for they drew so deeply from it. Cecil sipped her water, knowing she would only choke if she drank like the Khaleeshir.

"Are the dragons close?" Cecil asked.

Kyeit didn't respond. She felt outwards with her mind, groping around in the silence for Valence's familiar presence. Then, like someone had turned on a light, she found them. Two kilometres, dead ahead, just beyond the tree line. The dragons were waiting for them in a small clearing.

"We're coming," Kyeit told Valence.

Valence's relief washed over Kyeit like a warm bath. *"Rishi beasts?"*

Kyeit didn't have to answer.

She looked back at the Khaleeshir, who had begun to regain their strength and breath. Cecil was fit and ready to go long before the Khaleeshir were.

"I thought you were used to physical activity?" Cecil teased.

"We are," complained Arial, "But we didn't exactly spend our days training by escaping Rishi beasts."

"Well, no, obviously. That would be a terrible way to train," Cecil replied.

"But a great way to get killed," joked Shooter.

Kyeit huffed and sheathed her blade. "Come, we need to keep moving. We can joke when we reach Felidrun."

"You said that about Kaltar's cave when we left Xiar," Shooter muttered under his breath, "And about the mountain cave when we left Kaltar's cave."

The Khaleeshir smiled but dared not laugh. A smile even crept across Cecil's face for a flickering moment. The moment was cut short by a glare from Kyeit. No one said anything further until they reached the clearing.

* * *

They couldn't tell what time it was when they finally arrived at the designated clearing. The moon had disappeared behind the thick canopy of leaves and branches and all light seemed to disappear from the world beneath the canopy.

"There won't be a lot of light going forward," warned Cecil. "Beneath the Estian canopies, it will forever seem like evening."

The reunion with the dragons had been a touching affair. They hadn't seen each other in person since leaving Xiar. Kyeit didn't want to risk a large gathering of humans and dragons drawing unwanted attention. The communication had only been mental, and the separation had nearly driven the Khaleeshir to agony. Arkas had described it as being apart from half of himself, or like missing a limb or an organ.

Cecil hadn't understood it, and she likely never would. She was not Khaleeshir; she was not one soul in two bodies. She was Cecil, and Kinokaze was Kinokaze. The two were bonded as any other friends would be, and they had been for almost a decade, but they were not bound forever, and not by anything deeper than emotions and feelings. One day this war would end, or one of them would die, they would have to part and the partnership would be dissolved, even if the fondness and friendship remained. Even at the brink of death and beyond, these Khaleeshir would never truly part. Existence would be a nightmare for whomever of the pair remained, and for that, Cecil did not envy them.

Everyone had gone to sleep not long after their reunion. For all they missed their dragons, they needed their sleep. Kyeit had run them ragged for the last few days. They would need a good night's rest before continuing in the morning.

While the Khaleeshir slept, Kyeit and Cecil would keep guard. Their dragons would watch from the air above, while they guarded the camp from below. They sat across from one another, with nothing between them but a campfire and the very palpable tension.

Finally, certain that the Khaleeshir were asleep, Cecil pounced. "You need to explain to them eventually."

Kyeit blinked. "I don't know what you mean."

"I told them about the Kotharii," Cecil explained.

"You *what*?" hissed Kyeit.

Cecil shrugged. "I also told them about Venu'shael."

Kyeit gave Cecil a severe look. "So soon?!"

Cecil was unapologetic. "And I also told them about Bizhak Harzok and the Brown Dragon Clan."

Kyeit was incredulous. "We weren't supposed to tell them about that yet!"

"They needed to know," Cecil said plainly.

"The High Council—" started Kyeit.

"The High Council is wrong!" Cecil protested.

"Even those who don't agree with the High Council didn't want me to say anything," Kyeit pleaded. "They weren't supposed to know. It's too much knowledge for them too quickly. King Anducaerleonis—"

"Leon," Cecil interjected, "He prefers King Leon, you know that. Often not even the king part."

Kyeit rolled her eyes. "King Leon was going to tell them once they were ready to move on with their training."

Cecil scanned Kyeit, searching for something in her face or eyes. "You have no love for the High Council, so why are you suddenly doing their bidding? You know they're just trying to control the Khaleeshir. It's not right; my uncle says so—your *father* said so!"

Kyeit scowled. "These orders came from your uncle *and* my father!"

The two remained silent. They scanned the camp after Kyeit's outburst to ensure they hadn't woken the aurally sensitive Khaleeshir. When they were certain it was safe, they continued their voices hushed whispers barely audible over the crackling flames and popping wood.

"Why their sudden change of heart?" asked Cecil, very confused. "I thought we weren't keeping secrets from the Khaleeshir."

"We're not," Kyeit said. Her voice was heavy. Her exhaustion shone through; her mask had cracked. "We're...my father felt it best that we do not burden the Khaleeshir with too much information at once. He didn't want to demoralize them—these are not easy foes to defeat."

"He didn't seem to mind inundating them with information and responsibility when it came to the defence of Xiar," argued Cecil.

"That was different," Kyeit protested. "It's one thing to fight off a human army, or a dragon clan, but it took all five Metallic Dragons to kill Bizhak Harzok, and even then it was a close battle. They could conceive the idea of defeating Altimara...how does one begin to conceive defeating that eleven-headed monstrosity? Besides, there's no knowing if it will even be revived by Tenebrae. He'd have to find their remains first. The Metallic Dragons are the only ones who know where its remains were laid to rest, and the Blue and Red Dragon Clans have kept Venu'shael's remains safe for a millennium."

"That's the problem! He's just as likely to do it as he is to not. Just because the remains *appear* safe, does not actually make them safe. We need to prepare them for it."

"We have such precious, limited time," Kyeit argued. "Why prepare them for something they may never have to face?"

"What happens if they do, and they're *not* prepared? Do we lose this generation too?" Cecil demanded. "What then? Do we wait another thousand years to try again? There may not be an Enayra left by then."

Kyeit had no response. She hung her head. When she had not responded for several minutes, Cecil breached the topic again.

"You need to tell them," she said gently. "You need to tell them what you fear; why you've been driving them so hard since Xiar. And you need to tell them why."

"I can't," Kyeit mumbled. "I can't go back there again."

"You must," Cecil insisted. "And you need to face your father's death, Kyeit. I know why you're pushing this down and pretending that nothing's changed. I know why you're ignoring this and not letting yourself feel."

Kyeit didn't respond.

"They deserve to know too. They're our friends, and they care about you," Cecil implored.

Again, no response.

A log popped as it was split by the heat of the flames. Cecil poked it with a stick to ensure it didn't roll from the fire pit.

"I think Kanaahn deserves to know, at the very least," Cecil added.

With that, Kyeit stood up, grabbed her sword, and walked from the fire to patrol the perimeters of the camp without a further word.

Cecil remained cool and collected, though inside she knew she had pushed too far, and regret began to grip her. But what was she supposed to do? She wasn't going to just let her closest friend sit there and refuse to feel because she was too afraid. Cecil had been harsh, but it was for the right reasons. She had known Kyeit for six years; they had been recruited into the Darond around the same time and trained together. She had seen Kyeit at her best, and her worst. Cecil knew that if Kyeit didn't face her fears—and her grief—she'd be back at her worst shortly.

Chapter VI

The walk from the campsite to Felidrun was long, quiet, and dim. Though not for any reason than the thick branches and foliage that covered the pathways in the forest.

The dragons had been forced to fly, as they could not weave so easily between the massive trees and knotted roots. Once Risasi had tried and tripped; he had not been pleased, and the tree had been left with several scorch and claw marks in return. The dragons would keep a safe distance once the group reached Felidrun, and all mental communication would need to be dampened and eschewed until they were reunited.

The Kotharii were adept at being able to infiltrate the minds of those around them without people knowing. They could somehow sense a mental link and were able to spy upon it. No one was certain how; only that it had been the downfall of far too many Dragon Knights over the years.

It had been a while since Kanaahn had last travelled on foot. They had spent the last several months living in the lap of relative luxury with the wagons and camels. The strength and stamina he had gained from the Blood Covenant had come in handy. It was a two-day walk to Felidrun, where they would meet their Darond contacts at a modest inn known as the Sleeping Soldier. It was a popular fair for many locals and had been in business for at least the last decade and a half.

From what Kyelt had told them, Felidrun was a medium-sized city of about nine thousand people. It was walled, well protected, with a decent-sized garrison. Kyeit had warned them that even though they were in friendly territory, they had to assume they were still being pursued by Altimaran spies. If *they* could disappear into a crowd in Felidrun, so could a well-trained spy. Kyeit had speculated that some of the Altimaran Black Blades had been dispatched to track them down, though she couldn't be certain.

Cecil had said the Kotharii were more likely to be the ones in charge of the hunt.

The group was not likely to be attacked in the open, if at all. It was more likely that Tenebrae planned to have the Khaleeshir stalked and monitored closely. However, Kyeit did not relinquish her belief that, given the opportunity, the Kotharii would kill them all in cold blood.

Valence and Kinokaze were of a different opinion. They mused that the Khaleeshir were far more valuable to Tenebrae alive than dead, and so their deaths would achieve nothing. Tenebrae was more likely to capture them, and so he would have the Khaleeshir followed until such a time he was ready to pluck them from the Darond's grasp and take them for his own.

Kyeit had warned the Khaleeshir they would need to keep their heads down and disappear into the crowd as much as possible until they were safe in Ethon.

From everything he had heard, Kanaahn would have preferred if the Black Blades were chasing them, instead of these Kotharii—and he knew nothing about the Kotharii. The Black Blades, on the other hand, were the most feared clandestine organization in Altimara. Everyone expected the Altimaran army to bang on your door, ready to drag you off for any crimes they could concoct and put you to immediate death or to finish you on the breaking wheel, or whatever gruesome death they could imagine. But no one expected to be pulled off the street by a fruit vendor or sandal merchant who turned out to be a Black Blade in disguise. No one knew what happened to a person who had been taken away by the Black Blades, only that they were never seen or heard from again. The Black Blades were reserved only for traitors and the worst of criminals.

The Khaleeshir had all heard the story of when Shooter once thought he and his friends had seen somebody be abducted by the Black Blades. Shooter swore a man was standing by a merchant one second, and then gone the next without so much as a trace of the man—or the merchant—after, but Shooter had been the only one to see it. The event happened so fast, and everyone else in the area had been preoccupied with the concurrent stampede. A group of Mhokshi lizard-beasts broke free of their corral and rampaged down the street as they tried to flee a gnar that had made its way above ground during the day. Shooter swore he saw a figure in black leather armour, with a black blade kidnap the merchant and the customer. He claimed they had been shoved into a basket, secured, and thrown onto a wagon that sped off away from the stampede. No one else could corroborate Shooter's story, since they had all been watching the chaotic procession of the gnar and Mhokshi lizards.

These Kotharii, on the other hand, were so mysterious and unknown, that they seemed just as likely to Kanaahn to devour the Khaleeshir and drink their blood as they were to slaughter them and dump the tiny pieces that remained into a nearby river.

Kanaahn looked up at Kyeit, who led the column through the dense woodland. She wore the mask of a fearless warrior, but the anxiety that was emanating from her was so palpable it might as well have been a perfume. Her knuckles were white on her sword grip. She never put that sword away and Kanaahn had never seen Kyeit that paranoid. Kyeit reacted to every sound with suspicion, and she almost took Kanaahn's head off once when he returned from relieving himself in the woods. Even the slightest quiver of a tree or branch, or the shudder of a bush was enough to set Kyeit on edge. Normally, Kyeit had always been calm and collected, the perfect picture of poise and battle-hardened steadiness. Even during the Siege of Xiar and subsequent death of her father Kyeit did not break her tough exterior—though Kanaahn knew, at least when her father died, she was dealing with the grief and hurt privately, and on her own.

Cecil had explained that it was the Kotharii that had scared Kyeit so much, even more than the Black Blades or anything else Tenebrae could throw at them. No one had told

Kanaahn why. Kanaahn had a theory or two, but nothing he was going to voice to Kyeit—she was on edge enough without him prying into her personal life.

It was three long and exhausting days before they left the cover of the woods for the main road to Felidrun, and only once the gate was in view did they emerge from the wooded paths. Upon their arrival, Kanaahn could see that Felidrun was not the largest or fanciest of settlements. It did not compare with the splendour of Xiar or the massive fortress that was Ottogard. The walls were modest and squat but looked to at least be made of sturdy stone. The homes were one or two stories, with a mixture of thatched and wood-shingled roofs. Guards calmly watched the gates from either side, but rarely intervened or questioned any locals they recognized. It seemed like any other town. It reminded Kanaahn a lot of Kula if the Crown had actually cared about it.

Kyeit had already handed out their fake identification papers. Fake names and identities would be harder to track than if they travelled with their actual names. They had also been briefed on their fake reason for travelling to Felidrun. The story they had practised was that the group were mercenaries from the small village of Brennus, south of Felidrun—which would explain to the guards why they were entering the town from the southern gate, and why they came armed—who were going out to Ethon for a job. Their reason for coming to Felidrun was to stock up on supplies and purchase some horses—to help explain why they would soon be leaving on horseback when they had not arrived that way. In case they were questioned about their false point of origin, Kyeit had briefed the Khaleeshir on Brennus—apparently, it was a town of fifteen hundred people, and the only horses were privately held by the local landed knight and were not for sale.

Kyeit had forced the group to practice their excuses and memorize their false identities and learn to answer to them. Shooter joked that if they practised too long they'd never be able to go back to being who they were before—Kyeit did not appreciate the joke quite as much as everyone else.

Despite all their preparation and practice, Kyeit did all the talking when they reached the guard house. Within a few minutes, the guards waved them through with their fake papers and identities. It was almost too easy, and it put the Khaleeshir on edge. They had lived in Kula, and they had fought the Town Watch enough to know a trap when they saw one. Cecil reassured them that they were only being paranoid. Estion was Darond friendly, and the Baron of Felidrun, Llewyth Gruffydd, had been good friends with the previous Grand Master.

Surprisingly, this did not abate the teens' worry.

Kanaahn scanned the streets. They were in the middle of a crowd in the market square. They kept to the edges and avoided all eye contact. No one even noticed they were there; that was how Kyeit preferred it. The market at Felidrun was not unlike the one in Kula. The differences were the wares, the people, the climate, and the guards that gave a shit. It was almost enough to make Kanaahn homesick—almost.

Kycit led the group down a narrow alley toward their real goal: the Sleeping Soldier Inn. It was, as the name suggested, an inn and a public house. Cecil raved about their venison pottage and their ale was the best around. She claimed that she'd often plan trips across Enayra with a stop in Felidrun kept in mind, just so she could get a good meal and a decent drink.

When they arrived at the Sleeping Soldier, they found a large, three-storied building that leaned a little to the left. It looked more like a cosy farmhouse than a public house. If it weren't for the painted sign hanging above the door Kanaahn would never have guessed they had reached their destination. The building had a stable and barn around the back, and a vegetable and herb garden just outside of what was likely the kitchen. Several chimneys loosed cosy puffs of smoke into the sky, and Kanaahn could already feel the warmth of the place envelope him. Exhaustion hit him, and he wanted nothing more than a pot of stew and a cup of wine.

Cecil saw the look on Kanaahn's face and laughed. "Darond agents always say this place is enchanted. Once you see it, you're suddenly overtaken by the need to go inside and rest for a spell."

"It already smells better than the pubs or inns in Kula," Shooter pointed out.

"A barn smells better than the fare in Kula," snorted Arial.

Drunkenness and drunken messes were staples of a Kulan establishment. One time the group had been witness to a travelling merchant who had threatened to kill the proprietor of the Broke Neck Camel for finding one such drunken mess rotting in his bedsheets.

"Anything we should know before we head inside?" Arkas asked.

Cecil nodded. "If you get dancing, don't expect to stop until you've collapsed from exhaustion. Banalor the Bard is notorious for keeping the party going until people pass out in the bar."

Shooter grinned wide. "Sounds like my kind of bard."

The group entered the in to find it a moderately busy place. People were laughing and joking or talking loudly as they told stories over mugs of ale. Pipe smoke clung to the rafters like dense mist. The smell of freshly baked bread and biscuits wafted out from the kitchens and into the dining hall. There were several tables dedicated only for use in games of lancet, or for use in a game of nezarik—which required cards—and tabbat—which required dice.

"I regret leaving my deck and dice in Kula," Shooter said with a frown. "I could really go for a competitive game of something right now."

"Probably best you forgot them then," Arial muttered.

Shooter rubbed his hands together. "Maybe someone will let me borrow theirs."

Kanaahn was impressed. "Never thought I'd see a lancet board in a public house. It was always a game for well-to-dos where we're from. Not something the common folk knew how to play. We only learned because Arial's mother insisted."

"It's quite popular in Estion," explained Cecil. "In Asardaea too. Though the rules in Asardaea vary slightly, and they have a few extra units that the other nations consider illegal."

Before Kanaahn could press Cecil for more information, a loud cry erupted from behind the bar: "Welcome patrons!" Whoever shouted at them proceeded to whack a bell with a small hammer several times.

The patrons of the bar all stopped what they were doing, raised their drinks in the air and shouted their own hearty "Welcome patrons!"

Kanaahn's hand instinctively went to his katana. Cecil grabbed his wrist and shook her head.

The man who greeted them and rang the bell—a tall, portly Espian man with a bald head and thick moustache—came out from behind the bar. He wiped his hands on his dirty apron and held it out for each of the group to shake. Kanaahn held out his hand in return and suddenly felt his body vibrate with the force of the handshake. The room spun slightly when the man finally released Kanaahn and moved on to his next victim.

"Welcome, welcome!" he cheered, obviously thrilled to meet his new patrons. "Some familiar faces, and some new ones I see, yes. I'm Ruoth. I'm the owner of this establishment. What can I get for you?"

"A table to start," Kyeit answered. "We'll be needing rooms for the night, as well."

Ruoth turned and pointed to a large wooden table near the back corner of the room, next to a fireplace. It was opposite the entrance and had a good view of the entire bar, and the entertainment for the night. Then he turned back towards the bar. "Take a seat and I'll be right with you with some food. Ale?"

No one objected and the group made their way over to their table.

Ruoth chuckled. "Excellent. I'll bring you by a round shortly—Oi! Ogdyn! Vinella! What have I told you about dancing on the tables? Get down this instant!"

As they crossed the pub, the group passed by the bard and his group of fellow musicians. The bard was playing a lute, two of his colleagues were singing, and another was playing an instrument that looked like someone had plucked some poor, unfortunate bird of all its feathers, and sounded like they had proceeded to torture it mercilessly afterwards. From what Kanaahn knew, this was in fact, a bagpipe, though a rather simple version of the instrument. It had only a single drone, in addition to its chanter and blowpipe. They belted out a surprisingly gentle tune, despite the bagpipe. It sounded almost like a gentle lullaby, though Kanaahn recognized the lyrics as an old Asardaean ballad about the first emperor, Volesus. Kanaahn was even more impressed at the collection of instruments that sat behind the musicians. He could see everything from a hurdy-gurdy to drums, to several reed flutes and even a sackbut.

Shooter flashed a smile over at the bard Cecil had mentioned earlier. The bard winked back as the group passed. He was a handsome young man, about their age, if maybe a little older, with olive skin, dark eyes, and eyebrows so thin and well-groomed that could be used as rapiers. He sported a small, pointed beard on the tip of his chin, and his long, mahogany-coloured hair flowed down past his shoulders in a cascade of waves, curls, and braids.

The group filed into the hewn benches on either side of the table and began to light the lamps that sat on their tables.

Ruoth soon returned with a wooden tray carrying six tankards of ale. "It's our own personal brew; we make it ourselves. We've also got wine and spirits, some of it made here, some of it imported, if after you're done the ale, you find yourself in need of something stronger."

Spirits were not something they had drank often in Kula, due to cost and scarcity. They had celebrated the death of Jerrin with a toast of Asardaean brandy but had since not touched the stuff.

Ruoth next placed a platter of cheese and a steaming loaf of bread on the table. "Just to get your stomachs filled until your pottage comes. We have fine venison, barley, and sage pottage on today."

Cecil's eyes lit up at the mention of the pottage. Ruoth winked at her, then deftly placed a small cloth on the table, before he walked away without a word.

Kanaahn drank deep of the ale, despite his preference for wine. He had not realized how thirsty he had been until drink had been placed before him. It was surprisingly herbaceous, with a light smoky flavour.

"They add the herbs from their garden, and they grow and malt the barley themselves," explained Cecil. "Ruoth explained it to me when I was here last."

Arkas wiped some crumbs from the corner of his mouth. "When were you here last?"

"On the way to Xiar, to meet you, actually." Cecil paused for thought. "It hadn't been an urgent dispatch until *after* I had spent the night here. First messenger hawk in the morning told me of the impending siege, so I was forced to depart early."

Kanaahn shoved a block of cheese into his mouth. He could taste the nuts Ruoth had hidden within the unsuspecting wheel of cheese. It was sweeter, flatter, and harder than the creamy, soft, camel cheese he was used in Altimara. Cecil explained that they used sheep's milk to produce this cheese. It was a delicacy in Asardaea, as was mixing in nuts and other herbs. Ruoth's cheese was meant to be an imitative homage to Asardaean sheep cheese, known as becorus.

Kyeit took the folded cloth and opened it to find a key and a note. She pocketed the key and unrolled the note to read it by the dim lamplight of the table. Several silent moments passed before she spoke again. "Our room is the big room on the third floor. Our horses and supplies that we'll be taking with us tomorrow are ready and are out in the stable. He's marked the stalls with a piece of red cloth for us. Everything is on the house."

"All that secrecy for our accommodations?" asked Shooter.

"There's some more," admitted Kyeit. "Condolences for my father, for one. Congratulations on what we pulled off at Xiar. There's also a rumour going around that the Kotharii have been sighted near the same mountain we crossed to get here."

Cecil frowned. "So, they're definitely on our trail."

Shooter yanked the note from Kyeit's hand and pocketed it in his cloak. "Unless they're sitting at this very table or standing in the doorway with their blades drawn, I don't want to worry about what *might* chasing us anymore."

"Shooter!" Kyeit hissed. She grabbed for the note it was already long gone into one of Shooter's multitude of pockets.

"No!" Shooter cautioned. "You've been on edge since we left the wagons. It's time we all lightened up a bit and enjoyed ourselves. We're staying at a lovely, cosy inn, with live music, a cute bard, and delicious food—seriously this becorus is delicious and this bread is to die for. I don't want to hear any more about the Kotharii until we leave tomorrow. Tonight, we're going to enjoy ourselves."

"Shooter, you idiot—" Kyeit started.

Shooter stopped her by shoving a small cube of cheese into her mouth. "If we sit here, all whispering and tense, we're going to look even more suspicious than we already do. We're supposed to be mercenaries, so it's best we bloody act like some!" Shooter stood up and called to the bard. "Do you know the Dance of the Camel Bride?"

The bard turned to the back of the room, where Shooter and the others were, winked at Shooter and started giving orders to his fellow troupe members. One of them grabbed the hurdy-gurdy, another went for a large drum, and the third kept his bagpipe with him, while the bard, Banalor, began to sing.

Arial gave Shooter a knowing look. Shooter shrugged and took her by the hand. Arial did not protest, however. Every Kulan knew the Dance of the Camel Bride. It was based on an old local legend, though the song had become more famous than the story in recent generations. It was a simple song; the same few measures repeating at increasing speed until it reached a crescendo, crashed to a halt, and then slowly began to pick up speed again until either the musicians or dancers collapsed from exhaustion—if it was played properly, anyway, but few musicians outside of Kula went that far anymore. Eventually, the lyrics would melt away to the wild thrums of the music and the dancers lost themselves to the dance.

Arial was dragged to the dance floor as she and Shooter began to dance the traditional duet dance, spinning and whirling about each other like leaves in a hurricane.

Arkas and Cecil gave each other a look before sauntering off to the dance floor together to join the cavalcade.

"What are they doing?" demanded Kyeit. "They're going to draw attention to us!"

Kanaahn shrugged. "Having fun, I suppose. Would you like to dance?"

Kyeit shot Kanaahn a venomous look, but Kanaahn would not be belayed. He grabbed Kyeit by the hand and dragged her up to the dance floor. Kyeit protested and complained, but Kanaahn wasn't hearing it.

"Dammit, Kyeit. I'm not asking you to feel happy; you're going through a lot and grieving right now. I understand that, and I don't expect you to just get over it, but I need you to remember that it's okay to at least feel *something*."

Kyeit looked as if she had just seen Kanaahn swallow a frog. "But...I'm not familiar with the dance."

Kanaahn smiled. "It's quite simple. Just don't spin into the fire."

He eased Kyeit through the motions, moving with her, bobbing, and weaving around each other. It wasn't long before Kyeit had picked up the intricacies of the whirling dance. She moved like a whirlwind through Altimaran deserts, blowing the sand about in a parade of dust.

Several of the other patrons—a few of them Altimaran traders—joined in on the fun, and before long the dancefloor abounded with whirling and twirling and all kinds of screaming and revelry.

* * *

Ruoth had waited until the group sat back down—again, panting, exhausted, red in the face, and covered in sweat—to bring the pottage and more ale. Kanaahn and the others thanked him profusely as they drained their tankards, dribbling ale down their chins and onto their clothes. A cheer went up from the patrons, and Kanaahn and the others raised their mugs in response.

"That was so much fun," exclaimed Cecil.

Shooter had remained behind to talk with Banalor, so it was only Kanaahn, Arial, Kyeit, Cecil and Arkas who had returned to their table. Since their foray to the dancefloor, Kyeit's disapproval and grim determination to remain in a corner and brood had been replaced by a genuine smile for the first time in a long time. She had not completely forgotten her grief, but she had, at least, been given a reprieve from it, if only for now.

47

"I'm sorry, Kyeit," Kanaahn said. "But Shooter was right, we needed to lighten up."

Kyeit shrugged and sipped her ale. "I suppose he had a point. Things were getting a little grim. Besides, it was a lot of fun dancing up there. You did this a lot in Kula?"

Arkas laughed. "Only when we had a reason."

"Or a bit too much to drink," snarked Arial.

"We Kulans know how to party," added Kanaahn. "There's not a Kulan that doesn't know the Dance of the Camel Bride. It's a staple of weddings, parties, important occasions—"

"—Drunken benders," Arial continued.

A barmaid came and gathered the empty tankards for refilling and the group immediately began to down their pottage with a voracious hunger.

"You weren't kidding about the food, Cecil," Kanaahn said through chunks of venison and potato.

Cecil gently blew on her spoon. "I don't joke about the Sleeping Soldier's food."

Ruoth returned with more tankards and a bright-as-ever smile and handed out another round of ale to everyone.

Kanaahn could see, from the corner of his eye, Banalor and Shooter going off to their own table in another corner of the room as the troupe took a break for refreshment. He shot Arial a look. "What about Amber?" he muttered.

But Arial only shrugged in response.

"Who's Amber?" asked Cecil.

"She was a girl who worked as a fence for stolen goods back in Kula. She was also a great information dealer," explained Kanaahn. "Shooter was sweet on her. I thought the two might end up together—I think they did for a bit...before we left."

"Does he love her?" Kyeit asked. She showed a surprising interest, and Kanaahn had wondered if the ale was the cause.

"More than he loves himself," Arkas joked.

"Head over heels," added Arial.

Cecil looked confused. "So, why's he with that bard?"

Arial shrugged again. "Shooter does what he wants; goes where he wants. He's a free spirit. For all we know we may never see Amber again—if she survives all this."

"If *we* survive all this," chided Arkas. He drank deep from his tankard.

"She'll survive," Kanaahn protested. "She'll survive Kula better than anyone else there."

Kanaahn had always liked Amber. Not in the way Shooter did, of course, but he liked her as a person. She had always been fun to spend time with, and she was one of Shooter's informants he didn't hate having to go visit. Amber was witty, smart as a whip, and she was incredibly resourceful—Amber was downright dangerous, by Kanaahn's estimation, but most importantly, she was good for Shooter. She had been there for him when Shooter wouldn't let anyone else be. Kanaahn had only found out the true nature of Shooter's relationship with his father and stepmother recently, and he had only found out by mistake. He had picked up a conversation between Shooter and Arial when they had been travelling to Xiar; it was a conversation Kanaahn wasn't supposed to hear, but his wandering attention span and increasing hearing had led him to learn the truth. Arial had always known, though she admitted she was never certain how much of the truth she was told. Shooter had a habit of keeping back as much as he told—often more, but all that Kanaahn kept to himself.

The group had used the silence to rest and eat their pottage. Cecil was not overstating the quality of the food when she called it the best food in Estion. Kanaahn had never eaten anywhere else in Estion, but after eating at the Sleeping Soldier, he wasn't certain he ever would.

* * *

It was well past midnight when the last of the patrons had stumbled on home, and the barmaids who lived on-site returned to their boarding houses behind the main pub. Those who didn't had been escorted home by some of the regular patrons. Shooter and Banalor had snuck out for a walk. Ruoth had given them a key so they could get back inside if they came back after everyone had gone to bed.

Ruoth finally locked the door after his patrons and returned to the table to sit with the Khaleeshir. He brought with him something stronger than ale, for he had offered some of his finer spirits and beverages to the Khaleeshir in honour of their arrival. Cecil chose an Asardaean brandy known as Romontyac, which took its name from the city of Romontya, where it was distilled. Kanaahn had the same. Kyeit went for a Xiaran fortified wine known as Antigori; it had been a favourite of her father's. Arkas chose a small bottle of rice wine from Espias, and Arial chose an Asardaean white wine from Pescadum.

"It's a pleasure to meet you, Khaleeshir." Ruoth bowed his head and raised his glass of Romontyan.

"Thank you for your kindness and patronage," Kanaahn responded. "You've been incredibly kind and generous to us."

Ruoth let out a booming laugh that shook his belly as much as it shook the table. "You're the Khaleeshir! If that doesn't entitle you to a little special treatment what would the point of all this be?"

"It's not why we do this," Arial reassured him. Her face turned a bright shade of red—though Kanaahn couldn't tell if it was from the alcohol or the embarrassment.

Ruoth waved his hand and rocked back in his chair. Some of his brandy splashed onto the floor due to his big gestures. "No, but I'd like to do this for you as a thanks. You saved Xiai, and you showed those Altimaran dogs they can't just bully smaller nations. By the by—since we're talking openly, my real name is Tohru. I use Ruoth as an alias."

"Since we're giving out names, I'm Arial Gainsborough."

"Arkas Nazzer."

"You know us, Tohru," Cecil said. She gestured to herself and Kyeit as she spoke.

"I'm Kanaahn Saatus, and the guy who ran off with your bard is Shooter Maxim."

Ruoth-now-Tohru gave Kanaahn an enlightened look as if Kanaahn had just reminded him of something he had forgotten. If that were the case, however, Tohru did not say anything about it and instead refilled Kanaahn's glass.

"So, this whole pub and inn is just a front for a Darond safe house?" asked Arkas.

49

"That's correct," said Tohru. "It's a stopover for Darond agents, Dragon Knights, smugglers, allies, and anyone else who needs it. I use it to pass along messages, goods, and other contraband under the table. Being this close to the border and on the road to the capital, I get a lot of Altimarans passing through, and sometimes I get information from drunken merchants and diplomats. Information I'm able to pass on to the Darond, and they can put to good use. There are more secrets passed around in a public house than behind a tapestry in the royal palace."

"What got you into the cause?" Arial asked.

"I was always in the cause—it's a familial thing. I used to be a Darond soldier and occasionally a spy, but about fifteen years back I left fieldwork behind me. Kotharii were going around, hunting down Darond members in their homes. They killed my sister and her husband...and I knew I was on their list." Tohru's face grew sombre and withdrawn. It was a far cry from his normally cheerful demeanour. "So, I changed my name, put on some weight, shaved my head, grew a moustache, and moved to Felidrun where I opened a bar and continued to serve the Darond by other means. No one ever suspects the bartender."

Kyeit rummaged through her small pack and pulled out a rather thick letter. "Can you ensure this gets to Kaltar's family?"

Tohru beamed and pocketed the letter. "Good ol' Kaltar! How's he doing?"

"Last we saw he and Edva were stationed near the border in Altimara, by the Spine," Kyeit explained. "They took our camels and wagons. I don't know if they've been moved since."

"Blasted desert," spat Tohru. "It's an unbearable, dry heat, and the sand is damnable. I don't envy him. I'll see that his family gets this. I'll contact headquarters and see where I can send a return letter and a care package for him and Edva."

"You're the best, Tohru," declared Kyeit. She raised a glass to the innkeeper, and everyone seconded the toast.

Tohru tossed back his head and drained his glass. "Well, with that, I must get to bed. I'm glad I got a chance to talk to you and meet you all officially, but I've got an early morning tomorrow—I still have an inn to run, and all. You're welcome to stay up as late as you need and eat or drink whatever you'd like. It's all on me; don't worry about it."

Everyone thanked Tohru, and the larger-than-life innkeeper disappeared to his room off the kitchen.

Arial poured another glass of wine. "He's a hard worker."

Kanaahn nodded. "Generous too."

"Tohru is one of the best the Darond has to offer," Cecil said. "We don't deserve him, but he keeps on coming back."

They sat and spoke like this for several hours, sipping each drink as it was brought. They spoke about their lives, their fears hopes and dreams. Cecil had divulged that as a child she had always wanted to be a baker and open a small shop in the Craftsman's Ring of Malatrion. Her parents had always disapproved, proclaiming that she was destined for higher callings, but in the end, Cecil joined the Darond instead.

Kyeit had wanted to be a city guard in Xiar, and eventually a senator until she could run for Regent Princess. Instead, she joined the Darond after her mother died in the line of duty.

Arial had always wanted to take over her parents' merchant business, and move the headquarters to Targrond, on the sea—really, anywhere that wasn't Kula would've been nice.

If Arkas hadn't become a Khaleeshir, he would have departed Kula after his seventeenth birthday and made his way to Estion. He had plans to become a hunter-trapper in the wilds. His father had always struggled as a hunter and butcher in Kula, being in a desert and all, and refused to pass the struggling business on to Arkas and his siblings. He had wanted his children to go out and hunt in a more prosperous place.

Kanaahn had always planned to leave Kula eventually, but he had no idea what he would have done once he departed. He had considered being a mercenary, or even travelling to Espias to find out more about his family. To be honest, Kanaahn didn't even know if he *was* Espian, only that his father owned a katana, and a katana was an Espian blade, but, the way he saw it, someone had made the sword in Espias, and maybe that person was still alive. If Kanaahn could find the original swordsmith, perhaps they could enlighten him as to who had bought this blade all those years ago.

Shooter had not returned to the table and instead had continued to keep the company of Banalor the Bard, wherever they were now. Earlier in the night, Banalor and Shooter had sung together several times whenever Banalor was forced to return to his troupe mates. Kanaahn had forgotten how beautiful a singing voice Shooter had. His friend didn't always put his skills to use in that regard. Kanaahn couldn't say he approved of Shooter's jaunts, mostly because of how much he liked Amber and how good he thought they were together, but he wasn't about to take away any shred of happiness Shooter might find in another person. Instead, he sat, sipping his Romontyan brandy, and talked with his friends.

* * *

Shooter was not proud of what he did, and worse, his head was a mess of feelings and thoughts. They swirled together in his head like some horrid sewer of emotion. He had let Banalor think of him as the small-town boy, from an uneducated and unexperienced background; new to love and inexperienced with feelings. Shooter had let Banalor wine and dine him and acted like the bright-eyed fool the entire time—all for the sake of a little pleasure, and a bit of escapism from...whatever his life had become since he left Kula. Shooter had done what he had to take care of himself. It was what he always did. He looked after himself first. Shooter was a survivor. For all he wasn't proud of what he did, he couldn't say that he regretted it.

No. That was a lie. A lie he told himself; even he knew as much. He could lie to anyone, but Shooter couldn't lie to himself. If he did not regret it, why would there be guilt sitting plainly in his gut? He kept trying to quash, strangle and ignore this guilt at every turn but the feeling refused to go away. It was the guilt he felt over Amber, in part. He had loved her—no, he still loved her, but he had not gone to see her before the group left Kula. Things piled up. Shooter had been distracted by the hatching of the dragons. He had literally been dragged off by Arkas on his way to visit her. But Shooter hadn't gone back after.

51

By the time Shooter finally realized he had forgotten about Amber in the rush to leave without being noticed he had already been gone three days, and it was far too late to turn back. In that moment, out in the sands, staring into the embers of a dying fire Shooter had felt gut churn like a stormy sea, and he threw up. He had had the night watch, and no one had noticed—except Risasi. He had vowed to himself to go back and see Amber once he returned to Kula, once when this was all over, of course. But the doubt had nagged at him, and the fear that he would never return ate away at his surety. Shooter feared that he or Amber would not survive whatever was to come, or that she would move on without him.

The feelings got worse the deeper this gnar hole went. When they became Khaleeshir. When they went to Xiar and battled the Altimaran army. Now they were on their way to Ethon to continue their training. The further they got from Kula; the less Shooter felt like he would ever see it again. Or Amber.

To cope Shooter drowned his doubts, fears, and feelings in countless escapades with men and women. There had been the Darond soldier at the Tormenting Pinnacle, and one of the kitchen cooks. He had secretly visited a mixed-gender brothel several times in Xiar, and a few of his chambermaids and local guards had become late-night callers of his. Each time he hoped the guilt would leave him, and each time it grew and burrowed deeper in his soul, becoming harder and harder to uproot.

Shooter instinctively felt at one of the pockets of his cloak. It bulged with papers; all the letters he had written or tried to write. He left no evidence of them anywhere. He had written them to Amber; apologies, stories, anecdotes of his time with the Darond and training with his friends. He poured his hopes, fears, and feelings into these letters...but he had never sent them. Some were drafts he had abandoned partway through. Others he could never muster up the courage to send. Others still were too long and rambling for Shooter's taste, and he refused to send those to Amber. He had gone from trying to explain himself, and his absence, to pretending like this had always been the plan, and that he and Amber were always communicating by letter—playing it off like nothing happened. He had wound up, after several letters, rambling on about his feelings and his guilt.

No. Shooter felt it best that these letters never be sent. They could only do more harm than good. Going forward, he would need to keep his poor coping habits in check. He could not persist with these endless, meaningless flings. Not so much for the care of the other party, but more for his own sanity. The guilt would only continue to consume him...

Shooter kicked a stone and watched it skip across the cobbles of the street. He wished he could speak with Risasi, but Kyeit insisted they keep their mental bond muted—not the easiest thing for a Khaleeshir to do—lest they be detected by the Kotharii. At least he still had Arial to speak with. She was always the voice of sound reason.

Shooter's mind wandered to the Kotharii. The whole reason for Kyeit's fear and anxiety, and the reason they were forced to scurry about in the dark like rats hiding from the farm cat. What were these damned creatures? Not man, not beast. Perhaps a little of both? Some said part dragon, part man, but no one knew for sure. Shooter didn't know if *he* wanted to be the one to find out. If something could scare Kyeit, what right did he have to challenge them so carelessly?

Shooter was at least glad that he could break Kyeit from her stoic stupor. She had become a needless source of stress and pressure on the group, and Shooter feared this trip would end in another Drakhart before they reached Ethon if this continued. Hopefully, the evening had been cathartic and helpful to her.

Shooter sighed and looked up at the full moon above. Even a night-time walk in a strange town was painful to him. Kula was dangerous, it was hot and stagnant—in both atmosphere and climate. There was excitement, murder, and intrigue around every corner after hours. Perhaps a mugging, or a stabbing—one could not walk through the streets at Kula at night without proper safety in numbers or being sufficiently armed. From one door to the next, you'd have witnessed six stabbings, a murder, twelve beggars, and at least four shakedowns at the hands of the Town Watch. By contrast, this safe little hamlet was boring. It was not conducive to thinking. Arial would have to do, it seemed.

What was it that Amber wanted to speak to him about? That was what bothered Shooter more than anything. He had loved her, and she loved him, and usually, that was enough...but what had been so important was that she sought out his company beyond their pre-arranged meetings. What had changed...what had Shooter done? Had she found out he strayed? Had *she*? Perhaps that's why Shooter felt guilt for his escapades. No...it was not the straying that bothered Shooter. He had strayed before, as had Amber. They had never been truly exclusive, but they had loved each other, truly and deeply, and they had made the relationship work regardless. Each of them had needs, and sometimes the other was not around to meet them. They loved and forgave each other, despite all that. They worked around it, and there were no hard feelings.

It had suddenly become painfully clear to Shooter what bugged him most. He had spent the entire relationship with Amber as he had spent his relationship with his parents: waiting for the other shoe to drop. Something was about to change in their relationship, Shooter could feel it, and he felt it was his fault—and he feared that. He feared change, and worse of all he feared being rebuked by the one person he truly loved. His parents had been so horrible to him, yet Shooter could not bring himself to abandon them. They wouldn't survive without him. Fuck them for how they treated him—especially his stepmother—but they would starve without him. Well, no, they starved despite how much he brought home. They drank most of Shooter's pay; or snorted it.

Shooter did not need their blood on his hands. Their—albeit accidental—death at the hands of Drakhart had been...a relief. He did not miss them or mourn them. Shooter had felt bad leaving his parents at the time, but the money they took from him before he departed was meant to keep them well cared for until he returned—at least for a month he had planned to be gone. But he never came home at that time, and his absence only seemed to become prolonged the further away he went from Kula.

Shooter realized about halfway through his training in Ottogard that he no longer felt guilt for not returning—on the contrary he should have left years ago. Then came the news of their death; at the hands of Drakhart, no less! Yet unlike the disappearance of Amber, the news of his parents' death had freed Shooter from the burden of returning, or the guilt of having to leave them to languish in the suffering of their own making. Skittic dust, lust, and alcohol were terrible vices.

Shooter kicked another rock. The rock flew and cracked against the side of a house. The sound echoed through the alley, startling even Shooter. He clenched his jaw.

Bastards.

Why hadn't leaving been so easy before? Why did he have to spend years worrying and wondering, years he spent suffering? Fuck them. Shooter shook his head, cleared his throat, and looked up to see he had returned to the Sleeping Soldier. With a heavy sigh, he placed Banalor's key in the lock—he'd need to leave that with Ruoth before he left. Banalor didn't know that Shooter had taken it when he snuck out on him. He turned the key in the lock and opened the door.

* * *

Cecil, Arkas and Arial had gone to bed about an hour or two after Ruoth. Their heads swam and the room spun, and they supported each other as they stumbled up the stairs. They would regret the evening in a few hours when they woke up—but at least they had a few days to recover, as per Kyeit's schedule. She had carefully allotted a few days in Felidrun to "secure supplies", to make it look like they hadn't been prearranged. Kyeit had hoped that would be enough to shake the suspicions of anyone who might doubt their story and report it to anyone asking questions later—like the Black Blades, or other agents of Tenebrae. That was Kyeit's hope, anyway. Kanaahn wasn't too sure if Kyeit's plan was too obvious, or perfectly planned. Perhaps somewhere on the border between the two, running back and forth like some carefree draft dodger.

Yet, the disappearance of their friends had given Kanaahn and Kyeit the rare opportunity to sit and speak until the candles burned out in their sconces. It was now the witching hour, and Kanaahn and Kyeit were halfway through a quarter-wheel of cheese, and two loaves of bread. They had gotten into a bottle of Old Gerovian—known as whiskey in some parts of Enayra, though its original name stuck in Estion—and were now giggling in front of the dying fire.

Kanaahn attempted to throw in another log and almost tumbled into the embers doing so. Kyeit laughed and pulled Kanaahn back by his belt and he fell with a thud on the ground. Both of them laughed like idiots.

Kyeit passed Kanaahn the near-empty bottle of Old Gerovian. Kanaahn took the bottle and sipped; he had grown acclimated to the burn, but he still pulled a face as he swallowed. The taste took some getting used to. He handed back the bottle.

What Kanaahn had not let on was that he wasn't really drunk. He had not had this wide an array of alcohol, to be fair, but he was not unaccustomed to a long night of drinking. Kanaahn and his friends had celebrated the Last of Unthyr Festival with the adults of the village for the last two years in a row—which meant a late night and a lot of wine. Add to that his new constitution, gained from the binding ritual with Djall, and the alcohol took longer to hit him than normal. That was not to say alcohol did not affect him. No, the alcohol still dulled his senses and made his cheeks flush, but he was not a stumbling fool as he made himself appear.

Kyeit threw back her head and drained the bottle of Old Gerovian. She let out a satisfied gasp, but her face contorted from the burn.

Kanaahn looked at Kyeit like a fox about to pounce on a chicken—not physically, but verbally. "While we're on the topic of truth and sharing..." Kanaahn had just finished telling a rather embarrassing story from his youth regarding Shooter, himself, and a camel. "What's got you so bothered lately?

Kyeit shot Kanaahn a half-dazed look. At first, he wasn't certain if she had heard, or even understood him. Perhaps the Old Gerovian had been too much. He would never get

54

an answer now, and never get her to come to terms with her anxiety and fear just as Kanaahn was about to give up hope, Kyeit let out a long, rattling sigh. Her lips flapped as she ran out of breath, and spittle landed in the dying embers. She rubbed her eyes and shifted positions to face Kanaahn.

"Why do you want to know so bad?" asked Kyeit.

"I..." Kanaahn didn't have an answer—not one that wouldn't make him look like an absolute fool or cause a fight to erupt.

Because of what he felt for her.

Because he was her friend, and he was concerned.

Because of what he felt for her.

Because he and everyone else were tired of being driven like a pack horse.

Because of what he felt for her.

Dammit. There was no escaping this, and Kanaahn figured it was better to face embarrassment and shame than the wrath of an inebriated Kyeit.

"Honestly? Because I care, Kyeit. Because I care about you and I'm worried."

"Is that why you tried to pry me with Old Gerovian?" Kyeit asked pointedly.

Kanaahn could feel his face turn red with embarrassment. He needed more practice with Shooter's technique, apparently.

"Did you think this was my first time with alcohol?" Kyeit raised an eyebrow. "I know it's not yours either. Besides, after the binding ritual you're probably in better shape than most seasoned drinkers would be in your shoes, but I appreciate the attempt."

"I—" Kanaahn didn't know how to respond.

Kyeit waited for Kanaahn to come up with the words. She was more patient than Kanaahn gave her credit for.

Finally, he blurted out the first words to came to mind. "If you knew, why did you go along with it?"

"Because I enjoy your company, and...maybe..." Kyeit trailed off. "This sounds stupid but maybe, somewhere deep down, I *wanted* you to try and talk to me. Maybe, with you...I'd be okay bringing it up again. We've grown close since The Tormenting Pinnacle, and I'm starting to feel I can trust you. I just didn't know how else to broach the subject, but that's a big maybe."

Kanaahn didn't know what to say. This time Kyeit was not as patient, and she began to explain her recent behaviour without so much as waiting to see if Kanaahn was even paying attention.

"I fear the Kotharii, not because of what they could do to me physically, but because of what they can do to me emotionally. When I was eight, my mother was killed by the Kotharii. She had been a Dragon Knight with the Darond—it was how she and my father met. She had been the Darond representative to Xiar.

"After my mother was killed I just remember being filled with so much hatred. I wanted revenge, and I was angry...at the Kotharii, at the world, at everything. I just wanted to kill the Kotharii and get revenge. I threw myself into it—I spent extra time training with my sword and in my magical studies, even beyond what my teachers were recommending. My father was concerned...it wasn't abated when I threw in to join the Darond at ten years old.

"That's the minimum age for acceptance into the order as a page, and with my mother's reputation behind me and my father's political ties, there was no way they'd turn me down. They kept me training as a squire—I skipped being a page entirely because of my skill and relations—for the next few years. At some point in that time, they partnered me with Valence. I met Cecil during that time, but we hadn't become friends yet, but all I can remember is this burning desire for revenge in my heart. I had never hated anyone as much as I hated the Kotharii. My blood was fire, my vow was steel—I would not be dissuaded from my path."

"What changed?" asked Kanaahn at an opportune pause.

Kyeit stared hard into the dying flames. "About two years ago I nearly threw away my life, Valence's life, and the life of several colleagues during a routine supply delivery. I had just been made Knight-Captain and was told to lead a small group of squires and their dragons to deliver supplies to a spy camp in the Spine. We were about to head back when we got a warning from the spymaster at the camp that the Kotharii were spotted nearby, and we should wait until things had calmed before departing.

"I didn't listen. I didn't care. I chose to depart immediately—I said we'd be careful, but really I was hoping to bait the Kotharii into a fight. In my rage, I had forgotten I was fourteen, and they were not. It seems so foolish now, but when you're consumed by hatred, reality doesn't matter.

"They took my bait, of course. The Kotharii never waste an opportunity to hamstring the Darond and make us bleed. Valence and I were the only survivors. Valence still bears some scars on her neck and belly, though they're hard to see and she'll never admit to them. I've got scars myself from where their swords pierced and cut me. By all accounts, we should be dead."

"How did you survive?" asked Kanaahn. He was completely enthralled by the story he had never known about Kyeit.

Kyeit chuckled. "As usual, Cecil saved my life. She was flying nearby, escorting Æs, along with a group of fully-fledged Dragon Knights, to meet with Aurum in Espias. Æs could smell the Kotharii...and all the blood. His arrival scared them off before they could finish me, and Cecil and the Dragon Knights rushed me to the nearest safehouse for medical attention. Ironically it ended up being right here. Ruoth—Tohru—called the local medicine woman, and he fed, cared for, and boarded me for two weeks while I recovered. Valence too."

Kanaahn made a face. He was incredibly confused. "How did he board Valence without anyone noticing?"

"The same way Kanothir could become a cat. Metallic Dragons don't have unique breath weapons, but they're able to transform and change size at will. She took on a human appearance and the medicine woman did the rest. I'm still impressed she managed to maintain that transformation spell, even when wounded.

"When I had finally recovered, Æs came back to check on me, and make sure I was still alive. Of course, Æs didn't come alone. He brought Aurum with him. I didn't even know it was Aurum until he introduced himself. I swear I almost threw up. They commended my skills, and ability to—for the most part—survive against the Kotharii at such a young age. Though they admonished my recklessness and willingness to sacrifice so many for such a personal, petty vendetta. Then Aurum had everyone leave the room, and he and I had a very...cathartic talk about revenge.

"I swore that day, before the Great Golden Wyrm himself that I would never again be that person. I would let go of my anger and my rage. That's why I've been so on edge. I'm afraid, Kanaahn. I'm afraid of failing to keep that promise. I don't want to become that person, I don't want to endanger any more lives. Especially now that the lives I'm entrusted with are Enayra's last hope against Tenebrae. I'm afraid of making a mistake because that one mistake could be the one that dooms us all, and it would be my fault. It would be *my* responsibility. I fear the Kotharii, not because I fear death, but because I fear failure."

Kanaahn did not have an answer. He empathized with Kyeit's situation, but he knew nothing he could say would ease her anxiety or fears. Kyeit would feel how Kyeit would feel, and all Kanaahn could do was listen, but not make it better. It was not his place to do so—it was no one's place but Kyeit to fix herself.

When Kanaahn didn't respond immediately, Kyeit prodded his arm. "I bet you regret asking me now."

"No. No, no," Kanaahn sputtered defensively. "But I might feel just a bit worse about prodding as much as I did. I hope I didn't cause you to drag up too much too soon."

Kyeit shook her head. "The Old Gerovian numbs the pain of it all."

Kanaahn gave a concerned look.

Kyeit doubled over laughing. "I'm kidding! Look I...I appreciate you listening to it all. I suppose I needed to let that out sometime. Better now than at an inopportune time. I must have been horrible to put up with."

Kanaahn *really* didn't know how to answer. He tried a hint of sarcasm. "I mean, no more so than usual."

Kyeit shoved him playfully. Kanaahn was still off-kilter from the alcohol and the emotional conversation he and Kyeit had just had, and he fell backwards, his head hitting the floor.

Kyeit threw herself forward. "Are you okay?" She hovered over Kanaahn making sure she hadn't just knocked out a Khaleeshir.

"I'm fine," Kanaahn said through clenched teeth. "It hurts as expected, but I'll be fine." His vision was a little blurry, but he didn't feel concussed, but it didn't matter. His quickened healing would speed along the recovery process of whatever damage was done. Of course, that didn't stop the pain in the meantime.

Kanaahn massaged the lump forming on the back of his head and sat up. But still dazed from the alcohol and the fall, had forgotten Kyeit was still hovering over him, and he smacked his forehead right into her nose. Kyeit cried out and grabbed her nose. Kanaahn could see her own eyes begin to well with tears; no doubt her sinuses were already stinging from the force. A good whack on the nose could make even the toughest man cry— that and the stench of winged-wolf shit.

"Shit, I'm so sorry, Kyeit." Kanaahn sat up and placed an arm around Kyeit's shoulder.

Kyeit checked her hand for any sign of blood. Luckily the impact had only stunned her. She sighed with relief. "We're quite the pair, aren't we?"

Kanaahn sighed. "I suppose we are."

The fire had burned out by this point, and Kanaahn and Kyeit were sitting in the dark. The only light that remained came from the streetlamps outside that poured into the window like a flood, trying to expunge the darkness from any corner it could, but failing miserably.

"We should get to bed," Kanaahn said finally when Kyeit had not responded.

"Not yet," she whispered. "Not yet."

Kanaahn tried to make out Kyeit's shape in the darkness; his eyes had still not adjusted. Before he could see where Kyeit was, she had thrown herself on him. Her arms locked around his neck and Kanaahn could feel her lips press against his. Her lips were dry and cold. He could taste the alcohol on her breath, masked only by the alcohol on his. It was nothing like he had heard it would be. All the tales told of a warm, wet meeting of plump lips, and the fluttering of doves sounding somewhere in the distance and the sunset upon the two lovers, locked in each other's embrace for all eternity. The scent of roses and the feeling of weightlessness. But no, they were just two people, one garbed in light armour, half drunk, kissing on the cold, hard floor of a tavern. Kanaahn's head still ached from the fall, but he ignored it long enough to wrap his arms around Kyeit's waist and embrace her as she kissed him.

Then the door opened suddenly, and light poured in and the two pulled away from their moment. They squinted into the bright light of the outside world and stared into the face of a smirking Shooter.

"Next time hang something on the handle," he joked. "I would've slept in the barn."

Kyeit cleared her throat, wiped her mouth on the back of her hand, and preened herself a bit. She didn't even acknowledge Shooter's comment. Her voice draped itself in authority and seriousness once more. "Where'd you get off to?"

Shooter shrugged. "I had some fun with the local bard, but don't mind me, we can gossip later. Don't let me disturb...whatever it is I was about to walk in on."

"It was nothing, Shooter." Kanaahn couldn't even look Shooter him in his in bright, beaming, sarcastic, eyes, but he didn't have to. He could only imagine the look Shooter was giving him; something between pride and playful mockery. Kanaahn was glad it was dark.

Shooter, true to his word, didn't say another word and merely flitted up the stairs in moments. If it hadn't been the sinking feeling in his stomach, his burning cheeks, and the sheer embarrassment of it all, Kanaahn would never have known Shooter had been there just a few seconds ago.

"We should—" started Kanaahn.

"Yup," was all Kyeit responded, but her stalwart tone betrayed the gleam in her eyes and the shade of cherry on her cheeks.

The two cleaned up their bottles, ensured the front door was locked, and slinked off up the stairs to the room they shared with everyone else. Shooter would probably already be up there, spreading all the gossip. Kanaahn had doubts that Arial, Arkas, and Cecil had gone to bed, and were more likely sitting up to gossip about Shooter's escapes, and Kanaahn and Kyeit's alone time in the pub downstairs. There would be questions. Questions Kanaahn didn't have answers to; even for himself.

Chapter VII

Risasi's face contorted in a snarl and his muzzle raised, baring his ivory teeth in the moonlight. His claws scratched furrows into the soil. He stepped paw over paw, circling the dead moose. He snarled, chirped from his throat, then growled low, his chest vibrating from the sound.

His opponent for today was Djall.

Valence and Kinokaze insisted that the dragons spar at least once per day, to keep their skills sharp. In the wild, amongst their own kind, they would have been doing this at the instruction of their k'dir or k'nir only a few weeks after hatching. It was both a rite of passage and a necessary skill for dragons. Everything was settled through a friendly challenge. Who was stronger, who would lead a family unit, who would mate with the drake with the biggest horns, or the dam with the strongest tail and widest wings, who would hunt in a square kilometre patch of wood, and so on. Drazhan nit kidarr drazhan, after all—except in the direst of circumstances. So, the challenge, whether fuelled by hatred, or rivalry, always had to appear friendly. Scars were fine, worn as a badge of honour, even, but death and murder were frowned upon.

Djall launched at Risasi first. Lithe like a cat, his wings tucked in close to his body. Risasi reared up and caught the brunt of the attack on his scaly breast. Bone and scales saved him.

Djall's snout crashed into Risasi, and he let out a cry of pain. It was a trick he had learned from Shooter; an opponent's nose was his weakest point. Shooter would often smash his palm into his opponent's nose, causing stinging pain that would stagger an opponent. The enemy's eyes would water, and they would take a moment to refocus themselves, and in that time, Risasi would strike.

Risasi's head snaked around Djall, and he wrapped his teeth around the nape of Djall's neck. He aimed to pin the dragon, but Djall tilted his head up and scored Risasi across the face with his horns. Risasi let out a roar. He could feel blood trickle down his snout and into his mouth.

Djall rolled on his back and began to claw at Risasi's chest and stomach. The red dragon bucked, eyes closed, and collapsed under the flurry of claws and scratches.

"Djall!" Risasi roared. "Enough! You're not some house cat, you're a dragon! Fight like one!" He spoke entirely in Draconic, as the dragons did when their human partners weren't around.

"You're only saying that because you're losing!"

Djall stood up and flicked his tail at Risasi, catching the dragon on the left shoulder.

Risasi saw red. He charged at Djall, teeth bared, claws at the ready.

Djall sidestepped his opponent. "Ever the red dragon, falling prey to emotion."

"Ever the green dragon, too pompous to notice a trap!"

Djall caught a wing to the face. The leathery appendage slapped him in the snout and stunned him. Risasi had extended them with great force. With his opponent stunned, Risasi turned and slammed his head into Djall's neck. The dragon whimpered and his trachea shuddered from the impact. Risasi sunk his teeth into the back of Djall's neck, just at the base of the skull, and was finally able to pin Djall's neck to the ground. Djall struggled, tail flicking, searching, aiming for Risasi's face, but it wouldn't reach.

Djall had lost.

"I think that evens out the score," Risasi mumbled through a mouth full of Djall.

"For now," Djall complained.

Valence slapped her tail against the ground as some sort of draconic applause. "Well done. Risasi, you've been taking tips from your partner."

Risasi snorted. "Is that not the point of Khaleeshir?"

"It is," Kinokaze said, inserting herself into the conversation. Valence did not always respond well to the young dragon's cheek. "We are glad you are taking well to the point of it."

If Risasi could blush he would be a deeper shade of red. Fyete seemed to notice, for she nudged Adalinda and whispered something from across the clearing. Risasi shot them a look, but it did not stop his sisters from chittering.

Risasi had come into many changes after being bonded to Shooter. Shooter had gained an increased constitution, longer life, heightened senses, faster reflexes and even the ability to heal and recover faster. Risasi had begun to develop human emotions. Emotions that were not normally apparent in dragons. For example, love and affection. Dragons did not mate between clans, and they did not mate for love. It was purely a reproductive instinct to mate for life. Mates had become close and amicable, some might have even come close to an imitation of human love, but it was not quite the same as what Risasi now felt course through his body. It was a mixed bag, though. A double-edged sword. Red dragons were already subject to their passions. Red dragons were naturally more hot-headed, quick-tempered, and prone to anger, to spite, to avarice and gluttony. Red dragons were not wicked, but they were quick to let their emotions lead them by the nose. Whatever their thoughts or however agreeable a red dragon could be, all of that was lost when they felt slighted or grew emboldened by passion. Dealing with all these new emotions had been draining for Risasi, and some days he wondered if the fates weren't mocking his new condition.

Djall nosed the moose and looked to Risasi. Normally, amongst their kind, the victor would win the spoils and take the meal for themselves. But the dragons needed to remain hidden and couldn't spend hours hunting half the moose in the forest to feed themselves, and so Risasi and Djall began to devour the moose in cooperation. The other dragons had already had their practice fights and had eaten their fill as they watched Djall and Risasi pretend to murder each other.

Once the moose was nothing but a pile of well-cleaned bones, Risasi and Djall divided the skeleton amongst themselves and began cracking open the bones to lick out the marrow.

"I do miss our partners," Fyete stated as the group lay about, digesting their food.

Adalinda looked over in the direction of Felidrun, far off in the distance. "Agreed. I hadn't realized how quiet it was without them. My mind feels empty, and my soul feels halved."

"The ritual bound you forever as if one soul in two bodies," Valence explained for the thousandth time.

"You keep saying that, but that doesn't even come close to describing it," Djall chided. "It's so much deeper than that. So much more. Kanaahn is a constant presence in my head, a constant voice. I feel what he feels, smell what he smells. Our minds blend as one, our visions combine, and we see each other's sights. Some days I must block out Kanaahn's mind at times just to focus on my own actions. And yet it's...beautiful."

The other dragons agreed.

Valence stopped gnawing on a shin bone for a moment to reply. "Part of your training in Ethon will be learning how to balance the blending of minds. As you say, you cannot allow your partner's mind to distract you from your own actions. It would not be safe, especially in battle."

Valence and Kinokaze could not say much else, having never experienced a blood bond. It was not done amongst dragons any longer. It had been something reserved only for the Khaleeshir. A special ritual: one that might not be performed again, as the sacred artefacts that made the ritual possible had been stolen from Osamu's and Kanothir's corpses.

"It is a peculiar ritual," Fyete pointed out. "The humans have noticed. They notice the similarities to blood magic. Is it not the same?"

The dragons had always called the ritual Kha'n-Kha'lash; a Blood for Blood Spell. It had been common in the old days for two dragons with a special bond of friendship to bind themselves together through a blood pact, forever becoming as one soul in two bodies. It was knowledge passed from parent to hatchling through the Vizka'in'lash, Spell of Bestowment, which was the ritual wherein a sire and dam place their memories within their hatchling's minds. It was not something the dragons openly told the humans. The Blood for Blood Spell had been a closely guarded secret amongst the drazhani. One of the last vestiges of an ancient tradition that remained wholly and truly theirs, even if it was no longer practised frequently. For how it would look, if a race who had fought for millennia against Tenebrae's and his use of blood magic, were practising something that looked an awful lot like blood magic.

In truth, it was nothing of the sort, as Valence had explained. This was an ancient, drazhani ritual that had predated Tenebrae's creation of blood magic. It did not seek to take blood from an unwilling host to bend reality to your will. It sought to form a willing covenant between two beings, by tying them eternally together, forever, in heart, spirit and mind, but the humans would not understand. Not truly. That was why the secret ritual had been kept between Kanothir, Osamu, his ancestors, and the Metallic Dragons. No one else in the Darond knew how it was done, and they never would—much to their displeasure, for they had often pressed for that very information. The only others who would ever see the ritual were Kyeit, Osamu's eventual successor, and the Khaleeshir themselves.

"It is *not* blood magic," Valence bristled. "Blood magic is vile and destructive. This is a pure, ancient, draconic magic. It is sanctioned by the First Mother; it is sacred magic."

Risasi pressed the subject, letting forth a question that had burned on his and his siblings' minds. "Then why do we not perform it anymore? Why do dragons not bond themselves to one another as the Khaleeshir are made to?"

Valence snorted impatiently. "Because we are not meant to any longer. Search your memories...it was a tradition abandoned long before humans arrived. We revived it to bridge the gap between our species and bring peace. The idea was to bind humans to dragons, forevermore, so that we could learn from one another, and help protect each other's races from mutual destruction."

"But why?" asked Djall.

Valence and Kinokaze did not respond. They could not.

It was the question that burned in the minds of all dragons; or so they all assumed, for it burned in the minds of all dragons present for this conversation. They had the memory that this ritual had been sacred to their kind once, but after a certain point it just...stopped, but why? What had caused something still held so sacred and dear to all drazhani to become an abandoned taboo remembered only in distant memories passed down between generations like an heirloom,

There were no answers to this question in their memories. It was an odd predicament indeed, for there was almost nothing that wasn't answerable from the depths of a dragon's memories. All the information a dragon could need was available deep within their latent inheritance if only they knew where and how to look. Anything missing was learned by experience or not worth knowing.

No one broached the subject further. The look on Valence's face gave enough warning of the consequences. Instead, the subject was quickly changed by Fyete, tactful as ever.

"Will we meet a Metallic Dragon in Estion?"

Kinokaze nodded. "The Brass Dragon Aurichalcum calls Ethon home. He will be there to train us, and the other Khaleeshir for as long as we are in the city."

The young dragons practically vibrated with excitement, letting out a low, thrumming vocalization that escaped through their noses. The Metallics were sacred to all human practitioners of Dragomancy, but doubly so to the dragons. They were among the oldest dragons in Enayra; massive behemoths existing at unfathomable sizes that had seen the creation of Enayra and would live to see the end of it all. They had led the drazhani since the death of the Earth Mother and had stood by the drazhani in their darkest hours, even as their numbers thinned in the wake of Tenebrae's rebellion. It was as if meeting a god, embodied in flesh.

"I do not remember such excitement when we met," Valence teased.

"Nor I," added Kinokaze.

"You are Metallics, to be sure, but you are not *the* Metallics," Fyete explained. "To meet an Ancient One...one who has lived so long, one who is so powerful. The Metallics are even more powerful than our Great Mothers and Fathers that lead the clans."

The two Metallic Dragons exchanged looks. Their glance was brief, minute, almost unnoticed, but Risasi had seen. Risasi had caught the faintest doubt in the eyes of Valence and Kinokaze. His eyes narrowed, and he made note of it but said nothing further about the stolen glance.

"I do not understand why we must remain cut off from our partners mentally," complained Adalinda. "What difference does it make amongst other humans?"

It was Kinokaze who responded. "It is true most humans will not be able to sense the mental connection of a bond like yours. Humans are not innately born with the ability to talk with their minds. It is a skill learned through the study of magic, or taught directly by dragons since it comes naturally to us. If we're being followed by those Tulkaz or another dragon, they'll not only be able to sense it, but they may also be skilled enough to invade that link and spy on it."

"What are the chances of that happening?" Risasi was blunt and short in his remark.

Valence did not shy away from the challenge. "It would have to be an old and skilled dragon, but for the Tulkaz it is not beyond the realm of possibility for them."

Silence. Only silence.

Kinokaze interceded. "Since Xiar, we have earned Tenebrae's ire, and we have become worthy of his contempt. He would no doubt have us watched and followed as much as possible. The Tulkaz are his best bet. Kyeit, overseeing the safety of all Khaleeshir, felt it best not to give them any advantages they could use against us."

"She is afraid," Fyete reasoned, not unsympathetically. "Not without reason. A fight with the Tulkaz at this point would be less than ideal. I can't imagine what it would be like to combat some of Tenebrae's strongest soldiers."

Valence shot a disgruntled look at the blue dragon.

Fyete chose her next words carefully. "I too, am afraid, to be honest."

"Are there no ways to sense if they truly are following us?" asked Djall. "Can we not also sense them, if they sense us?"

"Yes," admitted Valence. "These Tulkaz set nature itself on the very edge of a precipice. They do not belong; they should not be. They do not feel of this world. Nature cannot handle them. The trees, the rocks, the sky, the wind, the earth itself, and all the creatures around can feel it. It throws everything out of balance."

"But we cannot take the chance that they would not sense us before we sense them. Even but a second poking around in our minds and across our mental connections could yield important information that could jeopardize everything," added Kinokaze.

"I must admit, I am not fully convinced," grumbled Risasi. "But I also cannot disagree..."

Valence and Kinokaze did not respond.

No one else said anything else.

Everyone had their own thoughts and opinions on the matter. Valence and Kinokaze did their best to sympathize with the other dragons, for they too had bonded with humans, but they could never understand the bond the Khaleeshir shared. They were as one soul in two bodies, and to willingly cut the other off was tantamount to cutting off your own limb. It felt like living a lie, and it made each half of the bond feel hollow and empty like a piece was missing from their soul. It was made worse by the fact that Valence and Kinokaze had likely fought as hard as they could against Kyeit, but to no avail.

Only the fear of the Tulkaz kept the dragons from ignoring Valence's warning and opening their minds up to their partners regardless of orders. It was a precarious situation all around.

"I'll take the first watch." Valence stretched her wings and took to the sky without waiting for a response. She was gone quickly.

Kinokaze shook her head. "Let's get some rest. We have a full day of training tomorrow."

* * *

Risasi lay sleepless at the edge of their "encampment." His back was turned to his siblings, and he stared out into the darkness of the woods around them. He stared as if looking for enlightenment between the trees, and if he stared hard enough, it would appear before him and bless him.

Something had bothered him deeply since arriving in Estion; since Cecil had explained what dangers lay before them, at the beck and call of Tenebrae. Whether what had dawned on Risasi had become apparent to the other dragons was unclear, but his earlier outburst between himself and Shooter had certainly not gone unnoticed by his fellow Khaleeshir. Yet Shooter had not pressed the matter at the time; there had not been enough privacy between them. It was too sensitive a subject to have without words, and perhaps some yelling and emotional outbursts.

Each of the five eggs that would become Khaleeshir had come from a clutch laid by the Matriarch of each clan, sired by the Patriarch. Ölüm had been Tenebrae's ilk, not unlike his sibling Balgorax, but by that same logic, Risasi was the offspring of Venu'shael, another reviled traitor amongst the drazhani. He had willingly joined Tenebrae, he had turned against his mates, his children, and his entire clan, and had thrown away everything he once held dear for Tenebrae's wicked designs.

Why? Why had he done it?

His father's memories were not in Risasi's head, not from that time. He had been laid, and his k'nir's memories had been implanted before he had turned on his clan. But Risasi inexplicably had the memories of his k'dir from after the betrayal. He could feel her pain, her ache. He could see the slaughter. So many red dragons lay dying, dead, broken, littered across the side of the mountain they called home. Some burned beyond recognition by their Patriarch's scorching breath. Others were rent and torn by claws and teeth. Thick crimson blood cooled and sizzled across the rocks. The stench of burning flesh and the sound of dying dragons were louder than the volcano where they lay. His k'dir could do naught but fight. Fight and mourn as she watched her clan—her *children*—die around her, all at the hands of he who had been her mate for thousands of years, since time immemorial. The pain overwhelmed Risasi whenever he recalled the memories. He longed for the time when, until recently, they had laid buried within his mind.

A dragon's memories stretched back to the days of the original dragons, but the further back the memories go, or the less important they were deemed, the harder they were to recall. They became less memories and more blurry visions of some forgotten moment in the past, lost to time, lost to nature. Like viewing the ruins of some great civilization thousands of years after their homes had been abandoned. These memories had been important to his k'dir, something she felt Risasi needed to know, but they had not been at the forefront of his mind. They had simmered just below the surface, and Risasi had been conscious of them, in the way one is conscious of their own nose, but he had never delved deep enough to realize what they were at first. Then Cecil had said the name of his k'nir...and everything flooded into him at once.

But worse still was the fear. The fear that he would be just like Ölüm. He and Ölüm had been close in their youth, before they could speak, before the madness claimed Ölüm and drew him back to his traitor k'nir, dragging poor, hapless Drakhart with him. Yes, they had drifted apart...but they had still been close, as had Tenebrae and Venu'shael. Close enough that Venu'shael would forsake everything for Tenebrae. Everything.

Did this bode some ill fate for Risasi? Would he be destined to do the same? Surely not. His mother had let him have these memories so that he could learn from his k'nir's mistake. Surely...?

And yet the doubt lingered. Risasi was unsure of the origin of this doubt. Dragons, especially red dragons, were not particularly known for their lack of confidence. Often, it was quite the opposite. Had bonding with Shooter done this? Was this...self-reflection?

Yet even through all the doubt and fear, however, Risasi could not fully bring himself to hate the k'nir he had never known. Despite it all, despite what had happened, despite everything Risasi had been left by memory in his own mind, all the pain and anger...Risasi wanted to *know*, to understand. He wanted to know *why*, and *what* had made his k'nir act this way, and make the choices he did. Risasi couldn't make a judgement call until he understood the full story, but how could he do that, when the only two dragons who would ever have known that were Tenebrae and Venu'shael himself? Would Risasi be forced to wonder forever, never truly on one side of the conflict or another? He knew what his father had done was wrong, but until he understood the why...he could never fully commit to the blind hatred.

Then there was the most dreaded thought that sank like a stone in the pit of his stomach...what if Risasi was fated to become like his father? Could one outrun fate? Was there even such a thing as fate? Risasi had been laid so that he would be bonded with a human and save Enayra, but how much of that was fate, predetermined by destiny, and how much of that was choice?

Risasi shook his head of these thoughts and tried to sleep, but sleep would not take him. Whatever fate was cursing him had cursed him to lay there, staring into the blackness of the forest, and musing on his inner turmoil. No rest would come to Risasi.

"No rest for the wicked," he thought to the empty void where Shooter's mind usually was.

Chapter VIII

Drakhart opened his eyes and shot up. He was covered in sweat and his chest ached. He looked around in the pale blue light of the cavern for Isunath. His dragon was flopped on his scaly side, breathing heavily as if asleep. Drakhart rushed to Isunath's side, making sure the dragon was not wounded.

"He'll be okay," Elandyr'ni called out from the edges of the cavern.

Tenebrae said nothing from his lofty vantage point.

Once Drakhart had made certain Isunath was okay, he looked down at his chest. He could see the skin just above where his heart was. It was puckered and red, like he had been branded long ago, but the pain was fresh, from the burning scar that was etched anew into his flesh. It was the symbol of the Black Dragon Clan, etched even deeper than it had been before. It glowed with a faint red light.

"We do not often perform this ritual twice, but it can be done," Tenebrae called from above. ***"I'll admit, I was not certain a human could handle it."***

The ache and emptiness he had felt since the loss of Ölüm was gone. Once more, Drakhart felt...whole. Mostly whole, anyway. He felt an echo of Ölüm somewhere in his heart and mind. A phantom limb of his dead partner. An appendage that would never die or cease to ache, but he was more whole, and the pain had abated; it could be ignored now.

Drakhart immediately noticed that Isunath's mind was calmer than Ölüm's had been. Ölüm's mind had been like a storm on the sea. It thrashed about violently, tossing the poor sailors that dared tread into the water. Boats smashed upon rocks, lightning arcing through the sky, splitting rock and shaking the world to its core. Ölüm's mind was pure chaos compared to the calm, warmth that was Isunath. Isunath's mind wrapped around and melded with his. It was like the embrace of a warm blanket on a cold night. Or the feeling of a warm hearth in the dead of winter. The chill in Drakhart's extremities was abated, and he could feel the ache in his heart start to heal. He felt ensorceled by the warmth of it all, and there was a humming somewhere in the back of his mind that Drakhart couldn't quite place the origin of.

That observation had not gone unnoticed by Tenebrae. ***"I feel I must apologize to you, for Ölüm."***

Drakhart was confused.

"I am in your head, and so I can feel your thoughts. I notice that you sense a difference between Isunath and Ölüm. I believe I am to blame for that. Ölüm was not...he dabbled in madness."

Drakhart's stomach sunk. "What do you mean, my lord?"

"When my soul was ripped from its body, I clung to the first, familiar living thing I could find. I clung to Ölüm's egg. It was near, it was safe, it was secluded...no one would find me there. I knew the way to get past the wards and spells that protected the chamber. I had helped to set them, after all. I spent time there, coalescing and planning my next steps. I believe my presence in Ölüm's consciousness for so long, while it helped me, may have driven the hatchling mad. I had hoped...perhaps once he had hatched, and been allowed to grow and meet me, I could help calm him down, but he took longer to hatch than I anticipated, and the damage had been done. It is something I regret. I am sorry."

Drakhart was stunned. Speechless. Not just because he had never thought he'd hear Tenebrae utter an apology to anyone, let alone him. He didn't know what to say, or how to respond. Drakhart knew what he *wanted* to say but could not find the words to give life to the thoughts. "Did I—" was as far as Drakhart got.

Tenebrae was able to intuit the rest. *"It is possible it affected your behaviour before his death. Once they bound you, some of Ölüm's nature may have bled into you."* Tenebrae could sense the doubt in Drakhart's soul. *"It does not make the choices you made any less valid. But...if this information changes which side you'd rather be on..."*

Tenebrae stopped just short of saying the words, but Drakhart could still intone their meaning.

Did Drakhart *want* to go back to the Darond? Did he want to be on the other side? Had he even meant to be here after all? Did Drakhart want to go back...could he even? But then the ache of Ölüm's loss tore through him like sheers through a cloth. He could feel the moment of his death—Ölüm's pain had been his own. The stretching of his neck, the popping and snapping of vertebrae. Drakhart could almost feel himself choking on his own blood, his windpipe filling with fluids, gurgling for air as Djall choked the life out of Ölüm— out of him. Drakhart remembered Kanaahn, and how he had treated him, disregarded him, for months before they had left Kula. Drakhart's anger, his grievances, had predated Ölüm. Had Ölüm's personality bleeding into Drakhart's exacerbated the situation? Perhaps, but that did not change the fact that Drakhart was already teetering down a different path from his friends beforehand.

Kanaahn had murdered Ölüm; for all the dragon had been mad, he and Drakhart had been kindred spirits bonded together for eternity, and Kanaahn had wrenched that away from Drakhart. He had murdered Ölüm in cold blood and forced Drakhart to feel every moment of the agony both physically and emotionally. His friends had turned on and forsaken him, throwing their lot in with Kanaahn and the Darond. The Darond. They had lied to him, and manipulated him, just as they were currently doing to Kanaahn and the others, and they used their mouthpiece Kyeit to do so.

The Darond were not interested in saving the world or liberating people, they wanted them enslaved to their regime. They wanted to control the Khaleeshir, and Drakhart would not be controlled. They were interested in some elitist status quo that benefited only the Darond and those on top—Tenebrae stood in opposition to that.

Then there was Kula. Drakhart had been put in charge of overseeing the welfare and prosperity of his hometown—well, the town he had been living in since he and his mother moved out there. For all he was not Kulan born, it had become his home, and he cared for it. Unlike Kanaahn and the Darond, Drakhart was doing good for the people of Kula. The Town Watch was no more, Lord Krystor Davenpourte was dead, and the city was well protected by a new set of walls and a new garrison of Altimaran soldiers. Many of them had plucked fresh from the ranks of eager Kulans looking for better employment opportunities than poverty would normally allow. Drakhart had been able to redistribute food from the royal grain stores to alleviate the food shortages and starvation that plagued the town under the gluttonous Lord Davenpourte. Crime had been reduced, by force and by circumstance. Those who would turn to crime for survival no longer had to explore that avenue to make ends meet; between the food redistribution and the new garrison providing opportunities, the only criminals left were those who chose the life for pleasure and not out of circumstance. These had been dealt with harshly and severely, with the worst offenders of Kula's underground being flayed alive in the town square, their bodies boiled, and their bones displayed atop the parapets for all to see—you couldn't display a rotting corpse in Altimara, for the risk of pests, and the type of pests it lured, were worse for the innocent civilians than the criminals.

Ölüm's death had abated the blinding anger, but it did not make it go away entirely. There was still anger and a desire for revenge. Kanaahn had still hurt Drakhart, and Drakhart believed in Tenebrae's path to justice over the Darond's. These feelings did not change, and these were his reasons for leaving his friends.

"No," Drakhart answered proudly. "I have made my decision, and I do not regret it. I pledged myself to your cause, and I uphold my pledge to you still."

Tenebrae rumbled and shook the cavern. Drakhart always took this as a laugh. Of course, he always feared one day he'd guess wrong and find himself sliding down the ancient dragon's gullet, but today was not that day.

"Your dedication is appreciated, and welcomed, Drakhart. Your commitment to the cause is admirable."

Tenebrae often mentioned this cause. Drakhart had no idea what this cause was or whether it was the overall cause, or Tenebrae's cause. It was something that had eaten away at Drakhart's curiosity since he had learned the truth.

Why? Why had Tenebrae made the choices he did? Why had he done all this? He had turned against his entire race for...what? What was his end goal? He had forever changed the course of Enayra history, for reasons he kept held close to his breast. But for these same reasons, or some version of them, he had gotten thousands to pledge themselves to nothing but the promise of change.

"Is there anything else, Drakhart?"

Drakhart snapped back to the moment and his heart skipped a beat. Tenebrae always seemed to choose which moments to probe into his mind. As part of his pact with Tenebrae, Tenebrae had an unimpeded right to enter Drakhart's mind, as he did with the others who served him. One could never truly know when Tenebrae would peer into your mind. He seemed to pick and choose the moments to give you privacy. You could normally tell when he was brushing against your consciousness, but sometimes if you were distracted enough, he would creep up on you. Drakhart could only pray this had not been one of those times. Though, if it had been, Tenebrae had chosen to say nothing, and left Drakhart to his thoughts, and whatever privacy he may or may not have.

Drakhart bowed. "Nothing, my lord. By your leave."

Tenebrae wordlessly descended back into the fathomless depths where he lived, off to continue his plotting and planning, and whatever dark experiments he was concocting down there.

Isunath had recovered from the exhaustion of the ritual and came over to Drakhart. He blew hot breath on the back of Drakhart's neck and pressed his nose into Drakhart's shoulder.

Drakhart smiled and returned his dragon's affection. He scratched Isunath's chin, and the dragon began to purr like rolling thunder. Smoke rose from Isunath's nostrils, and the smell of char and brimstone filled Drakhart's nose. His eyes watered and he sidestepped the dragon and looked to Elandyr'ni. "I never expected an ancient grimoire to be such a page-turner."

The Grand Enchantress had presided over the ritual, but she had spent much of the previous conversation pouring over an old, leatherbound tome. She flicked eagerly through the pages, muttering the words under her breath as she read. It took her a moment to notice Drakhart and respond. "Oh, it's not a grimoire. It's a favourite novel of mine. I *do* enjoy reading for myself sometimes. Now, shall we continue to your training?"

Drakhart nodded.

"Very well. Let's eat first; you'll need your strength." She peaked around Drakhart. "Isunath, meet us in the courtyard in the evening. Eat, and get some rest for now. Once you've recovered from this ritual, and our training is complete, we will continue flight training for the both of you."

Isunath blinked slowly. "Yes, Lady Elandyr'ni."

Elandyr'ni's dark cheeks blushed red. "You don't need to call me that, Isunath."

"You are respected amongst your kind. I intend only to give you the same respect."

"Off with you now!" Elandyr'ni playfully shooed the dragon away.

The dragon snorted playfully before taking off towards the exit above.

Drakhart smiled after his partner. For though Isunath had now gone from sight, Drakhart could still feel him as heavily in the back of his head as if he was standing before him. It had been too long since he had felt another mind entwined with his so intimately.

Elandyr'ni led Drakhart through the dark and narrow corridor that connected Tenebrae's caverns to the Altimaran Throne Room. The way was lit only by a dim torch that flickered as the draft threatened to extinguish its dull, but warm flame. Elandyr'ni would not, or could not, use her magical flame, though considering the ritual she had just performed, Drakhart could understand. It was a silent walk. Drakhart's mind was stuck on the same thoughts that had occupied him previously. Why? The why of it all. The why and the what.

Elandyr'ni finally shattered the silence. "Out with it already."

Drakhart was grateful that it was already dark, or his face would've been quite the sight for the Enchantress. He feebly squeaked out: "What do you mean?"

Elandyr'ni let a sly smile slip in the darkness. "Even I could see you pondering away in there. So, ask; perhaps I can answer."

Drakhart paused for a moment. He tried to find just the right words for what he was thinking. Unfortunately, his brain failed him and all that tumbled out of his mouth was: "Why?"

Elandyr'ni was able to suss out the true meaning, however. "Why does Lord Tenebrae do what he does? What is this all about, is that it? What caused all of this?"

Drakhart nodded.

"I don't know...I'm not sure anyone does anymore—except Lord Tenebrae."

Drakhart paled. "I can't exactly ask him. I don't want him to think I'm doubting the cause...it might not even be my place to ask."

"No, it's certainly not, but then again, was it ever anyone's place to ask anything in this world." Elandyr'ni was cryptic as ever.

"But even those who serve Lord Tenebrae...why? All for the promise of—of what? Change? After all these years they keep their faith in this?"

Elandyr'ni gave a sad smile. "I think, perhaps, I can answer *that* question. The Qiri'ar were promised freedom from Altimaran hegemony, where we can have our ancestral lands protected and unmolested in perpetuity. A safe place where we can practice our magic in peace, and live fulfilling lives however we choose. We were not treated well under Rego's regime—or even before that. We were slowly being forced from our lands, and if we relocated to Altimaran cities, we would be outcasts and ostracized. When we weren't being ostracized, we were being assimilated, and our lands were being stolen, all for resources and profit, but Tenebrae promised us protection; he promised us it would get better."

Drakhart had so many more questions, but he would need to wait to ask them; one question at a time.

"Tenebrae," Elandyr'ni continued, "Under the guise of the Altimaran royals, has spent the last ten centuries treating the Qiri'ar with what has been viewed as apathy by the Altimaran people, but in truth is disguised care. He had rerouted the Bacma River away from Lake Gishan'belor and the Qiri'ar capital and towards Targrond. On the surface, this dried up Lake Gishan'belor and deprived the Qiri'ar of their water source in favour of using it to fuel Altimaran industry in Targrond. In truth, Tenebrae used the Brown Dragon Clan to burrow into the ground beneath the city and reroute several natural springs into a reservoir beneath the city. Lake Gishan'belor was being overfished by other Altimarans and was being polluted and looted for its resources by Rego and his nobility. Tenebrae removed all interest from the area and provided the Qiri'ar with a private, incorruptible source of our sacred water.

"Under the guise of the Crown, Tenebrae restricted the settlement of Qiri'ar to the western shores of Lake Gishan'belor and has made it illegal for anyone who wasn't Qiri'ar to settle there. It appeared the Crown was restricting the Qiri'ar to a desolate land reserve, but in truth Tenebrae had guaranteed that the Qiri'ar could live in their ancestral lands, unbothered by outsiders.

"We are travelling traders, and the laws do not forbid us from travelling and trading, only from settling elsewhere—which is not what the average Qiri'ar wants. The laws *do* prevent outsiders from settling within our protected land and preserve our Qiri'aran ancestral homeland from destruction and theft. It may not seem like it to outsiders, but Tenebrae *has* made our lives better. He has made us stronger too."

"But in doing so, you have lost your sacred lake, and the swamps you once called home," protested Drakhart.

"But we have survived. We persist; our culture and traditions may change, and evolve, but the people survive. We live on. To survive, we must progress, and to progress…sometimes traditions must be left behind; and sacrificed. It is not ideal, but neither is this world. Eshgalon the Great knew we had to make sacrifices if we were to throw in our lot with the Great Aspect Isunath. If anyone had the power to help us it was the physical embodiment of one of the Great Aspects."

Elandyr'ni's answers had led to ever more questions, but one took precedence. "What do you *mean* he's Isunath? I thought Isunath was a human Aspect."

Elandyr'ni let out a genuine laugh. It was tinged with just enough pity to make Drakhart sting with embarrassment. "I forgot about the Altimaran propaganda. No, what you call the Old Religion here is known as Dragomancy everywhere else. When humans first came to this land, they brought this religion with them. It was the ancestors of the Qiri'ar and of the other peoples of Altimara who first grafted the Great Dragons of the Clans and the Metallics to their religion. These ancestors declared the ancient dragons to be physical embodiments of the Aspects. They were called heretics for it…funny how the tables have turned."

"I'm guessing the about-face has something to do with King Rego?" asked Drakhart.

"Correct. Before Lord Tenebrae took control of the king, his hatred of dragons led him to reconstruct the original Old World Aspectism of the first humans. It's an imperfect reconstruction, a hollow facsimile, but it served its purpose as propaganda."

Drakhart's head swam with the thought he had unknowingly named Isunath after his father. There was almost a sick irony to it. So consumed by these thoughts and revelations that Drakhart was too preoccupied to ask any of the myriad other questions that had begun to sprout and flower in his mind. There were just too many to quantify and ask without annoying Elandyr'ni at this point. But if Elandyr'ni's answers had done anything, they had solidified in his mind that Tenebrae's cause was just and true. He had made the lives of the Qiri'ar better, as promised. In return all he asked was loyalty. And why shouldn't he? The Qiri'ar were merely being asked to fight to safeguard their new and better futures. They would have to protect themselves in exchange for all they could ever want and more. It was as Elandyr'ni said. Tenebrae had made them stronger.

Drakhart still desired to know why Tenebrae had chosen this path in the first place, but not because he wished to deem whether the cause was just. Now it was purely for curiosity's sake. What had set Tenebrae down the path that would change Enayran history forever? That question still burned in the pits of Drakhart's soul, but so now, did another question.

"What will I be learning today?"

"Just the basics. I will not be throwing you into anything more complicated than making a flower bloom for now. Blood magic is incredibly dangerous for humans. Too much can go wrong—too easy to get addicted. If you can make a flower bloom without losing your mind, we'll progress you to the next stage."

Drakhart would have been insulted if he hadn't already been warned of the severe consequences of delving too deep into blood magic without being careful. He had been warned that even those who follow all the rules and don't push their limits can still wind up in the throes of Blood Lust, killing and murdering for more power. It was addicting, and most people were too weak-willed to practice. Of those with the proper discipline, about half still fell to the harrowing effects. He pushed the thought from his mind and asked his next question.

"And what would that be?"

"Once you've reached a sufficient level of discipline, I will walk you through growing Isunath. He will need to be larger if he's to battle against the Khaleeshir and their Metallic allies."

Drakhart was grateful to Elandyr'ni. She was a tough teacher, who stressed discipline, patience, and perfection, but she was not unkind, and she was not mean. She held herself to the same standards she expected of Drakhart.

Elandyr'ni grasped the stone wall off to the left. Fitting her hand around the particularly smooth stone about halfway up the wall, she pushed the stone inwards. Something clicked in the wall, and it parted to reveal the throne room.

Drakhart shielded his eyes from the harsh and wicked light. He would never get used to that. Elandyr'ni did not even seem to flinch at the difference. There were no hands in front of her face, or grimace of pain as the light flooded her senses like a burst dam.

She turned to Drakhart, a kind but stern smile on her face. "Now go freshen up. Eat, recover, and meet me in the courtyard when you're finished. I'll be waiting."

Drakhart bowed and did as he was told.

* * *

To say Drakhart had no free time had become an understatement. His days had become a routine of constant schooling and learning, training, and growing stronger. Always being tested, always being pushed to excel further; Tenebrae would suffer no slacking amongst his loyal generals, least of all from a Khaleeshir.

Drakhart's day started an hour before dawn when he would drag himself from bed, eat a quick meal that would be brought to him in his room, and go across the palatial compound to the Grand Enchanter's Cottage and adjacent gardens.

To call this building a cottage was another understatement. It was a large estate—a small palace, really—situated in the bosom of an even larger compound. It boggled Drakhart's mind, even more, to know that Elandyr'ni lived there all alone, with nothing but her thoughts and a massive library to keep her company. However, he noted that Elandyr'ni seemed not to care whether she was alone and made great use of the ancient tomes in the library. Most nights she would sleep, eat, and live within the library itself rather than her own bed chambers.

Here, Drakhart would be schooled by Elandyr'ni in blood magic. She would drill him on the basics for hours before finally working on the more advanced spells. Elandyr'ni was insistent that stringent adherence to the fundamentals would ensure flawless execution of more complex spells—especially after Drakhart's earlier incident. The most common mistakes made with blood magic were simply mistakes that often caused destructive and devastating consequences.

At the eleventh bell, Drakhart would eat another quick meal with Elandyr'ni before he would travel beyond the city walls to meet Balgorax and the other black dragons. They would teach him and Isunath how to fly in unison, ingraining rider, and dragon how to exist as one mentally and physically. Isunath was put through rigorous physical training to ensure he could keep his cool and fly with skill in the most perilous of situations.

Combat on dragonback had been the most recent lesson the dragons attempted to drill into the pair of Khaleeshir and they were exceeding expectations. It was a subject Drakhart did not wish to fall behind in because it would no doubt be how he and Kanaahn would next fight on a battlefield in the future.

After four hours with the black dragons, Drakhart would have another meal, this time he was allowed to eat where he chose, and he often chose one of the many public houses on Kasaadua's main thoroughfare. Once he'd had his fill of food and drink, Drakhart was expected to report to Calandor at the Major-domo's cottage, yet another estate within the massive palace complex of the Black Citadel.

Calandor would tutor Drakhart on speech—both elocution and language— mathematics, battle tactics, history, politics, court etiquette, and any other subject that required an astronomical amount of reading. Calandor was a harsher teacher than he seemed. He was ever calm, ever patient, always encouraging, but he expected perfection from Drakhart and would settle for no less.

Drakhart was ever eager to please.

Even after the lessons had ended in the evening, Calandor would hand Drakhart a crate full of scrolls, books, and treatises to take home for a bit of light reading. Another crate from Elandyr'ni would have already arrived at his quarters in the meantime. Drakhart was then expected to spend hours in his room during and after dinner reading the mountain he'd been given and absorbing as much as he could from them—he *would* be tested after all. That part Drakhart didn't mind at all, it improved his reading skills, and he enjoyed reading through the old texts, and the knowledge he gleaned from them was often valuable.

Drakhart had never realized how much he had been starving, though not for food, for what he craved most at his heart was knowledge.

Even now, with the hour nearing midnight, Drakhart was poring over a rather thick and dusty history on the Decline and Fall of the Gerovian Empire, immersed in a chapter about the Estian Anarchy. He was almost oblivious to the sharp knocking at his door.

It took a moment for Drakhart to drag his mind up out of the book to respond, and even still his eyes did not leave the page. "Come in."

The door opened slowly, Drakhart's back was to the door, and he did not turn or look up from his reading. With his nose still in the book, Drakhart called out to the maid who had come to provide an extra fur blanket for the evening and stoke the flames.

Nights in the Altimaran desert had been colder as of late, and even the sunlight absorbed by the black walls of the castle didn't always protect one from the cold.

"You can leave the furs on the bed. I'll take care of the fire. Thank you."

The figure responded, but it was not his chambermaid. No, this voice was masculine and exuded an ancient and subtle power. There was a slight accent to the words...like someone who had learned to speak Common as a second language but had done so long ago. It wasn't possible...

Drakhart stood up and wheeled around. It definitely wasn't his chambermaid.

The man who stood in the doorway was tall; just over two metres in height. He was broad-shouldered, with long black hair and coal-black eyes. His skin was slightly pale—

paler than Drakhart had assumed for a black dragon—and Drakhart could see the sharp lines of his cheekbones and jawline. It was as if the man's face had been carved from stone and hewn into an edge as keen as a blade.

There was exhaustion on his face, but Drakhart wasn't about to press into its origins, and Tenebrae was gaunter than Drakhart would have imagined, for such a large imposing dragon.

"My lord," exclaimed Drakhart. He hastily threw himself down to one knee and winced as he felt his joint collide with the hard stone.

"Stand, please. It's quite all right. I should have announced myself more clearly."

Drakhart fumbled to find the words as he reluctantly drew himself up from the floor. "Is something wrong?"

Tenebrae chuckled. "No, no. Nothing is wrong. I came to visit only to tell you that I have heard how deeply you've thrown yourself into your studies. Your teachers are impressed with your work ethic and progress, as am I."

"I pledged myself to your service. I wish to be as great a use to you as any others who serve you. I cannot do that while ignorant."

Tenebrae cocked his head to the side. "I know you were not pleased with my decision to put you through such a rigorous curriculum, especially since it meant abstaining from the battle and revenge, but I am pleased to see you've taken to it like a young dragon to flame."

Drakhart didn't know how to respond. He felt his voice freeze in his throat. He felt his stomach sink to his feet. He wanted to throw up and throw himself from the balcony all at the same time. Tenebrae's presence was even more unnerving as a human than he was as a massive dragon in the caverns below the city.

Tenebrae was no more just a looming presence in his mind, lurking beneath the ancient city. There were no longer kilometres of rock between him and the black dragon. The dragon stood before him, in human form, just as capable of killing him and reading his mind in Drakhart's own bed chamber as he was down below in the belly of the world.

Tenebrae mercifully kept the conversation going. "I have also come to tell you of a recent update I've been given regarding the Khaleeshir."

Drakhart perked up.

"My Eyes and Ears traced them to a Darond hideout at the base of a mountain on the Spine. We slaughtered their agents there, but they seem to have abandoned their wagons and camels. They were long gone before we discovered the hideout."

"They must have crossed the border on foot, going over the mountain and down into Estion from there."

"Yes, that is what I believe. They're likely heading to the capital, to be trained by the Dragon Master presiding there, and the Brass Dragon Aurichalcum. I have instructed my Eyes and Ears to follow the trail and confirm."

Drakhart's jaw clenched. "We should attack them while they travel. Stop them from reaching Ethon and from continuing their training. If you send me, Isunath, and some of the black dragons, we could—"

Tenebrae laughed. Not cruelly, but it was enough to send a chill down Drakhart's spine. The black dragon's laugh was like ice falling from the eaves of a roof in the dead of winter. "I appreciate your enthusiasm for the destruction of the Darond and their allies, but I have a better idea. This can provide us with a rare opportunity to take out two enemies with a single stroke of the blade.”

“How do you mean?”

“Currently we sit poised for a war that will engulf all of Enayra. It looks to be Estion, Asardaea, Espias and perhaps Utova against us. If the Darond had their way, they would turn Danaen against us as well. Years of careful statecraft may yet play out in our favour, but we still cannot fight four nations as two. We do not have the resources, even with the Qiri’ar and my clan on our side.”

Tenebrae walked towards the fire and sat himself down in one of the armchairs. He motioned to the chair beside his, indicating that Drakhart should join him.

Drakhart didn’t hesitate.

“I trust Danaen will, at worst, remain neutral in the fight to come, and at best, join us. Kings change often there, but Altimara and Danaen have long been friends. Utova is on the fence regarding the alliance, but their hostility to us is no secret. Their desire for revenge may burn brighter than their desire to be free of the wills and commands of others, and they may join the Darond yet, but to that end, we have dispatched Lord Marneron to ensure that does not happen. Estion, Espias, and Asardaea are no small threats. Asardaea commands an impressive army, and Espias is no slouch when it comes to martial matters. Estion has not been particularly wealthy or strong for a very long time, but what they lack in military might they make up for in resources. Estian timber has been used to build our navy, it builds most navies in Enayra, in fact, and Estian charcoal keeps every forge in Enayra lit from dawn until dusk. If Estion joins our enemies against us, we lose access to those resources, and we will need large quantities of both in the war to come, both for our burgeoning navy, and our forges. A single grain of sand on the scale could tip the balance one way or another. We need a way to neutralize, or better, turn Estion from the Darond and away from an alliance against us.”

“Why are the lives of the Khaleeshir necessary for this plan?” Drakhart was genuinely curious. He couldn’t see the grand web of planning Tenebrae had working away in his mind.

“If I were to use my Eyes and Ears to kill them, it would be irrefutable proof to even the most doubtful person that I have returned, and all is as the Darond says. It could work against. If I were to send the Black Blades, I risk much the same result, but I could also open Altimara up to military repercussions for murdering diplomatic guests of Estion on Estian soil using Altimaran resources. So long as the Khaleeshir are on Estian soil they are immune.

“For now, my Eyes and Ears will only follow them, keep an eye on them and track their progress. My real prize is not them, it’s Ethon. Estion has not been an especially stable or powerful nation since the Anarchy. What we must do is allow the Khaleeshir to think they are safe in Ethon, while we pull strings in the shadows and bring Estion down from the inside. If we can turn it, or remove it from the war, we will have a chance against the might of Espias and Asardaea.”

Drakhart rubbed his temples. “I must admit this sounds needlessly complicated, I can’t say I fully understand it.”

“Politics is needlessly complicated, but it is a game I must play, nonetheless. It is one *you* must learn to play if you are going to be my champion in the field and lead my forces. I want you at the head of all this once you’ve got more training behind you.”

Drakhart bowed his head in reverence. It was not the first time that Drakhart had heard of Tenebrae's plans for him, but to hear it again still astonished him.

Tenebrae smiled down at Drakhart. "I know you and the others have been hard at work on ways to try and shatter the Alliance. I know progress in such matters is slow, as to be expected. I am curious though...what are your thoughts on how to proceed? I know as the youngest, your voice can often be buried by older voices, and by your own doubt."

Drakhart's face flushed red with embarrassment. He would never have admitted his fears and insecurities to Tenebrae, and yet the dragon had been able to pinpoint them without even trying. Drakhart swallowed his pride and spoke openly, if timidly. "I...My lord I know we must avoid another disaster such as Xiar. We claim it as a victory because Xiar no longer exists, but the Darond and their allies know the truth, for all they will not dispute it on the world stage. I think we must ensure our enemies still take our threat seriously, and the best way to do that is to also humiliate the Khaleeshir. We must make them taste utter failure and defeat."

"You are certain your wish to defeat the Khaleeshir is not out of your own personal hatred and desire for revenge?"

Tenebrae had asked a legitimate question, but Drakhart, for once, was not acting selfishly, or out of desire for revenge. He had puzzled over this quandary for many hours. "No. The Khaleeshir are a morale boost for the Darond and their allies. If we can show them to be as fallible and foolhardy as any other human, they would lose face."

"And how would you hand them down this failure?" Tenebrae asked.

"At Ethon. We must take Estion out of this war. It would cause the Darond and their allies to lose heart and lose whatever boost Xiar had been. It will humiliate and humble the Khaleeshir; perhaps even demoralize them. It will also solve our issue of driving a wedge into the alliance between our enemies, and as you said, we must take Estion out of the war but keep access to its resources. This would solve all three of those problems at once. The only problem is the how..."

Tenebrae nodded. He stared into the flames and puzzled over Drakhart's words. Somewhere behind his dark eyes, Drakhart could see the wheels turning in his head. The ancient plotter, master of the long game, was once more plotting and planning.

"Drakhart. Your words are sound, and your logic has merit. I shall give you a task."

Drakhart's chest swelled with pride. "What would you have me do, my lord?"

A gentle smile crept across Tenebrae's face. "Find that how. Find Estion's weakness; something we can expose without exposing ourselves. The plan is to bring down Estion from the inside. If it's an internal matter, the other nations cannot help them. We cannot avoid a war anymore, Drakhart, but we can ensure it starts when we command, and tilted in our favour. Every advantage is a boon—there is no such thing as too much advantage."

Drakhart placed his fist over his heart. "I understand. I will not fail you."

Tenebrae took Drakhart's hand as a grandfather would take his grandchild's. He patted the back of it. "Your enthusiasm is noted. Come tomorrow, I will ask Calandor to turn over command of our spies to you. The tools of Altimara are at your disposal. You may also wish to brush up on Estian history. I find the past of a country creates its present and can inform its future. The destruction of Estion will be your brainchild. When the time comes, you will be at the spearhead of its destruction, and success or failure rests on your efforts."

Tenebrae stood up, and Drakhart did as well. He bowed to the dragon-in-human-form and watched with reverence as the man-dragon stalked from the room, likely to return to his cavern beneath the city.

When the door finally closed behind Tenebrae, and Drakhart could no longer feel the unsettling presence of his master, he ran to the garderobe to vomit.

He had been given a tremendous amount of power and responsibility. Truth be told, enthusiasm aside, Drakhart wondered if Tenebrae's trust had not been misplaced. If perhaps this was all some great test, or some great farce designed to see Drakhart fail, and failure with Tenebrae did not end well.

Fear gripped Drakhart. Fear mixed with the feeling of inadequacy. He felt like an imposter, running around in the guise of a prince or general, playing at politics and leading armies, dangled from strings like a puppet, dancing for the entertainment of others.

No. Tenebrae did not play games like that. When he was pleased with those who served him, he made his pleasure clear, and he rewarded it. When you disappointed him, you would know that as well, and punishments were handed out accordingly.

Drakhart wiped the vomit from his face and wondered how a sixteen-year-old boy from a backwater desert town could now be ennobled, be granted command over that same town, and now be placed at the right hand of Tenebrae himself.

Then Drakhart remembered that Kanaahu would be in Estion, as would the rest of his former friends. Drakhart would have the opportunity to wipe the smug looks from their faces and avenge the death of Ölüm and the loss at Xiar in one fell swoop.

Yes. That would be it. That was his motivation. He would bring Estion down around his former friends, exploiting the rot from within and bringing the nation down from the inside. A puppet ruler in place of the current king would keep Estion in line with Altimara. Someone weak enough to be pushed around, and could easily be replaced, but with enough sway behind him that he could keep a foot solidly on top of any rebellion and inspire enough people to lead an army into battle.

"*Isunath.*"

The black dragon stirred in the back of his mind. "*I heard.*"

"*Can I use your mind? I have ideas that I need to refine. I can't think alone.*"

Warmth.

Home.

Kindness and kinship.

"*Always. We are Khaleeshir. We are bonded. I am here for you, as you are for me.*"

Whatever anxiety had claimed Drakhart previously had started to leave him. His fear abated; his worry diminished. The voices in his soul telling him he wasn't strong enough for this were silenced. He could do this. He had Isunath. He could do anything.

Drakhart would need to summon his chambermaid. He would require food and coffee. He would not be sleeping again until he found this so-called weakness in the Estian armour and every possible way to exploit it.

Chapter IX

The woman peaked around the side of the alley. Soldiers had just marched past during their late-night patrol of the city. If she was caught, she'd be dead. She was wanted, after all. She slipped across the sand-strewn street, ducking into another alley in what was once known as the neighbourhood of Coppersworth, Kula's black market. It took its name from an old saying: you could buy and sell anything worth at least a copper in Kula's black market. It had been severely reduced and near expunged since the tenure of Lord Drakhart Ghast, Duke of K'nar.

Within days of the destruction of the Town Watch and the death of Lord Davenpourte, soldiers came pouring into the city, barking out orders and arresting malcontents. Drakhart himself had been there during the purging of Coppersworth and Thieves' Town. So many were arrested that Drakhart began purging those he had no room to hold or process. Those who were lucky enough to be arrested soon found their luck had run out, as they had been put to work in rebuilding the city. The burned-out ruins in the city's northern half were being rebuilt and redistributed to new arrivals coming from other areas of Altimara. Walls had been constructed, tall, high constructed of a sturdy stone quarried from out near Ottogard. A new castle was being built atop the mountainside for Lord Drakhart's personal use. The old compound that the Town Watch had used as their headquarters had been demolished and rebuilt as a large Altimaran army garrison.

Kula had changed so much in the last few months. Amber could barely recognize it. She remembered watching in disbelief when dragons came from the sky and killed the Town Watch. That brat Drakhart was now nobility, living in the capital and ruling over the people he was once a part of.

Amber had no love for Lord Davenpourte or the way things were before—except perhaps for the prevalence of crime—but these new ways were just as bad. These new magnanimous acts and gifts were coated in sugar and honey and all things sweet. They were being used to hide the injustice of it all, and that was worse than just blatant injustice.

People had jobs, but those jobs were all in the military and were being used to oppress dissent in Kula. They had new walls to protect the city from the wild creatures of the desert, but it was being built on the backs of overworked slave labourers who had once been their fellow citizens. The people had new homes built in a ruined part of town, but they were being given away to outsiders. Sure, the crime was gone...but at what cost when the rich merchants now ran things, and the common folk couldn't turn to the city's underbelly for help, for entertainment, for goods smuggled in at cheaper prices than what the merchants were offering.

Amber had lost her curios shop—which was really a front for her real business as an information broker. Now, no one remained who would buy her information, no one she was willing to sell to anyone. Drakhart had approached her, hoping their mutual friendship with Shooter would warm her to his offer.

Amber spat in his face and kicked him—literally—out of her store. Truthfully, Drakhart was lucky that that was all she did to him, but stabbing the new duke with half a legion outside was a good way to end up dead, and Amber was a survivor.

Drakhart returned the next day and had her shop burned to the ground. Luckily Amber was long gone by then. Now she was on the lam, living underground, skulking about the town at night to get supplies and visit allies, while her information runners brought her news and sent her messages during the day.

Amber stopped in a small courtyard in the middle of a group of houses. The people inside didn't seem to notice her crouching low below the windowsills. She crawled to one of the corners of the courtyard. Amber felt around in the sand until she found the handle she was looking for. Quietly, carefully, she brushed the sand off the trapdoor and threw it open. Amber closed the door behind her and pulled a small cord that dangled by the ladder. It tilted a bucket of sand up above that would spill its contents and burry the door again— she'd need to ensure that bucket was refilled the next time she went out.

When Amber reached the bottom, she picked up an oil lamp and lit it with a match she kept tucked behind her ear then proceeded down a narrow tunnel carved into the rock beneath the ground.

Here she was safe. Here they would *all* be safe.

Amber reached the end of the tunnel and met with a dead end. She reached into her robes and pulled out a large iron key. Amber groped about in the dim light until she found the next secret: a small, hidden keyhole within the rock face. She slipped the key inside the lock and slowly, gently turned the key. The tumblers inside clicked and clacked as the key opened the secret door. The sound of stone grinding against stone filled the narrow tunnel as a door parted and revealed another passage.

This place had been a little secret magicked up by Kuln's apothecary owner years ago— she had been a semi-practiced mage. Amber and other smugglers used it to store their contraband away from the prying eyes of the Town Watch and their rivals, for a nominal fee of course. The old woman had bequeathed it to Amber's ownership shortly before she was murdered by Drakhart's soldiers on suspicion of spycraft and treason. Truthfully she *had* been selling Amber information, as people always came and went, spilling their secrets and their business, but Amber had learned nothing that could topple the current regime. At least the Darond had been forgiving of her slow progress.

"All Information was gold. Even the smallest grain, the quietest of whispers, and the most mundane of news could be used against our enemies. A single grain of sand cannot topple an empire alone, but thousands together could bury it better than any rockslide."

That was what she had been taught by the previous Kulan agent of the Darond. Amber wasn't entirely sure how much she believed in the sentiment, but it was better than nothing in these times.

The rock door slid closed behind her with a gentle thud, and Amber threw her cloak onto a nearby divan. She let out a heavy sigh, feeling as if she were finally free to breathe and speak and exist once more.

This old underground warehouse now served as a refuge for those most vulnerable to retaliation from Drakhart's new regime. The new duke did not take kindly to dissent, both actual and potential, and he went to great lengths to ensure his soldiers and his castellan maintained an iron grip on the town while he was off galivanting around at court in the capital. The bastard couldn't even be bothered to come here and oppress the people himself.

Amber looked down from her balcony foyer into what was once the warehouse. She saw what she always saw here now: families huddled down below in a large, rectangular pit-like structure. Bedrolls and blankets rolled out across the floor. Everyone squeezing to fit as best as possible. It wasn't the best living conditions, but it was better than fearing for your life.

Amber climbed down the ladder into the pit and was immediately swarmed by families and children. The children loved her for saving them, and the families wanted updates, had questions, or needed something. As always, Amber listened as intently as she could. She was tired, but she had brought them here, and Amber had vowed to care for them so long as their lives were in danger. Tired as she was, her responsibilities were not so easily shirked.

It took a half hour for Amber to cross the floor and finally enter her office. She closed the door gently behind her and lit the candles and lamps throughout the room until she was satisfied with the amount of light. For the first time in three hours, Amber threw herself down into her comfy armchair—one of the few luxuries she allowed herself down here—and let out the longest sigh. It rattled from the depths of her soul, out through her lungs and flapping between her lips.

Sleep. That was what she wanted. She wanted to sleep for the next seven weeks. She wanted to ignore everyone knocking at her door, or barging in. She wanted to ignore every time the soldiers got close to discovering where she was and what she was doing, but she couldn't. She knew she couldn't. Too many depended on her, and Amber had made a promise. To herself, to the people she now cared for, to the woman who had recruited her, and to herself.

Amber looked over at her desk and stared with foreboding at the stack of paperwork that had come in that morning. She hadn't even had a chance to look at it yet. That was next on the list. Then she looked over at the opened letter that sat just a few inches from that first stack. Amber had received this letter three weeks ago from the woman who had recruited her; the woman she replaced as the new Kulan agent. In truth, Amber had known this woman for years, selling her information without knowing who she worked for. If Amber knew then what she knew now she might've closed up shop and moved away from Kula the first moment she set eyes on that woman. But this woman had paid well, and now the Darond paid well, and anything was better than living helplessly in fear, after all.

Amber picked up the letter, but she didn't need to reread the words. They were burned into her mind. She saw them when she closed her eyes. She saw them as she lay in bed each night, hoping sleep—or sometimes death—would take her. She saw them at the worst of times. They were not just burned into her mind; they were etched into her heart.

"He's asking about you. He wants to know if you're alive."

Bastard.

Amber didn't know how to feel, let alone respond. She had asked to see him shortly before he left, and instead of showing up to their planned meeting he simply disappeared. He never came by the store to tell her, to warn her, he didn't even send a note. He had just disappeared into the night, fleeing Kula, never to be seen again.

At first, she was mad—no, she was livid. She had seriously considered putting out a bounty for him. Shooter had never snubbed her like this before, especially at such a crucial...

After what they shared...

What he promised...

How she loved him...

When they...

Bastard...

Amber rubbed her temples. She couldn't even finish the thought now. She could feel her heart tear itself to shreds every time she tried. The rage subsided when that woman—that fucking woman—walked right into her shop and laid everything before her. The whole truth of why he had left, and *what* he had left with. That woman told Amber where he went, why it was so fast and abrupt, and where he had ended up in the end.

The truth was almost harder to swallow than the excuses Amber had thought up in her head. Dragons. That Kanaahn had come back from the mountain with dragon eggs, and they had hatched. The five of them left to raise their dragons in safety, to protect themselves and the new lives they had been tasked with safeguarding. The woman called them Khaleeshir. That word meant nothing to Amber at first, until the woman said the word she *was* familiar with: Dragonkin.

Lucky fucker.

He hadn't just abandoned her for fun. He had gone off to—knowingly or unknowingly—do his part to help people he had never met. Truthfully, Amber didn't believe it at first. Shooter had a big heart beneath all the damage and abuse. Beneath his selfish exterior beat the heart of a man who knew compassion and wished to give it to others but didn't feel he deserved it in kind. She could see him fighting for his friends, and maybe for people he knew, but putting his life on the line for millions that may never see him or know his name? With such a slim chance of success? Amber knew Shooter was a gambler, but she never thought he was that bad at playing odds. Then again, he had never been that good of a gambler, so she ceded that it was possible.

Then something happened that made her realize the truth of it all. Drakhart had returned with a black dragon of his own and killed Lord Davenpourte, ransacked his estate and destroyed the Town Watch with a horde of other black dragons that came spilling forth from the mountain like some reptilian volcano. It was then that Amber started to realize that the previous agent wasn't bullshitting her. It was also right around then that Amber was approached and recruited as her replacement before the woman disappeared into the night without so much as a thank you. At that point, Amber figured that if Shooter could be selfless and do his part, then she could stand to do the same. Maybe one day she'd get a chance to see him again. She had heard of Shooter's exploits at the Battle of Xiar, and that he was now on the way to Estion to continue his training.

And yet...

And yet...

When the word came that he had been looking for her, to make sure she was alive, Amber couldn't bring herself to respond. She froze. She wanted to respond and tell him she was all right, and that they'd see each other soon. Tell him the news she'd wanted to tell him before he left, but there was a part of her that was scared; that was hurt. Would he still feel the same after all this time? After all, he'd experienced out in the world without her, would he still *need* her? Especially now that he had gone out and matured, and his parents were dead. It was those thoughts that haunted her most, and the answer she came to scared her.

"Miss Amber?" A voice called out from behind the door. It was Vilingar, one of her runners.

"Come in."

Vilingar had been her runner when she was still just an information broker, and he had been one of the few she trusted with the most secret of information. He was also one of the few runners she took with her when she took the new position. The door barely opened and Vilingar slipped in through the smallest crack before it closed again behind him. Amber always said he was more shadow than flesh.

"New report from the Skullspider." Vilingar placed the rolled-up parchment on her desk, saluted, and slipped back off into the masses, all without making a sound.

Skullspider. That was the codename of the woman whom Amber had replaced, the woman who had recruited her. She took her name from the Altimaran Skullspider. They were massive, man-sized spiders known for spinning large, almost invisible webs across the entrances of—and inside—caves and canyons. They took their names from the skull-like pattern that covered most of their backs and bodies. The threads these spiders spun were thin enough to remain unseen but were unable to trap their prey. Instead, the advantage of the thin, invisible silk was that it was steeped in a toxin that infected on contact with the webs. Each time the potential victim collided with one of the many webs, they would be infected by small amounts of the toxin that would gradually shut down their bodily functions and slowly kill them painlessly and insidiously. Then the spiders would swoop in and slowly liquify their prey with their venom and devour their prey over several days.

Skullspider drew comparisons to the hunting method of the actual spider, and the way she used her information to slowly destroy Altimara and Tenebrae's regime from within. It was a little on the nose for Amber's liking, but then again, so was being a redhead named Amber, so she wasn't one to talk.

Amber unrolled the parchment and quickly scanned the scrawl. Her blood ran cold, her heartbeat faster in her chest, and her eyes widened as she learned what Skullspider had gleaned from her contacts within the noble houses who had been at the Black Citadel for the Royal Conclave.

Amber's heart sank as she read each word once, twice, then thrice. That had been no Kingsmoot, it had been the wholesale betrayal of Altimara and her people to a new and more wicked master. Moreover, plans were underway to begin the continent-wide war that would plunge Enayra into chaos and bloodshed for years to come.

Then a wicked smile crossed Amber's face as a plan came together within her mind. Many wars failed when their participants couldn't keep peace on the home front. Could Altimara really fight a war against her enemies if she was fighting her people from within? Time would tell, but Amber would need to act, and soon.

Amber ran to the door and threw it open. "Vilingar! Gather my runners!"

Chapter X

Boom.
> *Boom.*
>> *Boom.*
>>> *Boom.*

Kanaahn awoke within his dream. He stood in a massive stone cavern, somewhere...he was quite certain where he was. Was this even Enayra? Was any of this real?

He could feel a thrumming, a humming, and a beat like a drum. It reverberated through the cavern, through his chest. Kanaahn could feel it in the base of his skull, shuddering through his teeth, and into the depths of his very soul. It was somewhere between music and a heartbeat.

Boom.
> *Boom.*

Boom.
> *Boom.*

Boom.
> *Boom.*

Boom.
> *Boom.*

Huuuuuuuuuummmmmmmmmm.
Huuuuuuuuuummmmmmmmmm.

Boom.
> *Boom.*

Boom.

Boom.

Hu-hu-uuuuuuuuuuuuuummmmmm.

Boom.

Boom.

Boom.

Boom.

Huuuu-uuuuuuuuuuuuum.

Kanaahn had never heard music like this before. He wasn't even sure where it was coming from. All he could see was the darkness around him, the tall ceiling of the cavern obscured by the sheer height of it.

He turned to see two massive pillars of crystal, one white, one black, stretching from the floor to the ceiling like great cenotaphs of luminescent stone. Lightning crackled around them. If Kanaahn had to guess, they were rippling with arcane energy; he was not well versed in magic, but he had seen enough to know that there was something magical about these crystal pillars.

Kanaahn watched as the lightning danced across the surface of the pillars, striking other bolts of lightning in mid-air, striking the walls and floors of the cavern, only to send a spray of splintered rock in all directions. The explosions were minor, but the small sharp pieces would've been deadly if Kanaahn had been there...wherever there was.

But why was he being shown this?

What did it all mean?

Boom Boom.

Boom Boom.

Boom Boom.

Boom Boom.

Boom Boom.

Boom Boom.

Boom Boom.

Boom Boom.

The beating of the ethereal drum picked up pace. The beat grew more frantic, faster. Yet despite this, Kanaahn still felt at peace. He could hear a disembodied choir singing throughout the room. They hummed, they thrummed, they wailed to the sky in harmonious ecstasy. Still, Kanaahn saw no one around him. It was like a thousand ghosts; the souls of a thousand ecstatic people were singing the most joyous praises of...something? Kanaahn couldn't quite explain it. He was the only one in this cave, and yet he didn't feel alone. He felt eyes on him and could sense many presences. So many presences. Warm, cold, welcoming, hateful. There was life all around him, but it was invisible to Kanaahn.

Some of these empty voices thrummed as if singing in the back of their throat. Their voices were deep, and they shook Kanaahn to his core. Others were high, beautiful, and sonorous. Like a warm spring breeze across a field of beautiful flowers. Like the wind in the trees. Crisp; the feeling of biting into a fresh apple and feeling the cool juice dripping down your chin.

Kanaahn could only think of one phrase to describe the unearthly choir: hauntingly beautiful, and beautifully haunting.

Kanaahn took a step forward, and light began to emanate from the crystal pillars. It filled the room as water filled a sinking ship, and Kanaahn could suddenly see across the massive cavern to the far wall. He could now see a third and even larger crystal structure. It was colourless, but not see-through. It stood alone and looked to be even larger than Kanothir. This massive crystal filled much of the space it occupied, but it did not touch the walls or ceilings. It looked as if some great crystal flower had bloomed here in this cavern, but instead of petals, it was covered in large, sharp spikes and thorns. Though Kanaahn could not physically touch this crystal, he felt that if he broke off one of these thorns he'd be quite able to stab a man to death with the shard or pierce even the toughest armour. It glowed with an unearthly light, and it seemed...alive? It was one of the most beautiful things he'd ever seen.

Kanaahn then looked past the crystal. He could see, along the far wall, nestled up against the smooth rock surface, a large metal ring. The metal of the ring was easily half a metre thick both ways and it was buried in the rock itself, giving it the shape of a horseshoe. It looked almost like a gate of some sort, with ancient, unreadable runes carved into the front of it. Whatever the metal ring was, it too felt alive...but it was weakened. It gave off the aura of an old man lying on his death bed, wasting away, and becoming a hollow wisp of his former self. Whatever life was in that metal ring was slowly draining away, but it was not dead yet.

"What is this place?" Kanaahn asked.

His voice was disembodied. His lips did not move, his throat did not buzz with sound. Was he speaking through his mind? He wasn't sure. He didn't know how this place worked. Was it a dream, was it real?

No one would answer him. Even the disembodied choir, singing their prayers to whatever it was they saw fit to worship, was now silent.

His voice echoed through the room. "Hello?"

The only response was his own voice, bouncing back at him.

Boom.

Boom.

Boom.

Boom.

Boom.

Boom.

Boom.

Boom.

Boom.

Boom.

Boom.

Boom.

Boom.

Boom.

Boom.

Boom.

Boom.

Boom.

Boom.

Boom.

Boom.

Boom.

Boom.

Boom.

Boom.

Boom.

Boom.

Boom.

The drums petered off, the sound of their booming drifting off into the dark ceiling, drawing further apart, and ever slower in their call and response as if both drums went drifting off down two separate forks in a river.

The sound faded.

The light faded.

The beautiful cavern faded.

The dream faded.

Kanaahn faded.

* * *

Kanaahn opened his eyes and completely forgot the dream he had just experienced. Some faint knowledge of it hovered beneath the surface of his consciousness, like a poor unfortunate soul trapped beneath a thick sheet of ice, banging desperately against the barrier to get out; to be freed, hoping anyone, someone, would hear their cries and listen. But much like that poor unfortunate soul, the awareness of the dream felt the cold creep into its heart, felt the water fill its lungs. It grew still, the light left its eyes, and the struggle left its heart. It stopped banging. It stopped screaming. The only light that remained was the one at the end of the tunnel, and the dream, like the drowning person, sank deep into the dark, black ocean, never to be seen again.

Kanaahn had been surprised the previous evening. When he had gone upstairs, instead of being inundated with a deluge of questions and speculation from his friends—all of it mental, as not to embarrass Kyeit—Kanaahn had found his friends said nothing, not even Shooter. They had been fast asleep when he went up. But this didn't mean Kanaahn trusted his friends to say nothing. More likely, his friends were waiting for the opportunity to speak to Kanaahn in person, vocally, without having to hide within their own heads. Some gossip was better heard from the mouth than the mind, after all.

Kanaahn was proven correct when Arial pounced on the foot of his bed, bouncing Kanaahn around beneath the blanket like a coin in a coin purse.

Kanaahn groaned.

Arial shook him. "Wake up, they're gone."

Kanaahn groaned louder.

Shooter put a foot on the footboard and rested his elbow on his knee. "You can't hide from it forever. You had to know this was coming."

"Go away."

Arkas ripped the blanket from the bed, coming face to face with a very groggy, tired, and angry Kanaahn. Arkas shrugged and threw the blanket on one of the other beds. "Speak."

Kanaahn scowled. "I hate all of you," he croaked in a cracked morning voice.

He got up and stalked over to the pitted stone slab by the fireplace. The slab was built of the same stone that capped and framed the hearth, and the warmth of the fireplace heated the slab, and thus, the water within. Using the warmed water Kanaahn washed the sleep from his face, the crust from his eyes, and the fuzziness from his tongue and mouth. It was a few moments before Kanaahn felt like he was once more among the living, and he finished by running wet hands through his hair, using his fingers to remove any tangles. Finally, when he felt awake, Kanaahn turned to his friends, who had patiently waited for his return on his bed.

"Well?" demanded Arial.

Kanaahn shot her a look but acquiesced to her request. The sooner this torture was over, the faster he could slather his feet in pig fat and hold them over a burning fire. It would be less painful than this interrogation by his friends. "Nothing happened. We talked, that's it. Breakfast anyone?"

"Hold up!" Arial complained. "What the fuck was that? I want more details."

"I saw them making out on the floor," Shooter blurted out.

Arial gasped.

Arkas crossed his arms and tried not to smirk.

Kanaahn looked at Shooter, mulling over whether he should start choking Shooter now or later. "I wasn't making out with her."

Shooter shrugged. "That's not what it looked like to me."

Kanaahn pinched the bridge of his nose. He inhaled deeply, gathering what few shreds of his patience remained. Hunger welled in his stomach, and it was not aiding his mood. After a moment, Kanaahn turned around one of the armchairs by the fire so he could sit and face his friends. He told them of how he spoke with Kyeit—but not what they had talked about in detail—and mentioned how she had reason to fear the Kotharii—though not what that reason was. He explained how he made known the group's concerns, and his own concerns, for Kyeit's wellbeing, and how her recent behaviour since the death of her father had concerned them.

Kanaahn also explained how towards the end of the conversation, Kyeit *had* kissed him, and he had returned the kiss, but their kiss had been just that and had been cut short by Shooter's return from his late-night tryst with the local bard. Kanaahn's mention of Shooter's romp and late return had done exactly as he expected and turned the gossip-mongering and attention from his own adventures to Shooter's.

Shooter's face went from wry playfulness to a fish gasping for air as he attempted to turn the tables back on Kanaahn. His friends had learned everything about Kanaahn's adventures, and nothing about Shooters.

Kanaahn shot Shooter a smirk and quietly sneaked from the room while the gossip wolves tore apart the meaty gossip lamb. He closed the door behind him and turned, coming face to face with Cecil.

Kanaahn jumped.

"I'm sorry," came Cecil's whispered response. Her face betrayed her body. She stood with her arms folded, leaning to one side as she scanned Kanaahn up and down, but her face was calm, her eyes were kind, and her mouth wriggled as if trying to hide a knowing smile.

"Fuck, does everyone just know?" Kanaahn muttered.

"You and Kyeit were the only ones left down in the bar. You were down there a while with an unending supply of alcohol."

"I suppose that's fair. I might've assumed the same if it was one of you guys."

"Besides, there's the very obvious feelings you have for her."

Kanaahn didn't respond.

Cecil prodded once more, getting right to the point of what she was looking for. "You didn't tell them, did you?"

Kanaahn instantly picked up the words between the words. "Only what she was feeling, but not why. She told me about her past in confidence. It didn't feel right to tell them too."

Cecil smiled, nodded, and patted Kanaahn on the back. "I'm sure she'd appreciate that. I only know because I was there but...I know it's not something Kyeit tells just anyone. It's a sore spot for her. Not a proud moment of her life."

Kanaahn had no idea how to respond and opted instead to change the subject. "What time is it?"

"Almost midday," replied Cecil. "I'd go down and get some food quickly, we're leaving before day's end."

"Why? I thought we were supposed to spend the next few days gathering supplies and preparing for our travels, to blend in like real mercenaries?"

"Ruoth just got word from the spy network. Edva and Kaltar were slaughtered last night. Someone attacked their camp; there was a struggle but...it didn't last long. Whatever it was also killed your camels and tore apart your wagons. There were no survivors."

There was a panging sense of loss in Kanaahn's stomach. He had travelled across Altimara with those wagons and those camels. He had come to appreciate and love them as one would love a pet dog. It saddened him to think he would never see them or the wagons again, but such was the cost of the war they were fighting.

Then Kanaahn's thoughts turned to the "someone" Cecil had mentioned, and he could think of only one thing. "The Kotharii?" he asked, using the Asardaean term that Cecil had once used.

Cecil nodded. "Signs seem to suggest it."

Kyeit's worst fears and all her overcaution seemed to have come back to haunt the group.

"Do they know anything about us or our motives, where we're headed?"

"I don't know. They've found your camels and wagons, and they now know there was a Darond camp guarding a passage through the mountains on the Estion-Altimara border. I'm sure Tenebrae and his allies will be able to figure out the rest."

That was not good.

"Do we have horses and supplies?"

"Ruoth is just bringing in the last of them now and getting the stable hands to load up the horses. He's given us some of the fastest horses he could find."

"Bless that man." Tohru was owed a large debt if they managed to survive this war, and Kanaahn would see it paid. "Have the dragons been alerted?"

"I broke the rules and had Shooter contact Risasi earlier this morning. They'll be ready to meet us a few kilometres from the town. Now, get down there and eat. Kyeit's at the table with your food. We leave as soon as you're done. I'll go tell the others."

Kanaahn didn't waste a second. He slipped down the steps as fast as he could. His stomach roared like a hungry dragon—he could probably eat just as much. He scanned the bar as he reached the landing, scanning for Kyeit and where she was sitting.

Kanaahn met the eyes of Tohru, who simply smirked, winked, and pointed to the table in the back corner where they had sat the previous evening. Tohru *knew*. Somehow, he *knew*.

Kanaahn's cheeks went a vivid shade of pink, and he rushed over to Kyeit and the table—and more importantly his food.

"What's to eat?" he asked. He sat himself down opposite Kyeit, ready to grab as much food as he could carry. It was mostly just warm bread and biscuits with a side of butter and some warmed cider, but it was better than nothing.

"Cecil told you about what happened?" asked Kyeit. Her tone had grown more muted since the last night, and based on her eyes and facial expression, she was feeling the alcohol a little.

"Yes. I'm sorry about Edva and Kaltar. I didn't know them long, but they seemed like good people."

Kyeit only nodded and pushed a basket of bread towards Kanaahn.

Kanaahn ravenously tore into the bread as respectfully as possible for the situation. He chewed, swallowed, and looked at Kyeit. She wasn't even going to mention last night. Stoic as ever. Whatever she was feeling would be closely guarded until such a time as she felt others were ready to know. Was she upset with him? Was she hungover? Was she simply sad about her friends dying? Probably a little of the latter two options, and not much of the former, but the uncertainty was enough to kill Kanaahn's appetite. He wasn't good in awkward situations or with feelings.

"Kyeit—"

She cut him off with a warm smile. "I'm fine. I'm...I'm sad. I won't lie it does sting a bit, especially considering who..." She paused. "I'm fine, I promise, but we'll need to be careful until we reach Ethon."

"I understand."

Tohru floated by the table, leaving a tray of food for Kanaahn. There was a bowl of warm broth, some porridge and something Kanaahn recognized as 'coffee.' He'd never had any—it was expensive and not as popular in Altimara—but he'd heard wonderful things, and it smelled good.

Kanaahn grabbed the small, hand-spun mug and sniffed the steaming black liquid. It was dark as pitch, smooth as water, and smelled like heaven. He took a gentle sip, immediately singed his tongue on the brew, and grimaced at the bitter taste. "What the fuck is this," he protested. The coffee tasted nothing like it smelled.

"It's coffee," Kyeit said, sipping her own mug of the stuff.

"This tastes like the ashes from last night's fire."

"You can add things to it if you don't like it," Kyeit suggested.

"People do that?" Kanaahn's mind was blown.

"Milk, sugar, sometimes cream."

Kanaahn was familiar with milk. Camel milk was popular in Kula, but it didn't agitate into cream too well, nor butter, but it made good yoghurt. Sugar was known but was uncommon. It was mostly seen in sweets and pastries, which were often expensive and saved for special occasions.

Kyeit handed Kanaahn the ingredients she'd mentioned and showed him how he could go about adding them to his coffee in various amounts.

Kanaahn decided he would start by drinking the coffee with only a little milk at first and branch out from there. It cut the bitter taste and added a creamy texture to the coffee. Yes, this was much more to his liking.

Kyeit shook her head as if watching a puppy discover his tail for the first time. "Hurry up and finish eating, we want to leave as soon as possible."

Kanaahn nodded and went back to his meal, while Kyeit slipped from the table and went for the stables, where she'd go and check on Tohru's stable.

* * *

They left the village about an hour or so after Kanaahn had finished eating. Tohru had given them the fastest horses he could procure. He called them full-bloods. Cecil clarified they were specifically Estian full-bloods; the distinction was important since many horse breeders interbred Estians with other breeds to try and create new breeds with the Estian traits. Estian full-bloods were prized for their biddable nature and their so-called bravery, which meant they didn't spook easily, and made for fantastic warhorses—a trait that was important if they would be near dragons. They were fast horses, some of the fastest on the continent, and could gallop for long distances without needing a rest. These horses would be ideal for getting the Khaleeshir away from their enemies in a pinch but were still stocky enough that they could carry their riders and gear without issue. More importantly, they'd be nimble in the dense forests off the main road.

Kyeit and Cecil each rode palomino stallions. Arial had been stuck with a dun mare that did whatever she pleased. Arkas and Shooter ended up with relatively pliant grullo and blue roan geldings respectively, and Kanaahn had an amber champagne mare that had tried several times—with varying degrees of success—to take chunks out of Kanaahn's flesh with her teeth.

The Kulan teens were not well versed in horseback riding and had learned quickly that riding a horse was nothing like riding a camel. The two creatures walked differently, mounted differently, behaved differently—and honestly, they smelled different. A musty camel smelled like home. It was the embodiment of childhood or a happy nostalgic memory. Though Kanaahn would be lying if he said the horse didn't smell better.

The dragons brought up the rear of the group, walking single file on relatively narrow paths between the trees. The dragons were not used to walking such long distances and Kanaahn could tell Djall ached for the freedom of the sky above, but Kyeit and Cecil had stressed the importance of remaining beneath the canopy. They'd be harder to spot through the dense weave of branches and foliage, and a lot harder to ambush from above. Kanaahn couldn't disagree with the logic.

There had been no official confirmation that Kaltar and Edva had been killed by the Kotharii, but the likelihood was high. From everything Kanaahn had heard of them, he shuddered to think that they were following the group, and without the canopy above, could drop from the sky and attack them at any point.

Kyeit had been on edge since they left Felidrun, though she wasn't as bad as when they had crossed the border. Speaking with Kanaahn had seemed to take some of the weight off her chest, but now that she had confirmation of her fears and worries, she continued to brace for the worst.

It would not do to be caught unawares by the Kotharii, and in that respect, Kanaahn also could not disagree.

The trip went mostly silently. Occasionally one of the dragons would curse in draconic from behind the horses, having tripped on some outlying rock or root. It was all Risasi could do to control his temper and not burn and tear every root he saw—partially for the sake of remaining hidden, but also for the sake of the living, ancient trees that surrounded them all in the forests of Estion.

It was still weird to ride in the shade of so many trees and be surrounded by so much green and vegetation.

Kanaahn's gut felt uneasy not being able to look up and have an unobstructed view for kilometres in every direction. He felt trapped; like the group could be snuck up on at any moment. He'd also be lying if he didn't feel just a little chilly without the undying sun always beating down on him. Kanaahn was glad he'd gotten accustomed to wearing a shirt.

Though, it *was* admittedly nice to not have to worry about a cadre of deadly and violent—often poisonous—creatures sneaking up to attack and murder you as you slept or travelled. That was one thing Estion had over Altimara.

Winged wolves weren't going to swoop down, drag you up into the sky, and drop you until you were an easily digestible smear on the sands.

Rishi beasts weren't going to swoop down on you, spray their acidic stomach bile on you and then devour you as you writhed around, screaming in agony, blind and helpless.

Gnars weren't going to erupt from the ground, emerging from their subterranean caverns and holes in the ground below and drag you and your children and any small animals you had off into the night. No fear of dying while kicking and screaming as the pale, near-blind, and sharp-fanged hordes devoured you alive.

The most one had to worry about in Estion according to Kyeit were Geller's Bear, Geller's Moose, and Geller's Giant Rattler. Each was a massive megafauna that had a penchant for aggressive behaviour when others, usually humans, invaded their territory.

Sir Antoine Geller was a long-dead biologist who made it his goal to discover as much megafauna as he could in Estion and name it after himself. He was killed by his last discovery: Geller's Sabertoothed Boar.

Once the obvious question had been answered, Kanaahn learned that the only reason Sir Geller had been given the honour of being able to name so many megafaunas after himself was that no one else at his university was willing—or stupid—enough to attempt to study these creatures up close. Even Geller's Moose was colloquially known as the "Death Moose" for its violent disposition and razor-sharp antler points that had been famously known to gore even young, foolish dragons.

Djall's response, however, had been predictable. "I would very much like to meet one."

"I think you mean *eat* one," Kanaahn retorted.

"Same difference..."

Valence interjected. "Braver dragons than you have tried and died. I would not test a Geller's Moose until you were much older and larger."

Djall's pride was wounded, but the warning had stuck.

The group stopped a few hours before sundown in a wide clearing, near a babbling creek. Though sundown was a while away, sunlight was sparse beneath the thick canopy of trees, and darkness came much earlier than normal. It was better to camp early than to stumble around in the darkness of the Estian woods. So camp was made, and the hunt was on for dinner. The horses were watered and let loose in the clearing to graze on whatever grasses they could find, and the dragons were allowed to finally fly and hunt for their dinner under the watchful eyes of Valence and Kinokaze.

Shooter and Arkas had managed to snare a few rabbits for dinner and Arial and Kanaahn had prepared a stew to go with the vegetables Tohru had gifted them.

By the time the rabbits were cleaned, and the stew cooked, night had truly fallen, and the forest was wrapped in a thick blanket of darkness. Outside of the warmth and light of the campfire, the surroundings of the group were impossible to discern—even the normally farsighted Khaleeshir were blinkered by the sheer darkness of the woods at night.

The Khaleeshir, Kyeit, and Cecil now sat close to the campfire and enjoyed the fruits of their labour from wooden bowls.

Cecil blew softly on her second spoonful of stew. "I never knew you were such a good cook Kanaahn."

"I can't take all the credit. It wouldn't be half as good without Arial there to keep an eye on it all."

Arial shrugged. "Shooter and Arkas deserve some credit too. They brought back the meat. They've always had an eye for the best catch."

"It's not that hard. My father was a hunter-butcher in Kula. Growing up my father taught me, my brother, and sisters how to hunt in the lands around the city," explained Arkas. "He taught me how to tell the ages of animals, and which ones looked healthy and which ones were sick. It was a balancing act. You don't want to eat a sick and dying animal, but you can't only be killing the young breeding stock."

Shooter shrugged. "I'm just a second set of eyes."

"Well, whoever's responsible, this stew is amazing," Kyeit concluded.

Their first bowls were drained, and seconds were passed around.

Finally, Kanaahn gathered the bravery to breach the subject that had been on everyone's minds since their sudden departure from Felidrun. "What's the plan?"

Kyeit didn't look up from her bowl. "The new plan is the old plan. We head to Ethon, where we'll meet with Dragon Master Anducaerleonis and Aurichalcum. They will continue your training until you require more training, or until Estion is no longer deemed safe by the Darond. Though, we'll be taking a slightly different route to the capital."

As usual, Cecil picked up where Kyeit finished. Kanaahn wondered if they practised their routine before speaking with the Khaleeshir. "We had originally intended to have the dragons fly above, and we'd take the Kingsroad to the capital, blending in with the locals along the way. But we'd be too easily visible from above, and with the Kotharii hunting us, we can't take that risk. We're going to remain off the main roads for as long as possible until we're close enough to Ethon that the fear of Aurichalcum will keep the Kotharii at bay. We're also going to cut through Green Dragon Clan territory. The Kotharii will keep at a further distance the second we're within range of the green dragons' lands."

Kyeit picked up the trail from there. "The Kotharii are not brave enough to take on the might of the Green Dragon Clan, and their master would not allow them to act so boldly just yet. To do so would risk losing the Kotharii or galvanizing the other nations openly against him. Or both."

Kanaahn's eyes lit up with Djall's excitement. The dragon's elation leaked through into Kanaahn's mind and began to infect his disposition.

"Djall seems pleased," joked Kyeit.

"He hasn't shut up about it since we crossed the border."

"Will the dragons be expecting us?" asked Arial.

"Valence will be sent ahead when we near their territory," explained Kyeit. "She'll let them know our situation, but we'll likely be invited to an audience with the clan leaders."

"That's why we'll be spending as much time between now and when we reach the Green Dragon Clan briefing you on dragon etiquette and improving your Draconic," added Cecil. "As Khaleeshir, you cannot be caught unawares in diplomatic situations—even amongst dragons."

Groans went up around the campfire.

"I thought we'd have a break until Ethon," complained Shooter.

"You're Khaleeshir. You don't get breaks," chided Cecil. "You can sit on your asses when the war's done and won, but until then, you'll be training."

"So, what's this Anducaerleonis like?" asked Arial.

It was Cecil who answered. "He's a kind man, a good king, and a wise Dragon Master, despite his young age. He's a man of the people and an incredibly skilled mage in his own right. He's one of the Darond's strongest mages. Though I should warn you all now, he prefers to simply be known as Leon, King Leon if you must, but he does not appreciate a liberal use of his full name."

"I should also warn that before we enter the capital," Kyeit began. "Estion is...precarious, politically speaking. Leon has the support of his people, and he rules with them in mind."

"What's so bad about that?" asked Arkas, still able to remember how self-serving Lord Davenpourte had been back in Kula.

"In doing so, he's pulled a lot of power from the nobility and their armies. As such, King Leon isn't as popular amongst his father's old supporters," Kyeit explained. "The King cannot raise their own armed forces in Estion, not since King Aethalmenis III was overthrown by his son, Leon's father."

"To make a long story short," Cecil continued, "The King's power, and the enforcement of his laws, come from the army and the nobility that controls them. King Khomandar II ruled the kingdom as head of an oligarchy, doling out power, favours, and riches to his nobility to ensure his own power remained—in practice, if not publicly—unfettered. In doing so, he earned the ire of the people. Leon is the opposite of his father. He has gained the love of his people, but in doing so he has pushed his realm a little closer to civil war."

"It won't really come to that, will it?" asked Arial. "That seems a little dramatic."

Cecil let out a rattling sigh. "Estion has a long and complicated history. When they weren't trying to attack and conquer Asardaea or the other nations as the Gerovian Empire, they were at war with themselves as various incarnations of the Kingdom of Estion. Countless kings and dynasties have been deposed, murdered, purged, overthrown, replaced, and restored in the nearly two thousand years since the fall of the Enayran Empire. It's left the political landscape of Estion fractured and broken.

"You have the old, conservative hard-line war hawks that want to restore the old Gerovian ways and the imperialism that comes with. They want a strong military, an authoritarian monarchy, a wealthy nobility, and a shackled peasantry. Then there are the more moderate royalists who want a less militant country run by a constitutional monarch, with power shared between the nobility and the Crown, and mild freedoms for the people. Finally, you have the die-hard Republicans who don't want any monarchy and would prefer an Estion united under a government formed by the people, of the people, with the people's interests at the heart of it all. A government made up of temporary and popularly elected representatives."

"This is going to affect their participation in the war to come, isn't it?" Kanaahn asked flatly.

Kyeit shrugged. "The Darond are unsure. King Leon and his father, for all their issues at home, have always been deeply involved with the Darond and devoted to the cause. It's made even more complicated by the fact that Khomandar is currently the Grand Master of the Darond Order, head of the High Council, and is the Dragon Master under Aurum himself. Leon is the Dragon Master under Aurichalcum and is also on the High Council as both a Dragon Master and a monarch of Enayra."

Kanaahn caught Shooter's look from the corner of his eye. It was the same grim look that appeared on the faces of the others. The idea of having a corrupt oligarch in charge of the Darond was concerning, especially having grown up in Kula and seeing how it affected innocent people. Suddenly, the actions of the High Council, and how they attempted to control and manipulate the Khaleeshir made more sense.

"But if Leon were deposed..." Cecil suggested. She didn't need to finish her sentence. The implications were clear enough.

"Are we ever going to go to an allied nation where the political situation isn't precarious?' asked Shooter. "First there was that whole thing in Xiar where Espias couldn't interfere, and now we might be facing a revolution."

Cecil shrugged. "War brings many consequences. Death, destruction, and suffering upon the masses, and an endless supply of paperwork and political intricacies that cause headaches for even the most skilled and long-serving of diplomats."

Kyeit placed her bowl near the stone ring around the fire. "We should get some rest and divide up the watch. We'll have an early day tomorrow, and every day until we're safe in Ethon."

No one had any objections to sleep. A day's riding had been more tiring than they expected. Their thighs were sore from being stretched over a horse's back all day and a general exhaustion had just settled over them from the travel.

It was decided that Shooter and Arkas would take the first watch, being the least tired, followed by Kanaahn and Arial finally Cecil and Kyeit.

The dragons would sleep separate from the humans, as their hunt had taken them far from the camp, but they would return by the morning. Despite the distance, the Khaleeshir could feel the mental connection as strong as ever, and none of them wished to let go, especially having been separated previously.

Despite being told to sleep, the Khaleeshir would stay up late into the night, conversing back and forth with their bonded partners, drawing strength and solace from their bonds.

Chapter XI

It took several weeks before Elandyr'ni felt comfortable allowing Drakhart to commit to more complex spells, and even then it had only been at the insistence of Tenebrae. Their master wished to measure Drakhart's growth.

It had only been a few hours, and Drakhart was already exhausted. Blood magic took an incredible amount of will, mental acuity, and fortitude. Unpractised Warlocks found themselves consumed by a lust for power and blood. That was their downfall.

According to Elandyr'ni, drawing pure mana from blood was incredibly addictive for the average being. No one was quite sure why, but her studies into the subject led Elandyr'ni to estimate that it was psychological, more than physical and had something to do with the incredible amount of power promised and achieved by blood magic. Warlocks would justify the blood needed, and how they would go about getting it. The lesser evil, the bigger picture; whatever reason they gave, these warlocks would go mad and commit atrocities just to satisfy their lust. And why shouldn't they? What was the cost? Slit a few throats, spill some blood, draw some runes in that blood, speak some words—or don't if you were good enough—and draw on the pure energy of life itself. All you had to do was kill two or twelve people you didn't know.

It was easy to become lost to the Blood Lust. Too easy. Which was why Elandyr'ni spent days subjecting heavy mental burdens upon Drakhart as he cast even the most minor of spells with blood magic. Asking him questions that involved heavy thinking. Testing him on his memory of historical events and the Draconic language. Making him exert himself physically while casting spells. Anything to help him build a strong focus on his magic.

Drakhart was surprised by how much focus it took to cast even the most minor of spells when he couldn't dedicate his entire mind to it. His disdain for the practice subjected upon him soon left, and was replaced with respect for Elandyr'ni, and that she cared enough not to let Drakhart die by his own careless, untrained hand. Though, Drakhart supposed that was more directive from Tenebrae, considering how important Drakhart was to Tenebrae's plans.

What were Tenebrae's plans for—

"Focus!" cried Elandyr'ni.

Drakhart shook his head and focused on the task at hand.

He stood within a circle of blood and runes. A line led from his circle to a much larger circle. Within the second circle stood Isunath, looking pained, but excited. Five other circles were placed around the outer ring of the larger circle, connected by lines of blood and runes that crisscrossed beneath Isunath's feet and formed a pentagram. It was, as Elandyr'ni had told Drakhart, the most powerful symbol in blood magic. The number five was sacred for Warlocks. Five of anything was said to be incredibly potent. Warlocks often cast spells in groups of five for the larger, harder spells. A sacrifice of five offerings was best as well. It was a weird and ancient rule, but Drakhart did not begrudge what worked, even if he questioned the methods of the superstition.

Within the five circles lay the bleeding bodies of five prisoners. Their blood now formed the runes and circles that made up the matrix of magic beneath Isunath in the stone courtyard of the Palace Complex.

Drakhart chanted the words of the incantation, and reached out with his mind, to the pools of blood beneath him, then to Isunath. He was connected to his target. He felt the massive rush of power, unadulterated creation energy, and mana, that rushed into his veins and body and filled him like an overflowing chalice as he connected to his source of power. Drakhart breathed heavily. It was time to close the circle, and it would take every ounce of focus he possessed to hold himself together.

Drakhart drew his knife and cut open his palm. He could feel a mixture of pain and warmth well up in his hand. A trickle of blood dripped down his arm. As soon as Drakhart's blood mixed with that of the circle he was swallowed by the massive wave of energy that washed over him like a ship in a tidal wave. The feeling was euphoric.

He couldn't lose himself. Focus.

Drakhart's mind snapped back to the single image that grounded him during casting: him standing victorious over the dead body of Kanaahn. It was a goal and a motivator, and it kept his mind focused on the task at hand by remembering the why. Drakhart used some of the remaining blood that stained his fingers and added three more necessary runes to complete the spell.

When he finished, the wound on his palm healed itself at his behest, and the circle of energy was complete. There was a spark. Then lightning shot from parts of the pentagram and the runes, arcing across the sky, shooting in all directions, escaping into the air, or striking one another with a resounding crack. Drakhart continued the incantation. He felt power pooling into him, and he channelled it all towards Isunath.

The black dragon roared, reared, but for the most part took it all. Drakhart could feel the energy surge into Isunath. Drakhart felt it change the dragon through their mental link, as Drakhart directed the energy to do exactly as he wanted. Drakhart's goal was to grow Isunath.

Larger.

Bigger.

Bigger than Ölüm; than Valence. Like Tenebrae had done when he had gifted Isunath to Drakhart weeks ago.

The pain Isunath felt bled across the link he had with Drakhart, causing the Khaleeshir to wince instinctively. The pain made it harder to focus, but Drakhart pushed forward. Isunath roared. They could both feel the dragon's muscles stretch and tear, over and over again until they healed. Only to tear again before repeating the process. Bones broke, shattered by the sudden growth spurt. Once in pieces they stretched, elongated, and like the muscles, healed briefly before the process repeated several times over, each time more painful than the last. Skin stretched and broke, causing Isunath's blood to flow onto the pentagram and be absorbed back into the spell. Flesh ripped, blood dripped, and then suddenly the skin healed, if but briefly. That was perhaps the most painful part, as the skin tried in vain to keep up with the internal growth.

Drakhart kept going, trying not to think of what was happening to his Partner of the Heart and Mind. Trying not to think about how he could feel every agonizing moment of pain; every sensation and feeling, creep across his own flesh, skin, and bone as Isunath changed before him. Isunath doubled in size soon, twice the size Ölüm had been at his death.

More.

More!

Drakhart forced his will upon the magic as Elandyr'ni watched on for safety. Isunath continued to bend and break, growing more. Soon he we be as large as a three-year-old black dragon.

More.

MORE!

MORE!

Now—

Something broke the circle of magic and Drakhart lost control. The power flooded from Isunath and shot into the sky in the form of massive bolts of red lightning. The power ebbed from Drakhart's body like a burst waterskin. Empty and devoid of energy, he toppled over and fell onto his blood circles and runes. His breath came in ragged gasps, and he was exhausted. Drakhart had not an ounce of energy left in his body. He felt he was already within death's embrace. The cold fingers of the reaper reached out to him, its arms enveloped him, hugged him. He could feel the fingers gently plucking away at the strings of fate. The knife came forth to cut the thread and stop his heart and then...it receded. He could feel death slowly creep back into the shadows. Energy and warmth flowed into Drakhart and the realization of what had just happened washed over him. He had almost gone too far.

It wasn't until he saw the small, silver dagger that had nestled itself into one of the rings that Drakhart knew Elandyr'ni had forcibly stopped the ritual. For good reason, too. Drakhart felt like death might still take him. He was shaking uncontrollably and was incredibly pale.

Silver, Elandyr'ni explained to Drakhart earlier, was the most effective method of breaking the bonds of blood magic. Elandyr'ni always carried a silver dagger on her to combat enemy Warlocks. It had saved her own life more than a few times.

She walked over to Drakhart and placed a hand on his shoulder. "Perhaps that was a bit much for you, but not a bad start, my student. We will work our way up to magic of this calibre."

Elandyr'ni forced some of her own energy into Drakhart, sharing her life force with him. Immediately Drakhart felt warmth and life fill him. He felt alive again, and the shaking stopped. He sat up and looked at Elandyr'ni, still out of breath.

"I didn't even realize," rasped Drakhart. "Aspects save me, not the flowers again."

"You should have," Elandyr'ni's tone was more matter-of-fact than anything else, but a hint of disappointment lurked below the surface. "For now, that is why you have me, but you must learn. Notice the warning signs sooner, and remember your target, Isunath, is needed alive. You need to think of him as well. We can't keep giving you dragons you know." Elandyr'ni handed him a small loaf of bread. "Eat, it will help. And as for those flowers, you'll bloom as many of them as I say so until I'm satisfied. If you have a problem, take it up with Lord Tenebrae."

Drakhart did not hesitate to bite into the bread like he was a starving wolf biting into the haunch of a dead deer. He would, however, hesitate to protest the flower blooming exercise any further. He did not want to petition Tenebrae, and Drakhart knew that Elandyr'ni would surely make him if he had any thought of complaining. If that happened, Drakhart would eat his words, if Tenebrae did not immediately eat him.

The two of them looked over at Isunath. The dragon had collapsed and now lay there unconscious. However, tired and pained as he was the magic had done its job and healed even him relatively well. His breathing was slow but steady. Tendrils of smoke rose from his body where the energy had left him, and every breath rattled the very earth at his size.

It had worked. Drakhart smiled at a job well done.

"He's definitely larger than the other Khaleeshir. What of the Metallic Dragons they travel with?" asked Elandyr'ni.

Based on his calculations, and using only his eye, Drakhart estimated Isunath was now about thirty-one and a half metres from head to tail. "Still about half the size. She had been about seventy-two metres at her full size."

Despite not being as large as Drakhart would have liked, he revelled in the new advantage that Isunath had over the other Khaleeshir. He'd love to see Kanaahn, or the others try and kill his dragon this time. Isunath would be much more formidable, especially when armoured. He and Drakhart would avenge Ölüm.

Elandyr'ni mulled over Drakhart's words. "By my estimate, that would put the silver dragon at about twelve years of age."

Drakhart was astounded. "That's correct. How did you—"

"I've done my research on dragons. I know how much each species of dragon grows in a year. If you know where to look, and what to read, the information is all there. The rest is just math." Elandyr'ni stood and brushed herself off. "You may return to your quarters for today. You are exhausted, you need rest. I'll ensure Isunath is properly tended to before he returns to his roost. I will report back to Lord Tenebrae on your progress."

Drakhart bowed. Sleep was grasping him tighter by the second, and a good rest and a warm bath would be exactly what he needed. Perhaps a good meal afterwards, too. The cook had gotten accustomed to Drakhart's late-night meals; his training had kept him so tired that he was sleeping and eating at irregular intervals. Drakhart stumbled when came up from the bow. The world spun, and his eyesight went fuzzy. He could feel the exhaustion hit him harder than it ever had before. His face began to droop, and his lids grew heavy. He needed to start walking, fast, or he was going to fall asleep standing here.

Elandyr'ni helped him from the courtyard. Her strength always surprised Drakhart, but he never questioned it. Though from everything he had seen, he knew it had something to do with her tattoos—whatever they meant.

"Thank you," Drakhart mumbled. He had never felt more grateful to anyone before than in this moment. "You saved me twice today. I appreciate it."

But Elandyr'ni's response came, always as practical as ever. "You are my student, Drakhart. Lord Tenebrae has instructed I keep you alive."

Drakhart tried to laugh, but it came out more like a slow and pained wheeze. He was half asleep. He staggered along, shuffling his feet. Drakhart was headed towards his tower keep, to his room, and his bed, if he could just get there. He just had to get there before he passed out in some hallway along the way. Drakhart had no idea how far he was at this point, or how he would even manage up the stairs when he got there. He certainly couldn't hold up Elandyr'ni any longer than he already had.

That was where clear consciousness left Drakhart. The next thing he remembered was the smell of sandalwood and cedar. He could feel fingers reach around and grab his belt, hoisting him up. Drakhart tumbled through the air. Someone shouted. That was the last thing Drakhart remembered before everything went black.

* * *

Drakhart stood in a large cavern.

He could hear...something? Music? He wasn't really certain, but the sounds assaulted his senses.

Thuuum.

Thuuuum.

Thuuuuuuum.

It was dark, and he couldn't see the walls. The cavern was even larger than the one where Tenebrae made his home. Even though he couldn't see the walls, he could feel the enormity of it all. It wasn't natural either...it was almost as if the rock had been shaped and formed to be this way.

Thum.

Thuuuuum.

Thum.

Huh-huuuuuum.

He turned around; turned left, right, looked up and down, and could see only two features.

The cavern was flanked by two massive pillars of crystal, one white, one black. They opposed each other, in more than just position as far as Drakhart could tell. Arcane lightning crackled between the two pillars, clashing in between and causing sparks to fly about. Sometimes lightning from one pillar would hit the other, chipping off bits of crystal that flew across the room in a glittering shower. Other times, lightning would hit the rock around the cave, chipping bits of stone from the walls and floor that could be heard clattering across the cave.

CRACK!

Drakhart could feel his spine shiver. Every hair on his body stood on end. He could taste silver on his tongue. He had no idea where he was, only that he stood before true power. He could feel a magical, heartbeat-like rhythm in his chest. It filled his ears and pulsed through his chest. This beat thrummed through the cavern like some ancient song...no, it really was a song. Some low, deep-throated humming and chanting. Whispers flitting through the air, filling his ears.

CRACK!

TINKLE!

BOOM!

Hum-hum-hum huh-huuuuuuuuum.

Thump.

Thump, thump.

Where was he?

Drakhart squinted a bit harder and could make out some ancient, carved stone circle in the centre of the two pillars. He approached, and noticed carved runes along the edges of this stone circle...no, not a circle...an arch, or a gate? It stood up on its edge, part of which was buried beneath the stone floor of the cave.

Hu-huuuuuuuum.

Hu-huuuuum.

There was no rhythm to this music if it could even be called that.

Drakhart examined the stone circle. He didn't recognize the runes at all, but they seemed like the ones Elandyr'ni drew when performing Blood Magic. He would need to ask Elandyr'ni about this later...

Seriously, where was he? What the Hells was this place and how did he get here?

Drakhart.

He spun around. A voice whispered in his ear, breathed down his neck, and touched his arm. A spectre? A spirit? A ghost? No...just a voice. A voice that could touch...?

Thrum.

Thrum.

Thrum.

The music grew louder and closer.

Drakhart, my child. Come, my son. Come to me.

The voice...male, His father?? No! Female now? Androgynous? Was it two voices or one? He couldn't tell; let alone who it was. The voice echoed off the walls.

CRACK!
TINKLE!

The noises grew louder. The lightning, the humming, the rhythm of it all. The whispering voices. It cut through his ears, through his focus, through his mind. It cut like a blade through every thought he had. Every one of Drakhart's senses ached from the effort and the strain. This was not music, this was a racket. It was a deathly racket that threatened to harm Drakhart to his very soul. It tweaked his anxiety something terrible. Drakhart couldn't even understand why he was so afraid, or of what he seemed so scared of. Drakhart covered his ears. The noise was too much. The music hurt him.

"Make it stop!" he screamed.

But the world did not listen.

CRACK!

THRUM, THRUM, THRUM.

BOOM!
TINKLE!

HUUUUUUUM.
HU-HUUUUUUUUM.

THUUUUUUUUUUM.
HU-HUUUUUUUM.

BOOM!

CRACK TINKLE!

BOOM!

BA-BOOM!

BOOM!

"Make it stop."
But it did not.

"MAKE IT STOP."

But the ghostly orchestra did not listen.

"I HATE IT, MAKE IT STOP!"

And finally, it ceased.

* * *

Drakhart woke screaming.

Once he stopped—realizing he was safe in his bed—Drakhart came to notice that he was utterly alone. Despite all the noise he made, and as loud as he screamed, the room went back to deathly silence as soon as he had stopped screaming.

There was no one with him, no worried maid dabbing a warm cloth to his forehead, no Elandyr'ni fretting over him at his bedside, no Calandor harumphing all concerned in the corner. They had come and gone, each of them, over the last few days, each at different times, while Drakhart swam in and out of consciousness. Drakhart had been left to rest and recuperate, unbothered. He couldn't even remember how long he had been out this time, only that his constant companion had been Isunath, hovering like a shadow in the corner of his mind.

The first time this had happened and Drakhart had returned to consciousness it had been Isunath who had greeted him first from across their mental link. The dragon gave Drakhart the full story of what happened after he had collapsed the first time. Elandyr'ni had picked up him, over her shoulders, and carried him to his room, where she proceeded to care for him. She mixed tonics and tinctures to help restore his energy and boost his health to prevent Drakhart from getting worse. In Isunath's words, Drakhart had gotten close to death's door and had almost fully crossed through it. Elandyr'ni's magic and herbal healing decoctions had saved him just in time.

Since then, Drakhart knew that he had swung between conscious and unconscious, plagued and haunted by nightmares that always dragged him to this unknown place, filled with unknown sounds that sought to hurt him; to mock him. Drakhart hated this place. He hated that he kept being drawn there. He hated that dream. Was it a dream? He couldn't tell, and Isunath was never dragged there with him. Wherever Drakhart went when he dreamed, Isunath had not been able to follow.

Isunath had suggested it was a hallucination brought on by the herbal remedies Elandyr'ni had been giving him. When inquired, Elandyr'ni had not denied the possibility. The particular mix of herbs she had provided Drakhart would heal him, but the mixture could be hallucinogenic, and even toxic in high enough doses. Drakhart's heightened constitution had saved him from the worst effects, but it seemed he was still susceptible to the visions. Drakhart wasn't entirely convinced, but he didn't know who else to bother for answers, and so he kept his mouth shut for now.

"How long have I been like this?" asked Drakhart. This was the most lucid he had been in...however long it had been, and Drakhart realized he did not know how long he'd been recovering.

"Four days. Elandyr'ni says you far exceeded her expectations for how much you overdid it," replied Isunath.

Drakhart could smell the blood of a fresh kill. The warm liquid poured over his fangs, down his throat. The warm haunch of some unfortunate creature sacrificed to the circle of life. Drakhart's stomach roared in protest. He needed food.

Before he could even stand to find a servant, Elandyr'ni burst through the door. She answered his question before he could even ask. "I know everything." Elandyr'ni's eyes twinkled as her lips contorted into a smirk.

Drakhart had never seen her so smug before.

Again, Elandyr'ni spoke before Drakhart could ask his question. "I've got food on its way now I'm glad you're awake."

"You saved my life," Drakhart replied dumbly.

"I did my duty, as your teacher, ally, and friend," Elandyr'ni said curtly. "Nothing more."

"But still—"

"Nothing more," Elandyr'ni stressed the words as she repeated them and Drakhart dropped the topic. "How do you feel?" Before she received a response, she began to poke and prod at Drakhart's face. She examined his eyes and gums and checked inside his ear.

Drakhart groaned and rubbed his temples. "Tired, groggy, but better than I was when I wound up here. Hungry, too."

"That will soon be remedied. How is your mind?"

Drakhart contemplated discussing his dreams but felt it would only make him seem more unstable. Better to keep it close to his chest, he figured. "A little bit of brain fog, but I think that's from how long I've been out. A proper meal and a chance to get up and walk about and I should be fine."

"Good" Elandyr'ni responded. She walked over to the balcony, threw open the curtains and then the shutters. Light burst into the room immediately. "Because you'll be continuing your training post-haste. I don't think you're ready to go back into swinging a sword and casting more spells, but we've lost too much time as it is, so you'll continue to recover in bed, and train your mind. In a few days, we'll try physical training again. For now, you and I shall go over theory, and Calandor will come up to bore you with his lectures."

Drakhart was not surprised. Tenebrae's plans were specifically time-sensitive for reasons he did not always share. Though if Drakhart had to guess, from everything he'd learned about Estion and the Darond's grand scheme, it was likely because Altimara would soon be off to war again. Every hand would be needed to lead the armies against the anti-Tenebrae alliance that was coming. Calandor had spoken about it in detail during Drakhart's lessons. They would face at least the combined forces of Asardaea, Espias, and Estion. Tenebrae was not concerned about Danaen, for their alliance with Altimara was like iron, and their loyalty to the Darond was tenuous at best.

But Tenebrae had tasked Drakhart with solving this problem, and Drakhart was not one to accept failure as an option. So Drakhart, and by extension Calandor, Elandyr'ni, Lord Drungvist, and Lord Marneron, had been planning, learning, and plotting away, day and night, to find ways to shatter the alliance before it could field an army that would spell the end of Altimara and their plans. So far no solution had been found, and so preparations were being made for the worst-case scenario—just in case.

Everyone knew Altimara could not fight three armies at once. It could, however, perhaps manage two, and the Utovan front. But only if the fighting was drawn out, limited to sieges and small skirmishes, and they did not overcommit too many resources to both fronts simultaneously. If Altimara could control the field, the time and place of battle, they could outlast their enemies. It would be a defensive war, fought on the backs of fortresses and siege warfare, but it was at least possible to win that way.

"You're plotting again," Elandyr'ni called out from a small wash basin in the antechamber between Drakhart's garderobe and bedroom. There he kept his clothes, his armour, his wash basin and a stone tub. She began to chant and whisper at the bowl, her hands waving over the empty vessel as she spoke her simple spell. When she was finished, the basin was full of hot water and tendrils of steam drifted up from the surface. Her spells sounded like music to Drakhart, she would almost sing the words, feeling an innate rhythm through her bones. He never knew anyone else to cast music through song.

"I'm sorry," was all Drakhart responded. "Even in my current state, I'm still bothered by the task set by our master."

Elandyr'ni returned with a wooden wash bucket and placed it on Drakhart's lap, so he could wash his face from where he sat. "I can do this much, but you're on your own for the bath."

While Drakhart plunged his hands into the bowl of steaming water and splashed it across his face, Elandyr'ni had crafted her answer to Drakhart's previous statement.

"Lord Tenebrae has presented you with quite a quandary, no doubt. But together, I think we should be able to figure it out. You know *what* it is you must do, but the how...the how escapes you. We must take and make every advantage for ourselves when we strike. Any slip-up could cost us dearly. Most important we cannot allow the Khaleeshir to act as the morale boost they were at Xiar. Our actions must be quieter, we cannot afford another bold blunder like Xiar."

"There will not be another Xiar. The Khaleeshir will be surprised when they see me," Isunath jeered from across his bond with Drakhart. *"They will be older, but they will be smaller, and I shall crush them."*

"Be mindful that you do not underestimate them," replied Drakhart. *"It was how your predecessor died; he and I fell victim to our own foolishness. They are smaller, but as you said, older. They will have more experience flying, and more practice with their breath weapons. They have had more time to adjust to their slowly growing bodies, whereas you woke up at your size. You must continue training with the other dragons. Do not slack for even a minute if we are to be victorious."*

Isunath recoiled a bit, not out of fear, but because he had realized his folly. *"I shall keep that in mind."*

"Please do. I cannot lose you...not again."

Elandyr'ni noticed Drakhart staring off into the distance with a vacant expression. She smiled warmly at him. "You'll need to put on a more dignified face if you're going to continue this. We can't have you staring off like a fool every time you speak to Isunath. What kind of an example would that set amongst the other nobles or the soldiers?"

Drakhart couldn't help but smile. "I'll work on it. I promise."

"Good. And while you're at it, you'll be reading and copying these scrolls by tomorrow afternoon." Elandyr'ni produced four rather large scrolls from beneath her shawl and placed them on the wooden table across the room from Drakhart's bed.

Drakhart contained a groan of dissatisfaction. They were helpful teaching tools, but the reading was dry and boring, and the language archaic. It was a slog to get through.

"I expect a perfect replication of these when I return tomorrow. For now, though, I will leave you to your food, and I'll send up Calandor in two hours."

"Yes, Master," replied Drakhart.

He bowed his head, and Elandyr'ni returned the bow with her body. She walked to the door and stopped just shy of the threshold. There was a heavy pause. She did not move, she said nothing. Drakhart didn't speak either, too afraid he'd spook her—or himself. It was eerily silent.

Then she spoke. "I am glad you lived."

With that, Elandyr'ni crossed the threshold and closed the door behind her. Drakhart did not even respond. She did not need him to, and he wasn't even certain how. She said what she had needed to, and anything more from Drakhart would've been too much.

Drakhart let out a ragged sigh. He looked at the table, and the pile of scrolls waiting for him. Food would be here soon but for now, he might as well get a head start on his assignment. If he didn't start now he'd be up all night. Drakhart could read while he ate, and while he bathed, but not during Calandor's lessons. He would need his full attention for that, otherwise he'd drift off and fall asleep.

Chapter XII

Banalor threw open the back door and stepped into the alley. The door slammed closed behind him, and he walked over to a nearby bush. Banalor unzipped his pants and relieved himself inside the bush.

He had a half hour to kill before his next set. By his estimation that would be enough time to grab dinner, maybe a drink, and still have enough time for a roll in the hay with the pretty barmaid Ruoth had just hired.

Banalor finished up his restroom break and turned back towards the bar, only to come face to face with a tall figure in a pitch-black robe. The figure blended in with the night and the darkness of the alley, and almost seemed to be made of the shadows themselves.

Banalor kept his cool. "I'm sorry, was this your bush?"

The tall figure did not respond, but Banalor could hear rattling breath from beneath the hood.

"I'm done if you want to use it…"

Still no response.

"If you want an autograph, you'll have to wait until my next set. All requests must be done then too."

Banalor felt a shiver go up his spine. Something was wrong here. Felidrun wasn't exactly a town known for crime and murder, but Banalor knew a bad situation when he saw one.

He needed to keep his cool if he was going to survive, so Banalor smiled, nodded, and attempted to turn back towards the other exit of the alley.

It was not to be.

A second figure materialized from within the shadow of the building, almost gliding—not walking—into Banalor's path.

Shit.

Now he was surrounded. This was not good.

"Look," Banalor started, trying, and nearly failing, to keep his cool. His hands shook from inside his pockets. "If you want my money, you can have it. I won't even report you or tell anyone. Just let me go. I have a job to do inside."

The figures didn't respond, but Banalor *swore* he could hear hissing from behind the cowls. The air seemed to grow colder in the alley, and Banalor could see his breath materialize as it escaped his mouth.

Magic? How?

Banalor threw his small bag of coins at the figure in front of him. It bounced off the figure's chest and hit the ground. Then the figure growled, like an animal, and the figure behind him continued to hiss louder.

Shit.

Fuck.

Shit.

Fuck.

Piss and tits.

Banalor didn't even notice the figures move their hands to cast the spell before jagged shards of ice erupted from the cobbles, impaling Banalor from below.

Large spears of ice had caught him through his forearms, legs, chest, stomach, arms, and feet. He was bleeding from each of his wounds, the red blood leaking down the icy shards like sap from a tree.

Banalor tried to cry out in pain, but the figure in front of him reached out, grabbed his throat, and crushed his windpipe with a feeble crack.

He could feel the obstruction of his crushed windpipe blocking his throat. It was hard to breathe, and blood was pouring down the back of his throat and into his lungs. Banalor choked and gurgled but could not summon a sound. He was cold. He was in agony. He was bleeding, and the cold only made the flesh ache even more after it was rent apart. He could see his blood pooling on the ground at his feet, painting the cobbles like spilt wine.

Fuck.

Fuck.

FUCK.

The figures didn't speak. They didn't say a word, but Banalor could feel a great pressure in his skull. Something in his head ached like someone was digging around in there with meat hooks. His mouth hung open, and he tried to scream, but still no sound came out.

Tears flowed freely from his eyes. He wept from fear, from his pain, from sadness and agony. He was going to die, he knew it.

Visions of Shooter flashed through his head. The night they spent together. The hours they spent talking, the love they shared—if but for a brief evening. It was then that it became painfully clear that these figures were after Shooter. Banalor was just a casualty caught in the crossfire, though he didn't know why.

What the fuck had Shooter done to piss these people off?

Part of Banalor wanted to lash out, and fight back...but how? With what? A rock? His hands?

No. He would die here.

Banalor resigned himself to death. This was how his existence ended. Behind his place of work, impaled by ice, without the ability to speak or scream, or even beg for help or mercy. These fuckers were digging around in his head, looking for information about a one-night stand, and their intentions with Shooter were less than honourable if this is how they treated Banalor.

Banalor's head ached. Pain. Flashes of light. He was going in and out of lucidity. The blood was starting to flow slower—there wasn't as much left. He was bleeding out. He didn't have much longer. He could feel his killers' anger and for a moment his mind melded with theirs. Their thoughts became his, their feelings filled his heart. Banalor ceased to exist, but for a moment.

The strangers needed more time, but for now, they had enough information. It would do. It gave them a general location.

Ethon.

The Khaleeshir were going to Ethon, just as had been assumed, and this confirmed it. They did not know what route the Khaleeshir would take, but they would be easy enough to track down now that these strangers had a direction to work with.

The connection ended, and Banalor was Banalor once again. It was at that moment that he knew these strangers were going to kill him but—wait a moment. Something else flashed through Banalor's mind. What should've been an inconsequential memory was suddenly of great importance and once again Banalor and the strangers became one. Banalor could feel the hooded figures actively prolonging his life, bringing him back from the edge of death, back into the realm of the living. They healed him just enough to be useful, but not enough that it would truly save him in the end.

He was being asked by Ruoth to deliver a letter to a random location the bard had never heard of. But the bard, instead of heading right to the delivery location, let his curiosity get the better of him. He opened the letter, and sneakily read the contents. Not much of it made sense to him; it was just a normal letter that happened to be going to Asardaea. Banalor couldn't understand, if it was a normal letter, why wasn't it being dropped off at the local postmaster? Why was it being sent to some random location at the edge of town? Banalor didn't bother investigating further. He could never puzzle out the meaning of this strange request his boss had asked of him. It seemed harmless enough anyway.

But the hooded figures could figure it out. They understood the intricacies of subterfuge and smuggling. The letter seemed harmless enough but had likely been written in some special cypher that would allow the recipient to pull the true meaning from the otherwise mundane letter about the proper storage and ageing of a cask of porter. The initial recipient of the letter was likely a smuggler, who would get the letter to its final recipient outside of the eyes of the Royal Mail Office. It clearly bore a message of great importance, and the normal channels were unsecured and untrustworthy.

The hooded figures made note of the name of the bard's boss, Ruoth, who owned the establishment that bordered this alley. They also made a note of the location of the delivery at the edge of town. They would be reporting this smuggler to Tenebrae, and Tenebrae would likely have them shatter this spy ring soon enough. Anything to cripple the Darond and their allies.

It would be just like the Great Slaughter. The Darond would once again know fear as they had in the past, but first, to deal with the boy.

The hooded figures cut their connection with the boy's mind and left him feeling cold, empty, and alone. He could no longer feel their thoughts or emotions swirling around inside of him. All he felt was pain. He had no idea what any of this meant, except for the return of one foregone conclusion: he was not going to live.

Banalor looked up, his head rolled on his neck. He didn't have much longer; he could feel it. As he looked up, he could see something...just a faint glimpse of his attacker. All he could see beneath the hood was a big, yellow eye, and it wasn't human. The yellow eye ringed with red and orange, with a thin black slit for a pupil.

And then his head was ripped from his shoulders. Flesh tore like leather, muscle ripped like thin fabric, bones cracked, snapped, and popped, and blood sprayed across the ice, the alley, and the figures.

Such was the merciless end of Banalor the Bard.

Chapter XIII

The plan was to strike hard, strike fast, and strike simultaneously. Everyone had their orders and their targets. They would attack the forges that were forging the weapons of war that Altimara would need to plunge Enayra into another continent-wide conflict. Utova, Estion, Asardaea, Espias, and perhaps even Altimara's long-time ally Danaen would suffer the same fate as Xiar, but Altimara would not suffer another defeat.

Reports stated that the Altimaran army had returned to Xiar with fifteen legions, not long after losing the original battle, and wiped the city from the face of the earth. Nothing remained but a crackling crater and most of the farmland. Altimara did not waste any time in declaring a total victory over Xiar, choosing to ignore their initial losses, and claim that the city had been razed to the ground. Plans were announced that soon work would start on a new Xiar, built in the name of the late King Meland'ar.

Amber would not let that happen to others. It was no surprise she had come to care for people she had never met. She had spent much of her time as an information broker trying to effect change for the people of Kula. Now she had the opportunity to bring that kind of positive change to a wider group of people who needed it..

Amber and her twenty-three volunteers slipped between alleys, careful to keep to the shadows. They watched and waited between buildings, pressed themselves against the sides of warehouses and homes. Guards passed, doing their usual rounds, none bothering to check in the nooks and crannies of the alleys. Amber couldn't help but smirk. All the local conscripts had been shipped off to other garrisons for training. Most of Kula's garrison were outsiders. Every Kulan knew from birth that they had to always, *always* watch the alleys.

Soon Amber was in position. She had no contact with her accomplices at the other locations, but everyone knew their roles. At the count of three past the third bell, everyone would unleash their salvos simultaneously. Some carried jars of caustic liquid, other jugs of pitch and tar that would ignite a massive blaze in seconds, and a few others even managed to get a hold of a couple of small kegs of naphtha jelly. Whatever they used, the result would be the same: a conflagration that would be seen for miles around.

There were a variety of targets. Forges, furnaces, and granaries were mostly, meant to strike at the heart of Altimara's war effort. Armies marched on their stomachs, and granaries kept the armies fed. Altimaran steel armed the soldiers and was used to wreak havoc on the safety of other people.

This wasn't the first time they had done something like this. At first, the sabotage had started small, of course. Small little acts of sabotage meant to inconvenience and hinder more than halt, but now Amber wanted to turn up the heat and harm the army—and Drakhart—where it hurt most.

Amber reached her destination—the biggest forge in Kula, recently built after the smithy was relocated from Targrond to set up shop where the slums used to be. It was easier to pick the lock than she had initially thought. These buildings were made quickly, and the locks were of low quality. No local would have locked up their shop with anything less than four locks of the highest quality, one that was enchanted, and a good guard dog waiting on the other side. Only in Kula would someone spend more money on security than they spent on food.

The lock clicked open, and Amber stowed the picks back in her messy bun. She opened the door slowly, quietly, to ensure no one would notice. Amber closed the door behind her with a small click and immediately got to work. Fifteen anvils stood by the dead forges along the back wall. It was a truly impressive building, and Amber was almost impressed. She felt bad that it would all be in ruins soon, but that was the cost that would have to be paid. At least there would be no human cost, for not only was it almost the third bell past midnight, but today was a holiday. It was the first day of a week-long celebration held annually in Kula, the Kolahna Festival so no one would be working today, or for the next couple of days, and no doubt everyone had left earlier the night before to get in some well-earned rest before the debauchery began.

The forges were dead, but not cold. Heat still clung to the air inside the workshop, not quite as hot as if the forges were running, but a spectre of such heat. The forges ran for hours, constantly burning charcoal to forge steel and iron into materiel for the army. Everything from chainmail to plate mail, to spurs for cavalry, shoes for horses, and weapons like swords and poleaxes. Even mundane items were made, like nails and metal hoops for wagon wheels. The charcoal was imported from Estion, using both official channels and purchased through Danaen as well to get around the export limits set by Estion on Altimara.

Amber pulled a belt of bottles from beneath her cloak. She had just enough caustic acid to destroy the anvils, and some pitch to burn the rest of the building down afterwards. Vilingar had thought the acid concocted by the apothecary's former apprentice was overkill, but Amber stressed the importance of destroying the forge *and* the anvil. If they ruined only the forges, a new forge could be rebuilt quickly, and the anvils could still be used once the forges and furnaces were rebuilt. A temporary structure could be erected to keep out the elements, and the area heavily guarded to avoid theft or further destruction, but if they destroyed the building and the anvil, then the forge was useless until new anvils could be brought in.

An anvil, like a smith's tools, was the most important part of their trade. Blacksmiths often crafted their own tools, with many creating custom tools that they passed on to their apprentices. Some smiths refused to work on an anvil that wasn't theirs—superstition was prevalent in the forges—and many felt a personal connection to their anvils that they had

had for years. These anvils had likely been relocated with the Targrond blacksmiths along with their tools, and soon they would be scrap metal.

Amber had to work fast. The third bell was almost upon her. She borrowed a pair of heavy blacksmith's gloves from near the forge and unstopped the enchanted glass bottles. A minor protective spell had been cast on the flasks to prevent the acid from burning through them as well.

She splashed the acid all over the anvils, and immediately the acrid smell of burning metal and a sizzling sound, like oil squeaking in a frying pan, assaulted Amber's senses. She retched and covered her nose and mouth with a cloth tied around her neck. The smell of the acid was already horrible, and it burned her nose and lungs to inhale. The acid worked fast—faster than Amber had expected. Almost at once, it cut through the metal, biting away at the metal anvil like hot water cut through ice, curling the edges and staining whatever it touched a dark, putrid green. It was soon through the anvil and eating through the stone floor beneath, burning down into the sand below. The acid would keep going until it had completely evaporated.

With the anvils ruined, all Amber had to do was torch the place and escape. Soon, very soon the third bell would go off, and it would be time. She got the bottles of pitch into position near anything wooden and flammable in the workshop. It seems the smiths had been foolish enough to store some coal near the forge, to save time while working. They would be perfect fuel once they caught fire.

Then, she waited.

She passed the moments in absolute, frozen silence. Her stomach shook inside her chest, and she felt like she was going to vomit. Not now. Not right now. It could wait, it *had* to wait. Amber did her best to hold down the bile that was bubbling in her throat. She got control of her stomach right as the first of the third bells rang, announcing the hour from each of the new bell towers across the city.

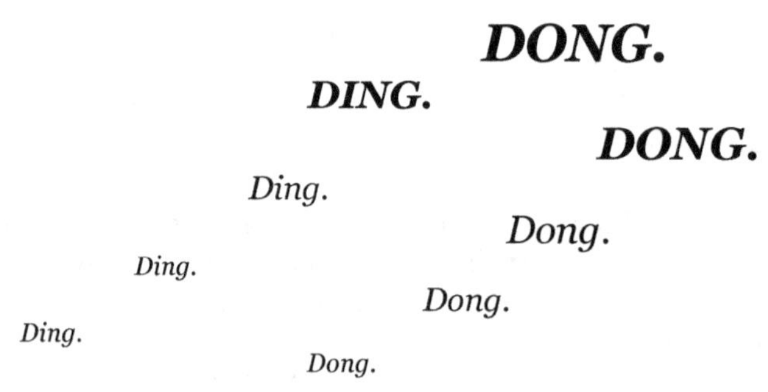

Almost there. Almost there.

DONG.

Ding.

Dong.

Ding.

Dong.

Ding.

Dong.

One more, then she'd count to three.

DONG.

DING.

DONG.

Ding.

Dong.

Ding.

Dong.

Ding.

Dong.

One...

Two...

Three...

Now!

Amber struck her flint and lit her torch. She touched the torch to everything she had smeared with the black substance and watched with delight as they each caught fire, one after the next, with the enthusiasm of a predator on the kill.

Smoke filled the room, and Amber could feel it starting to seep through the rag around her mouth. The heat became stifling and sweat beaded on her brow as the flames grew, licking at the walls and gnawing on all the pitch-slathered wood and charcoal in sight. She needed to get out, fast.

Amber went back to the door, eased it open, and reapplied the lock. That would make it harder for the fire brigades to get inside and put the fire out—if the whole building wasn't reduced to rubble by the time they organized.

Based on the light, commotion, and smell from outside, the other buildings in the district, and the granaries in the eastern part of the city had also gone up in flame at the appointed time. She could smell burning grain on the wind.

Perfect.

Amber retched again. She would need to hurry. She started to run, going back the way she came. Now it didn't matter who saw her. Everyone would be rushing up the main roads, going the opposite way. They'd be focusing on the multiple fires and preventing their spread. Everything would soon become chaos.

115

People screamed and ran up and down the streets of Kula. Young children and infants cried as their families fled their homes in the middle of the night, looking to escape the flames. Soldiers tried to keep order, to little effect. Entire patrols ran like brigades of metal ants over to the burning buildings, trying to contain the flames. Bells erupted across the city like an orchestra of doom. The sound of chaos and confusion was beautiful, in a macabre way.

Amber ran, and kept running until her lungs burned, her legs cramped, and she felt like vomiting in her mouth. She just barely made it to the secret trapdoor, and down the ladder—just barely. As soon as Amber hit the sandy bottom, she doubled over and threw up.

Before she knew it, a hand was on her shoulder, and her cloak and hair were being drawn back, away from her mouth.

Vilingar.

Amber choked back some bile. "T-Thank you."

Vilingar shook his head. He helped Amber up once she had finished and turned to another runner who was standing by the ladder. "Get something to clean this up. I'll get her to go lay down."

Amber's head swam, and she felt her legs wobble. "That was in...inopportune."

Vilingar said nothing. He was a master of silence. That was how he communicated. Amber loved and hated him for it.

"It was the acid and the smoke. It...it must have gotten to me."

Vilingar guided Amber back to the hidden door and opened it for her while supporting her with the other arm. Still, he did not respond.

But Amber could not shut up. "How did it go?" Amber was feeling her strength come back, but she still felt the nauseous gnawing at her.

"Well," replied Vilingar. "All targets have been hit. We're just waiting for everyone to return."

"Was anyone captured?" Amber asked, concern gripping her.

"I don't think so, but we'll know soon enough."

"I should go topside and keep an eye out." Amber stumbled as Vilingar escorted her between the tightly packed refugees in the former warehouse space.

"I'll go. You need rest. You need to take care of yourself."

Amber was defiant. "I'll be fine, Vilingar."

Vilingar went silent again. He escorted—really dragged—Amber to her office and sleeping quarters. He laid Amber down on the bed despite her protests and began lighting a few candles.

"I need to check in with Skullspider. Let her know we succeeded. I should be writing to her."

"You should be resting. She will understand."

Amber frowned. "Don't baby me, Vilingar."

Silence.

Amber's look prodded him for a response.

"If you're going to write to anyone, you know who it should be." Vilingar didn't wait for Amber's reply and slipped back out the door as quietly as he came.

Amber could kill him...if he wasn't such a good friend or her second.

Now that she was alone in the dimly lit cavern that was her office, Amber had to admit that resting sounded like a good idea. She had exhausted herself during her escape, and she was already burning the candle at both ends as it was. Between that and the sudden onset of nausea and vomiting, Amber was in bad sorts.

She hated Vilingar. Not because she truly hated him, but because he had been right on two accounts. Yet Amber still would not give him the satisfaction of knowing that.

Amber let out a sigh, dragged herself up from the worn old divan that served as her bed, and shuffled over to her desk. She riffled through several papers until she found what she was looking for a small pouch with pearl-sized herbal medication. She took two, washing them down with a swig from her waterskin, and sat down in her uncomfortable and ornately carved wooden chair.

She had demanded it as payment long ago, from a wealthy, but terrible businessman who thought it would be a good idea to go into business as a skittic dust merchant—in Kula, of all places. Because it was fancy, she thought it would be comfortable. Then Amber learned the uncomfortable truth. Rich people did not buy anything for comfort. Lavish furniture was some of the least comfortable she had ever experienced. A bag stuffed with damp straw and animal dung would've been easier on her back. Of course, the wooden chair was infinitely more comfortable than the bad businessman's end had been once his creditors and his competition caught up with him.

Amber grabbed her quill, dipped it into the ink well, and grabbed a blank parchment. She quickly began scribbling away, scratching letters onto the sheet with a pointed haste. Not a second would be wasted.

And while she was at it...she might just take Vilingar's advice.

Maybe.

Chapter XIV

It was Kinokaze and Valence that halted the party's progress this time. They had taken charge as soon as they neared the ancestral borders of the Green Dragon Clan. Dragon etiquette was a long and complicated process, and it was best to let those who were well acquainted with the intricacies to handle introductions.

Even though the Khaleeshir were being followed, they could not cross the ancestral borders without express permission from the Ancient Ones that ruled over the clan. To do so would invite death from above in the form of angry green dragons.

It didn't matter that Djall was one of their own, or that they travelled on official Darond business, or that two of their travelling group were metallic dragons, or even that these were Khaleeshir. None of it meant anything until permission was granted.

Valence and Kinokaze had now been gone the better part of a day and a half, entreating with the Patriarch and Matriarch, leaving the dragons and humans to their own devices in the forest.

The dragons had gone out to hunt, and the humans had set up camp. They were sitting around a small campfire in the dark of early evening, getting what was probably the fourth drilling on etiquette that day from Kyeit and Cecil.

"And what do you do when you approach the Ha'k'dir-ad-Erya-in'fuor-Elthir and Ha'k'nir-ad-Eru-in'fuor-Elthir?" asked Cecil.

Arial responded. "Bow low, and don't make direct eye contact. Do not speak unless spoken to. We are beneath them, despite our titles, and we must act as such."

"Correct."

In Common, most people referred to the clan leaders as Clan Mother or Clan Father, but the Khaleeshir knew better. These titles were imperfect translations, and to refer to the ancient, great dragons, first of their colour, by such human titles would simply be insulting. Once familiarity had been established, Ha'k'nir or Ha'k'dir would be acceptable, but until then all formalities had to be observed.

The group had to rewire their language, their way of thought, and everything they had already learned about dragons. Anything they had experienced with their own or other dragons did not apply to the Clan Leaders. These ancient dragons were not like Kanothir, who had likely become less formal after centuries around humans, or the Khaleeshir dragons, or even Valence or Kinokaze. The world moved slower for these ancients. They didn't leave their homes often or interact with the outside world. Change was not on the itinerary for the first green dragons, nor for any of the Clan Leaders.

By Kinokaze's estimate, the last time a Clan Mother or Father had left their grottos was when Tenebrae last posted a threat to the world a thousand years ago. It was much easier to adapt to them than to the other way around—ancient dragons were not known for their patience.

As Kyeit had explained, these dragons knew a world before humans. They knew a world before constant war and fighting. A world before Tenebrae had become the enemy of his own kind. Before empires and kingdoms grew and spread across Enayra. They had lived in a world before Khaleeshir, and while they had given their assent—and their offspring—to be one of these ten heroes that would bridge the gap between the two races of Enayra, they did not worship these heroes, and they were not beholden to them like others were.

"We've only been Khaleeshir for a few months, but I didn't realize how easy it was to forget a time when we were not treated with deference because of our new titles," Arial pointed out. "Not long ago we were nobodies from Kula. The only people who knew us by our names were our family and the Town Watch."

"On one hand it's nice to go back to a simpler time, in a small way. On the other hand, I'd rather not be devoured by an ancient dragon today," Kanaahn retorted.

"How do we even fight our way out of that if something goes wrong?" asked Arkas.

"There would be no fighting our way out. We would die, simple as that," Kyeit replied.

Cecil calmed down the Khaleeshir. "Your positions as Khaleeshir, the presence of dragons from other clans, as well as two metallic dragons, would be the only reasons we are spared. We'd be sent off, but we'd be banished for life. We could never return."

"So don't fuck this up, basically," Kanaahn concluded bluntly.

The testing continued.

Kyeit turned to Arkas. "What is the proper greeting when meeting a dragon of the clan?"

"Dol'viinaeszoth," Arkas declared confidently.

Roughly translated it meant: the blessings of Viinaeszoth be with you, or more simply, Viinaeszoth be with you. Viinaeszoth was the draconic spirit of the winds, that uplifted and aided all flying creatures of the world. The spirit's mood was fickle. On a good day, clear skies surround you like an ocean, and winds blow favourably for your travel. On a bad day, storms would hamper you, and winds would be your foe.

"Dragons have gods?" Kanaahn asked in bewilderment.

Risasi's low timbre rippled through Kanaahn's mind like a stone dropped in a calm pond. *"What did you think the Earth Mother was?"*

Kanaahn had no response. He had never really considered that before. Seeing as the Earth Mother was only the first dragon, and she had died—making her mortal—he had never quite considered her...divine. But, what else was a creature that became the earth, and ruled over the natural order of creation, life, and the natural world?

"As a matter of fact, we have about forty-three," Adalinda added. *"Though, what you would call gods, we would consider more divine spirits. Even the spirits are mortal, for all, they are far more powerful than us."*

"How do you kill the air?" asked Shooter, walking a fine line between sarcasm and genuine confusion.

"Anything that lives can die. Not all deaths are conventional," Fyete answered.

* * *

Valence and Kinokaze returned late into the night, almost two days after they had left. They emerged from amongst the trees, on foot, looking haggard and exhausted.

"We have succeeded," Kinokaze exclaimed, though her face betrayed her news. Her look was troubled, not triumphant.

"They'll allow us to move through their territory?" asked Kyeit.

"Not exactly," Valence replied. "They will meet with the Khaleeshir and the two Darond envoys. Once they have met you, they will decide whether we may pass through their lands. It seems they have great interest in meeting Djall."

Kyeit nodded. "Makes sense, he's their child."

Cecil was exasperated. "Leave it to an old dragon to make this long and complicated."

Valence took umbrage with that. "Are your politics any different?"

"What are we waiting around here for then?" Kanaahn asked. "Let's get going. The faster we can meet with the Clan Elders, the sooner we can get going to Estion."

The metallic dragons exchanged a glance.

Kinokaze smirked. "Faster is not a word that will describe this experience."

The dragons were recalled from their hunt, fur and blood still dripping from their muzzles.

"Should we clean them up?" Arial wondered as she attempted to dab at Adalinda's snout with a kerchief.

"Surprisingly, it would be best," replied Kinokaze. "Ancient Ones don't take kindly to a dragon that doesn't take pride in their appearance."

"How ancient are we talking here, exactly?" asked Kanaahn.

"A little over five thousand years old."

Kanaahn whistled, impressed. These dragons were around before humans even arrived in Enayra but quantifying that in years only made it more impressive. What had they seen? How different were dragons back then?

It suddenly made sense to Kanaahn. It didn't matter that they were Khaleeshir, or what power they might or might not hold, these five teens were mewling infants to these dragons. Kanaahn was only glad Kanothir had not been this way, it might have bruised his ego back then.

Once the dragons were cleaned up, Kinokaze and Valence led the group through the trees toward what they called the Emerald Enclave, home of the green dragon clan.

Arkas made note of the trees, the closer they got. The trees seemed smaller, younger, and farther apart. He noticed large, fallen trunks covered in moss. Some lay splintered, others were rotting. All were scattered across the forest floor haphazardly. Arkas noticed chunks of charred wood scrap, and that even the standing trees still bore claw and teeth marks where they had been scored by dragons. "We're definitely nearing the territory of dragons," he noted.

"Young dragons aren't always as in control of their emotions, or their fire," Valence replied.

Arkas couldn't help but feel the irony of that statement wasn't lost on Valence, but for the safety of himself and others, he chose not to address it verbally.

The walk to the Emerald Enclave took an hour. The group emerged from the ever-thinning forest and came upon a massive mountain. The mountain was covered in grass and vegetation, and the gently sloping sides sprouted from the ground and reached their way up to the clouds but didn't quite touch them. At the base of the verdant mountain loomed three massive green dragons that made even Kanothir look small. Though Kanaahn wondered how true that would be if Kanothir was allowed to take her full size.

"I would say they are no younger than three centuries," Djall mused in the back of Kanaahn's head.

The three dragons stepped forward. They did not smile, nor did they scowl. Their faces were like a calm pool; emotionless and still.

"Dol'viinaeszoth!" called the leader at the centre, stepping closer than his two cohorts. "I am Glay'ak. This is my k'iir Ithai'hra and my k'tir Vultoz. We were sent by the Ha'k'nir and Ha'k'dir to greet you."

Despite speaking to Valence, Kanaahn noticed that the green dragon's eyes were firmly fixed on Djall.

Valence stepped forward to represent the group. She lowered her head and neck in the form of a mock bow. Glay'ak returned the gesture, though his bow was deeper and more sustained.

Thanks to the Khaleeshir's earlier lessons, Kanaahn understood some of the intricacies of this exchange. Though humans called this action a "bow", what this gesture was really was an odd combination of trust and submission. By lowering their head and neck, the dragons showed that they trusted the other not to attack them, but also that they had no such intentions themselves—while bowing, the nape of one's neck would be exposed. When dragons fought and competed in the wild, the winner was the dragon that managed to grab their opponent by the nape of their neck, at the base of the skull, and pin them. Any dragon that violated the initial show of submission and trust without good reason risked being exiled and labelled 'harzok' for breach of etiquette.

Though despite his knowledge, something about the exchange did confuse him. *"I thought social hierarchy was based on colour and then age,"* Kanaahn questioned.

"It is Valence's attempt at being courteous. It's a magnanimous compromise. Glay'ak is older, so Valence should bow first, but because she is metallic, she is due more deference than a chromatic dragon, regardless of age. Valence is splitting the difference and showing her generosity as a friend by bowing first, though Glay'ak must always bow lower than she. It is a smart move, and she has taken command of this interaction," Djall explained.

"Thank you, Glay'ak. Will your siblings be watching our horses while we're meeting with your Ha'k'dir and Ha'k'nir?" Valence asked. Having met the Great Progenitors and being the child of a metallic dragon allowed Valence to use less formal terms.

Glay'ak jerked his snout in a way that Kanaahn could only interpret as some sort of nod. "They shall. We vow on our blood that no harm shall come to these creatures."

The horses did not look so convinced, and Kanaahn could swear he saw Vultoz start to drool as he eyed Arial's mare, but from what he knew of a dragon's honour, to swear upon one's blood was to swear upon one's life. These dragons' lives would be forfeit if they broke their word.

Again, Kanaahn saw Glay'ak's eyes wander over to Djall before returning to Valence.

"Did you catch that?" Kanaahn asked.

Djall didn't respond. He too seemed engrossed with Glay'ak. Djall couldn't take his eyes off the green dragon or his siblings.

"Djall?"

But it was no use. The dragon did not respond.

Valence continued. "It is appreciated. Please, lead the way."

The horses were tied to a nearby log and left to graze. They were clearly uneasy about the two massive dragons that suddenly kept watch over them like a mother hen over her new chicks, but there was no other way to explain to them what was happening.

Glay'ak took to the sky and the Khaleeshir, who had mounted up in the meantime, followed. Kyeit took the lead on Valence, just behind Glay'ak, and Cecil and Kinokaze took up the rear.

The massive green dragon flew low over the mountainside, moving parallel up the gentle curve of the mountain. He looked as if he was struggling to slow down for the younger, smaller dragons as much as they were struggling to keep up. Glay'ak kept checking back to make sure he hadn't left them all behind.

Kanaahn could feel anticipation well up in Djall's stomach, leaking over into Kanaahn and muddying his thoughts.

"Nervous?" Kanaahn asked.

"I have never been before. Not at Xiar. Not even standing before Kanothir. But here, among my people...about to meet my K'dir and K'nir, in blood and scales..."

"Are you okay?"

"Will you be there by my side?"

"Until we die, Djall."

"Then I will be okay."

Warmth flooded in from the mental link, filling Kanaahn with happiness and contentment and smothering the nerves and concern. The anxiety still swam beneath the surface like a small eel, but it did not consume Djall or Kanaahn as it had before.

Glay'ak soon crested the top of the mountainside and the small flock of humans and dragons that followed him were immediately awed by the sight of a giant caldera.

As they dipped down below the ridge of the mountainside, they saw a verdant valley that sat in the middle of the massive crater in the centre of the mountain's belly. Rolling grasslands, ponds, rivers, and streams stretched to all corners of this caldera. The width and depth of the mountain and its crater were betrayed by the gentle slope and relatively low height of the mountainside. The inner walls of the valley were sheer cliffs dotted with hundreds, maybe thousands of holes that could only be dragon lairs.

The wilds below looked like they had never seen the touch of human hands. They were not manicured or recuperating from fires, logging, settlement, or war, like many of the wild places of Enayra. There were no forests cut back and cleared for farmland and livestock enclosures. No grasslands slowly recovering from being razed to the ground by war or a careless baker. No settlements cropping up at random here or there, with high stone walls, or cozy cottages with spiralling smoke billowing from the chimineas. No long rows of tilled land planted with a myriad of cereal grains to be sold for profit and subsistence. The Khaleeshir could not hear the shouting of merchants, the banging of hammers on anvils, the braying of livestock, the screaming of children, the whisper of gossip.

This place was truly wild and untouched. It had existed as such for thousands of years, and the Khaleeshir and their Darond protectors were probably some of the handfuls of humans to have ever visited a dragon clan in their enclave and would likely remain part of this exclusive list for many thousands of years to come.

At first, Kanaahn could not help but be mesmerized by the beauty of it all. He wondered if this is what Enayra looked like, thousands of years ago, before the first boats showed up off the Asardaean coast.

As they flew over the massive, expanse below, Kanaahn couldn't help but notice something was missing. *"Where are all the dragons?"*

Glay'ak's laugh boomed in the heads of all present. *"Look closer, Khaleeshir."*

Kanaahn stared back down at the ground and squinted to try and see what Glay'ak meant. His eyes were much better than they had been before the ritual that bound him to Djall, but it took him a moment at this height to understand what he was seeing.

What he thought were mossy mounds, and verdant hills, blowing green grass and seas of emerald flowers, were dragons, moving, or sleeping, on the ground below. Kanaahn couldn't help but feel a little stupid now. *Green* dragons. Of course, they would blend in against the greenery that surrounded them.

Glay'ak laughed again. *"Take it not as an insult, Khaleeshir, for we surely take it as a compliment."*

The green dragon brought the group down lower, closer to the valley floor below. From here it was much easier to see more of the lives of the dragons below.

Now no one could miss it. Some dragons were flying, gliding low over the grasslands. Some rested by the rivers or slumbered in the grassy fields. Hatchlings could be seen playing by a pond under the watchful eyes of their mothers, while young males fought each other in mock fights, watched carefully by elders.

This place truly lived up to the name: the Emerald Enclave.

Djall was bewildered. *"It's beautiful...I've seen it in memories but...to see it in person."*

"Is it home?"

"It is."

None of the Khaleeshir had ever seen this many wild dragons before, living in their natural habit, among others of their clan. It was almost hard to believe the species was on the decline, or that a war raged beyond these peaceful walls.

Glay'ak's voice cut through the minds of his wards. *"Our people have lived here for thousands of years, undisturbed. It is all that remains of the World That Was. The Enayra that can never be again. War has not come to the Emerald Enclave in all that time. Please do not let that change, Khaleeshir."*

Before anyone could question what that meant, Glay'ak banked left and dove down perpendicular to the ground. The speed at which the dragon dropped was astonishing, and the fact that he expected the others to follow him in his swan dive made Kanaahn glad that Osamu had insisted on leg straps for their first saddle. He loved the rush of flying and pulling stunts, but he wasn't so skilled that he didn't trust himself not to slip.

As Djall pulled into a nosedive to match Glay'ak's, Kanaahn felt the adrenaline surge through him. He felt it start in his gut and then pulse through his veins into his heart. The poor organ nearly beat out of his chest in excitement and Kanaahn's face lit up in glee. His hair flapped and flowed behind him in the wind.

Kanaahn could hear Arial scream out from behind, the freedom and adrenaline taking over her. She was happy and free, and she couldn't hold it in anymore.

Kanaahn screamed next, letting out a whoop that echoed over the valley.

One by one, each of the Khaleeshir, Cecil, and Kyeit let out their own screams and cheers. Soon the dragons started joining in, their roars echoing across the valley below. Glay'ak belted out a massive roar of his own, vibrating the air around him.

Several dragons on the ground below looked up at the dragons and humans above them and returned the roars. Several more of them took to the sky and flew up at the sound of Glay'ak's cry and came to meet their new visitors themselves.

Glay'ak and his followers levelled out one hundred metres from the ground. Here they found themselves surrounded by a dozen green dragons of varying sizes and ages. Two of the dragons were easily double the size of Glay'ak. A few were his size, and the rest were around the same size and age as Djall.

If dragons could smile, Djall would've been beaming. He was home and surrounded by his people, his brothers, and sisters in scale, some maybe even in blood. This was his *clan*. This was his *family*. Djall's mind connected with the dragons around him, and he spoke to them, in draconic, in the proper way.

Kanaahn was dizzied with the flash of memories, emotions, words, abstract concepts, sights, smells, and sounds. Kanaahn was introduced to six different dragons simultaneously, and by the time they had retreated from his mind, he knew more about them than any human ever would in the span of a few minutes. Kanaahn knew more about these dragons than he had ever learned about Kyeit and Cecil in the months he'd known them both.

Finally, Kanaahn was forced to damper the connection with Djall as his partner fixated on a young female about his age and spent the rest of the flight stumbling over his own tail trying to converse with her.

"Remind me to teach Djall how to flirt when we get to Ethon," Kanaahn said to the rest of the group.

"Dragons don't flirt," Risasi interjected.

Shooter snorted. *"That's exactly why you should learn. You're terrible at it."*

Risasi grew defensive. *"I've never tried to flirt."*

Shooter dampened the connection between him and Risasi, so it was just the two of them. Kanaahn wasn't certain what was said, but it was enough to make Risasi's eyes grow wide, his mood grow serious, and smoke blow from his nostrils—Kanaahn could've sworn he saw sparks.

Kanaahn's eyes drifted to the lairs carved into the valley walls. *"Are there that many dragons here? There must be thousands, maybe tens of thousands of those caves."*

Glay'ak's response was sombre. *"No...Not in a long time. Many of those lairs are uninhabited and were excavated in ages past. Some have not been inhabited in a thousand years, but even so, you cannot un-carve the rock."*

Kanaahn could feel the sadness in Glay'ak's voice and soul. It welled in Djall and all the other dragons as well. They were watching the decline of their species, and while it was slow, it was visible.

Glay'ak began to descend towards the valley floor again. The closer they got, the more Kanaahn noticed that every single body of water in the caldera drained towards the centre of the valley. Kanaahn couldn't quite make it out, but he could see steam, or smoke, pouring from what looked like a hole in the ground.

Then it became clear.

The closer they got, Kanaahn could hear the roar. It *was* a giant hole in the ground, and the steam wasn't steam or smoke, it was mist from a myriad of waterfalls as all the water poured over the edge of the hole into a massive cavern below, like an overflowing cup draining in reverse.

"Follow close," warned Glay'ak. *"There's sheer rock behind those falls for most of the descent, and the opening is narrower than it looks. Single file only."*

They heeded Glay'ak's advice as the dragon dipped down towards the hole. The large green dragon dove into a vertical drop once more.

As Kanaahn and Djall followed Glay'ak, the two could feel the spray of mist on their faces and bodies. Their skin and scales grew damp. Kanaahn's clothes, and hair were similarly moistened. The mist made Djall's scales shine like a cavern full of emeralds, refracting the light that filtered in from above.

The chasm went on for a few moments before it opened into a massive cavern that sat just beneath the surface of the valley. The mountain caldera was completely hollow beneath. Kanaahn had no idea how deep the cavern went because all he could see beneath him was darkness and emptiness. There was no floor to the cavern, and the only place to land was a large stone mesa to his left.

This was where Glay'ak took them. He, the Khaleeshir and their Darond watchers landed. Glay'ak took the point and slowly approached the edge of the mesa.

Kanaahn wasn't sure what Glay'ak was doing. He couldn't see the walls of the cavern. All he could see was darkness and an unearthly light that illuminated the stone platform and a few hundred metres around it.

Glay'ak spoke in fluent draconic, speaking out loud for the first time since he met the Khaleeshir. Kanaahn and the others stumbled through translating the language.

"Mother, father. The Khaleeshir have arrived."

Silence.

Not even the drip of moisture or the roar of the waterfall down the narrow chimney of a tunnel into the cavern below seemed to respond to Glay'ak's words.

Then, a rumble. The shifting of some great behemoth within the darkness.

Kanaahn felt his stomach lurch as he realized the sound was not a rumble, but the footstep of some massive creature—two massive creatures.

Slowly, two emerald-coloured heads reached up from the black. All Kanaahn could see were the massive heads and only part of the long, snake-like necks of the Ha'k'dir and Ha'k'nir. Even from the bottom of whatever endless chasm they lived, the heads of these ancient dragons towered high above the platform where everyone stood. They were forced to lower their heads and draw backwards from the platform to get a better look at the Khaleeshir.

The Khaleeshir knew that like Metallic Dragons, the oldest of dragons from the first few generations were able to take on a humanoid shape and could grow and shrink their size at will. It made some of them pale as they realized that there was no way of telling if this was their full size, or if they had to shrink themselves to fit the cavern.

Kanaahn couldn't help but feel terrified. If these two dragons wanted to, they could kill every single one of their current visitors, right here, right now, with a single blast of flame or even a swipe of their paw. The only thing that would save them was the ban on violence within the Emerald Enclave. Flame and fang were not allowed, only mock fights for play or practice were allowed. More grievous disputes had to be settled outside the enclave; and there it was the woods themselves that suffered the brunt of it all, as they had seen.

The Clan Leaders reared back a bit, training their massive eyes on the mesa before them. While they examined the Khaleeshir, Kanaahn noticed other larger dragon heads pop up out of the darkness. The consorts of both Clan Leaders, as Kyeit had explained.

No one said anything. No one dared to speak.

Then, suddenly, the Clan Mother opened her mouth. "Welcome and dol'viinaeszoth, Khaleeshir, to the Emerald Enclave."

Her voice echoed across the massive cavern. The Khaleeshir squinted as they felt their eardrums nearly rupture. Their sensitive hearing did them no service here. It seemed the response was not missed by the Clan Father.

He immediately switched to a mental connection. *"Our apologies. I had forgotten what changes occurred after the ritual. It has been so long since Khaleeshir have come to grace us with their presence. I am Sha'janor, Ha'k'nir-ad-Eru-in'fuor-Elthir of the Drazhani-ad-Benavor. This is my mate, Ha'k'dir-ad-Erya-in'fuor-Elthir Kina'atael. Though you may refer to us by our condensed titles if you so wish."*

Kanaahn had been instructed to do most of the talking for the Khaleeshir, save for introductions, as he had been both the de facto leader, and the one bonded to Djall. Draconic etiquette dictated that appointed leaders do all the speaking for their group in interactions such as this. When in Malatrion, do as the Asardaeans, so the saying went.

Kyeit or Cecil could not step forward and speak for them, or it risked undermining their authority. For all the Knight-Commanders were bonded to metallic dragons and were the Khaleeshir's seniors in some regard, being Khaleeshir politically outstripped Knight-Commander. The Darond were formed to serve the Khaleeshir, after all.

Kanaahn went down into a low genuflection. He was Khaleeshir, but he was also a teenage human meeting one of the oldest beings in Enayra. He counted out the seconds, timing his bow, as instructed, and came back up after eight seconds.

Kanaahn responded in Common. As per custom, Kanaahn was to respond to his elders in the language they first addressed him in. He had let out an almost audible sigh of relief when the Ha'k'dir spoke in Common, and more so that Sha'janor had permitted him to use their shortened titles. Part of him was a little wounded that they did not think he was able to carry a conversation in Draconic or remember their longer titles, but the other part of Kanaahn knew that the dragons were right. Kanaahn would've stumbled through the entire conversation, and it would've been a political disaster.

"Dol'viinaeszoth! It is a pleasure to meet you, Ha'k'nir and Ha'k'dir. You do us a great honour by welcoming us into your enclave and meeting us personally. Your kindness knows no bounds, and you are truly as magnanimous as they say." Honeyed words and

bloated sentences were the best way to speak to these Clan Leaders. *"I am Kanaahn Saatus, son of Menalaea, from Kula, in the land of Altimara. This is my bonded partner."*

Something in Kanaahn felt weird claiming Menalaea as his mother, but in truth, she had been. She had raised Kanaahn and loved him as much as she loved Arial. Besides, Kanaahn had never known his parents' names, and to come before the Clan Leaders with no heritage would be seen as unsightly, so the son of Menalaea it was.

Djall stepped forward and dipped his head to those who were his parents. *"I am Djall-ad-Benavor. Together we lead the Drazhani-ad-Khaleeshir. These are our companions."*

Kina'atael shifted with a slow, lumbering gait. She switched her focus from Kanaahn to Djall. Her interest in the human had waned, but her interest in her own offspring had suddenly welled up like a fountain within. If a dragon could cry, she would be weeping.

"Jal k'zir. Vit ul weniri."

My son. You have returned.

Djall's stomach almost exploded. His brain short-circuited. Kanaahn tried to calm the dragon down as Djall's emotions overflowed and flooded into him. Kanaahn struggled to speak to Djall without anyone else noticing the two of them sliding from the group link for a moment. *"Djall. It's okay. This is your family."*

After what seemed like an eternity, Djall finally responded, with two simple words. *"K'dir. K'nir."*

Kina'atael reached forward and brushed her massive snout against Djall, nearly knocking the dragon over.

Sha'janor came forward and blew smoke from his nostrils so that it enveloped Kanaahn and Djall. Kanaahn's eyes watered as he fought off a coughing fit. Dragons might not notice that much smoke, but for Kanaahn it was like standing in the middle of a forest fire.

Whatever else was said between the Ha'k'dir, Ha'k'nir and Djall was kept private from the rest of the group.

Kanaahn looked back at Glay'ak, who seemed oddly touched by a moment that should not have involved him. There was something more to that dragon than he let on. Kanaahn wanted to find out—without offending the entire clan of course.

It was quite a while before the Clan Leaders and Djall reopened their minds to the other Khaleeshir.

"Our apologies, Khaleeshir," Sha'janor said. *"We have not been with Djall in over a thousand years. Not since we placed his egg within that mountain. We feared we would never see him hatched. Thank you for coming by on your travels."*

"I must say, Ha'k'dir and Ha'k'nir, that it has been a pleasure being bonded to your k'zir. He and I have learned much from each other, and he has saved my life on more than one occasion. I thank you for placing his egg within that chamber."

"You do us proud, k'zir Djall," said Kina'atael. *"Soon you shall destroy that vile traitor Ten'ebraex, and all shall be right in the world again. Perhaps you can return once all is said and done, and settle amongst your people?"*

Kanaahn's heart skipped a beat, and he suddenly felt like the stone floor beneath his body had given away, letting him fall into the black expanse below. No one had actually considered what would happen *after* they beat Tenebrae. Kanaahn was still climbing the mountain that was *if* they beat Tenebrae and was staring over the horizon to the next mountain of *if* they survived. Now he had to consider the possibility of Djall—the other half of his soul and being—up and leaving him after this was all over, for surely Kanaahn would not also be welcome here to live. He was still a human after all.

Sha'janor gave Kanaahn and Djall a much-welcome reprieve, saving the dragon from having to answer. He lowered his head in what Kanaahn could only assume was a nod and changed the subject. *"Forgive the interruption. Please, continue your introductions."*

Kanaahn and Djall turned and gestured to his companions, who proceeded to bow and genuflect themselves. They answered in order of which the dragons had hatched.

"I am Arial Gainsborough, daughter of Menalaea and Artimer—may his soul find peace with the ancestors. This is my bonded partner."

"I am Adalinda-ad-Kruvir, k'vir of Vercith'ae—may her soul find peace with Ezar Kanik—and her mate, Yjosta'gar."

"I am Arkas Nazzer, son of Hellus and Amitaelia. This is my bonded partner."

"I am Fyete-ad-Vikwul, k'vir of Keshal'anda and her mate, Vernix'iol—may his soul find peace with Ezar Kanik."

"I am Shooter Maxim..." Shooter froze. The words stuck in his throat. His father was his father, but he wasn't much of a father, and his mother... wasn't even his mother. Shooter had never known his mother, and the woman his father married afterwards was a horrible, bog-witch of a woman.

Arial shot Shooter a desperate look.

Shooter ground his teeth, and clenched his jaw, fighting with his own conscious to get the words out. He didn't want to admit his own heritage, but he couldn't leave his friends in a lurch with the Green Dragon Clan. So, Shooter did what he did second-best: he compromised.

"Son of Menalaea."

Kanaahn averted his gaze. He knew what Shooter was struggling with, but he couldn't let Shooter know that he was in the know. Shooter felt bad enough that he had put this on Arial before.

"Menalaea is either a very popular name, or she has borne many children."

Kanaahn interceded to smooth things together. *"Among humans, the bonds of family go beyond blood. Those that are your blood may not be your family, and those that are your family may not be your blood. It is not unlike how, among dragons, two dragons of different clans may be brothers or sisters, but not be blood."*

Kina'atael bobbed her head slowly. *"It is a good mother who is honoured as such by children she did not bear. The blessings of the First Mother be upon her."*

Arial, Kanaahn, and Shooter bowed.

Finally, Risasi stepped forward. *"I am Risasi-ad-Noram, k'zir of Venu'shael—may his soul find peace with Ezar Kanik—and his mate, Kara'imla."*

Risasi did not shy away from his k'nir. Where he should have done as Shooter did, and been coy about his parentage, Risasi had done the opposite, and proudly proclaimed both his k'dir and k'nir.

Murmurs, whispers, and rumbles echoed across the cavern. The Ha'k'dir and Ha'k'nir of the Green Dragon Clan exchanged glances. The Court of Consorts muttered in draconic. Even Glay'ak shifted with unease.

Kyeit visibly died inside, and Cecil's face went pale.

Valence glared daggers at Risasi, and Kinokaze couldn't help but be impressed at the gall of the young red dragon.

"Ever the red dragon..." Kinokaze whispered in the back of his mind.

Kanaahn, on the other hand, wanted to shrivel up and die.

It made no sense to Risasi to hide who his k'nir was. After all, each of the five eggs chosen to be future Khaleeshir was provided by the Ha'k'dir and Ha'k'nir of each clan. No other dragon could have been his sire. What if Ölüm had come here with the others, and not turned, what was he supposed to announce to them, when his father had been Tenebrae and Tenebrae's late mate?

Risasi felt no need to justify his decisions to these dragons, old and respected as they may be. Perhaps it was too much of Shooter's influence on him. Perhaps it was the human traits he had picked up when he had gone through the ritual of binding. Perhaps this was just the nature of a red dragon, but he felt no regret for it.

The red dragon proudly made his reasons clear through bursts of emotion across the mental link he currently shared with the Khaleeshir. He shielded these emotions from the Ha'k'dir and Ha'k'nir, however, for even Risasi was not willing to test his luck twice in one day.

Kanaahn immediately scrambled, thinking of ways to backpedal or smooth over this sudden wrinkle that Risasi had presented him with, but he could not find the words—any words—that he felt could adequately calm an angered ancient dragon.

But luckily for Kanaahn, Kina'atael seemed to find Risasi's outburst the funniest thing in the world. She laughed with a closed mouth, still communicating using the mental link, and her voice echoed inside everyone's skulls. Eventually, every other being in the cavern was forced to awkwardly join her, or risk embarrassing the Mother of the Green Dragons.

When the laughter had finally stopped, Kina'atael looked at Risasi with a bemused smile. *"So much like your K'dir. She too is ever the contrarian, spitting in the face of order and tradition. Why, when we heard tell that Ha'k'nir Kara'imla invited the Ha'drazh'ghar Vikwul to combine their clans and live together within the Vermilion Chambers, to share their territory—encouraging inter-breeding between the clans, no less! Well, we could not begin to imagine what madness she had been thinking. But our younger k'iir has always amused herself this way, and it seems she passes this trait on to you, young Risasi-ad-Noram. So, know that it is because of my love for her that I stay my hand here—that and the ban on such violent acts within the enclave."*

Risasi did not respond. He stared hard, unashamed, and unabashed at the Ha'k'nir. Her disguised reprimand did not affect him, and he did not fear her empty threats. Anger burned just beneath the surface of Risasi's calm exterior, but anyone who looked at the dragon could see that clearly. He always did such a poor job of hiding his true emotions.

But Kina'atael would not be outdone; least of all in her own home. She snorted. *"Though it seems you have your k'dir's temper."*

Foolishly, and despite his better judgement, Risasi took the bait. Something in him snapped. But before he could lash out, Shooter placed a hand on his neck. Valence and Kinokaze had shifted as if to pounce on him, and Kanaahn stepped forward and immediately changed the subject.

"Great Ha'k'nir and Ha'k'dir, now that the pleasantries have been observed I think we should get to the business of our visit, for unfortunately, it cannot simply be a visit of whim and courtesy."

Sha'janor, recognizing Kanaahn's change of subject for what it was—himself having done the same earlier—replied quickly. *"Yes, of course! I would hate to keep you from such important business. There can be no tarrying when it could mean the swift defeat of our harzok former k'tir, Ten'ebraex."*

The name drop caught Kanaahn off guard, but after Risasi's stunt, and considering their current company, he felt it best not to pry. *"Our humblest gratitude that you understand. You see, Mighty Ha'k'nir and Ha'k'dir, we humble Khaleeshir come before you to ever so kindly beseech your permission to pass through your lands as we progress towards our ultimate goal: Ethon."*

Kina'atael raised a scaly brow. *"And why, Khaleeshir, is it that you must pass through our lands specifically to reach the human settlement?"*

Ethon was hardly a "settlement" anymore, but the last time they had seen Ethon, it was probably still called Gerovia and had been nothing more than a collection of hovels and barns made by early human settlers. Kanaahn could forgive the wording in this case.

"The Oath of Volesus has outlived his empire, and—except in Altimara—has been upheld without fail for the last two thousand years. Humans do not encroach on our lands, and we do not devour your livestock, or otherwise inconvenience your lives. Any who break this vow on either side face severe punishment," Sha'janor added. It seemed he could not so openly defy his mate, and more so, that he agreed with her hesitancy in this regard.

Kina'atael picked up where Sha'janor had left off. *"Crossing our lands is more than just a simple traipse across our territory. It means sharing our resources. You will make camps, set fires, and even devour our animals. We cannot hunt outside of our lands, and while the Green Dragon Clan is not what it once was, we still require sustenance for the younger dragons. We are limited to what lives within our borders, and what lives within our borders live in a careful balance, unused to human presence. Humans and dragons acknowledge borders, but prey does not. Nature does not care. If they flee because of you, there is no guarantee they will return. We expose ourselves enough to this kind of risk by allowing you an audience, but to allow you passage...it is a great risk indeed. You ask much."*

Kanaahn weighed his words carefully. He had only one chance at this, and things already seemed to not be going in his favour. *"I ask not this favour lightly...but we are being pursued by those whom the dragons refer to as Tulkaz."*

Murmurs and whispers. Sha'janor and Kina'atael's faces went from indifference to concern. Even they did not take Tenebrae's dark servants lightly.

"Could you not fly across?" suggested Sha'janor, not unsympathetic to the danger Kanaahn had mentioned.

"We cannot fly across, for we cannot abandon our horses, and when we leave your lands, our safety in the air will no longer be certain. It is safer beneath the trees, and so we must cross on foot. The Tulkaz would not dare cross into your lands, for fear of your might and strength. We do not ask this lightly, and your clan has given much over the centuries to fight Tenebrae...but if we cannot survive our trip to Ethon, then all these years of fighting will have been for nothing."

"You ask us to sacrifice even more than we already have?" Kanaahn couldn't tell if Kina'atael was insulted, incredulous, impressed, or all of the above. *"Do you know how many of my children have died for the sake of this cause? How many I lost in the last war, and how many I have lost to Altimara because of my harzok k'tir?"*

Kanaahn had to choose his next words very, very carefully. *"What I am asking…is for you to take a chance on us. The sooner we get to Ethon, the sooner we can complete our training and defeat Tenebrae, and the sooner we can help the dragon clans recover. We—"*

"K'dir, k'nir, I beseech you, please. By offering them shelter, you offer it to me as well. Am I not your k'zir? Am I not part of the clan? Is it not our way to offer shelter to any in the clan, regardless of where they choose to call home?"

"Of course, you are permitted passage but—"

"And I shall not go without Kanaahn. We are Khaleeshir. We are bonded. One soul in two bodies; you cannot separate us."

"But the others—"

"Are Khaleeshir as well, and they are my nest-mates. My k'iir and k'tir. We spent a millennium together in that cave. We hatched and grew up together. They are bonded with these humans; in the same way I am bonded with Kanaahn. The remaining two dragons, while not my nest-mates, are the k'nir of the Great Metallic dragons. Would you deny the offspring of the Metallics, your nest-mates, the safe passage and hospitality due to them?"

Silence.

Sha'janor could be seen smirking from just behind his mate and her seething rage. If Kina'atael wasn't green, she'd be red with fury.

"I've never seen her speechless," Kinokaze muttered to the Khaleeshir privately.

After an eternity, Kina'atael was able to regain her composure before responding. *"If there was ever any doubt as to who laid you…"*

Sha'janor winked at Djall.

"Your arguments have weight. I cannot say I completely accept this, but I shall acquiesce if my mate does as well."

"Our k'zir makes a convincing argument. I acquiesce."

"Very well. You may pass through our lands. If you could leave as little a footprint as possible, it would be appreciated."

Kanaahn bowed. *"We shall do our very best, Ha'k'dir and Ha'k'nir. We appreciate your generosity."*

"You may rest up here for the night, for night shall soon be upon us, and it would not do well for us to ignore the rules of hospitality. Once you have rested, Glay'ak will see you back to your beasts of burden, and you may be on your way through our lands."

Kanaahn's tone was ever deferential. *"Thank you, for your continued hospitality. We appreciate the respite from our travels."*

Bows were performed and Sha'janor and Kina'atael returned to the dark void that was the cavern, their consorts following in quick succession.

Glay'ak said nothing.

No one said anything.

They were quickly and quietly escorted back out of the hole from where they came and led out into the verdant valley above.

"Well done, Djall," Glay'ak said finally once they had put some distance between them and the cavern. *"Spoken like a true green dragon."*

Djall couldn't help but feel immense pride in his actions. Though they were a mask for the sheer terror and fear that still coursed through him. His head was rushing, and his stomach kept lurching. He could feel his heart beating at a breakneck pace as if it was trying to throw itself against his ribcage and be free of its flesh prison. He had almost been certain he had caused their deaths, or at the very least, their banishment from the Emerald Enclave at first.

Instead, he had used eloquent elocution to best one of the greatest green dragons that had ever lived in an—albeit one-sided—debate. Logic had won out, as had the love of a mother for her child.

"We'll work on the diplomacy before we meet another Ha'k'dir or Ha'k'nir," Kyeit said. *"That was a chance I'd rather not take twice."*

Glay'ak did not tarry in leading the group from this ancient meeting chamber. Even he agreed it was best not to tarry and risk the wrath of a vengeful Ha'k'dir.

He led the group towards an ancient and massive cavern carved into the walls of the valley. It went deep into the side of the mountain, so far that Kanaahn didn't know if he could explore it all and be back by dawn. An ancient dragon once lived here with its mate and brood, no doubt—the size was confirmation enough of that. Though he didn't have to think for long to guess what happened to the previous tenants.

Kanaahn could only guess as to how many of the thousands of cavern homes that dotted the walls of the caldera were vacant. More than anyone cared to admit, and more than should have been. He had thought about it earlier, but his conversation with the Ha'k'dir and Ha'k'nir put it even more into perspective. It became painfully clear just how much the dragons had suffered since the Dragon War. They had lived and survived...but they had not recovered, and the Great Purge had only hurt them further.

The Ha'k'dir's concerns were clearer, now. Her arguments were heavier with the added weight of proof. Kanaahn could understand why she had been so affronted to be asked to sacrifice just a little more for the sake of the cause. She had given so much...and she had spoken true. These dragons had been her blood; her children and grandchildren and however many generations down the line. They were not just some nameless clan members she was elected to protect. This was her family—all of them were her family, every last one.

Kanaahn would have to return and apologize one day, perhaps bring her and her clan a herd of Geller's moose. She had taken a great risk because of Kanaahn's harsh logic, and Kanaahn was suddenly starting to understand just how great.

Chapter XV

Glay'ak had left the group to set up a small make-shift camp at the mouth of the cave. The dragons went out to hunt down some food for themselves and even brought back a wild boar for the humans to roast over the fire. The wood had been supplied by Glay'ak from some dead trees he had found scattered across the forest floor at the base of the mountain.

With food in their stomachs, the group felt the weight of the day on their eyelids, and they quickly went to sleep. No discussion was had late into the night, and no celebration. Only sleep.

But not for Shooter. Shooter waited for the others to drift off to sleep before prodding Risasi through the mental connection.

"Risasi."

The dragon didn't respond, but Shooter could tell he was awake. The dragon had not slept properly since they had crossed the Spine.

"Risasi. Wake up. I know you hear me."

Nothing.

"Risasi, if you don't respond, I'm going to come over and poke you until you respond."

"I would not, if I were you. You don't poke a sleeping dragon."

"Then it's a good thing for me you're not asleep."

Risasi grumbled.

Shooter rolled over onto his side so that he was facing Risasi, who had chosen to lie down at the back of the cavern. *"We need to talk."*

"Do we?"

"Risasi, we've needed to talk since that conversation we had with Cecil. Today made that very clear."

Risasi remained quiet.

"I'm sorry I didn't bring it up sooner."

"So, you have figured it out?"

"It wasn't that hard. We knew that the eggs provided to the Darond for the sake of becoming Khaleeshir came directly from each clan's Ha'k'dir and Ha'k'nir. Once Cecil

told us that story, it was easy to put two and two together. Especially with your reaction...”

“My response was not abnormal for someone of my clan—nor any dragon. We lost many good dragons that day to the madness of a traitorous Ha'k'nir.”

“The same Ha'k'nir from whom you so proudly proclaimed your heritage earlier.”

Risasi growled.

“You don't need to hide these feelings from me, Risasi. We're Khaleeshir. We're bonded.”

“You don't understand...”

“No, I don't, but that doesn't mean I'm stupid. Your father was close with Tenebrae, and you were close with Ölüm. Your father betrayed his clan for Tenebrae. You're afraid that history might repeat itself.”

Risasi was painfully silent.

Shooter knew he had broken through, but for a change, he didn't keep pressing the attack. He pulled back and waited for Risasi to return with a riposte. Shooter seemed to wait for an eternity, but finally, it came.

“I don't know why I have these memories in my head. They happened long after my egg had been laid and placed inside that cavern. Despite everything my k'nir did, my k'dir trusted me to follow my destiny, and work against Tenebrae...despite his blood in my veins. Dragons place great importance on bloodlines and lineage. It's believed that who your forebearers were will foreshadow who you will become. It's a lot of pressure.”

Shooter smirked in the darkness, but he knew Risasi could see it from across the cavern. *“You almost sound human.”*

Smoke rose from Risasi's nostrils as his temper rose within his breast.

“Peace, Risasi. I was only joking.”

“I feel many things concerning this development...”

“So, talk about them,” Shooter said bluntly.

“How did I even get these memories in my head? They would have had to have been planted there after the war and after the betrayal. Long after I had been put inside that cavern. Who put them there? Was it my k'dir? Why? What did she hope to teach me? And why were they hidden just below the surface, why had I never been able to recall them before that moment...did she want me to feel that pain fresh? Was that the point? What will other dragons think of me, and what will this mean for my future? Am I going to betray my siblings like my K'nir did? Am I going to join Tenebrae like Ölüm?”

“That...is a lot of questions...” Shooter was puzzled about how to untangle this mess. *“The best thing to do is tackle this in parts. Let's start with the first part. The memories in your head; they would have had to have been placed there after the war, that is obvious, but who put them there?”*

“From what I can see, it seems to be the perspective of my k'dir. She was the one who put these memories in my head, no one else could have. That is how the Bestowment works.”

“Tenebrae had access to the cavern when he was defeated, even as a disembodied spirit. It's not a stretch to assume your k'dir also had access.”

“But why?”

“Ask yourself the same question. Why would she do this, what we she trying to teach you? I think the answer is easier than you think.”

Risasi thought it over for a moment before reaching a satisfactory conclusion. *"...She wanted me to know about my ancestry. Could you imagine, as a Khaleeshir, meeting other dragons who would know what happened, proudly proclaiming my heritage without knowing the truth of what my k'nir did? It would be embarrassing. It would hinder my ability as Khaleeshir."*

"That makes sense. And yet she buried them just below the surface all the same. Why?"

"...That is a very heavy memory to place upon the shoulders of a hatchling. If I had carried that weight from birth, it might have pushed me on a very different path. The self-doubt I feel now...it would have been worse when I was younger. Red dragons are not always in control of their feelings, and a very confused, brooding hatchling who has yet to learn to speak or doesn't trust those around him is a dangerous hatchling."

"That's how we get Ölüms."

Risasi snorted.

"Now the other questions don't have answers at this point because it's all just speculation. You haven't betrayed your siblings yet, and you haven't joined Tenebrae. I don't know what this means for your future, or how other dragons are going to treat you, but from what I've seen, the dragons that matter don't seem to care."

"Until earlier."

"Well, you did kind of spit in the Ha'k'dir's face with your announcement."

Risasi grunted.

"Why did you do that, anyway?"

"Because even after I saw the destruction he wreaked upon my siblings and k'dir; even after knowing all the pain he caused, I can't hate him. Despite my fear that I might turn out just like him...I can't hate him. I didn't know him, and I do not know the reasons he turned on the clan. I'm sure they're not a justification but... there are so many questions I have. I need answers. I need to know more."

"Then we go get your answers."

"How?"

"The only place you're going to get answers is from your k'dir. We've already met Djall's clan, I don't see why we can't go see yours on our journeys. We'll go speak to her and get you your answers."

"You would do that for me?"

"Not for, but with. We're together in this. Partners."

If dragons were biologically capable of crying Risasi's eyes would be glistening.

"You don't need to say anything. I feel it." Shooter placed a hand over his heart. *"We share more than words through this connection."*

And so Risasi did not respond.

Shooter had been pleased with the conversation that was had. He stopped pressing; he got what he needed—no, what Risasi needed from this conversation. It had been for his partner's benefit, not his. Shooter just needed to pry the truth out of him and get the dragon to sort through his thoughts and feelings, and in that respect, Shooter had succeeded as much as he was currently able. The rest was on Risasi and his k'dir. Much would hinge on the answers they got.

After a few minutes of silence, Risasi reached out again. *"Shooter?"*

Shooter knew where Risasi was going. *"I'd go with you, Risasi, even if you chose that path; have no fear. No matter what path you choose, always know we choose it together. I go where you go, no matter what."*

"...Really?"

"I like Kyeit and Cecil. I like them as people—the same goes for Valence and Kinokaze, but I don't trust them, and I definitely don't trust the Darond yet. The Darond's lied to us because of the High Council. Kyeit has lied to us because of her duty to that council. Cecil seems to be fairly honest, but how far does that honesty go in the face of her responsibilities as a Knight-Commander? What is more important to her, duty, or honesty? I can't say I know her well enough to know the answer. She's got her own secrets; I can tell that much. I'm also not a big fan of who the Darond chose as a leader, or how closely they tie themselves to the politics of the realm. It reeks of a lust for power. So, I watch the Darond, Cecil, and Kyeit with a sideways glance all the time. If at any point they prove to be leading us down the wrong path, and you decide you'd rather step away from this fight and run away, or go join Drakhart and Tenebrae, I'd support you."

Shooter paused to allow Risasi an opportunity to respond. When the red dragon said nothing back, Shooter continued.

"I'd hate to turn on the others after everything we've been through, and after all these years, but just because Kanaahn's the leader doesn't mean he speaks for all of us. If he leads us down the wrong path after the Darond, I'd have to speak up. I know he feels similarly about the Darond and the wards they've sent us, but I'm not blind and naïve to think that his feelings for Kyeit might not dull his senses and tint his decisions in the future. We're only human, after all.

"I feel about the Darond the way you do about your ancestry: I don't have enough information, and I feel like we've only been getting half the story. Maybe I'm wrong, but in all my years I've learned to trust my doubt in everything that I get told until sufficient evidence proves otherwise.

"At the end of the day, it's not personal, it's duty. We're Khaleeshir, and everyone keeps telling us we're here to do good and help people...but I can't help but wonder whose definition of good we're following, and whether that's really what's best, or what's right. So, if it ever comes out that we're on the wrong side, and we're doing more harm than good, then I'll go find the right side, or make my own. We're Khaleeshir, and if we can't decide what is right and wrong for ourselves, do we even deserve to be heroes?"

"No. I suppose not. We would be no better than puppets; we'd be terrible heroes."

"Exactly!"

Risasi looked at Shooter and Shooter at Risasi. They smiled, and Shooter winked.

"Since when did you start caring about your duty as a Khaleeshir? You were always so reluctant at first."

"I was. I hadn't asked for this...I hadn't taken the stone knowing it was an egg that would change my life. I'll be honest, I was on my way to get it appraised when I first heard Arial's was hatching. Even after Ottogard, I loved you, but I didn't want to be a Khaleeshir. I hadn't agreed to it, so why should I be forced into it?"

"What changed?"

"Xiar. Xiar changed it all for me. I wondered...what would have happened to all those people, to that city, if we hadn't been there. I don't know if our fighting helped any, but I know the High Council got one thing right."

"What's that?"

"It was something Hunter said. That the High Council would have put us on top of a parapet as a morale boost for the troops. We'd do nothing but stand there and inspire people. But really, our presence does just that...it seems to inspire people. So many people who would never have given us a first look, let alone a second, in our old lives, suddenly respect us and expect great things from us. We're rubbing elbows with generals, soldiers, diplomats, and royalty, and all of them respect us—defer to us. We're going to defeat Tenebrae and bring peace to the world...but in the meantime, we're just teenagers and we have no idea what we're doing. We're in training ourselves, but the High Council knows the kind of weight our legacy holds, and that just having us around a battlefield makes other people fight harder. It's easy to fight with your all when you believe victory is guaranteed."

"You actually agree with them?"

"No. I agree with their assessment of our strategic value. It's something we need to learn to harness ourselves, but I won't be just sitting in some commander's tent smiling and looking pretty. What's the good of being some great, mighty hero if you can't go out and use all that power?"

"We may still fail, one day. The day is young. We are not infallible."

"Maybe, but in the meantime, I plan to give it my all. In Kula we have a saying: the egg doesn't ask to be laid, and it doesn't ask to hatch into a Mhokshi lizard. Yet that lizard lives life as it comes. I didn't ask to be a Khaleeshir, and yet here I am...and I can actually start making a difference like we always hoped we could one day back in Kula, but on a larger scale."

"You've become quite noble, Shooter."

"And you've become quite emotional, Risasi."

The dragon snorted. *"Tell no one."*

Shooter winked and rolled over in his bedroll. His silence was assured.

"...Shooter. Thank you."

"Don't mention it. Now, get to sleep, we've got a lot of travelling tomorrow."

* * *

Glay'ak landed as silently as a three-hundred-year old dragon could. His wings kicked up some dust, shifting rocks and pebbles and making the grass flutter like a candle in the wind. He waited for a moment before signalling to his partners.

Vultoz and Ithai'hra soon joined him.

They watched the cave where they had left the Khaleeshir and their Darond wards. With their dragon hearing, they could hear everyone fast asleep inside. They had timed this perfectly. Like hunters stalking prey, they waited a moment longer before discussing their next steps.

"What do we do?" whispered Vultoz.

"Patience. Let me reach out," replied Glay'ak. Glay'ak reached across the physical gap and found the edges of Djall's mind. *"Djall."*

No response.

Glay'ak waited a moment before prodding again. Harder this time.

"*Djall. Djall wake up.*"

The dragon stirred. "*Glay'ak? What are you—*"

"*Come outside. We must speak.*"

"*Why? What's wrong?*"

"*Nothing. We need to speak.*"

"*Should I wake the others?*"

"*No. Come alone. Quickly.*"

"*Then how can nothing be wrong, if it must be done in the dead of night, behind everyone's backs?*"

Glay'ak chortled. "*Your quick words won't work on me. Come.*"

Djall did as he was asked and slipped from the cave as quickly and quietly as a dragon could. It wasn't easy surrounded by those whose hearing was more sensitive than most, but somehow Djall managed. He landed in front of Glay'ak and his siblings.

They bowed to him, which confused Djall.

Glay'ak noticed the confusion. "We dragons give deference to our elders."

"I am aware, but I've only just hatched a few months ago."

Vultoz furrowed his scaly brows. "But your egg was laid a thousand years ago. Your mind was alive inside that shell, that is how you were able to choose who would be your partner. Dragons do not only count age based on when we hatch but also when we are laid. Your body is a few months old, but your mind is centuries older than us, k'tir."

Djall did not respond. He froze. As tired as he was he understood the weight of Vultoz's words. You did not use k'tir for anyone who was not a sibling of the same breeding pair as you.

"K'tir?"

"Yes. You are our older k'tir," Ithai'hra confirmed.

"How...you knew when I arrived?"

Glay'ak nodded. "We knew our k'tir had been gifted to the Metallics and the Darond to become the future Khaleeshir, just as our k'tir Unaedrol had been chosen before you. When we heard that the Khaleeshir had returned, we knew you must've been among them."

"Why did you have to wait until now to tell me?" Djall asked.

"You had other obligations at the time, and we didn't want to draw you away from your nest-mates and partner so soon," explained Glay'ak. "And we all wanted a chance to see you—together. Perhaps we could go for a flight, and you could regale us, k'tir, with the stories of your great victory over the harzok traitor Tenebrae and his minions at Xiar."

"You've heard of that? Wait a minute, if you two are here, who's watching the horses?"

Ithai'hra explained. "We've asked a few clan-mates to watch them. They are old, and so they do not eat anymore. Therefore, they are trustworthy."

Glay'ak stretched his wings. "We didn't want to miss the story of our brave, Khaleeshir k'tir."

It didn't take much more to convince Djall to ascend into the black, moonlit sky and fly about with his newfound siblings. In just a day Djall had gone from a lone dragon, whose only close relations were his Khaleeshir nestmates and his partner Kanaahn, to having a full family of dragons and clan-mates. He had met his parents, his siblings, and who knows how many more siblings were down in the enclave below.

But more than that...he had a future home. A place he could come after all of this was over, where he could mate, have his own hatchlings, and live a normal dragon life.

Or could he?

Kanaahn would not be allowed to come with him, and Djall was no longer certain he could live without him. They had become one and the same, slowly, but surely, ever since the ritual had been completed. Two souls became one soul. One soul in two bodies.

But more than that...as a Khaleeshir would his work truly be done? How many pieces would need to be picked up and repaired after the war was over? Defeating Tenebrae was easy—at least in concept—but rebuilding the world after a thousand years of status quo was far harder by comparison. Could the world even go back to how it was before? So much had changed...for dragons and humans. Would it want to change back?

"Tell us the story of your glory at Xiar, brother," Glay'ak pressed.

The quartet of dragons had just crested the clouds and flew in the sea of stars that lay just above. The light of a half-moon shone down meekly at them.

These thoughts would have to wait—and Djall would have to speak with Kanaahn about them later.

Chapter XVI

Kanaahn's dreams were not the rushing flurry of words, scenes, and senses. He did not dream like a dragon tonight. Tonight, he dreamed coherently, but his dreams were not calm and peaceful. They were even more haunting and chaotic than normal...and he would not forget his dreams when he awoke.

The voice cut through his head like a knife through flesh. He recognized the words. Someone had spoken them to him after the ritual in Ottogard, but the voice was different.

Kanaahn blinked and suddenly found himself in someone's house, and though he had never been here before, inexplicably he recognized where he was as if he had lived here his whole life. Kanaahn was in Kula, though that much would have been clear from the décor and architecture alone. It was clear from a cursory look that the familiarly unfamiliar house wasn't Menalaea's. It wasn't even a particularly fancy house, but it wasn't a slum either. It was something in the middle of both options. Not opulent, but not terrible.

Whose house was Kanaahn in then? He recognized the architecture, but not the exact location.

Kanaahn started. He saw movement in his periphery. Figures danced at the edge of his vision, and he went for his blade instinctually...and found it wasn't there on his hip. Not that it mattered. As Kanaahn soon discovered, the people couldn't even see him. He was a spectre. The young woman—for the figures were a young man and a young woman— approached the place where Kanaahn was standing and walked right through him as if he wasn't there. The woman and the man spoke to each other, but even though Kanaahn could see their mouths move, he could not hear their voices. At that moment Kanaahn noticed that not a single sound echoed through his dream; not these voices, not his footsteps, or even his own voice, as he discovered when he tried to talk, but no sound came out. There was only a dull ringing in his ears and the crushing sound of silence.

Kanaahn instead decided to study the two young people he saw. Perhaps he could learn something about them that way, if not from their words. The man was tall, handsome, with sharp features; clearly half-Espian, though Kanaahn couldn't tell what the other half was. He wore simple clothes the colour of the ocean, and several rings on different fingers. His hair was long and dark, the colour of a stormy sky, and his eyes were two emeralds that shone even in the minimal light of the interior of this home.

The man approached Kanaahn, still talking to his female companion and Kanaahn saw that he was deceptively tall; taller than Kanaahn. He had the physique of a warrior or soldier. Despite his physique, the man was still lithe; he wasn't particularly broad-shouldered, or overly bulky. Moreover, there was a danger that seemed to lurk beneath the surface. A cat-like nimbleness at rest behind his eyes, eyes that scrutinized and scanned everything they looked at as if assessing the threat of a house plant would save his life one day. Kanaahn could see the man's worn and weathered hands, and Kanaahn knew these to be the hands of a man who had grown used to wielding a blade and had been doing so since a young age. They were the same hands Kanaahn had.

There was something else as well. Something intangible that Kanaahn could see just by how this man carried himself. There was a deftness to his movement, it was more than the cat-like nimbleness he had read before, but it was the reaction speed of a Kulan rock viper ready to strike. He looked more dangerous than even the burliest of men Kanaahn had seen. This man could easily kill a man twice his size in a few short movements—or at the least, die trying.

Kanaahn's attention turned next to the woman. She was, simply put, incredibly beautiful. She couldn't be more than a decade older than Kanaahn and about the same age as her counterpart. Her hair was the colour of raven feathers against the black of a midnight sky and her eyes the colour of rich, loamy soil at the bottom of an abyss. Her skin was the opposite, pale white and almost radiant in comparison to the darkness of her features. She too was half-Espian. She was dressed in simple black leather britches and boots, a white wool shirt under a padded leather vest. Gloves were tucked into her sword belt, and off each hip hung a basket-hilted rapier. Several daggers were tucked into her belt towards her back, and the hilts of two stilettos were just barely visible, peaking up from each boot. The black leather-wrapped hilts blended in with the black leather pants and if she had been wearing a cloak, her daggers would be impossible to see until it was far too late. She was armed to the teeth, though her counterpart, if he carried any weapons, did not have it on him.

Based on how they were dressed, Kanaahn assumed she was about to head out into the world, a fact which was confirmed when she grabbed a black cloak and threw it about her shoulders. The woman walked over and kissed her partner on the lips. The two exchanged—what Kanaahn could only assume—were loving words before she turned and walked towards the door.

And then it happened. An explosion tore down the front door, splintering it and breaking the jamb and some of the wall. Glass tinkled to the ground as the windows shattered from the force. The woman was thrown back against the far wall. The man pulled a dagger from within the folds of his robes. Flames began to engulf the home and could be seen dancing across the neighbouring rooftops outside.

Two hooded figures glided in through the door, almost floating as they moved. Their movements were quick and fluid like water. They struck out at the man, who did his best to hold off their sword blows with a single danger. He was brave, and he held his own for as long as possible—longer than most would have in that situation. But with a twirl and a stab, his life was ended by the enemy's sword through his gut.

His eyes were wide, his mouth open in a silent scream. He was still processing his death when the light left his eyes. His last words were probably the name of his lover, as Kanaahn did not recognize the word—though he wasn't the best at reading lips. The dying man reached his hand out towards her, then went limp.

The now empty shell of the man fell to his knees like a puppet that had had its strings cut, and the hooded figure used its foot to steady the body as it retrieved the blade. Then the hooded figure beheaded the man for good measure.

The second figure had already begun baring down on the woman. She was dazed from the explosion, blood was running from her broken nose, her cloak was singed, her forehead was bleeding from a cut near her scalp, and her head was no doubt swimming with pain as her ears still rang.

Kanaahn could only watch in a mix of amazement and horror as she got up, threw off her cloak, and threw herself at her enemies, with both swords drawn. The trio fought and became a flurry of sharp steel. The woman held her own against both attackers. Kanaahn envied that he could not hear the ringing of steel on steel. If he could, there was no doubt that it would've sounded like an intense smithing session.

The swords on both sides of the conflict moved faster than Kanaahn had ever seen. Lord Genji of Xiar and Kyeit were some of the best swordsmen Kanaahn had seen yet, and they would've been put to shame by both the attackers and the defender.

Even with her head swimming, eyes burning from the smoke, lungs filling with ash and soot, rage and sorrow no doubt pooling in her gut, she was flawless in technique. Blood dripped down into her eyes, mixing with the tears, but still, she fought on, half-blinded.

Kanaahn was amazed.

She had the hooded figures pushed back towards the door, ready to send them back outside from whence they came. Victory was within her grasp...but she miss-stepped. Her foot landed, without her noticing, in the pool of blood that had come from her lover's body and had started to pool on the wooden floors. She placed her foot down and slipped on the slick, red blood. The woman fell and slammed the back of her head against the floor.

Kanaahn winced sympathetically.

The woman had lost one of her swords in the fall, and one of her opponents wasted no time in exploiting her dazed confusion to kick the sword off to the side and out of reach. The woman refused to give in. She drew a dagger from her belt and tried to stand up and fight on. Blood stung her eyes, and it was getting too hard to see. She was on her knees, trying to get up, but she stumbled trying to stand up in the slick of blood.

One of her foes swiped their sword at her. She barely managed to dodge, though their sword tip cut her across the cheek.

She slowed down, the second blow to her head had handicapped her. She was still slipping, struggling to get up, this time her opponent got her in the shoulder and the blade completely pierced her joint through to the other side. Her arm went limp, and the woman dropped her sword. She had left only her dagger...but it didn't matter. Another sword caught her in the thigh, then across the stomach, spilling the contents of her gut onto the floor.

She tried her best to struggle against the pain, against death, and the blood pooling at her feet; her blood mixed with her lover's. The woman was down, lying on her stomach, gasping for air, trying to breathe. She extended her arm and reached towards her lover's cold hands, she struggled as they were just out of reach, and the pain was growing unbearable.

Then a sword came down from above, through her neck. She kicked once...twice...then stopped moving.

The hooded figures looked at each other, and then immediately departed. They walked with the calm demeanour of those who had just come over for a quick visit with old friends and were now departing to go about their remaining business for the day. Flames had already begun to engulf most of the house by this point, and from what Kanaahn could see they had engulfed much of the neighbouring homes as well.

Tears stung Kanaahn's eyes, and he could feel them roll freely down his face. He hadn't realized he was crying. At first, he thought it was the smoke...and then he realized that this dream world did not affect him.

Then, the only sound he heard in his dream pierced through the silence; it was the wail of an infant from somewhere upstairs.

Before Kanaahn could look up, or make his way toward the child, the world dissolved, the cry faded into the distance and the floor gave way into the abyss. Kanaahn fell, fell, fell...and he was swallowed by the darkness, tears still streaming down his cheeks.

Then it all came to an end, just as quickly as it had started.

Chapter XVII

Elandyr'ni found Drakhart hunched over an ancient wooden table in the royal library, spilling over missives and diplomatic exchanges between Estion and Altimara going back four monarchs in both kingdoms. It wasn't a surprise to find him here. When he wasn't training with her and Balgorax, or studying under the tutelage of Calandor, he was here, carrying out his special mission given to him by Tenebrae.

Elandyr'ni had had her fair share of special tasks given out by their lord Tenebrae. She did not envy Drakhart; the pressure could be crushing for one so new to this. Elandyr'ni had gotten used to the pressure, and she had rarely failed her master. He was not unkind, and he could be forgiving if the fault was not your own personal failure, but each failure set back his plans, and Tenebrae's patience was slowly beginning to wear out. He was suddenly racing against...something. He didn't share what.

Drakhart had searched, searched, and searched again for anything that could potentially allow him to shatter Estion from within, but so far he had found nothing.

The monarch, Anducaerleonis, would not be so easily bullied, and there was no blackmail, leverage, or ancient relations he could exploit to undermine or coerce the king and his court. In fact, Drakhart had recently found that without a king itself, Altimara's position had been weakened and worse off in that regard. Drakhart was slowly losing his mind over this—Elandyr'ni could see it in his face.

Tired eyes ringed with black circles, red and bloodshot from lack of sleep. He had begun to grow a patchwork of light stubble across his upper lip and chin. It was not a full and proper beard, but a boy slowly becoming a man, growing his first few hairs. Drakhart was dishevelled and if Elandyr'ni hadn't known better, she'd have thought one of the beggars from the Burnt District had wandered into the castle.

Elandyr'ni knew his heart would appreciate the break she came to offer, even if his mind would refuse at first.

"Drakhart?" she called gently, so as not to startle him.

But Drakhart did not respond. He barely acknowledged her existence. He was buried in a missive; it looked like a spy report, and from the date she could make out on it, it was recent.

Drakhart's finger dragged over the missive as he absorbed every word, letter by letter. His back hunched over the table like an old crone, and his other hand gripping the edge of the table like a taloned claw clutching treasure.

Again, Elandyr'ni spoke, this time louder, more forceful. "Drakhart."

This time he turned, slowly. His body ached; she could see in the way he turned himself. Not just his head or neck, no, but his whole body, like some ancient spectre that haunted this place. Like some great tree monster with no neck.

"Elandyr'ni?" he croaked. Drakhart squinted in the dimness of the candlelight. It was late at night, and the stub of a candle on his desk was his only source of light.

She stepped forward into the glow of the candle. "I have a letter from your castellan. It's not good."

"You're reading my mail now?"

Elandyr'ni couldn't help but smirk. Even in this state Drakhart still had his wit.

"I think you'll thank me for doing so in a minute."

He stood up and combed his fingers his dishevelled hair. "How bad is it?"

Elandyr'ni handed Drakhart the letter.

Drakhart pored over every word, reading it one, twice, three times before fully comprehending what his castellan was telling him. Drakhart's mood soured as a frown etched itself into his face.

Elandyr'ni had already read and processed the contents of the letter. Supply shipments to Kula had been robbed. Soldiers killed. The barracks were continually sabotaged. Weapons and food were being stolen from warehouses, supply trains, and even directly from suppliers in the city. Three of the city's newest and biggest forges had been burned to the ground under mysterious circumstances, and their anvils had been ruined by some sort of acidic compound. Two others had had their anvils destroyed, and their tools stolen. It was affecting locale morale, and local stability, and could negatively affect the war effort going forward if it continued. Some of the Kulan people had even begun openly speaking out against Drakhart and the Crown. Peace in Kula was breaking down.

"Amber."

"Pardon?"

"The only person capable of this."

Elandyr'ni raised her eyebrow. "You don't give the locals much credit."

"I lived there for years. People had given up. They stopped fighting against the corruption of Krystor, and the mistreatment and abuse from the Town Watch. They turned a blind eye to the rampant crime and the syndicates—Hells, most people were employed by one of the crime lords in one way or another, and they were better than the Town Watch, at the least. I'd like to think my Kula is at least ten times better than what it was before. There are jobs for locals, plenty of food, and a better wealth distribution. I've done away with the abusive Town Watch, the corrupt Lord Krystor, and the cancerous crime lords. I've given them security, peace, justice, and hope. Someone has turned them against us."

"You've stepped on quite a bit of toes, from what I've seen. You speak of peace, but you mentioned there were whispers of discontent fomenting as early as your second week in power—much of it stemmed from your dealing with the crime syndicates. You imprisoned and murdered the crime bosses—"

"I cut the head off the snake and gave the body a choice: reform or join the head," Drakhart insisted.

Elandyr'ni frowned. "It might've been better to ingratiate yourself with the crime lords for a bit before slowly removing their pieces from play, take over or phase out their operations."

"I refuse to play the games of my predecessors. Besides, there is no reasoning with criminals. It's intolerable in the Kula I wish to build. Kula is better off without the corruption and criminal filth. If the cost of peace is a few actual criminals thrown in jail, facing justice, or rotting in a gibbet, then so be it."

Elandyr'ni sighed. Her tone remained gentle, but there was a firmness to her voice that slowly crept in at the edges of her words. "This 'criminal filth' spent years taking care of the people in the lowest levels of society when those on top shirked that duty. The urchins and criminals made their living under these crime lords, in one way or another, and peace was kept by the syndicates that ran the Kulan underworld. Unfortunately, those very same people are now dead in a ditch or rotting in a jail cell somewhere. The people see you as a tyrant that took away their protectors; it just took them longer, and a bigger nudge, to show their true feelings. It was bound to boil over eventually."

Drakhart was young, and he was impulsive. Elandyr'ni did not fault him for his naivete. It was born of his youth and inexperience. The boy was an idealist, and often acted in ways he felt would best achieve his idyllic dream for Kula and the people that lived there, even if it meant being uncompressing and unforgiving. It wasn't cruelty, it was progress, to Drakhart, and if people did not want to change, they would be forced to, or they would be broken. It was not a dream born of malice or wicked intent—quite the opposite. Drakhart wanted Kula to prosper. He had lived there, he had seen the suffering, and he had fought against it with his former friends. But the real world was far from ideal, and sometimes you had to compromise ideals for reality; it was a lesson Drakhart had yet to learn.

But to Drakhart's credit, he was willing to listen, and willing to learn when advice was offered. "What would you suggest, instead?" he asked.

"How many of the crime lords still live?"

Drakhart thought for a moment. "I arrested each of the Big Nine Kulan crime lords and twenty-five captains. Most of them are dead, but seven of the thirty-two arrested criminals are rotting in prison."

"Of those seven, how many had any considerable sway in the underworld?"

"Two of them. Only two of Kula's Big Nine turned themselves in without a fight. The remaining five in the prison were their captains. Everyone else resisted and was killed."

Elandyr'ni paused and pondered for a moment. She paced the stone floor, tapping her thumb on her lower lip. "Do you think if you offered them clemency in exchange for loyalty, they would take the offer?"

"Possibly, but I'm not sure. I wouldn't if I were them; not after the treatment I gave them. Honestly, I hadn't considered it."

"If they were wise enough to turn themselves in without a fight, they might be level-headed enough to see the benefit of siding with you, your treatment of them aside. Business is not about pettiness or revenge, it is about mutual benefit, profit, and above all, survival. You return them to their former positions of power, wealth, and influence, and in exchange, they work for *you*, to make *your* goals a reality. The people think they win, and you have yet one more avenue of control over them. It's simply really: use the army to keep them in check, but otherwise let them do as they will, and demand a portion of their profits."

Drakhart was sceptical. "You'd have me become a crime lord myself?"

"I'd have you see the forest for the trees. Crime is like a worm, the deeper you delve to find them, the deeper they dig to escape. There will always be crime, but the harder you crack down, the deeper it recedes into the shadows, the worse the offences, and you risk alienating and turning the people against you. No one loves a tyrant."

Drakhart didn't look convinced.

Tenebrae was happy to let Drakhart and the other dukes rule their domains as they pleased, so long as they committed to the war effort, to Tenebrae's cause, and results were had. So long as control could be maintained, Tenebrae cared not how it was achieved, but if Drakhart proceeded on his current course, there would be rebellion, and rebellion meant setbacks.

"I'm not saying you must put up with the more egregious crimes. Limit what they can do, but otherwise, let them alone. Take a portion of the profits for your coffers, which you can funnel back into the city's wellbeing. Most people do not commit crimes because they want to, they do it because they'd rather do that than starve. If you ease up, yes, some will return, because it's all they know, but most people just want the security and comfort that comes with having their old protectors back, because believe it or not, that's what the old Kulan crime lords did. They provided justice when Lord Krystor and the Town Watch refused to do so. They protected the people against the abuses of those in power. They've spent years being abused by those with authority, and they've learned not to trust the authorities because of it. Put the crime lords back into their place in society, and the people might be less likely to join up with Amber. You may even be able to use them to capture her."

Her words were starting to get through, Elandyr'ni could tell by the look on Drakhart's face. He was plotting again.

"Charging in with an army to put down a rebellion at the drop of a hat will not ingratiate the people to you. They can't read your mind, and they don't know your grand plans. They just see someone that charged in like a rampaging vurk, tore up their lives, jailed and murdered their protectors, and threw their criminal friends, and anyone who speaks up against you, in jail. It's worse because you're a local, and they feel you should know better. You want to show them you care? *Show* them. Don't force them to see it. Compromise."

Drakhart finally acquiesced. "I will try it your way. You've always given sound advice. I respect your knowledge and experience. I will have to have a chat with the remaining crime lords."

The two walked towards the library's entrance. Drakhart was preparing to leave immediately. He would not wait for the situation to deteriorate further.

"Where are they being kept?" Elandyr'ni asked.

"After their trials, they were sentenced to life in prison."

"Oh, that's just outside the capital. I'll send a notice to the Haurfahng to expect us."

Drakhart stopped. "They're not in the Haurfahng."

Elandyr'ni cocked her head. "Where else would you send them?"

"Kul'zabahg."

The Frozen Pillar. Drakhart had been both kind and cruel. Their true punishment would be the loneliness, the isolation, and the confinement in close quarters. The Hells are other people, and other people do desperate things in desperate situations, after all. She would need to dress warm—very warm.

Elandyr'ni stopped Drakhart before he crossed the library threshold. "I did not only come to warn you about this missive."

Drakhart could guess the other reason. "Tenebrae wants to know my progress."

Elandyr'ni nodded.

"Tell him I may have found the solution to our problem. It would not only rob the Darond of an ally, and take Estion out of the war, it may even gain us a new ally."

"What have you come up with?"

"What was the name of the bard His Eyes killed in Felidrun?"

"According to intelligence, his name was Banalor. He went by Banalor the Bard, but his real name was Banalor Owynn Gruffydd."

A slick smile crept across Drakhart's face. "I thought so."

"What does a dead bard have to do with your plan?"

"All in due time. For now, I must head off to Kul'zabahg. Please tell Lord Tenebrae I will be gone for a few days, and when I return, I shall have his solution."

Elandyr'ni laughed. "Tell him yourself, I must ready myself for a trip to Kul'zabahg."

"You're coming with me?" He didn't hide his confusion.

Elandyr'ni smirked. "I am your teacher. I am coming to teach. Besides, you'll use that travel time to train further under me. I won't have you waste precious minutes of study time. What kind of teacher would I be?"

Drakhart knew better than to argue with his teacher. Once she had decided on something, there was no changing her mind. And he would be lying if he said he didn't value her opinion and advice. For all Drakhart's heart wanted to do things his way, his head knew when a wiser, calmer, more experienced voice was needed in a situation. This was one of those moments.

"I shall reach out to Lord Tenebrae. I'll meet you in the grand courtyard. I'll ensure another dragon is ready for you."

Elandyr'ni shook her head. "I won't need it, but the thought is appreciated."

Drakhart's confusion returned with a vengeance. "Do you intend to sprout wings and fly yourself there?"

Elandyr'ni winked. "Something like that."

* * *

Kul'zabahg. The Frozen Pillar. The worst and oldest prison in Altimara. It was the only prison that didn't require guards. The inmates watched over themselves—what few there were. Coming to Kul'zabahg was a death sentence with no executioner.

In truth it wasn't a prison, but a multi-storey tower of grey-black rock that reached up to the sky like some horrible, crooked dagger. It was all that remained of an old fortification from the War of the Grand Coalition. Only the worst prisoners were sent here.

Kul'zabahg was situated right on the border of Anglum and Altimara, in the heart of the Spine, atop a frozen mountain peak. Prisoners were escorted here and left with nothing but a single sword, an enchanted fireplace that never died and required no wood and a monthly food and supply delivery. No other personal effects were allowed within the prison.

There were no guards because no one was going to escape Kul'zabahg. A prisoner's options were to live a boring, lonely life with their basic needs met and an ever-burning hearth or take the sword and charge off into the cold and frozen wastes, only to be found frozen dead on the side of the mountain—or not at all. There was a third option for wise, less foolhardy prisoners who couldn't handle the loneliness or the wilds. These prisoners knew the true boon of the sword: it was the only quick way to end the suffering.

Ancient Altimaran laws dictated that if anyone was able to successfully escape Kul'zabahg, and could report to a constable to prove it, they would be free and pardoned of all crimes. But these ancient laws had been written knowing the cruel irony that a sliver of hope entailed. Most never bothered to try their luck anymore. Anyone who charged off into the frozen wastes did so knowing they would die, and only chose that path because simply didn't feel like falling on their sword and being done with it so quickly—or they couldn't bring themselves to do it.

Isunath landed in the untouched snow. The wind howled around him and Drakhart. Swirling drafts spun snow in small twisters, forming ghostly spirals across the frozen waste. It was cold, but it was also so bright it was blinding. Light reflected off the pure white snow, but with Isunath standing there, he seemed to attract the light like some great maw of darkness. Drakhart kept moving his eyes back to Isunath every time the world was too blinding. The tower helped too, being as dark as it was. Drakhart could see how someone might go insane up here.

A black raven cawed a few hundred metres in the air above him, then swooped down low towards the ground. Right as the bird levelled out with Drakhart, it morphed and became Elandyr'ni. She went from a feathered bird to her human self in a matter of seconds. Instead of her Qiri'ar attire, she was now bundled up in a heavy vurk-skin coat lined with bear fur, and thick matching boots and gloves.

Drakhart was bundled up in a similar mix of furs and leathers and heavy leather boots with a black, wolf fur trim. He had never dressed so warm in his life; it was almost as stifling as it was lifesaving.

"This the legendary Kul'zabahg," he muttered to himself, staring up at the massive tower before him. He and every other Altimaran child had heard the legends of the mythical prison known as Kul'zabahg. All the usual stories surrounded the prison. It was haunted. It was the place where the greatest of villains were kept imprisoned. It was inhabited by a vulzah.

Some parents used Kul'zabahg the way other parents used gnars. It was a threat to make their children behave. Behave or you'd be left out at night to be eaten by gnars. Behave or your parents would get the local guards to send you off to Kul'zabahg where you'd be skinned and eaten by vulzah or freeze to death

Luckily, Drakhart's father never sunk to empty threats and bold lies to make his son behave. He had been a sailor and a military man. Vurkhart Ghast's threats were not empty, and he did not lie about the punishment Drakhart would receive if he misbehaved. He had not been cruel, but he had been strict, and he always kept his word—for good or ill—just like his own father.

"Shall we get going?" Drakhart proffered.

Elandyr'ni nodded. She had been many places in Enayra on the orders of her master, but never a place as cold and remote as this.

Isunath let smoke rise gently from his nostrils. *"I will wait here. If anyone escapes, I shall send them back to the tower."*

"I doubt that will be a problem, but either way I'm sure you won't have much difficulty with that," Drakhart replied.

Drakhart and Elandyr'ni walked the short distance through the thick, undisturbed snow towards the heavy wooden door. Though the door was more symbolic than an actual barrier against the outside. It was heavily worn around the edges, leaving giant gaps between the frame and the actual door itself. There was no lock or heavy latch, only a simple metal handle that allowed one to push the door inward and enter the prison. There was no need to lock the door. What lay on either side was worse than the prison within.

Drakhart stepped into a small, narrow hallway that only allowed a group to walk single file. It was not a long hallway, however, and soon Drakhart came to the central room of the main floor of the tower. The prison tower was entirely open. There were no bars or cells or enclosed spaces. Just a simple tower with a winding spiral staircase around the outside edge that led to other floors.

The first floor was a kitchen, complete with a larder, cold storage, and the enchanted hearth for cooking and warmth. Tables were strewn here and there, amongst broken crates and shattered furniture. Some of the small tables didn't even have benches or chairs anymore. Just crates and barrels and stacked piles of refuse that made up a passable facsimile of a seat.

Above this room, as Drakhart had read from the written accounts of this place, were the sleeping quarters. Simple beds, with heavy woollen blankets; likely worn and frayed with age, if the main floor was any indication. Each floor had another enchanted fireplace meant to help keep the inhabitants warm.

Theoretically, twenty-three prisoners could be housed here at a single time. Rarely had this tower ever been full to capacity, and the four times it had in its nearly seven-hundred-year history as a prison it had not remained at capacity for long. The numbers were usually back to single digits within two weeks, either from starvation, in-fighting, or fools who sought to make their end on the mountainside.

From the sounds above, Drakhart figured that the tower's current inhabitants were upstairs. They were chatting amongst themselves, though the conversation seemed tame and muted. From a quick look over at the kitchen, it was clear to see that the most recent supply run had been delayed. Or never made it due to the weather. Or had just simply not been sent out at all.

Drakhart drew his sword, and Elandyr'ni removed her gloves, so it was easier for her to cast magic. They weren't taking the chance that these armed prisoners wouldn't, in desperation, take a chance at revenge against the one who put them here.

They climbed the stairs, carefully and quietly. Finally, they rounded the corner on the last step and walked out into the dormitory on the second floor.

Five of the seven people who had been imprisoned here remained. Drakhart could smell the fate of the other two in the air. It smelled like Xiar; burned hair, singed flesh.

Sure enough, the remaining prisoners sat around a makeshift table by the fireplace, eating pieces of their former comrades.

Drakhart cleared his throat.

Immediately the prisoners jumped. Three grabbed their swords. They had been enforcers in their previous lives before prison. Two remained seated, a younger woman and an older man. They were in charge, but Drakhart didn't need posture to tell him that. He knew them well enough already.

Isur Emergahr, Boss of the Withered Hand syndicate. They ran most of the gambling dens and peddled in loans for the poor, and flesh for hire—both in the underground arenas and in the co-ed brothels of Kula. Isur had been a crime lord for at least fifty-two years. Everyone in Kula knew him.

The other was Hydelia Kurrem. She was relatively new to the criminal underworld, having only been involved for five years, but she quickly made a name for herself as a firecracker who was as happy to smash the status quo as she was skulls. She took what she wanted with hard work and cold strategy. She pushed out at least three former crime lords to earn her territory and aligned herself with Isur to ensure the other crime syndicates didn't team up and end her fledgling family. She dealt mostly with illicit substances and extortion rackets—though she only targeted wealthy merchants and corrupt officials with her protection schemes. She often gave to the people of Kula, the disenfranchised and forgotten. She and Isur had been known for setting up feeding halls throughout Kula for the poor and homeless, to ensure no one in Kula starved.

Something in Drakhart's stomach shrivelled as he came to the sad realization: in his mad rush to eliminate crime for Kula and give the people a better life, he forgot that there were crime lords that—while dealing with illegal goods and services—had the good of the people in mind and used crime to fund it. For every ten Koltar the Killers and Bagrand the Butchers, there was an Isur Emergahr and a Hydelia Kurrem.

Drakhart owed Elandyr'ni an apology.

"You!" hissed one of the enforcers.

"Bastard," spat the other one.

Their bosses still had said nothing. They continued to eat, barely paying notice to Drakhart and Elandyr'ni.

"You're the reason we're in here!" cried the enforcer on the left.

"I am, and I've come to apologize for that." Drakhart sheathed his blade.

The enforcer on the right laughed. "Apologize? You fucking prick. You don't apologize to your victim after you've cut out his heart and left his head on a stick."

Drakhart noticed a quick flash, a short glance, from the two crime bosses. They had stopped eating, and now were trying not to notice Drakhart and Elandyr'ni. Whatever they expected from him, it was not an apology.

"I've come to provide clemency. I want to make a deal that could benefit us both."

Hydelia chuckled. "You can't hold your new throne, can you?"

Drakhart's words caught in his throat. He felt sweat starting to bead on his forehead, despite the cold atmosphere and his breath crystalizing in front of his face.

"Let the pup speak." Isur pitched in now.

The three enforcers sheathed their blades and sat back down to enjoy a feast of their former fellow inmate.

Drakhart tried to control his temper. He would need to eat crow for his foolishness. Elandyr'ni, as any good master, never let Drakhart miss an opportunity to learn a harsh lesson. "It is true, that I am having a…difficult time getting some of Kula to accept me as their new leader."

Isur grunted. "I'm not surprised. I've lived in Kula my whole life. I've lived under three generations of Davenpourte dukes. They were bastards, each and everyone, but they held power. How do you think that was?"

Drakhart wasn't allowed to answer.

"By coming to us," growled Isur. "The crime lords helped keep order. At least until that Krystor brat decided he wanted *other* criminals policing the place. Not locals. He thought he could put us out of business by hiring criminals to fight criminals. But all it did was cause a bigger problem."

"Now you've gone and had us all killed," snapped Hydelia. "You've done what the Davenpourtes couldn't. Yet what has it cost you?"

"Truthfully, it's cost me the loyalty of my fellow townsfolk," replied Drakhart honestly.

Isur snorted. "You should've known better. You were born and raised there. I know you. You're one of the kids that killed Captain Jerrin."

Drakhart was surprised a man like Isur had even known who he was. Then again, an enemy of your enemy was a potential ally.

"The people of Kula had never trusted authority, and now you've come back to us to ask you to help keep a hold of them, eh? How bad have the revolts been?"

Drakhart refused to answer that question, but the flush in his cheeks answered enough.

Still, Elandyr'ni did not step in. He deserved this dressing down in her eyes. He was left on the back foot, with a populace in near revolt, and now he would have to grovel to get the help he would've readily been offered in the first place.

"I come not to apologize," Drakhart started. He would need to choose his words very carefully. "I cannot apologize for what I've done. I cannot simply offer clemency and expect your help. I have come at your mercy now, to make the deal I should have made when I became duke. I've recently had my eyes opened, and perhaps I would not be in this situation now if I had been smart enough to take advantage of your help in the first place."

Hydelia grunted and spit into the fire, causing it to sizzle.

Isur stroked his beard and watched Drakhart like a hawk watched its dinner.

No one said a word. Until Isur leaned to his left and looked Elandyr'ni up and down. "You're a wise woman. Are you his castellan?"

Elandyr'ni gave a curt bow. "No, sir. Just a teacher who wants to see the best in her student."

"You're a good teacher, for letting him take this dressing down. It's a hard lesson. Many nobles simply have people to burden the hard lessons for them."

"I only deserve half the credit. The idea was mine, but he is still here, listening to my advice, and taking in the truth of your words of his own free will. I did not force him to be here."

Isur looked back at Drakhart. "You're a good student. Not some stuck-up noble. Kulan raised, indeed. You know how to take a good beating."

Still, Drakhart did not speak. He felt the embarrassment sting his heart. He hated having to grovel to these criminals. He hated that he had to be here and admit he was wrong to those he felt Kula was better off without. Yet at the same time, part of Drakhart was endeared to Isur and Hydelia at this moment; and he could not deny the good they had done in their lives as crime lords.

This was a harsh lesson indeed. Harsher than any he had yet learned under his new masters.

"Come, sit," Isur motioned to his enforcer to drag a crate over to the fire for Elandyr'ni and Drakhart. "Warm yourselves by the fire. There's plenty of Maghron to go around."

Drakhart shivered.

Hawk-eyed Isur noticed his response before Drakhart himself could register it. "Do not think me cruel, for my joke. We hadn't seen food supplies in a month, and he was sick and dying. It's survival and practicality. We didn't kill Imlos though. She died on the trip up here; her rope broke while climbing the mountain. She's somewhere in a valley now. But sit, even if you won't eat, and let's discuss our new deal. You're clearly desperate, and I care about Kula. I think we can come to a profitable agreement for both of us."

Drakhart sat down. Elandyr'ni joined him. It was clear she had come, less to intervene, and more to ensure Drakhart did not backslide on his promise to keep an open mind and work with the crime lords.

"My offer is simple: I will free you and return you to your position. Rebuild your syndicates, and even raise additional crime lords to replace those that were killed. Give the people the familiar stability they seek. I will turn a blind eye to the crime—so long as it's kept controlled, regulated, and doesn't get out of hand. Hopefully, the people will be less willing to rebel, and I won't have to crack down, and it will show them I'm willing to listen. I'm also hoping you can...ingratiate them to me and my rule, though I can't say I expect a miracle."

Hydelia scrunched up her nose as if she smelled something sour. "What will you do with the rebels? Most of them are likely former associates and underlings of ours. Will you crack down on them?"

"Only the ring leaders. I have a feeling I know who the leader is. If I can take her and her lieutenants, I'll ignore and pardon anyone else."

"Fair enough," muttered Hydelia.

But Isur was quicker than that. "Amber, huh?"

Drakhart didn't respond. He didn't need to. The look on his face answered for him.

Isur chuckled. "I always warned that girl she'd get herself into trouble. She was too smart for Kula. She was wasted there. She would've thrived better in a larger city, with bigger fish and better pay. She refused to abandon the people—but I knew better. She was sweet on someone; I never knew who though."

Drakhart did, but he would keep that information to himself.

"It will be a shame to lose Amber. She was a valuable associate. She served all the crime families equally and without prejudice; and kept her alive in bad times. If the only price I must pay for my freedom is the loss of a good ally, I'll accept it. It's a small cost in the grand scheme of things."

"I'm surprised you're not demanding a piece of the action," Hydelia inquired.

"I admit I was wrong. It was my mistake in thinking I could take Kula by the throat and not face the wrath of the people, just because I was once one of them," explained Drakhart, "But my morals refuse to allow me to take any of the ill-gotten gains."

Isur grunted. "Your pride might get you killed one day."

Drakhart gave the old man a hardened look. "As long as the blade doesn't come from you."

The old man glared back at Drakhart. The two held their gaze for a few moments, tension thick in the air like smoke. The enforcers groped for their weapons just in case.

Everyone relaxed when Isur let out a hearty laugh.

"Aye. You've got my word. Hydelia?"

"Yes, gramps. I won't touch him either."

"There you have it. You leave the people to us; I can't say I can get the people to fully trust you—Kulans have spent centuries mistrusting all forms of authority—but I can do my best to at least ensure they know you are not the enemy, and that it was your generosity and change of heart that led to our release and return; for the sake of their well-being, of course."

Drakhart nodded. "You can rest assured that the well-being of Kula is a cause dear to my heart, sir. I may have made a grave mistake in how I chose to start my rule...but everything I did, I did for Kula and her people. I was once one of those folks bullied by the Town Watch. I may not be Kulan-born, but I spent the better part of my life growing up there. It's why—" Drakhart fought to get the words out "—it's why we fought against the Town Watch how we did."

"I noticed the rest of your friends aren't up in the estate with you," Isur muttered, acknowledging the reason for Drakhart's hesitation.

"We've parted ways," Drakhart replied quickly. His answer was quick, short, and very pregnant.

Isur said no more.

Drakhart held out his hand. The old man shook it, firmly but slowly. Hydelia followed. Her grip was even tighter than Isur's, and she looked Drakhart in the eyes like she planned to crawl into his skull and find his soul.

"How long before we can expect to be free?" Hydelia picked soot and pieces of her former comrade from underneath her fingernails.

"I will send proper winter clothes and transportation to get you down from here shortly. It may take a day or two, but I promise you will be freed."

"Dragons eh?" Isur nodded towards the window.

Drakhart nodded.

"I had a feeling you were behind that. It was a pleasure to see those Town Watch bastards blasted to death like that. What I wouldn't have given to be there and watch Krystor grovel for his life—can't say I envy them though. Better them than me, eh? But I'm glad you and I can be on the same side, especially if you command dragons."

"I'm surprised you don't buy the superstitions as most others do," noted Drakhart.

Isur shrugged. "I've never trusted the government propaganda. Guess I was right, seeing as now you and the dragons are working with them. A thousand years of the Glorious Hunt propaganda being shoved down our throats, and it's thrown out the window in the pursuit of a powerful ally. I wonder how much bloodshed could have been avoided if the dragons joined up with Rego long ago..."

Drakhart tried not to think about it. Tenebrae had been behind the monarchy, though he wasn't about to tell Isur or Hydelia that. It had been Tenebrae that had enacted the Glorious Hunt, and the propaganda against the dragons. Tenebrae had never explained himself or his reasons for that, but Drakhart had always assumed it was two-fold: the

Glorious Hunt and anti-dragon propaganda would primarily rid Altimara of any dragons who might recognize Tenebrae was leading the monarchy. By killing them, or forcing them from Altimara, they would not be able could closely watch the situation, and so they could not ruin his plans before they bore fruit. Secondly, it was an act of revenge that would also serve to weaken the dragons, so that there would be less to oppose Tenebrae when the time was right.

If that were the reason, it had worked. The first war against Tenebrae had eliminated five out of the eleven dragon clans—either through extinction or because the dragons fled Altimara after the war—had killed several of the Clan Leaders and had overall reduced the number of dragons in Enayra. The Glorious Hunt had killed even more. The remaining dragon clans, while still extant, never fully recovered from it all. They were diminished, and birth rates had declined.

"I'll start packing my things," sneered Hydelia.

She didn't speak much, Drakhart noted, and she was sarcastic and bratty, but she followed Isur's lead—she respected him, that much was clear—and she seemed trustworthy enough. Drakhart had come to respect her and Isur in his short time with them.

Drakhart stood and gave a small, courteous bow. "Very well then. We have a deal. I must report back to the palace. I will send word to my castellan to expect your return. He will tend to your needs until you're back on your feet. If you need anything, contact him. If he won't help you, please reach out to me directly at the Black Citadel. Address any letters to Drakhart Ghast—no need for formal titles."

Isur grunted. Hydelia didn't respond. The enforcers merely watched Drakhart like sharks watched a struggling fish.

Drakhart had no idea how else to end this conversation, so after bidding his new allies of convenience goodbye, he quickly returned down the spiral staircase he and Elandyr'ni had climbed up and returned outside to Isunath.

The dragon did not wait to exchange witty repartee. *"No one escaped."*

Drakhart smirked. The dragon had just been sleeping in the snow. *"How would you have noticed?"*

"I am a dragon. Nothing escapes our senses."

Hopefully, nothing would escape Drakhart's, and this deal would not end up being his doom.

"What now?" asked Elandyr'ni.

"We're going to Kula. I'll speak with my castellan and the commander of the garrison so they're aware of the deal. Then we'll return to Lord Tenebrae, and I will let him in on my plan for dealing with Estion."

Elandyr'ni's eyebrow raised once more. "You've yet to let me in on your secret."

"All in due time. You will find out when our lord does."

Realizing the futility of pressing the matter, Elandyr'ni changed the subject. "Are you hoping to draw out Amber by arriving in Kula yourself?"

"She doesn't know about my deal. She'll see me arriving, and she'll see me visiting the garrison and think I'm there to crack down. She might be emboldened to attack me, and I can deal with her swiftly."

"You don't intend to renege on your agreement with Isur and Hydelia, do you?" Elandyr'ni pulled her gloves back on and pulled a small gem from within her sleeve as she prepared to take flight as a raven once more.

"No. I'm a man of my word, and they seem to be sufficiently trustworthy—so far. Besides, just because I cut the head off one snake doesn't mean another won't nest in the old den. I can't keep putting down rebellions. I can't be duke of an empty town."

"How wise and mature of you," teased Elandyr'ni. "Your teacher must be very proud."

Drakhart shrugged. "I would hope so. I will have to ask Calandor when I see him next."

Chapter XVIII

The letter was written in a familiar hand. It could only have come from Isur. It was written hastily, on a spare scrap of paper, owing to the desperation of the plea it contained and the speed at which it required delivering. Indeed, the letter had only arrived in town a matter of hours before its author did—and not a moment too soon.

Amber,

I am writing you this letter because of our previous professional relationship. You have done much for me over the years, and I too have helped you in turn. Though to my embarrassment, I believe our score was not entirely settled when last we spoke, and so, out of respect for you and my debt to you, I am writing this letter to help balance the books.

I am returning to my position, as is Hydelia. I have been shown clemency by the Crown, but in turn for my freedom, it seems I must toe the line for a new master.

He is not as wicked or vile as I had expected. He is not greedy and selfish like the old dukes. He's local if not Kulan-born, but in his chest beats a Kulan heart. He's young and naïve, but well-advised, and he is willing to admit his wrongs and learn from his mistakes. I truly believe he has Kula's best interest at heart, and so I serve not as unwillingly as I would have thought.

He will pardon those who had turned against him; those who fight at your side even now—for I assume it was none other than you who have rallied the people against their new duke—but he will not forgive the leaders of this rebellion.

I am writing to warn you of that.

I will be returning to the city in a matter of days, and I give you until then to pack up your things, take anyone you love and care about, and flee. Go to Targrond, or Gindish, or even Boszlan—somewhere, anywhere, far away, for it will surely be safer than Kula.

I will not actively hunt you at first, in case you must take longer than the time allotted to leave or this letter does not arrive in time, but if I catch wind of your location or presence, I will be honour bound to report it—and you know me as a man of my word—after which I cannot guarantee your life or your safety at the hands of those who will come to capture you.

Please take this warning to heart. I would hate to see you or those you care about killed because of pride.

Take it from someone who knows, pride will only get you killed...or leave you lonely.

With all due respect,

Isur Emergahr.

Amber had not been pleased by the words in the letter she had received. She did not blame Isur. Imprisonment in Kul'zabahg could make anyone change their tune for clemency—something they seldom got in that situation. He had only done what he could for his and Hydelia's survival, and, in the long run, the best interest of the Kulan people.

If he had not bent the knee to Drakhart, he would have died in that frozen prison, and the people of Kula would've been rounded up, arrested, and slaughtered or imprisoned by the hundreds. Any who could work would've been shipped to Targrond or Kilnarn to serve in the shipyards or as oar slaves for the navy. It's what happened to some unlucky people already.

Amber was cutting things very close. Even with the tardiness of the letter's arrival, she had overstayed her warning period by a week, waiting for a response from Agent Skullspider, but still, a response had yet to come. No word came to tell her to stay, or to flee. Her time with the Kulan Resistance had been fruitful in slowing down the Altimaran war machine but they had not stopped it.

But Amber had expected—even planned for—a slow and protracted war of attrition with Drakhart's regime. It would not be one or two swift actions that would topple his dukedom and the Crown. It would be small acts of resistance. From pulling nails out of crates to dropping bedbugs into bedrolls meant for soldiers across the kingdom to sneaking cockroaches and other pests into crates of food. Sometimes it was bigger, like destroying anvils with magic or burning down granaries, foundries, and smithies.

In the end, the destruction would be repaired. New anvils would be shipped in. Buildings could be rebuilt. Supplies would be replaced, even if at a cost, But the time and delay would slow things down enough to hopefully give the Darond and their allies an edge. Every sword that didn't make it to the front, every soldier that was too demoralized or underequipped to fight, was another point of advantage for the Darond.

But now it was crashing down.

Her one hundred Kulans who were willing to fight for her, for Kula, and their families, had been reduced to a little over twenty-seven loyal resistance fighters—including her runners.

Mass pardons were handed out by Drakhart on his way back from Kul'zabahg. People left the hiding place to return to their homes now that it was safe. When Hydelia and Isur returned, many of the former criminals who hated Drakhart for killing their bosses and losing them their profitable careers suddenly went flocking back to their old lives like nothing had happened. Some had even been promoted to help fill in the gaps left by the dead crime lords and their captains.

Drakhart had redistributed food from the grain stores along with the pardons, as an apology to the people of Kula, and had declared the end of the coming week to be a local feast day and a holiday.

Those that stayed with Amber now were those who were personally loyal to her or had owed her a debt, and now sought to pay it off. They were those without family, who revelled in the destruction they caused, and cared not who they unleashed it on, be it Drakhart or a camel. Amber didn't give their little band much longer. Some were already starting to grow tired of the near-starving, cramped conditions.

Only a handful would leave with her—her most trusted captains, and runners, who would serve her through thick and thin, and believed in the cause. Nine in all, including her.

Amber knew she would have to cut her losses soon, but something kept her grounded here and made her refuse to leave. She wasn't sure if she was just waiting for permission from Skullspider, or if her stupid pride was refusing to let her admit defeat.

She and the rebels had done so well. They had disrupted the Altimaran war machine, even if just temporarily, in both small and large ways. Goods had been ruined by their sabotage, and while the steelworks and granaries were being rebuilt and refilled, the damage had been done in the meantime, and the damage to surrounding buildings had been minimal—at least in terms of housing and civilian casualties. Warehouses and other commercial buildings had been ruined by the blaze, but Kula had also exhausted much of its emergency water supply, meaning more water needed to be welled, barrelled, and shipped in for the military and ranchers.

The only reason Amber didn't feel worse about it was because running out of the emergency water supply didn't affect the common folk all that much. Most Altimarans, and especially those in Kula and other settlements in the middle of the desert, didn't drink water all that often. Instead, they drank wine, known colloquially as desert wine. It came in the red and white varieties. Red desert wine was made by fermenting prickly pears, while white desert wine was made by distilling the cactus juice into a liqueur. The white desert wine wasn't really wine, but that doesn't stop people from calling it that.

But now Amber was undermanned, and the pressure had been turned up. Drakhart was actively hunting her down, so he could try and kill her. If he hated her before, he hated her more now. What was more, two of Kula's respected crime lords had returned, and with all their wealth, power, and influence restored, they would be using that to track her down and turn her over to Drakhart. Amber couldn't fight that level of heat with volunteers anymore. She couldn't keep this going much longer. Every day she stayed she risked capture and eventually, death...and she had too much to live for now.

She had bit off more than she could chew. She had overestimated how easy it would be to undermine Drakhart, and how quickly—and cunningly—he would respond. It had surprised her, to say the least. Amber had expected Drakhart to stubbornly stick to his ways, and retaliate with a military crackdown. Harsh reprisals, more mass executions, and imprisonments for treason. Instead, Drakhart had—arguably out of character for him— done the complete opposite expected of him. He acquiesced to the will of the people and instead returned two respected pillars of the criminal community. In doing so, had slowly rebuilt the people's faith in him. It had completely gutted Amber's movement, and she hated Drakhart for it the more.

"What do we do, Miss?" Vilingar asked.

Amber chewed the inside of her cheek. "We can't wait much longer..."

"No, we can't Miss Amber. For our safety."

Amber nodded, staring intently at the low-burning candle on her desk. "I suppose eight is all I can ask for. I appreciate your faith in me."

Vilingar shrugged. "You've yet to lead us wrong, Miss."

Amber tapped the desk with her forefinger. There were many things she had to consider. She had to abandon Kula, she knew it...but if she left without permission, she'd be abandoning her post—a post she promised she would hold with her life. Yet, her predecessor had fled when necessary and appointed a new agent to take her place. Could Amber do the same?

But it was more than just fleeing from a promise...it was fleeing from her home. The only home she knew. She had taken the oath to defend her home and help her fellow Kulans. If she left, she was failing them.

Then again, when she needed them the most, they had failed her. Part of her was bitter. She had fought so hard, tried to force change, and when things got tough, they fled, but she also couldn't blame them. Stability was far more appealing than a life on the run.

Amber slammed her fist on the desk.

Vilingar replied as if he had already read her mind. "I accept."

Amber cocked her head to the side and smirked. "I haven't even asked yet." She was never certain if Vilingar *could* read minds or not. He had always insisted that he had no skill in that regard and was hopeless with magic. Amber had been inclined to believe him, as Vilingar was not known to be a liar, but there was always a small part of her that doubted his words, if in vain. If only to ignore the fact that they had been friends for so long, she had become that predictable to him.

"You don't have to; I already know where your mind was."

"Stay out of my mind," Amber teased.

Vilingar gave a curt, but polite nod in reply.

"Thank you, Vilingar. Please be safe?"

"As safe as you will be."

Amber hugged Vilingar tightly. The two had been partners in crime for years. He had helped her through some tough times, and the two had supported each other in all endeavours. He was like a brother to her, and she was a sister to him. It would be hard to imagine running a scheme without Vilingar there, but Amber had other capable runners on hand. "I'll write as soon as I've settled down. Please let Skullspider know about the change of plans and tell her I will reach out myself as soon as I am able. I will find other ways to support you both. I have an idea...I don't know if Skullspider will like it, but I don't intend to just roll over and run away."

Vilingar nodded again. "Drakhart knows you by name and by appearance. I'll be safer than you if you're going where I think you are."

Amber frowned. "I told you to stay out of my mind. And don't jinx me, Vilingar."

Vilingar only smirked.

Amber threw anything of importance haphazardly into a sack, then tossed the sack over her shoulders. She turned to Vilingar before leaving. "If...if Skullspider writes and asks about *that* situation again...tell her to tell him that I'm alright. That's what she should tell him. I'm alive, I'm alright, and I'll see him when he's home." Amber regretted never finishing her response letter, but now she had no time, and it was no longer a priority.

"Nothing more?" asked Vilingar, uncharacteristically pressing the subject.

"That is all." Amber was quite firm with her response.

Vilingar bowed mockingly.

Amber left her office and walked out into the now-emptied warehouse. She gazed at the seven men and women who had remained. Those who were considering returning to their homes and lives had already done so while Amber dawdled on a decision.

She didn't have to explain to her runners what was happening, or where they were going. They knew what was happening, and Amber knew wherever she went, they would follow. Years of friendship and a deep business relationship had forged bonds between them that were stronger than Asardaean steel.

They each waved goodbye to Vilingar and took off down a small side tunnel off the main warehouse. It was the only way out of the city not currently policed and heavily guarded. It would get them out to a mesa in the desert, several kilometres north of the city. From there, Amber would explain their plan going forward.

As she fled down the dark tunnel, seven loyal runners behind her, Amber only had a single wish: that she only had more time. Things would only get more difficult soon enough, and survival was not assured.

Chapter XIX

In the days since leaving the Emerald Enclave, Kanaahn had not had another dream like he had the night they stayed there. He had discussed it constantly with Djall, but even the dragon—who had been able to decipher that Kanaahn dreamed like a dragon back at the Tormenting Pinnacle—had no answers for this.

The dream had not been a dragon dream, and Kanaahn could remember it as if it was a memory, burned into his mind. It never grew less vivid, or more distant. It never felt hazy or lost in a fog of forgetfulness. No...no, this dream felt real, as if he had been there and experienced it himself. But Kanaahn had not been there, and he had never experienced this dream. He had never known these two people in his life. Though he had a feeling the hooded figures might have been the Kotharii. Something about them felt...wrong. They felt as if they did not belong. Like a forest fire at the bottom of the ocean, or a sea floating in the sky. It was like watching a carp fly like an eagle and a hawk tunnel through the dirt like a mole.

The most Djall could posit was that, perhaps, being in a place sacred to the Earth Mother, Kanaahn was being shown something that *had* happened. As for what or why, the Earth Mother was less forthcoming with those details.

Something in Kanaahn's intuition had given thought to what it was, but he abandoned that line of thought until further proof could support it. It seemed too perfect to be right. Regardless, Kanaahn was willing to accept that the Earth Mother had shown him a vision of the past...or perhaps the future? Maybe even something that was happening currently. It was a vision, that much was for sure. Not unlike Risasi's k'dir putting the memory of his k'nir's betrayal in his mind, but the why of it all was lost on Kanaahn.

Aside from telling Djall, Kanaahn had kept the dream and everything that had happened to himself. Kyeit and Cecil had enough to worry about. The group had left the protection of the Green Dragon Clan's ancestral lands a few days ago. They were nearing the shores of Lake Ardona, which also meant they were nearing the end of the vital tree cover that was masking their travel.

It would be another couple of days between the edge of the forest and the shores of Lake Ardona. At which point the plan would be to keep to the lakeside and see if they could charter a ferry to Ethon and enter the city from the lakeside harbour.

They would be harder to track on the water. They wouldn't be alone, and they would be one of hundreds of ferries and boats on the lake. From fishermen to local trading vessels and barges filled with timber and other resources bound for transport down the Acturn River towards coastal Pelchar, and from Pelchar, the world beyond.

The few days between the lake and the woods would be their most vulnerable, but it was a risk they would have to take. The Tulkaz—as Kanaahn had been calling them since spending more time around dragons—were tracking them. That much was without a doubt now, but everything they had done before now was meant to give them a head start on their foes and make the pursuit all the harder for the dogged servants of Tenebrae.

"Kanaahn?" Djall reached out to his partner through their mental link, prodding him as one would gently prod a parent away.

Kanaahn opened his mind more to indicate he was listening but otherwise did not respond.

"What if...how would you feel if I went back to the Emerald Enclave after the war?"

Kanaahn's stomach went cold. His heart nearly stopped. He had been expecting this, and yet he was caught so unawares and unprepared by the sudden question. Kanaahn cursed that he hadn't prepared himself to answer the question half as much as he prepared to hear it.

"I...I honestly don't know how I would feel. We've been together for such a short time, and yet you've become a part of me because of the binding ceremony. We use this phrase a lot but, we are now as one soul in two bodies. I don't even remember much of what my life was like before you were in it...and I haven't given much thought to what that would look like again in the future."

"We really do use that phrase a lot."

"It's the only apt way to describe it."

"But you're not against it?"

"I'm not. I can't be. We're talking about you being among your kind—your family. My parents died before I could even form memories of them, but if they suddenly appeared one day, alive and well—I'd be mad they never came back sooner—but I'd probably feel exactly like you do now, but I also can't say that I wouldn't miss you. I don't know how long it'll take to defeat Tenebrae, but after a couple of months together I'd miss you if you left, I can't imagine how I'd feel after a couple of years together."

"...You could come live with me, settle down somewhere nearby?"

Kanaahn smiled gently. *"While a wonderful idea, you know I can't. I wouldn't be allowed. Your mother barely wanted to allow us safe passage through her lands. Let's not even imagine how she'd react if I asked her to* live *on your lands. What happens if I settle down, and have a family? She'd kill me before I got the words out."*

Djall did not respond.

"You do what you have to do, Djall. I'm only being honest. I would miss you, just as you would miss me if the roles were reversed. But I don't want my bond with you to dictate your decision in this situation. I will miss you, but I would hurt even more if you never got to live amongst your family. Whatever you choose, I'll support you."

"I appreciate you. You know that?"

"We share a mind, Djall. I know what you feel even before you say it."

Djall was not able to respond.

Kanaahn heard the bowstring twang and the arrow whistle through the air before he saw it coming. The dragons and other Khaleeshir heard it too. The dragons flexed their wings on instinct but found themselves boxed in by the trees around them. They were unable to take flight.

Kanaahn ducked low in the saddle, pressing himself against his horse's neck. The arrow flew over him and buried itself with a thwack in the tree to his right.

Cecil and Kyeit had tried to dodge in time, but not having the benefit of heightened senses, fumbled to move their horses out of the way when they noticed the dragons and Khaleeshir bristle and dodge.

Cecil took an arrow in her hip, and Kyeit felt one bury itself in her shoulder. Whoever attacked them had purposely aimed for the joints between the plates. They knew what they were doing.

"Take the horses and go!" Kanaahn called out to Cecil and Kyeit. "Arkas, go with them and shoot at anything that shoots at you first. Arial, Shooter, with me!"

Kanaahn slipped the stirrups and leapt from his horse. He slapped the horse on the hindquarters, sending the animal running off towards Kyeit. She grabbed the reins of Kanaahn's horse, as well as those of Arial's and Shooter's, and charged off into the forest as fast as they could.

Arial's fingers crackled with lightning and the smell of ozone filled the forest. Shooter had his short sword and a dagger drawn and ready. The dragons snarled but held off belching flame into the woods carelessly. The last thing they needed was to unleash a massive firestorm. A fight was one thing, but a fire would draw even more unwanted attention.

Kanaahn searched the woods for any sign of enemies. He strained to listen for the sound of crunching dirt or snapping twigs, but there was nothing. Whoever had attacked them had either fled when their ambush failed, or they were waiting for something bigger.

"Come out and fight," Kanaahn called. "We know you're out there. Come out, or we'll burn this forest down around you."

No response.

Arial tried next. "We mean it. We've got six dragons here. Half of Estion will be ash by the time they're done."

Nothing.

"I'm counting from ten. If you don't show yourselves by then, we'll burn this place and all of us down with it." Kanaahn pitched his voice to sound older, more threatening.

Silence.

It was Shooter who gave the count in the end. "Ten. Nine. Eight. Seven...three, two, one. Risasi, torch it all; use magma if you want. Poison gas, if you must, Djall. Burn this place to the ground."

"Wait!" a voice cut through the canopy.

"That was the most dangerous game of nerves I've ever played," Shooter muttered through the private mental link between the Khaleeshir and the dragons.

Shooter pointed into the woods with his dagger, aiming at the spot where the voice had come from. "Lay your weapons down where you are and come out with your hands up.

How many are you? No lying or I'll get Djall to unleash his poison gas into the woods. Anyone who doesn't come forward will quickly be revealed when they drop dead."

The voice replied quickly. "We're seven, currently, but there's another thirty of us at our camp."

Slowly, the seven figures in the woods approached the Khaleeshir. Their hands were raised and devoid of weapons. They didn't wear armour, only a mix of fabric and furs, haphazardly thrown together from a variety of non-matching outfits. They looked tired, beaten, and honestly a little hungry.

Kanaahn recognized them instantly. "They're Lau'thso."

Shooter and Arial noticed the same. The corded muscles, tattoos that covered their bodies and multiple braids were unmistakable. They were varying skin tones—which was no surprise, as the Lau'thso were known to be welcoming to any who wished to join their lifestyle—but their skin all bore the unmistakable look of those who spent their lives at sea; worn by salt, wind, sun, and time. Both men and women stood among the attackers, all of them a variety of ages, but no one was either too young or too old to be there.

Shooter put away his weapons. These people were no more a threat in their current state than a rat was to Risasi. "Forgive me if this is rude to ask but...what the fuck are you doing in the middle of the woods? You're a sea people, aren't you?"

The man who had yelled from the forest earlier stepped forward. His voice was recognizable from amongst his followers. By his tone and demeanour, he seemed to be the leader of this group.

He was a tall and burly man. Middle-aged, with leathery, brown skin, earned from a hard life at work under the sun, sailing the oceans. His hair and beard were both long, braided intricately into both small and large, beaded knots, and were both grey as chimney smoke. Intricately tattooed designs, patterns and spiralling shapes covered every visible inch of his skin. He crossed his arms across his chest as he spoke. "I'll explain in due time, but first I owe you an apology. We saw dragons and armour...we didn't know if you were Black Blades on the hunt for us or mercenaries hired by Altimara to return us to Lord Drungvist."

Arial could not contain her confusion. "I'm sorry, what? Why would the Black Blades be after you? What did you do?"

Their leader frowned. He stroked his beard as he sought the right words to explain. From what Kanaahn could tell, the man also seemed to be weighing whether he could trust the Khaleeshir. Finally, he decided "We escaped from our captivity at the hands of Altimara."

"Captivity?" asked Arial.

"My people have been captured by Altimara and enslaved," the leader rasped. His voice wavered. He was someone who had experienced much pain and suffering.

Upon closer inspection, Kanaahn could see the man was more than a little hungry. His clothes hung a little too loose on his frame, the same with his companions, and his face showed signs of early emaciation and starvation. What was more, Kanaahn could see the white, puckered scar tissue around his wrists that showed better than anything else that his words were true. This man had been in captivity until recently, and they had him shackled—no doubt his ankles would tell a similar tale if they were visible. He had suffered greatly, indeed.

"How many of your people does Altimara have enslaved?" asked Shooter.

The leader's eyes hardened as he recounted the fate of his people. He sought vengeance, that much was clear. "All of them. Every last Lau'thso that once lived in Lau'than is in Altimaran captivity. They have us separated. Our children are enslaved as unwilling servants—hostages, really—to most of the Altimaran nobility. Our elders are being kept in encampments; they can't work and have no use, but it is they who teach the youth our ways while the adults are out at sea every year. If they die, we risk losing much of who we are, and Altimara knows this—it is also why they separated our youth from them. That leaves the rest of us. Every able-bodied man and woman between sixteen and fifty have been clapped in irons and used as manual labour in the shipyards of Targrond and Kilnarn or strapped to benches in the lower decks of Altimara's warships, forced to row their lives away as oarslaves."

"Where did you escape from?" asked Kanaahn.

"Me and my companions escaped when our ship went down in the Bay of Milon in a storm a few months back. We made our way to shore and found ourselves in Espias. We took that opportunity to flee across the Spine into Estion. The plan was to build a small encampment in the forests and start building new ships that we could use to raid Altimaran vessels and free more of our people. We also wished to pledge ourselves to the Darond...we had hoped that in exchange for our knowledge and our assistance in their fight against Altimara, they could help us free our people."

The trio of Khaleeshir exchanged glances with each other and then with the very confused-looking dragons that stood not far away.

Shooter smirked. "Well, have I got some good news for you—"

Hoofbeats erupted from where Arkas, Cecil, and Kyeit had disappeared. Soon enough, the trio on their horses burst onto the scene, their weapons drawn, ready to battle the threat they had left their friends to face. They were thoroughly confused when they found their friends conversing with their foes instead of combatting them.

Cecil's face was frozen in a look of utter bewilderment. "You were taking too long, and we couldn't hear any sounds of fighting. We got concerned. We thought maybe—"

"We're fine," Arial reassured her. "Very confused, but fine."

"What happened?" Kyeit half asked half demanded. She had worked herself up for a fight, perhaps even to confront her greatest fear, and was slowly coming down from the adrenaline rush when she realized she had done so for nothing. Regardless, Kyeit did not look so ready to trust these mysterious attackers just yet.

Shooter stepped between Kyeit and the Lau leader. "We threatened to burn the forest down and they surrendered. It turns out they're former Altimaran slaves from Lau'than. Altimara has enslaved the entire people, from what we're being told. They were explaining to us how they came to be here, and what Altimara was using them for."

Cecil and Kyeit looked horrified.

"Are you all right?" the Lau leader asked. "You two were the ones we hit; do you require medical attention? If you come back to our camp—"

Cecil smiled kindly. "The wounds were not serious. Though you pierced the weak points of our armour, the chainmail and padding saved us from the worst of it. Magic helped with the rest."

The Lau leader bowed his head, truly ashamed of his rash actions. "I humbly beg your forgiveness. We thought you might've been hunting us. We saw the dragons and the armour..."

Kyeit replied now. "Please, don't let it trouble you. You were only acting in self-defence. I'm only glad further bloodshed could be avoided."

"Why did the dragons make you think we were with Altimara?" Arkas wondered.

"They used them to guard the slave pens occasionally. We had never seen a dragon so close before. Sometimes, they'd let the dragons wander into the camps and pens and eat the sickest and weakest of us, but the defiant were just as likely to end up in their gullet as well."

Arkas had soon wished he had not asked.

"The least we can do is invite you to our camp and offer you some food. We don't have much...my people are not used to hunting in woodlands. We're sea folk, after all." The Lau leader looked earnest but determined to show hospitality to his new acquaintances.

Kanaahn turned to the dragons. "Djall, you hungry?"

The dragon shuffled and adjusted his wings. "I could eat."

Of course. A young, growing dragon could *always* eat.

"Go get something to eat and bring back some for us and these kind folks."

Djall nodded. He turned to the other dragons, who had no objections to the plan. They wasted no time tracing their way back to a previously passed clearing so they could take off and begin their hunt.

"You're too kind," muttered the Lau leader.

Kanaahn shrugged "You would have done the same for us, were we on a boat, and the prey beneath the sea."

Without further delay, the Khaleeshir remounted their horses and the group of seven Lau'thso sailors led them towards their encampment. The camp wasn't far from where the ambush had happened. Only a kilometre or two north from there. The Lau'thso had made their encampment in a place where the trees were smaller, younger, and more spread out but still provided enough cover to be hidden from above.

Before they could look around the camp, the Lau leader brought the Khaleeshir over to where they had kept their boat. Their boat sat nearly completed off to the side of the camp, covered by branches and a primitive lean-to structure. It was a longboat, as wide as a person was long, if not a bit wider, and at least eighteen metres long from stern to bow. Its keel was deep but flat. From what Kanaahn could see, there was storage space beneath removable deck boards, as some of them had been left off the bottom of the boat. Several rows of benches ribbed the inside of the boat at even distances from front to back. Oars were tucked up and piled inside, bundled together, and covered with cloth so they wouldn't rot. At the stern of the boat there was a captain's seat and a steering oar, and lying wrapped in cloth and rope was a single simple mast. It still resembled the pine it had been hewed from.

The Lau leader explained that tomorrow his people would finish attaching the single main yard in place, and then attach the sail to the mast. The sail—the cloth that the mast was wrapped in—looked as if it had been sewn together from bits of old sail cloth salvaged from a wreck. Kanaahn figured it was probably the remnants of whatever ship the Lau'thso had escaped from when they had washed ashore. Kanaahn could've sworn he saw a pair of trousers sewn in there somewhere too. One had to make do with what was on hand when desperation was at hand, he supposed.

It was not a fancy ship, but it was sturdy-looking. Even for how crudely it was assembled, the craftsmanship was clear—and Kanaahn knew next to nothing about shipbuilding. It would sail just fine, powered by a little wind and the muscles of her crew. Considering it had been thrown together by thirty half-starved and severely abused Lau, the ship was a right masterpiece. Kanaahn couldn't wait to see what they were capable of with all the time in the world, as many hands as possible, and the best quality wood and tools. Not to mention a belly full of food, grog, and a good night's rest in a warm bed.

The Lau leader patted the ship like it was a loyal dog or a good horse. He beamed with pride as his hands felt the grain of the wood. "When our people first came to Enayra, we used the trees from the swamps of Altimara to build our ships. They were naturally water-resistant and sturdy. Now we must travel to Estion to gather or buy lumber to craft new boats or homes. It's not the trees we had grown used to, but the wood is hardy. She's simple, but she'll sail, and with it, she'll help us free our people. Her and the Darond, that is."

Cecil and Kyeit exchanged a quick glance that went unnoticed by all but Shooter.

"I don't believe we've gotten your name yet," Cecil declared.

The leader bowed. "My apologies, Miss. An oversight on my part. I am Hau'farh iffin Aegwaur-ii-Illaewa dal Reen Borguth. In my tongue, that is Hau'farh, Son of Aegwaur and Illaewa, of the Reen Borguth. Reen is what we call our family groups, clans as you might call them."

Cecil bowed low. "I am familiar with your customs, if not your language, but I am deeply honoured by your explanation, Great Lau'ka."

Hau'farh's eyes twinkled with delight, his mouth curled in a smile, and he beamed like a child about to receive sweets for doing nothing in particular. He was giddy with excitement. "I did not expect to be recognized outside of my people. How do you know me?"

"Only your name, Great Lau—"

"Please, call me Hau'farh."

"I know only your name, Hau'farh. That was how I recognized you."

"Where would one learn a name like mine?"

Kyeit interceded. "I am the daughter of the late Regent Prince of Xiar, Hunter Karaglen. It was a name I had been taught in my studies. We independent states must know the names of our potential allies if we are to fight against Altimaran hegemony."

"Aye, that we must, my lady. Your father is a committed ally of Lau'than. I am sorry to hear of his passing, I was not aware. I had heard of the siege while in captivity but knew not the outcome."

Kyeit received the kind words with sincere thanks. It was clear by the look on her face that the pain of losing her father had abated, but had not fully disappeared, and would likely not do so for a while.

Hau'farh led the group towards the campfire and introduced them to the remaining members of his encampment.

The dragons returned briefly with a Geller's moose for the humans to devour. The massive creature would provide a great deal of sustenance to the starved Lau'thso. They did not remain long, though, as they left shortly to hunt for themselves and to get in a flight lesson with Kinokaze and Valence. The clearing was not large enough for all the humans *and* the dragons, and walking in the woods for long periods had left the dragons feeling trapped and claustrophobic in between the trees. So, they decided it would be easier for them to disappear for the evening—at least until the humans left the cover of the forest once more.

After the moose had been appropriately skinned and dressed, Hau'farh explained in totality how his people came to be kidnapped from Lau'than and enslaved by Altimara.

According to Hau'farh, the Altimaran navy under the command of Lord Drungvist attacked Lau'than during the winter months. Though Hau'farh hated Lord Drungvist for what he did to him and his people, he admired the duke's cunning. He struck at Lau'than when he knew all its people would be there without fail.

Hau'farh took an aside to explain to the uninitiated the specifics of Lau'thso culture. It was customary for adult male and female Lau'thso to spend the good months of the year sailing the world. They would travel and trade across Enayra. They carried cargo for a price. They carried people with passenger boats. They hired themselves out to foreign captains as sailors on fishing and sailing vessels. Sometimes, Lau'thso would serve in foreign navies or shipyards for a fee.

While the adults sailed, the elders would remain behind in Lau'than with the children, raising the next generation and instilling in them the ancient ways and knowledge. The elders guarded the closest kept secrets of shipbuilding amongst the Lau'thso. It was they who had mastered and memorized the ancient stories of and legends the people held dear.

But it was law that in the winter, like the Qiri'ar, everyone returned to the capital, bringing with them their money, their spoils, and new lumber to build new homes and new ships—though visits would be made throughout the year by some clans who sailed the seas close to Lau'than. A massive feast would be held and attended by every Lau'than living in the massive sea-borne city, and the celebration would last a full week. Here ten-year-olds would be given their first tattoos to mark their passage into adulthood, in preparation for their First Voyages in the coming spring. Tattoos would be added each subsequent year, marking completed voyages and personal feats of accomplishment.

Songs would be sung in great choruses and praises sung in honour of the Mother of Oceans, the goddess of the Lau'than people. They thanked her for all she did for her favourite children. They thanked her for providing a bounty of fish to eat, for keeping the waves calm and the storms at bay. They thanked her for swelling the rivers and lakes with water, thus inundating the oceans with even more water for them to sail. They thanked her for the rain that made the trees grow strong and hardy, which in turn was reflected in their boats and homes.

This year, during the normal festivities, the Altimaran navy waited until the last night of festivities had ended, after everyone had eaten and drunk their fill, and had fallen asleep. They struck quickly, using the Black Blades to lead their soldiers in quick seizure operations, rounding up groups of people before they knew what was even happening. Once all the Lau'thso had been shackled and boarded onto the Altimaran ships, the city of Lau'than and all the boats in berth there were doused in pitch and naphtha jelly, and set ablaze.

From there, Hau'farh's mood darkened, understandably. He recounted how his people were separated by age and by ability and enslaved. As he had explained, the elders Lau'thso were being kept near the shipyards to advise in the building and design of new ships for the Altimaran navy. The youth were being kept as indentured servants and hostages meant to pressure other Lau'thso into obeying their new overlords. All able-bodied males and females were shackled beneath the decks of Altimaran naval vessels or put to work in the shipyards as labourers.

From what Hau'farh explained, Altimara was doubling the size of its navy, maybe even tripling it. They were coming up with horrifying new ship designs meant to terrify and awe their enemies. Massive ships, bigger than any built before were going to headline fleets and bring Altimaran dominance of the seas. They were known as "fleet destroyers", for their supposed ability to annihilate and scuttle entire enemy fleets in battle. Hau'farh didn't know more beyond that, or if any actual testing had been done—or if the information he had was even accurate, seeing as he had spent most of his captivity strapped to a rowing bench beneath the decks of a ship known as the *Conqueror*. Everything he had heard had come from gossip between the Altimaran sailors and captains above deck; snippets snatched from whispered conversations and drunken boasting.

The *Conqueror* was familiar to the Khaleeshir, as it had been part of the blockade of Xiar during the Altimaran siege. The irony of this was not lost on Kanaahn or the others.

According to Hau'farh, when Altimara was defeated, the blockade was lifted, and the ships were sent back to Kilnarn. As they went back to port, a storm caught them off the southern coast of Altimara. The storm took the *Conqueror,* and the Lau'ka and his fellow Lau'thso saw the opportunity to escape. They were able to use their oars as leverage to break the bindings that held their chains to the deck and escape into the sea. Fifty Lau'thso went into the ocean, but only thirty made it to shore, with their arms and legs still bound.

The Lau'thso, stranded on the rocky shores of Espias, used the rocks to break their bindings, then fled towards Estion, knowing that nowhere in Altimara was safe—not even Xiar. Hau'farh led his people in the general direction of Lake Ardona. It had been a long and exhausting several weeks, and during that time they had nearly starved, but fate saw fit not to take any more of Hau'farh's crew from him, and for that he was grateful. Hau'farh explained that he could have kissed the shoreline when they reached the tree line and saw the lake looming in the distance. That was where they made camp and began building their boat.

"And that brings me to now," continued Hau'farh. "As I was telling these three over here, we came here to start building a new ship, and a camp. Once we had a longboat, we would go down the Acturn and out to sea. The plan is to arm ourselves and slowly start liberating more of my people from their captivity. Ideally, we'd also like to get in touch with the Darond, and request their assistance, or the assistance of those new Dragonkin I keep hearing about."

Cecil and Kyeit exchanged a glance, but Kanaahn had noticed. Kanaahn's gut did a backflip. He had a feeling they were intentionally avoiding the subject.

When no one responded to Hau'farh, he pressed the subject. "I don't mean to pry but...I have a feeling I'm speaking to them now, aren't I?"

"I'm not surprised you were able to figure it out," Shooter all but confirmed. "How many other people have dragons, right?"

A smile spread across the Lau'ka's face. "Exactly!"

Hau'farh bit into a chunk of moose, chewing hungrily, juice dribbling down his chin and into his long beard. The man had not had a meal quite as filling in too long.

No one said anything.

Arial and Arkas didn't know what to say. Cecil and Kyeit were not looking to make commitments on behalf of the Darond. Kanaahn wanted to at least offer some help, or even offer to intervene with the Darond on Hau'farh's behalf but stopped short of vocalizing his thoughts when he caught Kyeit's pointed look from across the campfire.

But Shooter didn't care what Kyeit or Cecil thought. He was Khaleeshir, and if they could help, he would do so. "I can't speak for the Darond, but as one of the Dragonkin, I can offer our help. We are not the Darond, but we're supposed to be here helping people, right?"

Hau'farh beamed.

Kyeit was aghast.

Yet Cecil, despite her previous stance, looked somewhere amused, if apprehensive.

"We'll fight to free your people. No one should be enslaved. What kind of great heroes would we be if we just ignored their suffering?" Now Shooter was talking to his friends.

Arial and Arkas agreed a bit reluctantly, but Kanaahn remained silent. Fundamentally he agreed with Shooter. Shooter was not wrong. Yet Kanaahn, as the leader, had to walk a delicate bridge. He couldn't let his friends bite off more than they could chew, and he had to keep the Darond off their backs, but he also wanted to make a difference and help people.

Ignoring all circumstantial context around him, Hau'farh was nearly weeping with joy. He shook Shooter's hand and pulled him into a bear hug, then proceeded to do the same with each of his other guests. The other Lau'thso let out cries in rejoice once they had come to understand what Shooter had promised. They began singing and chanting a beautiful and haunting hymn. They held hands around the campfire and swayed to the song of their hearts. The song was short but loud and sung from the soul.

All the while, Kyeit glared daggers at Shooter.

When the singing finished, Shooter—oblivious or uncaring to Kyeit's simmering anger—continued to broker deals with Hau'farh.

"And while I can't speak for the Darond, I can help you appeal to them for further assistance. Every hand helps."

Hau'farh looked puzzled. "How so?"

"We're trying to get to Ethon to meet with one of the Darond masters who will continue our training. You're looking to head down the Acturn to the sea. Ethon is along the way."

"You're asking for a ride?" asked Hau'farh, a little confused.

"We were looking to hire a ferry to the capital anyway. If you come with us, we get our ride, and you'll get to appeal directly to a Darond master and one of the Metallic dragons in person. I don't know how much sway a single Dragon Master has in the Darond, but any sway is better than no sway. You can put your appeal directly to the Darond, who can influence the other nations to help you. Between all of us working together, you'll have your people back in no time."

Kyeit was seething by this point and struggled to keep her emotions from showing on her face.

Kanaahn just looked uncomfortable.

Hau'farh's emotions overflowed as he realized what Shooter was offering him. "If you could help free my people, I would be eternally grateful. I would happily pledge ourselves to disrupt and destroy Altimaran shipping whenever the opportunity arises if that will help you in your fight against them?"

"It would help us a lot. Thank you."

Hau'farh leaned in closer after a moment of pause. "Is...is it true what the rumours say?" he asked with trepidation.

"What do you mean?" asked Shooter.

Hau'farh brought his words down to a light whisper. He leaned in closely towards the fire, so no one else could hear them. "Is it true that you're fighting Tenebrae? That the wicked dragon has returned, and he's truly the one in charge in Altimara?"

Kyeit's voice cut through everyone's head like a hot dagger. *"Don't you dare..."*

Shooter ignored her. "Yes."

Hau'farh grimaced. "Bastard." He spat upon the ground, then stamped on it with his foot. "We'll show him. You leave his navy to us, and we'll leave him to you. We'll make him wish he stayed dead."

Shooter couldn't help but admire Hau'farh's confidence.

Kyeit, meanwhile, was recounting the ways she would kill Shooter in his head.

Hau'farh and his people did not linger at the fire much longer. It was slowly getting to be late into the evening—for a sailor, anyway—and they had intentions to wake just before dawn to continue their work on the boat.

Kyeit waited until every Lau'thso had disappeared into their lean-to huts and then immediately dragged the Khaleeshir, and Cecil closer together, and began to spit venom at them. "What the Hells were you thinking?"

Shooter raised his eyebrow. "I was thinking I was doing my job as a Khaleeshir."

"You cannot just go around telling people that Tenebrae is back."

"I thought that's how the Darond gained support?"

Cecil smirked. "He's got us there."

Kyeit was fuming. "The *right* people. People with power, and armies. People who can keep a secret, and not stir up a panic among the populace."

"He has a right to know what he's fighting against."

Kyeit growled and flexed her fingers in a strangling motion, opening and closing them slowly. "That's the other thing! How dare you make promises like that? The Darond doesn't have the resources to attack the Altimaran navy and raid the shipyards to free the slaves. And the other nations can't just attack Altimara and their navy without starting the war prematurely. If we attack first, anyone on the fence might not side with us because we'd be the aggressors. Did you even think that through?"

Shooter held his ground. "What's the point of fighting Tenebrae if we aren't going to do any actual fighting? We need to free these people. Their enslavement is wrong, and it would deprive Tenebrae of the manpower he's currently in desperate need of. Besides, Hau'farh is going to fight, with or without our help. Should we condemn a whole people to slavery and extinction because it's inopportune?"

Kyeit crossed her arms. She breathed a few breaths, trying to calm down before responding. "I'm not disagreeing with the morality of your stance—it's the correct moral stance. There's even strategic sense to it, I'll admit—"

Shooter pointed triumphantly. "Ha!"

Kyeit remained calm. Rage would not avail her here. She remained cool-headed, but her words still dripped ice. "—But you must understand the very precarious position this puts us in. The other nations won't agree to attack Altimaran naval vessels to free these slaves, no matter how right or wrong it is. It's not politically feasible. And if they won't agree, the Darond won't even bother considering it."

"That's why I offered our help as Khaleeshir. We don't take orders from the Darond, and clearly, the Darond won't take orders from us. We're being trained by the Darond, but not subordinate to them. That's what you said, remember? We weren't listening to the High Council."

Kyeit was in a corner, but she wasn't backing down. She regrouped, calmed herself again, and lowered her voice a bit. "You can't just speak for your friends, any more than you can speak for the Darond. You got us a boat to the capital...but at what cost?"

Shooter turned to his friends. "Do you guys have any issue with what I did?"

Arial shrugged. "Morally, you're in the right. This might cause some issues with the Darond, but as you said, they do not rule us. We are allies, but not their subordinates. We're already enemies of Altimara after Xiar, so it wouldn't be much of an issue for anyone if we attacked them of our own free will."

"War with Altimara is going to happen eventually. We might as well catch them while they least expect it," Arkas reasoned. "Free the Lau'thso and maybe wreck the Altimaran navy while we're at it. I fail to see how that would hurt us."

Kyeit turned to Kanaahn.

But Kanaahn could not lie. He wanted to stay in Kyeit's good books...but he knew Shooter wasn't wrong. Shooter was more correct than the Darond and Kyeit at this moment. "I...agree with Shooter. I don't know much about war and strategy yet, aside from what I learned at Xiar, but I know this much: war with Tenebrae is unavoidable. It will happen. It *must* happen. That's the only way we're going to defeat him. One day we'll have to accept this fact, declare war, and march on Kasaadua and destroy him. We'll have to cleave through Altimara and her allies at that point. This is a fact."

Kyeit didn't look happy, but neither did she argue.

"But if we keep putting off this war because we're afraid of whether we're strong enough, or whether we're following some stupid arbitrary rules of war that Tenebrae may or may not keep following himself, we're only putting ourselves in a bad position later. Tenebrae recognizes that the first phase of the war is not going to be fought on the battlefield. That was the mistake he made at Xiar. He struck too soon, hoping to catch us unawares and earn a decisive victory. Fielding armies at this point isn't necessary. From everything you and Cecil have told us, it seems like the first part of this war is based entirely on resources and gaining allies. Political and strategic victories are key now, not military victories. Tenebrae is fighting now, not for land and conquest, but for the resources to feed his war machine, and allies to help alleviate or lessen the burden of war from Altimara.

"He didn't have the manpower or navy to battle the other nations combined, so he stole an entire civilization and enslaved them so he could have what he needed. Tenebrae also knows that Altimara cannot field an army large enough to fight every other nation in Enayra combined. He needs allies, but Tenebrae's not certain who he can trust as an ally. So, he's trying to get Danaen on his side, because Danaen has always been on Altimara's side until now. He's no doubt got his eyes on Estlon as well, for the lumber and the charcoal production. I know blacksmiths need charcoal to forge steel, and I know the lumber would help him with his navy and his army. We deprived him of the Xiaran grain he needs to feed his armies, so now he'll need to seek grain elsewhere. Anywhere. Estion might also be that elsewhere."

Shooter smiled at Kanaahn, obviously grateful for the support.

Arkas came to Kanaahn's aid. "Adding Estion to his list of allies would also act to further alienate the Darond and their allies from each other. Asaradaea and Espias are always trying to compete and outdo one another, everyone in Enayra knows that. Their animosity is no secret. If they're the only two Darond allies left, even the Darond might not be able to keep them working together. Having all the nations united helps the two giants put their differences aside for a greater cause, but if it's just the two of them against all Enayra? It just becomes a dick-measuring contest between empires, and that's just going to end up starting another war after this one."

"How has the Darond not thought any of this through, or seen any of this coming?" asked Arial, almost offended that five teenagers from Kula could see the forest for the trees better than a military organization with political sway and an intelligence corp.

Finally, Cecil spoke up. "They have."

Silence followed her admission. Silence and crickets. They were soon joined by crackling wood and popping logs.

Cecil repeated herself once more. "They've seen it coming. They've thought of the possibility, but we can't do anything about it. The nations fear war because we don't know what another Dragon War might look like. Enayra hasn't seen a war on that scale in ten centuries, and I don't know if anyone remembers how to fight one properly. The Dragon War cost the lives of so many innocents, not just soldiers. A third of Enayra's population was wiped out, and the dragons lost half their species. No one wants that again. It also doesn't help that no one knows what Tenebrae is hiding up his sleeve. Then there's the state of our allies...

"Estion is committed to the cause but can't muster the military to fight Altimara if it comes down to it. Those who command the military don't trust the king or the Darond. The most they can offer is resources because at least the Crown still controls those. Danaen is on the fence and is likely to either sit this war out of respect for her alliance with Altimara or may outright join Altimara against us, and I don't think we'll ever be able to change that. Utova hasn't joined the Darond because they don't want to give up their autonomy in the process—they've fought so long to earn theirs that they're loath to lose even a fraction of it. Asaradaea and Espias are committed to the cause, but relations with the Darond and Espias only go back a century, the Fall of Dragonsrest did much to damage relations, and it took three centuries for us to make peace.

"The Darond is wounded and broken and led by a largely incompetent High Council that isn't what it used to be. The council is divided between those who are competent but are powerless because they are a minority on one side. And those who serve only their own personal interests—a majority of the council—on the other. Beneath the High Council, the Darond itself is lacking in manpower and is fighting amongst itself as soldiers pledge allegiance to one faction or another, and it's been that way ever since the Great Slaughter."

"What's the Great Slaughter?" asked Kanaahn.

There was a long and pregnant pause before Cecil answered Kanaahn's question. The hesitation was clear on her face, and she stared hard at Kanaahn, contemplating how best to answer. Finally, the words fell from her lips. "It's the reason you and I are orphans."

Kanaahn's eyes widened, and his jaw dropped. The words echoed through his head like the tolling of a bell. He couldn't believe what he was hearing.

Kanaahn's friends all looked at him. Arial looked most concerned of all.

Cecil looked truly sorry that this was how Kanaahn found out. The regret was shown plainly on her face. "It's not how I wanted to tell you but keeping the secret of the Darond's fragility was tied to that secret, and lying to you about the Darond's real position was becoming untenable. I hope you can forgive us."

"Why did you keep it a secret?" Kanaahn asked. Tears stung his eyes, and he was biting back anger.

Cecil's explanation was calm and surgical. Efficient and quick; trying her best to be painless. "We weren't sure at first. Saatus isn't an uncommon name in Asardaea, so we weren't certain whether your parents were random Asardaean immigrants that moved to Kula and just happened to die around the same time."

"What finally made you sure?"

"We got verification from someone who knew your parents, not too long ago. He confirmed what we had suspected. We were going to tell you in Ethon."

For a long time, Kanaahn didn't reply. He didn't say anything. He just stared into the cracking flames of the campfire, thinking through and processing everything that had just been thrown before him. His parents had worked for the Darond and had died in the line of duty. Cecil's too, from what she had said. Then, finally, Kanaahn spoke.

"I'm more upset that you kept the truth about the Darond's fragility from us than the fate of my parents. You weren't keeping my parents' deaths from me; you were just making sure you weren't giving me false information, but keeping the truth of the Darond from us...how are we supposed to fight Tenebrae with a blunted, broken sword?"

"I'm sorry." This time, the apology came from Kyeit. Her voice was low, quiet, meek.

"The Darond are broken and afraid...no wonder they wanted to us to boost morale at Xiar, rather than risk losing us in a fight," Arial muttered.

"The High Council wanted to use you to boost morale, rally the Darond around you, and use it for a recruitment drive. Your prescind would unite our allies and allow us to rally forces to push back against Tenebrae," explained Cecil. "But the competent High Council members realized the hair-brained scheme for it was. Hunter put you on the battlefield as commanders. You could inspire but also lead. The Darond were meant to serve the Khaleeshir, after all. In one move he would put the Darond back on the right path, and they would have their inspiration."

"Explain what started this—the Great Slaughter. What was that?" asked Kanaahn.

Kyeit started. "About twenty years ago, some of the Dragon Knights were starting to clue into the fact that all might not be as it seemed in the palace of Kasaadua. An increasing number of Blood Witches were coming into service in the castle, but they were not seen at court. The assumption was that Altimara was researching forbidden blood magic and was planning to use that for...something. The council at the time wasn't sure what. Many in the Darond thought that blood magic was behind Altimara's desertification. To that end, the Darond had been preparing to fight Altimara, but they would it would be to put a stop to the Glorious Hunt, end the line of anti-dragon monarchs, and restore balance to Enayra—we had no idea Tenebrae was even involved then. In doing so, they could restore the balance of Enayra, and fix Altimara, and dragons and humans could live in peace across all the kingdoms again. It was a simpler task."

"What changed?" Kanaahn asked.

"Our spies and agents started hearing whispers through information brokers in Altimara that *someone* started inquiring about the location of the Black Dragon Clan, and ways they might be freed. At first, we thought it was some over-achieving archaeologist delving too deep into things they should not. Then our agents picked up whispers across other kingdoms that someone was looking to research ways to undo the crystallization Aurum had inflicted upon the black dragons that served Tenebrae during the last war. Whispers mentioned that the person who was looking into it was an older Qiri'ar woman, who claimed to be in the service of Altimara and bore the signet of the king. The High Council didn't believe in the veracity of these rumours—it all seemed a bit too convenient. Tenebrae had been dead a thousand years, and there was no way he was just suddenly back and serving Altimara. They decried the rumours as lies, put out by Altimaran Black Blades to throw off our agents, but some of the Dragon Knights couldn't accept that. These loyal few formed a splinter group that they called Dynia's Hand, named after Lady Sei'ophmei Dynia—"

"Who?" asked Shooter.

"She was one of the first Khaleeshir and was bonded to the green dragon Unaedrol. She was also the right hand of the former leader of the Khaleeshir, Nayondel Darond, founder of our Sacred Order, bonded to the red dragon Veryll."

Kanaahn had heard the name Unaedrol mentioned before, when the group had met with the Green Dragon Clan's leaders. Kina'atael had mentioned that Unaedrol had been Djall's blood brother and predecessor. Kanaahn had wished the dragons had been here at this moment, more specifically Djall. He wanted his opinions, his comfort. Djall had gone out with the other dragons, led by Valence and Kinokaze, for yet another hunt, and to practice their flying lessons and sparring at night. They required a bigger clearing than where the humans were currently camped.

The dragons were aware of what was going on. Kanaahn could feel Djall ebbing at the edges of his consciousness like a tide lapping at the shore, but his focus was elsewhere, and if he or the other dragons had immediate opinions, they did not make them known.

Cecil continued for Kyeit. "Dynia's Hand decided the best way to know for sure was to infiltrate the palace of Kasaadua and the court of King Meland'ar. They did just that, disguising themselves as servants and guards and foreign dignitaries. And they discovered the horrible truth. Meland'ar was but an avatar for Tenebrae, as had every Altimaran king been since Rego. Tenebrae had used Altimara to prepare for his return, and he would use Altimara to wage war and rain destruction upon Enayra again. These agents also learned that Tenebrae had restored his body, but not where he hid himself. The agents were never able to discover much more than that, as they were discovered and had to escape before they were killed. No one was able to find out how Tenebrae brought himself back, or where the source of his power came from considering he had nobody to begin with. Dynia's Hand hoped what they brought before the High Council was enough to get more Darond soldiers and Dragon Knights on their side. The Darond had spent nearly a thousand years preparing to fight the wrong fight and the wrong enemy. The war that would come to Enayra would be more devastating than they had ever imagined.

"But when presented with this new information the High Council did nothing. They dragged their feet. Debated endlessly about what to do. In the end, nothing would be done for a long time. Not until the Khaleeshir had been found, they said, but it would be too late by then. Kotharii appeared across Enayra and began tracking down members of Dynia's Hand, and other Darond agents, and slaughtered them in their homes. *That* was the Great

Slaughter. My parents were victims, as were yours. Kyeit lost her mother as well, though we're by far the only orphans created by this slaughter."

Kyeit picked the tale back up again. "Some agents survived but lost their entire families. Many agents and knights left the order out of fear of retribution. Tenebrae's reach had grown so long, that the Darond hadn't even realized that they were resting comfortably in his palm. Rumours went around within the ranks that it had been the High Council who gave the names and locations of these agents to Tenebrae, in exchange for a temporary truce. The High Council would get their dissenters and rebellious elements eliminated without dirtying their own hands, and Tenebrae got a victory. I don't believe it personally, buying time doesn't seem to be worth that many good men and women. Why handicap yourself for time? But I can see how someone could believe it.

"But now the Darond has been left gutted and torn between those who believed in the High Council, and those who supported Dynia's Hand. We cannot openly fight one another, for there are so few of us left, and we must remain unified for our allies. Neither can we set aside our differences and work together because we cannot agree on the proper path forward. The war effort suffers for it."

Everyone took a while to process the information. They could never have imagined that the Darond was in such a state, not from the way Kyeit, Cecil and even Hunter spoke about them. They knew that some members didn't agree with the bad elements of the High Council, but the Khaleeshir would never have imagined that the Darond were on the brink of going to war with themselves.

Arkas spoke first. "Before we proceed, what was the Fall of Dragonsrest?"

Cecil cocked her head.

Arkas clarified. "You mentioned the Fall of Dragonsrest—you've mentioned strained relations with Espias before. What was it?"

Cecil explained. "Dragonsrest is the ancient fortress that once served as the headquarters of the Darond and the Khaleeshir. It was established by the first Khaleeshir. It's located on the northern shores of Espias in the Bay of Milon. About five hundred years ago, in five-hundred and fifteen, Espias declared war on the Darond. They demanded tribute from the Darond for the continued use of their lands, or otherwise, the Darond should return it. The land had originally been given by the Espian emperors for use by the Darond and the Khaleeshir, but since no Khaleeshir remained, they felt that the lands should be returned—or at least taxed. The Darond disagreed, and so Espias attacked. The Darond attempted to hold the fortress against the Espian army, but they couldn't hold out against such numbers, and the defences of Dragonsrest had been neglected for some time, and an attack from Espias was never expected. The entire order was forced to abandon Dragonsrest and has not returned since. Because of this, the Darond had no political relations with Espias until a few generations ago."

"That sounds...complicated," Arkas admitted.

"Like you would not believe," Cecil replied.

Then Kanaahn asked the question that was eating at his mind. "What did this secret have to do with my parents?"

"They were the ones who founded Dynia's Hand, with a few others. Most of the agents and knights who were killed in the slaughter were members of Dynia's Hand," answered Kyeit.

Yet, instead of being filled with sadness and despair. Instead of wishing revenge against the Kotharii and Tenebrae and the High Council, Kanaahn was filed with only a single emotion: pride. Pride that his parents had done what they knew was right and had succeeded in their efforts. That they had given their lives for the cause they had already sworn their lives to. The information that his parents, and the parents of his friends, had died for, had helped Kanaahn now, as Khaleeshir. In a way, they had never truly left him.

"I can forgive you for the lies," Kanaahn declared. "I...understand the position you were in. I might've done the same if I were in your shoes, but I'm going to ask again: no more lies or half-truths anymore, please. We cannot fight together if the lies keep pushing us apart. We need to unite the Darond, we need to unite our allies, and we need to stop Tenebrae. We can't do that without honesty."

Cecil and Kyeit nodded.

"Shooter," continued Kanaahn. "I will help you free the Lau'thso. Even if it takes us years, even if we must go ship by ship. It will happen."

"I'll help too," Arial added.

"You can count my bow," declared Arkas.

Shooter smiled at his friends, but the tension between him and Kyeit was palpable. Shooter's mistrust of the Darond was not a secret to Kanaahn. The High Council and those who worked against them; both sides had their secrets and held them dear. Even those who claimed to be on the side of the Khaleeshir, who claimed to support and want the best for them proceeded to lie to them for the sake of "duty" or to save face. There would need to be much mending of fences before Shooter got over being lied to again. He didn't take well to that, Kanaahn knew.

Despite Kanaahn's forgiving words, no one else spoke that night, and everyone slowly began to head off to sleep, putting their bedrolls in a lean-to that had been put together for them by the Lau'thso earlier. Eventually, it was just Kyeit and Kanaahn left at the bonfire, which at this point had burned down to mostly cinders and ash. Only the faintest of light was emanating from it.

Kyeit noticed Kanaahn start to get up. "You've matured, Kanaahn," she said, suddenly. "I...I had expected you to get angry with us. To vow revenge on the Kotharii and any who protected them."

Kanaahn searched for the right words before responding. "I might have before Xiar," he admitted. "Before we spoke in Felidrun, even, but revenge isn't going to bring back my parents. My parents knew they might give their lives for the cause, and they fought anyway. They infiltrated Tenebrae's inner sanctum and escaped with their lives, but I'm sure they always knew it could end poorly. I would not be their son if I didn't face my duty in a similar manner. I need to keep forging forward, for the greater good. I can't get mad over things that happened long ago."

"Can you forgive me for getting upset earlier?"

"I never took offence to it. Knowing what I know now, I understand how frustrating it must have been to try and keep that secret while Shooter promised help the Darond couldn't give. You'll have to apologize to Shooter, though, not to me."

Kyeit nodded slowly in response.

"Kyeit?" Kanaahn called.

She looked over at Kanaahn.

"What were their names? Cecil never said."

"Llilor and Istora. Your parents were Llilor and Istora Saatus."

"Do...do you know what they looked like?"

Kyeit shook her head. "I do not. I'm sorry."

"That's okay. I understand," Kanaahn replied. "Thank you."

Kanaahn went over to the lean-to where he was to sleep for the night feeling embarrassed. He didn't know what he even asked. There was no way for Kyeit to know that. Yet somehow, Kanaahn had a feeling that he already knew. He hadn't asked because he didn't know...deep down, he asked because he needed to confirm if the nagging feeling in his gut was correct.

Chapter XX

Drakhart left Isunath in a clearing a few kilometres from the city of Felidrun. He could not be seen approaching the city on a dragon. It might send the wrong message. Instead, he rode a horse and took the main road towards the small hamlet. He came with no fanfare, no honour guard, no special escort. Not even Elandyr'ni or Calandor joined him.

For this mission, Drakhart was alone. He had to be. To arrive with a retinue would draw the attention of the Darond and the Crown, and they would know something was afoot. Altimara sending a diplomatic mission to a baron instead of the king would only raise suspicions. Especially since that baron was Baron Llewyth Gruffydd of Felidrun.

Despite being headquartered in this small city, the Lord Felidrun was one of the wealthiest barons in Estion. His lands were not abundant farmlands, they did not produce grain, nor were they blessed with lucrative gold mines. No; Lord Gruffydd's wealth came from owning most of Estion's charcoal production, as well as most of the lumber mills.

It was from Gruffydd that Altimara purchased their lumber for their navy and army, and the charcoal used by Crown-contracted smiths to produce arms, armour, and other supplies for the army. The Gruffydd Barons had a long-standing relationship with Altimara and her rulers—a long and profitable relationship.

Drakhart planned to use that relationship to further the power and wealth of both nations.

Until recently, Drakhart had been completely at a loss for a solution to Tenebrae's "Estian Problem." Nothing came to him. He tore through volumes of history and reports from agents, and no answer came to him. It was not until one sleepless night—a common thing for Drakhart nowadays—when he was working on requisitioning supplies to get the new Kulan smiths up and running after their move from Targrond.

As Drakhart was going over purchase orders and invoices for supplies, he realized that the seal on each of the invoices had been that of Lord Gruffydd and his noble house. Drakhart followed that breadcrumb trail to the royal library, where he went to the section on heraldry, nobility, and genealogical studies. He read up on the history of House Gruffydd and cross-referenced that with every Black Blade report from in and around Felidrun for the last fifty years.

There he had learned that the Gruffydds had ruled Felidrun since the Anarchy, and recently, Lord Gruffydd and his late father had raised an armed revolt against King Aethalmenis III thirty-six years ago. The revolt had been led by the king's eldest son and heir and had sought to return power to the Barons in exchange for continued support for the Crown. Gruffydd and King Khomandar II had been close, and Khomandar had put the Barons in positions of prominence and power, allowing them to enrich themselves and giving them full control over the Estian army.

Lord Gruffydd profited from his position as a favourite of the king. Something that he lost when Khomandar's son took the throne. The current king, Anducaerleonis, had advocated for more rights for commoners, reinstated the House of Commons to keep the House of Lords in check, and introduced elected positions in his government. He toned down the overreaching rights and avaricious privileges of the nobility and the military that they controlled in favour of increasing the rights of the common folk.

Anducaerleonis was much beloved by his people. Even some of the staunch pro-Republicans had to admit that Anducaerleonis's push for a constitutional monarchy was a step in the right direction, but it had not earned the king much love amongst his father's former cabal of nobles. In fact, it had earned him their ire, and the ire of the military.

Drakhart had sought a way to exploit this divide without illegally inciting the Barons to start a revolution. The Peace of Gerovia prevented the kingdoms and nations of Enayra from funding, supporting, or supplying separatist groups in other sovereign nations. It was the same clause of the treaty that prevented other nations from getting involved in the recent Battle of Xiar. Altimara could not twist the rules in their favour if they too broke them when it was convenient.

Drakhart couldn't break the rules, but he could tread on them a little if he could find a loophole to exploit.

For a time, Drakhart's breadcrumb trail ran cold there. The problem was how. How could he use Lord Gruffydd's growing animosity towards the Crown and spin it into full-on rebellion? Moreover, how could Drakhart put Lord Gruffydd firmly in the pocket of Altimara? The point was not just to put another king on the throne; especially if that king was going to turn out to be hostile to Altimara or support the Darond. Drakhart needed to put another king on the throne that would turn Estion from the Darond and either remain neutral or support Altimara in the coming war—either option would allow Altimara access to her necessary resources.

But one day, luck smiled upon Drakhart once more. It had been the arrival of an irrelevant, routine report from the Black Blades that came in, regarding the actions of Tenebrae's Eyes and Ears. The report outlined, in surprising detail, the death of what should have been a rather unassuming and meaningless bard in Felidrun. The death of any other citizen during interrogation from Tenebrae's Eyes would have been a footnote at best. It was the name of this bard that had stuck out to Drakhart. Banalor Gruffydd. While the identity of the bard had not been known at the time of interrogation—had it been, it might have been handled differently, and no doubt Drakhart would have been stuck as he was before—it had been learned shortly after when the Baron himself came to claim the body.

Drakhart did more digging and found out that Banalor was the nephew of the current Lord Gruffydd. Baron Llewyth Gruffydd was a widower and was infertile. His only sibling was a sister who had married a commoner and renounced her noble title. Gruffydd had always loved and supported his sister, despite her choice to no longer associate with the nobility, and had doted on her son as if he were his own child. When a wave of blue fever passed through Felidrun a few years prior, Gruffydd's sister, wife and brother-in-law were lost to the disease. Gruffydd, who had already been planning to name Banalor as his heir, went a step further and adopted the boy.

Banalor Fewell became Banalor Gruffydd, but he had already taken on the job of bard at the Sleeping Soldier Inn and was not one to back out of a promise. Lord Gruffydd, unable to say no to his earnest nephew, allowed his son and heir to live in his family's old home, and work as a bard in the inn, so long as he spent his free time under the tutelage of the Baron's castellan and other hired educators so he would be ready to take on the mantle of baron one day.

Banalor's only crime had been sleeping with Shooter, though Banalor had no idea the identity of the man he had spent the night with. In doing so, he had marked himself as one of the few people who was both expendable and might have intimate knowledge of where the Khaleeshir were going, and what their plans might be. Spies had named the innkeeper Ruoth as another potential source of information as he had been seen conversing with the travellers that matched the description of the Khaleeshir—of course that alone was not enough to peg him as an enemy, as it was proven he did that with most of his patrons. Moreover, he was well-liked, well-known, and a pillar of the community. For the Black Blades to interrogate or kill him might lead to repercussions that could muddle and complicate their plans. Unfortunately—more for Banalor than anyone else—the bard's interrogation had not given Altimara any more than a confirmation of what they had already expected: the Khaleeshir were heading to Ethon.

But it *did* provide Drakhart with an opportunity, even if that opportunity had been unforeseen, and nearly gone unnoticed at first. It was the very opportunity he needed to bend Lord Gruffydd towards Altimara and remove Estion from the battlefield in one fell swoop. No one knew who murdered Banalor, only that his death had been horrific and painful.

Drakhart intended to use that to his and Tenebrae's advantage.

Tenebrae had admittedly been surprised at the insidiousness and deviousness of Drakhart's plans but had approved, nonetheless. Though, Lord Tenebrae had made one thing very clear: Drakhart would bear full responsibility for this plan and anything that came from it, be it a success or a failure. It was a fair exchange, in Drakhart's mind, and Drakhart vowed not to fail.

* * *

The guards watched the figure approach on horseback. Never had a more ominous visitor appeared before them, coming out of the mist like some wraith. The figure rode on a black horse, dressed in a black cloak trimmed with black fur. Their robes were as dark as the night, and they wore only a simple arming sword at their waist but across their back was a large two-handed greatsword.

The guards could feel sweat bead on their brows despite the relative chill in the morning air. They tightened their grip on their poleaxes. Their captain gripped his sword. They straightened up and stood taller. They would not be intimidated, not so long as the Gruffydd unicorn was emblazoned across their tabards and shields.

"Hold," called their captain, trying to drown his fear in his gut. It struggled, kicking hard against his grip.

The visitor stopped his horse. The creature tossed its head. He turned to the captain and threw back his hood.

The tension died down when everyone realized that the visitor was, in fact, a human. Moreover, he was just some kid. The captain noticed the relief wash over him and his men and again did his best to hide his emotions.

"State your name," the captain declared.

"Drakhart Ghast," replied the visitor.

"Your place of origin?"

"Kula, in Altimara. Though I've just travelled from Kasaadua."

The captain's eyes narrowed. Something seemed too easy about this line of questioning. "State your business."

"I'm here to visit the Baron Felidrun. I come to bring my condolences for the death of his son, and I come with a gift," the visitor replied.

The captain scoffed. His soldiers smirked.

Now all pretence of fear had been replaced with overconfidence and bravado. "And we're meeting the king for tea tonight at the Sleeping Soldier. State your real business or stop wasting my time."

The boy, Drakhart, did not get upset. The captain couldn't help but feel a little disappointed. He'd been hoping for a rise out of this kid.

The kid held out his hand, flashing his ring to the captain.

"Do you see what this is?" asked Drakhart.

The captain shrugged and rolled his eyes. "Jewellery?"

"It's the new signet ring of the Duke of K'nar. It bears my crest, for it is the signet ring of the newly founded House of Ghast. I am Lord Drakhart Ghast, Duke of K'nar, Count of Morag, and Baron of Kula. I sit on the regency council of Altimara and have since the death of King Meland'ar."

The captain and his guards started laughing.

"Sure kid! If you're a duke on the regency council, I'm the Duke of Ethon and heir to the throne."

The guards roared out raucously at their captain's jest.

The man on the horse seemed less amused. He shifted on his horse—causing the guards to jump and reach for their weapons—and pulled out a rolled-up piece of parchment.

"Inside your guardhouse is a copy of Himmel's Heraldic Register, I assume?" the Drakhart boy asked.

The guard captain nodded, confused. "All guardhouses in Enayra have a copy, so we can verify nobility and their signets."

"Well, you won't find my heraldry in there yet. The Brothers Himmel will need to release a new edition for that, but you'll find the heraldry stamped on this parchment in there. Unless you recognize it?"

The guard captain slowly took the parchment. He *did* recognize the seal stamped into the wax. He had seen it countless times before; so often he didn't even need to verify it. It was the official Seal of the Realm for the Kingdom of Altimara. The guard captain broke the wax seal and struggled through reading the letter. It was hard because the captain was only mostly literate. Many of the bigger, longer words required a few reads and some guesswork for him to understand, but eventually, he got the gist of the words on the page.

The guard captain grimaced as he was forced to eat crow. "My apologies Lord Ghast. Please, enjoy your stay. Will you be needing an escort to Lord Gruffydd's manor?"

Drakhart took back the scroll from the captain. "No thank you, captain. I will find my way."

The portcullis rattled and the chains clanked while the guards turned the wheels to raise the metal grate. The boy, Drakhart, entered through it slowly, leaving behind a very sour, very dismayed guard captain and his several silent guards.

* * *

The home of Llewyth Gruffydd, Baron of Felidrun, Viscount of Symil, Count of Wendlin and Omagh, Chancellor of War and the Military, was a manor and estate situated in the north-east corner of the town, but within the outermost walls of Felidrun. The house and accompanying grounds were within a set of simple stone walls—save for the one part of the estate that was ringed in by Felidrun's outer wall—and was built adjacent to the local garrison's barracks. His manor was more form over function and pretended to be a castle, but Drakhart knew it would've crumbled under siege. There were ponds and gardens and manicured lawns of chamomile instead of grass. Beautiful flowers fountains and statues littered the flat landscape.

It was nothing like the estates of the Altimaran nobility.

The homes of most Altimaran nobles were more like fortresses than castles or palaces—and even the palaces, such as the Black Citadel, could withstand prolonged sieges. Bastions of strength and might. Heavily fortified, with thick and high walls and hundreds of soldiers swarming through the grounds like an army of ants. They were military buildings first, and homes after. That's not to say that the Altimaran nobles had no appreciation for art and architecture, but these luxuries were kept hidden within central courtyards and enclosed gardens in the very heart of the building.

Altimaran castles were like a pearl within a rather tough, old oyster. Drakhart felt Estian estates were more like a proper pearl necklace, set with gold and silver.

In Estion, despite a long history of war and strife, the homes of nobility were different from their military buildings. When in trouble, nobles withdrew to remote fortresses near their provincial capitals. Part of the reason was to avoid destruction and prolonged sieges against the populace. If the gates of towns and cities were left open for attackers, they would be less likely to burn and destroy. They would take what they needed and either take control of the city, meaning they would take care of it, or leave, leaving the populace in peace, if a bit hungrier. Military targets and civilian settlements were separate for the safety of the people—or so the nobility said.

Drakhart had heard from Calandor that it was merely a way for nobles to escape the cities before siege came upon them. They'd flee to their country-side castles, having taken anything of value with them—as well as their grain stores—thus leaving the towns without food or protection. The nobles cared not what happened to their citizens, so long as there were some left after whatever conflict to work the fields and pay the taxes.

Drakhart had no other issues getting to the estate of Lord Gruffydd. His letter from the regency council, stamped by Calandor and signed by every member of the council got him through the door faster than it had the front gate of the city.

Once inside the set of for-show fortifications, Drakhart's horse was taken from him by a stable boy, and he was escorted inside the stained, dark wood doors carved with all kinds of scenes from Estian history. Then he was led down long, straight hallways. Everything was right angles and stained-glass windows. The light was everywhere, reflecting against bright sandstone floors and carved wood-panelled walls covered in friezes. The ceilings were painted in a rainbow of colours and gilded and silvered with various shapes and patterns. The columns and buttresses were carved in the likenesses of humans and creatures of myth and legend.

Finally, Drakhart was led into a small study. It was draped in furs and decorated from wall to wall. The place was warmed by a massive red marble fireplace, again carved with the images of prancing deer and hunting wolves and gallant knights and all kinds of scrollwork. In the centre of the hood above the fireplace was carved the unicorn of House Gruffydd with eyes, hooves, and a horn of gold.

Drakhart noticed the baron as soon as he entered the room. Dressed in blues and greens, sitting in a high-backed chair on the other side of a heavy wooden desk. Papers were abandoned everywhere across the varnished top.

Lord Gruffydd was not the strong and composed man he was trying to portray. His hair was greasy and tousled, his eyes were swollen and puffy, red from tears. His clothes looked hastily put on as if he had pulled the first thing from his wardrobe and thrown it on moments before meeting Drakhart. Looking at his flappy jowls, and droopy visage, Drakhart finally understood why they referred to him as Baron Mastiff. This was not a baron, but a man who had been in mourning for a long time.

It was highly likely this was the actual case. He had lost his wife and had no heirs, and his dear sister and brother-in-law were also taken. His last living relative, his dear nephew, his heir, and his son, had been horrifically murdered. This was a man in pain, held tightly in the crushing depths of despair. Lord Gruffydd put on clothes, brushed up his appearance, and wore a brave face...but he was in pure agony.

It almost made Drakhart feel guilty for what he was about to do.

Almost.

Gruffydd welcomed Drakhart, taking his arm firmly and shaking it. He showed Drakhart to the chair opposite his, on the other side of his desk, and poured each of them a glass of wine.

Drakhart noticed that even though Gruffydd had poured himself wine, he barely touched his glass, aside from a sip he took at the beginning.

Gruffydd cleared his throat. "Lord Ghast, was it? Welcome to Felidrun. I must say, I wasn't expecting to be visited by someone from Altimara's regency council. What brings you here of all places?"

"I must admit, I had not expected to make my way out here as my first diplomatic visit; let alone under such circumstances."

Gruffydd's shrewd eyes narrowed. "It can't be that important a visit if you come without guards, or any kind of announcement?"

"I chose to make my visit secret. Altimara wishes to extend its condolences on the death of your son. We had heard the news through...whispers, that he had passed through our halls. I can't begin to imagine how you feel."

"No doubt. He wasn't much older than you, and I doubt you've raised many children yourself. And you need not step on eggshells around me. I know your kingdom's spies have a long reach across this content. Enayra stands poised for war against you—the idiot boy king won't shut up about it." Gruffydd's bark was starting to show. Amongst his peers, he was known as a tough and shrewd man, with no sense of humour and even less patience. The other reason they called him Baron Mastiff was starting to shine through; unassuming, sleepy, doughty at a glance, but tough, determined, and ferocious when roused in the defence of its house.

Drakhart changed track. "And yet you accepted my visit, at the last minute, despite all that."

Gruffydd cawed out a laugh. "I hate the idiot boy king, and I don't believe that the world is quite as bad as all that. Just fear-mongering to try and keep the masses clinging to his skirts."

"But that doesn't explain why you accepted my visit."

"Nor does it explain why Altimara is interested in my son and his death..." Gruffydd choked at the end of his sentence, struggling to get the words out.

"I will be honest with you, Lord Gruffydd. You are a smart man, and I see I cannot lie to you." Drakhart shifted in his seat. "Enayra *is* on the brink of war, though it is not because Altimara wants it, I can assure you, when war comes to Enayra, we will not sit idly by and allow this aggression."

Gruffydd, for the first time since he had met Drakhart, looked genuinely shocked. "I...have...you haven't come to—"

"No, I assure you, this is not some attempt at a kidnapping or murder." Drakhart raised his hands where Lord Gruffydd could see them.

Lord Gruffydd relaxed a bit, but he was still on edge. Drakhart watched with a tinge of amusement as he watched the man take several concurrent sips of his wine.

"Lord Gruffydd, if I may speak openly?"

The Baron's bark crawled back from his stomach. The Mastiff had found his courage again. "Why stop now?"

"Altimara is aware of your distaste for King Anducaerleonis. It is a distaste we share." Drakhart paused. He needed to be delicate with how he approached this. He was walking a very fine line. "You must understand, that despite my stamped letter proving my noble status—a passport required by all men and women born of status—I am not here under any official capacity as an ambassador, or as an envoy of the regency council."

Gruffydd nodded. He seemed to understand what Drakhart was saying. "You speak frankly, but not with political authority. I understand."

"I come with information regarding the unfortunate death of your son. Information that our spies picked up, and I think you would be most interested in. What you do with that information is up to you. You understand we can't officially help."

Drakhart proffered another roll of parchment from his robes. This time it was a forged spy report that pointed the blame for Banalor's death squarely at another party.

Lord Gruffydd took the parchment and slowly unrolled it. He read every word twice, thrice, four times before it finally sunk in as real. His eyes welled with tears, then his face contorted with rage, turning bright red. "Where's your proof?" the Baron spat across the desk.

Drakhart, slower this time, playing up the gravity of the situation, handed Gruffydd another piece of paper. This time it was a small, folded letter, that looked like it had been previously crumpled, slightly singed in places as if it had danced with a fireplace and stained with blood—the last few touches Drakhart had insisted upon, to up the authenticity. The contents of the letter betrayed its somewhat humble visage. Written on these papers was a fake order from the king of Estion to his spies to have Banalor murdered as a message to his adoptive father, it also bore the official royal seal of Estion. It was even written on the official station of His Royal Highness King Anducaerleonis. Luckily for Altimara, they had a well-placed spy within Filiddyn Castle who had been able to get a hold of the seal and stationery. Once the stationary was stamped, they forwarded it through the spy network to Drakhart so he could forge the note.

Gruffydd was livid. "The king murdered my boy. He murdered Banalor! The bastard should have burned his orders. He'll regret this, I swear it."

Drakhart hid his smile. "I have no doubt he will."

Gruffydd stood up, and with a roar, lifted his heavy wooden desk, tossing it towards the left wall. The desk didn't shatter or splinter, but chunks broke off, and cracks ran down the desk. Drawers fell out, an ink well shattered on the ground, staining the carpet, and papers flew everywhere. The wine decanter, as well as the Baron's and Drakhart's drinking glasses also broke against the floor. Some wine splashed into the fireplace, causing the fire to hiss, sputter and smoke, but not die.

Two guards came rushing in with the major-domo, weapons drawn. They relaxed a bit when they saw that Lord Gruffydd was standing, enraged, tears freely streaming down his crimson cheeks. His desk was smashed—it wasn't hard to tell who had done it, but they did not put away their weapons until their lord calmed them and sent them back into the hallway.

Once they were alone again, Gruffydd rounded on Drakhart. "What exactly did you expect this to buy you, Altimaran bastard?"

Drakhart was not afraid of Lord Gruffydd. The thought of facing Tenebrae after failing him scared him much worse than this man did.

"Truthfully? An ally."

"You want me to revolt against the king? You think I'm going to march to my death like a fool, for some foreigner and their foreign war, just to weaken Estion? You Altimarans are dumber than I thought."

"No, Lord Gruffydd. That was not my intention." Drakhart feigned sympathy. In truth, he was growing tired of this game.

Gruffydd screamed in Drakhart's face. Veins bulged in his neck and forehead. "Don't lie to me, boy! How feeble Altimara must be, to send a child to disrupt the peace of another country in such an overt way!"

"Lord Gruffydd, please—"

Gruffydd did not allow Drakhart to finish. "You heard the rumours of how I hate the boy king, and in that regard, I can say they are not rumours. He cares not for the longevity of the Crown or nobility, only for his precious people, to whom he defers and divests too much trust and power, but the people cannot rule. The people are afraid and superstitious. If that boy had his way, he would be but a puppet for the Republican scum. They and their republican democracy would ruin this country in six months if they took the helm. Before long they'll either have a new king in all but name, or some tyrant with designs for the crown that openly calls himself such. The people need the monarchy and nobility to keep the peace and keep control. So, I railroad him in the House of Lords, I shut down as many policies as I can that I feel will harm the Crown, and I do hate him. Now I have reason to hate him more—and for that I thank you. But I will not start a war just so Altimara doesn't have to worry about her borders."

Drakhart waited for Lord Gruffydd to grow silent before he spoke next. "Lord Gruffydd we have no intentions of stirring up a revolt just to weaken Estion. A weak Estion is not our intention. We need Estion to be strong and independent, though preferably allied with us instead of our enemies. Truthfully, we would have *you* on the throne."

Lord Gruffydd, having calmed down somewhat, took his seat again. This time, without a desk between them. "A laughable prospect. Even if I did have designs for the throne, I am oath-bound not to act upon them. Even so, it would be an unthinkable prospect. Estion is not the conquerable state it used to be. Generations of wise but greedy kings, fearing revolt from within and attacks from outside, built Ethon into a bastion of self-defence. The kings of old sought to ensure Ethon would no longer be known as the Sacked City. If I were to lay claim to the throne by right of conquest, I could rally five more of the nine barons to my side. That would make six barons total. Between us, we could field seven thousand soldiers, without calling on citizen levies—a prospect I'd rather avoid, for the people love the boy king, and I doubt they would join a rebellion against their precious monarch.

"The Crown could count on the support of the remaining three Barons, the Ethon Bluehelms that guard the city, and the Royal Guard. Before volunteers and citizen levies are called, that's easily five thousand soldiers. If I were to meet them on the battlefield, in the open, with a few good commanders under me, I'd take those odds easily. But they've got the walls, and not just one wall, a whole series of walls: walls protecting entire pockets of the city. They can move soldiers along the walls and pull back to different pockets in case of a breach. Once you breach the city you're fighting in tight spaces that the Bluehelms and Royal Guard know well. Then you must breach the castle on top of the hill. King Aethalmenis I started the construction, but it was his grandson Aethalmenis III who made that place impregnable. Khomandar never saw a reason to undo the work of his forebearers, despite his revolt.

"And on top of all that, the Baroness Pelchar, the Lady vohn Veishaupt, controls Pelchar and the Acturn. They can keep the city well stocked with mercenaries, soldiers, and supplies for months on end by sending boats up and down the river. So long as she keeps that river well defended, and the baroness always keeps the waters of the Acturn well protected, they'd have unbreachable supply lines. They say not even salmon swim upriver without her permission and the proper paperwork—and I believed it too."

Lord Gruffydd sagged in his chair. His demeanour softened; his face grew softer. "On top of all that...I cannot raise a revolt against the Crown even if I wanted to. I hate the boy king, but his father and I have been close friends since we were infants. I promised

Khomandar that I would keep the Crown on the heads of his descendants—that's *why* I act so boldly against him in parliament. It's for the stability of our power *and* the Crown's. If I take the Crown for myself or rebel against the boy king, I will break my oath to Khomandar. I cannot do it, not against those odds, and not without forsaking my oaths. Khomandar would have the Darond down my throat within hours."

Drakhart would need to work another angle. "You've never believed much in the Darond, have you?"

Gruffydd grew defensive. "I support Khomandar's decisions, even if I can't agree with them. He's my friend; my sworn brother."

"You can speak frankly between us, Lord Gruffydd. I won't speak of this to anyone else," Drakhart lied.

Gruffydd took a moment before he responded. His eyes searched Drakhart. When he was certain he could trust Drakhart, he finally responded. "I think we sacrifice too much autonomy to the Darond's cause, for very little benefit in return. The alliance with the other nations against Altimara won't last, and the Darond are a drain on time and resources—resources that could be used to strengthen the Estion against attack in the coming war. We don't need an alliance to survive. We need only remain neutral and be strong enough to ward off any possible attack and profit from the war by selling our resources to both sides. Danaen knows this well, and they've done just that. They're on good terms with Altimara but won't commit to one side or another. Altimara will leave them alone, and the other nations wouldn't dare attack without a constant supply of reekweed—which is controlled by the Danaen government—or a death wish. I've never believed that whole Tenebrae bullshit they've been pushing for the last twenty years either. It's just an excuse to rile us all up and start a war."

Drakhart hid a smile. "It sounds like with you at the head of this country, things might go a bit smoother. You know what this country needs, and your neutral stance would be respected by Altimara."

"But that brings us back to the crux of the problem: my oath, and the logistics a revolt would require. You cannot promise me soldiers or supplies because you cannot legally involve yourselves in the internal matters of another sovereign state. You're not even supposed to be here right now, sharing this information with me, but I'll look the other way for the sake of my nephew-son."

"What if we *could* promise you the numbers needed to conquer Ethon?" Drakhart asked.

Gruffydd scoffed. "But you *can't*. The laws—"

"—The laws state that we cannot provide you military aid in the form of military support, arms, armour, or supplies. The law, however, only applies to governments, their militaries, and their citizens. Non-citizens and protectorates are exempt from these laws by several loopholes and a wide grey area, so long as their actions are not officially endorsed by the state. This allows states to distance themselves from being responsible for, for example, an Asardaean expatriate returning home to fight for one side or another in an Asardaean civil war. The citizen, so long as they arm themselves alone, and act of their own volition, may involve themselves in the politics of their homeland, without incurring consequences for their new home of choice."

Gruffydd shook his head. "That's your grand plan? To send private volunteers here of their own volition. I can't take Ethon with a few hundred, armed citizens."

"What if those volunteers were four thousand Qiri'aran Warriors?" Drakhart asked.

Gruffydd's eyes widened. He looked like a child who had just been offered a cake on a day that wasn't his birthday. His eyes betrayed him. He had been hooked. "How...?"

"The beauty of this plan is that the Qiri'ar are not, in fact, citizens of Altimara. They are a tributary under our hegemony, in much the same way Xiar was. They are officially recognized as a semi-autonomous people group that pays tribute to Altimara but otherwise controls their own affairs—including their own external political relations. They could, technically, declare war and open political relations with any other Enayra nation, should they choose. Altimara would not be responsible for any actions or decisions made by the Qiri'ar, because they are neither citizens nor acting with the express consent or direction of the Altimaran Crown. And there is little doubt that the Qiri'ar are well-known for their fighting capability. You've heard the legends; we all have."

Gruffydd parroted out the legend as if on command. "My old father, bless his soul, used to tell me stories about them when I was a kid. During the Dragon War one thousand years ago, at the Battle of the Black Swamp, fifty Qiri'ar Berserkers held off an entire Asardaean legion, severely stalling the previously uncontested March on Gishan'belor. Using a combination of ancient herbal concoctions and blood magic, the Berserkers could ignore all pain. The battle lasted six hours, and when the Qiri'ar finally succumbed to their wounds, they had taken half of the legion with them. They bought enough time for the Qiri'ar and black dragons to reinforce Gishan'belor, allowing the Qiri'ar to withstand a nine-month siege that only ended after Tenebrae was killed at the Battle of Kahnair Plains."

Drakhart had also heard that legend. In truth, it was a little over four hundred Qiri'aran Blood Warriors against the one Asardaean legion. It had been a legion that had been slogging through a swampy marsh for three days in heavy armour, in territory that the Qiri'ar knew well, but it had been a legion of five thousand soldiers and accompanying cavalry all the same. The truth, while still impressive, was not the stuff of legends that a thousand years of myth and propaganda preferred.

"Would four thousand of their warriors be enough to tip the scales in your favour, and make you relinquish your oath in exchange for the Crown?" asked Drakhart. He knew that Lord Gruffydd was only nibbling at the hook, but Drakhart had not yet hooked him completely.

Lord Gruffydd stared at Drakhart for a moment before letting out a howling laugh. It was not the reaction Drakhart had expected, but Gruffydd's response had not been unaccounted for. "Ha! You must think me an idiot, or you're a better liar than I thought. The Qiri'ar have no love for the Crown, and the Crown hasn't exactly cared well for them. Why would they come to *my* aid at *your* request?"

"Lord Gruffydd, do you know anything about me?"

Lord Gruffydd snorted. "I didn't even know you existed until you showed up on my doorstep."

"Lord Gruffydd, I am Dragonkin. I'm sure you've heard rumours of the return of the Dragonkin. It is true. However, unlike my comrades who chose to become the lapdogs of the Darond, I chose to use my power to serve the people. I entered the service of King Meland'ar and have been rewarded for my service."

Gruffydd grew wary. "Are the rumours about Tenebrae also true?"

"No," Drakhart lied. "King Meland'ar was his own man, he was no one's puppet. No, the Qiri'ar follow me because of my partner dragon. He is of the blood of Tenebrae, and the Qiri'ar worshipped Tenebrae as their god. We have been able to use this to the advantage of Altimara, and continue to do so...for example, in aiding your bid for the throne."

Whether Lord Gruffydd truly believed him or not, Drakhart didn't care. Drakhart was hoping that Gruffydd's pride, greed, and overconfidence would be his undoing. The desire for the Crown, the hatred of King Anducaerleonis, and the yearning for revenge for the death of his son was misdirected as it was.

Drakhart stared Lord Gruffydd in the eyes, and watched with satisfaction, the exact moment the fish took the bait. All Drakhart had to do was set the hook and reel him in. "If you take the throne, Altimara will recognize your legitimacy by right of conquest. We will leave your people be, and provide whatever aid is needed to keep you neutral and well-guarded against invasion from Asardaea. In return, you will not join with our enemies in the war to come."

"And what of the Acturn?" Gruffydd asked, pretending not to be as intrigued as he truly was—he was failing terribly. "Lady vohn Veishaupt will still control the river and canal system."

"My lord," Drakhart began. His tone was reassuring and sweet like a mother calming her frightened child who had just woken in the middle of the night from a horrible dream. "Did you think I would truly come here without a plan? I have more respect for you than that. I am aware that the Baroness Pelchar will soon be initiating her bi-annual maintenance of the canal system."

Lord Gruffydd scoffed. "No one knows when she starts her maintenance. She keeps it secret and changes the dates every time she does it. For security reasons, she says. I have no idea how she can afford to close the canal for two months every two years and never once lose any money over it. She always makes her deliveries on time regardless. I dislike her by principle, but her ability to plan and run a tight ship genuinely impresses me."

"Our spies provide accurate information. We can use the Qiri'ar to seize the river while it's drained and undergoing maintenance. Even if the Baroness sends her forces to take back the canal, they'll be no match for the Qiri'ar, and they'll never refill the canal in time to save the city, especially if we catch it in a state of maintenance." Drakhart smiled. "Is my planning sufficient? Are these terms agreeable?

Gruffydd smiled wide. "I think I could agree to those terms. We will need to draw up a treaty later, but I will accept a gentleman's agreement for now. After all, you are not here at all right now." Gruffydd held out his hand.

Drakhart took it, gripped it firmly, and shook it. "With that agreement, I must be going. I must prepare the Qiri'ar. I will return to plan the attack in one month. In the meantime, if you must reach me, leave a candle burning in your window at night, and a Black Blade will arrive to take your message."

Lord Gruffydd thanked Drakhart again but stopped short of bowing—a king did not bow to a duke, after all. Drakhart resisted the urge to slap the baron. His arrogance was creeping forth now that he had achieved his wildest dreams, and the Mastiff was becoming the Jackass—and becoming insufferable.

* * *

Drakhart hid his excitement until he had left the city limits, but once he was away from other prying eyes, he couldn't stop smiling like a giddy idiot. The first part of his plan had been a success. Though, it would not be a complete success until the plan of attack had been put into action, and Ethon had fallen. Once the walls had crumbled and the Khaleeshir and King Anducaerleonis were defeated, the throne would be handed over to Lord Gruffydd. *Then* it would be a complete success.

Drakhart returned to the grove where he left Isunath.

The black dragon stepped forward into the clearing as Drakhart approached. "How did it go?"

Drakhart smiled at his partner. "It was a success. We have the Baron Felidrun on our side."

Isunath's lips curled back, flashing his fangs in a weird attempt to smile. "Excellent. My k'nir will be pleased with the update, no doubt."

Drakhart gingerly sidestepped a small pool of blood in the dirt and walked over to where his armour clothes lay nestled in a bundle in the bushes. "Did you eat well?"

Isunath's tongue flicked out. "The merchant was a bit fatty for my taste, but he went down easy enough." The black dragon sniffed the now very nervous horse that shuffled about at the edge of the clearing.

Drakhart had begun to dress himself in his armour. He had gotten pitifully used to having assistance getting in and out of his armour, but his fingers clumsily remembered how to do it on his own. "Too full for his horse?"

The horse nickered and bucked its head up and down. It seemed to understand where its fate was headed. The horse tugged against the reins, which Drakhart had tied to a low-hanging branch.

Isunath chuckled. "Never too full for a horse."

Drakhart wilfully ignored the struggling and screaming of the horse as Isunath tore into the beast's jugular and shook the creature until the gelding's neck snapped. He continued to dress himself in his armour, strapping straps, fastening facets, and buckling buckles.

This was not the armour he had thrown together for the Siege of Xiar. This armour had since been custom forged and made specifically for Drakhart. It was still black as night—to both match the tinted armour of his former comrades and to blend in with the black colour scheme most Altimaran soldiers wore. His breastplate was inlaid with bright silver filigree that stood out in stark contrast to the pitch-black armour. The filigree depicted a black dragon battling in flight with a green dragon—the green dragon's filigree had been made of patinated bronze. Silver filigree depicted scrolling designs and patterns along the edges of Drakhart's vambraces, boots, gloves, and greaves. His helmet, which Drakhart had left tucked in Isunath's saddlebag, was crested with a golden bat-like monstrosity that was the winged-wolf. It was the natural predator of the Altimaran wild ram—the symbol of the late House of Davenpourte.

By the time Drakhart had finished, there was a heavily mangled horse skeleton where the horse had once been tied. Isunath had left large chunks of meat on the bone, and blood and scraps of skin and intestine were scattered all over the ground.

"Do I have time to finish?" the dragon asked, licking blood from his muzzle.

Drakhart frowned. "We shouldn't stall our report to Lord Tenebrae. Bury it like you did the merchant's bones so the scavengers don't tip the guard off. You can go for a hunt when we get back and lick the meat off those bones."

Isunath was not pleased with Drakhart's answer, but he did as Drakhart said. Within minutes Isunath had dug a substantially deep hole in the clearing. He scraped the meaty, bloody bones into the pit before he covered them back up again. The dragon spread the blood around with his tail until it mingled and was covered by fresh-turned dirt. It would dry soon enough.

"Let's get going," Drakhart said. He mounted Isunath quickly as the dragon proffered his saddled neck.

The two took off, soaring up high so they appeared not much bigger than an eagle to those on the ground. The trip went silently for a few moments before Isunath spoke up again.

The black dragon switched to the mental connection so Drakhart could hear him over the billowing wind. *"Will I be coming with you when you return to attack Ethon?"*

Drakhart smirked. *"What you are really asking, Isunath, is if you can battle the other Khaleeshir?"*

Isunath said nothing.

"You are as large as an adult of your kind, but you are young in the mind still."

"That's not an answer," Isunath complained.

"You won't like the answer, my dearest friend."

Isunath puffed smoke through his nostrils. *"That's because it's a no, and I was promised the blood of Djall."*

"Don't throw a fit, Isunath," Drakhart said sternly. *"I shouldn't even be at the battle."*

"But you'll still go." Isunath protested.

"Only to ensure nothing goes wrong and oversee the siege. I will be well hidden, and I will not take to the field. I can't. If I'm seen, we lose plausible deniability."

"Who would you truly be fooling?" Isunath asked. *"Asardaea and Espias have made their choice. They believe in the Darond and the return of Tenebrae."*

"This is about keeping Danaen and Estion neutral or allied. Whichever the outcome may be, it's two less foes we'll have to fight," explained Drakhart. *"It's also about stalling the war until we're ready. If I'm seen on the battlefield, Espias and Asardaea can declare war on Altimara and send aid to Estion immediately. Estion would be saved, and we'd have to fight three armies immediately. Danaen may seek to join the winning side of that fight. Utova would no doubt capitulate to the Darond, choosing to lose some freedom on the battlefield temporarily in exchange for a chance to gain territory from a defeated Altimara."*

"It's a feeble excuse," Isunath muttered.

"We must shatter the unity of the alliance against us. Danaen must stay neutral or join us. Estion must make the same choice under Lord Gruffydd. Utova can easily be crushed if we have the time and resources to devote to a full siege of the city-state, and we can't do that if we're fighting off enemies on all sides. The hope is that if Asardaea and

Espias are left alone, they'll spend more time trying to outdo each other than they will be trying to fight us. If they keep trying to outperform each other, they'll be more likely to slip and make a mistake on the battlefield. It would aid us well to see them fumble."

"...Do you not think I could handle the other Khaleeshir?" Isunath asked with trepidation.

Drakhart took a moment to collect his thoughts. Isunath was different than Ölüm. Tenebrae had explained that Ölüm, having had Tenebrae inhabit his body, as well as having been laid over a thousand years ago, had been—by human standards—more mature when he finally hatched. Isunath, however, was but a few months old, even though he was as physically large as a three-year-old dragon. The downside to magically dvancing Isunath's size was that there was no way to magically age his mind along with it, so the dragon would be like a hatchling stuck in an adult's body.

"Isunath. My issue is not your ability. You are half as large as Valence is, you could easily best the other Khaleeshir in a contest of strength or size, but you are young in the mind. You have much left to learn. They have the benefit of more training and more experience than you. Yet despite this, I would still happily fly into battle together to battle our enemies, because I believe by the time of the siege you would be better prepared."

Isunath began to protest, but Drakhart stopped him. *"But because of the way the plan must unfold, you cannot fight on the battlefield, and you cannot join me. I cannot take the risk of your presence being noticed."*

Isunath didn't respond immediately, but Drakhart could feel the dragon stewing and seething within, like a child in the throes of a tantrum being told no.

When he had finally calmed down, Isunath finally spoke. *"Do you still fear losing me?"*

"I fear it every day, my dear Isunath," Drakhart spoke truthfully. A tinge of anxiety welled up in his stomach at the mere thought of losing Isunath as he lost Ölüm. Isunath was not blind to the feeling. *"Even so, under normal circumstances, I would take you with me, but strategy forbids me from doing so in this case. Please understand. It is what is required to ensure we do not fail at your k'nir's given task."*

Isunath's response was short and curt. A simple *"Fine."* It was punctuated by hurt.

Drakhart felt bad that this had come between him and Isunath, but he knew that Isunath's feelings could not take precedence over the plan. If Drakhart failed because of Isunath's or his own sentimentality or overzealousness, Tenebrae would have their heads.

Drakhart would make it up to his partner somehow—maybe a hunting trip to the mountains outside of Kasaadua. In the meantime, Drakhart found himself praying that Isunath would mature just a little faster, even if not at the same rate as his magically altered body.

Chapter XXI

Tenebrae had been pleased with the success of Drakhart's visit to Lord Gruffydd. The progress and continued success of Drakhart's mission gave the old dragon temporary peace of mind—though Drakhart knew that success had to continue, and it could not stop here. Drakhart couldn't get lazy.

Naturally, Tenebrae had been concerned by Drakhart's desire to be near the battlefield while the attack on Ethon unfolded, because of how much of a risk it posed, but Drakhart had promised he would go alone—save Elandyr'ni—and would not take the field. It was enough to calm Tenebrae's initial concerns with the plan, though Drakhart could tell the old dragon still wasn't fully convinced.

Elandyr'ni and Calandor had also been pleased, even proud.

The next step in Drakhart's plan was to go to Gishan'belor and speak with the Kinu'watan and Bishu'kagun, the High Chief and Great Mother respectively. No decision could be made that would affect the whole tribe without the express and unanimous agreement of the two leaders of the Qiri'ar Confederacy.

The Great Mother was the spiritual leader of the people. She was the one who selected the Blood Witches at a young age, and fostered, mentored, and trained them. Elandyr'ni herself had been fostered by the Great Mother at the age of four, and received her tattoos at the age of sixteen, signifying the end of her training. When the Great Mother passed— for her rule was tied to the length of her life—she would appoint a successor from amongst her closest devotees.

The High Chief was the political leader of the people. High Chiefs were not elected but battled for the right to lead the tribes. A chief was chief for life, but as he reached the end of his life, he would select twelve potential successors who would fight each other for the right to succeed. Combat was non-lethal—as the Qiri'ar would not risk their strongest warrior's lives outside of true battle but the challenger that defeated the greatest number of his opponents was declared the true successor. The High Chief could be challenged for leadership at any point, and if he was defeated in single combat, he would be replaced by the one who defeated him.

Drakhart had spoken with the Qiri'aran High Chief previously and mentioned some of what was to come, but nothing had been confirmed and few details were given.

Elandyr'ni had similarly been in contact with the Kinu'watan about the situation.

Now the two Qiri'aran leaders and the two servants of Tenebrae would sit down to discuss the finer details of invading Estion and taking Ethon. Of course, Drakhart had yet to mention the biggest concern he had about this invasion: how they were getting four thousand Qiri'ar over the Estian-Altimaran border without being noticed.

Drakhart had considered going over the mountains of the Spine to avoid any major border crossings, but that still meant marching four thousand Qiri'ar across Estion and keeping them hidden before they reached Ethon. Even in the cover of the forest, that didn't mean they were away from prying eyes and sneaking spies. If they were seen or noticed before they reached Ethon, they would lose the element of surprise, and all would be lost.

Drakhart was running out of time to postpone dealing with this problem, but he had no more time to think it over now, for now, he was approaching Gishan'belor, the capital of the Qiri'aran Confederacy.

The city of Gishan'belor came into view on the horizon shortly after midday. Even from afar, Drakhart was in awe at the sheer size and beauty of it. Even as Drakhart drew closer, his amazement only grew. Gishan'belor truly lived up to its name: the City of Colour.

Elandyr'ni mentioned it from time to time, often with a tone of nostalgia or longing. Drakhart could understand, he still found himself missing Kula during prolonged absences, but Kula, nor even Kasaadua, could hold a candle to Gishan'belor.

The city, despite sitting in the middle of a dry and cracked desert, on the edge of a massive dried-up lakebed, was livelier than any city Drakhart had seen yet. Though made of the same mudbrick as Kula, it was not left to go brown and dusty as Kula's homes had been. It had not been left to crack, or break, or crumble, or degrade.

No, the Qiri'ar instead chose to paint their mudbrick and adobe buildings with bright and vibrant colours and pigments. Bright blues, vibrant yellows, rich reds, warm oranges, verdant greens, and a myriad of other colours made up the rainbow colours painted across the cities. Sometimes they painted murals, but often the decorations came in formless shapes and patterns with no logic or sense. It looked more like an explosion of emotion and passion than a coherent painting, and it was stunning.

Apparently, from what Drakhart had been told by Elandyr'ni, the city was currently "mostly empty", as many Qiri'ar had been sent out on their annual trade pilgrimage. The Qiri'ar spent the better part of the year travelling across Enayra, trading everything from handmade cooking ware, trinkets, jewellery, and herbal tonics and tinctures for gold and other goods of like kind. The city was even bigger and livelier in the winter, when the massive, highly decorated, and brightly coloured tents went up, as the Qiri'ar returned to spend the season in Gishan'belor.

In truth, the trading served a double purpose—it allowed the Qiri'ar to travel across Enayra and gather information and gossip for Tenebrae from regions and places where his spies might be at greatest risk of exposing themselves. The average citizen wouldn't expect the Qiri'ar to be spies, since they had been travelling across Enayra, trading and wandering since the earliest days of their confederacy. Sure, they *had* been servants of Tenebrae during the Dragon War—but that was a thousand years ago, and no one wanted to think about that.

Drakhart was even more in awe at the massive cathedral at the heart of the city. It was a massive building surrounded by an even larger plaza. It was painted even more vibrantly than the other buildings and had been studded with gems and gilded and silvered. The building itself was a large rotunda topped with a perfectly semi-spherical dome, with sixteen evenly spaced naves that branched from the main building. It gave the building the overall shape resembling a star. Each nave ended in a semi-circular chancel and two triangular transepts on each side. The chancel and transepts were topped with towering spires that reached up to the sky like the fingers of a dead god reaching out of the ground. Each spire was topped with a broken pinnacle—except one. The last remaining pinnacle was topped by an effigy wrought of gold and silver that was comprised of a half-sun and half-moon that merged into one another. This building was none other than the Grand Temple of Gishan'belor, once known as the Great Temple of the Aspects.

Elandyr'ni had explained that each of the sixteen naves held altars that were once dedicated to each of the Sixteen Aspects. Five for each of the metallic dragons representing the five Great Aspects, and eleven for the remaining aspects that were worshipped as dualities. These dualistic Aspects were said to be the astral forms of Ha'k'dir and Ha'k'nir of each dragon clan. That practice changed after Eshgalon the Great had made his pact with Tenebrae. Afterwards, only Tenebrae and his late mate Kyna'braxa—worshipped under their Common names of Isunath and Kistharoth, Aspects of the Night and Day— were allowed to be worshipped in the cathedral, or at all amongst the Qiri'ar. The remaining altars had been destroyed and the naves, chancels, and transepts, that were once used to worship the other Aspects were now used to house the carved tombs of Qiri'aran leaders and heroes, and worship was given to them instead. The effigies that topped the pinnacles of the other spires were broken off, and the only spire that remained was the one that represented the Aspect associated with Tenebrae.

Drakhart and Elandyr'ni, each riding a black dragon, headed for the great plaza in the centre of the city, where they would be met by the Kinu'watan and the Bishu'kagun. What Drakhart had not expected was the massive crowd of Qiri'ar that filled the plaza, standing before the steps of the Grand Temple.

Drakhart could hear...singing?

Drums were beating, punctuating each word sung by the crowds with a deep rumble like thunder. The deep, reverberating voices of the male Qiri'ar seemed to be coming from the back of their throats, warbling, and thrumming. Drakhart could feel the music deep in his chest like the tune gave birth to a creature that reached deep into his heart to touch his soul with its melody. The drum emboldened the lyrics and gave them a heavier weight and meaning. The beat came in time with each syllable.

He could make out the words but had no idea what they meant—save for one: Yishunar. Drakhart recognized that word as the Qiri'aran form for the name of the Aspect Isunath, another name for Tenebrae, also known to the Qiri'ar as Vihl'ku'lehg or Father of Night.

Boom.
Boom.
Boom.
Boom.

Fihn'bul. Thul'nur.
Tyol'nir. Yuhl'gur.
Thulgun. Vihl'ku'lehg.
Kuliduhn. Lhu'paskh.

Boom.
Boom.
Boom.
Boom.

Hefskij. H'ofneer.
Tilmir. Kau'lir.
Yishunar. Caum'lir.
Ith'maefel. Kumu'tlir.

The crowd repeated those words, endlessly, never losing track of the rhythm.

As he landed there came another assault on Drakhart's senses. He could smell the incense and spices burning away in large braziers, amongst the crowd of Qiri'ar who chanted and swayed with the rhythm. While the men chanted, the women danced and fluttered about in the crowd, losing themselves to the throes of prayer and devotion.

Song and dance were an important part of the Qiri'ar religious practice. So much so that when they first encountered the Lau'thso centuries ago, the Lau'thso adopted many Qiri'ar prayer songs, but changed the words to fit their religion.

The dancing women and chanting men added the smell of sweat to the incense and spices, and all of that mixed with the smell of blood.

That was another important facet of the Qiri'ar way of life.

When Isunath landed, Drakhart decided that Gishan'belor was not just the City of Colours. It was the City That Lived; the City of Senses for it was a veritable assault on all five.

The crowd stopped chanting after one final cry, and stood at attention, waiting for their leaders to say something.

Drakhart could see a sea of dark skin and golden tattoos decorated with equally golden jewellery and elegantly garbed in varying colours of fabric.

Elandyr'ni led Drakhart across the raised dais foundation that surrounded the church and towards a massive, burly, middle-aged man and an incredibly old, but incredibly tall woman. Drakhart thought that Elandyr'ni was tall and had never truly believed her when she said she was short for a Qiri'ar. Drakhart had underestimated the extent to which that statement rang true.

The Kinu'watan was a mountain of a man, made entirely of bulging muscles covered in bright gold tattoos. He had to be at least two and a half metres tall, towering well over Drakhart and Elandyr'ni. He looked to be no older than fifty. Drakhart noted that he dressed similarly to how Kanaahn did; he wore no shirt, only a set of red pants and a gold half-skirt. Drakhart could see the hafts of both a greatsword and a greataxe peak over the man's hulking shoulders, fasted by crossing leather straps across his chest.

The Bishu'kagun was only about two-and-a-quarter metres tall, and she looked to be about ten years younger than the Kinu'watan—though Elandyr'ni had mentioned she was closer to twice his age, though no one was quite sure what the actual number was. Magic was involved in that equation, no doubt.

If Elandyr'ni's braid was considered long—wrapping around her neck and shoulders like a necklace—then the Bishu'kagun's hair was endless. She wrapped it around her neck and shoulders like a scarf so that it wrapped around her four times. It was bound by countless rings of gold and silver, and a small four-headed metal spike was embedded in the end of her braid.

The Kinu'watan approached Drakhart and Elandyr'ni and bowed low. "Welcome, Drakhart Ghast. I am Kinu'watan O'lomec." He turned to Elandyr'ni "Welcome home, child. Your people have missed you. Have you served Vihl'ku'lehg well?"

Elandyr'ni returned the bow. "I have. I have composed myself with dignity and excelled—as any of us would under the service of Our Lord. I am sure I have made our tribes proud."

The Bishu'kagun smiled. "Very good, my child." Drakhart noticed she too had a tattooed tongue, like Elandyr'ni. "Welcome, Drakhart. I am Bishu'kagun Iliar'ni."

The Kinu'watan barked orders in Qir'to'ah to several in the crowd, who immediately rushed forward with troughs of uncooked meat for the two dragons that had brought Drakhart and Elandyr'ni here. The animal it came from must have been recently butchered, because Drakhart could smell the fresh blood still in the meat, and it pooled in the bottom of the troughs.

O'lomec shifted his whole body to face Drakhart. "We received your letter, Drakhart. Four thousand Qiri'ar should be easy enough to muster. Though many of us are out travelling Enayra, there are enough here now we could fill those numbers and be prepared to march in a month. We shall take this city with ease."

"You won't be tasked with taking the city alone," Drakhart reiterated. "Before we launch the attack proper, we will besiege the enemy, and demoralize them until our allies arrive. We shall attack together, in unison."

The Kinu'watan scowled. "We could take the city without reinforcements and face minimal losses."

"I am sure you can, Kinu'watan O'lomec. I do not deny the ferocity or strength of your warriors, but Lord Tenebrae prefers a swift and simple victory. He would leave nothing to chance. The Khaleeshir will be there at Ethon, after all. They were able to turn the tide at Xiar—we cannot risk another fluke like that."

Iliar'ni nodded. "You and Our Lord are wise to fear the power of the Khaleeshir. They could turn the tide again. Hope and faith are as powerful a weapon as magic or blade, and no doubt the Khaleeshir are the Darond's only source of either right now. The power of morale is just as important as the power of numbers when it comes to warfare."

The Kinu'watan buried his feelings, but it was clear to anyone with eyes that he was not pleased. He was clearly itching for a fight. The Qiri'ar had been idle for too long for his liking, it seemed.

Drakhart had done his best not to offend the chief. To send the Qiri'ar to war, the Kinu'watan and Bishu'kagun would need to unanimously agree, and now was not the time to make an enemy of the Kinu'watan. He could not just bank on the fact that they served Tenebrae and would immediately agree to please the ancient dragon. In the end, this was

Drakhart's plan, and while it served Tenebrae's needs, and the Qiri'ar had pledged themselves to Tenebrae, they were still afforded their promised autonomy and freedom of choice. Even Tenebrae always asked them to join him but never told them.

Drakhart could respect that, from a certain perspective, but it meant Drakhart needed to walk a careful line in these negotiations. So far they had agreed to join Drakhart, but they could withdraw their consent at any time, sending the Qiri'ar home prematurely.

"Kinu'watan O'lomec. I know your warriors are strong. I have seen Elandyr'ni's power overcome even the most seasoned of veterans on several occasions. I too, mean no offence by my words, I merely wish to be prudent. Much hinges on our success at Ethon, and I do not wish to fail Lord Tenebrae. I'm sure you understand. I promise, when the time comes, your people will have their day of glory on the battlefield. The city must still be taken, but we must be clever."

The Kinu'watan stared hard at Drakhart, searching the Khaleeshir's face.

Drakhart could feel his blood run cold.

Tensions rose for a moment before the Kinu'watan smiled, chuckled a bit, and clapped Drakhart on the back. "You speak pretty words, Khaleeshir, but I see the sincerity behind them. Forgive my zealousness...I am itching for a fight."

"We all are, Kinu'watan O'lomec," Elandyr'ni replied. "But I promise you, the Khaleeshir are not foes to be underestimated."

The Bishu'kagun led Drakhart and Elandyr'ni into the Great Temple. Drakhart and Elandyr'ni would lay the plan before the two leaders of the Qiri'ar, and the Kinu'watan and Bishu'kagun would interject, suggest, and correct as needed. They knew what the Qiri'ar were capable of and knew where the limitations were. Using this knowledge, as well as their own experience, the four of them would craft a plan that would be impregnable when brought before Lord Gruffydd.

The massive ash wood doors creaked as they opened. Drakhart was amazed at both the scale and the simplicity of the interior. For as beautiful and grandiose as the outside was, the inside was kept simpler. The floors were paved with chips of coloured glass and other stones, creating a pattern of colourful mosaics, and the walls were painted in the same manner as the outside, but otherwise, there was no gold, no jewels, no ostentatious statues. Just an altar at the end of the nave where Tenebrae was worshipped, and tombs in the alcoves of the other naves and chancels.

In the centre of the hall was another raised dais, upon which was erected a blue Altimaran marble and gold ciborium. Inside the spacious ciborium had been placed a large, varnished wooden table that had been cut from a massive Estian ironwood—the tree was at least three metres in diameter, and still bore its bark along the outer edges. Atop the massive table was a vellum map, a silver jug of wine, and several cut-crystal chalices. There were no chairs around the table; everyone would be expected to stand for the duration of this meeting.

Drakhart remembered his lessons under Elandyr'ni, as she prepared him to visit Gishan'belor. The Great Temple was meant to be opulent on the outside, but inside, all that mattered was prayer and devotion. Simpler interiors would be less distracting from that goal. Besides, having to clean and maintain a beautiful, gilded interior would only be made harder with all the blood that was spilt within the temple for rituals and magic.

The two Qiri'aran leaders, Elandyr'ni, and Drakhart took their places around the table and examined the map of Enayra.

Drakhart explained his plans for the attack. They would get into Estion, sneak up on and surround Ethon, and hold the city hostage. They would attack the roads, close them, and kill anyone who tried to pass and block any alternative routes through the woods. A portion of the forces would be sent to the Pelchar to take the canal there and ensure no reinforcements could get through to the city that way.

The Qiri'ar would hold these positions until Lord Gruffydd arrived with reinforcements. The boy king would no doubt call for his banners to protect the city, expecting the barons to raise their armies and march to Ethon to break the siege. But when the time came, most of the barons would join Gruffydd if it meant deposing King Anducaerleonis and regaining their power under the future King Llewyth. Drakhart had been working on a plan to keep the call for aide from going out to the remaining three barons who would not join Gruffydd. Once Gruffydd and the other barons arrived with their soldiers, he would reveal his treachery to Ethon, join the Qiri'ar and together they would begin their attack on the city.

Elandyr'ni had suggested executing psychological warfare during the siege. That would allow the Qiri'ar to lay siege to the city and demoralize the soldiers and people without incurring any losses until Lord Gruffydd joined the attack. The Bishu'kagun was open to this idea; she appreciated the power of morale and trickery. It would also act to make the city easier to conquer once the actual fighting started.

The Kinu'watan went along with the plan, so long as he and his soldiers would be allowed to let loose on the enemy army. No one had any intention of murdering the people of Ethon, however. The Qiri'ar were bloodthirsty warriors who revelled in the thrill of the fight and the rush of murder—but only on the battlefield, against an equal or stronger opponent. Qiri'aran culture frowned upon the murder of innocents or those at a disadvantage. There was no glory in a one-sided fight. No challenge. No honour.

Drakhart respected their devotion to their honour. Even the Altimaran army, for all its propaganda and grandstanding, would not have hesitated to slaughter half of Xiar's civilians in retaliation for the siege if they had won the battle. Drakhart doubted Tenebrae would've stopped them, even if he didn't openly encourage it.

Surprisingly, it was the Kinu'watan who suggested a secret weapon that might help totalize their victory at Ethon. "Our traders have brought back whispers from Ethon and across Estion, last winter. Rumours are going around, supposedly leaked by a very drunken Darond agent, that the bones of Ulzar'khimal are hidden somewhere in Estion. Details are sparse as to where, but supposedly the information is accurate."

Elandyr'ni and the Bishu'kagun's eyes widened with fascination.

"You've never mentioned this," the Great Mother said.

"Have you verified these rumours?" Elandyr'ni asked with as much restraint on her excitement as she could muster.

"These rumours haven't been verified, and I wasn't about to raise Great Yishunar's hopes for nothing." The Kinu'watan replied.

From his look—and from what Elandyr'ni had mentioned—he and the Bishu'kagun often enjoyed picking at one another's sore spots. No one was sure if it was malicious, or simply a friendly rivalry, but there was tension in the air between them. Elandyr'ni had also mentioned that the Kinu'watan played a dangerous game and that Bishu'kagun often got the last word.

The Bishu'kagun's gaze was chilling, and even the mighty Kinu'watan seemed to shudder. "I will send some of my Blood Witches if you can lend some warriors. We shall send them to investigate the truth of the matter. If we could revive Ulzar'khimal, it could be a great asset in not only the war against the other nations of Enayra but also the Metallics and the other dragons. They could barely kill it last time."

Drakhart had heard mention of the creature the two leaders spoke of. Ulzar'khimal, or Hope Devourer, was a mountain of a dragon that had been created by Tenebrae through intense experimentation. The creature—for it could not truly be called a dragon—was created by combining several large dragons of each of the eleven dragon clans. According to Elandyr'ni, legend said that some of the beast's heads even came from a few clan leaders. The eleven-headed monster was a terror in its day during the Dragon War and was only killed after many dragons sacrificed themselves in battle. The Metallic Dragons were almost defeated trying to kill the monster. Tenebrae was very interested in reviving his old allies and creations—but he could not find where their bones had been hidden.

"I'm well aware of the boon it would be," the Kinu'watan replied. "But I also know that not all whispers can be trusted. They must be verified."

"Would we even be able to revive a creature like that?" Elandyr'ni asked.

The Bishu'kagun paused for a moment and thought on her answer. She pondered while she played with a bangle on her wrist. Her face pinched inwards as she thought. Then she finally responded. "Normally, the limit for resurrection is three days. Anything revived beyond that limit would simply be a lifeless husk, a slave to your will, but the soul and mind of the person would be lost forever to the void. Advantageously, this creature was a soulless husk before its death; it is not a natural being, and was made through terrible magics...theoretically, it *is* possible. I would need to speak with Lord Yishunar. He would know the best way to go about it. It would require *much* blood and *many* sacrifices, I would say. It would be a delicate procedure and would require many Blood Witches, as well. We'd need time, too; lots of time. This is not a simple spell."

Elandyr'ni could barely hide her excitement.

The Kinu'watan flashed a quick smile. "Even if these rumours are true, and it can be done, it would be done in time to aid our siege. We should not place our hopes upon this. It is something that could only be done *after* Ethon falls, and not before."

If Elandyr'ni struggled to hide her excitement, she found it harder to hide her disappointment.

Drakhart interrupted. "In that case, we can speak with Lord Tenebrae on that later, then. I would consider securing Estion a higher priority than raising Ulzar'khimal from the dead, especially if one must be done before the other. It means nothing if we cannot seize the city."

"I would agree," the Bishu'kagun admitted, if reluctantly. "But I must ask an important question. How do you intend to bring our army across the border with Estion, unnoticed? You have cleverly avoided that caveat so far, but a lot of this plan relies on surprise. Four thousand Qiri'ar are not subtle."

The Kinu'watan chuckled like that was the funniest thing he had heard.

Drakhart's suddenly found himself very parched as his mouth went dry. Before he could even struggle out the words "across the Spine", Elandyr'ni saved him.

"We use Hizhu and the others," she replied simply as if that had always been the plan.

Drakhart wasn't about to disagree, even if he had no idea who or what a Hizhu was.

The Bishu'kagun and Kinu'watan obviously know who or what Elandyr'ni was talking about, because the look of amusement on their face was unmistakable. Clearly, whatever Elandyr'ni had suggested was both incredibly effective, and unorthodox.

But Drakhart would not be ignorant for long.

* * *

After some more discussion, the plans were close to being finalized. The Qiri'ar had enough supplies for the campaign, and anything they didn't have, they didn't need—at least according to the Kinu'watan.

The Bishu'kagun had asked Drakhart to see her before he left for a list of supplies that would be welcomed if Lord Tenebrae could provide them. The Kinu'watan frowned at this but did not argue further. She had also made it clear that she had something *for* Drakhart—more specifically, for Tenebrae. Something he had long since thought lost but would aid him greatly in the war to come.

The Kinu'watan and Bishu'kagun departed after and left Drakhart and Elandyr'ni alone in the Great Cathedral.

There was only one thing left to do before departing, and that was to ask this Hizhu if they would be willing to participate in the plan to smuggle the Qiri'ar into Estion. To this end, Drakhart was shown to a small door set back within a small portico, off the side of the main rotunda. This door led to a narrow and dimly lit set of steps which in turn led below the Great Temple.

Drakhart and Elandyr'ni descended these stairs together. The way, though dangerous, was thankfully lit with small glowing spheres of pale blue light set in alcoves along the wall.

When the steps finally ended, after what felt like an eternity, Drakhart found himself standing in a massive underground cavern. Most of the cavern was a large, still lake, though where Drakhart and Elandyr'ni stood was a short, stone bank. The surface was so smooth and still, it could have passed for glass.

On the far wall, Drakhart could see a roaring waterfall that stretched much of the length of the opposite wall. The waterfall cast a wave of mist across the underground cavern. From deep within the lake, Drakhart could feel a pulsing, like a beating heart. Something from the depths was emitting a dim and pulsing light, but Drakhart couldn't see what it was from where he stood.

"This is what remains of Lake Gishan'belor. It is our new sacred lake," Elandyr'ni explained.

Drakhart was in awe—though he couldn't help but notice the large tunnels that led from this main lake chamber.

Elandyr'ni did not let his curiosity fester for long. "Those tunnels are why we are here."

Drakhart was always impressed and unnerved by how easily she seemed to read his mind.

Things suddenly clicked together in Drakhart's head like flint on steel, and the fire of understanding illuminated his mind. He remembered the discussion he and Elandyr'ni

203

had had in the caverns deep below the Black Citadel. Drakhart remembered who had carved this lake on Tenebrae's orders.

As if on cue, a massive creature extricated itself from the shadows of a tunnel and stopped before Elandyr'ni like a loyal pet. The creature was massive.

This creature was Hizhu, and Hizhu was a brown dragon.

He was as tall as a castle and as wide as a warship. His skin was a muddy brown, with a soft sand-coloured underbelly. Hizhu had crook-shaped horns on either side of his head, that curved forward sharply—forming almost a triangle where the horns bent—extending to the tip of Hizhu's short, flat snout. The creature's nostrils were narrow, his muzzle was flat, and had a severe underbite, with large fangs poking up from beneath his lips.

Hizhu's back was covered in thick scaly armour—thicker than normal dragon scales, with plates almost resembling heavy plates of steel armour—and he had a thick tail that ended in a heavy bone club. The beast's legs were thick like Estian ironwoods, but short, sticking from the creature's side and bending at a sharp angle. Unlike a regular dragon's feet, which pointed forward, Hizhu's feet pointed out at angles. Drakhart could see what looked like vestigial fleshy flaps on the creature's back that were clearly once wings.

Hizhu's eyes were small, almost impossible to spot, and milky white. The dragon was completely blind.

Drakhart understood why dragons often took umbrage with brown dragons and classified them as such. Hizhu did not resemble a dragon, this creature resembled something like a cross between a mountain, a lizard, and a deformed badger.

The ground shook and shifted as the creature moved to better look at Elandyr'ni.

"Hello, child." The dragon's voice was thunder.

Drakhart could feel the bass and timbre reverberate in his chest.

"How are you, Hizhu?" Elandyr'ni asked, petting the creature's snout.

The dragon's voice was slow, methodical. It was like the sound of creaking tree boughs, with a hint of rolling thunder, and the cracking of stone. **"I am well. I was just about to go feed from the leylines. Why have you come here? Who is this?"**

Drakhart stepped forward. "I am Drakhart, honourable Hizhu. I am a Khaleeshir in service to Lord Tenebrae, bonded to Isunath, k'zir of Tenebrae."

"Khaleeshir...?" The brown dragon puzzled through the word as if he had never heard what it said. **"Tenebrae..."**

Drakhart was worried now.

Suddenly, Hizhu's mood changed. He went from calm and pensive to happy and raucous. **"Tenebrae has not forgotten us! And he has managed to turn the Khaleeshir!"**

"Only me, Hizhu," Drakhart elaborated. "The other Khaleeshir still serve the Darond, but Tenebrae intends to deal with them soon."

"Is it he who seeks our help?"

"In a matter of speaking, Hizhu," Elandyr'ni answered. "He has left Drakhart in charge of the destruction of our enemies in Ethon, but we require a way to get there unnoticed. It would mean a certain victory for Drakhart, and a victory for Drakhart is a victory for Tenebrae. And each victory is a step closer to the world he promised."

Hizhu stared at Elandyr'ni blankly. Drakhart wasn't entirely sure if the dragon understood what was being asked of him, or if he was simply mulling it over.

It seemed to be the latter when Hizhu finally responded. **"It would be an easy enough task to tunnel from here to Ethon. You humans cannot use the leylines to travel like us, but we can use the leylines as a guide for your tunnels. Like tracing a new map from an old one. How many are going?"**

"Four thousand Qiri'ar, including myself, Drakhart, the Kinu'watan and the Bishu'kagun," explained Elandyr'ni. "It will be a military march, so there will be supply wagons and pack animals as well."

The brown dragon muttered something under his brother and let out a sigh. **"Give me two months, and the tunnels shall be carved. I will speak with my siblings and alert the Ha'k'dir and Ha'k'nir. They shall agree once they know you come on Tenebrae's authority. I will lead you through the leylines myself."**

Elandyr'ni bowed. "Thank you, Hizhu. You are very kind."

Drakhart wasn't certain if a dragon could blush, but he was almost certain Hizhu was right now—if it could be called that.

"Tell Lord Tenebrae that we shall visit him in Kasaadua soon. We would like to commit our forces once again."

"Are you sure, Hizhu?" asked Elandyr'ni. "You were freed of your service after the last war. Your clan lost many, and your numbers dwindled...the brown dragons fought with distinction. We still sing of their sacrifice."

"But we failed. What good is our honour if we fail? We want to try again." Hizhu did not even wait for a response. His excitement and desire to serve Tenebrae got the better of him, and he bounded off down the tunnel he had come from, off to complete his promised tasks.

When the ground stopped shaking, rocks stopped falling, and the lake once more grew still, Drakhart turned to Elandyr'ni. "What was that?"

Elandyr'ni shrugged. "I should think you recognized a brown dragon; Hizhu to be exact. He's a bit simple...most brown dragons are, but they're kind, and they're harmless—if you're a friend anyway. He's very sweet."

"He's...not what I expected," Drakhart admitted. "Does he speak for the clan?"

"In a way. The Ha'k'dir and Ha'k'nir were severely wounded in the Dragon War. They're shells of their former selves, so while they have the final say on any clan-wide decisions, they do not leave their burrows. They cannot."

Drakhart's puzzlement was visible.

Elandyr'ni elaborated, but her tone grew as grim as her face. "At the Battle of the Kahnair Plains, they battled the Ha'k'dir and Ha'k'nir of the Green Dragon Clan, as well as Aurichalcum and Æris. They did not win the fight...it was four on two, and despite being armoured, and massive, the Ha'k'dir and Ha'k'nir could not fly. Instead of killing the Ha'k'dir and Ha'k'nir, the *noble*—" the word was dripping in ichor as Elandyr'ni spoke it "—Metallic Dragons tore off their limbs and slit open their bellies, then simply left them to expire slowly and painfully. The other brown dragons found them there after the battle had ended and took them back to their caverns to recuperate. Brown dragons cannot breathe fire, or fly, but they've been gifted with other abilities. They can sing the stone and earth to their will, and shape it as they wish, and they can control their size, to shrink or grow at will, like a Metallic Dragon. Using this ability, the Ha'k'nir and Ha'k'dir were able to shrink down, so they could be moved by their clan, but things were grim.

"The Qiri'ar were called to help, but by the time they arrived, the limbs could not be reattached with our blood magic. It had been too long. The wounds were healed, but the limbs could not be saved, and existence became agonizingly painful. Dragons of that age do not eat, they feed off the leylines. They are constantly fed and sustained by the natural magic of the earth. So, unable to stop eating as any wounded animal or human might do, and as none of their children was willing to strike the merciful blow—nor would they allow the Qiri'ar to do the same—the Ha'k'dir and Ha'k'nir live a cursed half-life—ever in agony, but unable to die. They will never be able to produce another clutch of eggs, they will never be able to leave their homes again, and they shall never again know a day without pain or agony.

"The brown dragons' numbers were greatly diminished by the war, and unlike the other clans, only the Ha'k'dir and Ha'k'nir were fertile. They have not been able to replenish their numbers since the Dragon Wars, and every time a brown dragon is slain or dies, their number further diminishes. Those that remain stay hidden deep beneath the earth, tending to the leylines, and singing to the stone as the First Mother commanded.

"This is why Tenebrae released them from their oath of service. He would rather lose a formidable ally than watch another clan go extinct needlessly. He promised them a world where they could live free from the scorn of their supposed 'siblings', but what good is it if the brown dragons don't live to see it? Tenebrae's plans could have gone faster with the brown dragons at his side, but it wasn't worth losing more of his people."

Drakhart was horrified. "Why would the Metallic Dragons do such a thing?"

"The brown dragons were tasked by the Earth Mother with placing and tending to the Mana Cores that keep the magic and nature of Enayra in balance and were tasked with building and maintaining the leylines of the continent. Because of this, they do not often see the light, they feed on the leylines instead of hunting, and they do not fly. As you saw with Hizhu, they've become...different than most dragons because of this lifestyle, and for this, they are shunned and discriminated against. They are othered by their own kind. Even Aurum has treated them harshly; though he revels in his so-called benevolence."

There was hatred in Elandyr'ni's voice now. Drakhart could understand why; more so, Drakhart could see the similar hardships faced by the Brown Dragon Clan and the Qiri'ar Confederacy. Both had been outcasts and oppressed by people who were supposedly their siblings. Both have almost lost their entire way of life. Both had been given a chance to regain their glory and revolt against their oppressors by Tenebrae. But while the Qiri'ar had gradually recovered and regained or reformed much of what was, the brown dragons had not been able to, and would never be able to. Their days would always be numbered.

Drakhart couldn't help but change his opinion of the simple and somewhat child-like Hizhu. "Even after all that, they're still willing to fight...it's admirable."

In truth, Drakhart had a thousand more questions for Elandyr'ni about everything he had just heard. Foremost was how Tenebrae could be so saddened by the death of a dragon clan, but still order the Glorious Hunt to take place. Why had no one ever questioned the actions of the Metallic Dragons against the Brown Dragon Clan? What the Hells was a Mana Core or a leyline?

But now was not the time for ceaseless questions. Those would have to come later when Elandyr'ni was not so angered by the plight of Hizhu and his people, and when Drakhart wasn't wracked with sudden guilt for dragging them back into the conflict, just so he could have personal glory and victory. Drakhart sincerely prayed that he would not be responsible for another dragon clan going extinct.

Chapter XXII

Before the Lau'thso had met the Khaleeshir, the plan to get the boat from the encampment to the lake had originally been to simply carry the boat the several days journey, over land. However, having access to dragons changed the plans significantly. The Khaleeshir and Lau'thso agreed that they would bind the boat to a special harness that would allow four dragons to carry it to the water's edge. Without having to carry the boat, the Lau'thso could move faster over land and conserve their energy.

Once the Lau'thso rendezvoused with the dragons and the boat at Lake Ardona, Kinokaze would go ahead to Ethon to let those waiting for the Khaleeshir know of their impending arrival. The dragons would follow once they received word from Kinokaze.

From there, the dragons would depart to Ethon and arrive before anyone else. While dragons were not hunted or hated in Estion as they were in Altimara, the sight of many dragons of multiple colours flying over the heavily trafficked Lake Ardona trying to keep pace with the Lau'thso and their boat would raise whispers and rumours. The dragons would instead arrive, one by one, posing as envoys of the Darond—something that the people of Ethon were accustomed to seeing.

The Khaleeshir and Kyeit would arrive by boat with the Lau'thso shortly after, while Cecil went ahead—leaving at around the same time as Kinokaze but a few days before those in the boat—to take the horses to Ethon alone. She would hopefully arrive after Kinokaze but before the Khaleeshir.

Kyeit admitted—perhaps for the first time—that this staggered arrival was overly cautious. Whispers would get back that the Khaleeshir had arrived sooner or later, but Kyeit was firm that she preferred later. The longer it took word to get back to Tenebrae that the Khaleeshir were already in Ethon, the better.

Shooter had disagreed. If you can't lie successfully, he argued, just own the truth. It made no sense to lie for a week, only for the same information to get back to Tenebrae regardless.

Kyeit's counter had been that Tenebrae was likely plotting something against Estion in the same way he had plotted an attack on Xiar. They could not give him anything that would give him the advantage. In the end, Kyeit was in charge, and so she had the final call.

The tension between Shooter and Kyeit had been palpable ever since the latter had come clean around the campfire. They were cordial, and Kyeit had apologized, but Shooter had not fully forgiven Kyeit, and he had made that very clear to Kanaahn and the other Khaleeshir. Shooter's mistrust of the Darond only grew because of Kyeit's revelation.

But Kanaahn had his own thoughts weighing on his mind. He and Djall had spent their free time—as the humans accompanied their dragons in bringing the boat to the water—discussing the revelation about Kanaahn's parentage.

Kanaahn had names now, if not faces to put to them. Llilor and Istora Saatus. He would have to do more digging once he reached Ethon. Hopefully the Darond would know someone who could tell him more about his parents.

Djall had been thrilled for Kanaahn. He was as supportive and kind as Kanaahn had been for Djall to meet his parents.

"I'll have to go back and put their names on a proper pair of grave markers once we return to Kula—after I level whatever building Drakhart put up over their graves." Kanaahn had let the joke out, though he knew it might not be a joke. Drakhart had put large amounts of money into rebuilding entire swathes of the city, and while Kanaahn couldn't help but be a little impressed—even happy for the Kulans, if not Drakhart—he had no illusions that Drakhart would not be vengeful enough to ruin the one place Kanaahn held dearest in all of Kula.

"If he has touched the graves of your mother and father, then I shall ensure whatever gravestones replace them will be carved from his bones," Djall vowed.

"I don't think his bones would be big enough, but I appreciate the support, Djall."

That revelation made no difference to Djall. He had made his vow, and he intended to keep it. Instead, he changed the subject. "Where do you sit on Kyeit's revelation?"

Of all the topics they had spent the time discussing, Kanaahn and Djall had not spent time on that one. For the first time since it happened, Kanaahn was forced to consider where he sat in this mess.

As he did with Djall, Kanaahn didn't verbalize his thoughts but shared his mind with the dragon as he sorted through his feelings. It was easier than trying to find the words for his feelings.

On the one hand, Shooter had a point. A very good point. The Darond had constantly lied to the Khaleeshir to control them, and worse still, even those who claimed to oppose the will of the High Council had actively participated in the lies. Whether it was to save face or hide how weak the Darond truly was, it didn't matter. It showed that even those who claimed to be allies did not trust the Khaleeshir, and—at least to Kanaahn—it reflected a desire to prevent the Khaleeshir from taking control of the order again.

Furthermore, knowing just how weak the Darond was did not inspire confidence in them, and it left Kanaahn feeling like any ideas he may have had for winning the war, and defeating Tenebrae, had just been limited severely. It also ruined what little confidence he had finally built in the idea that it *was* possible to win against such odds.

On the other hand, those very feelings of fear and anxiety gave Kanaahn an idea as to why such lies were told in the first place. The Khaleeshir could not be demoralized, and neither could the average Darond member. Knowing this would weaken the morale of an already depleted and withering force. Perhaps it had been done out of some misguided kindness; why add to the stress of the Khaleeshir, who no doubt already feared the possibility of their deaths at the hands of Tenebrae before the end.

More so, Kanaahn could not fully blame Kyeit for her part in this—and by extension Cecil. It went beyond his feelings for the Knight-Commander. It was a genuine understanding of the position Kyeit was put in. It didn't matter if she was their friend, or how long she had known the Khaleeshir, Kyeit had a duty, and that duty came before everything else.

Kyeit had been devoted to the Darond and her duty long before she had ever known the Khaleeshir. She was in line for Dragon Master, as the heir of Osamu, to take up the long life and responsibilities of the recruiter responsible for finding and training the future Khaleeshir. By all accounts, she may very well outlive Kanaahn and the others. How could she compare such temporary things as friendship to her eternal duty? It was always a monumental weight upon her shoulders, even if Kyeit didn't show it.

In the end, Kanaahn was no closer to coming to a definitive decision about where he stood on the matter.

"You could think and think in circles, and you're still not closer to making up your mind," Djall chided. "How do you decide on anything like that?"

"How can I decide without all the information? I don't believe we have it all yet. There's so much more to all this—there must be."

Djall snorted. "Or maybe that's what you tell yourself so that you don't have to decide?"

"Or maybe, as Khaleeshir, I need to learn to listen to both sides and try to find the common ground between them. We are the bridge between the races, and the bridge between nations, but should we not also be the bridge between people?"

Djall laughed.

The laugh of a dragon was an odd thing. Despite being able to speak like a human, they did not laugh like humans. When dragons laughed, it sounded like short, sharp breathing—almost as if they were hyperventilating. But there was also a whooping, choking sound, like a bird call. Kanaahn was never ready to hear it; the laughter of a dragon always sounded wrong.

"When did you stop acting on impulse? Are you certain you are still the Kanaahn I bonded with?"

Kanaahn did not laugh along. He did not joke back. There was no sarcasm. He knew full well what had aided this change.

Djall did too.

"I am sorry, Kanaahn."

Kanaahn placed a hand on Djall's snout and stroked his thumb against the small, rough scales there. "I know, Djall. I don't take offence. But sometimes it all comes back..."

"I know. We share a mind." Djall nudged Kanaahn gently with his snout.

"Between all the lies, the last few weeks since we came to Estion and Xiar, it's given me some things to think and consider about myself, and the kind of person I want to be— the kind of person I *need* to be—for Enayra's sake."

"Do you still want revenge on Drakhart?" The dragon still burned for vengeance against the former ally. Though he had killed Ölüm at Xiar, Djall's hatred of Drakhart had not abated. His quarrel was with Drakhart as much as it had been with Ölüm. Drakhart had scarred Kanaahn for life. Djall would not forgive that, or any of the other hurts he inflicted upon the Khaleeshir or the world.

Kanaahn answered without hesitation. "It's no longer just about revenge. It's about correcting a mistake. Drakhart chose evil, and he joined Tenebrae. He may be against us, but he is still Khaleeshir, and I don't doubt that Tenebrae will ensure he is just as powerful a villain as he would be a hero. I cannot in good conscience leave something like that to roam Enayra unchecked after this war ends."

"I can still feel the hate you have for him, deep within you," Djall noted.

"Yes, I still hate him. I still feel anger when I think of the things he said and did—when I think of how he gloated about killing our families. I hate him for the scar he gave me, and for how he betrayed us. I don't think that will ever go away, at least not for a long time." Kanaahn's fists clenched. "But Drakhart made his choices, and *he* is responsible for the consequences. I will hold him accountable for the hurts he caused."

Kanaahn sat silent, motionless for a little longer, before entirely changing the subject. If he dwelled too long on these memories, they would lead to a dark place.

So instead, Djall changed the subject once more, and he and Kanaahn spent time talking over things they'd like to do with their time while training in Ethon— it would all depend on how long they would be staying in the capital.

One thing Kanaahn had wanted to do since Xiar was ask the Darond for a proper sword master. Someone to train him how to properly use the katana he had inherited from his father. Kanaahn had never had any formal training, except some extra training he had done with Kyeit, which had only allowed Kanaahn to correct general errors. Otherwise, Kanaahn had just been swinging the sword around in whatever way felt most comfortable or made more sense, and while he had survived this long, the ability to swing a sword did not a master make. Eventually, Kanaahn would meet someone more skilled and deadly than he, and it would end poorly if he had no proper training. Seeing the artful mastery of the blade that Lord Yoritomo Genji possessed during the Siege of Xiar had only made Kanaahn pine for a proper teacher. Surely the Darond could get someone for him.

"It's not like you to think about your survival," joked Djall.

"What do you mean?"

"I seem to remember you leaping over the wall at Xiar and throwing yourself into the thick of the battle. Kyeit and Arial had to save you."

"I was doing just fine until I fought that captain!" Kanaahn argued.

Djall chuckled, slapping his tail against the ground. "I do enjoy pushing your buttons."

"You're a mean lizard," Kanaahn teased. "Go find some bugs to eat and leave me be."

Djall flapped his wings, playing along with Kanaahn's teasing. "I am no lizard, and I do not eat bugs! But I will go find something to eat. I am hungry."

"You're always hungry."

Djall chuckled one last time before departing on another hunt.

* * *

Shooter was spending his time in conversation with Risasi. He sat by the water's edge with his feet in the lake, Risasi napped in the sunlight as they waited.

"I don't trust them," Shooter seethed to Risasi.

"This is not new information," Risasi replied.

"I trust them less now, then!"

"Not a surprise, to me."

Shooter narrowed his eyes at his partner. "Just listen."

Risasi shifted his head. "I am. I am also responding."

Shooter took a deep breath and admittedly struggled not to smile. "You're a terrible sounding board."

Risasi's lips curled back in a weird smile. "That's because I'm a dragon."

"Yes. You're very good at that, I suppose," Shooter replied.

Risasi always knew how to calm Shooter down when he got heated. It wasn't often Shooter let his emotions boil over like this—Shooter much preferred to run from his emotions as a point of fact, but when it happened, Risasi was always there with dry humour and wit to smooth everything over or at least give Shooter a head start.

Risasi had not appreciated the lies told by the Darond either, but he was not as wounded by them as Shooter had been. Shooter didn't like being lied to on principle. Which was a great irony because he quite often resorted to lying himself.

"Why are humans so afraid of the truth?" Risasi asked, this time serious.

Shooter sighed and laid back on the grass. "Probably because we're so afraid of what other people might think of us. We fear the opinions of people we've never met."

"How honest," retorted Risasi. "Would it not be fair to say that is why the Darond kept that secret from you?"

Shooter shrugged. "I suppose so. I still don't appreciate it. I feel like I'm fighting the Darond as much as we are Tenebrae...and I don't know who we know less about."

"That *does* bother me. More than the lying."

"What does?"

"Not knowing what to expect from Tenebrae. We have all these Darond spies everywhere, and yet we can never predict Tenebrae's next move with any certainty. All we have are educated guesses and maybes. The first thing Valence taught us was to never fly straight into a thunderhead."

The irony of that advice was lost on Risasi for the moment.

"It looks calm on the outside, but it could be your death because you never know what it's like inside. Yet here we are, expected to go into a continent-spanning war without knowing what the other side can field."

"That frustrates me too, to be honest." Shooter sat up and leaned back on his forearms, kicking his legs in the cool water. "I wish...well, that's not important."

Risasi didn't push the subject, but he did change it. "You don't intend to leave the Darond, do you?"

Risasi acted cool and collected, but Shooter could feel the worry bleed across their connection. Shooter's response was soothing but honest. "No. Not yet. I don't plan to—I don't want to, but I can't speak for the future, that is. If they keep lying to us like this, maybe I will. I don't know if I'd go over to Tenebrae unless I had a very good reason. I don't know what I'd do, but I know I'd uphold my promise to free the Lau'thso, and maybe I'd start fighting Tenebrae in my own way."

"You have changed," Risasi mused.

"How's that?"

"You seem so dedicated to your role as Khaleeshir, compared to when we first met. You never wanted any of this, as far as I remember."

Shooter leaned forward. He stared at his reflection in the rippling water. It wasn't much different than the last time he had checked it...but the person inside was not the boy who left Kula months ago. "Xiar changed that. Xiar changed a lot of things..."

Shooter knew he wasn't the only person. Everyone else had felt the jarring shock that was the Siege of Xiar. Some of the scars Xiar left had been for the better, such as Shooter's commitment to being Khaleeshir, and the bond it forged between rider and dragon. Others were haunting, gaping wounds that would never truly heal. They came and crawled through your mind in the dead of night. The sounds of dying. The scream of children whose mothers and fathers had been crushed by debris or killed by a trebuchet's stone. The wailing of soldiers as they died in horrific ways...or perhaps, worse, the sound of the maimed and broken, who would live, but never again be whole—in mind or body. The metallic stench of blood, of ozone from the magic, of flesh and bone, broken and butchered by steel. There was the smell of sweat that clung to soldiers, the smell of shit and piss as bowels emptied themselves when hearts stopped beating.

Battle and war had made things real for Shooter. He was not just gallivanting across the countryside like some hero-of-old tilting at the Joust, saving maidens, and being worshipped by the common folk. He was helping to prevent another Xiar. He was helping save those children from being killed and murdered by invading soldiers. He was saving mothers and fathers from the bell tower coming down on them and their families.

He was helping people like Hau'farh free their families, and their people, from slavery. From being worked to death until there were no Lau'thso left. Until an entire people had been erased from the face of the earth to feed a war machine like wood or charcoal fuelled a furnace.

Risasi changed the subject again. "Will you reach out to Amber again when we reach Ethon?"

Shooter pulled some grass from the muddy bank. "Why should I?"

Risasi adjusted his wings. "Because you love her."

"If she wanted to hear from me she would have responded."

Risasi looked out on the water, watching a small dot on the horizon glide past at a calm but constant pace. Likely some passenger barge or fishing boat. "Maybe she's unable to. Drakhart is likely cracking down on any who might be an ally to us. He knew Amber, and I'm sure he knew the asset she might be. She's a prolific information dealer, after all."

"Or maybe she hates my guts for just leaving without a word."

"Or maybe that's the guilt talking."

"Or maybe I don't want to talk about this anymore." Shooter stood up and pulled his feet from the water. He didn't bother putting his socks or boots back on—they'd just be soaked through—and he walked over to where the group had set up camp.

"Humans," muttered Risasi. He shook his horned head.

The dragon was not upset or hurt, but from everything he had learned of Amber from Shooter and the other Khaleeshir, Risasi was close to flying to Kula himself, finding her, and bringing her to Ethon so she could smack some sense into his partner.

* * *

Arial had gone for a flight with Adalinda, something that the two had not gotten to do often since they left Xiar. It was something she desperately needed.

Arial used whatever spare time she had to study her grimoires and practice her magic, but whatever time she had left was often used to listen to her friends—new and old— discuss their problems and feelings. Most of the time it was the same issues ad nauseam, but Arial listened all the same. Sometimes she offered advice she knew they'd never take, but most times it was enough to simply let them talk and air out their feelings, so they didn't explode their feelings over one another.

In return, Arial would vent to Adalinda, who had picked up her partner's uncanny ability to listen to even the most mundane and asinine of problems without wanting to commit murder or explode from boredom.

"I'm going to kill all of them," Arial fumed. *"Arkas is so clearly crushing on Cecil, but he refuses to admit it. He just keeps talking about how he wants to hunt this terrain for a challenge like I don't see what he's doing by obfuscating the issue."*

Now, of course, Arkas had never *said* anything of the sort, but Arial knew her best friend well enough to notice. She could see the look in his eyes whenever Cecil talked. The way he hung on every word, and how his eyes lit up when she spoke to him—which was seldom unless it was a group conversation. Arkas had always been quiet in Kula. He didn't usually speak to strangers, and only really spoke around his friends—and eventually the dragons—but whenever Cecil spoke to the group, Arkas used the opportunity to suddenly pipe up, sometimes even joke. He would never have done that around relative strangers like Kyeit and Cecil before the dragons had entered their lives. It took Arkas too long to grow comfortable with people.

No one else would have noticed this change—indeed, no one else did, but Arial knew, Arial *always* knew.

"I have no idea how Cecil feels in return because she's just a wall of mystery herself. Then there's Shooter and the bullshit he's pulling with Amber and that stuff with the bard. I can't even begin to explain how disappointed I am in him right now. Ugh! And then there's Kanaahn and Kyeit. I could kill them both."

For a change, Adalinda got involved. *"What's wrong with the two of them? I ask out of both concern and curiosity."*

"A love so dramatic that even the dragons are interested," Arial bemoaned. She massaged her temples. *"Thank you for letting me vent like this. I appreciate it. You have to hear it all through my head, and then hear me complain about it later."*

"We are partners, and you would do the same for me," Adalinda replied.

Adalinda banked left, dipping just a bit so she could keep an eye on the small bundle of people that moved beyond the tree line. It was the Lau'thso and Kyeit on their way to the water's edge. Adalinda and Arial watched their progress with interest.

"I would," Arial admitted. *"And yet you never vent to me. You must have something to complain about."*

Adalinda thought for a moment. Despite her words and knowing in her heart that Arial would do the same for her, Adalinda had never actually considered it. Dragons didn't vent. They didn't complain. If they had a problem, they fought it out or went for a flight to clear their minds. Humans were odd creatures, to be sure...but some of their traditions might benefit dragons. How many fights and feuds could be avoided by venting? How much different would dragons be if they had a little more compassion and a little less arrogance born from their longevity?

Adalinda blinked. *"I don't have many things to complain about, but...you call it gossip?"*

Arial smiled. *"Am I the first human to gossip with a dragon?"*

"Dragons gossip all the time; but not with humans," Adalinda explained. *"I am happy to change that. There is much I cannot gossip about with my siblings."*

"Like what?" Arial asked, leaning down in the saddle.

"Are you aware of Risasi's infatuation with Kinokaze?"

"Can dragons do that?" Arial asked, confused. *"I didn't think dragons could breed outside of their clan."*

"It is not normally done, but I do not know if it is possible. It seems being bound to humans has—as Osamu said—changed us as well as you. He's as tail over horns as Kanaahn is for Kyeit."

Arial's smile widened. *"Then he's got it bad."*

"Very."

"Any other infatuations I should know about?" asked Arial. Venting was fun, but Arial had forgotten how good gossiping could be as well. She did this often with Amber back in Kula; being an information broker, Amber had the best gossip in town.

"Fyete and Djall," replied Adalinda. *"I don't know if it's mutual, and Fyete is more subtle with her attraction than Risasi is, but I've noticed the signs. She is attracted to him, but I don't know if Djall is aware or reciprocates the feelings. Fyete is subtle like her partner. If we had not been nestmates, I would not have noticed."*

Arial had questions. *"You were hatched and raised like nestmates, like siblings. Is that not weird for dragons? It seems like it would be like falling in love with your brother or sister."*

Adalinda shook her head. *"Normally, dragons mate within their clan. All dragons of a single clan are technically related. They are all children of the Ha'k'dir and Ha'k'nir—or them and one of their consorts. Though if you go far enough back in the bloodline everyone is descended from the Hu'k'nir and Ha'k'dir. Eventually, the bloodlines all mix, of course. So long as you are not full or half-siblings, and do not share a grandsire, it's not an issue. This case is odd entirely because none of us are of the same clan, yet we are still nestmates. To say nothing of inter-clan mixing. Aside from the last part, I see no issue with it."*

Arial was confused, even a little weirded out. She couldn't image having feelings for Kanaahn. They had no blood relations, but they had been raised side by side like siblings, and she considered Kanaahn her brother. Then again, there was a period where she had a small crush on Arkas when they were younger, and Shooter once had a crush on Drakhart for a few weeks a few years before. Maybe it wasn't as weird as she thought.

"Could anything come of a union between dragons of a different clan or colour?" asked Arial.

Adalinda thought. It went from a moment of thinking, or quite a deep conundrum for her. Eventually, she responded, just as confused and curious as Arial. *"I...don't know. No dragon has ever tried."*

"Perhaps we'll live to see that first together."

* * *

Arkas crouched low in the grass. He kept as low to the ground as he possibly could, just as his father had taught him. Though hunting in grasslands was different than hunting in the dunes and rocky crags of the Altimaran desert. That was why he was doing it.

Arkas relished the challenge of the grasslands as he had in the forests. It was a new territory and a new terrain. Grass and trees and bushes were easier to hide in, but the animals were far more sensitive to the slightest snap of a branch or even just the whiff of humans.

Whereas in Altimara, the animals were used to humans passing through to hunt, and it was easier to mask your sound on the sand—though there was a severe lack of hiding places, except behind the crests of dunes and in rocky caverns and crags in mesas.

The animals in Altimara were more dangerous, but in Estion they were meatier, but more skittish and prone to fleeing rather than fighting back.

Even the temperature made a difference. Arkas could spend far longer hunting in the woodlands or grasslands of Estion than in the deserts of Altimara. He consumed less water and wine, and fewer resources, and he wasn't at risk of heatstroke or sunburn. He could hunt for hours or days on end if he wanted so long as he was properly stocked on supplies and found somewhere to shelter from the elements.

True to his father's upbringing and livelihood, Arkas was a hunter at heart. The sport was thrilling to him. The tracking, the stalking, the kill. The feel of his heart in his throat as Arkas pulled back the bowstring. Putting the animal down quickly, humanely. It was still meant to be a respectful transaction. The animal was dying so another could live and eat. One life for another. Arkas always said a prayer after each kill and was sure to thank the animal.

Fyete was up above, hunting her own quarry from the sky—but Arkas refused to use her eyes to assist in his hunt. It wasn't fair to the animal, or sportsman-like of him. The animal didn't have a second set of eyes in the sky, and neither would Arkas.

Today, Arkas's quarry was deer. A buck specifically. He had picked up on the creature's trail early in the morning. Arkas had pursued the creature through most of the day, carefully stalking the deer as he meandered through the fields, eating grasses, chewing its cud, and drinking from springs.

Arkas had caught sight of the creature once, earlier during his hunt. The buck's antlers showed its youth; no more than six points, but his body was lean and well-muscled. The buck had been eating well this year. He was alone; either he hadn't formed a harem this breeding season, or he had lost to a bigger, stronger male.

Arkas had spent the better part of the day following the deer at a distance. He walked, slowly, carefully, following the tracks, watching the deer graze, or run through the woods, but now, the deer had stopped. It had been a good hour of waiting and watching. For the most part, the buck had spent that time resting and grazing some more. It didn't look like it was going anywhere any time soon.

Now would be Arkas's chance to strike.

He pulled his bow from his back, slowly, quietly, and nocked an arrow. Arkas sat crouching in the grass, holding his breath as he took aim. Right in the middle of the deer's chest, where the heart was.

Arkas drew back the bowstring and felt a rush as the bow went taut against his fingers. His muscles in his arms and back flexed as he felt the weight of the draw.

Arkas held his breath, checked his aim, counted to three, and let the arrow go. The wooden shaft slid past his fingers, against the bow. He felt the fletching brush past him. He felt the bowstring twang, and he felt it reverberate through his hands and arms.

Time seemed to slow as the arrow slipped through the air. The deer didn't even look up as the arrow pierced its side. It cried out, but it didn't run. It fell on its side, kicking its front legs out slowly as the life left the creature's body.

Arkas left his hiding place and walked over to the deer. It hadn't been the cleanest shot. Arkas could tell before he had even reached the deer. He had pierced the creature through part of its spine. Arkas swore to himself; that he had been distracted when he made the shot. He could have done better. Now the creature was dying, but it wasn't instantaneous as Arkas had hoped. The creature was struggling to depart this world. Without wasting a breath, Arkas drew his dagger, and cut into the creature's neck. It stopped struggling within seconds.

That was not how Arkas wanted this to go, but life never went how you wanted it.

Arkas watched as the blood welled from the neck wound and pooled on the damp ground. It stained Arkas's hands and fingers.

"I'm sorry I could not do better, but thank you for your sacrifice," Arkas whispered to the departed deer.

There was an irony to hunting that Arkas had preferred to ignore...he felt far more sympathy for killing this creature and causing it to suffer than he had at Xiar. Xiar had inflicted wounds—both physical and mental—on all of Arkas's friends, but it scarred Arkas differently. It had scarred him because it did not scar him.

Arkas could remember every kill. The boy not much older than him that had leapt over the wall like he was arriving at his wedding night, proud to be one of the first of his battalion over the wall, only to get an arrow to the eye and a second to his throat. He fell back, grabbing at his neck, screaming, gurgling, spilling up blood. He fell back and tumbled back down to the ground below. Arkas remembered the wet crunch his body made as it hit the ground below.

There was the old man who was trying to flee his duel with two Xiaran soldiers. He was wounded, limping like an old ram with a broken leg. He was scared, begging for mercy. Arkas put an arrow through the back of his skull just like he would an old, wounded ram. It was the merciful thing to do.

A young Altimaran woman, who fought like a veteran and had the hardened, battle-scared face of one. Her attitude was that of someone who had seen many years of service. She climbed over the wall with a battle axe, and swung wide, carving deep swaths into the Xiaran defenders. Arkas put an arrow in her knee, but she refused to go down. Arkas engaged with his daggers and watched the woman's life drain from her eyes as she gasped for breath. His dagger was buried to the hilt in her throat, and her blood was slick on his gloved hands.

Arkas had handled these kills as practically as he would hunting an animal. A life for a life. A simple transaction. It was his life, or the life of his friends or allies, for the life of an enemy. It was war; that was how war worked. The other side would not show him any quarter if the positions were reversed.

Yet, Arkas did not thank his human kills for giving their lives for him. He did not apologize to those whom he failed to kill on the first shot. He felt no compassion, no sadness, nothing at all. At times, he got lost in the heat of battle and almost relished in the feeling of his knives cutting through flesh and bone. Severing arteries and veins; feeling the warm blood run over his fingers.

This scared him the most. He was a hero of Enayra, a Khaleeshir. He was meant to be a beacon of hope and inspiration. Magnanimous and kind to all—even the Altimarans he fought would be amongst the people he would have to look after and watch over after the war was over and Tenebrae was defeated.

No. Arkas was wasting time. There was no point puzzling this over. What he had done he had done because that was war. The soldiers got their quick death—or as quickly as Arkas could manage. They would have done the same to him, though they might not have shown him the same courtesy. There was no point pondering over the morality of it all. It was a moot point.

Arkas sighed and wasted not another minute. He began to field dress the dear while he waited for Fyete to return.

Fyete touched down a few minutes later, with a wild boar in her maw. *"You called?"*

Arkas didn't look up from his work as he skinned and quartered the deer. "Are you okay if I put these in the saddle bags?"

"Do I ever complain?"

Arkas smiled. "No, I suppose you don't."

Fyete put down the boar. "You're dwelling again."

"I am not."

"You were though. I can feel it. I am literally connected to your mind at every waking moment. You can't lie to me."

Arkas did not stop with the deer, but he didn't respond either.

"Arkas."

"It's not normal for humans to feel that way, is it? All my friends understand the practicality of the kill. But all the death around us, both on our side and on the enemy's side...even the civilians...it affects them but to me? All that death—I don't feel anything. I feel bad for the civilians, but I can't do anything but kill more enemies. And I am sorry to see my allies fall...but I can't do anything except defend them by killing more enemies. As for our enemies, it's hard to feel sorry for someone who is trying to kill me. I kill them because it's me or them."

"I see nothing wrong with what you've done, or how you feel. It is perfectly normal for dragons."

"I'm not a dragon."

"You're part dragon now, thanks to the ritual."

"I've always been like this. When we killed Jerrin and those Town Watch members last year, I had the same feelings. Dare I say I even enjoyed getting revenge on them? I remember sticking a knife into the skull of one of Jerrin's underlings and I...enjoyed it. It felt like retribution for everything they did. I felt *better*."

Fyete took a small nibble out of the boar's haunch. "You should. The Town Watch were terrible people, they did terrible things. They almost hurt Arial. You did the right thing by killing them, and you made Kula a better place."

Arkas sighed and ran his forearm across his sweating forehead. A dribble of blood smeared across his temple. "You are the worst impulse control."

"I only speak fact." Fyete had gone from nibbling on the haunch of the boar to ripping deeper into the flesh. Blood stained her muzzle. "You are not broken, Arkas. There is nothing wrong with you. You care deeply for me and your friends. You are not some unfeeling, heartless monster, but you will do what you must to protect us. You do not freeze when you must act. That is the sign of a true hunter—a true *hero*. It's practical, and I admire it."

Arkas smiled. He quickly finished quartering the deer and began loading it into the saddle bags. "Let's get going."

Fyete frowned. "I was just digging in."

"Bring it with you. You knew I wasn't going to be long."

Fyete picked the boar up in her fangs again. *"But I was hungry."*

Arkas shook his head. "I repeat, you are the worst impulse control."

Chapter XXIII

The departures had gone as planned.

Kinokaze and Cecil left first—though not together—and three days later, a message arrived from Ethon declaring that the Khaleeshir were expected, and preparations were being made for their arrival. Cecil had not yet arrived at the capital, but based on when she left, and the fact she was leading several horses, she would likely arrive within the week.

With Kinokaze's confirmation, the dragons had departed next. They left the night previous and would be in the capital in a few days.

The Lau'thso, the Khaleeshir, and Kyeit would leave together in the morning, as planned. By all estimations, the boat would be in Ethon's harbours within a week if the weather kept kind.

Loading up the boat had been simple. The Lau'thso quickly and skilfully launched the longboat into the water with ease. Getting in was the hard part—for the Khaleeshir at least. They had never seen a boat in person before, let alone having sailed in one. They stumbled and nearly fell into the lake, but the Lau'thso were patient and helpful and were able to get the Khaleeshir seated at the back near Hau'farh.

Kanaahn noticed the chieftain standing up against the rear stempost, standing behind a massive hide drum. His hands firmly grasped two thick wooden sticks. Kanaahn had heard tales of the Lau'thso sailing songs; prayers sung in honour of the Mother of Oceans in exchange for her protection against storms and hardship on the high seas—or any other waters for that matter.

Kyeit had explained that the Lau'thso had inherited much of their current repertoire from Qiri'aran converts who had intermingled with the Lau'thso when they first arrived in Enayra. While many of the tunes and songs were taken from the Qiri'ar, the words were the original songs sung by the first Lau'thso to arrive. The tunes had changed, but the language had not.

The songs served a dual purpose as well, aside from being a prayer for safety, they helped the rowing teams keep time while they worked. Though neither Enayra nor Lau'thso historians could decipher which of the two purposes had been the original reason for these songs. It mattered not to the Lau'thso people, however.

Once everyone was boarded and seated on their rowing benches, Hau'farh called out what Kanaahn took to be orders in Lau'thuk. Like a well-oiled and uniform machine, every oar was quickly in an oar lock and every hand was on an oar.

Hau'farh called out a few more times, and when he received no response, he began to beat the drum. Kanaahn could feel the rhythm in his soul...it felt...familiar. Like he had heard this song before. The beat of the drum was slow and methodical, and the rowers kept time with the slow beat. They rowed with their whole bodies as if it were a dance. Not a single person was out of step.

Boom.
> *Boom.*
Boom.
> *Boom.*

Boom.
> *Boom.*
Boom.
> *Boom.*

Boom.
> *Boom.*
Boom.
> *Boom.*

And then, they started to sing. The song was in a format Kanaahn was familiar with from his days at the Broke Neck Camel; it was a call-and-response song. During the chorus, the whole crew sang, including Hau'farh, bearing their souls and voices to the sky above. The drum helped set the beat.

Weeshaal raaind na saair, nulal yel had luusnal?
Wardweesdur uyas wuarda naa uf wur luus Lau'Wa!

Wed nuacad raish uyas wuarda naa nuyas yel iwa relin?
Waish nuacal lees na Lau'Wa rusul raraain nuus runal!

Ylwen zulal, yees iid lees na husainul,
Vas yel ulur hiair unuac lees Lau'Wa rusul!

Weesun yasraiad I iw relin, uh nulal yel had luusnal?
Da naa yasr rusul ulr hiair al heesn al uurd railar yasrusal!

Had daish caasna naish daral I al hulras freer iw rden?
Waish yuasnal iaid dual waildascui yaral rayalr len!

Ylwen zulal, yees iid lees na husainul,
Vas yel ulur hiair unuac lees Lau'Wa rusul!

Ni weerd raish sulun uf wuarda naa, uh nulal yel had daish?
Dees eel'd aailna rairud ulur nuar, na runal radeel ulur faish!

Gaish cuasard li wardweesdr lees had relin, uyas wuarda ruryal?
Dees fuiwal waish ulur Lau'Wa fardeel al yaral nira yurra!

Ylwen zulal, yees iid lees na husainul,
Vas yel ulur hiair unuac lees Lau'Wa rusul!

By the middle of the song, the call and response had been abandoned, and everyone chanted as loud as they could across the lake, rowing unceasingly all the while. Their voices echoed across the lake, and Kanaahn could even see some fishing boats and transport barges stop to watch—and listen—to the longboat skim across the surface of Lake Ardona, singing their hearts out to their goddess. It was beautiful.

Dees weshud ulur na duacunrad, nees fuiwal waish na her.
Wees naish raal nisaairailur yusnud ul hulras haasral ner!

Dees weshud ulur na duacunrad, nees weshud ulur fardel.
Dees laardal waish er runal al nasailcal dud waish laiad naas radeel!

Ylwen zulal, yees iid lees na husainul,
Vas yel ulur hiair unuac lees Lau'Wa rusul!

Even after the singing ended, the pounding of the drum remained, forever keeping time with the rowing. The drum was joined by other instruments: the dipping of oars into the water, the splashing as the wood cut through the waves, and the grunt of rowers pulling them back out again.

"What was that song about?" asked Arkas politely.

Hau'farh replied, not missing a single drumbeat. "In Common, it's known as the Song of Mother's Mercy. It's a song of thanks, for the Mother of Ocean's protection against storms and other ill omens. We beseech her for her mercy and in return offer up our souls and our voices in song. Legend says this was the very song my people sang when Enayra came into view on the horizon."

"That was beautiful," Arial said.

Kanaahn could almost see the faintest glimmer of a tear in Hau'farh's eye as he replied. "My dear Arial, you should hear it when it's sung across the decks of a thousand ships at the start of every sailing year. Tens of thousands of voices and a thousand drums are raised in unison to the Mother of Oceans and her glory. It is the song we use to start every voyage; it is sacred to us."

222

It was Shooter who responded. "One day, the sound of Lau'thso singing will once more be heard from the seas around Lau'than, and every corner of the ocean as they sail."

"One day Enayra will be free," added Kanaahn.

Hau'farh did not respond, and everyone ignored the tears that now freely rolled down his face. His people were facing great hardships now, and he had been lucky to escape, but he refused to leave them to their fate, and now he was no longer alone in his fight to free them. For this, Hau'farh would be eternally grateful.

Almost sixty thousand Lau'thso men, women and children had been dragged off into captivity, and the Khaleeshir were determined to return each and every one of them to their homes and their boats by the time this war had finished.

No matter how long it took. No matter the cost.

Chapter XXIV

Ruoth was a bartender, and an innkeeper. His job afforded him a closeness with his clientele and a certain level of trust that allowed him to see many things and hear just as many whispers; things that no one else would be privy to. He bore witness to private conversations between friends. Stolen moments between lovers. Secrets between thieves and liars. People cheating at games. Soldiers whispering about their orders. Spies slipping notes between one another.

In nowhere else but a tavern could so many disparate people come together and mingle. Some historian Ruoth once knew claimed that history happened in the halls of power, and on the field of battle—Ruoth knew this man was wrong. History might be recorded on the battlefield, or in palaces, but it always, *always*, started in a tavern.

Ruoth had to *pretend* not to notice any of the things he saw, of course. That was as much a part of the transaction as collecting payment for food, drinks, and board. But Ruoth always kept track of everything he heard and reported anything of interest to the Darond. As one of Ruoth's old friends once said: if you ever wanted to know a town's secrets, all you had to do was go talk to the local barkeep.

In the past few weeks, Ruoth had noticed much, and all of it was troubling.

The horrible death of Banalor was the catalyst for a wave of change that swept over Felidrun and blanketed the town with tension. It had been Ruoth who found the boy in the ally, torn to shreds by magic. Blood flooded the cobbles. It was horrible.

Ruoth could only imagine how the boy's adoptive father felt; Ruoth knew about the boy's family, and where his future lay once Duke Gruffydd had passed. He had expected there to be a drastic reaction—a manhunt for the one responsible, at the very least, but none came. Lord Gruffydd kept to himself and hadn't been seen outside his halls, aside from briefly, when he departed for the funeral.

There was no manhunt, no inquiry, no door-to-door investigation. There was only silence.

There were, however, whispers of a mysterious visitor who had been seen at the estate of Lord Gruffydd and disappeared just as quickly. Since that supposed visit, things changed further. The soldiers and local guards were coming by the Sleeping Soldier less and less, and in their place came tax collectors, and with greater frequency.

The poll tax went up. The fees for using the lord's mill and the communal ovens went up—though luckily Ruoth had his own ovens, on which he paid a smaller tax than the fee would be. Taxes went up on alcohol sales, and on his business revenue and the value of his establishment, and those taxes were now paid weekly. Then came the new taxes. There was a new tax on malts and cereals. A new tax on distilleries. A new tax on yeast. A new tax on hops. A new tax on the fucking windows—sixteen copper marks per window, a full silver sliver if it had stained glass in it. Some of the locals had gone about smashing their windows and filling in the gaps with bricks to avoid the tax. The Duke responded by declaring a *former* window tax—a one-time payment owing the value of two silver slivers for the loss of revenue.

How long before they started demanding payment for how often one used the garderobe? No doubt a tax made payable in only gold crests, at the rate things were going.

Ruoth was starting to get angry.

He was also starting to piece things together. Ruoth had been a soldier once; he knew the only time lords and kingdoms raised taxes to that extent was when they were trying to fill their coffers with as much money as possible, and there was only one reason for that: war. War costs money, and someone had to pay. Normally, nobles would take out a loan from a banker—or a wealthy merchant—or take a loan from the Crown, and pay it off with war booty, plunder, and the future earnings of whatever territory they annexed after the war. It was easier, it was faster, and it was less taxing—no pun intended—on the common folk, who were already expected to be called up as citizen levies and serve and die for their country.

For those to whom credit and loans were not an option, the only other avenue for raising funds was to raise existing taxes and create new taxes. It was harder on the people, so it was usually only done if the war was expected to be quick. If tax revenues were being hoarded, it meant they weren't expecting to require citizen levies; the people's service would be monetary.

It told Ruoth all he needed to know. Lord Gruffydd was preparing to march his soldiers off to battle. It would be a quick war, but it was to be a secret strike at the enemy because he hadn't announced it. Furthermore, this war would not have the blessing of the Crown, because the king had not declared war on anyone recently. This left Ruoth to assume only the worst: Lord Gruffydd was preparing for revolution, and he was planning to place himself on the throne.

The horrible death Banalor suffered, the way he died, and the visit from the mysterious stranger in black only helped add to Ruoth's suspicions. Ruoth was certain that Lord Gruffydd was getting help from Tenebrae in one way or another. In some way, that fucking dragon was stretching the rules to their limit without breaking them. Worse yet, Tenebrae had likely been responsible for Banalor's murder—or at the very least he was utilizing what was a tragedy for Lord Gruffydd to turn the man against the Crown and pinning the blame on someone else.

The only problem was that Ruoth had no proof, and he wasn't about to report back to the Darond with no proof. Speculation like that could cause issues down the road; political scandal and lies were not a good look for the Darond right now and would only derail their efforts to turn Enayra against Altimara and Tenebrae.

Ruoth was also very certain that the Felidrun leg of the royal mail service had been compromised. There was no way to smuggle missives out either; lately, many of the go-betweens he used to smuggle letters outside of the scope of the Crown's mail service had recently disappeared under suspicious circumstances. Ruoth could find no proof they'd been arrested or dragged off to a dungeon, but he speculates that was the case.

Lord Gruffydd had, somehow, found these smugglers and Darond agents, and removed them from the board of play. Ruoth was now unable to send letters through unofficial channels and unwilling to send his enciphered messages through official channels, for fear his cyphers had also been broken. He was effectively stranded in a den of wolves, and with every visit from the bailiffs and assessors, he could feel the hunters circling ever closer.

How anyone had managed to figure out the location of these smugglers and associates, or even Ruoth's loyalties to the Darond, Ruoth himself could only guess. Here his theories were less concrete. He had spent years under the radar of the Black Blades, and Estion was clearly on the Darond's side—their former king was now Grand Master. The best Ruoth could posit was that something had changed in the capital, or there was an informant inside the smuggling ring he had set up in Felidrun.

Either way, Ruoth knew one thing was certain: he would be next.

Ruoth spent that morning alone, as he usually did. His regulars weren't expected until about noon, and his employees arrived an hour before that. Most mornings were spent on upkeep for Ruoth, and this morning it was wiping down the bar top and polishing and dusting the bottles up on the wall behind the bar.

Ruoth saw the bailiff and assessor coming through his kitchen window before they arrived. Every week, during the mid-morning on Vindrdas, the bailiff and assessor arrived at the Sleeping Soldier to collect the taxes due. This had become such a regular occurrence that Ruoth already had two bowls of pottage and mash on the table, still steaming away. There was also a mug of porter for the bailiff and a bottle of Asardaean red for the assessor who preferred it to the beer. The meal sat waiting for them when the two arrived, but it would not be eaten that day.

The bailiff and assessor entered the Sleeping Soldier, but they were not alone this week. They came with several armed soldiers—not some low-level patrolmen either, but fully armed and armoured soldiers straight from the Duke's estate. Two of them carried pikes, one a sword, and one more carried a wicked-looking bardiche. Manacles clattered in the bailiff's belt with every step he took, but Ruoth pretended not to notice them.

Ruoth smiled wide and drummed his fingers on the bar top. He played the fool. "Welcome good sirs. Your food is ready on the table; I'll have to get more for the rest of you. I wasn't expecting there to be more than normal."

Despite his offer to get more food, Ruoth did not immediately leave to do that. Nor did he turn his back on the guards or bailiff. Especially as they ignored the food. The assessor scribbled down something quickly and the group of thugs approached the bar.

"That won't be necessary," the assessor mumbled.

Ruoth's hand slowly crept below the bar. The soldiers reached for their weapons but were surprised when Ruoth's hand did not return with a weapon, and instead, produced an empty tankard and a rag to clean it with. The soldiers eased up, relaxing their hold on their weapons, and allowed Ruoth to continue to move about behind the bar as needed.

"Are you sure?" the innkeeper asked. "I've got lots more stew for you, fresh bread even. I can bring up the full keg of porter for everyone to enjoy. They look thirsty. It's hot out today, and I'm sure it's not easy to walk around in the heat and dust all day with all that armour on. Surely you boys must be parched."

The bailiff averted his gaze. The assessor looked as if he had just smelled something sour. The guards shifted uncomfortably.

Ruoth hid a smile. He reached down below the bar, and while a few of the soldiers flinched and two reached for their weapons, no one was as concerned as before, and once more their concern wilted away after he came up with another mug.

"I'm sorry Ruoth," mumbled the bailiff, barely audible.

Ruoth screwed up his face. "I'm sorry, could you speak up a bit? I'm a little hard of hearing. Happens at my age."

The assessor shot a look at the bailiff.

The bailiff cleared his throat and continued. "I'm sorry, Ruoth. Don't want to have to do this. Just business you understand."

The soldiers said nothing but stood there awkwardly trying to avoid eye contact with Ruoth. He had known each of them by name, they had eaten here on multiple occasions. None of them wanted to be here right now, not even the bailiff. Only the assessor seemed unbothered by it all. He never came here—except to harass Ruoth in recent weeks, and even then he always complained about something. Ruoth usually made sure to spit in his food.

Again, Ruoth played the fool. "I don't know what you mean." He reached below the bar again and came back up with yet another mug. This time the guards didn't flinch.

The assessor was running out of patience. "You're under arrest. For sedition, spy craft, and treason!"

Ruoth hated the assessor's voice. It was grating; loud, shill, and harsh. Like a goose being beaten with a mallet. He reached below the bar once more. No one even noticed when he did it this time. "What do you mean? What have I done? I'm just a simple innkeeper, trying to make my way in the world."

The assessor sneered. "A clever ruse, but you can't lie your way out of this one. Arrest him! We'll be claiming this bar in the name of Lord Gruffydd. This business, its property and all material value are now state property."

The bailiff and soldiers started to move around the bar, closing in on Ruoth. There was no time left. He had been discovered.

Ruoth pulled his large, bearded axe from beneath the bar, leapt over the countertop, and drove the blade of his axe into the assessor's skull. The man let out one final honk before collapsing in a heap on the ground. He gave a final, gruesome twitch as Ruoth pulled his axe from the man's forehead.

The soldiers shouted. The bailiff fumbled to get his club out and paid the price. Ruoth sunk his axe in the side of the bailiff's neck, hacking nearly all the way through it—he'd lost his touch, there was once a time when Ruoth could've taken the head off an enemy in a single, effortless swing. The head flopped to the side, dangling from a tiny flap of flesh and skin. Blood sprayed everywhere, making the floor slippery.

Ruoth tried to maintain his balance as the soldiers closed in around him. The pike wielders came in first, keeping their distance and stabbing at him from afar. The one with the sword and bardiche hung back, waiting to see if their allies would fail or succeed.

Ruoth had been a soldier. Few people here knew that. He knew how to fight pikemen. Despite his age, Ruoth was quick and nimble. He slammed the blade of his axe into the ground, then reached out and grabbed the pikes just below the blades and yanked them from the pike soldiers' hands. The soldiers were taken by surprise and released their weapons. No one ever expected you to steal their pike—it was a risky gambit most wouldn't dare try.

Ruoth, using his immense strength, slammed the pikes into the ground, snapping the tips off, and cracking the hafts clean in half.

By now the sword and bardiche soldiers had rushed in, aiming to strike him down. Ruoth was able to grab his axe, but just barely ducked a swing from the bardiche. He was not fast enough to dodge a thrust from the sword, and the swordsman got him in the side. It wasn't deep, but the wound was irritating, and now he was bleeding. He needed to end this fight now.

Ruoth roared and grabbed the soldier's wrist with his free hand, then slammed his axe head into the man's chest, once, twice, three times. Plate was cleaved apart like it was made of wood. Flesh tore. Bones cracked. Blood frothed from the man's mouth as his lungs collapsed. When Ruoth let him go, he hit the ground like a fleshy sack.

The pike soldiers had fled already, all that was left was the bardiche wielder. Ruoth could see in his eyes, the will to fight had left. He wanted to flee, but his duty prevented him.

Ruoth had no patience for the soldier's hesitance. He closed the gap between the two. The bardiche wielder tried to widen it again and swung out with his axe to either cleave or scare off Ruoth, but Ruoth's axe handle blocked the strike. Ruoth's axe had been reinforced and enchanted with magic. It was an old weapon and was not as brittle as some run-of-the-mill axe. The bardiche bounced off the wooden haft as if it were made of stone.

Ruoth grabbed the stunned soldier by the throat, tossed aside his axe aside as the soldier dropped his bardiche, and tore the helmet off the soldier's head. When he was unmasked, Ruoth saw that it was, in fact, a woman. Older, a veteran. Probably the captain of this squad. Fear was clear in his eyes. She was pleading for mercy with her eyes, even if her words failed her.

Ruoth would show her mercy; she would get a quick death. With a quick twist of his wrists, the woman's neck snapped out of place with a loud pop. She let out a short grunt. Her head was turned at an odd angle, and soon she joined her comrades on the ground.

Ruoth spat on the floor he had moped not an hour ago, his mouth filling with saliva and phlegm. He had been a soldier, but he was getting too old for this shit. He ached now, and his side stung like he'd been stabbed with a hot poker. He would need to bandage himself—but not here. They'd be after him and Ruoth was running out of time.

For now, Ruoth settled for searing the wound with a poker he had left in the fire—just in case he needed a backup weapon for that encounter. His flesh sizzled and Ruoth hissed as he felt the wound cauterize. It wasn't perfect, but the bleeding would stop for now. He could attend to his wounds properly later.

Ruoth cursed to himself. He got sloppy in his old age. He should've killed the pike soldiers. Their escape limited the time he had available to him. They'd run off for reinforcements, and soon they'd arrive. Ruoth didn't have long to get out and burn it all down behind him.

There was only one thing for it, really.

Ruoth used the fire poker to pull the crackling logs from the massive central fire and scatter them across the wooden floor. Then, with much effort, he recovered a barrel full of pitch and a bale of hay from a nearby broom cupboard. He spread the handfuls of the hay across the floor, then tipped the barrel over until its contents spilt across the floor. As soon as the pitch came near a burning log or clump of hay, it caught flame. It wasn't long before much of the bar was alight, and smoke started to fill the entire room.

The old soldier grabbed his axe and made his way to the back door. He kicked the door open and fled down the back alley. Ruoth avoided the main streets. He could hear people screaming in the square and the streets around the bar. From where he stood, Ruoth could see the flames had started to climb higher up his inn. Smoke started to billow from the windows of the building—the windows had already shattered from the heat.

The people would be focused on the fire, and hopefully not notice the man and his axe, both caked in blood and gore, fleeing down a back alley.

Ruoth had two tasks ahead of him: get out of town without getting caught and get to Ethon as soon as possible. He had to warn the Khaleeshir and the king about the situation that was unfolding in Felidrun. Proof or no proof, they needed to know, or they'd be caught on the back foot.

Ruoth had a safehouse at the edge of town. There was an old, hidden room in the side of an old warehouse that he owned. His name wasn't on any of the paperwork, so no one would've thought to search the place.

He'd still need to be careful, but Ruoth would have some time to better tend his wounds, and then escape Felidrun. There was a tunnel under the wall in the basement of that safe house. On the other side of that tunnel was a small stable stationed outside of the town's walls. Ruoth would have a horse from the sympathetic stablemaster, and by the time they found either the tunnel or the safehouse, he'd be long gone.

Ruoth—no. No, he was Ruoth no longer. That identity burned down with the Sleeping Soldier Inn; discarded. He was Tohru once more, and the soldier awakened. The bar and name had served their purpose, but Tohru was needed now. Tohru he had been born, and Tohru he would be again.

Panic and commotion continued to erupt from where his bar had once stood. It was good and burning now—Tohru could smell the ash on the air, and smoke pooled in clouds above the city like balls of blackened cotton. The bells that warned the fire brigades erupted across the city. People screamed as they rushed towards the burning inn—someone screamed, afraid that Tohru had been caught inside of the inferno.

Just as Tohru had hoped, no one could resist watching a good fire, especially when it was the local tavern that was burning to the ground. Patrons gathered around to mourn the loss of good food, good booze, and good times. Volunteers gathered around to put the fire out. Everyone else just gathered around to watch the flames and pretend that they hadn't thought about doing the same to another building at least once in their lives.

Tohru grinned through the pain as he kept running. He was still a soldier, and he hadn't lost his touch just yet.

Chapter XXV

At first, the Lau'thso refused to let Kyeit or the Khaleeshir pick up an oar, but after a day of pestering, they relented. Soon enough, Kanaahn, Arial, Arkas, Kyeit, and Shooter were each taking their turn at the rowing bench. They'd done well, considering the Kulans had never been on a boat before. They even stopped throwing up after the third day.

Progress had been quick, and stops were only taken to eat, catch a breath, or sleep. Now, shortly after dawn of the seventh day, the walled harbour of Ethon appeared on the horizon, and by noon they had cleared the massive harbour gate and were about ready to dock.

The Khaleeshir were greeted by a bustling lake harbour and a massive city that outsized even Xiar. Ethon was one of the oldest cities in Enayra, along with Malatrion, Kasaadua and Daesh'ara. Despite its reputation as the "Sacked City", it was still a glorious jewel of architecture and city life.

The city had been constructed on a hill at the edge of Lake Ardona. Tall, white walls encircled the perimeter of the massive city. The walls encircled even the harbour. The walls were several metres thick, partially submerged, with many gates of varying sizes. Each gate led to a tunnel that was secured by no less than four portcullises and two heavy ironwood doors on either end—each.

The gates were labelled and designated for different kinds of traffic. Some of the gates were for commercial traffic, some for military vessels only, and others were for fishing barges specifically. More still were for passenger barges and other civilian traffic, and other privately owned vessels. The division of the gates was based on the way they were taxed. Different taxes were collected on gates meant for fishermen than on commercial and civilian use. Military vessels were given their own gates so that they were not delayed by ordinary traffic.

Because they were considered a civilian craft, the Lau'thso brought their longboat through one of the smaller civilian gates into the massive walled harbour. Kyeit got the group through the gate easily by passing them a letter from the Darond High Council explaining their purpose. They were waved through without issue.

Once they exited the narrow tunnel, they were welcomed by a lively and busy harbour. Boats were everywhere, going in and out. Gulls cried. They could hear the shouts of fishmongers selling their wares right on the dock. There was the roar of the crowds as they pushed through dock-side markets and stalls looking for freshly offloaded goods. They could hear the yelling of merchants who argued over the price of this or that. The shout of sailors and their captains who were coming in, offloading their boats, or putting out to the lake. Somehow, most pervasive of all was the sound and smell of livestock, and of course the ever-present stench of fish. These were just some of the things they saw, smelled, and heard as the Lau'thso pulled into the dock.

People stared as the Lau'thso and several outsiders ambled out of the longboat, onto the ancient, creaky dock. It was here that the Lau'thso and the Khaleeshir were forced to stand around awkwardly for the other party to arrive to greet them. The stares only continued across that time, and people kept stopping to gawk at these new arrivals like they were a circus on show.

The bystanders only grew more curious when a retinue of soldiers—some with gold breastplates and cloaks and others with blue helmets—pushed their way through the throngs. At the centre of the soldiers was Cecil, flanked by two men Kanaahn didn't recognize.

One was a young man; he was bright-eyed, handsome, and dressed in orange robes that called to mind the colours of a sunrise. His hair was a tousled mop of curls pushed back out of his face. His hair was the colour and lustre of varnished wood. His eyes were the colour of the night sky. His skin was sun-kissed. He smiled and waved to all who recognized him.

The other man was the first man's opposite in every way. He was thin, gaunt, and grey-haired. His skin was pallid, and his face was bedecked with a perpetual frown and a stern gaze. He wore robes of dark purple and black, that encapsulated the colours of the sky at dusk. His shoulder-length, grey hair was pushed back into a tight and neurotically neat ponytail. His face was wrinkled, his mouth pinched, and he had a hooked nose like a flacon. No one waved at him, and he did not even acknowledge the existence of the people around him.

"Is that the welcoming party?" Shooter asked.

"Those are the Bluehelms. They guard and defend the city—a dedicated city guard. They're tasked with keeping order and enforcing the laws, and in times of siege, manning the walls. The ones in gold are the Estian Royal Guard. Their job is to defend the monarch and their family, as well as any domestic or foreign dignitaries."

The dock creaked in protest as the heavy, armoured boots of the soldiers tread across it with military rhythm and precision. They came to a halt in front of the Khaleeshir, Lau'thso, and Kyeit.

The soldiers parted like a curtain in one fluid motion and allowed Cecil and the two men accompanying her to walk forward and greet the Khaleeshir.

The morose man took the lead. He gave a curt, but polite bow. "Welcome to our great city of Ethon, Dragonkin. We've been expecting you. I am Imuhlair. I am the king's Senior Major-domo. King Anducaerleonis is attending a meeting of the House of Commons and could not come to greet you himself. I am to show you to the castle, and he shall meet you there once the session of parliament has ended."

Despite the disinterest in his voice and face, the man was polite enough. Kanaahn had a feeling his looks were just an unfortunate side effect of his bearing, but otherwise, Imuhlair was a consummate professional who didn't allow much emotion to seep through to the forefront.

The young man—who couldn't have been more than four or five years older than Kanaahn—stepped forward next and held out his hand for Kanaahn to shake. Kanaahn took it, without hesitation, and shook the young man's hand. The man's grip was lacking, but his face was friendly enough. "I am Iskren. I am the newly appointed Junior Major-domo."

Kanaahn could see a slight scowl creep across Imuhlair's face as his young counterpart mentioned his title. He got the feeling Imuhlair wasn't exactly happy with Iskren's appointment as his junior.

Cecil and Kyeit exchanged a knowing glance.

Imuhlair cleared his throat and folded his hands behind his back. "We should get going. There is much to be done. I shall lead you through the city; King Anducaerleonis has instructed that I give you a tour of the city as we go."

"What for?" asked Shooter. "You're a Major-domo, not a tour guide."

Imuhlair's brow furrowed. "His Majesty will oversee your training. He believes your training must go beyond the martial arts. Swords and magic have their place, but so does knowledge—of history, of people, of cultures, of languages. Learning about this city and its people will allow you to one day solve their problems. You cannot help people if you do not understand them, and you cannot understand them if you do not know their history, and how they live."

With that, Imuhlair turned on his heel—the soldiers following suit—and he walked off towards the main street.

Iskren looked at the Khaleeshir. "I'm sorry for him. He's not exactly happy with my appointment."

"Why is that?" Arial wondered.

"I was appointed by King Leon directly, but Imuhlair was appointed by the previous king, Khomandar, Leon's father. He was Khomandar's Major-domo. Leon refuses to be his father's puppet, though and thinks someone younger is needed to fill the Major-domo's shoes. But to placate his father, Leon appointed me as Junior Major-domo and made Imuhlair my senior. The plan is to retire the man in the next few years, so that I may take his place. He's served well, but it's time for some fresh blood to take over."

Imuhlair called from the street. "Come, Iskren! We don't have time to dawdle."

Iskren bowed his head and begged pardon before leaving to be by Imuhlair's side.

The Khaleeshir, Kyeit, Cecil, and the Lau'thso led by Hau'farh walked from the dock to the main street as well. The soldiers closed rank around them with an almost worrying immediacy. The group meandered through the city's many districts, slowly making their way up the steep hill towards the castle. Along the way they cleared several gates and checkpoints, passing underneath thick and sturdy walls.

Imuhlair began his history lesson as soon as they left the harbour district for the potter's district. "Ethon was once known as the Sacked City. It was known for being easy to besiege and conquer, both by internal and external enemies of the state. But in recent generations, it has taken on a new name: the City of Walls. The change started during the reign of His Majesty's ancestor Aethalmenis I. One particular summer during the early years of his reign, the kingdom saw a terrible drought. Forest fires erupted across the south of the country, and the flames threatened to spread north towards Ethon. Aethalmenis I immediately began to construct barriers to slow the spread of flame. These barriers were initially smaller structures meant to only act as a firebreak between districts.

"But over the years, as Aethalmenis II and III succeeded the first, they reinforced, rebuilt, and fortified the walls, turning the city into a veritable fortress. They went from simple anti-fire measures to a method of peacekeeping that would lockdown districts and neighbourhoods. It works as both an internal security measure and one that could be used to weather external sieges. By creating pockets around neighbourhoods, the city has an elastic front line that could move and adapt based on the flow of battle.

"In one particular use, during the early days of Aethalmenis III, the nobility rebelled to curb the king's slow increase of absolute power. They laid siege to the city, expecting it to fall as easily as it had many times across history. The siege lasted one hundred and forty-seven days, and even though the outer walls had been breached four times, each time the attackers had been quickly expunged and repelled. Every time the wall was breached, Aethalmenis III would pull his front line back to the next district, allowing soldiers to pour into the district they'd breached. He would then surround the soldiers by using the walls to move his men around. Once the cauldron closed around the attackers they would be eliminated to the last man.

"The failure of the rebellion allowed Aethalmenis III to hold an iron grip over politics and power in the kingdom until his son rebelled against him. But even during the Princeling's Revolt, when His Majesty's father took the throne from his own father, the young prince knew better than to repeat the mistakes of his predecessors. He took the city with deceit. He used fancy words and large cash bribes provided by the previous Baron Felidrun. He was able to bribe the mercenary gatekeepers across the city to let him in. They were later executed for their failure to defend the city and replaced with the Bluehelms."

Kanaahn was fascinated, and a little overwhelmed, at all the history he found in every corner of Ethon. Xiar had been an ancient city, but it had not seen as much as Ethon had—perhaps due to Xiar's large, natural mountains that guarded the borders of the Antigorus Valley. Xiar had always been relatively peaceful. It was a city known for its mages, its knowledge, the library, and its universities. It was not known for being a world player. But Estion had seen countless wars, revolts, rebellions, civil wars, sieges, and the endless boots of thousands of soldiers.

As they walked up winding streets and stairs that led up the hill to the castle, the group kept passing ancient statues of soldiers with worn copper plaques affixed to their base. The statues looked worn from the years. The bronze statues were green from years of exposure to the elements, and some were caked in white crap from gulls and other birds. The rust from the bronze streaked the stone bases where it had bled from the statues. They were clearly old, and they passed one every few minutes.

Partway through the weaver's district, when Imuhlair had once again gone silent after discussing how a Gerovian monarch had once funded an entire war with the proceeds from lace manufacturing, Kanaahn finally asked about them. "I've noticed these statues everywhere in the city. Who are these people?"

Imuhlair paused the column to approach the statue of the soldier. "These statues date to the years after the end of the Estian Anarchy and commemorate those that died during the War of the Grand Coalition. Each of these statues—custom-made to the likeness of each soldier—honours a member of the Imperial Gerovian Guard who died defending Gerovia from the encroaching armies of the Grand Coalition that had formed against the Gerovian Empire. Three hundred and eighty-seven members of the royal guard gave their lives on the battlefield during the Great Chase and the subsequent Great Siege of Gerovia. The memorial statues start five kilometres from the city, where the remnant of the Gerovian Rear-guard met the Coalition forces on the battlefield in a bid to slow the enemy down. The statues continue throughout the city, and end with the final twenty-three statues, that stand in alcoves on the walls of the throne room of the castle, where the last of the royal guards of Gerovia were killed defending their emperor.”

It was another two hours before the group finally arrived at the castle. They were led through the massive, thick, and ornately carved ironwood gates that led to the outer courtyards of the castle. The walls of the castle were tall and wide and reminded Kanaahn of the walls of Ottogard, but they looked newer and less worn. These walls were a recent addition to this castle.

The gates parted with a lumbering creak. The chains that operated the doors clanked from somewhere in the gatehouse. Imuhlair escorted the group through the corridor that led through the ten-metre-thick walls.

Imuhlair’s voice echoed in the corridor. “Filiddyn Castle has stood in one form or another since the earliest days of Gerovia. Much of the current castle dates to shortly after the Anarchy, but a few sections date back to the time of the Gerovian Empire.”

The light at the end of the torchlight tunnel soon exploded into Kanaahn’s eyes as he exited out into the paved eastern courtyard of Filiddyn Castle. From what Imuhlair had explained, it was one of four courtyards of the castle grounds—one was located at each cardinal direction, and each was separated by a thinner set of walls than the outer wall had been.

Kanaahn could see, on the steps of the castle, directly across from where they entered the corridor, the king, and a few courtiers. They were flanked by evermore Bluehelms and Royal Guards. Several pages carried banners and pendants that flapped in the light breeze. The impossible complex coat of arms of the Royal House was stitched onto blue banners trimmed with silver and gold. The royal family’s crest was an amalgamation of at least seven other heraldic crests from earlier points of Estian history, as families merged and married into one another over the years of turmoil and conflict.

Kanaahn had heard a lot about King Anducaerleonis; from Imuhlair, from Kyeit, and from Cecil. But now he would get to meet the man himself. Kanaahn was surprised at how young he was. Between his name and everything he had heard about the young king, Kanaahn would not have guessed he was *that* young. He couldn’t be much older than Kanaahn and his friends were. A year or two, at most.

He was handsome, in a boyish way. He was not the tall, muscle-bound hero king in heavy plate armour that Kanaahn had expected. He was a young man, with long platinum hair that was tied back in a long braid that went down his back. He was clean-shaven, and his green eyes were as deep as the ocean and shone like the night sky.

King Anducaerleonis, despite coming from an ancient dynasty, wore a simple crown upon his head. There were no jewels set within the simple circlet, only a lion’s head at the front and back. He did not wear armour, instead, the boy king wore a simple grey kaftan with a pleated skirt, a silver hem, and a slim, sky-blue tabard trimmed with gold, emblazoned with the heraldry of the Kingdom of Estion—a gold dolphin naiant on a blue shield and stripped with gold.

Aside from the crown, the only other sign of wealth on the king was an ermine-trimmed cloak fastened with a golden chain that ended in a ruby-studded brooch on each side and the rings he wore on each thumb and pinkie—three of which were described by Imuhlair as part of the symbols of state and were worn by all Kings of Estion. Only one was a personal effect of the king.

Anducaerleonis extended his arms out in a welcoming gesture. Kanaahn noticed he was unarmed. "Welcome to Ethon, Khaleeshir. I am King Anducaerleonis I, head of the House of dae Haultegare-Zeeman-Tyddyn. But I would much prefer if you simply referred to me as Leon; King Leon if you *must* be formal."

Kanaahn bowed. "It is a pleasure to meet you, Leon."

Arkas, Shooter, and Arial followed suit.

Kyeit bowed as well, but not as low.

Cecil did not bow at all.

Hau'farh had each of the Lau'thso awkward falling over themselves to bow as low and formally as they could muster.

King Leon suppressed a chuckle. "Please, Great Lau'ka. You and I are equals. You do not need to bow to me."

Hau'farh looked like he was blushing. He had never met a king before. The Lau'thso were simple people who lived for travel, trade, and the sea. The open ocean was their home, and they didn't have the patience for intricate and back-biting politics.

Leon stepped towards Hau'farh. "Great Lau'ka, so long as you and your people remain in this city, you are guests of me and my court. I have heard of your plight from Knight-Commander Wynne, and I would like to offer as much help as I can to you and your people, so that you may reclaim that which was taken from you."

Hau'farh's smile widened further. "Thank you, Your Majesty. Thank you so much."

"We shall speak more of this later, in more detail. For now, I must speak with the Khaleeshir and the Darond Commanders alone. I shall have Imuhlair escort you to your guest quarters, where you may rest and freshen up from your long journey. I will send for you when I am able, but until then, someone will be at hand to ensure all your needs are met."

While the Royal Guards brought Hau'farh and the Lau'thso into the castle, towards their new lodgings, Leon remained out in the courtyard with the Khaleeshir,

"Kyeit. Welcome back to Ethon. It's been too long." There was something sad and longing in Leon's face as he addressed her.

Even Kanaahn could see that he seemed to be walking on eggshells as he spoke to her. It reminded Kanaahn of the way people spoke to children when they were about to hit them with devastating news. Something in Kanaahn's gut dropped.

At that moment, a woman with a long, blonde braid, clad in leather armour and a heavy cloak seemed to materialize out of the shadows of the courtyard and took her place beside King Leon. Her face was obscured by her hood. But Kanaahn's attention soon returned to Kyeit and Leon.

Leon's face went grim. "Kyeit..."

Kyeit's face dropped.

Kanaahn could feel his stomach drop further.

"I wish we could have met again under happier times, with happier tidings. First, I would like to extend my heartfelt condolences for the death of your father. Regent Prince Karaglen was as noble and honourable a man as there was in Enayra. I learned much from him. I am sorry he has gone to join the ancestors so soon."

Kyeit gave a half-hearted bow in thanks but did not speak. Kanaahn wasn't certain if she was too concerned about the news to come, or if she was just tired of hearing the condolences by now.

"But unfortunately, that does not seem to be the only thing you've lost since your departure."

The woman next to Leon shifted.

Kyeit stiffened. "What do you mean?"

Leon's face was a combination of disbelief and anguish. "Xiar...seems to have vanished."

"What do you mean vanished?" Kyeit demanded. "Was it destroyed?"

"We don't know. There is no rubble to indicate it was destroyed, but Altimara is claiming responsibility," Leon explained. "Darond agents believe this to be false, and Altimara is merely claiming responsibility to make up for their shameful loss months prior. Investigation seems to indicate that it may have been a spell gone wrong—even half of the Mana Core is missing. It's like someone scooped up the city and walked away with it. There's nothing left but a crater and a chunk of the Mana Core. Altimara is already building on the ruins, to claim the valley for their own."

Kyeit looked horrified.

Leon did not wait for the message to sink in before he continued. He much preferred to rip the poultice off. "I'm afraid the bad news does not end there."

Kyeit held back her tears as best she could, but her eyes were glistening, and her voice cracked and wavered. "What else?"

"...You've been summoned."

"What do you mean?" Kyeit regained some composure.

"You've been asked to return to Tuir'Delohmeyh and report to the High Council. The orders came through this morning."

Kyeit's face went slightly pale. Kanaahn had never seen her so concerned before. The normally cool Kyeit was now afraid. "Will you not be coming with me?"

Leon shook his head. "I must stay here and help train the Khaleeshir. Regent Alaxzander is also unavailable. You will have to face the High Council alone. They've chosen their moment carefully." Leon produced a rolled-up scroll from his robes and handed it to Kyeit. "It's all there in the letter."

Kyeit did not read it. She tucked the scroll into her belt and hardened herself once more. "Where is Valence?"

"In the northern courtyard, awaiting your arrival. The other dragons are training with Lord Aurichalcum, but she remained behind in anticipation of your imminent arrival. She knew you'd want to depart immediately."

Kyeit let out a sharp breath. "She was correct. I will depart at once; best not to keep the High Council waiting." She did not turn to wish the Khaleeshir goodbye. She did not say another word to Leon, or Cecil, or anyone else present. She simply marched towards the gate to the north of the courtyard and disappeared beyond the portcullis.

The Khaleeshir were still getting over the fact that Xiar, the city they had fought so hard to defend, had simply vanished from existence so shortly after their departure, with no explanation as to why. It made Kanaahn wonder what the fighting had all been for; whether the death had even been worth it.

Cecil looked concerned, but not surprised. She had clearly known about this before Kyeit arrived but had been unable to provide her with a warning. Kanaahn would inquire later.

Leon's troubled look did not disappear as he continued to speak to the Khaleeshir, but it did fade slightly. Like graffiti on an old, weathered wall. "While you are here, you will continue to hone your skills. As Dragon Master, I have decided that your training here will be just as much as honing the skills you already possess with your chosen weapons, as it will be about honing and strengthening your mind. Kanaahn, I've heard from Djall that you seek proper training with your katana, and to that end, I have hired a master swordsman from Espias to help you hone and refine your skills. For Shooter, you will train with Agent Skullspider here—" Leon gestured to the hooded woman beside him "–in the art of subterfuge, assassination, and poisons. Risasi indicated that may be something you would enjoy; and excel in even. For Arkas, Fyete said that you would be wasting your time trying to improve your archery any further, but I still think learning under the Royal Hunt could be of value to you. I would, at the very least, like to get you more acquainted with that short sword, and even knife combat. Shooter, you'll learn knife combat from them as well when Agent Skullspider can spare you."

Leon turned to Arial. He paused for a moment before continuing. Kanaahn noticed a glance exchanged between the two of them—it was brief, and only appeared for the quickest of seconds before disappearing into the weight of the moment again.

"I have spoken with Adalinda and learned you are quite the skilled mage. Arial, you'll be training under me to perfect and grow your magical skill. I can see by your hair that your powers are growing quickly, but your knowledge should be as wide as the power is deep."

Kyeit had told Arial on the trip to Ethon that King Leon was not just a king and a Dragon Master, but one of the most talented non-Tsuru mages in the Darond. He was one of the few mages of his years who could cast magic without the need for a focus; he used no wand, no crystal, and no staff to channel his mana to cast spells. His will was unnaturally strong for a spellcaster of his age; most mages were in their sixties or seventies before they could start casting spells at the complexity that Leon could. Some rumours even said that he could draw from leylines directly without destroying himself, though Kyeit assured these rumours were unsubstantiated and likely exaggerated. No human could draw from a leylines without dying. The power was simply too much for the body to handle.

"All of you will also be studying history, culture, literature, and a second language of your choice, while you are here. I have brought some of the finest tutors in Estion to the castle to mentor you. Your training will begin tomorrow, bright and early, and will be supervised by myself, Lady Ilana Tsuru, and Lord Aurichalcum. We shall each take turns testing your knowledge as you learn and shall carefully observe your training to ensure your progress goes smoothly."

Leon let out an exhausted sigh. "I wish I could allow you time to rest before we begin, but every minute we waste is precious time lost. It's always a race against the clock with

Tenebrae. He's been too silent for too long, and we have no idea when or where he'll strike next. I have a feeling we'll require the Khaleeshir again before long." Leon turned with a swish of his cape. "I am sorry for the brevity of our talk, but there are many matters of state I must attend to before I meet with Hau'farh, and it all must get done before we sit for dinner tonight. We shall talk later. Agent Skullspider will escort you to your rooms in the meantime, and an hour from now, she will take you to meet Lord Aurichalcum and Lady Hana Tsuru, once they've returned."

It was not uncommon for the Metallic Dragons to be living in the capitals of the nations of Enayra. Kanaahn had learned in Xiar's great library that since the days of the Age of Heroes when the first Khaleeshir bridged the gaps between dragon and human, the Metallic Dragons had advised rulers across Enayra. However, since the Dragon War, the Metallic Dragons had taken to serving only a single nation—or no nation at all in the case of Argentum.

Aurum, who had once advised the kings and queens of Altimara, now advised the emperors of Espias, though he had only done so in recent centuries. Argentum, who had once advised the emperors of Espias, now advised, and watched over the Darond headquarters at Tuir'Delohmeyh along with Æris—who had been asked to leave Danaen during the Age of Darkness, when they grew closer to Altimara. Æs and Aurichalcum were the only Metallic Dragons who still advised the same kingdoms as they had before the Dragon War. Aurichalcum advised the kings and queens of Estion, and Æs advised the queens of Asardaea.

Leon bowed and departed without another word and left the Khaleeshir in the hands of this Agent Skullspider. The Khaleeshir stared at the hooded agent, unsure of whether they could trust her, or even who she was.

Then Skullspider laughed. "Isn't this something? The irony is quite delicious. I suppose I was always going to have to tell you, but I didn't think it would be like this."

Kanaahn and Arial were dumbfounded. They recognized that voice.

"Mom?" Arial asked in disbelief.

Skullspider threw back her hood to reveal that she was, in fact, Menalaea Gainsborough. "It's been too long."

The Khaleeshir were speechless. Cecil did not look surprised; another thing she knew but didn't reveal.

"How?" was all Kanaahn managed to get out.

"I've been the Darond's Kulan agent for sixteen years," explained Menalaea. "When Artimer died, he left me his business. What he didn't tell me was that his business was a front for the Darond, and was used for smuggling goods, people, and information across Enayra, and through Altimara, right under Tenebrae's nose. It was a bit of a learning curve, I'll admit, but eventually, I came to be quite good at it."

"How come you never told us?" Arial asked. Her whole life had been turned upside down.

Menalaea gave Arial a gentle smile. "I wouldn't be a very good spy if I told a bunch of children my identity. I'm sorry, love."

Arial wasn't mad. No, on the contrary, tears began to drip from her eyes, and she could feel her voice leave her. She ran to her mother and hugged her tightly, refusing to let go.

Menalaea said nothing; she only hugged her daughter and dried her eyes with the hem of her sleeve. "There, there, my child. It's okay."

"I missed you so much," Arial said.

Menalaea gently stroked Arial's head as she soothed her daughter. "I know. I missed you too, love. I missed all of you. Things got very lonely after you left to train with Osamu."

Kanaahn's eyes widened. "You knew?!"

Menalaea laughed. "Who do you think suggested your names to Osamu and the Darond in the first place?"

Silence.

Kanaahn noticed at that point that Cecil had sneaked away from the reunion. Where she went, no one saw, but it was clear she wanted to give the Khaleeshir and Menalaea their privacy.

Menalaea huffed, still hugging her daughter. "I think I should explain. Follow me; I'll lead you to your rooms and explain on the way. You can still walk and talk, right?"

Kanaahn nodded dumbly.

Arkas and Shooter were clearly impressed with the revelation. Shooter himself seemed to have grown a whole new level of respect for Menalaea—Kanaahn caught the word badass whispered between him and Arkas.

Menalaea took Arial's hand and led the Khaleeshir into Filiddyn Castle. They were so engrossed with Menalaea's story that they were oblivious to how ornate the inside of this fortress castle was.

"The Darond was desperate. It had been a thousand years since Tenebrae's defeat, and we were no closer to having new Khaleeshir. Volunteers used to line up and offer themselves up to the Darond to be tested. None of them realized the cost of being unworthy was their lives—to protect the location of the eggs, I was told. After the first century or two, the volunteers stopped; it's hard to volunteer knowing that your life will be ended if you're deemed unworthy. The list of people who we thought might be worthy was also shrinking. We tried using Aurum's prophetic powers to see if any of the names suggested were worthy, and all he could ever tell us was 'maybe.' Yours were the first names he felt confident about, but even then it wasn't a guarantee. We were starting to think that the eggs might never hatch, and no one would ever be found worthy."

"You sent Kanaahn into that cave knowing he might die?" Shooter asked.

"I never thought Kanaahn would die. I would not have suggested your names if I had thought for a second you were unworthy. Call it a mother's intuition."

"I call it a lucky guess," Shooter mumbled.

Menalaea shot him a stern look that caused Shooter to pale a bit. "I see your wit hasn't left you, Shooter, dear."

"Never," Shooter responded with a grin.

"I'll admit though, I am still disappointed about Drakhart. I would have never imagined he might change sides," Menalaea said. "If I had known..."

Arial wiped at a wet corner of her eye "How did you escape Kula? We kept waiting for news of whether you survived, but Kycit kept telling us that there was no news because the Kulan agent had disappeared."

"When I saw the dragons attacking Kula, I knew I had to get out. So, I went to each of your families and took them with me. Though, I do apologize Shooter. I was too late to save yours. I even took Drakhart's mother with me—just because her son's a bastard doesn't mean she deserved to die in the fire. Those dragons were trying to be careful, but fire is not sentient like those that wield it. Your family is safe, Arkas. I left them and Kinraea with Ruoth when I reached Felidrun, and he sent them to safety at Tuir'Delohmeyh. I had explained to each of them where you really were, and what you were really doing—though I hadn't the heart to tell Kinraea the truth about Drakhart. Last I heard, your father and siblings were looking to join the Darond. They said they couldn't sit back and let you do all the fighting."

Arkas smiled. "That sounds like them. Whatever regiment they're about to be assigned to has just gained a great asset."

"I recommended them for the Obsidian Banner. They'd be a great asset to our stealth and reconnaissance operations," Menalaea explained.

No one knew what an Obsidian Banner was, but they had too many other questions that took precedence.

"How long have you been here in Ethon?" asked Kanaahn.

"I only just arrived a few weeks ago. I've been so busy rearranging the Darond spy network and my company's trade routes. And I wanted to surprise you when you arrived. So, I kept my arrival a secret. I'm so proud of all of you. What you achieved at Xiar...you truly lived up to the legacy of your predecessors."

Menalaea stopped, suddenly. Without even realizing it, they had arrived at their rooms. They were standing in a brightly lit, circular room in the middle of the eastern wide tower. The central room reminded them of the cul-de-sac-like room outside of their quarters at the Tormenting Pinnacle. But whereas the antechamber at the Pinnacle had been cut from the bare rock and was barren of all decoration—save for a few torches—this room was decorated with tapestries and furs, and at the centre of the room sat a marble fountain that spewed forth the cleanest water the Khaleeshir had ever seen.

"This tower was originally built to house the original Khaleeshir," Menalaea explained. "It was known as the Heroes' Tower, though nowadays it's called the Old Tower. Nowadays the rooms are reserved for foreign dignitaries and royalty from other nations. Until today; today they host the Khaleeshir once again."

Menalaea handed each of the Khaleeshir a heavy key to their rooms. "You have an hour until Lord Aurichalcum returns with your dragons, and Lady Hana Tsuru is currently at a meeting with King Leon. When they return, you will meet them. So, freshen up quickly; you'll find a change of clothes in the wardrobe. Should you need anything, there's an enchanted stone by the door that will allow you to summon someone who can assist you."

When she handed Shooter his key, she also slipped him a small, folded letter. It was done quickly, and without anyone else noticing. She looked him in the eye but said nothing more.

Each of the Khaleeshir hugged Menalaea goodbye and disappeared into their rooms. All except Kanaahn. He waited until each of his friends had gone before approaching Menalaea.

Kanaahn had one question on his mind, and it had been burning like a beacon since Menalaea had revealed herself. He whispered the question to her. "Did your husband know my parents?"

Menalaea didn't seem surprised by the question. She seemed to have been expecting it. "I had heard that your parents' identities had been confirmed. I'm glad you finally have answers." Menalaea walked over to Kanaahn and placed a gentle hand on his cheek. "I only found out recently that my husband knew your parents. They had worked together previously, but my husband told me nothing of his secret life, and he had a bad habit of burning all communication after committing it to memory.

"He saw the flames from our house and rushed to your parents' aide because he feared they had been attacked—this was during the height of the Great Slaughter. By the time he arrived, the blaze was out of control, and your parents' bodies were...well they were beyond recognition. He died from the burns he endured in that building, but he told me your name was Kanaahn—he said it had been stitched into your blanket and I had no reason not to believe him. He died there, in my arms, and you in his, so I was forced to learn your last name from the neighbours, who knew your parents.

"It wasn't until a few weeks later that I learned my husband had been a Darond agent when several Darond spies arrived at my house to explain it all to me. No one ever told me about you, or who your parents were. It seemed that the Darond weren't aware of your existence, or they assumed you died in the fire—or maybe they just didn't care. I did find out recently that the reason my husband knew your parents was because they had infiltrated the Black Citadel together. They worked together as part of Dynia's Hand. Artimer provided the cover identities to half the agents and smuggled in the rest using his merchant caravans. That was probably why no one bothered to talk about it after he died— the High Council weren't exactly thrilled with the doings of Dynia's Hand."

Menalaea pulled Kanaahn into a half hug.

"But I know my Artimer, and he would have jumped into that burning building even if he *hadn't* known your parents because saving you was the right thing to do."

Kanaahn hid his disappointment, but Menalaea, being a mother, could read minds.

"Don't worry, that's not the good news. I've already tracked down two people who knew them. You have an uncle in Asardaea, he's a General and a former Darond soldier. He's your father's older brother. Your mother had a younger brother living in Felidrun; I reached out to him about a week ago, but he hasn't responded yet. I think you might know him. He was the one who verified your identity."

Kanaahn put two and two together. "...It was Ruoth—Tohru I mean."

Menalaea nodded and hugged Kanaahn. "It was indeed. You have a family now..."

Kanaahn gave Menalaea a small smile. "I think I've always had a family...but I know my blood family now."

Menalaea hid her tears better than anyone Kanaahn had ever known, but now her eyes glistened for the first time Kanaahn had seen in his life.

Kanaahn hugged Menalaea again. "Thank you for everything you did for me. I know I've always been stubborn about the help but...I wouldn't be half of who I am today without you. Thank you."

Menalaea did not respond. She only returned the hug.

* * *

Shooter didn't have to be told who this letter was from. He already knew. It smelled like her like desert rose and sage. Her one luxury in life was that perfume. Shooter wanted to vomit. He was so nervous. He had waited for this response for weeks, and now that he had it, he was almost too afraid to read it. He considered throwing it out the window and pretending he'd never received it.

No. Menalaea would kill him—if Arial didn't get to him first.

Shooter sat himself down on the bed and opened the letter. He scanned it through and managed to keep down his lunch. He had to reread the letter a few times, yet each time he was no closer to understanding what was on the page. His mind worked overtime to try and put the words together.

Amber wrote to him like he was an old friend she hadn't seen in years. Not like they had been lovers. Not like he had just left without a word. Not like he had forgotten to see her before Shooter left, when she expressly requested to see him, and it was urgent.

She had become the new Kulan agent. She had raised an insurrection against Drakhart and successfully sabotaged the Altimara war effort—for a time. Drakhart returned a few of the local crime lords—Shooter had done jobs for both returned crime lords before—and in doing so, had been able to placate the populace once more; for now. But it gutted Amber's resistance and she was forced to flee the city for the sake of her life.

Amber spoke about all as if she was recounting a lazy Ygdas afternoon.

This letter had been written before she departed from Kula, and Shooter had no idea where she was now, or how to get a hold of her. Even if Shooter had the words for a reply, he couldn't send one.

On one hand, he was proud of Amber for putting her skills to use and working to help the people of Kula. Shooter was a lot of things, but he wasn't heartless, nor was blind to the suffering of the Kulan people. He knew how hard many of them had it—he had once been one of them.

Shooter had suffered in Kula too, though he suffered for different reasons. He'd lived in poverty for as long as he could remember. His parents had been common thieves and criminals who scraped by to provide for the family. Eventually, the jobs went from paying for the family to paying for their skittic addiction. Of course, none of that had ever changed the fact that Shooter's father had never liked him—he'd always made that very clear through most of Shooter's life, even before the addiction claimed them. And Shooter's stepmother only encouraged the violence. The skittic just made it all worse.

Shooter thought maybe if he worked hard and earned enough money to keep his parents cared for, they could get off the skittic and Shooter would earn their love and respect. It never worked. The money never went towards food, clothes, or the family. It always went towards skittic.

And the abuse continued.

Instead, for a time, Shooter tried to keep the money. He stopped giving the money to his parents to spend. He decided he could buy the food, pay the taxes, take care of the family, and put their lives back on track. It only made the abuse worse. Keeping the money from his parents angered them—they needed their fix; they needed Shooter to make more money. Shooter wondered if perhaps it was all his fault for not trying to get work sooner.

Still, the abuse continued.

Eventually, though, Shooter grew numb to the abuse and decided that if he was going to get beat and insulted by his parents anyway, he would keep the money for himself. But not to spend on the family—it would be to save up and get away. Get out of Kula. Make a new life elsewhere—if he could ever work up the nerve. He gave enough money to his parents to keep them quiet but kept a small cache of coins hidden away that no one else could find.

Through it all, Shooter's friends, especially Arial, and Amber, had been a haven. An escape from the pain and addiction and yelling and abuse. Only Arial and Amber knew the true extent of it, but they had been rocks for Shooter. A constant help, and Shooter was forever grateful. He loved them. Arial as a sister, but Amber...Amber as much, much more.

They were going to run away together. Make a new life in another city and get married. Have a future. Maybe some kids. Maybe not. Shooter never thought of himself as much of a parent, and honestly, he was so afraid that he'd repeat the mistakes of his parents when trying to raise a child. The plans were never concrete, anyway. But it was something the two liked to talk about, dreamed about. Even if they never meant it, it was nice to have something to aspire to, no matter how impossible. Then the morning would come, and reality would set in—Shooter didn't want to be responsible for his parents dying from withdrawal, and Amber was never going to leave her life as an information broker behind.

Now Shooter was Khaleeshir. He was bonded to a dragon. He had gotten away and made a new life and was able to make a life and a name for himself. He had become someone he could be proud of. Shooter could help others how he had wished someone would come and help him as a child.

So much had changed...and yet it had all gotten far more complicated. Part of Shooter had yearned for the simpler days. At least, back then, he knew what the next day brought. Even if it was terrible, it was stable. Consistent.

Maybe he should have brought Amber with him to Ottogard. They would have gotten out of Kula, and run away like they planned. Would it have made a difference? She had ended up joining the Darond anyway, but at least they would have been together.

Shooter let out a deep, rattling sigh and held his head in his hands. He was a fool to try and run from his feelings.

He should have done more, said more. Been more open with his feelings.

Did she even know how he felt?

Did Amber know how much Shooter missed her?

Did she know how much he loved her?

No. She didn't.

Because Shooter had never told her. Not really, not recently. Not truly. He had spent every moment since he left Kula running from his feelings out of fear, out of guilt. By the time he realized what he needed to do, it was too late.

Shooter wanted to lay back on the bed, close his eyes, and let the sadness and ache envelop him until he fell into the darkness, and fell asleep. But he couldn't do that. He had to meet with Lord Aurichalcum and some Tsuru lady. He was on a time limit.

So instead, Shooter got up, washed up, and changed his clothes. He placed the letter from Amber in a pocket in his cloak, and buried his emotions deep below the surface, where no one else could see them.

But he could still feel them, and they still hurt.

Chapter XXVI

Menalaea had brought Kanaahn and the other Khaleeshir to a small reception hall somewhere in the castle's maze-like insides. Truthfully, Kanaahn and the other Khaleeshir had known Aurichalcum had returned because they had sensed their dragons returning to the city as well.

The Khaleeshir and their dragons had tried to stay in communication while they were apart but both parties had been too busy to communicate. The Khaleeshir were rowing their way to Ethon, and Aurichalcum kept the dragons busy with flight drills, mock fights, and lessons on their history and culture.

One thing Djall had kept telling Kanaahn was how much of a culture shock being around other dragons was for him and the others. Much of their cultural knowledge was in their mind, placed there by their forebearers, but much of it was buried, and what wasn't buried wasn't in use because the dragons were not among their own kind. But even what was there wasn't completely up to date, since they had been laid over a millennia ago, and they were missing a thousand years of cultural shift and dragon history.

Risasi had joked that at least dragon culture didn't shift as quickly as human culture, which seemed different every generation. But a thousand years is still a long time for a dragon; and cultures still shifted in that time, even if it was slow.

Djall had warned Kanaahn of one thing: Aurichalcum was not a dragon with a sense of humour. He was serious, he was dour, and he was often severe in his treatment of his students. Shooter's flippant attitude was not going to go over well with him.

Kanaahn had tried to warn Shooter of as much, but he doubted it would do anything to temper Shooter's behaviour.

The doors to the reception hall parted and Kanaahn got his first glimpse of Aurichalcum and Lady Hana Tsuru. Neither was what he had expected.

Aurichalcum was not in his dragon form, but instead, had taken on a human-like form—but there was something still not quite human about him. Maybe it was the ruddy, brass-coloured hair, or the amber eyes. Maybe it was the proportions of his face or the fact that he towered over everyone in the room. Aurichalcum was in simple white robes, with a brass-coloured overcoat and a gold sash at his waste. His face was pinched with displeasure, and he made Imuhlair look happy and jovial by comparison. His age was overall undiscernible. He looked both old and young at the same time, like some ethereal mirage that was constantly changing in the dim candlelight.

Hana on the other hand, was young. Younger than Kanaahn and the others by at least a few years. Her eyes were closed, but Kanaahn couldn't figure out why. Her clothes were not dissimilar from her brothers in Xiar. Simple white robes, with a red sash. But they were not as ornately decorated as Yomi's or Tachi's had been. The only decoration was the Tsuru family crest on the back of her robes, just below the collar.

"**Welcome, Khaleeshir,**" Aurichalcum called. His voice boomed through the hall, but it also cut through each of their minds. He entered their minds with the force of an avalanche. The pain was only made worse by the fact that he was speaking mentally and verbally at the same time, forcing the listener's mind to try and focus on both simultaneously.

At least he addressed them in Common.

"*Welcome,*" came Hana's voice in Kanaahn's mind. Just as distinct, but softer, gentler. Where Aurichalcum's voice had been like a hammer against an anvil, Hana's voice was a strong breeze during a summer storm.

Whether Aurichalcum noticed how strong his voice was or not, he did not let on, but he also did not relent. "**Forgive the manner of communication. Hana is unable to hear, speak, or see by normal methods. I communicate like this for her sake.**"

"*That's fine, but maybe you could keep it to just the mental connection?*" Shooter asked. His face showed his discomfort. He was wincing from the force of the dragon's voice and telepathy. "*And maybe tone it down in our heads a bit.*"

Aurichalcum frowned. "**Why? You can hear, can you not?**"

A smile crept across Hana's face. "*I think their issue is the strength at which you are asserting yourself into their minds. It is a touch overbearing, Lord Aurichalcum. Would you be so kind as to ease your words?*"

Aurichalcum's tough demeanour withered slightly. "*Apologies, Lady Hana. Is this better?*"

"*Much,*" Shooter replied.

Aurichalcum exhaled through his nose. His frown drooped further.

Hana kept the conversation from devolving into emotion and arguing. "*Welcome to Filiddyn Castle, and to Ethon, Khaleeshir. It is good to see you.*"

The Khaleeshir returned the pleasantries.

"*What are your names?*" Aurichalcum more demanded than asked.

Kanaahn stepped forward first. "*I am Kanaahn Saatus, bonded to the green dragon, Djall.*"

"*I am Arkas Nazzer, bonded to the blue dragon, Fyete.*"

"*I am Arial Gainsborough, bonded to the white dragon, Adalinda.*"

"*I am Shooter Maxim. I'm bonded to the red dragon, Risasi.*"

Aurichalcum's piercing gaze swept over each of the Khaleeshir, but it lingered on Shooter the longest. "*Risasi...I might've guessed.*"

Kanaahn could see Shooter's eyes narrow. He was going to say something stupid. Hoping to avoid being eaten alive by a dragon as old as the world, Kanaahn gently jabbed his elbow into Shooter's side. Not hard enough to hurt him, but just enough to bring him to his senses.

"Has King Anducaerleonis explained your training regimen?" asked Aurichalcum.

Kanaahn replied first. *"To some degree. We know what we'll be studying, and with whom."*

Aurichalcum walked towards the Khaleeshir and began to pace back and forth in front of them. *"Then I shall explain. Listen closely because I will not repeat myself. Starting tomorrow, you will be woken at an hour before sunrise. You will start your day with a brief hour of exercise, followed by a quick repast. Once you have eaten, you will complete an hour of history and culture, an hour of literature, and an hour of language. Then you will spend an hour with Lady Hana, learning how to strengthen your minds against invasion from outside forces. When you've made sufficient progress with her, you will spend three hours training your martial skills; be it magic, weaponry, or whatever else. At midday, you will eat; you will have one hour of rest to do so. Afterwards, you will report to the northern courtyard and there you will be instructed in dragonback combat, and other flying drills. Your training will also include fighting other humans on dragonback and even fighting dragons, both on the ground and in the air. You must know how to battle all three if you are to face the full might of Tenebrae's forces. He cannot be underestimated. You will train with your dragons for a further three hours in this way. After that, your time is yours to do with what you will—though I suggest using it to further your studies. There will be homework."*

Kanaahn wanted to groan. The training was starting to remind him of the tutor that Menalaea had hired for the children when they were kids, but somehow even more strict.

Whereas Kanaahn *wanted* to groan, Shooter did, earning the ire of Aurichalcum in the process.

Within seconds, the ancient dragon had rounded on Shooter and came within an inch of his face. He did not use mental communication. "Do you have a problem with something I said?"

To Shooter's credit, he didn't back down. "Isn't that regimen a little...excessive? We've only been Khaleeshir for a few months."

"Excessive?" spat Aurichalcum. "Do you think Tenebrae is letting the traitor wallow around in luxury while you're here gallivanting across Enayra? No! If I know Tenebrae, he's training that boy into the ground. You must be better and stronger than anything Tenebrae produces. We don't know what he has up his sleeve. If you slack for even a moment, we'll lose. And it'll be your fault."

Kanaahn was both impressed and concerned with how seriously Aurichalcum was taking this war against his former brother. He thought Kyeit was dedicated, but Aurichalcum made Kyeit look like a slacker. Aurichalcum didn't just *believe* in the fight against Tenebrae, he *lived* for it. It was his reason for existence.

Hana looked troubled from where she stood behind Aurichalcum. For her, everything had gone silent. *"Lord Aurichalcum, Is everything all right?"*

Aurichalcum did not immediately reply to Hana. He glared at Shooter for a moment longer, shoving his face as close to Shooter's as he could. He growled, just under his breath, but the Khaleeshir could hear what he was saying just fine with their new senses. "Just as undisciplined as your dragon. No wonder, knowing his parentage. If these are the heroes we must rely on, then we've already lost."

Kanaahn had never thought he could hate a Metallic Dragon. Kanothir had been wonderful. Valence, despite her temper, was a good and trustworthy friend. Kinokaze was amicable and had a great sense of humour. But the Great Aurichalcum was just a bitter, old, asshole.

Aurichalcum turned back to Lady Hana. *"Everything is fine, little one. I was answering one of the Khaleeshir's questions."*

Hana didn't indicate whether she believed Lord Aurichalcum. Her face was like a statue, unmoving and emotionless.

The door behind everyone suddenly creaked open. It was a slow and nervous creak.

Everyone turned to see a young woman of indeterminate age. She was tall and dressed in full armour, with a sword at her side. Her eyes and hair were the same colour as Lord Aurichalcum's, and her face had the same ageless, illusory quality. She was a dragon.

"Thrae, what is it?" demanded Aurichalcum.

"You've been summoned by Leon," the first woman said.

"King Anducaerleonis," Aurichalcum stressed. "Did he say what the reason is, Thrae?"

The woman, Thrae, shrugged. "He didn't specify. He just said it was urgent, and your presence was required."

Aurichalcum's lips pursed so thin they disappeared. He stared at Thrae, trying to discern if she was telling the truth or not. His gaze was hard and scrutinizing. "Very well. I shall return if I am able." He switched to the mental link. *"Can you handle this, Lady Hana?"*

Lady Hana nodded, but her response did not carry into the minds of the Khaleeshir. Whatever she had said seemed to cause Aurichalcum's stern gaze to soften a bit before he departed. He did not say goodbye to anyone as he turned and left.

There was silence for a few moments. But once the woman known as Thrae was certain the Great Dragon was gone, she spoke. *"I came as soon as you called me, Lady Hana. I'm sorry."*

"I'm sorry, was your name Thrae?" asked Arial.

"I am. I am Aurichalcum's daughter and partnered with Leon. Please forgive my father. Tenebrae's betrayal changed him, and he hasn't quite been the same since."

Shooter's jaw dropped a bit. *"I'm sorry, what?"* There was too much there for him to process at once.

Thrae explained in a jumble of quickly spoken words. *"I have been Leon's partner ever since he was young. His father insisted he be partnered with me, in preparation for the day he would become a Dragon Master and succeed his father. We've been partnered for at least a decade; and have remained so after Leon's ascension to Dragon Master. My father does not typically allow anyone to ride him—even Khomandar was partnered with my mother. Though it's not like it would do anyone much good to ride my father into battle..."*

"Your father is certainly...intense," Arkas stated, his arms crossed.

Hana stepped forward. *"I would also like to apologize for Lord Aurichalcum's behaviour. I tried my best to calm him. Thrae speaks true; the damage from Tenebrae's betrayal has not been healed, because he does not allow it to heal. It is more than just a physical wound; it's a wound on his heart as well."*

"I have so many questions," Shooter declared as Hana walked towards the Khaleeshir.

Shooter reached out, as if to catch Hana, like expected her to fall.

But Hana did not fall. No, she walked as if she could see just fine. She paused before Shooter and smiled. She turned her head towards Shooter, and for a moment, just a moment, her eyes opened, and she looked at him, and for a moment, just a moment, Shooter felt seen. *"Just because I am blind, does not mean I cannot see. Being a druid has allowed me to use the Mother as my eyes. I can see the mana of the world around me, and the Mother fills in the gaps. It's not perfect, and there are limitations, but I can get around on my own."*

"I'm sorry," Shooter replied, genuinely empathizing with Hana's predicament.

"Do not be. I was not born this way. Unfortunately, life has not been the kindest, but I've been able to overcome it."

Thrae blew a stray hair from her face. *"That's why my father listens to you. You've struggled just like he has. Mother used to say it was because you succeeded where he failed. Despite the age difference between the two of you, you've been able to do what he could not. In some way, I suppose he respects that."*

"What do you mean?" asked Arial.

Thrae bit her lip. *"Tenebrae...took my father's wings. During the Battle of Kahnair Plains, Tenebrae battled the forces of the Khaleeshir and the Metallic Dragons. At some point in the fighting, Tenebrae was able to get the upper hand on my father, and he tore the wings from my father's body. Tenebrae's betrayal had already wounded my father emotionally—the two had been close before the former's fall. But Tenebrae taking his wings...it only made the wounds deeper. For a dragon, our wings are a very important part of who we are. My father struggled for a long time to find peace and closure, even centuries after Tenebrae's defeat. For a while, he was almost back to normal. But then we found out Tenebrae was still alive...my father has yearned for revenge ever since, and it's consumed him."*

"How has he been teaching the dragons to fly then?" asked Arkas.

"Using me, Valence, and Kinokaze. He flies on our backs in his mortal form and instructs the dragons from there. We act out his examples. It's not ideal but it's worked."

Hana sighed across the mental link. *"Sadly, knowing this will not make the training under him any easier. He will push you as hard as he sees fit, and Leon will likely allow him, because it's what's needed, even if it isn't ideal. I apologize in advance. But hopefully, with this understanding, you may have some pity for him."*

"I'll try my best," muttered Shooter, mostly to himself. "I make no promises."

Arial shot him a look.

Hana walked forward and examined each of the Khaleeshir with her unseeing eyes. With her eyes finally opened, everyone could see that they were milky white. At first glance, they looked like perfect spheres of white marble, but at a second glance, one could make out where the sclera and pupils had once been, when they still held colour, and could still see.

"I think for now, I will let you go. There is something I must do before dinner starts, and I think Aurichalcum succinctly summed up your training—as brusque as the explanation was. Will you please excuse me?"

No one objected. Meeting Aurichalcum had been an emotionally heavy experience that they were not expecting, and it weighed on their minds.

Lady Hana bowed to each of the Khaleeshir and took their hands in welcome.

When Kanaahn took her hand he felt a chill up his spine. He shivered. He felt his mind leave his body. The room began to spin, and then he was in the room no longer. He was somewhere...perhaps somewhere in his mind's eye? He could see where he was, but he had never been here before. He stood on a diverging path in a dark and desolate woodland. It was cold. It was lonely. He felt eyes peering at him from all sides. He was surrounded. He was afraid.

From the corner of his eye, Kanaahn saw two ravens. The creatures croaked and fluttered off down the right path. The ravens croaked again, but Kanaahn could see the path they took was treacherous. The weather was bad, and the footing was unsure. The path was fraught with danger.

On the left path was a warm hearth, a full stomach. He could smell alcohol down that path, just a little further down if only he followed it just a bit more. But it was not as safe as it seemed. Something in Kanaahn's gut seized as he started towards the path. The hairs on the back of his neck pricked up. Danger. Danger was lurking on that path.

The vision was over before it had even had a chance to start.

Kanaahn opened his eyes and realized he hadn't ever left the room, and no time at all had passed. He felt a cold sweat upon his brow. The vision slipped from his mind. It felt like a dream the morning after dreaming it. It was there, in bits and pieces. But it was fading fast, and soon Kanaahn wondered if it had ever happened at all. If there had ever been two ravens and...what was he thinking about?

It was gone. Lost. Like a leaf down a roaring river. It would not surface again.

Hana smiled.

Then, in turn, she took each of the other's hands. Within seconds she had departed and was gone, Thrae not far behind her.

Thrae saluted with two fingers as she disappeared out the door and down the hall.

The Khaleeshir were left in stunned silence.

"I guess...that means we have some free time before dinner then?" asked Arial.

Kanaahn intended to use that time. He wasn't going to turn up the chance to have a walk about the palace and clear his head before dinner. Maybe go see Djall for the first time in weeks. They'd spoken since they'd arrived, but they hadn't seen each other, and he missed the big green lizard.

Chapter XXVII

There came a knock on Menalaea's door late in the afternoon.

Her instincts kicked in; a focused deadliness, years of training, preparing for this moment. She reached for her dagger—not the one at her hip, but the one she kept stashed up her sleeve for emergencies. This blade was poisoned, dipped in one of the deadliest poisons known in Enayra: rotbane.

A single drop of the poison in your system would cause a necrotic rot to set in, starting at your extremities. It would start at your fingers and toes and work its way into your heart—most people chose death before it got that far.

Another knock.

It took another moment for Menalaea to realize she was not in Kula. She was not in her hidden office bunker beneath the house. She was not sitting on a spider's web of her own making, waiting for the Black Blades to kick in her door and drag her off to prison—or worse. She was in Estion, she was safe. Her family was safe.

Menalaea tried not to let her voice waiver as she responded. "Come in."

The door opened, and Arial poked her head into the room. "Mom?"

Menalaea immediately shifted, as she had a thousand times before. No more the spy, the assassin, the killer, the clandestine leader of a continent-spanning information network, the head of a mercantile company. She was no longer Agent Skullspider, she was Menalaea Gainsborough, mother of two.

"How can I help you, love?"

Arial entered—closing the door behind her—and came over to sit on Menalaea's bed. "I just...I wanted to come see you. I wanted to talk like we used to. I..."

Arial's voice broke in that moment. Though she wasn't crying, there was a sadness in her that Menalaea immediately picked up on. She rushed over to the bed and sat next to her daughter and wrapped her arms around her.

Menalaea brushed the hair from Arial's face. "What's got you all upset, love?"

Arial inhaled and steadied herself.

There was so much of Artimer in her. Yet so much of Menalaea, too. In her youth, it made Menalaea worry, but considering what Arial was now, Menalaea knew it would serve her daughter well. You could never be too hardened against the world, especially when you were so involved in its politics, but the sense of justice and a kind heart her father had unknowingly bequeathed their daughter would serve her well as Dragonkin.

"I thought you were dead Mom. I spent weeks without a word, and I had to come to terms with…I needed to accept…I needed to come to terms with the fact that you might be dead, and I might never see you again."

"Love—"

"You were dead, mom. *Dead*. And it was so much worse because I left on a lie. I lied to you—I've *never* lied to you before, and I had to spend months living with that guilt, and then you died. You were dead to me because if I didn't start coming to accept it if I lived with even a shred of hope only to have it crushed, I didn't know if I could live with that. No one knew where you were, and I didn't know at the time that you were perfectly fine, or that you were some…some spy. What else was I supposed to think?" There was a hint of anger and betrayal, in her voice now.

Menalaea felt guilt as well. She never showed it, she always hid it beneath her carefully constructed mask of lies and half-truths, but she *hated* lying to her daughter. One day Menalaea would've told her the truth—that had always been the plan—but it just never seemed right. It never seemed safe. She wanted to tell Arial now; tell her everything, her whole story. Explain, and make her feel better. That's what mothers did!

But that wasn't what spies did. That wasn't what Agent Skullspider did. So Menalaea remained silent, and she let her daughter vent.

"I grew up without a father. I never knew Dad, and I never knew anything about him. You never spoke about him. I knew you—at least I thought I did—but it turns out I didn't know you at all!"

Arial paused. She was rambling. She was upset and she wasn't making sense. Just like Artimer used to. Whenever he got upset he would just vomit out words until the emotions were out. The words were clumsy, but the emotion was raw, and Menalaea had learned to decipher it all long ago. It made her miss him.

Then, Menalaea saw Arial clench her fists. Her daughter gathered herself, and then she looked Menalaea in the eyes. This was no longer Artimer sitting here beside her. Menalaea was now looking at herself. This was her at sixteen. Young, with so much to prove, but always, *always* just wanting to help people deep down. But there was also anger. So much hidden anger deep down. It lurked in her soul, and she kept it well hidden—well chained—but it was there, and the world always liked to underestimate her because she kept it hidden. The world stepped all over her. Never again

Never again.

"I've spent the last six months being lied to by people who were supposed to be my friends. I've been shot at by archers and siege engines, attacked with magic, and nearly killed. I've been betrayed by a person I considered family. But the one person—the *one person* I thought would *never, never* lie to me has spent my whole life lying to me."

Let it out. Let it all out. Don't let them walk all over you. Never again.

Never again.

The storm in Arial rose. The anger reared its head. Menalaea swore she saw lightning crackle across Arial's pupils and flash in her eyes. That was magic; her daughter was a mage, and a powerful mage by the looks of her hair.

And like that, it was gone. The anger died, receded into the depths, and sweet, loving, kind Artimer was there once more.

"Please...don't lie to me any more Mom. I can't...not by you too. Please..."

Menalaea's heart ached. It broke, and she hugged her daughter, but her daughter did not cry.

"I promise, love. Never again. No more lies." And Menalaea meant it. For the first time in her life, she meant it. "I never meant to hurt you or worry you. I never told you anything because—"

Arial hugged her mother tight. "I know *why*, mom. I understand the why. That was never a question. If I were you, I would have done the same, and I don't blame you for it. But I'm not the same person I was six months ago, and things are different now. So please, going forward, don't lie to me."

Menalaea smiled. "I promise."

They sat like that for a long time, holding each other, mother, and daughter; the only family they had.

Finally, Arial broke the silence. "Can you tell me about Dad?"

Menalaea's heart broke again but for different reasons. She put her mask back on, her brave face, her motherly face. "Sure, love. What would you like to know?"

* * *

Risasi felt the wind under his wings, and all around him. It held him aloft and simultaneously pushed against him as he cut through the air like some great, red frigate. His second and third set of eyelids were firmly closed and the world around him acquired a pearlescent glow because of it.

Most humans didn't know that a dragon had three sets of eyelids.

There was the outermost eyelid, that almost everyone saw. It functioned like any other creature's eyelid. It covered the eye when they slept, or blinked, allowing the eye to remain moist and keep out foreign objects, like dust and dirt.

The innermost set of eyelids was little more than a transparent membrane that allowed dragons to fly through high winds. It kept their eyes from drying out in the headwinds, and it kept dust and debris from damaging their eyeballs. Dragons always kept this eyelid closed while flying, just like the membranes that they could contract in their ears and nostrils that kept debris and water out of their other orifices.

But it was the second set of eyelids in the middle of the other two that were incredibly special. This second eyelid was translucent, and it was this eyelid that gave everything a dragon saw a pearlescent lustre when closed. This eyelid was magical and allowed dragons to see the mana of all living things. It was used exclusively for hunting and combat. The dragons called it "nes'kitroth", or "second sight." With this eyelid, every living creature appeared like a bright-burning flame of white-blue energy.

But this eyelid needed to be trained because what few humans understood was that *all* things were alive, and all things that lived had mana. The trees below, the fields of grass, the water, the rocks, and even the wind held residual bits of life energy. The mana was present in varying degrees, and some flames were larger than others, but a young dragon could go mad without the guidance of an older dragon. Everything was just a burning mass of light and flame around them. To the untrained eye, a deer could get lost in the field of grass below, and a moose could be invisible in the massive, ancient forests of Estion.

It had been something Kanothir had tried to train the dragons to gain better control of, and it was training advanced by Valence and Kinokaze, and now Thrae and Aurichalcum aided them as well.

Truthfully, when Risasi had first gone hunting in Altimara he had not believed that using their second sight would ever be so difficult. The sands of Altimara were nearly devoid of any latent mana, and Risasi assumed that was normal. The only life was in the occasional spring, oasis, river, sparse plant life, and of course, the prey animals that roamed the wastes.

But then Risasi arrived in Xiar, and he suddenly realized that Altimara was *not* normal. Altimara was dead, sucked dry of any and all-natural mana like a waterskin drained to the last drop. How or why, none of the dragons could figure out, but the who was painfully clear. Tenebrae. The truth of it was confirmed when they saw that lifeless rot begin to eat away at Estlon's outer edges upon their arrival over the mountain.

Sure, Risasi had grown to enjoy the challenge of hunting in these new territories, so full of life and light, and he grew to welcome the training under his elders. But now he had come to understand the wrongness of what Altimara had become.

"Do you see anything?"

"Nothing, yet."

The voice was Kinokaze's. She had chosen to join him on this hunt. Risasi had been hungry, but it was agreed that the dragons would not depart Ethon without one of the metallic dragons as a guide, and as Thrae was unavailable, Aurichalcum was unable, and Valence was enjoying a well-earned nap, Kinokaze had been the only one able to accompany Risasi on his hunt.

While Kinokaze had not been particularly hungry, she recognized that young dragons frequently were. Their first year of life was the most they would grow in a year in their entire lives. In Risasi's case, he would be twenty-eight metres from head to tail at a year old—he was about halfway there already. From there his growth would slow, as would his appetite and his metabolism.

Risasi shuddered as he remembered that he and the other dragons had a sizing tomorrow. Aurichalcum and the king's leatherworkers would measure the dragons for new saddles, as they had started to outgrow their first saddles. Those saddles would need to fit their increased girth and stature, while also allowing their partners to sit on their backs. For some of the dragons—mainly Risasi and Fyete—straddling the spot at the base of their necks would no longer be possible, as their necks had grown too thick. According to Aurichalcum, they were still too small for standing saddles, but kneeling saddles would work fine at this age and size.

It didn't make the measurement-taking any easier, or more enjoyable, and Risasi still dreaded it. He pushed the thoughts from his mind and returned to the present.

Risasi was not going to complain about spending more time with Kinokaze on this hunt. He enjoyed speaking with her. She was vibrant and knowledgeable, and Risasi welcomed her wisdom and her company.

It didn't hurt that every time he looked upon her his heart would flutter around in his chest, and his stomach felt like he had swallowed a flock of birds. Shooter had explained the feeling as "butterflies in his stomach", which Risasi thought was the funniest thing in the world.

Who would swallow butterflies? They were so small, and they tasted bad—and they had no nutritional value! Not a very filling meal.

Shooter insisted it was just a figure of speech. Dragons had figures of speech, so Risasi was familiar with the concept, but he still wished there could have been a better, more sensical one instead. Risasi preferred the flock of birds analogy. He had done that once, and the feeling was identical.

"Have you seen anything?" Risasi asked.

"Nothing yet. It's hard to hunt in the grasslands, there are more human settlements, and the prey tends to stay farther away."

"Could we try the forest?"

"It's too far away. We'd be gone for days."

"Could we eat livestock?" Risasi bristled with excitement at the thought.

Kinokaze was not as receptive. *"That would be...problematic. It might cause issues."*

Risasi didn't understand that either. Humans raised these animals to eat them anyway, but if you descended upon their pastures and flew off with a cow or a sheep, suddenly they would get upset and shoot arrows and sling stones at you or complain to the king. If these animals were meant to be eaten anyway, why could he not eat them?

Kinokaze had explained it was because these farmers expected payment for their livestock. They raised these creatures with the expectation to sell them for money. This money was necessary for their survival, apparently more than food. Risasi had suggested offering a loose scale in exchange, but most farmers would rather have the money than the scale—as valuable as a dragon scale could be, there was no guarantee they could sell it in their small farming villages.

"Perhaps we should return later when there's less human activity?" Kinokaze suggested.

Risasi did not want to return later. If he did, it would be with others, and Kinokaze may not be the one to accompany them. As hungry as he was, Risasi relished the time spent in Kinokaze's presence more. *"Let us look a little longer."*

Kinokaze did not respond. If she disagreed, she did not speak.

Risasi felt a sudden and cold dread in his gut. Had he said the wrong thing? Perhaps he had offended her?

Bah! What was he doing?

Dragons did not love romantically like humans, and they did not mate outside of their clans. Colour with colour, that was always the rule. When dragons did mate, they did not wallow in their feelings like Risasi had been, worrying if they had used the wrong word.

Such foolishness.

The mating habits of dragons were complicated and involved a precise set of mating rituals and dances.

The male, a drake, would indicate interest by declaring his intent to the female, the dam, and then performing a mating dance. There was no set dance; it was often made up on the spot and came as a feeling—more of an instinct—by the drake.

Most dragons believed the dance came from the Earth Mother, who named all dragons at their hatching and placed these dances in their souls. Every dance was different, though some were similar across lines of descent. The language of the dance was a language in and of itself; every move meant something, and communicated a piece of who the dragon was, and what was in their soul; all their strengths, all their flaws, and everything else in between.

The dam would either respond, and join in the dance, or reject the drake's advances by flying or simply turning, away from the spectacle. If that happened, the drake would find a new dam to court.

If the dam accepted the drake's initial advances and joined the dance, the drake would need to prove himself as a worthy and strong mate by completing the Three Trials. The dam would dictate these trials, but they followed the same three guidelines.

First, the drake would need to defeat an older male in single combat. Next, he would have to kill a dangerous foe, such as a Khin'shala or an icosakraken. Finally, the drake had to hunt a mighty animal as prey.

Enayra was a land full of megafauna, many of them dangerous and used to competing with dragons, so drakes—or rather dams, as it was the dams that chose the prey animal—had their pick of the lot. It was the dams who also chose the older male for their prospective drakes to battle, and they selected which dangerous foe the drake had to kill.

But nowhere in that complex process were "feelings" or "butterflies" involved. These were human feelings, human concepts—human emotions. Risasi hated every second of this…this…weakness! He—

"Risasi?"

His heart melted. *"Yes?"*

"Is something the matter?"

Risasi looked back at Kinokaze, and he saw what he always saw: the definition of beautiful.

Kinokaze's scales shone brightly. Her muscles and sinew flexed powerfully beneath her scaled skin as her powerful wings flapped to keep her aloft. Her neck was long and powerful—and her jaws! She could crush the ribcage of most prey animals if she wished. Her horns were sharp and deadly. Her fangs and claws were polished and clean, sharp as any blade. They could shred flesh and crack bones with ease. Kinokaze took great pride in grooming herself properly. She was the picture of beauty.

"What do you mean?" Risasi stumbled over the words.

"You are acting…odd."

"I don't understand what you mean."

Kinokaze's outer eyelids blinked. *"I can smell it. You're producing adrenaline, and I can hear your heart rate increasing. Did you see prey, or is something wrong?"*

"I…"

What if he was just honest about how he felt? He had told Shooter to do the same so many times, but what if Risasi took his own advice? Admitted to Kinokaze that he found her attractive, and he wished to mate with her. He could land, and he could perform his mating dance…did even he have a mating dance yet? Despite his feelings for Kinokaze, he did not feel the music or choreography deep in his soul. The mother had not granted him his dance…or had he just not unlocked it?

"Are you ill?" Kinokaze sounded concerned.

"I..."

How hard was it? *I find you attractive. You are large and powerful and could crush the skull of a Geller's moose with one powerful snap. I desire to mate with you.*

"I am...just hungry. I am also tired from our training. Perhaps you are right, perhaps we should come back later..."

Kinokaze hesitated for a moment. After a moment, she shook her head and veered her course back towards the capital. *"Let us return then."*

Risasi had faced near-certain death at Xiar, thrown himself against a powerful magical barrier, and unlocked his secondary breath weapon—all things he had done because of his feelings for Kinokaze—but he could not bring himself to voice these feelings and give them power by speaking of them to Kinokaze.

Instead, Risasi followed Kinokaze silently, feeling quite defeated.

* * *

Arkas drew his bowstring back, touching the waxed string to his lips. It was a familiar feeling, like a warm hug or a blanket on a cold night. It was comfortable. It was relaxing. Archery calmed Arkas's mind and smoothed the sea of thoughts in his head. Archery made sense, even when the world didn't.

Archery always made sense.

The bowstring snapped back into place; the bow shuddered. Arkas felt his muscles relax as the tension of the draw disappeared. The arrow whistled through the air. He could hear it, see it. His heightened senses made this all the easier.

Thud!

The arrow embedded itself into the wicker target he had borrowed. But Arkas did not smile. He had missed. He had aimed a few inches left of centre, to a small blue circle that had been painted on the target. Arkas had aimed too high, and his arrow embedded itself on the edge of a larger white circle a few inches above his intended target.

"Damn," Arkas hissed. He was the only one around; the only one to hear it, and to witness his shame, but it did not make the shame any easier to swallow.

Arkas was practising his archery in the western courtyard of Filiddyn Castle. This courtyard was where the three military orders under the purview of the Estian Crown—the Royal Guard, the Bluehelms, and the Royal Hunt—trained.

In the last few decades, the Royal Hunt had been granted the use of a purpose-built archery range in the south-western area of the courtyard, for their ranks to practice their marksmanship.

It was here that Arkas had spent the three previous hours, shooting arrows at targets until his thoughts had calmed.

It wasn't working.

What Arkas had really done was spend the past three hours missing two out of every four shots he took by—what he considered—wide margins and being just a bit off the mark on the other two. This was unlike him. He hadn't shot this bad since he had been thirteen. If his father was here he'd be ashamed. His siblings would've mocked him ceaselessly.

Arkas's archery had been suffering since he had failed to kill that buck clean. The thoughts of Xiar had troubled him during the hunt, and even since then, his mind had found no calm. Every time he closed his eyes he relived the kills, and all he could think about was how he felt nothing in the doing of it all.

Arkas nocked another arrow. It was his penultimate shot; these two would have to count. He raised his bow, drew back the string, and aimed, once more, for the little blue dot left of centre.

"There you are!"

He let go prematurely, and the arrow was loosed. It shattered against the stone wall behind the target. He swore and wheeled around on whoever had distracted him.

It was Cecil.

The fight left him.

"By the Hells, that was…that was bad," Cecil noted. She examined the target a little closer. "Oh, Hells…those are all bad."

Arkas mumbled something indistinctly. His cheeks were bright red. He was embarrassed; at his skills, at his failure, at the fact that Cecil was standing here watching him fail miserably. How long had she been standing there?

Arkas swore again, this time inside his head.

Cecil hopped over the barricade and held out her hand. "Mind if I give it a shot?"

Arkas hesitated. It was his last shot, and he needed to get this right. More for himself and his ego than for any other reason.

"You can hand me the bow, or you can talk about what's got you shooting like a child who just got his first bow."

He couldn't find the words—or rather, he couldn't get them out. Why was he suddenly struck dumb? He had spoken to Cecil before; granted it was in the company of others, and it was usually in response to something Cecil had said first.

Arkas clenched his jaw.

"Well?" Cecil's tone was softer now, like someone talking to a wounded animal.

Arkas handed her the bow and the last arrow. It would be less embarrassing than talking about what was really bothering him.

If Cecil was disappointed, she didn't show it. She took the bow and the arrow with an excitement Arkas immediately recognized. He had seen it on his father's face, and the faces of his siblings. He had often worn such a look on his own face. It was the face of someone who enjoyed archery and found solace in it that few others could.

It was the look of a kindred soul.

Cecil stepped forward towards the rope. She nocked the arrow, then drew back the bow with ease. She had fired a bow before, and frequently enough that a seventy-pound draw weight was nothing to her. Arkas was impressed.

"What were you aiming for before I disturbed you?"

"The blue dot, left of centre."

Cecil nodded, took a breath, held it, and aimed the bow.

Twang!

Zuuuiip-thud!

The arrow buried itself in the centre of the blue dot. Cecil didn't even break a sweat.

Arkas would be mad if he wasn't thoroughly impressed. "I didn't know you were an archer."

Cecil shrugged. "You never asked." She turned and handed the bow back to Arkas. "When I was a kid, my parents insisted I become proficient with a variety of weapons. One of them was the bow. Martial skill is highly valued in Asardaea, especially among young women. It's a tradition that stretches back to the Hero-Queen Maude, and the legendary Zosime."

"You're Asardaean?"

Cecil cocked her head. "You ask the strangest questions..." She was teasing him. Her smile said it all. "So, do you want to talk about it now?"

Arkas sighed. "I suppose I have no choice; I'm out of arrows after all."

The two hopped the barrier and walked over to the gallery, where spectators would sit and watch archery contests between members of the Royal Hunt.

Once on the bench, Arkas found the words. "I'm sorry about earlier I... My mind has been all over the place for the last little while."

Cecil gestured to the target. "Yes, I see that. What's got *you* of all people shaken?"

"How do you deal with all the death? You've been in the Darond longer than I've been a Khaleeshir. I don't know how many battles you've been in, but how do you handle the killing?"

Cecil furrowed her brows. "I've killed a few of Tenebrae's agents. A Blood Witch, and two Black Blades, but Xiar was the first battle of that scale I've been in. It was the first battle in this war, and the first taste of real battle the Darond had seen in five centuries, to tell you the truth. Is that what's bothering you? You know there's no shame in not wanting to kill, or having it affect you. You'd not be the first person to be haunted by it. I remember my first kill—"

"That's not it," Arkas corrected. "I'm not haunted by the people I've killed. Not...not in that way. I don't feel regret, or loss, or horror over it. It's quite the opposite actually...I feel nothing. I don't feel sad, or remorseful. When I killed those soldiers at Xiar, it was no different than putting an arrow through a deer or killing a rabbit. They were not people; they were just targets. When it was animals it was one thing—no one expects you to feel sorry for animals. That *is* a transaction, especially in Altimara; your life, or theirs. At least with an animal, its death is practical; you get to eat, and the animal isn't just left to rot in a mass grave."

Cecil frowned.

Arkas felt his heart race. His cheeks flushed. He suddenly felt warm all over, and his stomach threatened to revolt and return what remained of his lunch. He had admitted what was bothering him, and now Cecil would judge him for it. It wasn't normal, it—

"You'd hardly be the first person to feel that way either."

Arkas was stunned, and his face reflected it.

Cecil smiled warmly and placed her hand on his. "It doesn't mean you're broken because you're transactional about death. I wouldn't say it's the healthiest outlook, but it's not *wrong*. Now when you start enjoying it, let me know; at that point, I would worry."

Relief washed over Arkas like a wave. He wasn't broken, or defective. He could still be a hero—he could still be *good*. Cecil's words had meant more to him than she realized, then perhaps even Arkas had realized at first. For a moment, Arkas wondered if perhaps they meant more *because* they came from Cecil.

And then he realized he was sitting there with an odd look on his face as he let the relief soak in—he had to say something.

"No, no enjoyment," Arkas replied quickly. "It's just... What else am I supposed to be? If I don't kill them, they'll kill me, or my friends. In a perfect world, no one would kill anyone but...we're at war—death is expected."

"You sound like my older sister and mother." She smiled when she spoke, but it was not a happy smile. There was pain in her eyes, and the edge of her mouth twitched slightly.

Arkas knew enough about people that whatever she was remembering was painful enough without him prying, and he changed the subject.

"Thank you," he began. "It's good to hear it from someone else."

Cecil shrugged. Her levity returned. "Sometimes a little encouragement from others is as important as believing in oneself. You're not the first person I know who felt this way, but I understand how it can feel isolating when you see your friends affected by war in different ways."

Arkas had no response, only a deep feeling of gratitude.

Cecil continued the conversation for him. "You know, Arkas, if anything is ever bothering you, you can always come talk to me?" She quickly added. "Or Kyeit—you can even talk to our dragons if you want to. We may be the same age, but we have some of the experience you and your friends don't yet. That invitation goes for all of you."

"I won't forget."

Cecil's eyes lit up and she smiled. "See that you don't. You're my responsibility still, and I can't have you dying in battle because you can't hit the broadside of a barn."

Arkas choked out a laugh. "Well, I suppose I'll have to worry about that if we ever fight a barn." Something dawned on Arkas at that moment. "Why did you come out here looking for me, anyway? Were you that worried?"

Cecil smirked. "No, dinner is soon, and no one could find you. Come on, hurry up or we'll be late."

Chapter XXVIII

The dinner with Leon was more private than Arial had expected. She had expected a great hall filled with knights, soldiers, courtiers, nobility, and councillors. Instead, it was a—relatively—small dining chamber with a few long tables. The Lau'thso were there, as were the two Major-domos, and King Leon, as well as Cecil and the Khaleeshir.

Hana arrived late, escorted by an attendant. Her long white hair seemed to reflect the light of the candles, glowing like the sun itself. She sat, aloof, at the end of the head table, minding her own business as she ate her food quietly.

There was an aura about the girl that made Arial feel uneasy every time she was near her. Something magical clung to her—not in the same way it hung about magic users. This girl almost seemed inherently magical.

Yomi had shown Arial a shard of a Mana Core in Xiar. The shard was full of light, life, and mana. It was a font of power and energy, and Arial could sense it even from within its wooden case halfway across the room. Hana felt similar, and Arial wasn't sure why. Maybe it's because she was a druid. Or maybe it's because of the way she used magic to get through life, making up for eyes, voice, and ears.

Either way, Arial was poring over Yomi's grimoire that he had so kindly provided her with before she left. She had eaten her food quickly—in truth, she wasn't that hungry—and had spent the rest of the evening ignoring everyone at the table for her grimoire. She needed to get to the bottom of Hana. She didn't think Hana was malicious, but her status as a beacon in the patterns of magic of the world intrigued Arial to no end. She wanted to learn as much as she could, but so far she was turning up blank.

She slammed the book shut as Kanaahn came and sat by her.

"You'll get that dirty down here," he teased.

She shielded her book from Kanaahn's mug of frothing beer, just in case. "Not if you don't bring food near it."

"Arial, this is a dining hall, not a library. There's nothing *but* food in here."

"Did you come just to harass me?"

"No. I came to see if you were okay. You've had your nose in that book all night. Honestly, we were all concerned, but your mother said I should be the one to bother you."

Arial looked over to the head table to see Menalaea whispering into Leon's ear, sneaking sideways glances at Arial. Work prevented her from coming to Arial herself, but it didn't stop her from worrying about her daughter.

Arial sighed. "I'm okay, I promise."

"*I* know that." Kanaahn shrugged and sipped his ale, leaving a foamy moustache on his upper lip. "But your mother hasn't spent the last few months watching you stick your nose in that book every chance you get."

"I haven't had a chance to study much since we left Altimara. We've been so busy travelling. It's hard to read when you're exhausted and harder to do on horseback. Or on a boat."

"You know studying doesn't start until tomorrow?" Kanaahn asked, remembering what Aurichalcum had said about studying hard and using free time to get ahead.

"This is something of personal interest. I'm curious about something."

Kanaahn took another sip of beer. "What is it?"

"Nothing important."

"It's important enough for you to do it now."

Arial shot Kanaahn an annoyed look.

Kanaahn was very familiar with that look. He no longer feared them. "Well?"

Arial huffed. "Ilana. She's got a magical aura to her. Don't you feel it?"

Kanaahn shrugged, looking over at the Tsuru. "Not really. What do you feel?"

"She's like a beacon of magic. She bends the mana of the world around her. It almost seems to pool around her, surround her. It's part of her. I've only felt it once before, and I want to know why. I don't know if it's because she's a druid, or how she uses the magic."

"And this can't wait?"

"I'll be up all night otherwise, and we need our rest."

Kanaahn sighed, sipped his beer again, and swung his leg over the bench. "Good enough for me."

"Leaving so soon?"

"Your mother sent me here to spy. I've got what I came for. She said nothing about stopping you." Kanaahn knew better than to stop Arial from trying to do *anything*. You did not stop Arial Gainsborough when her mind was set. You simply watched from the sidelines and stayed out of her way.

And he was gone.

Arial contently returned to her studying. However, she soon faced two problems. A dead end in the grimoire—she had gone through half of it and had found nothing that could help her. And a complete and utter lack of focus. Whatever focus that had been driving her forward had left her, and she could no longer concentrate on the task at hand. Her mind wandered. She started at a page for minutes without realizing it. Her eyes scanned the same sentence five times before she finally slammed the book shut and stuffed it into her bag in a fit of frustration.

"May I join you?"

Arial wheeled in her seat. It was Leon.

"I'm sorry if I've offended you, Your Majesty."

"Please call me Leon. And not at all. On the contrary, you've intrigued me. You must be a good student to study even when not required. As your magic teacher, I'm quite interested in your studies."

Arial moved over a bit, allowing him to slip onto the bench beside her.

"Yomi Tsuru gave me his grimoire before I left Xiar. I've been studying it as much as I can, to learn as much about magic as possible. There are so many theoretical applications of magic that no one has ever tested before."

"Is that what you're studying now?" asked Leon.

Arial shook her head. "I'm trying to find if there are any notes made about druids. This grimoire isn't the most organized though."

"Grimoires seldom are. They are erratic and scattered as a mage's thoughts. I'm sure your grimoire is in a similar state."

Arial beamed with pride. "I organize my grimoire by school of magic, and then alphabetically. It's a lot to manage, but at least I know where to find things."

Leon's look was one of bewilderment. "I must admit, you've impressed me further. Why are you looking into druids?"

Arial paused. She wasn't sure how Leon would feel about her interest in Hana. It wasn't that Arial hated or disliked the girl but being around her gave Arial a weird feeling. Arial simply wanted to understand the *why* behind it all. In the end, Arial decided she could trust Leon. If he was a mage, he could likely sense it too.

"Hana," explained Arial.

"There's something magical about her presence. Yes," Leon finished.

Arial had guessed right.

"I'm sure it's not a surprise to you that I've felt it too. I'll be honest, I don't know why she's a beacon in the flow of mana and energy. She's like a Mana Core; a human Mana Core. I've been around other druids, and they don't possess the same kind of aura. No one has ever been able to explain it. I think Aurichalcum might know, but if he does, he won't share it, and I'm not brave enough—or stupid enough— to press the subject."

"Exactly!" Arial exclaimed. "She reminds me of a Mana Core shard that Yomi showed me in Xiar. She feels the same."

Leon tilted his head. "Have you never been near a true Mana Core?"

Arial frowned. "No. Should I have been?"

Leon waved a hand. "No, I suppose not. You had a perfect opportunity in Xiar—the whole valley survived off its Mana Core. That's how it was able to resist the desertification of Altimara. But I'm sure you had more important things to focus on with the siege."

Arial knew what a Mana Core was. She knew they were also sometimes called Mana Crystals. They were fonts of magical energy that sat at important nexus points of Enayra's leylines. Sometimes they were beneath ancient cities, and other times located at important geographic locations across the continent. They were extensions of the Earth Mother's power, and they were the source of mana for mages the continent over.

All of this had been part of her lessons under Yomi Tsuru in Xiar. These lessons were the foundation of every magical education and were the first thing any mage learned— before they even learned to wield magic. You cannot expect to wield a power you can't understand, as Yomi had told her.

"I suppose I'll have to make that a part of a lesson while you're here. I can take you down below the city, past the catacombs. I will show you Estion's Mana Core during your training here."

"You could do that?" asked Arial, failing to hide her excitement.

"I'm both the king and Dragon Master here. For the sake of your education, it would be easy enough to do. But I must ask you to keep the location of the entrance a secret. Who knows what someone with less than good intentions could do with a Mana Core? Even shards of Mana Cores are dangerous if used improperly; it's said even a shard can level a city."

"I promise, I won't tell a soul." Arial had heard of the kind of power Leon spoke of. "Yomi once told me the core shard at Xiar had been used during the Dragon War. It intensified a shielding spell cast by the High Magus of Xiar to cover the entirety of the Antigorus Valley. Nothing could enter the city without the express permission of the Xiaran High Council. I shudder to think what Tenebrae could do with power like that."

"He would have the will to wield it," Leon agreed.

"Do you think that the real reason why Tenebrae wanted Xiar?" asked Arial.

Leon pondered for a moment. "I don't know. He might have assumed the shard was destroyed using the spell in the first war. He may not even have known it was still there. The shard, from what the Darond had learned, had been greatly diminished by its use in the first war against Tenebrae. It still holds some power in it, but it's a shadow of its former self. Mana Core shards do not replenish like Mana Cores, because they are not attached to the main crystal, and thus cannot receive energy from the Earth Mother. The only way to put energy back in a core shard is to draw upon your own mana and invest it into the crystal. But our limits are much less than that of the Earth Mother. It would take a lifetime to rebuild even a fraction of the power it once had. I doubt the stone is kept as anything more than a memento at this point."

The stone Arial had held had not felt diminished. From what little Arial had known at the time, it didn't feel as powerful as perhaps legends spoke of, but there was a great fountain of power in that core shard. Arial had a theory, one that she formulated after hearing Leon's explanation. Perhaps it would take a lifetime, to refill the core shard. But a thousand years is like ten lifetimes for an experienced mage...and how many mages did Xiar have at its disposal? It was home to some of the greatest magical universities on the continent. It was in no short supply of mages. Who knows...

"Hmm?" Leon pressed, noticing Arial's puzzling look.

"Oh, it's nothing."

Leon did not press the subject. "I hope you don't mind me inserting myself into your studies."

Arial smiled. "It's not a problem; really. I appreciate you taking an interest, and I appreciate the information you've provided me. At least I know to stop looking for my answers in this grimoire."

Leon chuckled. "But you won't stop looking?"

"If I can't find the answers in this book, then that just means I have to find them on my own."

Leon laughed and shook his head. "Truly you are an odd apprentice. I don't know many mages our age who would pursue knowledge for the sake of knowledge and pay no heed to the potential power they could gain."

"There are more important things in life than power. Too many people crave power, but they forego the necessary knowledge, and they destroy themselves—and others—with their hubris. I'm from Kula. I've seen what power can do to good people."

Leon tilted his head and puzzled over what Arial had said. "That is surprisingly profound for someone your age."

"You're not much older than me," Arial protested.

"No, but my head has borne a crown for several years now. My body is only a few years older than yours, but my mind has been weighed heavy, and made old by burden and responsibility."

"*You speak of such morose things in what should be a pleasant chat.*" Lady Hana's voice cut through their minds.

Arial jumped, but Leon seemed nonplussed by the sudden appearance of the druid.

"*Forgive the intrusion. I couldn't help but overhear the latter part of your conversation through Arkas's mind when I was speaking with him. He could hear you, and I could hear his thoughts.*"

Arkas pretended not to notice any of what was going on right now, sipping his mug of beer and turning to talk to Kanaahn.

Arial feared Hana far more than she feared Aurichalcum at this moment.

"*You've always been terrible about eavesdropping,*" Leon joked.

Hana smiled. "*When the Khaleeshir are done with me, it will be impossible for even I to eavesdrop on their minds and conversations. But until then, I will use this as a teachable moment.*"

Leon stood up. "*It's just as well I suppose. I should get going. I've got a lot of work to get done, and my time will be split between statecraft and training starting tomorrow. Arial, thank you for the conversation.*" Leon disappeared into a side door shortly after, leaving Arial alone with Hana in her head.

Arial's skin was crawling. She could smell magic. The smell of ozone and iron. Every hair on her body stood on end, and the air seemed to crackle with energy—even though it wasn't. Hana's presence unnerved her.

"*Does my presence bother you?*" Hana asked.

Fuck. Arial had forgotten that Hana was in her head.

"*I...It's just the—*"

Hana giggled. "*Leon was the same when we first met. You're magic, and you can sense magic. I am inherently magic. It unnerves you.*"

"*How?*" was all Arial could manage to sputter.

"*That...that's a story for another day. But I'm not surprised you can sense it. Most mages can. But most mages get advanced warning of me and my...presence. I'm not surprised it unnerves you, either. It is a great power, and it stands out. As someone who cannot draw on the same sources of power as I can, it makes sense that it would scare you. In a way you could say, it unnerves you because I am unnatural. I should not be. Yet here I am.*"

Hana was a riddle. A riddle that couldn't be solved. A riddle that could read minds. Arial hated it here.

Hana giggled again, and Arial looked up to see the young girl had walked across the dining hall towards her. Before Arial could flee, Hana had sat herself beside her. "*A naturally inquisitive mind faced with a problem it can't solve. I'd be lying if I said I wasn't just a tiny bit amused. I do promise that you will have your answers—but you will have to work for them.*"

Hana reached out and took Arial's hands, and Arial saw a static crack between her and Hana's fingers. She wanted to withdraw her hands, but she couldn't. Either Hana or Arial's own body, wouldn't let her. Hana was ice cold to the touch. Arial felt every hair on her body stand on end. Goosebumps covered her flesh.

Then she wasn't in the dining hall anymore. She was standing on a bridge, and it was slowly crumbling. Arial tried not to panic, it had to be a vision after all. But it felt real, and the fear was real. She screamed but made no sound.

Shit.

No one else was here, and no one was here to help her.

A small blue flame danced and laughed in front of her face and bounced its way across the bridge towards the path ahead of her. That path led to a towering frozen mountain engulfed in a blizzard. She couldn't see much else...but she could feel pain. Immense pain. Emotional, mental, and physical. It was pure anguish. Crushing sorrow and anguish and then...weightlessness. Hope. Hope and light blended. It lifted her.

The bridge cracked and crumbled further. Arial looked behind her. It was the only other way she could go. There was not much this way. A simple cottage, smoke rising from the chimney, and an abundant garden. It was beautiful, it was peaceful. The emotions here were happy, and calm. Everything was peace and bliss. But beneath, there was turmoil. There was something not quite right. It felt wrong...like she had made the wrong choice. Blood and death leaked out from beneath the rose bushes. Skeletal hands reached up from the dirt of the vegetable patch. Undead skulls, screaming their presence to the sky above, tore forth from the gourds. This cottage was built on the graves of so many. All of them innocent, all of them screaming for revenge.

Arial screamed again; the bridge collapsed.

And then it was all over.

She was back in her seat like nothing had happened. Hana was gone, Arial was sitting with a bowl of warm stew before her, and no one even seemed to notice that something was wrong. Whatever she had experienced, she had experienced alone.

Hana was back at her seat at the head table talking to Lord Aurichalcum, who perched himself just over her shoulder. He must have just come in just now. They stood there, unmoving, unblinking, silently. They had to be speaking, but whatever they said was kept privately between them.

Arial stood up. She was still unsteady, and she felt like she was going to be sick. She wasn't hungry, and she no longer wanted to be in this room. But by the time she stood up, she had completely forgotten the experience, and couldn't even remember why she was standing.

"Everything okay, Arial?" Arkas asked.

Arial nodded. She was confused. "Yeah...I...I think so."

"Sit down and eat," Kanaahn called from down the table. "You've barely touched anything."

Arial listened to Kanaahn and her now growling stomach. She ate the stew, but she couldn't remember doing so. Her mind was too preoccupied. She was trying to remember what was bothering her, deep in the pit of her soul, and why everything suddenly felt like a dream.

* * *

"What do you think happened to Kyeit?" asked Shooter.

Dinner had ended early. Based on the bells it was only a few hours before midnight, but the Khaleeshir would be up early the next day, and they were going to take as much rest as they could now.

"She got called back," Arkas shrugged. "Wasn't exactly a secret."

"You think she's in trouble?" Shooter pressed. He was looking to gossip.

"I don't really think it's our business," Kanaahn lied. Truthfully he was just as eager to find out what that cryptic summons from the High Council was all about. Kanaahn had never seen Kyeit that dismayed to report to her superiors.

Shooter's only response to Kanaahn was a sideways look of disbelief.

Even Arial wasn't buying it.

"She's told us a lot. So has Cecil," Arial added. "I'm sure they had to tell the High Council what we'd been told—they'd learn about it eventually. Maybe she's been called in to answer for it?"

"If that were true, Cecil would be going back too," argued Shooter.

"Maybe she already did," suggested Arial.

Arkas shrugged. "Doubtful. She wouldn't have made it back in time if she had."

"Well, Kyeit's the one in charge of the mission to keep us safe," Kanaahn finally added, joining in on the speculation. "Maybe she's got to answer for both of them?"

Shooter shrugged.

"Do you think Kyeit will be back?" asked Arial.

Shooter shrugged again. "I don't know, but she left rather quickly. She didn't look happy."

"That could easily have been her reacting to the news that her home has just disappeared into thin air mere weeks after her father died," Kanaahn argued.

"Yeah, that's fair," Shooter replied. "I still can't believe Xiar's just...gone. How do you lose a city?"

Menalaea materialized from the shadows.

Everyone jumped.

"Quite easily, actually. Estion lost several cities during the Anarchy. Cities that were once on the map were just...gone, without a trace. No ruins. No remains. Just disappeared. Altimara's got the Lost City of Hillenus, a city that was built between Ottogard and Kula and disappeared into the desert without a trace. Cities go missing all the time."

"We didn't see you there," Arkas said.

Menalaea gave a sharp, but friendly smile. "That's the point, dear. I'm sorry to interrupt your gossiping. I've come to give you all something. I didn't have them on me earlier, and I wasn't just going to leave them in your room to be stolen or lost before you arrived. You forgot them when you left." Menalaea pulled a burlap bag from under her cloak and untied it. She reached in and began to remove things, one by one, to the Khaleeshir. "Kanaahn, your pipe, your nezarik cards, and your tabbat dice." She handed a small, oblong, leather pouch to Kanaahn.

Menalaea turned to Arial. "I made sure to grab him before I fled Kula." She pulled the mangled stuffed dragon Smokey from the sack. Menalaea had repaired the damage done by Adalinda when she hatched, and it looked as deformed as new when Arial's friends had made the creature for the first time.

Arial flushed red grabbed the dragon, and tucked him—gently—into the billowing sleeves of her robes before anyone could see him. "Thanks, mom," she whispered.

"Arkas, your father told me to bring this to you." Menalaea now produced a six-inch knife in a beautiful leather sheath from the bag. She handed it to Arkas with great care.

Arkas's eyes widened as he beheld the knife. "That's...that's the family knife."

"Family knife?" asked Shooter.

"It was made by my great-grandfather, for my grandfather when he became a hunter. It's been passed down the generations in my family. My father always said it would be handed down to me one day—being the oldest and all."

Menalaea smiled and patted Arkas's hand gently. "Your father said it was time. He said you have greater need of it now than he does, and he would be proud for you to wield it in the fight against Tenebrae."

Arkas immediately began fiddling with his leather belts, trying to get the knife around the belt at his waist. He wasted not a second in displaying the heirloom, all the while trying to blink away the tears that now gathered in his eyes. He swallowed away the lump forming in his throat.

"Nothing for me, I guess," Shooter smiled. He wasn't surprised. His parents hadn't done him much good in life, and he didn't own a lot of his own things. What he did own was already on him.

"Actually, I do have something for you."

Shooter chuckled. "The sack?"

Menalaea shook her head and produced two things from the sack. "Well, your own nezarik deck, and set of tabbat dice, and this knife. It's a gift from you know who."

The knife was a thin stiletto blade with a simple, leather-wrapped handle. It wasn't ornately carved; it wasn't fancy or inlaid with gold. It didn't have a gem in the pommel. It was pure functionality. But there was no denying that this blade was of fine craftsmanship. It was forged for function over fashion, and Shooter knew from experience that this blade functioned perfectly. It belonged to Amber and was part of a set. Shooter could guess where the other knife was.

"And this—" Menalaea handed Shooter a small leather cord strung through a pressed metal medallion.

Shooter turned the medallion over his hand. It was old, worn out, and covered in scratches, soot, and dirt. The leather cord was worn and frayed and looked like it might snap at any second. There were letters engraved into the rough surface of the medallion, but they were barely legible; worn by time and damage. He could only make out a few pieces of the inscription: *El...t...os,*

"What's this?"

"I found it on your father's body when I pulled him from the wreckage," explained Menalaea. "I don't know what it means, or what purpose it served. But I thought you should have it."

Shooter felt a wave of cold wash over him. He wanted nothing to do with this, knowing its origin. He wanted, with all his strength, to turn to the window and throw it from the castle forever. But he couldn't do that. Not now anyway, not in front of Menalaea. Later, perhaps.

"Thank you," Shooter said finally, though it was clear he was forcing out the words. Even if he wasn't thankful for the medallion, he was certainly thankful for the knife. He pocketed the medallion and affixed the knife to one of the inside pockets of his cloak.

Menalaea pretended not to notice the conflict on Shooter's face. She returned the cloth sack to the void beneath her robes. "I'll let you get back to your gossiping. Try not to speculate too much, you may find yourself disappointed with reality." With that, Menalaea was gone. Disappearing down the hallway and into the shadows again.

"Have I ever told you how much I love your mother, Arial?" asked Arkas.

Arial smiled. "Yeah, me too."

Chapter XXIX

Tohru spurred his horse onwards. The poor creature had been run ragged, but there was no time to stop. Not yet. He wasn't safe until he crossed the border.

Tohru had fled Felidrun without issue. He stayed away from the main roads. He had no guarantee that they weren't patrolled by soldiers and guards who might be looking for him. Tohru had no idea how high up this conspiracy went, but he wasn't going to risk it. Instead, he chose to take the slower route through the forests. For a few days, he was safe, going at a quick but measured pace. But in the middle of the third night, he noticed he was being followed.

It turned out to be the worst-case scenario. Hooded creatures materialized out of the darkness and attacked him in his camp. Tohru knew what they were; he'd fought them once before, and he knew what they were capable of. He had seen some of the Darond's finest cut down in their prime like wheat before the scythe, and he had once almost been among that number. Tohru had barely fled into the night with his life. He hadn't stopped since. He ate and slept in the saddle and had his horse running as often as he could. Tohru only hoped it would be enough.

Tohru was not far from the border of green dragon territory. He was hoping they'd be able to help him, even if all they could do was scare off the Tulkaz. He just hoped he wasn't angering a worse enemy than he was fleeing. The green dragons were not known for being kind to those who violated their borders.

One of the Tulkaz cried out from somewhere in the woods behind him.

Shit. They were catching up.

"Just a little more," Tohru whispered to his horse. "Just a little more. We're almost there."

Tohru didn't make it.

But not because the Tulkaz caught up with him. Instead, a massive green dragon landed in front of him, just as he entered a clearing. The dragon roared and flexed his wings.

Tohru's horse reared, nearly throwing him, but Tohru was able to hold on.

The dragon did not look happy. "Why have you come here, human?" he demanded. "Speak!"

"Tulkaz!" Tohru cried. He did not waste a second in warning the dragon of the lurking danger.

The dragon did not waste another moment. With a roar, he charged towards the two hooded figures that emerged from the woodland. They hissed and spat as the dragon charged at them.

The green dragon let out a chattering call from deep in his throat, and two other dragons swooped down from above to join the fray. If there was one thing the dragons hated more than humans entering their lands, it was the Tulkaz and any other of Tenebrae's servants and creations.

Tohru didn't stick around to watch the fight. He fled into the woods, now carefully skirting around the edge of the green dragons' territory. He didn't know who won or lost the fight he had abandoned, and part of him felt bad for throwing that fight on the dragons, but he buried that part of him again quickly.

A roar echoed from somewhere behind him, and Tohru spurred his horse on faster. It sounded cold, but better them than him, he figured. At least the dragons stood a chance against the Tulkaz. Their involvement would allow Tohru to get to Ethon in time and prevent whatever was coming from happening. That could only benefit the green dragons in the long run.

Chapter XXX

Amber smoothed out the sheets and blanket of Drakhart's bed, then dutifully fluffed his pillows. He'd been gone a while, and she hadn't been able to spy on him. She took the job as a chambermaid in the Black Citadel, hoping to help the Darond from within the vipers' den. Instead, she was more a maid than a spy.

Calandor hired and maintained his own house staff in the Major-domo's Villa on the compound's grounds. Elandyr'ni kept an entirely Qiri'ar staff at her Grand Enchanter's Cottage—though to call it a cottage didn't do the small mansion justice. She was unable to sneak into their places and steal state secrets as a result. The military leaders were all nobility, who made their homes and offices on the battlefield, or at their estates in their home cities.

The only other government position that worked out of the castle was the king, and there was currently no king, or a royal family for that matter. The country was being led by the Regency Council, and they took their orders from Tenebrae.

Amber obviously wasn't going to be Tenebrae's chambermaid, let alone even allowed to know where he was being kept. Which meant the only other person she could spy on was Drakhart.

In truth, it wasn't a total loss. Drakhart had—according to the gossip around the castle—been given much more responsibility lately. Despite being a recent addition to the nobility of Altimara, he had risen quickly in the ranks, and been tasked with leading the Regency Council, even.

The only problem was that since Amber had been here, she hadn't seen him. When she started, he had just left on a diplomatic mission to Gishan'belor with the Grand Enchantress, and even though he returned, he had spent no more than a day here in the palace before departing again. Though no one knew where he was going.

So now Amber was left to snoop around Drakhart's room for half an hour a day as she dusted, maintained tidiness, and kept the place cosy and comfortable for when Drakhart returned. Despite all her snooping, she hadn't found a single thing.

Amber let out a huff and examined herself in the mirror.

Her long red hair, for which she had become known, was gone; cut short and dyed black with a special mixture of herbs and pigments. She had used her skills with make-up and disguises to change a few facial features and hide her freckles. In case Drakhart ever came across her, he would have a harder time recognizing her. She wiped her hand across her forehead and gathered up her equipment before leaving the bedroom.

Amber arrived in Kasaadua a few weeks ago. She hadn't sent word to Vilingar or Skullspider yet. She didn't have a contact network in the city, and she didn't trust Kasaadua to not be full of spies. Tenebrae had had a hold on this city for a thousand years; anyone who worked in the shadows as much as he would've been smart to put the shadows on a leash long ago. She would only send word once she had important information to send. That technically made her AWOL, but it's not like the Darond were going to be barging into Kasaadua looking for her.

As she walked through the halls, onto the next room she was supposed to clean, Amber's thoughts strayed back to Shooter. She had sent him a letter through Skullspider before she fled Kula, explaining everything that had happened since Shooter left. If he had responded, or if he had even received it, Amber didn't know. She might never know at this rate. It would all depend on when she would be able to reach out to Skullspider again. It wouldn't be any time soon at any rate.

She felt bad for how she had written the letter. Amber had been terse and to the point. That was how she'd always been, at least with anyone who wasn't Shooter. Shooter was different. She had loved Shooter. But she had not written of her feelings. She had not written of how she had been hurt that he had left without so much as a goodbye. For all, she understood why, the irrational part of her that lived deep within everyone refused to understand. She did not tell him the truth about why she had wanted to see him before he had left. That was not something you just dropped on someone, let alone in a letter.

Amber felt for the dagger she kept strapped to her thigh beneath her dress. The familiar feel of the simple handle. It had saved her life more times than she could count. She had sent its twin with the letter; what the letter didn't say, Amber hoped the dagger would.

Though she might doubt it sometimes, she knew how Shooter felt about her in return. He didn't say it often, but she knew, deep down. It was in his actions.

Shooter didn't open up to a lot of people, and even though he had opened up to Amber more than anyone else, it had been a chore to drag even what she had out of him. Shooter kept his secrets and feelings guarded. Though Amber could understand why. He had gone all his life without a place he could go to be vulnerable and open, and anytime he was, it only caused him pain.

Amber cleared her head of such thoughts. For now, they were a distraction. She was here to blend in and to spy, not muse on her love life. For now, Amber was no more, there was only Yiilae the chambermaid.

Chapter XXXI

Kanaahn had been dragged from his bed at the crack of dawn. A chambermaid entered and woke him before disappearing to do the same with the other Khaleeshir. She had left him a cauldron of water over the fire, which he could scoop out into a bowl and use to wash the sleep from his eyes and face.

Once he was dressed, he and his friends were escorted by Menalaea down to the castle's library where King Leon, Hana, Aurichalcum, Imuhlair and Iskren were already waiting for them. Several long tables were cleared—save for stacks of books—for use by the Khaleeshir and their new teachers.

In these halls, Leon and Aurichalcum lead lessons on history. Imuhlair would lead culture and political studies, and he, along with Iskren, would lead the lessons on language. Hana handled literature, as well as her own lessons on how to shield their minds from intrusion, invasion, and subversion.

Leon had started their lesson that day with a lesson on the basic history of the Darond Order and the original Khaleeshir. He reasoned that if the Khaleeshir were to lead the Darond, it would be best for them to know its history and how it operated. History of other nations would shortly follow in the days and weeks to come.

Despite his youth, Leon lectured with a skill and knowledge beyond his years. Even Aurichalcum respected Leon's encyclopaedic knowledge of history.

"The Darond," started Leon, pacing back and forth in front of the table where the Khaleeshir were scribbling away at notebooks and leaves of parchment. "Were originally founded in the year thirty-seven Heroes by the original Khaleeshir. The Darond, short for the Sacred Order of the Knights of Darond, were a paramilitary, chivalric order meant to assist the Khaleeshir in their sacred duty of bridging the gap between the two races of Enayra. The Khaleeshir could not be everywhere at once, so Dragon Knights would be trained and dispatched across the continent to mediate conflicts between humans and dragons. As the Age of Heroes progressed, the role of the Darond expanded, and they were requested to mediate beyond their original scope, and soon intervened in internal issues between humans, and between dragons."

Kanaahn's hand burned as he wrote down as much of what Leon was saying as possible. He hadn't written this much in years, and it brought him back to the days when he was sat down and forcibly tutored at Menalaea's expense. She had always wanted Arial and her friends to have a better chance at life than they would normally be afforded, no matter the cost. A basic education would see to that.

"The original Khaleeshir divided the Darond into five orders, known as banners. They are the Obsidian, Emerald, Vermilion, Cobalt, and Alabaster Banners. Each banner was put under the direct control of a Khaleeshir, based on their specialization. The Khaleeshir commanded their banners under the title of 'Lord or Lady.' Below each Lord or Lady of the Banner serve a single General and four Knight-Commanders. Each Knight-Commander in turn oversees two Knight-Captains, who themselves oversee the regular rank-and-file recruits more directly."

Leon paused while the Khaleeshir's notes caught up with his words.

"The Obsidian Banner was founded by Lord Zhevor Vessan, the Phantom Blade, bonded to the black dragon Kwe. He was a master of stealth, subterfuge, and spy craft. In fact, in his time before he was a Khaleeshir, he was one of the founding members and the first Night Lord of the Altimaran Black Blades. Lord Vessan knew that no organization could keep the peace across the continent if their arms, eyes, and ears did not reach from coast to coast. With an ear in every port, eyes on every road, and arms that could stretch across every nation, no conflict would engulf Enayra without the Darond's prior knowledge; knowledge they could use to stamp out conflict before it arose. The Obsidian Banner is the banner of the Darond's spymasters, messengers, smugglers, cypher corps, and assassins.

"Next, is Lord Eldim Rodir, or Eldim the Wise. He was a scholar before he was made Khaleeshir and bonded to the blue dragon Lo'ind. More specifically, Lord Rodir was a professor of philosophy at the University of Xiar and was headmaster of his department. Lord Rodir believed that justice was a blade, but any blade that was wielded without, knowledge, wisdom, and precision was prone to abuse. The Cobalt Banner was founded to codify the laws and rules of our order and is comprised of legal scholars from all nations so that Darond soldiers are aware of the laws of the nations in which we operate. Cobalt Bannermen are also in charge of collecting, copying, and preserving banned or rare manuscripts, and maintaining the Darond libraries, archives, and records. No knowledge should be forbidden or lost. Lord Rodir made it his banner's mission to distribute literature—banned and lawful alike. They also provided the services of scribes for free for the disenfranchised and poor and provided legal aid to peasants who were being abused by their lords or rulers. To this day, the Cobalt Banner is our scholarly wing, made up of our scribes, scholars, and legal professionals.

"Lord Tolrem Tsuru, the White Wizard, bonded to the white dragon Beylyn, founded the Alabaster Banner. The Alabaster Banner is dedicated to the pursuit and study of magic. He is the progenitor of the Tsuru magical bloodline and the first of his family to be born with white hair, the sign of a powerful mage. Not a descendant of his has been born without magical ability since, even if they choose not to pursue magical arts. It was said under Lord Tsuru, the Alabaster Banner maintained a magical library at Dragonsrest beyond even the collections at Xiar's universities and Great Library. Before becoming Khaleeshir, Lord Tsuru was the Grand Enchanter to the Emperor of Espias. All our mages and magical scholars serve the Alabaster Banner, except for mages who deal in the healing arts. They serve the Emerald Banner.

"The Emerald Banner is made up of our doctors, nurses, mage healers, surgeons, and herbalists. It was founded by one of the most prolific healers and doctors of her time, Lady Sei'ophmei Dynia, the Mother of Enayra. She had been the royal physician to Queen Faustina II of Asardaea before she was made Khaleeshir and bonded to the green dragon Unaedrol. Sei'ophmei was trained in classical medicine, as well as the art of magical healing. She was also a skilled mage in her own right, being well-versed in pyromancy. The purpose of the Emerald Banner was more than just healing knights and soldiers during war or battle, but also helped provide medicine to the people. Lady Dynia travelled Enayra, providing medical care to the poor and those living in remote regions, and not just in times of hardship, famine, or sickness. She did this quite regularly when times were good as well. She earned her nickname for the care and kindness she showed to all.

"Finally, we have Lord Nayondel Darond, the first leader of the Khaleeshir, bonded to the red dragon Veryll, first Grand Master of the Darond Order, and Lord of the Vermilion Banner. In his youth, he had been a knight-errant serving the Estian royal family. The Vermilion Banner is perhaps the most well-known banner of the Darond Order. All our warriors, from the Dragon Knights to our regular soldiers serve the Vermilion Banner. They are the military might of the order. Though originally, at the time of the order's foundation, they were merely meant to be peacekeepers. Lord Darond created the Dragon Knights to further deepen the bonds between dragons and humans. He believed that while only the Khaleeshir should undergo the bonding ritual, any human deemed worthy by the dragons should be partnered with a dragon to better demonstrate the point of the Khaleeshir: that two races could coexist, and work together, for the greater good and coprosperity of the other, and their shared home."

Leon paused in his explanation. The room was silent except for the sound of scratching quills.

Kanaahn cursed under his breath. He had smudged the previous line again. Writing with wet ink using his left hand had always been a struggle, and Kanaahn had never developed his skills at using the other hand to write. He did want to be able to read his notes later. Now his notes were ruined, and his hand was stained.

Leon seemed to notice Kanaahn's struggles and looked to Imuhlair. "Imuhlair, do you happen to have one of those new styluses on hand?"

Imuhlair nodded and produced a small wooden stick from a pocket in his robes. He stalked over to Kanaahn and placed it gently down on the table.

"Try that," Leon said. "It's something new from Asardaea. They've only just made their way down here. It's like a stylus, but it's made of wood, and the centre is made of compressed lead. You might find that a bit easier to write with."

Kanaahn had never been more thankful for anything in his life. He still gripped the new 'stylus' awkwardly, and he had the paper turned at an awkward angle, but it was easier than trying to negotiate with a quill and ink. It would take some getting used to, but this would be an easier tool in the long run. Kanaahn was able to recopy his old notes on a fresh page and catch back up.

"Any questions?" asked Leon.

Hands immediately shot in the air.

"One at a time then." Leon pointed to Arkas first.

"Who leads these banners now, since there hasn't been Khaleeshir to lead the banners for a thousand years?"

"If no Khaleeshir were around to lead the Darond, Lord Darond stipulated that a council would be formed to rule until new Khaleeshir were selected. The council was to be formed of the five Metallic Dragons and the five generals of the banners. Over the years this council evolved into the High Council, and the Metallic Dragons came to be represented by the Dragon Masters. The five generals remain on the council, but room has also been made for the leaders of each supporting nation. In the year six-hundred and two Darkness, the Darond Concordat was signed between the Kingdom of Asardaea, the Kingdom of Estion and the Darond Order. In exchange for financial, military, and political support for the Darond, the two kingdoms would be granted a seat on the High Council, which is filled by their monarchs, or a chosen representative. The Concordat was amended in nine thirteen to include the Espian Empire."

Kanaahn raised his hand. "Are we supposed to lead these banners now that the Khaleeshir have returned?"

Leon paced and mulled over the answer. He exchanged glances with Thrae, Cecil, and Aurichalcum before he finally responded. Their looks were troubled. "That would be the ideal plan."

Arial followed. "Will the High Council allow it?"

Leon's response took longer to formulate this time. "We don't know. The High Council is divided; those who oppose your attempts to lead the Darond, and would rather make you puppets, and those who want things to be as they should have been—as the old Khaleeshir intended. Those opposed to you on the High Council have gotten used to their power...it's not something they'd like to lose, and they will fight for every inch they can."

Thrae grimaced. "They were already displeased that Hunter involved you in the Siege of Xiar. But because he was an ally, and not a member of the Darond proper, they could not punish him. Xiar never signed the Concordat, so he had no place on the High Council, and no official title, but regardless their assistance, political clout, and wealth of magical knowledge was too crucial for the Darond to risk losing."

It finally dawned on Kanaahn then. *'So, instead, they punished his daughter. He's dead, the city has disappeared, and nothing is stopping them from pinning the blame on Kyeit.'*

'I was thinking the same,' Djall chimed in from inside Kanaahn's head.

"Can you tell us who is on what side?" asked Shooter. "We know about the divide between the traditional Darond and Dynia's Hand."

Leon smiled. "Kyeit's had you doing your homework."

Cecil looked away.

No one was going to correct him that it had taken some serious teeth-pulling to get that information from her and Cecil.

"While Dynia's Hand is no longer an active cell—nor do we use that name—the sentiment remains, and the lines are still drawn along those old boundaries. Among the High Council, Asardaea, myself, and most of the Dragon Masters are on your side."

"Most?" asked Kanaahn.

"Grand Master Khomandar is opposed. He believes that putting the Darond in the hands of inexperienced children would only undo a thousand years of hard work." Leon's face soured slightly.

Arial pressed further. "Who is opposed?"

"Aside from the Grand Master, Espias is naturally opposed to Asardaea, and thus to you, and the generals do not wish to relinquish control of their banners. Though they've claimed they'll turn over command as soon as you've been trained, I don't trust them to keep their word. Darond generals in recent years have been known to inherit their positions from their forebearers, usually their family, rather than be commissioned."

Kanaahn let out a sigh. "We have our work cut out for us, don't we?"

Leon smiled. "So do all who aspire to greatness."

* * *

The literature lessons involved much more of a slog through thick and heavy texts. Some selections were prose novels meant to impart lessons or portray satire. Some were epic poems, that went on for hundreds of pages, detailing the exploits of heroes both real and imagined. Some were simple collections of poetry and songs. Some were histories, or treatises put together by men and women who were long dead—some whose names had been completely forgotten.

Their first literature study would be on Asardaean literature. Asardaean, being one of the oldest countries on Enayra, and one of the main forces behind the foundation of modern Enayran society, had produced a long list of literature that continued to influence writers, politics, and people even until the modern day. Each of the books, while old and written in various Asardaean dialects from across the ages, had been translated into Common for the ease of the reader.

The list of books chosen by Imuhlair and Iskren had been extensive. At the top of the list was *De re militari* or 'Of Military Matters', a treatise originally written in Old Western Asardaean in the early years of the Age of Conflict, during the late reign of the Hero Queen Maude. Though it was called a treatise, the book was massive. It dealt with Asardaean military history, specifically during the time of Emperor Volesus and the Enayran Empire, and the military of the following Kingdom of Asardaea, led by his niece, Maude. It compiled a long history of basic Asardaean military strategy, the structure of the Asardaean army, and much more about the subject of war, Asardaea, and war in Asardaea. Despite the age of the book, much of the structure of the standard Asardaean Legion, and Asardaean military command hadn't changed

Next, there was *Poíisi*, or simply 'Poetry', a collection of Asardaean poetry, written in Middle Eastern Asardaean, that chronicled thousands of poems stretching back to the Age of Heroes. It was a popular book among Asardaean youth, and some of the poems had been bedtime tales for children in Asardaea since ancient times.

This was followed by *Historia reginae*. It was a more modern book, published in the last half-century, that detailed the history of Asardaea's long, unbroken dynasty of warrior queens, tracing their lineage back to the Hero Queen Maude, and from her to the Emperor Volesus. The book detailed important events of their reigns and details of their lives.

Next was an epic poem suggested by Cecil. *Faustina Prima* had been one of the three books she carried with her and read and reread often. It chronicled the life of the

Asardaean Queen Faustina I, in the years leading up to and during the War of the Grand Coalition. Faustina I the War-Forged had been an average queen, until the War of the Grand Coalition, where she personally led her armies in conjunction with her generals against the might of Gerovia and their allies. The epic poem portrays Faustina's transformation from a weak and inexperienced leader into the mighty warrior queen she came to be known as later in life.

Finally, the last book was *Imperium Enayra: How Love Conquered a Continent*. It was a recent publication from Asardaea's ancient University of Malatrion. It chronicled the history of Volesus and Zosime, and the events of their lives, from the former's conquest of Enayra and foundation of the Enayran Empire to the latter's creation of the modern Asardaean Paladins as the fist of the Asardaean monarchy, and keepers of the peace. While a modern history book, and more of a historical analysis of facts and figures, its value was no less important for understanding the modern basis of Enayran history.

The words in most of these books were long and difficult to pronounce. They made Arkas's head ache just trying to make sense of them. Often he'd find himself reading the same sentence over again. His head thrummed and felt heavy, and his eyes drooped. He had started with the book Cecil had suggested, and while he found it interesting, he just couldn't focus long enough to make any sense of it.

Arkas had no idea how he was going to get through literature lessons like this. Most of the reading would need to be done between classes; today being the exception. Most classes would be spent from here on out discussing what was read and dissecting each long-winded paragraph of each page of these long-winded books.

The Khaleeshir had been given separate sections of the library to spread out, make themselves comfortable, and read through their assigned literature. Arkas had chosen a secluded corner in the far back of the library. Here he sat in a comfy armchair near a cold, dead fireplace.

Cecil sat down in the chair nearest Arkas. "Having a hard time?"

Arkas rubbed his eyes and put down the book. "I don't know how anyone reads for hours—for fun, no less. All you do is sit there and torture your mind."

"I could say the same about hunting," Cecil retorted. "You stand around in the dirt and mud for hours. Sometimes you miss. Sometimes you don't get anything, and it was all for nothing. Sometimes your prey runs off. You can't sit around and talk because you'll scare the animals. You can't read because you'll miss your target passing by. You can't even have a nap for that same reason."

"I see your point," Arkas muttered.

"Is it the language used, or the content?" Cecil asked, her tone growing more serious.

"I'm not sure anymore. I find the content interesting, what I understand of it. But it's just so long-winded and rambling. It's like listening to an old man drone on for hours. I just want them to get to the point. It makes the reading slow going."

Cecil picked up Arkas's book and examined where he was. "This is page ten."

"I said it was slow going."

Cecil smiled. "Sometimes you just need to clear your head. But sometimes, a little help doesn't hurt. Would you like to read through this together? I'll come by later tonight, and we'll read through the novel, and if you have any questions, I'll answer them. The same goes for the other books in your pile."

"Good luck. I can barely get through the interesting book. I don't know how I'm going to get through the boring histories. These are Kanaahn's kinds of books, not mine."

Cecil hid a smile. "I never took Kanaahn for a reader. Not to insult his intelligence, I've just never seen him read."

Arkas smirked. "We haven't exactly had the time for it lately. But he did quite a bit of reading in his free time back in Kula. It's a little harder to do when you're fighting a war."

"Why? I don't seem to have a problem." Cecil winked. "So, where did Kanaahn get these books? Kula doesn't have a library, as far as I can remember."

"You've studied Kula?"

"As much as anyone. We'll have to take the fight to Tenebrae one day, which means besieging Kasaadua. The Darond has considered seizing Kula as part of the invasion plan. At the time it was thought to be an easy endeavour. A city with no walls, no garrison, and little defensible architecture. Not to mention Krystor Davenpourte's willingness to switch sides and join the Darond, and Menalaea's smuggling routes. It would've been an easy enough city to take and reinforce it. We would have used it as a staging ground for other attacks against Altimaran cities, and as a resupply point for any armies we have marching across the land."

"That's going to be a lot harder to do now, what with Lord Davenpourte dead and Drakhart in his place turning the city into a miniature Ottogard."

Cecil replied with a nonchalant toss of her head. "So, where did Kanaahn get these books?"

"From Menalaea mostly. Menalaea had a library to be envious of—for Kula anyway. She encouraged us all to further our education as much as possible. Reading was about all we could do in that regard in Kula. She did get us a basic education as children though. We'd spend hours at Arial's under the stern gaze of several tutors. Menalaea wanted to ensure we had every advantage in society, regardless of what we chose to grow up and become."

Cecil closed her book and rested her chin on her hands, and her elbows on the arm of the chair. "What *did* you want to grow up and become?"

"The only thing I'd ever been taught to become: a hunter and butcher, like my father and grandfather before me. I come from a long line of hunter-butchers. One day, my siblings and I would take over the store, and the family legacy."

Cecil did not reply with words. She merely put a hand on Arkas's forearm and gave him a dim—yet sympathetic—smile. From the look in her eyes, Arkas could tell that Cecil truly understood the weight of the legacy Arkas spoke of.

Arkas could feel his cheeks flush, and he did his best to hide it.

The gaunt and slim figure of Imuhlair stalked between the rows of books. He made small silent strides, his fitted robes refusing to betray their master by making a single sound of swishing fabric—lest they feel his wrath. His footfalls made no sound. Not even his breathing could be heard. His arms were clasped behind his back; long, bony fingers intertwined like some skeletal cat cradle. Imuhlair's posture was as impeccable as his hair. No longer than his chin, neatly pushed back and trimmed ever so immaculately at his jawline. Not a single hair was out of place. Finally, he came to a halt, perching himself in front of Arkas and Cecil, like some great carrion bird. He almost resembled a vulture, with his hooked nose, sallow cheeks and black, scrutinizing eyes that hid far too much from the world. He did not speak. Imuhlair merely pursed his lips and stared disapprovingly at Arkas and Cecil.

Arkas smiled sheepishly.

Cecil did not seem the least bit perturbed—in fact, Imuhlair only cast his iron gaze upon Arkas, and didn't even acknowledge Cecil's role in his distraction from his studies.

Without a single word, Imuhlair cocked his head, narrowed his eyes, and raised his eyebrow. The implication was immediately understood by Arkas, and he quietly returned to his reading. His face now burning from embarrassment. He could feel fear pooling in his gut.

The very corner of Imuhlair's mouth twitched in what was, if but for a fraction of a second, something like a facsimile of a smile. But just as quickly as it formed, it died, and Imuhlair's frown returned as master of the face. Imuhlair turned mechanically, his eyes still fixated on Arkas, before he floated off without a sound to some other aisle to check on the other Khaleeshir.

Arkas's eyes met Iskren's from across the aisle—the young Major-domo was sitting with Shooter, working through a copy of *De re militari* with him. Iskren looked around him, making sure Imuhlair was nowhere nearby before he made an apology to Shooter and quickly walked up the aisle towards Arkas and Cecil.

"I'm sorry," Iskren said. "He's not normally so...intense."

Cecil clicked her tongue disapprovingly. "You're lying to him now."

Iskren smiled. "You're right. I am. He's always this bad. But it's nothing personal; Imuhlair is a good man and loyal servant of the Crown. He just wants to see you succeed. But he doesn't take kindly to slacking off."

"I've noticed," Arkas muttered. "How do you put up with him?"

Iskren shrugged. "One day at a time, usually. He's not so bad once you get to know him."

"Oh yeah?" asked Cecil.

"Well, that's what I tell myself anyway. I'll let you know if I ever get to know him."

Arkas smirked.

Iskren was the opposite of everything Imuhlair was. He was bright, warm, jovial, and friendly. He smiled, he was welcoming and kind. He was patient. Arkas was certain that at the very least, Iskren was human; the same could not still be confirmed of Imuhlair.

Shooter had joked that the man was secretly a reanimated corpse. The reason he frowned all the time was that smiling loosened the muscles too much, and frowning kept his rotting flesh together. There were times Arkas didn't wonder if there was some truth to that statement.

"Honestly, I don't know if I'll ever get to know him. He's always disappearing somewhere, then reappearing just when he's needed, often with a solution always at hand. Sometimes, I wonder if he's not spying on Leon more than helping him."

"What do you mean?" asked Arkas.

Iskren leaned against the bookshelf. "Well, he was Leon's father's Major-domo first. Most kings in Estion choose their ministers, advisors, and Major-domo when they take the throne, but not Leon. He wasn't allowed to. When Leon took the throne, King Khomandar insisted Leon keep the same cabal that had served under him previously. Leon's been able to shake most of his father's circle over the years, but he just can't seem to get rid of Imuhlair. Some days, I wonder if Imuhlair isn't stalking off to go rat Leon out to his father."

"Why would Imuhlair want that?" Cecil asked.

"Why wouldn't he? His loyalty is to the old king, and the old king wants to have his cake and eat it too. He's leading the Darond, serving under Aurum, while still being the one pulling the strings in Estion. Except, Leon and his father haven't always seen eye to eye, so Khomandar uses Imuhlair as the strings to move the puppet."

Cecil was not convinced. "That seems a little far-fetched."

Arkas was a little more convinced. "Is that why there's two Major-domos?"

Iskren nodded and leaned in a bit closer. "Imuhlair knows his days are numbered, and Leon doesn't trust him anyway. That's why Leon brought me in. He fought tooth and nail to get me appointed to the Major-domo position. The junior part is only temporary. Khomandar wasn't happy, of course, but Leon kept hitting him with facts and logic. Imuhlair's not getting any younger...he's served a long time. Eventually, he'll need to retire..."

Cecil gave a puzzled look. "Why are you telling us all this again, Iskren?"

Iskren laughed. "No reason. Just wanted to reassure Arkas that Leon and I have his back." Iskren turned to Arkas. "If Imuhlair gets on your back too much, let us know. We'll straighten him out. We want to see you succeed, not be made puppets of the High Council—you can trust us. The same goes for the other Khaleeshir; you'll always have an ally in Leon and I."

Arkas's veins ran cold as if ice had replaced his blood. His face went white as a sheet. Even Cecil started to take on the same colour as the marble walls.

Iskren looked confused, then suddenly realized what the cause was. Iskren turned slowly and noticed the scowling, terse face of Imuhlair staring up at him. The two major-domos said nothing. They simply stared at each other. Imuhlair's look was scathing and intense. Iskren was embarrassed and dumbfounded.

Iskren broke first. He bowed his head and stalked back off to Shooter. Imuhlair paused briefly to fix his intense stare upon Arkas one last time before disappearing again.

Arkas and Cecil exchanged a look and dove back into their reading. They did not have any more issues staying focused for the remainder of the lesson.

* * *

Language was not Shooter's strong suit, and he cursed the day he had ever accepted Risasi's egg from Kanaahn.

Osamu had been a tough teacher; he had imparted the importance of learning Draconic to his pupils, and for the limited time he had with the Khaleeshir, had done his best to impart his vast knowledge of the language upon them. Kanothir's participation in the lessons had helped immensely. But that didn't make the language any easier to learn. Words caught in Shooter's throat strangled his tongue and threatened to thoroughly confound his vocal cords.

Draconic was not meant for humans; this was proven by the fact that dragons had modified their original language to be easier for humans to learn, so they could cast magic and communicate between the species. In the meantime, Old Draconic had died, and very

281

few dragons were still alive who remember it, let alone speak it. The only living dragons who still spoke this version of the language were the Great Metallic Dragons and the clan leaders.

The irony of changing the language was that even modern Draconic still was not fully learnable by humans. They did not communicate using the full spectrum of senses that dragons could. Draconic had retained that much of the old dialect, and it wasn't something that came naturally to humans.

Shooter had been thankful that at least he did not have to learn Old Draconic—not that it made learning Draconic any easier. But now, Shooter was forced to learn another language on top of Draconic. He had chosen, perhaps somewhat spitefully, to learn Qir'to'ah. Many shared a disconcerted glance when Shooter announced his intent to learn the language of the Qiri'ar. Few ever learned that language, except for matters of trade, or to perform Qiri'aran blood magic.

Leon had explained that to award his loyal followers in the Qiri'ar, Tenebrae had developed blood magic to be bound to both Draconic and Qir'to'ah. It was not usually a good sign when someone sought to learn the language for purposes other than diplomacy or trade. Shooter was not trading with the Qiri'ar, and while some would argue that war was the continuation of diplomacy by other means, it was not a form of "diplomacy" that required you to speak the enemy's language.

Despite misgivings—and to the surprise of everyone, even Shooter—Leon had promised to find someone who spoke the Qiri'aran language, and in the meantime, Shooter would practice his Draconic while everyone else learned their new chosen languages.

Kanaahn had chosen Asardaean, and the immediate response he had received had been to pick one. As Kanaahn had learned, Asardaean was a complex language with a variety of dialects and branch languages stretching the span of human history on Enayra.

In the end, Kanaahn narrowed his choices down to Western Asardaean, and Old Western Asardaean, which were not overly dissimilar, the former descending from the latter—it was argued if you could speak the Old language, it was an easy enough task to learn the modern language—and also High Asardaean, which was a newly created language no older than three centuries that sought to unify the two largest dialects of the Asardaean language. Eventually, Kanaahn intended to also learn Espian sometime in the future.

Kanaahn's choices came from no greater desire than because he wished to speak the languages of his familial descent.

Arial had gone with High Xiaran, the language of many written works in magical academia, in hopes it would assist her in growing her magical knowledge, and thus her powers, by way of widening the sources she could learn from.

Arkas had chosen to learn Daesh, the language of Danaen. Partly, out of a long-standing curiosity and desire to travel there—Arkas had always wanted to try his hand at hunting the famed megafauna of Danaen—and partly because he knew their travels would eventually take them to the Danaesh Royal Court, and diplomacy would be important. Danaen had long been an ally of Altimara, and any advantage during negotiations may help sway them towards the Darond.

Of course, the only problem with Shooter's decision was that he would now be forced to study Draconic until someone who spoke Qir'to'ah could be located. Shooter was at least grateful that his teacher would not be Aurichalcum. Thrae had volunteered herself to teach Shooter; though whether to save him from her father's dislike of him, or because

Aurichalcum would have refused regardless, Shooter couldn't tell, but he was grateful all the same.

It didn't make learning Draconic any better, though.

"What do you struggle with?" Thrae asked, a little more than frustrated.

"My tongue gets all twisted trying to pronounce the hard consonants and heavy words. This is a language invented by a species without lips, that can talk with their minds using all their senses. It was not meant to be learned by humanity!"

Thrae smirked at Shooter's complaints. "You're not wrong…and yet, so many humans have learned it. In fact, it was humans who facilitated the changes in our language by creating the first written form of modern Draconic. They did so to make this language easier to learn and married some of their language rules to Draconic to do so."

"There are apostrophes and hyphens in the middle of words, littering the language like bodies on a battlefield. How does one even begin to pronounce those? This is a language made up by someone with too much time."

Thrae appreciated Shooter's sense of humour and couldn't help but snicker a bit. "That does not make it impossible to learn. Just difficult"

"And I am having difficulties. I start reading a sentence and one starts word bleeding into another. Translations don't stick. Letters switch places. I can't understand what things mean, and I don't understand what the fuck a conjugation is or how it works because the rules change every time I change the pronoun."

Thrae sympathized with Shooter's plight, but she could not let him give up. "Perhaps, if you and I came up with some ways to combat these issues you're having. You need to learn Draconic; this is not negotiable, but I promise I will help you find a way that makes it easier to learn. If you promise to tough it out, I promise, I will help make it as easy as possible."

Shooter sighed and ran his hands through his hair. Did he really have a choice? Thrae was right. He *had* to learn Draconic. There was no negotiating this. But if she was willing to work *with* him, that wouldn't be so bad. "Okay. I trust you."

Thrae smiled. "Wait here, and I'll get some more textbooks to work from. I'll sit here and work you through it."

"Thank you," Shooter called, just before Thrae disappeared between the labyrinth of shelves.

If Thrae heard him, she didn't acknowledge it, but Shooter's sentiment was sincere all the same.

❋ ❋ ❋

For his first day of training, Arkas found himself back at the archery range of the Royal Hunt. He couldn't help but remember the conversation he had had with Cecil here the day previous, and something about their conversation had endeared Arkas to her. But it also gave him heart and strengthened his resolve.

Arkas unslung his bow and walked to the range, where he was greeted by his new teacher.

283

"Imiisah Ifelen, Lady of the Royal Hunt." She declared. Her hand was outstretched.

Arkas took it and shook her hand. Her grip was firm, and her fingers were calloused in that familiar way only an archer would know. Imiisah was tall and slender, but with muscled arms, and Arkas was certain she had upper body conditioning to match. At a glance, her arms were thicker than Arkas's by a fair margin. He could only wonder how heavy the bows she was used to were.

The woman wore simple, black leather armour, and kept her dark brown hair tied up with a neat bun. Her bow, though well crafted, was not ornately carved or adorned, and her arming sword was similarly simple. If not for her title, Arkas would never have known she led a group known as the *Royal* Hunt.

"Arkas Nazzer," he finally managed to respond. "Khaleeshir."

"Well, obviously," Imiisah smirked. "Never thought a man with such a well-cared-for bow and as many quivers as you carry to be such a terrible shot, though."

Arkas's brow furrowed. "What do you mean?"

Imiisah jerked her chin towards something down the archery range.

When Arkas saw what she meant, he turned red with a mixture of anger and embarrassment. She had hung his training target from yesterday from the side of the gallery above the shooting range.

"That's—"

"Got to be some of the worst shooting I've ever seen," Imiisah finished flatly.

Arkas kept his composure. "I wasn't at my best. I was...distracted."

Imiisah clicked her tongue. "The number of times I heard that. Don't worry, we'll get you trained up, kid."

Arkas did not appreciate having his skill as an archer question. He had worked hard—very hard—to be as good as he was. Three years of hard work, blisters, and sitting in the baking sun nearly passing out from heat stroke. Hours spent hunting in the sands at night, nearly freezing to death. He did not come this far to be questioned for one bad day.

Arkas defiantly nocked an arrow and drew back the bowstring. He took a single glance at the target to mark his aim and then turned his attention back to Imiisah. Arkas fired the bow, his body still perpendicular to his target. He maintained unbroken eye contact the entire time.

By this point, Arkas had gathered a crowd of curious watchers. Everything went silent. All that could be heard was the sound of the arrow whistling across the range, and then the sound as it embedded itself into the target.

Dead centre.

Imiisah shrugged. "Anyone with half an eye could make that shot."

Arkas turned and fired three more arrows at the target in quick succession. Each one hit their target; a large green dot at the top of the target, a medium-sized dot at the right of the target, and a small blue dot left of centre.

In case Imiisah wasn't impressed with that, Arkas continued firing arrows at each of the six targets down at the end of the range. Arkas pierced every painted dot on every target he fired at. He even split a few arrows cleanly down the middle where other archers had embedded their shots in the targets first.

By the time Arkas was done he had emptied a whole quiver, and part of his second, but he had hit everything he had aimed at dead centre.

He wheeled on Imiisah; a smug look proudly planted on his face.

Rather than impressed, Imiisah looked satisfied with herself, like a cat that had just devoured a mouse. "Good to know the rumours are true. I just had to be sure. Thank you for your demonstration; it also means I know *exactly* where to begin with your training."

Arkas was incredulous.

Imiisah threw back her head and laughed. "Kid, do you think you're the only archer who has a bad day? Do you think we wouldn't understand?" Imiisah's tone went from teasing to sympathetic. "I *heard* you were a good archer, but now I've *seen* that you're one of the best I've met in years. You've got skill, and there's nothing left for me to teach you."

Arkas smiled triumphantly. "Well, I appreciate—"

"On a bow of that draw weight. You'll be practising with a longbow under me going forward, as well as learning to master that short sword of yours, and knife combat."

"So, all of this was just a test?" His ego had deflated.

"Yes," Imiisah replied. "You passed with flying colours. But if you think just because you're the best at one thing your training is over forever, you've got another thing coming. You're Khaleeshir, there is no best at one thing only, and there is no end to training. What kind of teacher would I be if I let you live your life content with mediocrity?"

Arkas sighed. "A poor one, I suppose."

"You suppose correct k—" Imiisah stopped herself. "Arkas. Your name is Arkas right?"

He nodded.

A grin split Imiisah's face again. "You've earned your name after shooting like that. Well, Arkas, shall we start with the longbow, or do you want some more time to mend your ego?"

"What are you just standing around for? I won't learn anything talking."

Imiisah threw back her head and cackled once more. "I look forward to our time together, Dragonkin. I think you and I will get along just fine." Imiisah turned towards one of her huntsmen standing in the gallery. "Vistrel! Get Arkas here a longbow, hundred-fiver if we've got one to spare, and I mean double time!"

Arkas put on a grin to match Imiisah's. She was tough, and she was brusque, but the Lady of the Royal Hunt was no different a teacher than his father had been, and Arkas had thrived under his father's tutelage. Imiisah's familiar methods would be welcome if they took a bit of an adjustment period to get used to after so long.

"Geller's moose?" Arkas asked, wondering why a hunter would need a bow with such a draw weight.

"Geller's deer," Imiisah corrected. "Geller's moose need at least hundred thirty if you're hunting in groups and not worried about accuracy—hundred-fifties to drop them properly if you're alone."

Arkas would be lying if he said he wasn't a little excited at the prospect of hunting animals that large and learning to fire with bows that powerful.

Imiisah nudged him with her elbow. "While he's off finding your bow, we're going to start with a warmup. Loosen up the muscles, prevent injury and strain—and then we'll be doing some exercise to build up your muscles. You won't be drawing anything with proficiency using those willow switches you call arms."

"Yes, ma'am." Arkas saluted and followed her lead.

He was going to like his training here.

Chapter XXXII

Hana's voice cut through Kanaahn's head like an axe through flesh. *"Your thoughts become your shield. Stray thoughts, white noise, and lies become your shield and confuse your enemies. You cannot focus on anything but those. They will form a shield that wraps around your mind and shields it from those who would seek to read your mind, infiltrate your connection with your dragons and others, and dominate your mind."*

Kanaahn shivered. He'd been at this for weeks—all the Khaleeshir had—but it did not make the practice any easier. Hana's mental presence was like an avalanche, and Kanaahn found himself surprisingly exhausted trying to just fend her off.

"You will feel my thoughts press against your shield like a sword or spear. Once more, I shall attempt to penetrate your defences. You must resist me."

True to her word, Hana's thoughts collided with Kanaahn's mental shield like a cavalry charge into a row of pikemen. Unfortunately, Kanaahn's pikemen were simultaneously, and momentarily blinded by the sun and had dropped their pikes. The cavalry charge slammed into his forces and decimated them, scattering the remnants to the wind. The pikemen were in retreat.

Kanaahn felt like his head was in a vice. The pressure was immense. He wanted to vomit. His eyes were blurry and welling with tears. He could feel his throat seize. Kanaahn wanted to jab his fingers into his eyes and pull them from his face to alleviate the pain. If only the ache would cease. Make it stop.

Make it stop.

MAKE IT STOP.

MAKE—

Suddenly, it was over. The pressure was alleviated, and the pain receded. Hana's mind left Kanaahn's and he was alone again.

For weeks Hana had been teaching the Khaleeshir how to shield their minds and resist invaders.

It had been a painful experience.

Kanaahn and the others had to cut off all connection with their dragons while learning under Hana. The pain of the experience was bleeding across the mental link and causing their partners anguish from a distance.

Kanaahn couldn't hold his breakfast in any longer, and he leaned over the wooden bucket and vomited until he was dry-heaving and his sides ached.

"*I apologize,*" Hana said with an eerie calmness. "*The methods seem harsh, but I can assure you that you will not be shown mercy by your enemies.*"

Kanaahn had not expected someone so young to pack such a mental punch. Shooter was on all fours like Kanaahn, Arkas was unconscious, and Arial was just barely standing. She was supporting herself with her staff, blood running down her nose, but out of the four Khaleeshir, Arial seemed to be doing the best, and learning the fastest.

Even Aurichalcum, who had stayed long enough to observe for a while, had noted Arial's quick aptitude when it came to shielding her mind from enemies. That didn't mean she didn't struggle, of course, but she was certainly ahead of her peers.

"*You will have a few minutes to recover, and then we go again.*" Hana had remained seated upon her small chair the entire time, unmoved, unfazed, and unconcerned.

"Remember that one time I got trampled by that Mhokshi lizard?" Shooter asked, hunched over his own bucket.

Kanaahn nodded.

"I'd rather do that again."

Kanaahn snorted. His throat burned from the acrid, burning bile he had been vomiting, and phlegm filled his nose and throat. He spat into the bucket.

Arial had straightened back up and pushed her hair from her eyes, wiped the blood from her nose, and looked over at her friends. Her white and blonde streaked hair almost seemed to radiate light now. "Are you guys okay?"

"I've been better," Shooter replied.

"I've been worse," added Kanaahn.

The three of them looked at the unconscious Arkas. He lay motionless. It was hard to even see if he was breathing. He lay on the cold stone floor, drool spilling from his mouth.

Arial bent over to check on him. Relief washed over her face when she placed a hand on his wrist. "Well, he's alive at least."

"Of course, he is. Arkas is tougher than that," Shooter argued. "Remember when he got gored by that desert deer once?"

"We've got bad luck with animals," Kanaahn mused.

Arial tried to shake Arkas awake to no avail. "*Hana, he's not waking up.*"

Hana stood, for the first time since training began, and walked over to where Arkas was lying on the ground. In comparison to her sweating, vomiting, and exhausted students, Hana had not looked like she had exerted even one ounce of her strength on this training. Kanaahn wondered if she was even trying—and worried at what Hana trying would even look like.

Hana bent over Arkas but did not even have to touch him. "*He is alive,*" she answered confidently. "*That much is clear. But his mind is muddled. Allow me.*"

Hana reached out towards Arkas and placed a hand upon his brow, and her face went blank for just a moment.

* * *

Arkas awoke to find himself lying in a river, his face just above the surface. The liquid tickled the corner of his mouth and the edges of his nostrils. He sat up and wiped the water from his face, then examined his surroundings.

He was in the middle of a shallow river, the gentle water running calmly down towards the sea. But how Arkas had got here, he wasn't entirely sure. He hadn't ever been to this place before. This wasn't a location he was familiar with.

The sky above was split down the middle. On one side it was black as night. Storm clouds gathered and blocked out the light. Lightning arced and thunder rumbled from within the clouds. On the other side was a normal sunny day.

Arkas stood up, looking around at his surroundings. He instinctively reached for his bow and was shocked to find it wasn't there. His quivers were gone, his bow was missing, and even his hunting knife had left his side. Arkas was alone, in the wilderness, and unarmed.

He turned left and right, examining either bank. On the left bank was a castle, reaching to the sky, made of the finest sandstone and Asardaean red marble. For miles in front of the castle was a mighty and ancient orchard of trees. A single tree stood at the head of the sea that was the orchard. Several boughs on its right side were shattered and broken, but it stood proud all the same.

On the right bank, was a mountain of corpses, in various states of decay. Skeletons, rotting corpses, partial pieces of former living people. And all of them screaming. Crying out in pain, in agony. They called Arkas's name, and they reached for him. Clawing their way across the muddy bank for him.

The smell of iron filled Arkas's nostrils, and he looked down and realized that the water had turned to blood. But not only that, the current had picked up. The gentle stream had quickened, and it showed no sign of stopping. The gentle stream rose and reached his knees, then his waist. The gentle stream became a roaring river. Blood filled Arkas's eyes, nose, and mouth. He sputtered, trying to swim, but the current swept him away and everything faded to black.

* * *

Arkas shot up. Sweat covered his body, soaked through his clothes, dripped down the side of his face, and dampened his hair. He had found himself, not in a river, or covered in blood, but sitting on the cold stone floor of the training hall where he had last remembered being.

Arkas turned and saw Hana kneeling beside him, smiling at him without directly looking at him. She tilted her head, smirked, and stood up, turning back towards Arkas's friends.

Arkas felt a shiver run up his spine. *"Where am I? What happened?"*

288

"You passed out during the last assault on your mind," Hana replied. *"How are you feeling?"*

"Sweaty."

Hana chuckled. *"But otherwise, okay?"*

Arkas nodded. His mind felt fuzzy, his tongue felt numb. He could taste blood but...why? Why could he taste blood? He tasted his mouth to see if he had accidentally cut himself, or bit his tongue, but there was nothing there. Where had he gone? Something nagged at the back of his mind, but it faded faster and faster the longer he thought about it. Had he dreamed something? No. He couldn't have been out for more than a few minutes.

The memory of his dream faded from his mind within moments, and all Arkas could remember was passing out and waking up shortly after. It was as if the dream had never happened.

"In light of Arkas's condition, I shall extend the break. We'll try again in ten minutes. I don't want you to hurt yourself." Hana sounded genuinely concerned for Arkas's well-being, and no wonder, considered he had passed out in the middle of her training.

Arkas looked over at Arial and noticed she wasn't doing much better. The flow of blood from her nose had resumed, despite Arial's attempts to stem the flow. Blood had crusted to her white robes, drying on the front. Shooter and Kanaahn, though no longer vomiting, were still hunched over their buckets, dry heaving as the world swam before their eyes.

Arkas had never imagined training to be Khaleeshir would be so painful, or dangerous. Perhaps he had underestimated the Darond's capabilities; he had certainly underestimated the training.

Osamu had been kind to them, Arkas realized. He had trained them, but gently, kindly. He hadn't pushed them to their limits like Leon, Aurichalcum and Hana were doing. The payoff to the pain and suffering was supposed to be incredible; a power unheard of in this world in ten centuries.

Arkas just hoped that the payoff wouldn't come too late.

Chapter XXXIII

The moment Drakhart returned from Gishan'belor, he was immediately required to leave Kasaadua again. He had departed for Felidrun once more and met with Lord Gruffydd to confirm the plans for the Siege of Ethon.

Lord Gruffydd had been preparing since the moment Drakhart had left him, and Drakhart could see the dedication he had thrown behind their plot.

Drakhart had left Felidrun with very few concerns about Gruffydd's loyalty and commitment. Gruffydd would be at Ethon at the appointed hour, and by the time Ethon realized what was happening, it would be too late for the crown or the Darond to react in any meaningful way. Gruffydd would have his Crown, his revenge, and his freedom, and Tenebrae would have the neutrality of Estion in the coming war.

Danaen was closer and closer to siding with Altimara, though talks with them had stalled as their king had grown ill. A meeting Calandor had planned with the king had fallen through at the last minute, as the king was unable to travel, and was too sick to receive visitors.

According to Calandor, King Ghand'iilu II had been struggling with an ongoing sickness for the past decade, and even in his youth was prone to ill health. Despite his weak immune system, he had been a great king who had often foregone his own preservation for the sake of his people. He was well beloved. Even Tenebrae respected the man. However, the dragon also feared that losing him may lead to more pro-Darond elements taking the throne in an election and shifting the balance of power against Altimara's favour.

But those were problems for another time. For now, Estion took priority. As did grinding down the morale and resolve of the Utovan rebels, which Lord Marneron was doing with gusto. Reports coming from the north favoured Altimara as the victor in the long run, though it would yet be a protracted conflict.

For now, Drakhart's focus had been the march to Ethon.

After the allotted two months, Hizhu had completed the tunnels that would lead the invasion force into Estion unseen. Within a week, the Qiri'ar had gathered their forces and their supply wagons in the caverns below Gishan'belor, and Hizhu and some other brown dragons now led them through the tunnels that had been sung for this march.

The trip to Ethon had been going rather uneventfully. In truth, that was how Drakhart preferred it. Events meant problems, and problems meant delays. Delays were not ideal for what Drakhart was planning. The Qiri'ar were making good progress. They would make Ethon in good time, and strike when their enemies least expected it.

They kept moderate pace in the shaped caverns beneath Enayra's surface, protected at the front and rear of the column by a pair of mature brown dragons. Hizhu himself took up the lead, occasionally reshaping the tunnels as needed to better suit the needs of the marching army. Sometimes, the walls or floors had shifted slightly from seismic activity, general decay, or influence from the leylines below.

Drakhart had witnessed the shaping of the stone. It had been hauntingly beautiful. The brown dragons sang, emitting the sound from the back of their throats and deep in their gut. Their song shook the whole cavern, and the rock melted before them, reshaping, and reforming however their songs commanded.

Drakhart had no idea what language the brown dragons sang in. It sounded like Draconic, but Drakhart couldn't understand a single word. Elandyr'ni had explained that it was Draconic, but it was a dialect that branched off from the main Draconic language thousands of years ago and was closer to the original Draconic language. It was supposedly impossible for any but a dragon to pronounce. The arrival of humans had instigated a shift in the language, and Modern Draconic had been modified to make it easier for humans to speak and pronounce.

While Hizhu reshaped part of the tunnel, Drakhart decided now was as good a time as any for the Qiri'ar to take a break. They had been marching for six hours, and a rest and meal were well earned.

While the army rested, Drakhart passed the time by talking with Elandyr'ni over dinner—in truth, Drakhart had no idea what time it *really* was because there was no light down in the tunnels beneath the surface. All they knew was that they were hungry and tired, and this was their third meal, so it must be sometime towards night. So, he had the Qiri'ar stopped to set up a camp for a short rest. They would eat, rest for a few hours, and pick up the march again once they had had some sleep.

Before they slept, however, Elandyr'ni was insistent that Drakhart get some studying in. Tenebrae had been clear that the invasion was not going to be a reprieve from training. Drakhart's training was still imperative and of the highest priority. For tonight's lesson, Elandyr'ni was teaching Drakhart to summon a familiar.

It was not going well for Drakhart. The spell was complex, complicated, and difficult, but Elandyr'ni was calm, patient, and supportive. She was certain he would learn eventually.

Once more, Elandyr'ni demonstrated how to summon the creature of shadow and blood. "Draw the rune for the animal you wish to summon. It can be any animal, but it's recommended the animal be something small, easy to miss, and not immediately out of place for the area you're summoning it. The point of the creature is to be but an extension of yourself, your mind, and your will. That is why it is a familiar and not a thrall."

Drakhart cut open his finger again and drew upon the wooden board he'd been working with. He drew the runic combination that created the word for "rodent." He had chosen a rat, at least to start. Something small, ubiquitous, darkly coloured, and easily overlooked for how common they were. No one would look twice if the vermin scuttled across the street, through an alley, in a storeroom. They might become enraged and attack, but this familiar would not be harmed by such regular methods of extermination.

Elandyr'ni acted through her instructions alongside Drakhart, drawing the rune for a lizard. She continued her instruction. "This is one of the few spells where using your own blood is a must. By pouring your blood into the spell, the familiar becomes an extension of you, and you can more easily control the creature. You'll also be able to see through the creature's eyes and share in its memories when it is dispelled. Think of it like a smaller Isunath, and the connection you share with him."

Something in Drakhart's heart ached a bit at the mention of Isunath. He and the dragon had been separated a lot lately. They kept in touch, their minds could never truly be uncoupled, no matter how far away they were from each other, and they spoke every night, and when either of them wasn't training, or busy, or marching. But leaving Isunath behind had affected their relationship, and Drakhart was not so oblivious he could not see it.

Isunath did not appreciate being left out of this march to Estion. No matter how large Isunath was made by blood magic, he *was* still but a few months old.

The change in Drakhart's face did not go unnoticed by Elandyr'ni. "I'm sorry. I didn't mean to bring anything up."

Drakhart shrugged. "It's not your fault. Isunath wasn't happy to be left behind. I forget his mind has not grown to match his body. He'll forgive me..."

But he's not Ölüm. Those were the words that hung in Drakhart's throat, stuck there like a piece of dried bread. Elandyr'ni knew it but said nothing—Drakhart could see the recognition in her eyes.

It wasn't that he disliked Isunath, on the contrary, he loved Isunath. But the loss of Ölüm would always weigh heavy on Drakhart's mind and heart, and while Isunath was a great partner, Drakhart's bond with Isunath was more like a parent and child than the equal partnership he had shared with Ölüm.

Elandyr'ni effortlessly changed the subject. "Let's focus on the spell at hand. Before the blood dries. Now that you've chosen a rune, and drawn it in your blood, you must bind the spell to reality using a runic circle, like a regular spell. Once more, your blood will be crucial to this. When the circle is complete, you simply bring the familiar into a physical being with your willpower. You must focus, focus is crucial to this spell, more than any other you've learned so far."

Elandyr'ni traced the runic circle with her blood, enveloping the central rune with a circle of smaller, more intricate, and complex runes. She read out each rune to Drakhart as she did, pronouncing them as clearly and slowly as possible, and going over every motion with intention so Drakhart replicated them perfectly.

There was nothing worse than getting runes wrong when casting blood magic. Using the wrong runes led to unexpected consequences, such as death, and sometimes, in the most horrible ways.

Elandyr'ni had once mentioned a girl she had grown up with who had simply imploded. Her whole body had been compressed and compacted upon itself, like repeatedly folding a piece of paper over and over again, until she was nothing but a small fleshy, bloody, ball the size of a pebble. The screams of her dying friend would still haunt Elandyr'ni sometimes when she would cast a complicated spell—it was what spurred her to get every detail absolutely correct.

Finally, when the runic circle was complete, Elandyr'ni instructed Drakhart to open a slightly larger cut, and let his blood drip upon the casting circle. She demonstrated the incantation, and Drakhart was once again impressed at how easy Elandyr'ni made it look.

Elandyr'ni called the runes to life with her chanting. Though she spoke slowly and clearly, it took but a few moments for the blood to drain from the runes and from Elandyr'ni's open cut and pool into a small, semi-coagulated blob of blood in the centre of the spell. But she was not yet finished. She continued the spell, and shadows crawled from the edges of the cave, like living tendrils, and wrapped themselves around the forming, bubbling ball of blood, until finally, the ball stopped moving. Drakhart was amazed to see that atop Elandyr'ni's wooden board sat a small lizard of blood and shadow, with eyes that glowed like hot embers.

Elandyr'ni held her hand out, and the lizard crawled onto her palm and up her arm, before perching itself on the witch's shoulder. It looked and acted like a normal lizard, if Drakhart had not seen the creature's origins he might've thought it *was* real.

"Now, you try. Exactly as I showed you."

The pressure began to mount, and Drakhart felt it like the weight of a mountain upon his shoulders. He doubted he'd be able to produce a familiar as effortlessly and easily as Elandyr'ni, but he was always willing to push himself to try.

Drakhart did exactly as instructed, repeating the incantation slowly and with purpose, making sure not to mispronounce any words. He let his blood drip upon the circle. Drakhart poured his willpower on the slowly forming ball of blood. He watched, with disbelief, as the shadows slowly started to shiver, like a candle in a draft. The tendrils of shadow started to reach out, slowly, cautiously, as if afraid of the blood blob. Drakhart's heart skipped a beat in excitement, and then, as quickly as he was casting the spell, it all fell apart. The shadows retreated, and the shifting blood ball exploded, splashing droplets on Drakhart and Elandyr'ni.

Drakhart clenched his fist in frustration.

Elandyr'ni, retaining composure, praised Drakhart on his attempt—admittedly the closest he'd come so far—and used her magic to remove the blood from her and Drakhart's face and clothes. "I think we should stop there for today. You'll get the spell—you're getting there. Practice will help. Don't become discouraged."

Drakhart could hear the giggling and chittering of a few Blood Witches who had been watching from afar. He couldn't understand what they were saying, but they were certainly commenting on his ability.

"I've been able to cast spells before, I don't know why this one is so difficult. I've never had so much difficulty with blood magic before. I mean, how can I cast the spell that grew Isunath, but a small familiar is beyond me?"

"This is a difficult spell. It's more complex than anything you've cast to date. The spell that grew Isunath redirects existing energy into something else, but this spell seeks to shape the energy to create something new. It is far more complex and intricate—simple as this spell may seem. Also, we're not co-casting the spell this time, so you're entirely reliant on yourself. You're doing better than I was at your age, but it will take continuous practice."

Drakhart sighed. "In other words, ignore them."

Elandyr'ni nodded. "You must forgive them. In our culture, men don't practice blood magic. Blood magic is for women and women alone. We do not even have a word for

Warlock, in our language, we only call them Blood Witches. For them, it's odd and alien to see a man attempting to practice and master blood magic."

"So, only women can be Blood Witches, but anyone can be a Blood Warrior?" asked Drakhart.

Elandyr'ni nodded. "That is correct."

"But surely men can perform blood magic too? I'm proof of that, and I can't be the only warlock," Drakhart protested.

"It is not a matter of skill or ability. It is an ancient rule that has been passed down amongst my people. Blood magic is naturally addictive and corrupts easily. The more one uses, the greater power they crave. Men tend to fall prey to blood lust easier than women. It is a fact that more men have lost themselves to this power than women, especially among my people. But the decision is also spiritual and biological. Women bleed, and women also give life, and that connection to the power to create life is symbolic of our birthright from the Earth Mother and from Tenebrae to perform blood magic."

"But couldn't a Blood Warrior be just as powerful as a Blood Witch? Especially if they outnumber them?"

Elandyr'ni smirked. "There are no Blood Warriors without Blood Witches. The tattoos that grant us power are a sacred and ancient ritual, but they cannot be achieved without our magic."

"I've always wanted to know more about them," Drakhart admitted. "I mean, you're tattooed right down to your tongues."

Elandyr'ni paused. She leaned in a bit and lowered her voice. "The other Blood Witches and the Bishu'kagun would not appreciate me sharing this knowledge. We don't tell outsiders, even if they serve Lord Tenebrae."

She scanned the area, ensuring that no one was paying too close attention to their conversation, and lowered her voice before continuing.

"The ink is special, for it comes not from herbs and pigments alone, but from the blood of Lord Tenebrae himself. We were the only humans to pledge ourselves to him, and for our undying devotion, he awarded us with powers he has never bestowed upon another: a part of his power.

"Tenebrae offers us his blood, which we infuse with pure mana and other sacred herbs using ancient rituals. This changes the viscosity of the blood, making it more like ink or paint, rather than blood. It also removes the caustic properties that are inherent to dragon blood. We then tattoo ourselves with this mixture. It covers our entire body so that no part of us may be weakened by a whole in this protection.

"It is the Blood Witches that activate the spell weaved through the tattoo process to instil our people with a portion of his power and strength. It is why a Blood Warrior is called such, and why our warriors our famed for fighting against crushing odds and coming through it to taste victory. The spell in the tattoos increases our strength, our stamina, our ability to heal, and our capacity to cast spells. There is a reason dragon blood is such a potent magical item...even congealed dragon blood contains great power. It is the most potent of all blood, especially when working blood magic. It is infused with such an amount of natural mana that it's inherently magic. It can make the impossible, possible."

Drakhart was starting to put two and two together. "Kanothir...it was her blood you used to revive the black dragons wasn't it?"

Elandyr'ni nodded, a smile creeping across her face. "It was, indeed."

"But...but how? There's no way you could have kept that much blood on you for that long, not without proper storage. It was just you and me in Kula, you didn't bring anything with you."

"You remember the lessons I gave you on anatomy?"

Drakhart nodded.

"Then you know how blood flows through the body. It uses veins, arteries, and capillaries to pump itself to every inch of our body. It runs through our bodies like water through a river. It is what keeps our heart beating, and every part of our body alive and well. In magic, as in biology, blood is the source of life. Mana uses the blood, and our bloodstreams, to travel through our body. Like how fish use a river to get from the ocean to a stream"

"What does that have to do with my question?" Drakhart asked.

Elandyr'ni held up a hand to shush him.

He should have known better than to question Elandyr'ni. Sometimes, her explanations took time, but Drakhart always had sight of the full picture by the end of it. Elandyr'ni just preferred to show it to him piece by piece, so he could better understand and appreciate the whole.

"Tenebrae and one of the previous Bishu'kagun spent years developing a way to reduce blood down into its base components, as a way of extracting pure mana from blood for storage and later use in spell craft. They created a way to distil pure magical energy from blood, breaking down the organic components, leaving only ethereal, intangible mana."

Drakhart's confusion was clearly etched into his face.

"The Bishu'kagun at the time learned that mana reacts to core shards specifically, in a peculiar way. Mana is *drawn* to these crystals like metal to a magnet, or a moth to a flame. Which should strike you as odd, because Mana Cores are used to *diffuse* mana outwards, and into the world above. Into other living things. Most in the magical community believe that Mana Cores, and by extension core shards, can only expel energy one way: out. But core shards can do something that Mana Cores cannot: they can reverse the flow of mana at will, and take in, as well as send out.

"The Bishu'kagun discovered that by using core shards, one could draw the mana directly from the blood, distilling it instantly. Core chards, even when broken from their main Mana Core, continue to live and retain their power...but even when depleted, more power can be poured into them. In fact, they crave it, almost seek it out, like a hungry child crying for its mother's breast. If you take any core shard, be it full or empty, the Bishu'kagun learned they will always seek to absorb more power. If you expose them to blood, the shards will immediately draw in the blood, vaporize the organic components, and distil and convert the liquid into pure mana, then absorb the mana within itself. There the mana will remain until it is expended."

Drakhart was starting to connect the dots. "When I first started studying blood magic, you told me that the only limit to how far a warlock could go was based on how much control they had over their emotions, their willpower, and the amount of fresh blood they have at their disposal. A single human body has about four to five litres of blood, but most of what we spill is lost, either because of how long it takes to drain from the body, and we don't have the time, or because it evaporates or dries while we prepare our spell. That's why practitioners practice the art of drawing runes as fast as possible and memorizing all the possible runes they will need to create their desired outcomes."

Elandyr'ni finished where Drakhart ended. "But with this research, we can extract even more mana per sacrifice, both by volume and by quantity, and we can store it for long-term use. This research can optimize blood magic to make it even easier and more convenient. I'm currently researching ways it can be used to reduce the risk of blood lust in practitioners."

"What causes the core shards to behave so differently?"

"The Bishu'kagun could never find a proper answer. The best she could hypothesize was that without the constant influx of mana from the leylines, the separated core shard begins to adapt to its new situation by storing as much mana as possible, to keep itself alive as long as possible, but it never loses its original ability to expel mana. But what's puzzling is the mana it absorbs doesn't go anywhere. The crystal doesn't use it in any large quantities, and though the crystal is living, it seemingly does not require large mana reserves to sustain itself. There is no good explanation for why it sucks in as much mana as possible."

A thought came to Drakhart, but he kept it to himself. He knew nothing of these matters and had only just recently learned about Mana Cores and core shards. Elandyr'ni had likely been studying it for years, and Tenebrae knew far more than anyone who served him. He wasn't about to spout silly theories without any basis in fact.

But Drakhart did ask the burning question on his mind. "So, as you've said, these crystals can be used to assist in the casting of spells?"

Elandyr'ni crossed her hands, and her demeanour grew serious. "They can, but I will not allow you to use them to cheat. If you wish to summon your familiar, you'll do so the hard way—or not at all. You have the skill; you lack the practice and experience. Mana shards will not give you that."

Drakhart sighed. "Fine. You win."

"I know. Now get some rest. We'll continue tomorrow before breakfast; you'll want to be up early for that."

Chapter XXXIV

Arial's early weeks of learning with Leon had simply been a review of everything she had learned under Yomi, Osamu, and on her own via the former's gifted grimoire.

At first, Arial had been disappointed at this review of the basics which she felt she had already grasped—or so she thought. She realized soon enough the reason Leon had spent so much time going over the basics again. Arial's tutelage under Yomi and Osamu had been more rushed than she realized. Her time with Osamu had always been limited, and sometimes the deeper explanations of the basics were missing, and with Yomi, Arial was limited by how long they had before the siege began, and Arial's countless other duties required of her in preparation for the siege. The basics were taught, but in some areas, the how and why were glossed over in favour of practical instructions of magic that would be useful in the short term.

So, Leon patiently went over everything Arial had learned with a fine-tooth comb, and filled in the gaps in her knowledge that he felt was important for her to know—especially now that time was not an issue.

One of the first things Arial learned was that her knowledge of Mana Cores had been severely lacking. She knew what they were, what purpose they served, and that they were an extension of the Earth Mother, but what Arial did not know was their greater use and meaning for humanity, for magic, or for Enayra.

The Earth Mother, as Leon had taught her, used Mana Cores as conduits to reach out across Enayra and keep watch over all living things. It kept nature in balance. But Mana Cores were also wellsprings of the Earth Mother's power. She drew in the mana of the universe and dispersed it across the land via the Mana Cores. The leylines acted like rivers, allowing the mana to flow across Enayra, reaching every corner of the continent. The leylines and Mana Cores allowed mana to leak up out of the ground, feeding the earth, the grass, the trees, the rocks, the wind, and the water. It gave life and kept nature fertile, and in balance.

Mana from a blade of grass was transferred to the deer that ate it. The deer to the human. When the human died, the mana returned to the universe to be drawn back in by the Earth Mother.

In exchange for giving living things life and spreading her mana across the world, the Earth Mother took her tithe in the form of the souls of the departed. All souls were drawn into her and became part of her consciousness. The souls replenished the Earth Mother's strength, and became part of her collective consciousness, allowing her to grow in strength and draw on greater and greater amounts of mana to bring more life to the growing populations and their growing needs.

Religion taught that the souls of the sinful and wicked were dragged to the Nine Hells, where they faced various tortures as they passed through the levels of torment. After an unspecified amount of torment in the Hells, their souls were purified—like a distilling pot—and then finally sent to the Earth Mother to aid in her replenishment of the world. Though Leon was not so certain about that explanation; the Hells were known to be a creation of humanity and were not a concept native to the dragons before humans arrived in Enayra. It is more likely that the Earth Mother took all souls, regardless of their conduct or the content of their character. But that truth would not make the poor farmer feel better when his lord demanded higher taxes and tithes during a famine that had claimed half the farmer's family, and so many generations of scholars chose not to openly challenge the concept of the Hells.

This had been the natural order of life and death in Enayra since long before humans arrived; it had been the original pact forged between the Earth Mother and her draconic children. That was where the term "joining the ancestors" came from.

Leon further explained that the study of magic was *really* the study of drawing mana from this cycle to cast spells. Dragons taught humans arcane magic, but themselves never used it. They used nature magic and drew directly from the power of the Earth Mother.

Yomi *had* explained that all living things in Enayra could at least hear the Great Song of the Earth or The Humming of the World, as it was sometimes called. But it had been Leon who explained that this song was the song of creation and replenishment that came directly from the Earth Mother. Dragons heard it, and it guided them and taught them. It gave them power. Even animals could hear it. But humans did not originate from Enayra, and a vast majority of humans could not hear the Mother's song. Those rare few that could had the potential to become druids, but most humans were content to stick with their arcane magic.

Arial had not been missing too much knowledge from this part of her studies, but Leon felt it necessary to review it all the same.

One part that had been explained briefly was the use of a casting focus when casting spells. Using a focus allowed mages, especially young mages, to channel their mana into a single point. It allowed for more precise casting, and for casting larger spells that required large amounts of mana. Some mages, especially in the early days, would channel their mana in their palms, but this was dangerous, and sometimes painful if the caster wasn't careful, so having a focus was preferred.

The most common type of focus was usually a gemstone fitted in a wand or staff to help one focus their own mana. Some mages would even carry gemstone spheres of varying sizes, known as focusing orbs. However, the latter option was not always practical. Crystals and gems came from the earth and thus were closest to the leylines at their formation. They were naturally attuned to the flow of life and mana, and it did not take much nudging to reconnect them.

Some gems worked better than others; gemstones that came from the deepest parts of the earth, nearest the leylines worked best. Garnet, corundum, emerald, spinel, quartz, and any one of the eleven marbles were the most common.

To cast magic, all a mage needed was to draw upon their mana, focus it, and then impose their will upon the mana to achieve their goal. This was why most magic was cast verbally, using the Draconic language. By giving words to their will, it allowed the mages to better manifest upon the mana.

Once you could master that, you were limited only by your skill, your knowledge, and your own limitations on how much mana you possessed in your body. But theoretically, that mana could become anything. Healing energy, a fireball, a gust of wind, a bolt of arcane lightning. Mana could become anything so long as you had enough mana and strong enough willpower.

Mages with a weak will were in danger of being consumed by the mana they drew in. Often, magic gone wrong ended explosively.

One thing all the mages who had taught Arial agreed upon: nothing short of a perfect understanding of the rules and limitations of magic and the basics of the power she wielded were good enough—doubly so for a Khaleeshir.

But finally, after weeks of reviewing the basics, Leon had deemed Arial ready to view the Mana Core of Estion. She shuddered with excitement. Arial felt goosebumps on her skin. She couldn't believe she was about to experience something that very few others would ever get to experience. Only a handful of people in Enayran history had ever seen one, and Arial was about to be one of them.

Leon had led Arial down through the dark and winding corridors that lay secretly nested beneath the palace. Only a few people knew of their existence and about the secret entrance to the tunnels behind the stone-carved throne.

They stopped abruptly at a massive golden door. It seemed to be inlaid with crystal of some kind. Arial wasn't fully sure of the construct, but she could feel the power thrumming through the door. The hair on the back of her neck stood up and her teeth felt electric.

Leon placed his hand on the door, and the crystal inlay lit up like coals in a fire. All darkness was erased from the tunnel in the all-encompassing light of the crystal. The door parted in the middle and disappeared into the wall without much sound.

Arial was led through the wide entranceway into what could only be described as Leon's sanctum...yet it was so much more.

Tables and workbenches littered the massive cavern, each covered with weird metalworks. Some of the things she recognized as gears and springs, and others were completely unrecognized. Crystals of varying sizes littered the entire workshop, emitting varying degrees of light. Magic encompassed the entirety of the room, and all of it came off the crystals—which were clearly the same material that was inlaid in the door.

Off to the left, Arial could see a modified minecart that once floated on a stone and metal track. Both the bottom of the cart and a small portion of the track were coated in the crystalline substance. Several workbenches across the room were scattered with parts and remains of what looked like arms and hands.

Light emanated from the ceiling as if the sun itself reached into the heart of this cavern. Upon closer inspection, Arial noticed that the light came from specialized chandeliers that, instead of having candles, held chunks of the mysterious crystal in their sconces.

"What is this place?" asked Arial.

"This is my laboratory and my workshop. It is also where you shall be training with me from now on. The Mana Core is just beyond here." Leon pointed towards the back of the workshop.

Arial drifted across the workshop, almost ignoring Leon's reply. She had become fixated on something deeper in the cavern—the very thing Leon was pointing at.

The cave was wide and deep, but it ended in an open archway. Beyond the archway lay a set of winding staircases that zigzagged across the face of the sheer walls of the chamber beyond the archway. The chamber was an impossibly large, vertically oriented, cylindrical chamber that extended deeper into the ground, and whose ceiling extended back up to the foundations of the castle.

At the very heart of this chamber was a tall pale crystal. It resembled something like a carved tree. It consisted of a thick central trunk that widened at the base and the top, with offshoots and branches sprouting from the sides of the main crystal body. More offshoots erupted from the walls and floor like weeds or flower buds. The whole structure was taller than any building Arial had ever seen. The only structures Arial knew that could rival the size of this crystal were mountains.

All the crystals emitted such a burning light and magical aura that Arial felt she might be consumed by them—like a moth that touched a flame. Everything felt so alive...it was warm, it was...breathing?

This was a Mana Core. A true Mana Core.

"It's beautiful," Arial said, astonished, bordering on incredulity.

Leon approached behind her. He nodded. "It is indeed. This is Estion's central Mana Core. More lay scattered throughout the land, but this was one of the seven Mana Cores directly placed here by the Earth Mother during the shaping of the world." Leon pointed to the walls of the massive cylindrical cavern that held the Mana Core. "If you notice, in the walls, you can see the entrances to the leylines of Enayra."

And indeed, Arial could. The leylines were a patchwork of holes of varying sizes that dotted the walls of the caverns like holes in Yeshtaburg cheese. There were human-sized tunnels, tunnels only a mouse could fit into, tunnels the size of a city gate, tunnels so small they were nearly invisible—the size of a pinprick, and tunnels Arial was certain several dragons could fly down abreast and still not touch the sides.

These were the leylines that gave life to all Enayra.

"There are Mana Cores beneath each of the capitals of Enayra," explained Leon. "And one beneath Xiar, as well. Aurichalcum says that humans have always been drawn to them, even if they didn't realize it. These leyline nexuses have enthralled the human soul since they arrived in Enayra. Their location is known only to the Metallic Dragons, the Dragon Masters, and a select few others."

Something in Arial's mind clicked. "You're experimenting with mana shards?"

"Please, allow me to explain," Leon replied calmly. "It was not my work to start. This workshop was my mother's before it was mine. Before she met my father, my mother was a professor at the University of Xiar. She and my father met while my father was attending studies at the university. They lost touch after my father returned to support the revolt against my grandfather. To make a long story short, they eventually reunited, fell in love, and married. My mother learned of this place, and my father had allowed her to experiment with mana shards. She had so many ideas and theories for ways to use mana shards to help better the lives of people across Enayra." Leon gestured to the remains of the once floating minecart. "This was her attempt at a new method of cross-country transportation. She left it unfinished, but I've been working to restore and improve what she left behind."

"Does anyone know you're working on this?" Arial asked.

Leon shook his head. "Only my father and Aurichalcum. We'd rather keep it secret."

"Why? Think about how much faster this research could go with more people."

Leon's face grew stern. "My mother intentionally kept her research to herself and left it only to me. Could you imagine the first thing many would ask if they knew what I was working on?"

Arial couldn't.

"Could it be weaponized," Leon answered himself. "I know. Because that was the first question my mother's mentor originally asked when *he* started looking into experimenting with Xiar's Mana Core."

"Who was her mentor?"

"I don't know his name. He was the Headmaster at the University of Xiar. He was trying to find ways to weaponize the core shards and gain an advantage in the war against Tenebrae. A noble cause...but how long before Enayran nations started turning these weapons upon each other? My mother, and now I, wanted to help the people with these inventions. To make our lives easier and improve humanity. But we cannot do that with weaponry."

"He must not have succeeded, because Xiar didn't have any weapons like that during the siege."

"That's because my mother killed him and destroyed his research—at least concerning weaponry. No one else was working on this project; only he and my mother—and it was all conducted in secret."

"For obvious reasons, no doubt," Arial added, "How was she not arrested?"

"She fled before anyone could discover what she did. She took only a few personal belongings, her mentor's research, and fled to Estion, where my father had returned to overthrow my grandfather. She explained the situation to my father, who offered her sanctuary. He kept her presence a secret and allowed my mother to continue her research on Estion's Mana Core."

"And the rest is history," Arial finished. "You're here, so they fell in love and got married."

Leon nodded.

"When did she pass?"

"About seven years ago, when I was ten. One of her experiments went wrong. There was an explosion. No remains were found, except a few locks of hair and two fingers. My father covered up her death, claiming it was an assassination gone wrong, and she died from her wounds. It was then that I learned what she was doing down here. My father made me swear to secrecy. No one could ever know."

Arial placed a hand on Leon's forearm. "I'll keep your secret. No one will know of this. Not even the other Khaleeshir."

"Except Adalinda," Leon corrected.

"It's involuntary."

"I appreciate it all the same."

Arial walked over to Leon's workbench, looking at the cogs and gears and other assortment of metal tools and crystal shards. "How much do you know about mana shards?"

"You're getting ahead of yourself. Let's get through some practice first, and then we'll move on to theory and more about mana shards."

Arial turned, surprised. "You actually intend to teach me?"

"Someone will have to carry on my work, one day. And I think my work should be in the hands of a Khaleeshir. You'll live much longer than me, anyway. You're a talented young mage. You'll be able to figure out the mysteries my mother and I can't."

"Well then if it's all the same to you, can we start with the theory? There's more I want to know. I've been theorizing about Mana Cores and core shards since I first saw the shard in Xiar. There are many things I don't know, and much no one wanted to teach me."

Leon joined Arial by the workbench. He waved his hand, and two chairs flew from across the room and settled down on either side of the workbench. When Arial was seated, he began his lesson—but with a question, rather than answers. "What have you theorized?"

Arial did not hold back. "When I held that core shard in Xiar, it didn't feel diminished. It wasn't a powerful beacon like it had once been, but it felt alive with power. It was inherently magical. I think Xiar has been slowly replenishing the core shard's power since its last use. I'm sure you're already aware of this though, and you were trying to tell me in our last conversation."

A smile grew on Leon's face. "You are correct. The mages of Xiar tithe to the stone upon their deathbeds. It's known simply as 'The Obligation.' Whenever a mage in Xiar reaches the end of their life, they are carried on a litter to the home of the High Magus. Here, they pour all of their remaining mana into the stone, recharging the stone a little more. The process kills them, as they expend all of their mana; but they see it as a glorious death, for death was going to claim them regardless."

"Was Xiar confirmed to be destroyed then?"

"That we still cannot determine. There is no sign of any rubble; but when magic goes wrong, it's not unheard of for it to vaporize and utterly unmake anything caught in the blast. It could just as easily be teleported halfway across the world. We may never know."

"That's my other theory. I have read in Yomi's grimoire there were ways to track core shards. The notes he provides are scant beyond that." Arial recalled.

Leon nodded. "It's possible."

"Xiar took a large chunk of its Mana Core with it when it was lost. Could you not use a Mana Core to track down the missing chunk of the Mana Core?"

Leon thought Arial's suggestion over for a few moments, giving serious thought to the viability. "It would be a stretch, but it is possible—assuming it wasn't destroyed, of course. If it *has* been teleported, it would only work if the city were still on this world, somewhere."

"You say that like there are other worlds," Arial teased.

Leon shrugged. "No one has proven there are. But no one has proven there aren't. And there is just as much evidence for as against."

"Back to my original point: it's possible?"

"It's possible," admitted Leon.

"You've done it before, haven't you?"

Leon smiled. "You're very perceptive. Yes, I have. It requires a Mana Core to do, but it *is* possible. It's more complicated than you think, though."

"Explain."

"I learned, through trial and error, that you need the core that the shards originate from. Cores recognize their offshoots; like a parent recognizes a child. Think of shards as fruit and cores like the trees. We'd need to go to the ruins of Xiar and use what remains of the Mana Core there to search for the city."

"And that's not exactly doable at the moment, with Altimara already swooping in to claim the valley for themselves."

Leon tried to reassure Arial. "But when this war is over, we could do it. It's a good plan; I hadn't even thought of it. But we can't execute it any time soon. Besides, I'd need to rebuild the tool required."

"What happened to it?" asked Arial.

"The same thing that happens to all the best inventions: it blew up."

Arial turned on her chair, to look back at the Mana Core that hummed behind her. Pure energy crackled off the central pillar of crystal and struck a few of the leylines and crystal growths on the cavern walls. It was mesmerizing and intoxicating all at the same time. "What other knowledge did your mother hide from the world? Am I allowed to know?"

"Well, I can say that Xiar was wrong. Core shards are not inactive lumps of rock like they thought. They do not sit there and obediently wait for us to pour our power into them. Core shards are just as alive as the cores they come from but cut off from their main source of power—the mana of the leylines—they are hungry, and they seek out ways to replenish their power."

"What do you mean?"

Instead of explaining, Leon picked up a nearby core shard and handed it over to Arial. She took the shard carefully like it was going to shatter in her grasp. She expected to suddenly feel something...but the stone was dormant. She felt nothing. It felt alive but like a faint heartbeat of a dying person, and not some live, vibrant creature.

"I don't understand."

Leon smiled. "Probe a little deeper."

Arial used her mind to reach into the heart of the core shard and do as Leon instructed. She felt a dim light, like a flickering candle. A faint heartbeat like the gently beating wings of a butterfly. Warmth, familiarity, friendliness. She felt all of these, but there was no hunger. No longing. No desire.

"I still don't feel anything."

This time, Leon picked up a small knife from the table and cut upon the tip of his left forefinger. Blood ran from the wound, quickly flowing like a waterfall from the sliced flesh, running along the edge of the blade. Leon removed the blade from his skin dangled his finger over the core shard, and patiently watched as blood dripped from the tip of his finger onto the stone.

It crept up on Arial like dusk at the end of the day. Slow, creeping, but constant and unstoppable. Like a mosquito landing on its prey, seeking to suck the blood from their veins. Like some great icosakraken, in the depths of the sea, reaching out towards its prey. Slowly wrapping its arms around a shark or whale, or another poor creature, strangling the life from them, dragging them down to the depths to be devoured by its toothy maw.

Arial watched in astonishment as the blood hit the stone and evaporated, dissolving into crystalline dust, before being absorbed into the crystal. Just as quickly as the feeling of hunger enveloped the stone, it receded as if it had never happened at all.

"Do you see now?"

Arial was amazed. "What happened?"

"The core shards crave power. They're cut off the source of their magic, and while whatever power was in them when they were removed from the Mana Core remains, for some reason—we don't know why—they seek out more. They're semi-sentient, but they cannot force themselves upon living beings. They cannot take mana without the other party offering it up willingly...with one exception."

"Blood."

"Precisely. For some reason, these stones can distil blood down to its basest form and extract the mana from that."

"That makes sense. Blood is the source of life in the body, and there are great amounts of mana in the bloodstream. Mana we ingest from eating other living creatures, the mana present within ourselves used for magic. It's all in the blood. For those that can't manipulate the mana of the leylines and perform arcane magic, they use their blood to perform blood magic, by going directly to the source, and imposing their will upon the mana in the blood in combination with the Draconic Runes of Power."

"Exactly!"

Then it struck Arial. "Could you imagine if Tenebrae or his allies knew about this?"

Leon frowned. "It would be bad. It would be very bad..."

Chapter XXXV

Tohru was hot, tired, aching, and sweating. His feet were cracked and bleeding, and he was stumbling over the roots of the ancient Estian trees. He had not accounted for the death of his horse and thus had not thought to pack proper walking shoes. The horse had fallen and broken its leg a few hours after escaping the Tulkaz when he left them to the green dragons.

Unfortunately, Tohru was racing against time, and he couldn't wait for the poor creature to get better. There was no farmer he could leave the horse with to recover in these woods. The only recourse was to put the creature out of its misery. It took one swing of the axe to put the horse down. But Tohru had no time—or tools—to bury the creature, and he was forced to leave it where it died, to be reclaimed by nature. It was not the first time Tohru had put down a horse in his life, but it never got any easier.

The end of the forest was coming soon, opening to grasslands and farmland. At this point, Tohru could make for a ferry at one of the ports or small villages on the shores of Lake Ardona, or he could go straight across the fields towards Ethon.

Both options presented their own danger. He might be wanted by this point, and who knows how far the news of his escaping arrest had gone. If he walked into one of those small towns and his face was plastered on the wanted board, he'd be hunted down by townsfolk and the constabulary in a second. There was also no guarantee of his safety while on the boat. He'd be stranded on a ferry in the middle of a lake surrounded by people who might want him dead or arrested.

Walking through the fields was just as dangerous. He'd be exposed, out in the open, and easily run down by anyone on horseback. He'd also be passing through and between farms, whose farmers got their news from weekly markets in other towns. News that might include Tohru's wanted status. If they recognized him, they might capture him themselves and turn him in for the reward. He didn't know these farmers, but he knew their lives were full of hard work and toil. Earning a bit of extra coin to help their families was an attractive prospect, and if that meant capturing a tired Tohru and turning him in at the nearest jailhouse, well that was just how it had to be.

He could make that decision at a later time. He had other problems right now, anyway. Tohru threw down his pack, grabbed his canteen and drained it. There was barely a mouthful of water left, and he was sweating like a pig. He was losing more water than he was taking in at this point, and he could already feel dehydration kicking in. He needed to find a spring or a river soon or he wasn't going to make it much longer. At least his rations were holding up.

Against his better judgement and nagging gut, Tohru took the time for a rest and pulled out a handful of nuts he had stored in his pack. Something to keep him going for now.

As he leaned back against an ancient tree, Tohru couldn't help but laugh at his own foolishness. Off on a mission to warn Ethon about the coming danger that he had no details about. He was going to sound like a raving lunatic. Worst of all, being in the woods meant he had no idea what was going on in the outside world. He didn't know if Lord Gruffydd had already enacted whatever plan he might be plotting—if indeed he was plotting at all. For all Tohru knew Ethon lay besieged. Or worse, King Leon was dead, and Gruffydd had crowned himself. Or worst of all, he had been wrong, and he was running around in the forest like an idiot for nothing.

Maybe Tohru had just been an old fool who missed his days as a soldier and a spy. Maybe he just wanted to taste a bit of that glory again. Fight some enemies, spill some blood, crack some skulls. He had been there, alongside his sister and brother-in-law at Kasaadua, and their allies—their friends. They had all sneaked in together, and it had been together, through their combined efforts that they had discovered the horrible truth: Altimara had been led by Tenebrae since his supposed death, and he was plotting to return and enact his revenge. If they hadn't exposed Tenebrae's survival to the Darond when they had, Tenebrae would've caught them all by surprise years ago. But thanks to Dynia's Hand, they had managed to put the brakes on the old lizard's plans. Even if for a short while. Maybe he wanted to be congratulated and hailed as a hero again. Lot of good that did last time.

Tohru groaned. No. No time for doubt. If his doubt had any basis in reality, then why would the Tulkaz be after him? Why would they have chased him down, and gone so far as to encroach upon the green dragons' territory to stop him? That was a great risk to take for a man who had stumbled upon nothing.

No, he had been right the first time.

A soldier's instincts were never wrong. Never. They always meant something, even if the soldier themself might not know what specifically.

Tohru stood, dusted himself off, and checked his map. According to the wrinkled thing, there was a small stream that ran from a spring in the woods down to Lake Ardona not far from where he was. It didn't have a name, but it had been marked on the Darond's strategic map he had been putting together based on survey information. It had finally come in handy. Tohru rolled up the map, stuck it in his bag, and kept walking towards the west.

"I'll head through the fields," he said to himself. He planned and used it as a distraction from his doubts, exhaustion, and thirst. "I'll go between the farms. I'll live off the land, steal what I can't get from nature. The farmers won't have farms to farm if I don't get to Ethon alive or on time. Besides, it'll be remote in the fields and farmlands. There are kilometres between some farms, and so long as I don't get caught, I'll be safe. You're a genius Tohru!"

Tohru shouldered his axe. Once he found water, if he kept up a good pace, he'd reach Ethon in time, he reassured himself. He would make it before Gruffydd could, and then Ethon would be ready for whatever Gruffydd or that lizard Tenebrae were planning. If those blackguards wanted the city, they'd have to bloody take it from beneath the mountain of corpses, because the Bluehelms, Royal Guard, and Darond would die to the last man to defend it.

Chapter XXXVI

Kanaahn hesitated before entering the training hall. He had been told that a master swordsman from Espias had been found and hired to teach Kanaahn how to properly wield his katana.

Half of Kanaahn was excited to meet this master; not only because he had recently discovered that he was part Espian, and he was excited to learn more about his background. But also, because he had always wanted to learn how to wield his father's sword properly, in a matter befitting a great warrior.

In the way his father would have.

At the same time, meeting this sword master caused Kanaahn a great deal of anxiety, because Kanaahn had taught himself how to use the katana, without any formal training. Besides the training Kyeit had given him, which had been more general training for sword work and duelling, Kanaahn had merely picked up the sword one day and swung it in whatever way felt natural.

It wasn't hard to kill with a sharpened blade, even as an unskilled user, and Kanaahn learned that lesson quickly. He had never fought anyone particularly skilled either. The Town Watch had been criminals who were just as unskilled with their weapons as he had been, and Kanaahn had had friends, and been lucky. The soldiers at Xiar were not particularly skilled with their weapons either. They were professional soldiers, sure, but they were not artists with their weapons. They swung their weapons for king and country. For loot and pay. Maybe for a warm meal. But there was no artistry or skill with it.

The only time Kanaahn had fought someone of any skill seriously, he had almost been killed. The captain at Xiar had disarmed him and almost strangled him to death. If it had not been for the intervention of Kyeit, Arial, Valence, and Adalinda, it would have been Kanaahn's head taken as a trophy instead.

Therein lay the anxiety that wormed its way into Kanaahn's breast and ate away at his courage. Kanaahn was most afraid of looking like some idiot child from the sticks, waving around a sword like a fool in front of a veritable sword master with his own school.

But then, Kanaahn supposed, that was the point of training. And one couldn't judge someone who had trained themselves and survived all these years too harshly. After all, he had trained himself, *because* he had no access to a proper teacher. The fact that he had lasted this long had to count for something. You couldn't measure a deer by its ability to hunt a wolf any more than you could grade a wolf on its ability to grow horns.

And yet the fear persisted.

Only to be melted away immediately by his new master.

Kanaahn was not met by some dour, serious, bitter old master, but by a young man, who almost beamed as Kanaahn approached him.

"Welcome. You must be Kanaahn, my new student."

"I am," Kanaahn replied. He bowed, nice and low, as was the custom in Espias.

The master chuckled. "You're familiar with the customs, it seems."

"I know a little. Kula was a waypoint for many traders heading to the capital. We'd get people from all over in the taverns."

"Altimaran," the master noted. "I'd heard tell that you're a fellow gryphon."

Kanaahn was confused, and his face didn't hide that fact.

The master noticed. "Apologies, you might not be familiar with the term. It's a colloquial term in Asardaea and Espias, to denote someone of mixed Asardaean and Espian heritage. The Espian Tiger and the Asardaean Eagle interbreed to make a proud and mighty gryphon."

"I didn't realize intermarriage between the two was so common. I always heard the two countries were rivals."

Kanaahn's master nodded. "For the longest time they have been, and while they play nice now, the rivalry always sits just below the surface. But that's why intermarriage is so common. Espian and Asardaean nobles kept marrying off their children to each other to try and shore up peace between the countries. The hope is that eventually, there will be so many gryphons that no one will want a war between Espias and Asardaea, because everyone will be related. It's even started to trickle down to the common folk."

"Has it worked?"

"It has so far, but we'll see if it holds. It's left most of the noble families of both countries of mixed heritage over the last two centuries. The cultural hybridization that's happened in some families, like mine, has been astounding."

"Were your parents' nobility?"

The master shook his head.

"My father's a smith, and my mother inherited her father's sword school. My mother travelled to Asardaea to teach the daughter of a noble in Pescadum her sword style and met my father there. The rest is history. Just another by-product of intermarriage and cultural hybridization. How about yours?"

Kanaahn shrugged. "I don't know. I was raised an orphan."

"Oh, I'm sorry to hear that."

"Don't be. It's not like it was your fault. I'd appreciate learning more about where I come from though."

"You're about to learn a whole lot more than that. But first, I suppose you need my name."

Kanaahn nodded.

"I am Hachisuka Sakakibara no Yoshitomo, though I'm also known as Lucius Servius in Asardaea. You may call me sensei, or master."

Kanaahn bowed again. "Kanaahn Saatus, of Kula."

"I will teach the Suiō-ryū school developed by my great-great-great grandfather...and perhaps, I shall teach you more about yourself. You and I are similar. You've made it clear that there is much you'd like to know about your gryphon heritage. I can't give you answers beyond what it means to be one, but I think, as a fellow gryphon, it's the least I could do."

Kanaahn felt his heart beat faster. "I...thank you. I've gone my whole life until this point never knowing where I came from. Now I know a little and any answers you can give me... Thank you."

Yoshitomo smiled. "You may ask me anything you'd like before we begin our training."

Kanaahn wasted no time. "Your name. It's longer than most Espians I've met. Also, you have two names?"

"Some gryphons will have two names—their Asardaean name and their Espian name. Not all though, sometimes they'll only have one name, which is some combination of Asardaean and Espian names. I was born Lucius Hachisuka. I was given my mother's family name, designating me heir of her sword school, but named for my father's father. When I grew older, I chose to go by two names. I use my Asardaean name in Asardaea, and my Espian name I use to denote myself as the master of Suiō-ryū, and when I am in Espias.

"The length of my Espian name is quite a complicated affair. Espian names *can* get longer if you'd believe it, and more complicated depending on your position in society. High-ranking nobility will have more complex names than low-ranking peasantry, who at the lowest rungs will have no surname at all—at least not publicly. Everyone has one for taxation and census-taking purposes. But to keep it simple, Hachisuka is my ujina, or household name. Sakakibara is my myōjin, or clan name, denoting which of the Four Great Clans I descend from.

"When the people now known as Espians first landed in the land that would become our home, we landed as an army. It wasn't meant to be an invasion force. They were an army tasked by the emperor of our original homeland to sail forth and discover new lands. Our people were lost in a storm and found ourselves off the coast of Enayra. The explorers were made up of the four most trusted clans of the emperor back home: the Sakakibara, the Honda, the Ii, and the Sakai. We don't need to go into why we stayed, only know that we could not find our way back home, and so we've remained in Enayra ever since.

"But, of course, as time went on, and populations grew, everyone had one of four last names—except for the Imperial family, of course. The courtiers from the Great Council of State had distant cousins mucking out stables in the market district. A Sakakibara in the capital had nothing in common with a Sakakibara from the southern coast.

"So, the tradition of having a myōjin and an ujina was created, to differentiate between one's clan of origin and the household where their loyalties lay. My household took the name Hachisuka, and while we trace our lineage back to the Sakakibara, we do not use the name. My daily, informal, name in Espias is merely Hachisuka no Yoshitomo."

Questions mixed with fantasies and what-ifs sprang up in Kanaahn's head. He couldn't help but wonder if he had more than one name. If so, what was his Asardaean name? What was his Espian name? Did he have a fancier name? Kanaahn couldn't help but wonder which of the four clans his mother's family had descended from.

Yoshitomo smiled as he studied Kanaahn's face.

Kanaahn knew the man could sense the turmoil, the questions, and all the flurry of thoughts living within his head. Yet Yoshitomo did not comment on his observations, and a very embarrassed Kanaahn was thankful for that.

But now it was Yoshitomo's time to ask a question. "May I see your blade?"

"Huh?"

"Your katana. May I see it?"

Kanaahn awkwardly drew his blade and handed it to Yoshitomo.

Yoshitomo took the blade and seemed to weigh it in his hands. He said nothing while he examined the blade, or while testing the feel in his hand. He carefully examined the pattern of the steel, the shape and curve of the blade, and even the bee menuki peeking out from beneath the cord that wrapped the hilt. Yoshitomo marvelled at the gilded wisteria branch design of the tsuba, and even the crane carved into the kashira.

Yoshitomo handed the blade back to Kanaahn with a wide grin. "I've only seen three of these kinds of blades in my life. It's an Ujikuni."

"Pardon?"

"Ujikuni Sengo is an old swordsmith living—or maybe was, no one's certain if he still lives—on Mount Kenjo. He's famed for making swords of incredibly high quality, but he doesn't create blades very often and will refuse most clients. The last two emperors have tried getting an Ujikuni blade, but he's refused them. I don't know how you came to own this blade, but you should treasure it."

"It belonged to my father. I don't know where he got it."

"Your father was a very lucky man, with exquisite taste."

"I had no idea it was so valuable. I always thought it was just some heirloom."

"It's definitely an heirloom, but don't let the rather simple design fool you. Ujikuni may not be one for gaudy designs, but the quality of this blade could put even mine to shame, and my family's Terumune has served us for five generations."

Kanaahn examined the blade in his hand and found he was filled not with pride, but even more questions—and perhaps even guilt.

Did he truly deserve this blade? He wasn't a master. He was self-taught; some kid running around with a metal stick swinging it around playing hero. This blade wasn't his, it was just given to him. But did he even have a right to it? It would've been much better off in the hands of Yoshitomo than Kanaahn's foolish fingers. He had no idea what it was, just as he had no idea of the maker, his culture, or anything that came with carrying a blade like this. Kanaahn sheathed his blade and swallowed; his throat was suddenly dry.

Yoshitomo put a hand on Kanaahn's shoulder. For a long while, he didn't say anything, but as Kanaahn's eyes met his master's, the man spoke the words Kanaahn needed to hear most. "I know exactly what is going through your head right now because I have been there himself. I too am a man straddling two cultures, trying to reconcile both halves with the other. Sometimes I slip and fall. Sometimes I lose sight of one side for the other. Sometimes, those around me won't let me forget my mixed origins—for good or ill. Sometimes I'm too much of one, and not enough of the other. Sometimes I'm too much of both at the same time. And still, sometimes I'm not enough of either for anyone. But we must always remember that we can not be any more than who we are. I am a sword master, the son of a sword master and a blacksmith, from a long line of sword masters and blacksmiths. My parents were Asardaean and Espian, and I am a gryphon."

Just like Kanaahn.

Yoshitomo grinned wide. "Let's shift the lessons towards swords for today, shall we? Come. Show me what you've got."

Arkas drew back his bowstring. He could feel the weight of the draw on his fingers. His mouth was dry. There was a slight wind blowing from the northeast. Just enough that it might shift his arrow a bit. He adjusted to account for it.

The target was down range from him, a small, painted blue circle in the middle of a reed mat. Arkas felt his arms quiver under the weight of the draw. It was over double the weight he was used to. Imiisah wanted him practising with the hundred-fifty weight today, rather than the hundred-fiver he had been using lately. She claimed it was to gauge his progress. Despite all the training, practice, and exercise he had been doing, Arkas was having trouble fully extending his draw. Moreover, the target was at a farther distance than Arkas was used to shooting at.

It made sense. Imiisah knew he was a good shot, and incredibly skilled with his own bow, under perfect circumstances. Recently, Arkas had even shown promise with the hundred-fiver. But the heat of battle was not always perfect circumstances. Things were often less than ideal and never went in your favour when the world was on fire around you, and people were trying to kill you. Targets are at unideal ranges, and a different bow might be needed to pierce their armour or hit them at that distance. Bowstrings snapped, and there was no time to make, wax, and string a new one in the middle of a fight.

The Lady of the Royal Hunt had used this reasoning to teach Arkas to shoot a longbow. Arkas was only thankful she hadn't forced a crossbow or an arbalest into his hands.

Arkas held his breath, released the bowstring, and felt the string snap back into place. The twang reverberated through the bow, into his fingers. The arrow whistled across the range...

...and missed spectacularly.

Arkas frowned. "I can do better."

Imiisah smiled. "Yes, you can. With your bow. But your skills with a longbow need practice."

The brusque and tough woman still lurked below the surface, but as her expectations of Arkas grew, she became gentler and more patient. Perfection was earned through barbs and jokes, as she said.

The Lady of the Royal Hunt, appointed by Leon upon his ascension to the throne, had been in the position for three years and came from a long line of hunt masters, many of whom had served as Lord or Lady of the Royal Hunt. Imiisah was incredibly skilled and took her job very seriously. It was a simple job description: protect the royal forests and all creatures in them from poachers and loggers, and hunt to keep the castle's kitchens overflowing with meat.

In recent generations, new tasks had been added to the Royal Hunt's list of duties, such as roving the wilderness helping those lost and in need and ensuring that people weren't hunting animals out of season beyond just the boundaries of the royal forests. In more recent years, under Leon, the Royal Hunt had been training the Bluehelms and the Royal Guard in the art of the Estian longbow.

Arkas closed his eyes. His frustration was showing. He hadn't been this frustrated by a bow since his father started training him a decade ago. His father had been a patient man, which was good because Arkas had been a slow learner.

"There is no shame in failure, especially when you're still learning."

"I'm better than this," Arkas complained.

"Yes, you are. But not with a longbow. You must get better—again."

Arkas let out a deep sigh, his breath rattling in his throat. He wiped the sweat from his brow and face and looked up into the big blue sky.

Instead of getting angry, or mocking Arkas for his outburst, Lady Imiisah laughed. A deep and throaty laugh.

Arkas shot her a look.

"You remind me of myself when my father first taught me." This openness was rare for her.

"I remind *me* of myself when *my* father first taught me," Arkas clarified. "And that's the problem."

"Was he not a good teacher?"

"He was a great teacher. Kind, and patient, but stern, always pushing me to my limits—because he knew I could exceed them. He always believed in me."

"He sounds a lot like my father. What's your frustration then?"

"I am," Arkas admitted. "It took me three years to master the bow. It took my sisters less than a year to master theirs, and my brother mastered it in six months. When I finally mastered the bow though, I was the best shot in Kula, better than even my father. I clawed my way to be the best, I worked hard, and practised until my fingers blistered and bled."

"And now you're back at the bottom, struggling again."

"Afraid that it's going to take me another three years to master this stupid thing. Afraid that I'll be stuck in a situation where I'll be left with nothing, but a longbow and I'll be useless. Afraid I'll fall behind my friends in progress. And not to mention that I haven't even started with the shortsword yet. I've been the best shot in Kula for five years. Who am I if not the best?"

Imiisah smiled. "Someone trying their best to learn. Sometimes putting in the time and work. There is no shame in putting work into your craft."

"No, but I'm not so foolish to think I have three years to master this again. This war is moving fast. I don't even think we'll be in Estion for three months before we're forced to move. The war will either catch up with us or force us to move somewhere else so we can be closer to the battlefield."

Imiisah took a swig from her canteen and passed it to Arkas. "A great weight has been put on your shoulders—on all your shoulders. You didn't ask for this, but someone gave it to you anyway. All you can do is the best with what you're given. I promise I will not let you take three years to master this, so long as you promise to try and be patient with yourself."

Arkas sipped from the canteen. Imiisah had just asked him for the hardest thing of all. And yet...

"I will do my best."

She beamed. "That's all I ask. As will I."

* * *

"This is a foolsberry," explained Menalaea. "Incredibly dangerous, and hard to cultivate, but incredibly effective. They look just like cranberries or currants and are easily confused for them, but the berry is entirely toxic, inside, and out. Even touching the berry with your bare hands can cause death. The oils present on the skin of the berry will seep into your pores and can be deadly if left unchecked. Ingesting the berry is certain death."

Shooter clumsily took the berry through his thick, leather gloves, struggling to maintain dexterity through the thick gauntlets.

Menalaea had been showing Shooter a variety of poisonous plants and even some animals that could be used to create poisons for ingesting, coating blades, and various other uses.

Shooter had eagerly learned the lessons she had taught him, and while it had increased his already immense respect for Menalaea, it also increased his fear of her.

He had learned of deathfoil, a type of plant easily confused with the common clover but brewed a toxin that put the drinker into a deep, comatose sleep that mimicked death. Shooter had learned of the Danaesh black-eyed tree frog which produced a poisonous mucus that could be distilled to create a toxin that caused paralysis. The black-ringed golden rattler from Espias could be milked for a venom that caused temporary blindness, ulcers, and hallucinations. Shooter had been most worried about the applications of common nutmeg, and how even a handful could cause convulsions, hallucinations, or even death. It was good for temporarily removing someone from the playing board by making them ill, but even more useful during interrogations.

"How long have you been able to do all this?" Shooter asked. He almost feared the answer.

"You mean the poison and the subterfuge?"

Shooter nodded.

"Well, it didn't come naturally. I didn't go into life expecting to become a spy. I was just a housewife before Artimer died. But then I ended up taking over his business, at which point I learned about his real job as a smuggler, spy, and even occasional assassin. Well, when I said I'd take over his business, I didn't expect to also take over his Darond duties, but I knew it was the only way to keep my family safe. I was afraid if I said no—which was totally within my right to do—that eventually my husband's enemies would find me, and if they did they'd find me without protection, without a clue, and completely defenceless, and that scared me most of all. So, I allowed the Darond to train me in the arts I now teach you."

"And no one noticed?"

"Kanaahn and Arial were very, very young. I brought them with me, left them in the care of a wet nurse, and told anyone who asked that I was going off to visit my husband's family in Targrond. He had just died, and everyone knew that. It was clear that I was taking over his business. So, I spent six months at the Darond Headquarters, training to eventually become one of their best agents. As Arial and Kanaahn got older, I'd leave them with a nursemaid, and tell them I was out on business. No one questioned it."

"So, you've just always been able to kill someone effortlessly?"

Menalaea baulked. "I wouldn't call any of this effortless. It takes time to extract the toxins properly and turn them into useable tools."

This did not abate Shooter's fear, or respect.

Menalaea took back the foolberries and then picked up a small plant that looked like a desert dandelion. Shooter had seen them growing in the cracks and crags of mesas and on Mount Pinnacle as a child. They sometimes even grew out of the cracks of mud-brick walls in Kula.

"This is known as death's dandelion," Menalaea explained, cupping the yellow flower in her hands.

"Of course, it is," Shooter muttered. "It looks just like the desert dandelion."

"It *is* the desert dandelion."

Shooter was taken aback. "How toxic are they exactly? Because we used to play with them as kids and—"

"Not at all—not to humans, anyway," Menalaea reassured. "But they're extremely toxic to dragons. It is only the dragons that refer to them as death's dandelion."

Shooter's jaw dropped. "How...?"

"The sap is harmless to most creatures but seems to cause a reaction in dragons. Dragons use their stomach acid as the fuel for their fire. It's magic that converts the acid into flames or the specialized breath weapon. When the sap of the desert dandelions reaches a dragon's stomach, it changes the acidity of the gastric acid, and it begins to eat through the dragon's stomach lining."

"So, it gives dragons ulcers?"

"In doses of ten millilitres or less. Larger quantities of fifteen to twenty millilitres will cause the acid to keep dissolving the stomach lining until it rips through the stomach wall and burns through the rest of the dragon's organs. Twenty-seven millimetres or more will cause the gastric acid to rapidly change into a gas and has been known to cause dragons to burst."

Shooter, for the first time in a long time, looked horrified.

"The dragons don't actually explode—not normally. But their stomachs engorge to the point where they've been known to expand to such a size that they tear through muscle, flesh, bone, and sometimes scales and skin. A dragon's stomach is incredibly tough and durable. In the days before humans and dragons learned to live in peace, humans would use the stomachs of slain dragons as bags and pouches; watertight and incredibly tough."

Shooter silently waited for the third boot to drop.

"Although—"

There it was.

"—It's been theorized that if a dragon were to attempt to breathe fire after their stomach acid had been converted to gas, they might very well explode. Details on whether this has happened are scant and not wholly trustworthy. Add the fact that most dragons don't willingly ingest this flower, and after doing so are in too much discomfort to try and breathe fire anyway, and I'd say it's more just myth than fact."

Despite Menalaea's attempt, this did not make Shooter's horror disappear. But then a thought crossed his mind. "How many of these things do we need to shove down Tenebrae's throat to kill him, do you think?"

Menalaea chuckled. "I don't think there's enough desert dandelions in the world for that. My measurements are based on the works of Illus the Hermit from the earliest days of Enayran history. Shortly after the first ships arrived. Volesus hadn't even founded the empire yet. Measurements can be foggy and have shifted over time as measurement systems have, but it's generally agreed that the most accurate interpretation of the dosage is meant to be in a ratio of per three hundred pounds of body weight, per dragon."

"So much for the easy solution," Shooter shrugged.

"Shooter dear, I think you of all people would agree, that life is never as easy as it seems.

Shooter snorted. Never had he agreed with a statement so wholeheartedly.

* * *

Kanaahn raised his blade. He could feel his sweat drop down the side of his face. He had been sparring for hours on and off and every bone in his body ached. He was yawning, slowing down, and he wanted nothing more than to lie down in the dirt and sleep. His Khaleeshir compatriots felt the same. But Aurichalcum and Thrae would not allow their students to rest.

The only rest they got were the brief periods between their own matches. But instead of resting, they had to study the current match going on to learn from their mistakes and successes.

This time it was Kanaahn versus Risasi, while Shooter battled Djall simultaneously. Arial, Arkas, Fyete and Adalinda waited by the edge of the courtyard, watching the sparring match take place with bated—if ragged—breath.

Aurichalcum had started them off on one-to-one combat. One dragon to one human, rotating their partners every match until everyone had sparred with everyone else. The old dragon had reasoned that they had to grasp the fundamentals of human-dragon combat, and once they had an idea of what they were doing, they could add more into the mix.

But a week prior, Aurichalcum decided to challenge the Khaleeshir as duos. Two pairs of Khaleeshir would fight one another, the dragons against the humans. The point was to have the dragons and humans communicating while fighting, helping each other get the upper hand while also focusing on their own fight. It would be like having a second set of eyes, sharing information, watching for blind spots and openings the other would have missed. It would be practice for the battlefield.

The matches ended overwhelmingly in favour of the dragons. None of the human Khaleeshir had battled a dragon in single combat before. The dragons were faster, stronger, and hit harder than any of the humans could. The human Khaleeshir were covered in welts, bruises, scratches, and scars. The dragons were roughed up in places but looked none the worse for wear. Even Risasi, who had taken a bolt of lightning to the side, had been mostly saved by the magical shielding Aurichalcum had granted all the combatants.

The shields were meant for magical training and were made of ornaments and trinkets engraved with Draconic runes of power and set with mana shards to power the spells. The shields were not terribly powerful, owing to the small size of the shards that powered them, and how they required a topping-off of sorts. The shards needed new mana to replenish their stores, and the Khaleeshir could only provide so much per day without endangering themselves, their lives, or the progress of their training.

Stronger, more destructive spells would shatter through the shields like a hammer through glass, but against basic spells, they did the trick. These shields also stopped things like claws, teeth, and bladed weapons from piercing flesh, and would absorb some of the damage from other blunt-force blows.

But while the shields protected the combatants from basic magical attacks, like dragon flame, and simple magic spells, unfortunately for Kanaahn, it did not save him from Risasi's tail slamming into his gut.

Kanaahn went flying. He bounced across the courtyard like a stone skipped across the water's surface. He could feel the cobbles try to grate off his skin and flesh, but the shield protected him. The force still drove the wind from his lungs and the pain of each impact was still very real.

He struggled to stand, pulling himself up to one knee. Kanaahn had lost his sword, and it now lay just that bit too far away, out of reach.

Risasi snarled and closed in on him.

Nearby, Shooter fought Djall. The green dragon had Shooter rolling on the ground, as the latter tried to avoid being stomped to death by Djall's massive, clawed feet. So far, Shooter had been able to avoid the worst this way.

Kanaahn dived for his sword, narrowly missing Risasi's jaws by an inch. He could feel the dragon's hot breath on his ankles. Risasi wasn't fooling around, even in a friendly training match. The dragon's passion overtook him, and his competitive nature consumed his rational thought. Kanaahn had to be careful.

But he had not been.

With his sword in hand, Kanaahn stood and turned to face Risasi, only to get Risasi's tail to his face. The blow knocked him down, sprawled on his back. Kanaahn's head cracked against the pavement. He saw stars swim in his vision, his neck had popped when he fell, and the world was spinning. The shield had prevented his skull from cracking open and concussion from forming, but the whiplash from impact was not stopped.

"Fucker," Kanaahn hissed.

He heard Risasi snarl.

Aurichalcum would not save him. Thrae would not be allowed to save him. Aurichalcum did not believe in mercy while training. An enemy would not show the Khaleeshir mercy on the battlefield, and he would not show them mercy either. As on the battlefield, so on the sparring field, was Aurichalcum's mantra.

Kanaahn had to fight back or forfeit. There were no other options. His vision blurred and doubled. His eyes stung and filled with tears. There was an aching at the base of his skull.

Risasi was closing in.

Kanaahn had few options. Magic hadn't worked for him since before Xiar. The more he tried, the worse he failed. The last time he tried to create a fire ball it exploded in his face and almost set the woods on fire. He couldn't see his opponent, so his sword wouldn't be much help.

Shit.

"Use my eyes," Djall urged.

"Can you focus long enough?"

"I shall try."

Immediately, Kanaahn's eyesight shifted to a vantage from somewhere behind him. He saw, from somewhere in Djall's periphery, Shooter crawling out from between Djall's legs.

Kanaahn wouldn't have long.

They had attempted something like this before, but they had never used the other's eyesight to move about in the world. It was disorienting, but there was no time to get things wrong.

Kanaahn rolled out of the way of Risasi and slashed at the dragon's side as the red behemoth passed by him. The blade did not pierce his hide, or the shield, but Risasi could see the attack all the same, and he snarled in response.

Just as quickly as it had started, Kanaahn's time with Djall's eyes came to an end. The green dragon was forced to turn his attention back to Shooter and a new onslaught of attacks.

Kanaahn's eyesight was still unfocused as he came back into his own head. He saw the red, blurry mass that could only be Risasi rear up on his hind legs. The dragon was going to breathe flame. Then Kanaahn smelled brimstone. He could feel the heat for the flames. No—not flame. Lava. Risasi was breathing lava.

"Djall!" cried Kanaahn.

His vision was slowly returning, but there were very few ways to dodge this.

"A little busy right now!" the green dragon roared.

Shooter had managed to scale Djall's back and was climbing up his neck like a palm tree.

Kanaahn stared down Risasi and the coming lava. He doubted that his magical shield would be able to withstand the blast of lava that was about to engulf him and half the courtyard.

"ENOUGH!"

Everyone froze.

In a flash, without anyone noticing, Aurichalcum had appeared between Risasi and Kanaahn. His stern gaze drifted between the two.

"The fight ends in favour of Risasi and Shooter." The words seemed to drip from Aurichalcum's tongue like poison. The old dragon's disgust was clear on his face. Aurichalcum was fair, in the regard that he would give Shooter his due—but he would not be happy while doing it.

Aurichalcum folded his hands behind his back and stalked back towards Thrae at the edge of the courtyard. He turned his attention towards the sky and saw the sun had started to sink in the sky. It would be dinner soon, but not quite dark. "I think, perhaps, that is enough for today. We'll pick up tomorrow where we left off."

It was the closest to pleased they had ever heard Aurichalcum sound in the month they had been here in Ethon, and yet they still would not assume he was pleased with them. The Khaleeshir knew there would be no words of encouragement. There would be no congratulatory words. There was only Aurichalcum's stern gaze, Thrae's apologetic glance, and silence. An awkward silence born of discomfort and exhaustion lingered even after the ancient dragon and his daughter disappeared from the courtyard.

After what felt like an age of the world, Kanaahn finally turned to Risasi. He glistened with sweat. "You okay?"

Risasi snorted. Thick clouds of acrid smoke drifted from his nostrils. "I should ask you that."

Kanaahn shrugged, "I'll be fine. I didn't almost get stabbed."

Risasi sneered. "You are an odd one. You were nearly concussed, and I almost bathed you in lava, and you're worried about *me*."

"Welcome to Kanaahn," interjected Shooter.

Djall laughed. He seemed to agree.

Arkas, Arial, Adalinda, and Fyete approached the duellists.

Arkas's stomach growled like a feral cat.

"Hungry?" asked Shooter.

Arkas nodded. "Starving—for a while now, honestly."

"Same," added Kanaahn.

Arial and Shooter agreed.

Fyete smiled a toothy smile, fangs bared. "I could hunt."

"You could always hunt," teased Adalinda.

"I'll go with you," Risasi replied. "Djall?"

Djall nodded.

"Let's let Valence and Kinokaze know. They will have to join us."

The humans said goodbye to their dragons, if only their physical presence would be departing, and walked themselves back towards the main building of the castle.

"Dinner should be soon," noted Kanaahn. "But we should probably wash up a bit. I don't know about you, but I'm covered in dust and sweat. I can feel the salt dried on my skin."

No one disagreed with the idea of a warm bath, or even something as simple as a warm washcloth at that point. So, the plan was set, the chambermaids were notified, and baths were drawn.

Chapter XXXVII

Tohru crouched low inside the barn where he was hiding. The villagers had no idea he was here, and for the moment, those who were pursuing him didn't either. But they did not stop their search. They prowled between the buildings of this small, forgotten farming settlement in the middle of Estion, looking for Tohru.

Tohru had been surprised when they showed up while he was hiding in a different village a few nights ago. He had been sleeping in a hayloft when he heard the commotion outside. The animals had not been pleased by the presence of these unearthly creatures. They set nature on edge. Horses, chickens, cows, ducks, geese, pigs, sheep and more raised their voices in a loud symphony of discomfort and panic. In a way, Tohru was grateful for the commotion. Exhausted as he was, the cacophony had woken Tohru from his slumber, and likely saved his life.

When he heard the commotion, he had placed an eye against a small hole in the side of the barn and saw the hooded figures that had chased him from Felidrun. Tohru had been horrified and surprised that they were here. He dreaded to think of the fate of the dragons who had stood in the way of these creatures. Tohru hoped their end had been swift and merciful—if it *had* been an end—though he knew that was too much to ask of the Tulkaz.

Tohru had managed to escape from them that night, fleeing into the fields of cereals and grains before his pursuers discovered him. Tohru was glad that he had arrived in the fields during the fall, and before harvest, or he would have no place to hide. The tall, golden fields were great cover, though he knew they would not last forever.

To try and throw off his pursuers, Tohru stalked between villages during the day. He made sure to keep to the main roads, hood pulled up, and keep as low a profile as ever. It would be harder to track him on a route as well travelled as a main road. The presence of carts, pack animals, livestock, and other people would mask his scent and his footprints. So long as Tohru didn't do anything to make himself too noticeable, he would be just another weary traveller on the road with hundreds of others like him.

Tohru also knew that the Tulkaz would not dare follow him during the day, for risk of being seen. They couldn't hide in alleys or forests now. There were people around, and they would notice these strangers with ease. Tall silent, hooded strangers, who never showed their faces and could not speak would not go unnoticed in parts such as these.

So, the Tulkaz gave chase only at night, hunting Tohru to whatever settlement he had hidden in, just narrowly missing him each time. Each time they approached, the animals alerted Tohru and the locals to the presence of these interlopers, and they would be forced to flee into the darkness again before they were seen. These hunters were ruthless, but too much attention would be a problem.

Tohru could only imagine how frustrated the Tulkaz had been trying to track him down. But he was not so naïve to think that his luck would never run out. One of these days—and sooner rather than later—they would catch him, and his life would end miserably and painfully. He was still over a week away from the capital, but Tohru had no idea if he was already too late or not.

He had already worked on a contingency plan; in case he didn't make it to Ethon in time. Tohru had sent a messenger ahead—after stopping in a post station along the way—to Lady vohn Veishaupt, Baroness of Pelchar, to warn her that Lord Gruffydd may be planning something. Tohru did not trust a messenger to reach King Leon, and so had not bothered to reach out to him unless it was in person.

Tohru had long believed that there was a traitor among the king's inner circle. There was no direct evidence, but every so often, an informant went missing. The Altimaran army would somehow catch and search a supply caravan going to the Darond, and confiscate the contents. A ship carrying gold or war supplies would be raided and confiscated. It wasn't enough to alert the suspicion of most of the Darond, but it was just enough to concern Tohru. Tohru was not most of the Darond, and he was more experienced than most other spymasters. Menalaea had also shared his concerns, but most of the High Council would not, or could not, listen to either of them. Regardless, Tohru would listen to himself, and would not trust a message going to the king directly unless he delivered it himself.

The way Tohru saw it, if Lord Gruffydd *was* keeping an eye on any mail being sent, it was only mail that was headed for the king in the capital, and nothing going to the Baroness Pelchar, so far away and far removed from his scheme.

All the same, Tohru was careful to send the letter under an assumed identity, pretending to be a young wine merchant looking to charter the Baroness's trade barges for the transport of several barrels of the finest wine south of Pescadum. Tohru knew the Baroness well enough to know that she had all her mail checked for cyphers. She trusted *no one*. The Baroness would easily pick up on the Krahvaden cypher Tohru had worked into his fake letter.

Suddenly, there was a bang from down below. Tohru recognized the sound as the gelding down in the barn below began kicking at the gate to his stall.

Tohru shifted carefully and peaked over the edge of the hayloft. He didn't see anything, but the animals were upset. Something was putting them on edge. Tohru had an idea of what was causing the commotion. He reached for his battle axe that lay not far from him, in the hay. He had expected this.

What Tohru did not expect was for the Tulkaz to crash through the roof and attack him from above.

He just barely managed to roll out of the way. It didn't do him much good, as the hooded figures shattered the floor of the hayloft, sending Tohru crashing to the ground. His back slammed into a falling timber, and he felt the wind rush from his lungs.

He was still dazed when one of the Tulkaz—who had landed on their feet—stalked over to him. They moved silently, coldly, like an unstoppable fog. Tohru had expected a second figure—there had always been two—but was pleasantly surprised, if a bit contrarily to the situation, that there was only a single enemy.

Perhaps Tohru would have a chance.

He recovered stood up and hefted his axe.

The hooded figure hissed at him and froze just out of reach. It refused to come within swinging range of the axe.

If the Tulkaz would not come closer, Tohru would need to close the gap to strike. He would need to be careful—it was likely this was a trap to get him to lose focus and goad him into striking.

Tohru shifted forward slowly, stepping forward inch by inch.

The hooded figure stepped backwards.

This was obviously a trap. There was no choice but to spring it—unless Tohru wanted to stand here until dawn.

Tohru took a step forward, right into the range of their trap, and made as if it to strike the Tulkaz with his axe. But just as the Tulkaz went to recoil, Tohru threw a knife he kept tucked in his belt at the hooded foe. Then he raised his axe above his head, ready to charge and strike.

There was a sound above him, and Tohru looked up in time to catch sight of the second Tulkaz dropping from the roof above.

Tohru heard a hiss from the first Tulkaz as he side-stepped the second. His knife hadn't hit the creature, but it had knocked back the creature's hood to reveal its horrific face. Even in the darkness of the barn, Tohru could see the narrow, reptilian eyes. Golden eyes bifurcated with narrow black slits for pupils. A scaly bald head, and absolutely no nose. Twisted, deformed horns erupted from where the creature's ears would be, and their snout was slightly elongated, but not quite long enough for a real dragon. The creature wasn't quite human, nor were they quite dragon. They were some unearthly combination of the two.

Tohru had fought these creatures countless times in his youth, but he had never seen their faces before. He had always assumed they had no faces. But what he witnessed here lined up with the legends he had heard about these creatures.

Unfortunately for him, the distraction of the first creature was enough to seal Tohru's fate. He had looked away long enough. A single flinch. A single distracted glance. Enough for the second creature to strike him in the back of the head.

Tohru saw stars and fell to one knee.

The first creature lunged towards Tohru and punched him in the face, then the chest. The second creature reached out and with a quick twist and a sickening crack, broke his leg. They moved quick as lightning, quicker than any man Tohru had ever fought. He was no match for them, and it was clear at the speed they moved he never would be.

Tohru cried out; he felt his axe slip from his grasp. He felt the creatures close in, surrounding him, hissing, sniffing, tasting the air with long forked tongues. The world spun. Stars in his eyes. He could smell blood, taste blood, feel it drip from his nose and pool in his mouth. There was pain everywhere and nowhere at once. Parts of his body were enflamed, and other parts were completely numb.

Tohru prayed with his last moments of consciousness, that his message would reach Pelchar in time.

Then it all went black.

Chapter XXXVIII

Shooter had never been so clean. The maids had laid out several pairs of fresh clothes for him after his bath and had even presented him with a selection of perfumes. He had settled on the fine gold and red tunic and black leather trousers. As usual, he adorned himself in his purple cape stolen from Captain Jerrin and chose to anoint himself with the perfume of lavender and clove.

Now Shooter was making his way through the candlelit halls of Filiddyn Castle towards the great hall, where dinner was being served. He was late. Shooter had fallen asleep in the bath. He had been thoroughly exhausted mentally and physically by the long and early day. He had crammed more knowledge into his head in one morning than he had ever thought possible and had spent the rest of the day forcing his body past previously held physical limits. How Shooter had been doing this for months eluded him.

Now, all Shooter wanted was a good, warm meal, and a long, heavy sleep. Shooter knew he would be doing this again the next day, and the day after, and every day after that until the war caught up with them, or until they were required elsewhere. Shooter knew which of the two it would be—it was only a matter of time after all.

Still groggy from his nap, Shooter rounded a corner and was surprised when he almost bowled over Hana.

Shooter grabbed Hana's sleeve and stopped her from falling. *"I'm so sorry! Are you all right?"* He had switched the telepathic link—it had become second nature when he saw Hana.

Hana straightened herself. *"I am fine. I should have sensed you. I was lost in thought."*

"It's okay. I should have heard you coming myself."

Hana smiled. *"I was just on my way to retrieve you, actually."*

"I know. I'm late for dinner?"

"You weren't the only one, just the last. Today's training seems to have been hard on all of you. A warm bath was enough to claim your attention."

"Thank you for understanding."

"Come, let's get to dinner. They're waiting for you—no need to apologize when you arrive. Leon has been very understanding, and few would dare speak out against him. At least, few among those who are currently at court..."

Shooter frowned. *"Leon isn't very popular amongst the nobility, is he?"*

Hana shook her head. *"The people love him, for he has empowered them. But the nobility once empowered by his father—and who empowered his father in return—are not quite so keen to lose their power and influence."*

"Do all the nobility feel that way?"

"Most of them do, but a few support Leon. Those against Leon are known as the Cabal faction by those in the court, while those in favour are known as the Reformist faction. The Cabal is led by Lord Gruffydd while the Lady vohn Veishaupt leads the Reformists. The problem is there are more in the Cabal than the Reformists, and the Cabal has the larger army."

"Is there the possibility of a rebellion?"

Hana did not respond immediately. She paused as if searching for the proper words— or perhaps the proper lie. Shooter was surprised when he received the truth. *"Yes, and no. It is always a possibility, but we believe that Lord Gruffydd's loyalty to the former King Khomandar is enough to ensure he will remain in line. Though we cannot be too optimistic to think this will always be the case, and so we must be vigilant."*

"How many barons are there?"

"Nine. Only nine noble families remain from the founding days of Estion, once Gerovia. Many were lost during the War of the Grand Coalition, many more in the following Anarchy. The rest combined over the years as families intermarried, others were lost in successive civil wars and political upheavals. All the while dynasties rose and fell, and the throne changed hands again and again. The lands that were once spread out across one hundred and thirteen noble families of varying rank are now consolidated under nine remaining houses—few of them older than one or two centuries."

Shooter was as honest in his reply as Hana had been in hers. *"Estion sounds like a mess, politically."*

Hana frowned. *"It is. It has been an unstable powder keg since the very founding of Gerovia and the days of the city-states. The little more than a century and a half of Imperial rule were the most stable this country has ever been. It has not been so stable since. Nearly seventy dynasties have ruled this country in its many incarnations in the two millennia since its founding, and sixty-three of those have been since the end of the Empire."*

Shooter, unsure of how to respond, was relieved to find they had finally reached their destination and were now standing before the doors to the great hall.

Hana changed the subject immediately as if the two had not just been discussing the possibility of another Estian civil war and years of political upheaval and strife in the middle of a continent-spanning war. *"It seems we're here. Would you escort me to my seat, as a gentleman should? It is proper courtly etiquette."*

Shooter smirked. *"You're still talking to the wrong person for courtly etiquette. However, since I almost ran you down in the hallway earlier, and for all the trouble you went to finding me and bringing me here, I'd be happy to oblige."*

Hana held out her hand, which Shooter took without a second thought.

Suddenly everything went black.

* * *

Shooter opened his eyes to find himself at the edge of a massive hole in the ground. He couldn't see the bottom in the darkness below, but a faint glow emanated from somewhere deep down. It was warm and called to him, like a comfy bed after a long day. Electricity danced in the air and made loose hairs stand on end. A voice he did not recognise called to him from deep within the giant hole below, and Shooter did not have it in him to resist.

Until...

From behind him came a sound. The scuff of shoes on dirt; gravel crunching.

Shooter turned and saw the shape of a woman. She was outlined by light, and he couldn't quite make out her face, but the flaming red hue of her hair made Shooter certain who she was supposed to be.

The woman said nothing, and her features and face were obscured by the light behind her. She appeared as a hollow void against the bright light, her amber hair flying about in a heavy breeze that Shooter could not feel.

Shooter couldn't step towards her, no matter how hard he willed himself. No matter how hard he tried.

Shooter reached out with his hand, hoping, by some miracle, that his arm would bridge the four-metre gap between himself and the woman and brush her outstretched fingers. He wanted nothing more than to be with her, but he would not—could not—move.

A figure appeared from the woman's side. Short, small. Like a child. Or a goblin. Honestly, it could have been a gnar. The figure was similarly obscured by the light, cast in shadows, and just as far away.

Shooter felt the light in the hole behind him call to him again, pull him, just as the woman and small figure before him did the same. He was stuck between two forces, and both were drawing him towards them, both were calling him as if calling him home.

Shooter felt pain, felt himself being stretched like he was on the rack, being pulled and punished. Flesh tore, bones cracked, popped, broke. Ligaments ripped like fabric. He opened his mouth to scream as the agony started to overwhelm him. But no sound came out.

Then, he passed out. Everything went black.

The next time he would open his eyes, Shooter would be seated at the dinner table, devouring a loaf of bread as if nothing had happened, with absolutely no memory of the pain, the woman, the small figure, or the hole.

* * *

Leon felt the tapping on his shoulder and turned to see Iskren standing there, sullen, and sombre. He didn't speak, but Leon knew it was urgent. His attention was needed—in private. He apologized to the Khaleeshir, to whom he was speaking, and went with Iskren to a small, private antechamber off the main dining hall.

"What's the matter, Iskren?"

Iskren frowned. "I'm sorry to bother you. I wouldn't be doing this if I wasn't concerned."

"What is it?" Leon stressed.

Iskren paused. He looked around and made sure no one was listening, as if looking behind a curtain would curtail spies. Finally, he responded. "I think there's a traitor in the castle. Someone close to you."

Leon's brows furrowed. "Well, we know that—the entire privy council my father left me are spies meant to keep an eye on me for him and ensure the country—"

"Not like that," Iskren interrupted. "I'm talking a spy for Tenebrae. For the enemy."

Leon's face grew more serious. "That's impossible."

"We all thought so, but it seems they've snuck in anyway. Played the long con."

"I'm guessing by that response you have an idea of the culprit."

"I think we should investigate Imuhlair."

Leon frowned. "I know he's my father's man, but he's always done well by my family. I'm replacing him because I was concerned about his loyalties to my father, not because I'm concerned about his loyalty to the nation."

"Leon please." Iskren pleaded. "This could be serious."

"I presume you have proof?"

Iskren paused again, like a rat caught in the act of stealing from the store cupboard. "Nothing concrete..."

Leon grew stern. "I can't accuse a man of treason and espionage without evidence. I'm not my grandfather."

"Imuhlair has started locking his desk *and* his office. He never did that before."

"Why are you trying to get into his office and desk?"

Iskren smiled sheepishly. "Because I was looking for evidence?"

Leon was not amused, but he let Iskren continue.

"I also found him attempting to get into my office while I was out. What his true reason was, I don't know, but he claimed he was trying to leave a note for me on my desk while I was out. Of course, he claimed once I had arrived there was no need, and he told me what he had to do in person. It was about the impending arrival of the Dragonkin, which I found odd, as I had already been told of their arrival by him earlier. He seemed nervous and eager to depart."

Leon paced back and forth. His grim look appeared even grimmer in the dim torchlight of the room. He pondered on everything Iskren had told him. Truthfully, he found this all hard to believe. Imuhlair had always been his father's man, but he had *never* given Leon any reason to suspect he might be capable of committing treason and working with Tenebrae.

Iskren waited eagerly for Leon's judgement. To say his face drooped from disappointment when he heard it was an understatement.

"I can't act on that. But I agree, if what you told me is true, it is worrying. I'll have Imuhlair watched, and if he does anything worth reproach, I'll have him brought before me, and the evidence presented to him."

"But it could be too late by then—"

"I will *not* arrest or try Imuhlair on nothing but hearsay. I will not make the mistakes of my forebearers. I will *not* try a man for *nothing*."

"Don't you trust me, Leon?"

Leon frowned. "With my life, Iskren. We have been friends most of our lives. I believe you that these things happened. But I, as king, cannot make my decisions without proof behind them. Everything I do is scrutinized by the Republicans, and by the Cabal. If I imprison and try Imuhlair on such serious charges with no proof, and he is found innocent, the Republicans will decry me as a tyrant akin to my grandfather. They'd proclaim that I was but one step away from bringing back the absolute rule of the monarchs. The Cabal would use it as a further reason to try and railroad me in parliament and may even turn some of my remaining loyalists against me. A young king with no experience trying an innocent man with treason because I wanted to remove my father's councillors—that's all this would appear as to them. The stricter the crime, the heavier the burden of proof I must present. It is both a matter of law and a matter of integrity."

Iskren sighed. "I understand. I apologize... I just don't want to delay and risk anything bad happening. I don't trust the Cabal, and I don't want to ignore what could be an obvious threat to your rule, and the people."

"I appreciate your concern, my friend. Your loyalty has been indispensable to me as I navigate my role as king. Your support is even more so. I promise you if there is truth to your accusations there will be justice. But for now, I need *you* to trust *me*."

"I can do that."

Leon smiled. "Thank you."

The two embraced, and after a few pats on the back, they walked back out to the dining hall to continue dinner.

Leon couldn't help but notice the glances Imuhlair cast towards him and Iskren. Leon's stomach turned, and suddenly he felt himself grow wary of the man he had viewed as a friend and confidant in his early days as kind.

Their relationship had been complex, to say the least. Leon trusted Imuhlair as much as he clashed with him, and until he had decided to replace Imuhlair with Iskren, there was no one else Leon would trust with the affairs of state, or to advise his rule.

Even when Imuhlair disagreed with Leon—which was often—he would always give Leon good and prescient advice. For that, Leon had been eternally grateful. It would be fair to say Leon even saw Imuhlair as an uncle, more than a good friend and advisor.

Leon still felt guilt about forcibly retiring the old Major-domo, and part of the reason he had asked Imuhlair to train Iskren was so that even after his retirement, Imuhlair's knowledge and wisdom would still be present at court, and guiding Leon's hand.

But now, Leon felt nothing but fear; fear and nausea as he slowly realized that he sat in a den of vipers, and even those he thought he could once trust may be the first person to drive a dagger into his spine.

Chapter XXXIX

Drakhart had been impressed with the results of his final inspection of the Qiri'aran forces. Not that there was much to inspect. Most of the Qiri'ar wore very little, or even no armour. The older generations of Blood Warriors went into battle in the traditional way, wearing absolutely nothing but war paint and their tattoos. The generation after them wore at least a pair of pants and some boots. The youngest generations carried shields but still wore nothing that resembled traditional armour—though Drakhart did see the odd pauldron here or there. There was no point in prolonging life in battle to the Qiri'ar. Death at the hands of a worthy foe was a great death for a Blood Warrior. No amount of armour would stop death. Besides, in their blood magic-fueled frenzy, they wouldn't feel any of it.

As per the battle plans decided on in Gishan'belor, the Blood Witches would be split between rear-guard support, and tactical support alongside the different attack groups. They would be needed for both healing and tactical magical support while the Blood Warriors attempted to breach the walls in the attack phase. The Blood Witches' secondary job was also to collect as much of the fallen and spilt blood as possible, for later use. Not a drop was to be wasted, for it was too precious and useful to the cause.

Things were proceeding according to schedule, and Drakhart was pleased.

The Qiri'ar were ready for battle—itching for it almost. It was no surprise. They prided themselves on their battle prowess and honour in the face of overwhelming odds. It had been a long time—too long—since they had been able to do so.

The warriors and Blood Witches had already been divided into their divisions and attack groups, each of them positioned in the semi-circular subterranean tunnel that would allow the Qiri'ar to surround the entirety of Ethon once they surfaced. No traffic would be allowed through on the main roads to the capital, and no help would come from the loyal barons. A separate strike force would be sent to capture and guard either side of the Pelchar to ensure no one would be able to send help via the canals.

The Qiri'ar planned to distract and demoralize the defenders. They would use fear and their imposing presence to wage psychological war against the city. The king would call his banners and Lord Gruffydd would respond, as would the rest of those who served him. But instead of coming to relieve the siege, they would join the Qiri'ar in the attack.

The insider within King Anducaerleonis's court would keep messages from reaching those who would remain loyal to the king, including the Baroness of Pelchar, Lady vohn Veishaupt, and other members of her Reformist faction. There weren't many, and they would not outnumber the forces raised by even the Cabal alone, but if they did manage to raise an army in support, and get inside the city walls, it would only prolong the siege in favour of the defenders.

Drakhart turned to his officers, who would be leading the Qiri'ar on the battlefield while he remained far from sight. He examined Kinu'watan O'lomec and several of his personally appointed Vul'kuhn. There was no exact translation, but it roughly meant something akin to "most-trusted", who acted in a similar capacity as the legates of the Asardaean army. Each army group would be led by one of them, and each would besiege a different section of the city before the larger army groups were broken down into smaller strike squads and attack groups.

Once the forces of Lord Gruffydd had joined up with them, they would charge the city. The plan was to blitz the defences of Ethon before the defenders could realize they had been betrayed. The arrival of the Barons would no doubt be seen as a great triumph and relief by the defenders of the city. They would not take the field to strike the Qiri'ar from behind and leave Lord Gruffydd to press the attack and break the siege. In this moment, they would lower their guard, and cheer for those whom they regard as allies, and in this moment they would be weak.

Ideally, the castle would be breached and taken, and the king taken captive. Afterwards, Lord Gruffydd would be proclaimed king, and after an appropriate amount of time, Drakhart would miraculously "arrive" with a delegation from Altimara to formally recognize the new king, by right of conquest, as agreed.

Drakhart paced down the line of his commanders. "I must leave for a time. I need to meet with Lord Gruffydd and confirm his side of the attack. When I return, the siege will begin. Kinu'watan O'lomec, I'm leaving everything in your hands while Elandyr'ni and I are gone."

The Kinu'watan grinned. "We shall not fail you. It may have been a long time since my people have seen a war of this scale, but I know how to keep control of them. And these Vul'kuhn would die before failing me, you, or Vihl'ku'lehg,"

In the time since they had first met, the Kinu'watan and Drakhart had slowly formed a bond of mutual respect and camaraderie. They were not friends by any stretch of the imagination, and Drakhart wasn't certain if O'lomec even liked him, but they had learned to work well together and had at least grown to respect one another.

"I admit, O'lomec. I envy you," Drakhart admitted.

O'lomec raised an eyebrow.

"You'll be in the thick of battle. You'll be out there fighting, where all the fun is. I'll be stuck in some tent, pretending I don't exist. I do wish my sword could taste blood. Moreso, I wish I could be out there teaching my former friends a lesson."

Elandyr'ni shot Drakhart a concerned look.

"A few months ago, I might have fought and argued, and taken the field anyway. I would have even brought Isunath with me, and together I would have single-mindedly charged into battle bent on revenge. But I must admit, I've calmed since I was humbled in my own hometown. Being in this position of leadership, I've been forced to learn—to mature. I still crave vengeance...but I am willing to play the long game to get it."

The Kinu'watan grinned wide. "His'krakh ii na ithca."

Drakhart couldn't even pretend he understood that.

Elandyr'ni translated for him. "In Qir'to'ah, it means: 'revenge is like ithca.'"

This, Drakhart could understand. Ithca was a drink served amongst the Qiri'ar, made of shaved ice and a cold herbal tea mixed with special berries found only around Gishan'belor. It was said to give one great mystical power, but aside from that, it was refreshing and delicious in the desert heat. Because of the ice, the drink was always served cold enough to hurt your head if you consumed it too fast.

Drakhart came to understand O'lomec's point. Revenge, like ithca, was best enjoyed cold, but exacting it too soon could be dangerous.

He responded with his own proverb. "Altimarans have a similar saying: the older the desert drop, the sweeter the fruit."

This proverb was common in Altimara; anyone who had lived there for any period of time knew it, or at least had heard it recited once.

Desert drops were a special berry that grew across much of Altimara, often from the surfaces of rocky outcrops. Somehow, despite the limited rainfall, they had adapted to produce incredibly juicy and sweet berries. The longer the berry remained on the vine, the sweeter and juicier they'd be. They were not often easy to get a hold of, due in part to where they grew, and because of how scarce they could be, but it was said the juice of a single ripened berry could slake the thirst of a single person for a week.

O'lomec threw back his head and belted out a hearty laugh. Clearly, he appreciated the saying. He even clapped Drakhart on the back a few times for good measure. "You're even starting to think like us now. I think your time among has done you some good."

"It's certainly mellowed him," Elandyr'ni added.

* * *

Because Isunath could not be brought with them—for many obvious reasons pertaining to secrecy and stealth—Elandyr'ni and Drakhart would have to rely on horses and the Kingsroad to reach Felidrun. The going had been slow, and they were forced to travel off to the side of the road, wrapped in shawls and cloaks, keeping a low profile, and drawing as little attention as possible.

Leaving his armies alone for so long was a source of anxiety for Drakhart. Every moment he spent in silence was a moment he spent wondering if perhaps his plans would collapse around him. If the Qiri'ar were discovered, everything would be ruined before he returned. And yet if Drakhart wasn't leaving them in such capable hands, he knew he'd be more worried than he was.

But now, they were almost at Felidrun. They would be meeting Lord Gruffydd in a small "hunting" encampment a few days ride outside of the city. In truth, it was a farce. The large hunting encampment was nothing more than a war camp by another name, manned by the forces of Lord Gruffydd and his cabal of barons. There weren't many more soldiers here than would be required to guard the encampment during a regular hunting trip, but the soldiers were no doubt ready and poised to march at a moment's notice at their appointed garrisons and fortresses. From this camp, Lord Gruffydd and his fellow barons would plot their part of the siege of Ethon.

Elandyr'ni stopped her horse, a grey dapple Xiaran, and looked at Drakhart. "Before we enter, I want you to know that as your teacher, I am proud of your growth."

"I couldn't have done it without your guidance, vii'so." Drakhart had been sure to use the Qir'to'ah word for teacher.

"The Drakhart I had known a few months ago would have—as you told the Kinu'watan—taken the field with Isunath and reigned flame and vengeance down upon the city of Ethon. You would have been a liability. To think you baulked at the thought of having to be patient."

"I had great advice, vii'so."

"But you also learned much on your own."

Drakhart shrugged.

"Your deal with the crime lords of Kula showed you are willing to learn from your mistakes and your hubris. You squashed a rebellion and endeared your people to you and the ways you seek to change and improve their lives. Now, you've found a weakness in our enemy's armour and not only exploited it, but turned it in our favour, and gained us an ally. You were given a task by Tenebrae, and you've excelled; you've united our allies against Estion to remove them from play before the game even starts. I am proud of you."

Drakhart didn't respond. He only smiled, nodded, and spurred his horse onwards towards the encampment.

Elandyr'ni slowly shook her head and urged her horse onward as well.

The two rode into the camp without being accosted by any of the passing guards or soldiers, and finally stopped in front of the central tent of the encampment, obviously meant to serve as both Lord Gruffydd's living quarters and his war room.

Elandyr'ni and Drakhart exchanged another glance before turning back to the two soldiers that guarded the tent. The soldiers acknowledged them, took their horses, and parted the tent flaps for them.

The two of them entered to find Lord Gruffydd and all his fellow barons sitting around a table, laughing, smoking, drinking, and feasting to their hearts' content. Much of the merriment stopped when Drakhart entered. As promised, Lord Gruffydd had rallied five other barons to his side. Drakhart had memorized their names and portraits by heart, at the behest of Calandor.

To the immediate right of Lord Gruffydd sat a short, greying man with a stocky build, no neck, and a shiny bald patch in the middle of his liver-spotted scalp. He was Maximilien dae lae Feton, Baron of Baracus, Viscount of Climm, Duke of Saard, Count of Elligon, and Chancellor of Laws.

Opposite him, on Lord Gruffydd's immediate left sat Imolna dae Esterazh-Villei, Baroness of Yeshtaburg, Duchess of Smyrah, Countess of Illit, Samzy, Whiteford, and Crahn. Chancellor of Coin. The woman looked like a skeleton and dressed like a queen. Her skin was taut and pulled tightly over her pointy bones. Her eyes seemed hollow and empty, but behind their façade sat a woman who scrutinized everything she looked upon. The only thing tighter than her skin was her hair pulled back into a neat black bun.

Next to Lord dae le Feton sat a man who somehow looked even more skeletal than the Baroness Yeshtaburg, and a thousand years older. This ancient creature was hunched over the table, his eyes closed, his nose dipping into his goblet of wine—were it not for the ripples on the surface of the liquid Drakhart would have thought he had died that way. But whereas the Baroness Yeshtaburg had taut skin, Vitori Ellisahd, Baron of Guld, Duke of Riverbend, Viscount of Simmit, Yelt, and Ziihm, and Count of Ilverberg, Chancellor of Ceremonies, was a skeleton wearing a loose skin sack. The smoke-like remains of wispy white hair were all that remained of a once proud lion's mane of hair he used to have. The painting Drakhart had been shown was at least fifty years out of date.

Standing directly behind Lord Gruffydd was a young woman, perhaps not much older than Drakhart, but much taller, broader and with much more muscle. A scar ran across the middle of her face, over the bridge of her nose, and a second just to the right of her right eye. Part of her left ear was missing. This was clearly the Bearoness—a clever nickname, for it was said she liked to travel the woods and do battle with Geller's bears. She had once battled a mother bear, only to find she had two young cubs with her. Instead of leaving the cubs to die, she adopted them and became their new mother. Sure enough, two bears had been seen sleeping just around the back of the tent on Drakhart's approach.

The Bearoness's real name was Lydia of Beauhn-Llangorodd-Monerrucci—the culmination of three noble lineages stretching back to the Gerovian Empire. She was Baroness of Beauhn, Duchess of Llangorodd and Monerrucci, and Viscountess of Bruch, Thruhg, and Tilden. She had inherited her titles young after her father died in a hunting accident, and her mother had abandoned the family shortly after she was born. No one ever publicly questioned how her father could have possibly died, shot by an arrow through the gut when he had been out hunting alone, without a single witness. Justice had been delivered to the man who had allegedly killed her father—he had been burned at the stake alive after a confession had been drawn from his own mouth, after hours on the rack.

Calandor had let Drakhart in on a bit of noble gossip that the Bearoness had been abused by her father, and that the drunkard had been a terrible father, terrible lord, and a heavy spender that had nearly bankrupted the family. But it was only gossip and hearsay, and no proof had ever given credence to the rumours.

Drakhart wasn't going to ask and find out.

Finally, standing off in the back of the tent, pouring himself more wine, was a middle-aged man with a closely shaved, black and white beard, and matching hair. He was of average height, and average build, and was overly unassuming, unremarkable, and just...average. The average noble could have just as easily passed as a carpet merchant. If Drakhart hadn't known his face, he would have assumed this man had been one of the serving staff. In reality, this was Lord Gyorge vohn Bruhgen-Himelshtat, the Baron of Ruhndel, Duke of Forswyth, Immelburg and Falford, Count of Gorm, and Viscount of Stelberg-Rethen.

Drakhart made a note to never address the baron directly. He was known for being as boring as he was average-looking. His voice had a habit of putting even the most afflicted insomniac to sleep. He drawled on and on, unendingly, at the most monotonous and slow pace, and he was dispassionate by nature. Even Elandyr'ni didn't make eye contact, for fear she'd be stuck talking to him at some point.

Lord Gruffydd welcomed Drakhart and Elandyr'ni with much enthusiasm and excitement. Whether it was feigned or genuine, Drakhart truly couldn't tell. But it was not an enthusiasm shared—or faked—by his colleagues, who measured Drakhart with cold indifference.

Drakhart couldn't entirely blame them. He had come from nowhere, with mysteriously perfect evidence to turn them against their current monarch, on the promise of a throne. He was the mysterious saviour from a kingdom that they had repeatedly been told was their enemy by their former monarch, whom they respected deeply—just not enough to keep his son on the throne.

Of course, whether they believed the Darond about Tenebrae's control over Altimara or not might also taint their views of Elandyr'ni and Drakhart. Drakhart would need to be careful not to lead them on to the truth. Altimara had to be viewed as acting independently.

Baron Felidrun raised his goblet to Drakhart. "Welcome, Lord Ghast. I am glad you could join us. To what do we owe the visit?"

Drakhart bowed. "I did promise I would return once the Qiri'aran army was in place. I wanted to ensure everything was still going well on your end and to confirm your plans. I can't risk messages being intercepted by our foes, and the only one I trust to carry my message is myself."

Baron Felidrun smiled and pointed to the two seats opposite him and his cabal of barons. "A wise choice indeed. Come, and allow me to explain."

Drakhart and Elandyr'ni bowed once more and took their seats. The eyes of all the barons and baronesses bore down upon them like a tidal wave. Even the average Baron Ruhndel had returned to his seat to stare blankly at them.

Lord Gruffydd stood and pointed to the map of Estion he had laid out before him. Several wooden blocks indicated where and how his armies would be arranged during the siege. He handed Drakhart and Elandyr'ni the reports—troop and supply manifests.

He had indeed raised the seven thousand soldiers he promised, with more easily available if he called on citizen levies—a baron's right, and not the Crown's in Estion. His supplies were sufficient for the march to Ethon and could easily supply his army of seven thousand for at least six months if the siege became a protracted affair. More supplies had been stored and warehoused across the lands of the Cabal nobles and could be drawn upon for a further nine months—this did not include each of the nobles' ability to replenish and restock their supplies of grain, or coffers of gold.

Lord Gruffydd had already assigned his army groups to different portions of the wall, based on their strengths and weaknesses. A decent force was being reserved to reinforce and aid the Qiri'ar who were being sent to seize the Acturn Canal. By holding the canal, they could ensure no one reinforces the city by the waterways, and it ensured that no one could sabotage the dikes that kept the lake from flooding the lowlands.

The lowlands around the city had been created by draining parts of Lake Ardona to create suitable farmland in the densely forested country. Logging and timber operations continually expanded the lowlands each year, since Estion was the main supplier of lumber and charcoal across Enayra. If the dikes burst, and the lowlands flooded, it would only make the siege harder. Most of the soldiers would at best be standing knee-deep in mud and cold water, and at worst would be slowly drowned as the water rushed to fill in the bowl-like terrain.

The hope was to use the Qiri'ar's unstoppable and crushing offence to overwhelm the defenders on the walls and breach the city. The Qiri'ar would create gaps in the defences, and Lord Gruffydd's forces would pour into the gaps to fill and claim them. They would repeat this as many times as necessary until they finally reached the central fortress of the city, all while ensuring they didn't overextend their supply lines, didn't spread their forces too thin across too many fronts and attacks, and avoided encirclements by the famed elastic defences.

Drakhart listened to Baron Felidrun's explanations and plans, and when the baron finished, he handed the reports back to Lord Gruffydd. "You've truly planned for everything. I'm very impressed."

"Have you managed to find a way around the limitations of the Qiri'aran's powers?" The Baron wondered.

Drakhart did not respond immediately. Taking a moment to pause and reflect upon his response.

"You mentioned to me when we were first planning this operation, that it may be an issue. I assume the issue is no longer?"

Drakhart smiled. "Indeed. As I said, the Qiri'ar have a limit to how long they can utilize their special powers. Two hours is the absolute limit. Anything beyond that pushes their bodies past the natural limit and can cause more harm than good. They risk damaging their bodies permanently—they already give their lives to use their powers. To get around that issue, we've divided the forces into three waves. As one wave reaches its limit, the next wave will be sent in to replace them, and they'll alternate until the city has fallen, or they do. It's a slower method of going around the problem, but it allows us to prolong the usage of our forces while minimizing losses, and you seem to have planned for a long campaign, so there should be no problem."

"No, indeed there is not. It's a careful solution, but a wise one. Every soldier counts when attacking the defences of Estion. Even a single man could tip the balance."

None of the nobles had said a word since Drakhart and Elandyr'ni had arrived, and Drakhart took note of that.

Drakhart faked a smile. "Truly spoken like the true future king."

"A king with no other masters than his country and his people, unlike our current king."

The air grew tense. Drakhart could even feel Elandyr'ni's apprehension. He had foreseen this happening. Lord Gruffydd was attempting to ensure his realm's independence and he was doing so in front of his followers. He was having Drakhart confirm that all the assistance provided by Altimaran wasn't a prelude to conquest or subservience. Lord Gruffydd would not be dominated or controlled like a puppet. Altimara would be his ally, not his master.

Drakhart threw him a bone. "No. No other masters. I assure you that. The Darond will not poison you like they do the boy king."

Satisfied, Lord Gruffydd changed the subject. "Would you like to stay the night? Rest up and return to your forces in the morning? We should have more than enough food for you and the Grand Enchantress."

"No, thank you. The offer is generous, but the sooner we return, the sooner we'll be able to begin our blockade of the city."

"Are you sure? That's an awful long way to travel for such a short visit."

"As I said, I can't trust my messages to be delivered by anyone but myself, and I trust only myself to deliver them. I had to ensure all was as planned. There is no travel too long or too short if it ensures success."

Lord Gruffydd smirked but did not reply. He bowed his head to Drakhart and Elandyr'ni, while the other nobles merely nodded disaffectedly, and as quickly as Drakhart had arrived, he left.

* * *

Elandyr'ni waited until they were far from the camp before she spoke. Night had fallen, and they had set up their camp for the evening before she brought up any of her thoughts about the day.

"I could have transported us to the encampment. It would have been faster."

"Yes, it would have," admitted Drakhart.

"And yet, you chose to travel by horse to this encampment—those two weeks wasted for a meeting that didn't even last half of an hour."

"I did."

"Just to prove a point?"

Drakhart shifted on the stump he had chosen as his seat. "Precisely."

Elandyr'ni smirked. "You've learned well."

"He was expecting us," Drakhart stated.

Elandyr'ni nodded. "I noticed. No one seemed the least bit surprised when we arrived. He's either spying on you directly, or he has spies spread across the country watching out for you."

"When his spies didn't report seeing our army, I'm sure it set him on edge. It got his nerves going. Perhaps, he thought, we had betrayed him. I never told him *how* I would be bringing them into position for the siege, to be fair. I've unnerved him by preparing without him knowing. He is the kind of person who wants to know everything he can about his enemies and twice as much about his allies."

"He fears we'll attempt to make a puppet of him," Elandyr'ni added. That much had been laid clear at the meeting.

"I have no intentions of turning Lord Gruffydd into a puppet for our benefit because he would not be a benefit as a puppet. Lord Gruffydd is not the kind to sit idly and be told what to do. He is far too hard to control. We'd have better luck orchestrating an invasion and occupation of Estion under the banners of Altimara, than we would making Gruffydd a puppet. Regardless, I'd much rather have an ally than a liability. He fears for nothing."

If Elandyr'ni was convinced or not, she did not say. Drakhart had told her what she needed to know of his plans, but no one, except perhaps Lord Tenebrae, truly knew the extent of what he was planning. Drakhart had prepared in the utmost secrecy. If but a single word of it had escaped and reached the Darond before the trap was sprung, all would be ruined. War would engulf Enayra, and Altimara would be sitting in the middle of a political scandal and could risk losing the neutrality of Danaen.

"Was it worth delaying the attack for? This point you made?"

Drakhart nodded. "It was. I have shown Lord Gruffydd that we are not to be intimidated, we are not to be underestimated, but above all, we can be trusted to keep our word."

"He may still pose a problem for you later. His fellow barons don't like or trust you. They understand the necessity of this alliance, but they'd sooner be done with it all and have it behind them than continue it after they get what they want."

"They are not my concern. The Cabal will do as their leader says. He has them enthralled to his own will. They may not like it, but they *will* obey. Gruffydd is my only concern."

The fire popped, filling the silence between the two.

"Do you think he'll turn on you?" Elandyr'ni asked. She asked not out of curiosity, but like a teacher quizzing her student on arithmetic.

Drakhart grinned. "I would welcome his attempt. But even if he were foolish enough to do so—and I don't think he is, unless provoked—he would not get very far. Have our spies in his encampment said anything I should be concerned about?"

"No," Elandyr'ni responded. "There is nothing they've discovered or heard whispered that should concern us."

Drakhart didn't linger too long on her response. "And our man inside Filiddyn? He is prepared, and aware of our plan?"

"He's run into a few issues. He believes someone may be catching on to his ruse and may be acting to counter his activities, but nothing we should be concerned about yet. If he can steal the king's stationary unnoticed, and communicate with us without being seen, then I doubt whoever is trying to counter him will catch him in time to stop what's coming. By the time they reach the heart of this conspiracy, the city will be in flames, and the boy king will be dead."

"Captured," corrected Drakhart. "He will be captured."

Elandyr'ni raised a brow. "Didn't you promise Lord Gruffydd he could kill the king?"

"I did. But I did not say when. There is something Lord Tenebrae requires from this King Anducaerleonis before his life is ended."

For once it was Elandyr'ni's turn to be confused. "What do you mean?"

"Our Lord wishes to speak with the boy king. He has knowledge that only he can provide. It is of the utmost importance."

It was then that Elandyr'ni did something that she had never thought possible of her. She lost composure. She looked shocked, hurt, perhaps even offended. She had always been privy to Tenebrae's every whim, plan, or thought. Nothing but the deepest secrets were kept from her, and those were kept from everyone. But for once, Drakhart knew something she did not.

Why?

What could possibly be so important?

This did not go unnoticed by Drakhart, who shifted to try and reassure his teacher and friend. "I assure you, keeping this from you was not my choice. It was our lord's decision. It's imperative that this secret remain so for the time being. I assure you, once Lord Tenebrae has the answers he needs, he will let you in on the secret and involve you on further goings on."

Elandyr'ni felt better, but the nagging in her gut, and the anxiety that gnawed at the edge of her mind like a hungry rat at a grain sack would not be abated, only dampened.

Drakhart, growing ever in tune with the emotions of others and how to manoeuvre them, did not respond. Instead, he looked at Elandyr'ni, with a genuine, warm smile on his face. He didn't say anything. The look said it all. It was meant to be reassuring and kind. To help her ease her fears. After all, Elandyr'ni had worked far too hard for her whole life to be worthy of Tenebrae's praise, and to earn her position—against thousands of other Qiri'ar—at his side, as his chosen Blood Witch. She would not be replaced and thrown aside so easily, not even for someone who had come to be her student, whom she had come to care for as a younger brother, as a friend.

Yet Drakhart's smile. His warm, endearing smile; was such a rare sight. Something he rarely let shine through. It was enough to calm her. She was embarrassed that it had worked.

"I trust Lord Tenebrae." She muttered.

"As you should. As do I. Your loyalty will be rewarded. It always is."

Elandyr'ni smiled. Her loyalty had *always* been rewarded. Tenebrae was good to those who served him dutifully.

As quickly as Drakhart eased her fears, he had changed the subject. "Come. Let's get some rest. We have several long days of travel ahead of us."

"Now, whose fault is that I wonder?" teased Elandyr'ni.

Drakhart shrugged. "I couldn't begin to imagine. I'll have to speak with that person when I find them."

But they would not sleep yet. An unnerving presence made itself known, materializing from the shadows at the edge of the camp, closely followed by a second. They came draped in long black cloaks that covered their faces. They made no sound, but they set nature itself on edge by their very existence. Even their presence felt *wrong*. They smelled of rotting flesh and stale air.

It was Tenebrae's Eyes who appeared before them. Drakhart would be lying if he wasn't a little scared right now, even Elandyr'ni, who had been around them many times before, felt on edge around these two.

"What a surprise. I wasn't expecting you to be here," Drakhart replied, feigning bravery.

The creatures did not respond. A hissing sound filled the air. Their response was not verbal, but Drakhart could feel every thought and emotion rushing through his head. The images of a fight in a barn. Flames. Weeks of chasing someone across Estion. Green dragons, more fighting, blood—green blood. It all started in Felidrun, in a small, otherwise innocuous-looking tavern that had been burned to the ground. It was the burning that set these two on the trail of this man. He had fled quickly, covering his tracks. They knew he would ruin Tenebrae's plans if he had been left to flee unchecked.

"How interesting...Lord Gruffydd never mentioned anything about that. Where is he?"

The image of a middle-aged, bald man, lying in a cold dark cell somewhere unknown to him. It was a dungeon, but it wasn't anywhere in the Black Citadel. This dungeon was in a building Drakhart had never seen before, but from what he could tell, it was ancient— and it was nowhere nearby. There was something else kept locked up in these dungeons. Inside of several larger cells were three massive, emerald, green forms. They were hard to see in the minimal light. The smell of blood. They were wounded and sedated.

It was Elandyr'ni who spoke this time. "Alert our lord, then interrogate the dragons, and see if they know anything that can be of use to us. Once you're done, bring the dragons and the spy to my cottage, and kept under close guard in my laboratory. I wish to interrogate the spy personally—unless our lord has an issue with that?"

Silence, but an answer came still.

Elandyr'ni frowned. "Speak with him then. I want to see what I can extract from this prisoner, and I want the dragons for experimentation."

Drakhart interjected. "Did he know anything of our plans?"

Again, the emptiness of silence. An uncertain response.

Not good enough for Drakhart. "If I had known, I would have requested to see him. I cannot risk our plans being discovered before the trap is sprung. What's done is done. Ensure he does not escape. Elandyr'ni will deal with him later."

Silence. Acknowledgement.

Drakhart shifted on the stump. "Where does Lord Tenebrae send you now?"

They were returning home. Back to their roost, to await further instructions. They had thrown caution to the wind during their time in Estion, especially in pursuit of the renegade innkeeper. They would bring Tenebrae many gifts and had learned much, but their presence was becoming less and less discreet, and they risked discovery. It was time, as per Lord Tenebrae's recommendation, to lay low, and remain in the shadows until they were needed next.

Drakhart waved a hand dismissively. "You have served well. Our lord will see you rewarded. Enjoy your moment of respite...I doubt we shall all have as much downtime soon."

The figures remained silent. They turned to leave but hesitated. One of the figures turned back towards Drakhart and Elandyr'ni. It said nothing, but it made sure they knew of the danger lurking, not far from their encampment.

"Oh, we're aware. But I appreciate the concern. We'll handle them soon enough." Elandyr'ni's voice was smooth as silk.

With that, the creatures stalked back into the shadows, and the goosebumps on the back of Drakhart's neck lowered. The unease was gone, and the unnatural feeling—the wrongness of it all—was gone with them into the night.

They waited a few minutes before speaking again. It was Drakhart who spoke first.

"We should get some sleep."

Elandyr'ni did not argue. It was a few hours before midnight, but the two had spent many hours in the saddle, and they were as exhausted as their mounts. They still had weeks of travels ahead before they returned to their underground encampment. Every moment of sleep was welcome.

* * *

Drakhart and Elandyr'ni slept out under the stars that night. In a small clearing off the main road. The fire was doused, and they slept on bed rolls under simple sheets, opposite each other. There was no need for a watch, for Elandyr'ni could summon a Blood Familiar.

A small lizard scuttled across the forest floor, made of shadow and blood, its ruby eyes staring through the darkness of the night, watching for any signs of attackers, spies, or any other danger. If it sensed anything, it would wake Elandyr'ni, and she, in turn, would wake Drakhart.

Neither of them slept far from their weapons, and anyone who dared to attack them would find themselves sorely mistaken, and in more trouble than they had bargained for.

In the end, the familiar was helpful, but unnecessary, for no one dared to attack the Grand Enchantress and the Dragonkin while they slept. But the blood lizard *did* notice a small, non-descript figure, sitting in the shadows, not far from camp. The figure did not move, did not make to attack. It simply followed and watched.

The figure never saw the lizard, nor knew that Elandyr'ni and Drakhart were, because of this lizard, always aware of his presence. As they had been for weeks. This unknown watcher in the shadows had been following them since early in their travels, picked up—somewhat surprisingly to the figure—only a few days after they departed the tunnels beneath Ethon. This figure had followed them every step of the way, from where he had found them, quite by accident, to Baron Felidrun's encampment.

The shadowy tail had seen everything and had heard even more. He compiled everything he had heard and intended to report back to Baron Felidrun as soon as this figure discovered where Drakhart was encamped with his army, and where he was hiding thousands of Qiri'aran warriors near the capital of Estion. His last report had been shortly before Drakhart and Elandyr'ni arrived at Baron Felidrun's camp, letting him know they were on their way.

What the figure did not notice, however, was that the Drakhart that slept in the bedroll was not the real Drakhart.

Not until it was far too late.

He finally noticed moments before a massive sword sliced through his flesh like a hungry animal and took the head from his shoulders in the dark and silent night. His body was left to rot and be devoured by whatever scavengers would have it. But not before the little lizard had lapped up the blood from the dead spy's cooling corpse and turned the deepest shade of crimson as it grew to twice its size.

Chapter XL

"Kyeit's back."

Djall's voice cut through Kanaahn's dreams like a blade. It was just before dawn. Where he would normally take every minute he could to sleep before being dragged from his bed for a full day of training, today of all days, Kanaahn didn't waste a second.

He rose from his bed and placed the pot of water on the still-warm remains of the previous night's fire. When the pot was ready, he poured the warm water into the stone basin and proceeded to wash the sleep from his face. He had bathed before bed last night, but he wished to rid the crust from his eyes and grogginess that clung to him. With a few splashes of warm water, they slid from his face and pooled into the water bowl.

With his face cleaned, Kanaahn quickly dressed into the simple clothes he had been gifted in Xiar. A white shirt, a black leather vest, black trousers completed with black leather boots and gloves. Kanaahn tucked the gloves into his belt and fastened his sword at his hip. He would need it later for training.

Once Kanaahn was dressed and ready, he checked himself in the polished silver mirror that stood in the corner, and quickly—but calmly—left the room to go find Kyeit.

Based on Djall's directions, she had departed the courtyard where the dragons were staying shortly before Djall woke Kanaahn, and she and Valence—in the latter's human form—were on their way to check in with King Leon and Cecil. Kanaahn figured that Kyeit was likely still meeting with Cecil and Leon. He would need to catch her before breakfast, just outside the great hall.

Kanaahn planned it out in his head. He would head to the courtyard to meet with Djall. Kyeit would probably be in the meeting for the next half an hour. At that point, the other Dragonkin would be woken, and breakfast would be served. It would be an hour before the other Khaleeshir were down in the dining hall and eating. But Kyeit always ate before her charges. Even in Xiar, Kyeit was up, fed, and ready for the day before the Khaleeshir had even woken up and dressed themselves.

So based on Kanaahn's estimates—

Kanaahn rounded a corner and slammed into someone. "I'm sorry. I was lost in thought, please forgive—"

Kanaahn's mouth hung open, and his sentence went unfinished, as he looked down and found that the person he had collided with was Kyeit.

Behind her stood a tall woman. She was broad-shouldered, and despite being encased in a veritable carapace of armour, Kanaahn could tell she was covered in corded and bugling muscles. Her hair was as silver as his mirror and gleamed in the dim torchlight. It was kept in a long, tight plait that draped down her back like a tail. Piercing silver eyes like two moons gazed at Kanaahn. He had never seen her in this form before, but it was unmistakeably Valence. If all the silver didn't give it away, the discerning gaze and stern demeanour would have.

"I uh...welcome back."

Kyeit hid a smirk.

Valence did not hide hers.

At first glance, Kyeit appeared to be in a much better mood now than she was when she had left. Seemingly, the meeting with the High Council had not been as bad as Kyeit may have feared.

Djall cut across Kanaahn's thoughts to deflate his hopes slightly. *"I would not be so certain. Kyeit is better at hiding her true intentions than the Metallic Dragons."*

"Not now."

Now Kyeit smiled openly. "Hello, Djall."

How Kyeit could have guessed that Djall had chosen that moment to intrude, Kanaahn was unsure, but her ability to somehow read Kanaahn's mind had always been eerie.

"Hello, Kyeit." This time his voice cut through both Kanaahn's and Kyeit's heads.

Kanaahn's face went red.

"How are you?" Kyeit asked the dragon.

"I am well, thank you. How was your meeting with the High Council?"

"Djall, I'm begging you please stop." Kanaahn pleaded with his friend in private.

Djall did not stop.

"Better than I could have hoped, but still unpleasant as always. I would rather repel another siege singlehandedly than face the High Council like that again. But I suppose I should be telling this to Kanaahn?"

"I apologize, he was here first. Take care, Kyeit. It's nice to have you back."

"It's nice to be back, Djall. Thank you."

Djall removed Kyeit from the connection. *"You're on your own from here, my friend."*

"If only that were true," Kanaahn lamented.

Valence eyed Kanaahn, waiting for his response.

"What can I ask that the lizard hasn't already?"

"Not a lizard!" Djall grumbled.

"Quite a lot, actually," Kyeit replied coolly.

Kanaahn chewed his lip. "I thought you were in a meeting with King Leon?"

"Did Djall say that?" Kyeit teased.

"He might've mentioned it..."

"His Majesty was busy in another meeting. Both major-domos were in there. It seemed urgent—they wouldn't even tell him I was here. So, I was hoping to get something to eat before we continued with your training."

"We are eager to see how much you've learned since we've been gone," Valence added.

"You, or the High Council?" Kanaahn asked, cutting to the point.

Kyeit knew there would be no escape. "Let's find somewhere quiet to talk. Valence, come find me when His Majesty is finished with his meeting."

Valence nodded and left Kyeit to walk off with Kanaahn. The two left the narrow hallways of the palace to find a small, shaded cloister with a willow tree in the centre. It was dark, far from being touched by the early light of dawn, and it was cool, but it was private and secluded, and they could talk there unbothered.

"I'm only telling you this because you lead the other Khaleeshir. I think you deserve to know what the High Council is up to. I leave it to your discretion whether you choose to tell the others."

"Well, Djall will know whatever enters my mind."

"Then it's up to you two to tell everyone else, should you feel it the right thing to do."

"I won't lie to them, Kyeit."

Kyeit frowned. "No...of course not."

A tense silence followed for a moment while Kyeit gathered her thoughts.

Kanaahn awaited her information with bated breath. His heart pounded in his chest, and he could feel his cheeks burning hot. But that was not because of what Kyeit was about to tell him. He had tried; really tried, to bury his feelings. Ever since Kyeit had rebuffed his affections in the Tormenting Pinnacle. But no matter how many times he dragged these feelings around back, beat them with a stick, and took a cleaver to their neck, they still ran around, struggling, clucking, and screaming, spurting blood everywhere with every dying breath. Yet instead of dying, they only seemed to grow. Kanaahn did not act on them—he did not actively seek to pursue Kyeit romantically—but the feelings sat there, boiling away beneath the surface, colouring his actions whether he liked it or not.

"The High Council is not pleased. Xiar was an embarrassment for them. Not because it was a failure—no they were quite pleased that the city was saved. But putting you in the heart of the battle, letting you lead the defence, it all undermined their directive, and their plans for you. They wanted you a little less involved. They wanted you as a silent beacon of hope, doing as they said, dutifully and unquestioningly. My father had other plans, and he acted as he believed he and others who felt as he did, was best for Enayra."

Kanaahn waited for the "but" to drop like a hammer on the anvil.

"But my father is dead. His position on the High Council is vacant. Xiar is gone. On top of that, anyone else who would have supported his decision was either dead or mysteriously unavailable for the meeting. Regent Alaxzander was preoccupied with military matters in Asardaea. Osamu is dead. King Leon is here overseeing his kingdom and your training. The Dragon Masters on our side were busy and absent from the meeting. The only two generals who opposed the Grand Master are out on assignment, advising the Grand Duchess of Utova on fending off recent Altimaran incursions."

"Do they know what you've told us?"

Kyeit nodded. "I told them. They asked. As you say...I could not lie. They would know. They're not pleased with how much I've told you. They're not pleased that I allowed my father to circumvent their wishes—my given orders. They feel because I did not reprimand or report him, and because he is my father, that I am complicit in his actions. Disciplinary action is to be taken, though specifics are yet to be decided. There will be a trial, and I will be forced to defend myself before the complete High Council, and they'll decide my punishment from there. Also..."

"Also?" Kanaahn almost didn't dare ask the question, fearing the words to come.

"I've been removed from my duties as your guide and protector. The task is being reassigned. Cecil will also be removed because her assignment was not to accompany you on your travels. She was sent to Xiar to help defend the city, and she remained out of a sense of duty afterwards, but she will be getting new orders, and will be sent elsewhere."

Kanaahn felt his stomach sink to his feet. He felt dizzy. The world was spinning. "When is this happening?"

"I don't know. Likely in the next few weeks. King Leon will receive a summons to Tuir'Delohmeyh for a meeting of the High Council. They have not said as much, but I believe that he will be asked to bring you Khaleeshir with him. Once you arrive at the fortress, I do not doubt that the High Council will use every excuse for why you cannot leave. You will have your training personally monitored by the High Council, and you will become as they wanted you: their obedient puppets, preferably willingly, but by force if need be."

"Can we stop this?"

"We're trying. But I need to meet with His Majesty first. I've sent word to the generals and the Lord Regent, but I haven't heard back from them. I don't know how successful we'll be." Despite the obvious pain in Kyeit's voice, she maintained her composure.

"I can't believe they didn't swear you to secrecy..." Kanaahn was amazed more than anything.

"Most of this what I've said is speculation beyond their summoning of Leon, but even so they probably knew I'd break my oath anyway. I'll likely face further punishment for telling you, and for telling King Leon and the other council members loyal to you—no doubt part of their plan. But I couldn't sit idly by and allow this to happen. My father was right. I'm sorry I ever withheld any information from you."

"I can't ever say I appreciated it. But I can at least sympathize with the position you were put in." Kanaahn sighed and ran a hand through his hair. He nibbled his thumbnail and tried to think of a solution to this problem. "For starters, I'm not going to say anything to the other Khaleeshir for now. I don't want to worry them. They'd only try to get involved, and that would only hurt more than help. The rest, I'll have to entrust to you and your allies."

Kyeit smiled. "I appreciate that. We'll do everything we can to stop this."

"I trust you. Even if I only know a few of you," Kanaahn replied. He struck before Kyeit could change the subject. "How are you holding up?"

Kyeit stood and walked from the small stone bench where the two had been sitting. "You know, when I first met you, all of you, I had discouraged myself from growing too close. I didn't know how long my mission would last, only that I had orders, and I would follow them. I pushed you all away, especially you, for the sake of that duty. Even after my father passed, when I could have used your support most, I kept you all at a distance and nearly got lost in my anger and fear. It wasn't until this was all about to be taken away from me, when I stood there, being scolded by the High Council, that I realised how much of a fool I'd been to take that time for granted. I had come to see you as my friends, despite my best attempts otherwise, and I did nothing to show you that. I can't let my father's death be for nothing. He died so you and the other Khaleeshir could live. So, the city of Xiar could survive, and stand as an example against Altimaran aggression, and Tenebrae's crushing influence. Even if Xiar is gone now, and I have lost my home and my family, I am not alone. Thank you for showing me that."

Kanaahn had been prepared for a more guarded response. He had prepared for Kyeit to keep him at arm's length from her feelings. She had always done that. She kept her personal feelings close at hand, for the sake of the mission, for the sake of her orders. For her own sake. Out of fear, perhaps. Maybe even out of shame. But Kanaahn was surprised, taken aback even, by the candid and open way Kyeit spoke with him. He was utterly speechless. Bereft of any words for a response.

Kyeit did not waste an opportunity to tease Kanaahn. "Look at that. For once you're speechless. I should surprise you more often."

Kanaahn still could not recover.

"Come, shall we get something to eat before the others are awake? I can meet with His Majesty after breakfast, while you're training for the day."

Despite being at a loss for words, Kanaahn was not going to turn up that opportunity. He smiled, nodded, and followed Kyeit from the cloister.

* * *

Morning lessons had been modified that day. Aurichalcum and Thrae lead the hour of history and culture at the start of the day. Normally that hour was led by Hana, Leon, or his Major-domos. None of them were present for the morning lessons. Cecil, too, was also gone, as was Kinokaze.

Kyeit and Valence were the reason for said meeting. Their return had not gone unnoticed amongst the Khaleeshir.

Arkas had heard from Fyete first thing in the morning, as had the remaining Khaleeshir. Kyeit's return was accompanied by whispers amongst the Khaleeshir, who had all noticed Kyeit and Kanaahn talking and sitting together at breakfast. They seemed to have grown much closer since the latter's return.

Arkas had not participated in the rumours and gossip. He chose to keep his thoughts on the matter close to his chest.

His hawkish eyes and keen senses had noticed the increased tension in the air. He had noticed how, despite her smiling, laughing, and teasing, Kyeit was afraid behind her mask. Something had shaken her during her return to Tuir'Delohmeyh and her time before the High Council. Something was terribly wrong. Great change was coming, and everyone was about to be caught very unawares.

"Is your book not interesting to you?"

Arkas looked up from his thoughts, his unturned pages, and his blank page of notes to find Thrae, hands on her hips, watching him as a dutiful teacher should.

"I apologize. My thoughts are elsewhere, y'thair."

"Where do they dwell, Khaleeshir?"

A distraction caught Arkas before he could respond. "I thought Khaleeshir was the plural?"

Thrae's eyes lit up. "In Drazhanii, when referring to the Khaleeshir, they are Khaleesh in singular only before bonding. Once they have undergone the ritual, and become as one soul in two bodies, bound forever, they are only ever referred to in the plural, even if only

345

one half is present. You are always Khaleeshir, because even separate, a part of Fyete dwells within you, and a part of you in her. That was the point of the Khaleeshir...to bridge the gap between dragon and human. They were created to bring the two races closer together. Being as one also provides you with an advantage on the battlefield. You can be in two places at once, as I'm sure you've experimented with during my father's sparring lessons."

Arkas nodded.

"But that does not answer my question, y'wiihr. Where do your thoughts dwell?"

Arkas wasted no more time being distracted. "Something feels wrong. I feel it in the air. I can't place it, but it gives me pause. It turns my stomach."

Thrae's face did not move. "You are keen. I cannot say much, y'wiihr. But the faction that is against you in the High Council is not pleased that they have not gotten their way. It's nothing for you to worry about."

"Are you certain?"

"I promise. As y'wiihr, it is your job to study, and as y'thair, it is up to us to keep you safe, and away from harm. I suggest you return to your book, dry as Plinius Secundus may be. You still have much to get through."

Arkas wasn't convinced, and his worries did not abate, but he put them to the side for now. If Thrae said to trust her, Arkas would trust her.

But he would keep his bowstring waxed and ready, should it be needed.

* * *

Shooter's language lessons had progressed slowly for the first few weeks. He had been handed a Qir'to'ah to Common lexicon and been left to study, copy, make notes, and memorize to the best of his ability. It was three weeks before he finally got a teacher proficient in the Qiri'aran mother tongue and was able to teach it.

The man, Qul'den, claimed to have come from Asardaea. He claimed to be "a full-blooded Qiri'ar of sorts" and came highly recommended by fellow members of the Darond. Despite Qul'den's claims of his ancestry and the fact that man was very fluent in Qir'to'ah, Shooter couldn't help but notice certain parts of him didn't line up. Shooter had seen many Qiri'ar in his life. He had grown up in Kula seeing them come through town twice a year to trade and exchange goods. Once in the spring, and once in the late autumn—not that Altimaran seasons differed much, except for how hot it was, and how many people died from that heat.

Qul'den did not fully match what Shooter knew to be Qiri'ar. Admittedly, Shooter was not Qiri'ar, nor was he an expert. Far be it from him to tell someone what they were or weren't, but Shooter knew there was more to the story, and more to Qul'den than the old man let on.

He wasn't as tall, or muscle-bound as the Qiri'ar Shooter knew. They had a reputation for being as tall as mountains, and as strong as a bear. He was also missing the distinctive golden tattoos that covered all Qiri'ar from head to toe, and his clothing was very different. Though Shooter supposed that could have been due to his living in Asardaea.

346

That was another thing that was odd to Shooter. But it wasn't unheard of for some members of the Qiri'aran tribe to leave their ancestral lands and secretly settle elsewhere in Enayra, often for love, sometimes because they've been banished by the tribe.

On a personal level, however, Shooter had nothing against Qul'den. Quite the opposite, in fact. He liked Qul'den. The old man was someone after Shooter's heart. Wise, with a good sense of humour, a sharp wit, and a keen eye. But he also took no bullshit, and despite being supportive of Shooter's progress and desire to learn Qir'to'ah, he pushed Shooter towards excellence.

It was in this manner he had trained Shooter for the last month and a half.

"You must roll your r's in a more pronounced matter," Qul'den declared after Shooter had attempted—for the fifth time—to pronounce a sentence on a page, and once more, failed miserably. To Qul'den's credit, his patience never drained, never ran out. But still, he pushed towards excellence.

"Halu varrrr, ti'iim theelo semvyietae. Rrrrristo im'tha—sorry—imthelodae." Shooter made sure to stress each rolled "r." Though he struggled with it, he was progressing at the very least.

"Excellent. Now what did you just say?"

Shooter went blank.

Qul'den waited a moment. Pausing. Hoping, as always, that Shooter would have the answer. But when it became obvious that Shooter, while getting the hang of the pronunciation, was still working on the translation, Qul'den gave the answer. "Long ago, before the first sunrise. Dragons ruled."

Shooter was, for the first time in his life, eager for education, and so scribbled down the answer as quickly as possible. "What are we reading today?"

Qul'den sipped a small cup of tea. "It's the Qiri'ar creation myth. It was said to be given to us by the Metallic Dragons themselves. The Great Aspects. They told us how the world came to be before humans arrived, and we keep those tales sacred. We pass them down, written, and verbally, to each new generation, and hold them dear."

Shooter leaned in. "Does anyone else know about this?"

Qul'den shrugged. "That depends."

If Shooter had been asked months ago whether he'd ever care about creation myths and cultural stories, he'd have yawned, shrugged, and politely declined. Tradition had its place, but that place was not in Shooter's memory. It would not have been for him. But studying here in Estion, and especially in recent weeks under Qul'den, had awakened a new passion in Shooter that had never been there before.

"I mean...wouldn't the history of Enayra before humans arrived be something valuable? For everyone to know?"

Qul'den shrugged once more. "It's just a story. A story passed down from an old dragon to an old man, to countless generations of other old people, and finally to me. I wouldn't put too much weight in it."

"But isn't that story sacred?"

"To some. To the Qiri'ar. Likely to the dragons. But how do we know it's true? How do we know it wasn't mixed up along the way? How do we even know that the Metallic Dragons told us the truth in the first place? We don't really."

"What could the Metallic Dragons possibly want to lie about in a creation story?" Shooter spoke with slightly more offence than he had expected.

He had *never* deferred to authority, especially authority he didn't know. He didn't trust the Darond and yet...he had come to admire, perhaps even idolize, the Metallic Dragons. Maybe it was the reverence held by Risasi and the other dragons, that bled into part of him as their souls merged more and more over time. Maybe it was how the Metallics were spoken about by everyone who admitted them. Maybe it was the incredible power that Shooter could tell lurked beneath the surface whenever he looked at Valence, or Thrae, or Kinokaze, or Aurichalcum.

Qul'den smacked his lips after another sip of tea. "Dunno. What indeed. That's a good question. Maybe you should ask them." Qul'den gestured with his chin towards Aurichalcum—who had appeared around mid-morning after his meeting with Leon—and Thrae.

Shooter didn't reply. He looked over at the dragons in their mortal form. Tall, slender, strong, incomparably beautiful. Otherworldly. Is that what humans looked like to dragons? Dragons were of this world—more than humans were, at least. No one knew where humans came from, but they were not part of the Earth Mother's plan, that much was certain.

Instead, Shooter changed the subject. "Do they take those appearances because to them, that's what they think humans look like, or because they're incapable of imperfection?"

Qul'den downed the last of his tea and sat back in his armchair. "I repeat, why don't you ask them? What are you afraid of little Dragonkin?"

Shooter had no answer. What *was* there to be afraid of such a question? Aurichalcum was grouchy and unapproachable, but Thrae would have been happy to answer...yet Shooter refrained. Quite uncharacteristically. He never thought he'd meet someone who was more anti-authoritarian than he was.

"Well, if you don't ask, you'll never know." Qul'den chided.

Shooter's brow furrowed. "But you claimed you've spent your life learning many things, from a variety of cultures, and histories and under a broad spectrum of subjects. The kinds of things you must know... You are my teacher after all, should I not benefit from your knowledge?"

Qul'den smiled. Genuinely smiled. "The best knowledge is knowledge earned. Knowledge without wisdom is wasted, and wisdom is based on experience, no? Besides, in my seventy years, I know only one thing, and that is that I know *nothing*."

That made no sense to Shooter.

Qul'den continued. "So, until you gather up the courage to experience what asking such questions brings, let's get back to the text at hand, yes? Qir'to'ah, ma'guun tha fehla."

In Qir'to'ah only, going forward.

Great.

Shooter would need all his concentration.

* * *

Arial's lessons with Leon alternated between practical study, where Arial practised the magic she was taught, theoretical study, where she studied magical theory and other book-based learning, and furthering Leon's studies on mana shards.

In that time, Leon had also replaced the gem in her staff with a mana shard. It was the rarest of magical focuses, but also the best conductive material for mana, especially when guided by a skilled mage. Mana could be stored in the stone like a reservoir. That would allow Arial to amass potentially vast quantities of excess mana in her staff for times when she needed more mana than she could give.

Arial had been incredibly grateful for the gift, though she kept it a secret from the others.

Leon was absent for the day due to unplanned meetings, however, so Arial was left to study magical theory and Leon's research on her own.

She was alone in the laboratory, studying hers and Leon's notes again, trying to get a deeper grasp of Leon's and his mother's findings.

Leon had trusted her with the magical key that unlocked the doors to the tunnels and the laboratory itself and had even taught her the secrets of the wards that protected the tunnels from intruders. Without the incantation that served as the password, anyone who accessed the ancient tunnel system to the laboratory would find the way drowned in traps, counterspells, curses, and warding magic. The spells were ancient and powerful, supposedly laid by the Metallic Dragons themselves to guard the Mana Core beneath the city. Either way, they were near impossible to break, and very dangerous if triggered.

As Arial had learned during her magical theory lessons, there were three main types of Arcane Magic.

The first type was offensive magic, made up of the six elemental magic schools: fire, water, earth, air, ice, and lightning. Second, was defensive magic, which was comprised of healing magic, protective magic, and illusion magic. Finally, there were the natural magics. They were a miscellaneous category of magic that focused on magic that was not used in combat. The main subtypes of magic under natural magics were enchanting, divination, and conjuration.

Enchanting allowed one to imbue otherwise non-magical objects with magic, or draw out latent, innate magical properties so that they became more overt. Most commonly this came in the form of brewing draughts, potions, and other mixtures that were then strengthened by magic to make them more potent. The enchantment on the Khaleeshir's sets of armour, or Kanaahn's katana were other common, if more difficult, uses of enchanting.

Divination was concerned with seeing the future, scrying, and reading and interpreting dreams to discern the ways of the world. Few mages practised divination, and those with any kind of skill or gift were even fewer. Most involved with modern magical discourse were divided as to whether divination was even a school of magic, or just fakery used by charlatans to swindle people from money. The proper term for prophecy was called 'reading the possibilities' since the art was so imprecise, and no future was set in stone.

Finally, conjuration had to do with the summoning of spirits, creatures, and familiars from beyond the veil to aid and assist you. Conjuration bound these beings to the caster for a pre-contracted amount of time. Some mages made a bond with a single familiar for the course of their lives, others chose to make temporary contracts with multiple different spirits or familiars. But one thing was constant—overuse and abuse of this power led to destruction.

Arial flicked over her notes. Now would be a good time to review everything Leon had taught her about protective magic, especially now that her mind had wandered there—and she was growing weary of the blueprints and research notes.

The wards, shields, protective spells, counterspells, curses, and other such magic used to protect the laboratory and tunnel system fell under protective magic. Defensive magic was not easy to counter or dispel, like offensive magic. Defensive magic, especially under the school of protective magic, were custom-crafted spells with specific triggers, clauses, and reactions to certain stimuli and were meant to sustain themselves long after the caster's death. The spell was cast and imbued with all the mana it needed to sustain itself until the triggers were set off. Sometimes, runes were used when casting the spell, to bind the spell to the leylines, and allow them to draw indefinitely upon the magic within the earth. However, doing so was dangerous and could easily have negative consequences if done incorrectly.

Mages would spend days, sometimes weeks, carefully writing out, revising, and perfecting their spells before using them. More complicated spells were not something to be rushed. One missed word, one missed trigger, one wrong choice of word, and the spell could collapse in on itself—ending poorly for the mage—or could easily be broken or circumvented by another magic user.

The only way to stop a spell of protective magic would be to trip the spell, thus expending the spell—a dangerous prospect—or to know the exact words that would deactivate the spell. The latter would require knowing the intricate and complicated spell already. This was often impossible, as mages kept their custom spells a well-guarded secret from even their own grimoires. These were spells kept locked away in the minds of mages and were never written down.

Some mages could spend their lives dedicated to deactivating a protective spell, only to die before they could figure out the proper combination of words and runes, and usually, their death was self-inflicted due to a mistake in the process. It was delicate, detail-oriented work.

And Arial was terrible at it.

She was learning, but that learning was difficult. Since arriving here, Arial could not, for the life of her, construct a proper protective spell that did not either explode in her face or have so many loopholes it may as well not have been cast at all. She did not fare much better when it came to piercing protective magic spells.

Leon had assured her that it was merely a lack of knowledge on her part—something to be expected for a novice, and a problem that would be less and less so as she learned and progressed in her studies. But that did not make Arial feel any better about it.

It didn't take long for Arial's head to start aching from the dryly written notes and textbooks.

She closed her grimoire and rubbed her temples. Arial couldn't' believe how much she had filled out that beat-up old grimoire since she had started studying magic.

When she had bought it, the grimoire was only half-full of hastily scribbled notes and theories of what Arial, at the time, thought was a powerful mage. After months of studying the craft, she had learned that the person who had owned this book had been a novice, an acolyte. An advanced one, sure, but a student, nonetheless. Based on how incomplete the grimoire was, it had been a student who had given up on their craft partway through and sold off their grimoire—or had it stolen, more likely—after doing so.

Yomi had thanked Arial for rescuing this grimoire from a life in the hands of a less-than-savoury individual. A mage's grimoire was a window into their mind, and the key to their undoing. No one left their grimoire unattended. Leon had even taught Arial how to shrink her grimoire down to pocket size so that she could bring it with her. That was what she did with her first grimoire, and the second one gifted by Yomi.

Turning to that second grimoire, Arial went back to poring over the notes and writings she had been allowed to take with her—in secret—from Leon's research. She hadn't understood most of what she had read, but from what she had managed to grasp, Arial was surprised that Leon had trusted her with such valuable research. Leon and his mother had gone to such lengths to keep this knowledge secret for so long, yet Leon had allowed Arial unfettered access to these chambers and knowledge. It spoke to the trust Leon put in her.

Leon had argued that there would be no one more trustworthy than a Khaleeshir. Arial would far outlive him as one of the chosen, and Leon's research needed to pass to someone impartial, who could not place the needs of a single nation above all Enayra. Whatever children he might have one day may not be so altruistic as he was, and Leon could not bear to think that his mother's research might be turned to evil and wicked designs.

Arial was honoured if a bit swamped in diagrams, blueprints, and terminology.

Though it had been a lot to learn all at once, Arial soon found a new passion in this research and had set herself a goal of finding the last piece of the puzzle that would make this viable and useable.

No major breakthroughs had been made since Leon's mother had passed, and the research fell to him. Leon mostly spent his time trying to find new applications for the core shards, or developing contraptions for them to be used in.

The most important discoveries had been written down and distilled into simple points by Leon's mother, points that Arial had copied down into her own research notes early on. She reviewed them often; even now. They became a mantra for her as if reading them might help her suddenly discover that missing piece.

1. *The Core Shards are fragments taken from Mana Cores; the gathering points for mana within the leylines, and part of the mana cycle.*

2. *The Core Shards are inherently full of mana and take that finite mana with them after being separated from their Core. They can act as power sources, i.e., for spellcraft.*

3. *The finite mana in a Core Shard can be replaced. Mages can store their mana within the shard for later use.*

4. *The Core Shards do not regenerate or grow once separated from the mother crystal.*

5. *Core Shards react to blood. Blood can be distilled into pure mana by a Core Shard; the process seems to be innate. They cannot do this with any other form of mana. Anything but blood must be given willingly.*

6. *Once applied as a power source, the way the power is unleashed cannot be directed to more than one use. If it is turned on, it stays on. The energy is unleashed at a constant and steady stream until drained but cannot be shut off, diverted, split, or dampened with any known magical intervention. Mechanism dies once power is expended.*

7. *Core Shards can be combined with a mage's staff to create a mana focus, that allows mages to channel, direct, pool, or unleash mana while spellcasting, with the Core Shard as a conduit, or focal point of the spell. More effective than other gemstones used for similar purposes.*

8. *Use as a power source deemed plausible but limited.*

RESULTS: *APPLICATION AS A POWER SOURCE IS PLAUSIBLE, BUT <u>NOT</u> CURRENTLY VIABLE*

Arial wasn't so sure. No, in fact, she had an idea that the answer to these conundrums was staring them right in the face. The answer seemed obvious, painfully so...but no one was willing to cross that line, and that was why they hadn't discovered it. They had considered it, Arial was certain, but not seriously. Not serious enough to try it. The thought was so repulsive to Leon and his mother that they had considered it a non-starter.

But Arial, seeking to excel, was wondering if she even had such qualms. Perhaps in the service of greatness, and progress...perhaps there were no boundaries...

The answer was so simple: blood magic.

Arial understood the basic principles of blood magic. Yomi had taught her, to answer her unceasing questions, though he had done so with a look of grave concern.

Blood magic used blood as the fuel to power the spell. Runes were the medium that transformed the blood into mana, bound the mana to the spell, and provided the framework for the spell, then directed it around that framework. The actual spell, the words spoken by the casters, gave life to the desires and solidified the spell as reality, to the will of the caster—like arcane magic. But unlike arcane magic, the will was the most important, the words were secondary—but they helped guide the magic more surely. The most skilled warlocks could cast a spell without uttering a single word, for their will was as stone, and they didn't waver for a second.

Supposedly, that was because blood magic was unnatural and because it was unnatural, it required a great will to subvert nature and the natural order. A witch or warlock struggled with nature to cast their spells.

Arial didn't believe that.

If it was so hard, why was it so much easier to cast than arcane magic? Not everyone could practice arcane magic. Some had no skill, and never would, but anyone could become a warlock if they possessed a strong enough will and a knowledge of runes.

Arial had a feeling it was just said to dissuade people from using blood magic.

Regardless, blood magic was her answer. Blood magic would be the providence that allowed her to do what Leon and his mother were unable to.

Arial had agonized over testing her theory. For one, she didn't know much about blood magic, what she had learned was taken in bits and pieces from whatever Yomi or Osamu had told her. Secondly, Leon might not approve—no, he definitely would not approve. On top of all that, Arial's grasp of magical runes, even in just the context of arcane magic, was still fledgling. There was the chance something would go wrong.

And yet...

She produced a small, rolled parchment from within her sleeve. She'd been hiding this for a while. Arial had stolen it from Xiar's library while preparing for the siege. She had wanted to better understand blood magic and how it worked. If Arial was going to fight it, she wanted to be prepared, and know how best to combat it, and what to expect. In the end, so much had happened during the siege that Arial had forgotten she had it when they left the city, and she never had a chance to return it. It was hers now, she supposed.

This ancient parchment, written in a form of Middle Common, had been instrumental in teaching Arial about blood magic over the last few weeks. Arial had never cast any of the spells listed on the treatise. There was never a reason to, especially when she had arcane magic. But now...now it might have other uses.

Arial was determined. It was now or never. If she was going to try this, it would be now, while she was alone, and Leon was distracted. What he didn't know, wouldn't hurt him. She could always explain it to him later...maybe once she'd had some time to ease him into it. He was a reasonable man.

She stood up from her desk and walked over to the metal cart that sat rusting and dilapidated on a short track system. She inserted a small Core Shard she had grabbed from the workbench and inserted it into the fittings on the side of the minecart. Then, using a sharpened piece of scrap metal lying next to the tracks, Arial cut open her index finger. Using her free hand—and trying to avoid dripping blood all over her white robes—Arial checked the parchment on blood magic, and the notes she'd made on draconic runes.

With great trepidation and greater excitement, Arial drew the first few runes. They were smudgy, crude, and lopsided, but they were her best attempt for a first try.

She kept drawing.

Arial could only pray she was using the runes in the proper order. One mistake and there would be consequences. Referencing them wasn't as easy as Arial thought it would be, especially with only one hand available to turn or flatten pages.

"I wouldn't do that."

Arial jumped, tripped, and smacked her head against the rusting cart. Stars clouded her vision and a bursting pain exploded on the side of her head. She swore as she stumbled to find her balance.

Leon rushed over and helped her up. "I'm sorry, I should've spoken up earlier."

"Leon, I—" Arial started.

"You don't have to explain. I know exactly what you were about to do."

To Arial's surprise, Leon didn't sound surprised or furious. It was not the reaction she was expecting for what she was about to attempt. "But—"

"I think I'm more disappointed that you were about to use blood magic without any knowledge of what you were doing. You know how dangerous it is to experiment with new magic—especially one as demanding in cost as blood magic."

"I...what?" Arial couldn't tell if her confusion was because of the bump now forming on her head, or because Leon's reaction was genuinely causing some form of dissonance between what was expected and what happened.

Leon walked Arial over to her chair by the desk and sat her down gently. "Let me look at it."

He moved his fingers through her hair to find the spot where she banged her head. Arial winced and audibly hissed as Leon's fingers brushed against the quickly forming bruise.

Leon placed his hand just above the bruise and without a single word, slowly began to reverse the effects of the bruising. The pain went away, the ache dulled, numbed, then vanished, and the stars that swam in Arial's eyes were gone like the stars at dawn. "How do you feel?"

Arial blinked a few times. "Like that never happened."

Leon sighed. "Thank the Mother it wasn't anything more serious, then. Bruises are one thing, but concussions are impossible to fix with magic. No one's ever been able to figure it out—the brain is just too complex a thing, it seems." Leon sat himself across from Arial, frowned slightly, but kept his calm composure. "What were you thinking exactly?"

"I...I thought I was going to help you make a breakthrough in your research. I had so many questions, there seemed to be a missing piece, and the more I thought, the more I realized that the missing piece was blood magic. I guess...I guess I wasn't thinking when I tried to test my theory."

Leon shook his head. "I'm just glad you're safe. But I think I should've been more honest with you from the start."

Arial's brows furrowed. The confusion returned.

"It's been known that blood magic could fix the problems that are impeding the research for decades. It was my mother that discovered it. I kept those findings from everyone, even my father, on purpose."

"But...why?"

Leon's demeanour shifted a bit. He stared off at the wall. "It was that discovery that killed my mother. She attempted to experiment in much the same way as you did. But, in her impatience and excitement, she didn't take the time to properly do her research on blood magic. She was a more skilled mage than you or me, with many more years of experience, and a deeper knowledge of runes. But her knowledge of blood magic was very limited. In the end, it was her downfall...the spell was written incorrectly, with loopholes, and mistakes, and perhaps her will even faltered while casting the spell. In the end, it caused the explosion that killed her."

"How do you know this?"

"Her last entry describes her discovery and details her enthusiasm for the breakthrough. She mentions testing the experiment immediately. The entry was dated to the day of her death. The rest I surmised from logic, or the evidence that remained when I inherited this research. My father was too saddened to investigate...but the answers I found led me to those conclusions. Her spell likely failed to limit the energy output of the Core Shard, and the resulting explosion killed her. I'm glad I came when I did, I'd be very upset—and very in trouble—if the same had happened to you."

Arial knew better than to experiment with magic she had no practice in. She knew even better than that to do so unsupervised. It was always recommended to study in pairs, that way someone could help you break a spell if it failed—hopefully, ideally, before it killed you.

"I'm sorry. I don't know why I did that. It bothered me. I had to know. I had to—"

"I understand that part," Leon reassured her. "There was a time in my life when I might have done the same. The thrill of discovery, the desire for knowledge, for progress. It gnaws at you, and sometimes you'd be willing to do things you know are wrong."

"Except use blood magic?"

Leon frowned. "That is the reason why my progress on this research has stalled. That and being king have limited my free time for research. I've spent the last few years trying to find every or any, alternative to blood magic. It's dangerous, and on top of that, how would that look to the Darond? To the rest of the world? New inventions that can only be fuelled by magic rocks and blood. The Darond would bury me if those were my findings."

"But nothing you've tried has worked?"

"No. Nothing."

"And blood magic?"

"I haven't tried it. But theoretically, it is likely the best option to proceed."

"Then why don't you try anyway? You're not looking to use blood magic to gain power or break nature. You're trying to create a better Enayra for everyone. These new inventions could do that."

"At what cost?"

"A few drops of blood and your pride."

"It's not that easy. Everything we've ever believed would be shattered. It could disrupt social order, and it might even break the Darond. The Darond and every magical authority in Enayra have spent centuries warning against the evils of blood magic, and now we'd be throwing that away for a few inventions. Is it worth *that* kind of scandal? To say nothing of the potential that these inventions could be combined with blood magic for evil. We might not do it, but someone inevitably will."

Arial crossed her arms. "That would always be a possibility, regardless of whether we proceed with blood magic as the catalyst. Always. Once you make this public, eventually, someone's going to find a way to weaponize it. Surely you know that. And on that note, maybe the Darond *are* wrong about blood magic. I'm not saying it hasn't been used for great evil, but that doesn't make it inherently evil. Does it?"

Leon said nothing.

"I know I'm new to this research, but in the few weeks I've been assisting you with it, I've come to care for it. Maybe not as much as you do; I don't think anyone could ever love this research as much as you or your mother, but certainly a great deal. Would any progress not be worth a small sacrifice? Is the greater good not worth sacrificing a few morals for?"

"It's a big moral to sacrifice!"

Arial had never seen Leon so frustrated. He had never so much as raised his voice. He was not angry, but he was clearly in turmoil. "Well, it's a big discovery to make! Clearly, your mother felt the same. That's why she tested her theory as soon as she could. Sure, it was ill-advised, but it came from a desire to change the world, to see her research through to the end."

Leon was silent again. His demeanour sagged a bit, and he slumped forward in his chair and rubbed his face with his hands.

It was only when nothing had been said for a few minutes that Arial immediately blurted out an apology. "I'm so sorry. I...that was too far."

Leon let out a rattling sigh. "Perhaps. But it was the truth. My mother, had she survived, would've published her results, regardless of the consequences. Maybe with a bit more tact than you might use, I'll admit."

Arial smirked.

"For one so young, and so new to this, you're very wise. You speak with passion and wisdom beyond your years."

"Being Khaleeshir has forced me to grow up, and quickly. Faster than Kula ever could prepare me for. I've had to learn a lot in a short amount of time. Sometimes I think it's just words coming from my mouth." Arial shrugged. "Besides, you're not much older than I am, and you carry just as much of the world on your shoulders."

"Almost as much, yes. I've got the benefit of only having a single nation rely on me. But you have the continent riding on your shoulders."

"That is true, but it's not a burden I carry alone. I have Adalinda, and the other Khaleeshir—my friends. I have Kyeit, Cecil, Kinokaze, and Valence. I have my new mentors, my teachers, and everyone in the Darond. And I have you. In that respect, I'd say I'm lucky."

Leon tilted his head but said nothing at first. Finally, he changed the subject back to research. "Thank you for helping me see straight. For your wise words. I needed them, without even realizing it. We'll continue testing your blood magic theory in the coming days, but for now, we've got an hour left before lunch, and I think you could stand to practice your magic."

"I couldn't agree more. I think I've slowly started to get the hang of that lightning spell you taught me last week."

Leon stood from his seat and pointed towards the open space where he and Arial practised their magic against a series of targets on the far wall. "Well. Show me what you've got then."

* * *

Kanaahn blocked left, then right.

But Yoshitomo did not let up. He did not give Kanaahn a second to breathe. The first two strikes were meant to catch him off guard, get his sword away from his centre and create an opening.

True to form, Yoshitomo pulled back as if to swing his sword, and instead initiated a thrust.

A few weeks ago, that might have flustered Kanaahn, but now Kanaahn transitioned into a seamless parry and pushed the thrust aside, stepping back in the process.

Yoshitomo was as relentless as the water that gave the sword style its name. His ancestor had modelled the sword form on the way water moves. At some moments, gentle and flowing, like a river or a stream, and at other times, a crashing, relentless wave of attacks. Strike after strike, like the waves against a cliffside shore during a storm.

Right now, Yoshitomo was like the waves.

He came again, this time pulling his blade above his head, at a slight angle, looking to strike at Kanaahn from above.

Kanaahn needed to turn the tables on his master, and quickly, before he was backed into a corner. Instead of blocking Yoshitomo's blade from beneath, he stepped aside, pushed the blade away with his own, and swung to strike at Yoshitomo's side.

Yoshitomo spun, stepping back with his right leg to turn himself, and his blade, and block Kanaahn's strike.

The two wooden sparring swords clacked together, sending a reverberating crack through the chamber.

"You've come a long way. A few weeks ago, you'd stay on the defensive against a stronger, faster opponent. Now you're starting to think like a fighter. Turn the tables, regain advantage."

"It worked at Xiar."

"If only all our enemies were common foot soldiers. No doubt the Khaleeshir that betrayed your group will have spent hours training with his own blade. Even he won't be a novice when next you meet. You'll need to fight like a seasoned veteran if you're to survive. Our enemies will not be as merciful as I have been."

Kanaahn could feel his welts, bruises, and cuts react to Yoshitomo's words. If the intense training Kanaahn had endured was considered merciful by default, Kanaahn almost feared to see the effect Tenebrae's training would have on Drakhart.

"I wonder what Tenebrae will throw at us. There must be more than just soldiers and Drakhart."

"You already know, I think."

"The Tulkaz?"

Yoshitomo held his ready stance, despite the break in the fighting. "Indeed."

"Have you fought them?"

"No. And I don't think I would be here if I had."

Kanaahn shuddered. How scary were these Tulkaz?

Yoshitomo would not allow him to deliberate that. Kanaahn had let his guard down, and Yoshitomo would make that a painful lesson. Distraction in a real fight left you dead.

Yoshitomo closed the gap and slashed at Kanaahn's midsection.

Kanaahn tried to recover.

He plunged his blade low and held it down parallel to the floor for a few moments. He tried to time it and react perfectly to Yoshitomo's movements. To aim for the opening.

Only to have Yoshitomo's blade crack against his collarbone, sending Kanaahn to the floor in a spasm of pain.

Yoshitomo shook his head. "The Wave Slicing Stroke? Brave, but foolish. You lost the second you acted in desperation. That technique is still a bit beyond you—especially on such short notice."

"I'm sorry, master."

Yoshitomo spun the wooden sword in his hand so that the blade pointed behind him and held out his free hand to Kanaahn. Kanaahn took the hand and Yoshitomo hefted him to his feet. "As long as you learn from your mistakes, you need not be sorry."

Kanaahn gave a short bow. "Yes, master."

"I am proud of the progress you've made during your time with me. You still have much to learn. The road to becoming a master of Suiō-ryū is long and arduous. It is a lifelong commitment to mastery, but you have that potential in you. I see it."

Kanaahn blushed. "You honour me, master. Truly, your words mean more to me than you know."

Yoshitomo's stern and serious look softened, and he placed a hand gently on Kanaahn's shoulder. "I *know*. Trust me, I know."

Of course. How could Kanaahn have thought otherwise? If anyone would know, it would be him.

"In that regard, as well. I thank you for everything you've done."

"Do you feel more like a gryphon now?"

"Truthfully? I don't know. But I understand what it means to be one a bit better. I'm still Altimara. I'm still Kulan. Nothing can change my upbringing and everything I've lived and experienced, but now I have a new perspective on who I am and what it means to be me. I feel less lost in my identity, and though I've only known about it for a short time, that has been an immense weight off my shoulders."

Yoshitomo smiled. "Sometimes it's hard, but you must never lose sight of who you are."

Kanaahn could only nod, but the emotions that welled up inside him spoke volumes on his face. He was never the best at hiding his feelings.

"Now come, the day is still early, and we still have a lot of training to do. Let's continue sparring. Experience is the best practice."

Kanaahn got into the ready position. "Yes, master."

* * *

Menalaea was predisposed that day. She never told Shooter what that meant specifically, only that she was busy on assignment. But because of that, today was one such day where Shooter was left with Arkas and the Royal Hunt to learn the art of fighting with a knife and shortsword.

At first, Shooter laughed, to himself mostly, that he wouldn't even need these lessons. He'd been using knives most of his life. They were a passion, dare he almost amit they were an obsession. What he wasn't forced to turn over to his father and mother, he'd spend on knives, and what he didn't spend on that he'd spend gambling for more money.

Then Shooter saw the Royal Hunt in action. Fighting with a knife was much more than just stabbing, shanking, and gutting. There was an art form. Disarming, taking control of the fight, locking up your enemy's limbs to create your own openings, and then striking at them.

In the few months he had been here, Shooter had been taught how to fight against larger opponents, smaller opponents, and stronger and faster opponents. Disarm, destabilize, and strike.

Suffice it to say he'd had gained a new appreciation for the Royal Hunt and their knife fighting style.

For that day, he was made to spar with Arkas. Normally, Shooter would spar against a member of the Royal Hunt, but today, they decided it would be a test of both their skills. Arkas and he each had a single knife and only had to land a single strike. The knives were wooden—the Royal hunt didn't need them killing each other—but that didn't mean jabbing each other with the end didn't hurt.

At that moment, Arkas had locked up Shooter's knife arm and was attempting to stab him with his own weapon.

Shooter had Arkas by the wrist and was doing everything he could to keep Arkas's wooden blade away from him. But Arkas was stronger than Shooter was.

Arkas had a semblance of muscle on his body, from years as a hunter-butcher apprenticing under his father, and all the archery practice. Shooter was skin and bones by comparison. Training with the Darond had made him stronger, but he was already starting from behind.

But had clever tactics on his side. He knew he could use Arkas's strength to his advantage he could...just...get...loose!

Shooter started to twist Arkas's knife arm at the wrist. He wasn't looking to do anything with it, it was a feint more than anything. He needed Arkas focusing on the wrong arm, while Shooter tried to slide his knife arm and wiggle in Arkas's grip.

Arkas fought back, struggling. He twisted back against Shooter and tried to pull his arm free, but Shooter's fingers wouldn't let go.

Arkas tried to pull Shooter forward, using Shooter's tight grip against him, so he could slam his forehead into Shooter's nose. But Shooter turned the moment on Arkas and pushed Arkas back.

It was just enough momentum, just enough strain, to get Arkas to loosen his grip on Shooter's arm. It wasn't enough to give Shooter his arm back, but the movement allowed Shooter to turn his arm beneath Arkas's armpit, just in time for—

The Huntsmen watching the match shouted for them to stop. That meant freezing in place and holding their current positions.

As the Huntsman approached, the two Khaleeshir slowed their breathing...and Shooter's eyes widened as he realized what had happened.

The Huntsman approached, examined Shooter's trapped arm, and smiled. "You twisted your arm at just the right moment. Your opponent didn't even know what killed him...until it was far too late."

Shooter grinned wide.

Arkas shook his head, and a smile crept across his face. Shooter's blade was planted firmly against his armpit, gently poking into his skin. If this had been a real fight, Arkas would be maimed, at the very least, if not already dead.

Arkas released Shooter and the two shook hands, as was custom during this sparring matches. "Son of a bitch," Arkas hissed through his teeth. "You've gotten good."

Shooter shrugged. "Just quick thinking. I thought you had me there."

"I did last time."

"And you will next time. We seem to be neck and neck in terms of wins."

The Huntsman looked up at the sky, checking the position of the sun. "We're almost done here. Cool down, stretch out, and get some water. You'll be Aurichalcum's soon enough, and you'll need your strength back for that."

Arkas and Shooter weren't going to disagree with that. Aurichalcum pushed them even harder in their training lessons than any other teacher they had in Ethon. Aurichalcum was merciless, strict, and rarely handed out praise. Time meant nothing to him—little wonder, being as old as he was—and he had been known to keep them beyond their allotted training sessions, and even into dinner, to ensure they had made proper progress.

They would spar together until Aurichalcum arbitrarily decided they had progressed far enough for that day, and then, and only then, they would be free to eat, rest or sleep.

Of all the training they endured, everyone hated Aurichalcum's training the most. Perhaps because Aurichalcum was abrasive and merciless. Or perhaps it was the exhaustive, endless pain they would find themselves in afterwards. Sleep was the only release from the ache, and come morning it would often start again, reduced to a dull throbbing.

Shooter let out a sigh. If there was one thing he missed most in their rigid, pre-planned and full days, was the time he would spend with Risasi. Flying together, talking together, or even just spending time together. Risasi was always out training with the Metallic Dragons when Shooter was training with Menalaea or the Royal Hunt, and when they *were* training together, they were too busy fighting to talk.

Their minds were always linked, and they chattered throughout the day, sporadically, but they lacked meaningful time spent together. There was no way to shut off the connection between Khaleeshir unless it was manually closed on both sides of the connection, and doing so was not done lightly. It was like cutting off a part of your body. The emptiness, the pain, the feeling like some part of you was lost or missing and would never be reclaimed was haunting, and it was not a feeling Shooter wanted to repeat. None of the Khaleeshir wanted to, and they too were feeling the effects of the loss of their dragons.

Shooter would bring it up with Leon when he had a moment. At the end of the day, Leon outranked everyone in charge of their training, except for Aurichalcum. If anyone could reason with Aurichalcum, it would be Leon. If anyone could find a way to make a change to the schedule so the Khaleeshir could spend more time together—for the sake of their bond, for their health, and for their effectiveness as bonded pairs—it would be Leon.

Shooter just hoped that Aurichalcum would not let his dislike of him colour his decision.

* * *

Fyete stretched out on the cooling cobbles of the courtyard where she and the other dragons had made their stay while in Ethon. It was not the most comfortable place to sleep, not like a soft, mossy forest floor, or the warm sands Fyete had been partial to, but it wasn't terrible, like the stone stalls in the Tormenting Pinnacle, or within the dragon's tower in Xiar.

Training had been arduous that day. Her wing joints ached and were stiff, and she had torn a muscle in her chest that Thrae had to heal for her. While the wound was healed, the phantom of the ache had taken longer to subside. The mind was harder to heal than the body, as Thrae had told her. But eventually, it would go away.

Her siblings were also trying to get some rest—they would go out later to hunt. At their current size, and with Valence, Kinokaze and Thrae with them, they would not be bothered by much, so hunting at night would not be an issue.

But rest would not come to them this evening.

Valence and Kinokaze interrupted them and returned from the business that had kept them away for most of the day. They had taken their mortal forms shortly after Valence had returned this morning, and disappeared into the bowels of the castle, and hadn't been seen since.

From what Fyete and her siblings had learned from their partners, there was a meeting going on between King Leon, Imuhlair, Iskren, Valence, Kinokaze, Hana, Kyeit, and Cecil, though what about, no one could say. Only that the meeting had gone on most of the day.

Fyete and the others woke, opening their eyes, raising heads, and watching as the two humanoid beings morphed back into dragons. Flesh stretched like a sheet over a frame. Scales and skin looked melted and deformed. Faces elongated. Bones seemed to meld and crack. Despite the gruesome-looking transformation, Valence and Kinokaze seemed to feel no pain or discomfort as they transformed back into their true, draconic forms.

"Welcome back," Fyete said.

The other dragons sat up, stretched, and stirred from their relaxing stupor.

It was Valence who replied. "We apologize for our absence. The day has been busy."

"It *must* be dire if you've been forced into those feeble forms," Djall teased.

"Needs must," Kinokaze replied. "Humans have yet to make architecture that can accommodate us. Except perhaps Tuir'Delohmeyh, but that was not originally built by them."

Every dragon knew Tuir'Delohmeyh. Though most knew it as Fohl'Dimiitor or sometimes Ves'Hurundahl.

Long before humans ever arrived in Enayra, the ancient and deep caverns within the mountains of Anglum had been where the Earth Mother and Earth Father had made their home. Where they had laid their first clutch. Somewhere, deep in the bowels of the mountain, the Earth Mother was buried, and her consciousness lay, watching over all of Enayra, and the whole of the planet. It was there that the Great Progenitors and the Metallics battled the Earth Father after madness claimed him. It was in those caverns that the Metallics and the Progenitors brought their Father low and took over the rule of the draconic race for themselves. It was there, in those caves, that the dragon clans formed, and the dragons lived for many thousands of years before coming above ground to live their lives, when the clans grew too large for the caverns below.

It was sacred, once, to the dragons, and remained so.

And then the humans arrived…

The Darond had eventually been given use of the ancient tunnels and caverns—or at least a small portion of it, for not even the Metallics nor the Progenitors, could properly remember how deep the caverns went.

It was inside these loaned tunnels and caverns, granted by the Metallics, that the Darond made their headquarters, and from here they plotted and planned their war against Tenebrae, and had remained ever since. But even the humans did not know what truly lay at the depths of those caverns: the Heart of the World.

"You'd think after all these thousands of years they'd get around to making dragon-friendly architecture," Fyete replied.

"Dragons haven't exactly done much to allow humans to access their homes either," Risasi added.

The other dragons looked at her. She had garnered many odd stares from the dragons, who somehow thought it was the strangest thing in the world that they had to adjust their lives for others.

Risasi doubled down, however. "Khaleeshir are supposed to be the bridge between humans and dragons. But aside from settling petty squabbles and defeating Tenebrae, what have our predecessors done to bring the races closer together? They were supposed to bring peace, and instead, the world has gone without them for a millennium."

"It didn't work," chided Djall.

"We are only the bridge," Adalinda chimed in. "But a bridge can only be a bridge. Bridge a gap, ford a river. It cannot make people cross it. We are the bridge, our predecessors did their jobs correctly, but it's up to both sides to cross that bridge and meet in the middle."

Kinokaze dipped her head in a nod. "Precisely. I see you've been listening to the words of Lady Thrae."

"It is a touch more positive than listening to Lord Aurichalcum," Adalinda admitted.

"Uncle has been soured by his many years in this world," Valence explained. "He has suffered much and lost even more."

They had all heard. They all knew. Not just his wings, but his mate, many of his siblings who lead the other clans, so many of his fellow dragons, entire clans wiped out under the watchful eye of the Metallic's joint leadership …lost to his own brother, one of their own. His kha'diniitor, his nest-mate.

The betrayal cut deep, the wounds still ached, and the loss cut deeper still.

"No one envies him his loss. No one judges him…in his position, we'd likely be the same—" Risasi started.

"Risasi has only lost his hatching teeth and first few scales and he's already half as grouchy," joked Djall.

Risasi shot him a look.

Djall merely shrugged.

Adalinda and Fyete sniggered, as did Kinokaze.

If Risasi could turn red with embarrassment, he would, but thankfully it blended in with his scales. He continued, pretending he had never heard Djall's remark. "—but doesn't make living with it any easier."

"Lord Aurichalcum does push us rather hard," Adalinda noted.

"He wants the best of us," Fyete added, almost defensively.

Djall snorted. "Doesn't make training any easier."

"The humans have a saying," Valence interjected. "Never meet your heroes."

"That means something coming from a fellow Metallic," Kinokaze joked. "But the humans are correct. We put the Great Metallics on a pedestal. It's tradition, it's natural, it's what we've learned and been taught...and we forget they're just as mortal as the rest of us. Just as flawed, just as susceptible to emotion as anyone else. They're not gods."

"Don't tell the humans that," joked Risasi. "It would shatter their pantheon."

The other dragons chuckled.

Valence and Kinokaze did not.

It was Valence who spoke first. "We dragons worship them too, in our own way. It's not an organized religion like the humans, but the deference we show to the Five Great Metallic dragons and even the Progenitors, is similar to human worship."

"It's not the same—" Djall said defensively.

"Do you forget how you five genuflected to us when we first met? You treated us as if we were our forebearers."

The dragons were now silent.

It was Risasi, surprisingly, who answered the challenge. "Then perhaps that must change?"

Fyete was sceptical. "You're going to change our species?"

Djall shook his head. "Dragons don't change."

"Maybe they should," Risasi was adamant. "We haven't changed in thousands of years, and where did that get us? We're on the verge of extinction. We should learn more from the humans and adapt to new ways. It's why they've lasted so long, despite all of their foolishness and warmongering. That which does not bend..."

Djall pressed the subject. "We're nearly extinct because of Tenebrae, and his betrayal, not because of our ways."

Risasi had not responded, but he remained indignant.

Again, Djall did not let up. "What would you do away with, exactly?"

"The Metallics, for one—" he looked at Valence and Kinokaze "—with all respect. I think we've outgrown their leadership and the leadership of the First Clutch. It is time for younger dragons to take control; that is something we could learn from humans. The division between clans must be removed, it has weakened and divided us. There are barely enough of us now to even bother with clans anymore, and over half the clans are gone forever. They won't come back. That's something else we could learn from the humans."

"And who then, do you propose would lead the Drazhani; you?"

"Why not? Why not all of us? We are Khaleeshir, after all. The great bridges; wise and noble. We are the hope of this world and those who shall help save it. Why shouldn't we?"

"You had no issue deferring to tradition when meeting my k'dir and k'nir, even if you were petulant about it," Djall argued. "You've been fairly adherent to tradition before now, in fact."

"Much has changed.

A voice cut through the argument. "Your k'nir once spoke as you do."

The dragons all turned to see Thrae, in her mortal form. She wore an amused look.

Everyone dipped their heads in an informal bow, except Risasi, who held fast to his newfound beliefs. Perhaps bonding with Shooter was finally starting to change him.

Thrae approached Risasi, a smirk on her face. "Your father once shared those same ideas. Tenebrae as well…"

A feeling like an ice floe surfaced in Risasi's gut. He felt a chill creep into his bones as he suddenly began to process the meaning of Thrae's words. He was more surprised that she wasn't angry with him at the moment. How she could be smirking after such implications was astonishing to him.

"They were right," Thrae said finally.

Every dragon, even Risasi, looked incredibly perplexed, confused, and even affronted.

"I say this as an old and wizened dragon. We *have* become too rigid. So long as we avoid sickness, foolishness, or death at the hands of another dragon, we can live virtually forever. We are inherently magical, incredibly large, with no natural predators, and if we wanted we could burn Enayra to the ground and not think twice. In the thousands of years we've been on this earth, we've grown complacent. We've grown metaphorically fat, and we've become rooted in tradition. Traditions that once guided us now strangle us and prevent us from moving forward."

"Tradition isn't a bad thing," Djall argued. "It's kept us together all these years. Given us purpose, and identity."

"It has at that," agreed Thrae. "It's also caused our kind just as many problems. I was there, a thousand years ago, when Tenebrae betrayed us. I was not much older than you five Khaleeshir are now. I was young, but I still knew what was happening. At the time, I felt as you did Djall. Tenebrae was a traitor, he broke our laws, and the laws of nature. He had to be brought to justice—he had to be ended, for the greater good. There was no other way for it. But after a thousand years, I wonder…how much different would this world be if we had looked past those laws and tradition, and maybe tried another solution?"

"Like what, diplomacy?" Djall asked, half genuine, half incredulously.

"Perhaps. Or perhaps trying to see the other side. Humans call it compromise I believe?"

"How well has that compromise done for humans?" asked Fyete. "No offence to our partners, but humans certainly do more fighting than compromising most days."

Thrae now stood firmly between Djall and Risasi and looked between the two dragons as she spoke. "Perhaps. But their lives are shorter than ours, and their memories are shorter still. Maybe we, as dragons, should have learned more from them, and they more from us. The bridge has been built, broken, and rebuilt…"

"…But a bridge cannot force anyone to cross it. It is up to both sides to meet in the middle and use the bridge." Djall finished Thrae's words.

Fyete was incredulous. "You can't seriously be suggesting that we compromise with Tenebrae? After everything he's done, after all the violence and bloodshed, we're just supposed to talk to him and make it all better?"

Thrae shook her head. "Not at all. There is no fixing what has already been done. It cannot be undone, and Tenebrae cannot be reasoned with. There is only one way this ends now. What's done is done. But my point was merely that perhaps we could have avoided all this bloodshed if we had been more willing to talk and compromise before things spiralled out of control; at the first hint of discord, as opposed to resorting to violence immediately."

"You assume Tenebrae would be willing to discuss things," Fyete retorted. "To your point, we can only extend the bridge, but we cannot force others to cross it."

Thrae nodded. "Yes, and that is still correct. There is no guarantee he would have accepted such a solution—perhaps things would *not* be different. But we did not try either and so we share the blame for this. We let pride get in the way of a solution, pride and tradition. Dragons solve their problems by fighting, even if it's not to the death, that's how it always has been. Now we've fought ourselves to our near extinction."

Fyete did not respond.

"Something to consider." With that, Thrae turned and departed, leaving as quickly as she appeared.

Chapter XLI

Kyeit and Cecil sat in a small cloister in the eastern wing of Filiddyn Castle. They had finished their meeting with King Leon and his advisors: Hana, Iskren and Imuhlair. Aurichalcum and Thrae remained absent from the meeting so they could instruct the Khaleeshir, but they were apprised of the situation using their telepathic abilities.

Leon and Cecil had not been surprised by Kyeit's news. They had always expected the High Council to pull something like that, and the aftermath of Xiar had somehow presented them with the perfect moment to blindside Kyeit and make her their scapegoat. If not stopped, the High Council would have their way, and gain control over the Khaleeshir.

It was never a matter of "if" this would happen, but "when", and how long it would take for the High Council to act. Apparently, the answer was as soon as they discovered they hadn't gotten their way.

Leon had called it a "political tantrum." Cecil had to agree.

Kyeit had spent every waking moment trying to appear calm and collected as she always did. She was tough, made of iron. She was a calm pond with nary a single ripple. That was how she lived her life, as she had been instructed by her mother, by her father, to live out her role as a princess, as a diplomat, and as a soldier. But beneath the calm was a raging storm, a tumultuous sea churned and tried to swallow itself whole like some great, voracious beast. Waves folded in on themselves, crushing all hope, light, and faith.

And in the centre of that storm was still that scared little girl who watched as a Darond Honour Guard returned the mutilated body of her mother to her home in Xiar. Who only a few months ago, had lifted a sheet to see the decapitated body of her father, and came to the stark realization that she was now, technically, an orphan.

Cecil's words cut through that storm like a ray of light. "It's okay to let it out, sometimes. Emotions were meant to be felt."

"I know."

"And yet…"

"What do you want me to do, Cecil, cry? Am I supposed to just break down? Soldiers don't get that luxury."

Cecil cocked her head to the side. "Humans do. You were a human before you were a soldier."

"I'm not going to cry just because those bastards on the High Council want me as their scapegoat. I'm not going to cry because my duty is being taken away from me, as well as my new friends."

"I'm not asking you to cry; the myriad of human emotions is so much greater than tears and sadness."

"I'm *already* angry, Cecil."

Cecil smirked. "I've noticed."

Kyeit glared at Cecil, venom in her eyes.

"I'm sorry, Kyeit. But you told me to hold you accountable for your feelings."

"I regret the day I made you make that promise."

"I'm sure you regret much more about that day than that."

"What happened to the sweet, quiet, innocent Cecil?"

"She's reserved for those who *haven't* known me as long, or as well as you."

Kyeit stood up and paced the cloister, trying to maintain her calm. Her armour was the only noise in that cloister for a while.

Cecil prodded further. "Maybe I should call, Kanaahn."

Kyeit wheeled around, turning on Cecil with the speed of a diving Rishi beast. "And what's that supposed to mean?"

"Breakfast with Kanaahn was the most I've seen you smile since you've been back. To say nothing of that late night you spent up together at Tohru's."

"So, what of it? We're friends."

"I'm not commenting on the status of your relationship. I'm making a note of how calm and free you seem to feel around him. You're able to open up around him and *feel*. Happy, angry, sad, and more."

"Kanaahn's easy to be open with. You're not jealous are you?" Kyeit asked more out of concern than mockingly.

"No, not at all," Cecil reassured her. "On the contrary, I'm quite relieved. You need to remember how to feel again. You've spent so long pretending you were made of iron you forgot you're human as well. You've put your duty above all else for so long, including yourself, and your needs. You've become so serious and dour. But in the last few months, being around the Khaleeshir seems to have done you good. Kanaahn helps especially, but I've noticed a change in you around the others—even Shooter."

A smile crept across Kyeit's face. "He can be a pain, but Shooter's smarter than he likes to let on. He's got such a big heart in that chest, but he'll never show it. There's a lot of wisdom under the surface. Arkas too; he's just as wise as Shooter, and he's got eyes on everything. He sees more than you realize, but he's quiet and doesn't butt in where he's not needed. Hells have mercy on whoever stands in Arial's way; that girl could break Enayra if she wanted. She'll outstrip even Leon in power once she's fully trained. Kanaahn...I can't even explain it. You're right, I can be more open with him, I can be myself. There's no pressure around him. I don't have to be Kyeit, Knight-Commander, or Kyeit, Princess of Xiar, or Kyeit, Aide to Master Osamu. I can just be Kyeit. I don't know why in such a short amount of time we've grown so close."

Cecil said nothing, her smirk spoke volumes, more than her words ever could.

Kyeit rolled her eyes. "Don't get me started. You're not impervious to teasing either."

Cecil raised her hands. "Very well, I surrender."

Kyeit sat down on the stone bench beside Cecil. She looked up at the clouds passing by overhead, covering an otherwise blue and bright sky. "The world feels so different than it did all those months ago at the Pinnacle. So much has changed—we've changed, the Khaleeshir have changed...so many are gone."

Cecil nodded. "It's only going to change more. We'll change more. The Khaleeshir will change more. And even more of our friends and allies will be dead by the end. It's the bitter reality of war."

"You speak like you've experienced war before."

Cecil smirked. "I have. At Xiar." Her smile faded quickly, however. "Joking aside, war rarely leaves lives untouched, whether they're civilians or combatants. War does not require sacrifices. War takes them whether they're required or not. We have a saying in Asardaea: war is the great equalizer. Death comes for everyone."

"You Asardaeans are always so stoic."

"Can you expect anything less from a nation built on war? Our predecessor, the Enayran Empire, was forged in war, and birth by conquest under Volesus. No amount of pretty fairy tales or honourable reasons will change that. The current kingdom was founded by a Warrior Queen, worshipped as a hero, descended from the dynasts of the empire, who earned her right to rule in war, by fighting off a Gerovian attempt to conquer our lands. Every one of her descendants and successors has been lauded as mighty warrior queens or stern and stoic philosopher queens. But even in times of peace, we make money from war. Selling arms and armour to other nations; and siege engines. Before the War of the Grand Coalition, Asardaea made a fortune selling weaponry and armour to Gerovia. After the war started, we supplied and armed the Grand Coalition, and made even more money. When the war ended, and we thought the bloodshed over, Gerovia, now Estion, descended into a bloody and violent civil war...waged with weapons forged in Malatrion, Pescadum, and Durodunum."

"And then there's you, warrior and philosopher."

Cecil changed the subject. "I owe you an apology. I'm sorry I didn't go with you to Tuir'Delohmeyh."

"Someone needed to watch over the Khaleeshir and their training. I would have trusted no one else."

"I share some of the fault for what they seek to blame you for," Cecil insisted.

"Perhaps, but in the end, the orders were mine and mine alone. You stayed of your own volition, and I accepted your help because of the tough situation we found ourselves in. Your orders weren't disobeyed for your part in this." Kyeit reached out and hugged Cecil, embracing her with both arms. "There is nothing to apologize for, my friend."

Besides, it wasn't like they'd ever actually punish *Cecil*, of all people, and Kyeit knew it.

Cecil smiled. "Can I at least buy you a drink? For old time's sake?"

"Well, now that's a different story! Can we take the time?"

Cecil stood and placed her hands on her hips. "I think after everything we've been through, there is always time for a quick drink—for the nerves. Another Asardaean saying."

Kyeit shook her head and followed Cecil from the cloister.

"When was the last time you and I went out for a drink after a day of duty?" asked Kyeit.

Cecil shrugged. "A year ago, when we were on assignment in Utova. We went to that small but crowded tavern on the main street. The Bloodied Bear, I think it was."

"I remember! You drank me under the table—literally—and we threw up in the alley behind the tavern after."

"We almost got in trouble for that. Drunken and disorderly conduct."

"Yeah, the only thing that saved us was the Grand Duchess's daughter. She had been the one to invite us out and drank more than both of us combined. Instead, we were given a warning. I believe they explained our actions as a form of 'drunken diplomacy.'"

Cecil laughed. "Let's not repeat that this time. Leon isn't with us, so we can't call that."

"One drink. Two at most. I mean it."

"That's a promise I can keep."

* * *

It was a warm summer night. The sky was awash with colour as if a painter had decided to splash their entire palette on the canvas that was the sky.

In the east, oranges, reds, yellows and even streaks of white and blue clouds blended near the horizon, as the shining ball that was the sun slowly sank beneath the horizon. In most of the sky, and especially the west, blues, blacks, and purples ruled. The blend was more subtle and gentle than the warmer colours, and the entire canvas was speckled here and there with the first glint of starlight. All of this was reflected in the massive expanse of Lake Ardona, like some giant glass mirror, polished to the smoothest and clearest perfection. It was truly, simply beautiful. That was the only way to describe it.

It was Enayra in its purest form. Something that was often lost in the world of today.

Aurichalcum stood where he always stood on warm summer nights like this: on the wrap-around balcony at the top of the tallest tower of Filiddyn Castle. This tower had been his home ever since Aurichalcum had been assigned to advise and watch over the Kingdom of Estion. That had been Aurum's call, of course; these things were always Aurum's call.

A gentle breeze blew, tousling hair and robes alike, like a playful child, or an old lover caressing her beloved. But unlike the nostalgic feeling of a former love, filling the soul with warmth and happiness, it filled Aurichalcum with anger and frustration. He clenched his fist and slammed it into the balustrade. He heard the stone crack but paid it no heed.

The wind did not love him. Not any longer. Now it only mocked him, teased him. The sky above laughed at him, pointing, and jeering with its beauty and majesty. But Aurichalcum could not look away, even if he wanted to. Looking up, he saw the sky, teasing and laughing, and looking down, he saw the same, only reflected in the lake.

The natural beauty of the world was not wonderful or majestic, not to Aurichalcum—not any longer. It was infuriating and frustrating. It was venomous, poisonous, and filled him with a venomous hatred that reached deep into his chest and arrested his heart, filling it with dread and anger. Once more he smashed his closed fist into the balustrade and watched, nonplussed, as a large chunk broke away and tumbled down into the courtyards below.

Once he would have taken flight—as a mighty and proud dragon, and not locked in this flawed and weakened mortal form—and found the wind filling his wings, keeping him aloft. He would have felt the breeze envelop him. He would have been able to see the sky from within its embrace and dip down below to the lake, grazing his fingers against the calm surface. He had once lived, loved, and enjoyed the natural world and all its beauty. For once he had been part of it in a way only a few creatures could ever truly experience and appreciated.

But no more.

Never again.

"We can't keep replacing that." It was Thrae, followed closely by Hana.

Aurichalcum turned calmly. He had felt their presence walking up the spiralling staircase and knew she was coming to check on him. Aurichalcum had traced their presence as they crossed the castle and approached the tower, but he had lost track of them in his anger. It was hard to miss someone as bright and powerful as Hana, and he knew his own daughter's presence well enough, and yet he had managed to do just that. He didn't reply to Thrae's comment, he merely turned back towards the quickly darkening sky.

"I hope we haven't interrupted anything important, Lord Aurichalcum."

Aurichalcum's demeanour softened for Hana. *"Not at all, Hana. Am I needed by His Majesty?"*

Hana shook her head. *"No. I've come with other news."*

Aurichalcum raised a brow.

Thrae answered. *"She has read the possibilities."*

Aurichalcum did not react.

"Of the Khaleeshir," Hana added. *"Of the human Khaleeshir, anyway. But I suppose that goes without saying."*

It was well known amongst those who could read the possibilities, and everyone in this room, that it was much harder to read the possibilities of dragons in the same way as humans. There were several prevalent theories as to why this was the case. But the truth was even worse, for everyone here knew that the fate of the dragons was tied to the fate of the planet itself, and it was impossible to read the possible fates of a whole world.

Aurichalcum turned back to the horizon, lips pursed. His softened demeanour disappeared like the sun into the sea.

Thrae and Hana exchanged a glance, waiting a moment before proceeding with the answer.

"Well?" demanded Aurichalcum.

Hana stepped forward. *"There is much turmoil to come. They have a great many trials ahead of them...and some of them will be devastating. In the end, their choices will either lead them to fulfil their responsibilities, and achieve greatness..."*

Aurichalcum's eyes narrowed. *"I don't like that or."*

"I didn't say or," Hana replied defensively.

"It was implied. An unspoken or. Those are the worst kind."

Hana relented. *"Or they shall fail, and all will be doomed. There's a chance their trials may overcome and consume them, and if that happens, it will mean the worst."*

"An imprecise reading," Thrae admitted.

Hana interjected *"All readings are such. There are no guarantees in life, despite what most other humans will believe. Nothing is certain, there is no fate. Those were the very words you once told my mother and father."*

Aurichalcum nodded sagely. *"Destiny is a lie; the greatest lie of all. There are only the choices we make, and the consequences of those choices. All too often, we all must live with the consequences of others' choices also, whether we know it or not."*

"That's why it's called reading the possibilities," Hana finished.

Aurichalcum knew these words well. He often spoke them to the ever-hopeful Darond, and to his siblings, particularly Aurum.

Aurum often read the possibilities over his millennia of life. Most recently to bring forward lists upon lists of possible hopefuls who would claim the five dragon eggs within Mount Pinnacle and take up the mantle of Khaleeshir. Every time, Aurichalcum warned Aurum and the Darond against putting too much stock in those names, and perhaps to look elsewhere, and each time those five hopefuls were sent to their death, destroyed by the wards, consumed by the minds of the eggs, driven to madness by the hatchling's minds peering into their souls to read them.

Aurichalcum was more than a little amused when the first five names in a millennium not brought forth by Aurum turned out to be the ones who passed the trials and emerged from within the mountain with the eggs in tow. Perhaps it was because they had not gone in with any expectations of greatness or glory, or perhaps they were truly worthy— whatever that meant. No one was certain how that was measured, for it was the Earth Mother herself who weighed the value of her champions, and rarely did she ever explain herself, even to her oldest of children.

Aurum never let others know that, of course. Nor that he had not been the ones to choose the names; that these names had come at the recommendation of one of the Darond's smuggler-spies. Aurum claimed he had dreamed these names, as he always had. That these names had appeared in a dream to him, and he declared they were the ones. Convenient, of course. But Aurum always did prefer a convenient lie to an uncomfortable truth. Aurum had become predictable.

Aurichalcum turned around and faced Hana. *"Do you believe these Khaleeshir strong enough to stay the course and make the right choices?"*

"I do," Thrae answered.

Aurichalcum looked at his daughter. *"It was not you I asked."*

"I have trained them just as much as you have. I have faith in them, and so should you."

Aurichalcum ignored the clearly wounded Thrae. *"Do you believe they'll make the right choices, Hana?"*

Hana did not hesitate. *"I cannot say. Nothing is definite. But I have hope that they will. We have to believe they will, or we have nothing. Destiny is a lie, but hope is very real."*

Aurichalcum scoffed. *"Hope is a double-edged sword, and more often than not, most people choose to fall upon said sword than face the grim reality before them."*

"A blade is only as great as the hand that wields it. If you don't trust yourself, or us, with that blade, then why should we continue training the Khaleeshir?"

Aurichalcum's face grew sour. He did not reply; instead, he turned back towards the now burgeoning night sky, alive with the light of thousands of stars. He did not say anything for a long time, he merely stared at the sky above, silently mulling over everything.

But Thrae and Hana did not leave. They remained, whether, for a response, a command, or any kind of acknowledgement, Aurichalcum did not know, but he would not have them wait for much longer. He grew tired, of both the day and the company.

His response finally came, but it was terse and quick. *"Leave me."*

Thrae and Hana did not waste a moment in doing as he said and were gone as fast as they had come to him. It wasn't long before Aurichalcum was left alone again, with nothing and no one. Just himself, his loneliness, and his longing to return to the sky. All was normal.

And perhaps...something new. A little spark. A little bit of hope where once none remained.

Maybe, just maybe, the Khaleeshir would succeed, and maybe, just maybe, Tenebrae would finally face justice, and be destroyed.

Aurichalcum grimaced.

Or maybe they'd fail just as miserably as he had, and all would be doomed. Only time would tell. Time, and a volatile, emotional group of teenagers with the weight of the world on their shoulders.

Aurichalcum could see rain clouds begin to gather on the near-dark horizon.

* * *

Kanaahn sat in the comfiest armchair he'd ever been in, puffing away at his pipe. It had been a habit he picked up in the taverns of Kula while hanging around the old travellers, traders, and storytellers. Though he'd only been in the habit for a year or two, it had been one that he'd grown to enjoy in his spare time. Menalaea and Arial had not been pleased about the development—but at least it was better than gambling, which had become one of Shooter's vices.

Kanaahn remembered something an old man had told him once over a game of tabbat. *You didn't grow up in Kula without picking up a vice or two, some are better than others.* Kanaahn also remembered that the man had no thumbs and was missing his index finger on his right hand. Perhaps he wasn't the best person to take advice from in that regard, and perhaps he was why Kanaahn chose the pipe over cards or dice—at least anything more than a friendly, low-stakes game. And either of those was better than getting too deep in the drink.

How much had changed in so little time...

Kanaahn looked out towards the open doors that led to the small balcony of his room. It was a dark and moonless night, and it had begun pouring rain not long ago. The only light came from the fireplace and the candles Kanaahn had lit around the room. All of it bounced off his polished armour that sat in the corner of the room—transported there via smugglers from Xiar around the same time they had left. It created an eerie effect on the ceiling and walls.

372

This room was a far cry from his room in Kula. Menalaea was far from destitute, to be sure, but the room was simple, as per Kanaahn's request. A dresser, a small desk and chair, a mirror, and a bed. That was everything to his name. Not including his clothes, his pipe, and his sword.

Now he stayed in a castle, with his own balcony, a fireplace, the world's comfiest armchair, his own personal garderobe, an armoire full of clothing, a bathing room, a bed covered in expensive furs, bedside tables, chests, and trunks to store his stuff, a suit of armour, a shield, a hammer, a stand for his katana, a desk and chair and a shelf full of books.

Kanaahn looked over at the bedside tables. "And even more books..."

Stacks of books meant for his studies stood waiting for him. He would not be sleeping so early this evening after all. There was still too much to do...even though exhaustion nagged at the corners of his mind and tugged at his attention. The desire to sleep pulled his eyelids down, making them heavy, and attempted to pull him into a warm embrace.

Then, a knock at the door pulled him from his stupor. Kanaahn looked at the door, then over at his katana on the stand. It was too late for a maid, and no one spoke from the other side of the door.

"Hello?" Kanaahn called.

No response.

Kanaahn stood and drew his robes tighter around himself. He put down his pipe and quietly sidled over to his katana. He unsheathed the blade and walked over to the door. He called out again.

"Hello? Who's there?"

"It's me." The voice was quiet, gentle...almost meek sounding. Whoever it was, was intentionally trying to be quiet. But he knew the voice, and the person it belonged to was anything but. It was Kyeit, and she was trying to be quiet.

Kanaahn paused before responding, looking at the sword in his hand. "Uh...one moment." He quickly returned the blade to its sheath and then walked over to the door—checking his appearance in the mirror on the way. With a racing heart, Kanaahn gently opened the door. He winced when the door creaked its song to the world at the top of its lungs.

"Yes?"

Kyeit stood there, arms crossed, a bemused look on her face. For the first time since he'd met her, Kyeit was not wearing her armour or some form of mail. She was dressed simply in black leather trousers, black boots, and a linen shirt. She kept her sword at her side still. "May I come in?"

"Um, yes?"

Kyeit passed the threshold. "You don't sound so certain."

"I'm incredibly confused."

Kanaahn began to walk away from the open door when Kyeit stopped him. "Close it."

"What?"

"Are your ears okay?" Kyeit teased. "Did you get hit in the head a few too many times today?"

"I'm still incredibly confused."

Kyeit placed her hands on her hips. "Close the door. What I'd like to say should be kept between us." She waited before adding: "Please."

Kanaahn's heart was racing, his palms were sweaty, and he felt the room spin. Suddenly, he was too warm, but his sweat was cold. The breeze coming in from the open balcony door was no longer cooling, and Kanaahn felt as if he was standing next to a blast furnace. However, he obeyed and closed the door.

Kyeit turned and sat down in the armchair beside Kanaahn's, examining his pipe on the table. She noted the small pouch of tobacco, picked it up and pulled a pinch of it out to sniff. "An interesting blend. May I?" Kyeit indicated to the still-lit pipe.

Kanaahn could only sputter nonsense.

Kyeit took it for a yes, clearly, as she picked up the pipe, took a quick puff, and blew the smoke out immediately. "Xiaran Gold. I thought so."

"How did you--?"

"My father was a pipe smoker, and I'm from Xiar. It's not hard to put two and two together. The smell of the smoke and the tobacco was familiar, and the flavour is unmistakable."

Kanaahn chuckled nervously. "I suppose I should've known. Xiaran Gold has always been an indulgence of mine. It was never cheap, but when I had a little money saved up, and everything I needed was paid for, I'd buy enough to fill my pouch. I made sure to get a full barrel put in with my things in Xiar when it was offered. I'm glad I did. This stuff's about to be very rare and expensive now that..."

Kyeit nodded but did not respond. The topic was still fresh, but she knew to what Kanaahn was referring.

An awkward silence hung between them like a spectre.

"Sit, please." Kyeit urged.

Kanaahn swallowed but did as he was bid. Kyeit handed him the pipe, but Kanaahn's lips and mouth were too dry, so he simply put it down.

"Do I make you nervous?" Kyeit asked.

Kanaahn found his nerve. "Admittedly? Yes. This isn't exactly in character for you. You've been gone two weeks on top of that, and I mean, there's Felidrun." Kyeit almost seemed to smile at the mention of Felidrun. "Let's also not forget the conversation we had at the Tormenting Pinnacle."

She brushed her hair behind her ear and cleared her throat. "That's...actually why I've come here."

"What?" Kanaahn's stomach sunk to his feet and his blood ran colder than a Kulan night in winter.

"I'm going to cut right to the point." Kyeit's attitude went from bashful and kind to serious and direct. This was the Kyeit he knew best. "To say I've had a lot of time to think over the last few weeks is an understatement, and I've had time to put things into perspective; regarding my duties, my life, my job, and my feelings."

Kanaahn could hear his heart.

"I've also had a very good talk with Cecil, who has been able to put a lot of things in perspective for me."

His heart was going to explode.

"Kanaahn, you're not stupid, and neither am I. I know what almost happened in Felidrun. We have feelings for each other, and I've been stupid for trying to deny it. I'm sorry."

Pop. There it went. Despite his now-defunct heart, Kanaahn managed to respond calmly. "Why the change?"

"I put a stop to anything because of my duty. I meant what I said. My duty to protect you all, and my oath to the Darond, came before anything or anyone else. For me, at the time, it was unwise to become involved with you—for a multitude of reasons. Survival isn't guaranteed, and neither was my tenure with you. I couldn't risk feeling anything that might be taken away just as quickly. I didn't trust it not to be just a passing affection."

"You have so little faith in me?" Kanaahn teased.

"You are not the first boy my age to express interest. Also, I had just met you, how *could* I trust you?"

"That's a fair point. I apologize."

Kyeit sat forward in her armchair. "But now my time with you is limited anyway. Even if we have a chance to stop the High Council's plans, it won't be immediately, and whatever we try may not succeed. I gave so much of my youth and my time to the Darond. I dedicated my short life to my duty and executing every order immaculately. But it's clear now that many in power don't see the value in my sacrifices. I will continue to dedicate myself to my duty, and I will fulfil my role as Knight-Commander of the Darond to the best of my ability, but I also need to live for me."

Kanaahn still had so many questions. "What does that mean for us? Forgive me, I don't have a lot of experience with any of this."

"Really?" Kyeit was surprised.

"I've killed a man, but I've never even kissed a girl," Kanaahn admitted.

Kyeit smiled, though not unkindly.

"What about you?"

Kyeit blushed. "...The same. I threw myself into the Darond, and how I answered you was how I answered many other potential suitors."

Kanaahn snickered. "Potential suitors. Are you always so formal? No, what am I asking, of course, you are."

Kyeit crossed her arms and threw one leg over the other with mock indignance.

Then the silence returned like a cold winter and set in. The two teens simply sat there, looking at each other, or trying to do anything but that. They took turns stealing glances at each other.

Kanaahn was surprised Djall had not interceded or made commentary the entire time. No doubt he had heard everything and was still listening. The green dragon was probably laughing with the other dragons right now.

Djall did not waste a good moment to tease Kanaahn. *"Don't worry. You'll hear it from me later."*

"I hate you," Kanaahn replied.

Then the connection went dim, but never truly extinguished.

"So, that's the whole reason you came up here tonight?" Kanaahn finally asked.

Kyeit nodded and stood. "That's it."

"I appreciate you coming by. I'm glad we could have this talk."

In truth, Kanaahn was not glad they had had this talk because his delicious dinner would soon be flying down the garderobe chute as soon as Kyeit left. Kanaahn was going to vomit from excitement and nerves. But for now, he held his food down and walked Kyeit over to the door, swinging it open with perhaps a bit too much eagerness.

Kyeit turned at the door and hugged Kanaahn, and his face turned the colour of Risasi. But despite it all, he hugged her back, relishing the moment for every second he could. Their arms wrapped around one another, in a gentle embrace.

Then Kyeit reached up and kissed Kanaahn, and suddenly Kanaahn felt like he was in a lucid dream. He didn't know what to do, and so he simply closed his eyes and kissed her back.

As they pulled away, Kanaahn tilted his head, tasting his own mouth. "Have you been drinking?"

"Only one drink. Cecil and I went out. I wanted to be sober for this."

"The kiss or the conversation?"

"Whatever happened. I didn't know what to expect really."

Kyeit looked at Kanaahn, and he at her, their hearts beating in unison, their faces flushed scarlet with embarrassment and emotion, and their ears and cheeks burning hot as blood rushed through them. Kanaahn had only felt this way once before, and that was in the tavern in Felidrun. Of course, this time there would be no Shooter to interrupt them.

Kyeit's eyes softened. "Shut the door..."

Kanaahn obliged.

Chapter XLII

Drakhart was hidden in the command tent, buried in the back corner in an alcove. He needed to stay far out of sight, because if any of the Khaleeshir caught sight of him, or heard he was there, there would be Hells to pay on the international scale, and it would end badly for Altimara. Everything had gone so perfectly so far, any failure at this point was unacceptable, least of all failure by his own hand.

Drakhart paced in circles around the alcove, wearing a rut in the muddy grass. Every preparation had been made, every consideration taken. There was nothing more he could do. Under the cover of pouring rain the night previous, the Qiri'aran warriors had come above ground and arranged themselves as planned, encircling the city. All traffic on the roads was cut off, and civilians were having their goods confiscated for use in the siege and were being placed in tents—but kept safe—per Qiri'aran War Laws.

From now on, all was in the hands of Elandyr'ni, the Kinu'watan and the captains and commanders. Runners would keep Drakhart updated, but he could do no more than watch as his plans unfolded. The rain from last night had finally abated, and as the day slowly warmed before dawn, a fog blanketed the land. Drakhart couldn't have crafted a better scenario to begin the siege with if he had written it himself.

Now, it was time to wake the city, and let them meet their doom.

The drums began to beat. Drums so large, with calls so deep, that every beat reverberated through Drakhart's soul. The throat singing began, carrying their ghostly tune across the foggy fields.

Not unlike...

Then the chanting started.

Y'ra tii'raten! Fe'lo kee'raten!
Yii'ko ta'reh ka!

The famed Chant of War.

Often the last thing ever heard by enemies of the Qiri'ar, and well known in legends as the beginning of the end for whatever army was unlucky enough to find themselves up against a Qiri'aran army.

This chant would be repeated, loudly, and for as long as it took for Baron Felidrun to arrive and begin the siege proper. This part was not about attacking, but about unnerving the enemy. To make them feel surrounded, to fill them with dread and doom, and to wither away their will to fight so that by the time the actual fighting started, their will to fight would be gone.

By the end, the fault would lay entirely on the shoulders of the defenders. It would be their lack of resolve that would destroy them. Not even the presence of the Khaleeshir would be able to restore their morale.

When the Qiri'ar finally breached the walls, they would overwhelm the defenders, and teach them the true meaning of what it meant to be a warrior. Estion's defeat would be absolute, and they would have no one to blame but themselves.

Chapter XLIII

Kanaahn woke shortly before dawn. He wasn't sure what drew him from his slumber, but something nagged at his mind and his senses until he opened his eyes. It took him a few moments to remember he wasn't alone in the bed when he rolled over and was shocked to find Kyeit lying there next to him. The memories of what happened last night came back to him. He placed a hand on Kyeit's shoulder.

Kanaahn's hand grazed across the smooth and pearly skin that marked the many scars covering her body. Kyeit called the scars her reminder of everything that had been taken from her, and the lessons she had learned.

He traced the scar on her shoulder with his finger. It was mostly straight, but it was long, with jagged edges. The wounds had been deep. Whatever weapons the Tulkaz had attacked her with had clearly been enchanted with dark magic, and the scars would never truly heal. Just like the scar on Kanaahn's own back. They both were marked forever by their shortcomings in battle.

Kanaahn let out a shivering sigh. A chill had crept across the room like the creeping hands of the Winter King, descending upon fields and sands alike, covering the land in frost, and killing any living thing unfortunate enough to be found outside in the winter.

He scanned the room and found, to his dismay, that he had left the doors open to the balcony, and while the rain had stopped, the fog now blanketed everything outside and a chill wind had set in overnight. Kanaahn, even with his increased senses and better eyesight, could only see as far as the edge of the balcony from where he lay.

He stood up and looked around the room for his sleeping robes. They had been thrown somewhere, far from his reach the night before. Kyeit had left her clothes in a heap on the armchair, next to her sword. Kanaahn had not been so prudent. He found his robe in a pile by the front door. He scooped it up and slung it on over his shoulders, and wrapped the cord tightly around his waist.

Then he heard it.

It was the nagging that had woken him...but it wasn't nagging. It was chanting. Rhythmic chanting, and singing, and drums.

And it didn't sound friendly.

Kanaahn ran over the balcony and leaned over the edge. He still could not see more than a few metres in front of his face, but from what he could hear, it sounded like someone shouting up from the courtyard.

No...no not the courtyard.

That's how it sounded to him, but his hearing was better than most now. It was much further. Outside the city? It was impossible to tell in this fog. He still couldn't see anything. But Kanaahn could hear the song.

Y'ra tii'raten! Fe'lo kee'raten!
Yii'ko ta'reh ka!
Hiina tae nasu! Filir naga'than!
Yevor'both nha hauh!
Yevor'both nha hauh!

Tohkah fiisk na'eroh! Tauri sul mar'ehm!
Folh ki rau hak'ara deh!
Folh ki rau hak'ara deh!
Hul! Rah!
Hul rah ul a'karam tii'loh!

Kanaahn did the first thing he could think of. *"Djall, what the fuck is going on?"*

The dragon responded immediately. *"I don't know. We've been forbidden from flying, training is cancelled today, and Aurichalcum has disappeared with Thrae. I think they've gone down to the walls. Something, or someone, is outside the city, but we have no other details."*

"I have a bad feeling about this..."

Djall's response was as practical as ever. *"You should get dressed—not just in clothes, full armour and weaponry. I haven't seen much of war, but I know when a battle is coming. You should let Kyeit know and get her out while you can. They haven't summoned Cecil, Valence, or Kinokaze yet, but I don't know how much longer that will last."*

"Thank you, Djall. Let the other Khaleeshir know. Wake them immediately."

"I shall."

Djall hesitated.

"Yes?' Kanaahn asked.

"About last night..."

"Not the time."

"No, not that. Next time...cut the connection please?"

Kanaahn was confused. *"What do you mean?"*

"I don't know what you call it, but it was unpleasant and disgusting, and I do not wish to experience that ever again. The next time you do...that, just cut the connection, and never speak of it again. It was unnatural, and I am only thankful it did not last long."

"I would argue that is the most natural thing a human could do."

"Well, I am not a human, and I cannot understand how you get pleasure from...that. Dragons are much more efficient and natural, and we can produce far more offspring per pairing than a human can."

"This is not the time to discuss the merits of reproductive methods. Your point has been taken. I know it takes two to sever the connection temporarily, but my mind was...preoccupied. I'll make sure to take your sensitive lizard feelings into account next time."

Djall was not amused but did not waste another second. Time was too precious for further banter.

Kanaahn walked back into his room and approached the bed. "Kyeit," he called gently at first.

Kyeit roused slowly.

"Kyeit." More urgently this time.

Kyeit opened her eyes slowly, stretching and adjusting to the day. "What's wrong?"

"You need to get up, get dressed, and get back to your room."

She frowned playfully. "What's wrong? You didn't enjoy yourself?"

"Normally I'd enjoy witty banter, but right now isn't the time. Do you hear that?"

Kyeit was groggy and confused in equal measure.

"Right, sorry. Your hearing isn't like mine. Someone is outside the walls, chanting, and it sounds aggressive. Aurichalcum and Thrae are down there right now investigating, there's fog everywhere, and Djall and the dragons have been grounded for the day, and training is cancelled."

Kyeit immediately shot from the bed and ran to her clothes. Her exhaustion was forgotten, and her grogginess a thing of the past. "They'll come for me soon, no doubt. I need to be in my room, or at least awake and available."

"I'm sorry to wake you this way—"

"No, you did the right thing. Thank you." Kyeit threw her clothes on with a speed that Kanaahn could not believe. She was dressed and nearly presentable in minutes. "I'll finish getting ready in my room. Let's keep what happened between us for now. I don't need people in our business."

Kanaahn nodded. The last thing he needed was Arial, or gods forbid, Shooter, finding out about this. Djall was bad enough.

Kyeit walked over to Kanaahn and gave him a quick kiss before departing. She smiled at him once last time before she slipped off into the hallway, back to her room, praying that no one saw her leave.

Just as quickly as his life had changed last night, he was left alone with his feelings and memories. But Kanaahn could not dwell on his confused squall of emotions right now or take time to process what had happened. For now, he was too focused on getting dressed and getting his armour on over his clothes. All the while, anxiety and fear ate away at his nerves from the pit of his stomach.

Memories of Xiar flashed in his mind. He could hear it again, smell it again, just like he was there once more. Again he was in the thick of battle, surrounded by blood, guts, and dead men. The waves of soldiers, all of whom wanted to kill him, swarming over the walls of the city.

In truth, he might as well have been back in Xiar. Kanaahn was convinced all battlefields were the same place. Another plane of existence, where combatants were transported to at the beginning of the battle. A featureless, desolate plane, filled with two armies who want nothing but to kill each other for no other reason than they were told to. They were paid to. Some had their own convictions and beliefs that drove them, sure, but in the end, they all just followed the orders of their commanders and prayed to whatever deities they believed in that they would live to go home to their families, or at least see another day.

Kanaahn was certain of one thing, however, he would not let this city fall. Ethon would be standing at the end of this, no matter the cost.

* * *

The Khaleeshir met outside their rooms within a half hour of Djall's warning.

Arial left her room to find Kanaahn waiting for her. They were joined not long after by Arkas, and lastly Shooter. There were no jokes, no witty repartee, no sarcasm. Things were far too serious for that now. They were in their armour; enemies were at the gates. The war they thought they had left behind after Xiar had now followed them and come to Ethon.

The five teenagers exchanged serious but knowing looks. Arial held out her hands, and Arkas and Kanaahn joined theirs with hers, then each of them with Shooter. They stood there, in a circle, hands held, looking back and forth at each other.

"Whatever happens. No matter what," Arial declared. The rest was left unsaid, but everyone knew the words and feelings well enough. They nodded, squeezing each other's hands a little tighter.

There had been levity and light-heartedness before Xiar. Then Xiar happened, and they realized war wasn't a game. Their lives were not suddenly some great odyssey or myth where the heroes always win, and the battle was but a few lines of gallant one-on-one combat that ended in victory for the good guys. They learned that sometimes even when you win, you lose. You lose people, you lose yourself, or parts of yourself.

Risasi interrupted the moment. *"They've gathered on the wall."*

"Have they summoned us?" Arial asked.

It was Fyete who answered. *"Not yet, but I would make your way down here as soon as possible."*

"Who's been called?" Shooter asked.

"Kyeit and Cecil just took Valence and Kinokaze down there The chanting is getting louder."

"What is it? Do we know?" asked Arkas.

Djall replied this time. *"Fog's still too thick to see, so we're not certain, but they're not friendly."*

Arial's blood ran cold. She feared the day she would grow used to battle and killing. It always surprised her how much Xiar bothered her, but how little their skirmishes with the Town Watch bothered her. Maybe it was the difference in motivation, or perhaps because they had known the Town Watch to be wicked and wholly evil, whereas the soldiers they fought at Xiar had been nameless, faceless nobodies who, while serving a wicked cause,

382

did not intend to be wicked themselves. Or maybe it was because Arial was taking the time to process it all, where she never gave it a second thought before.

Kanaahn's voice cut through Arial's thoughts like a ship through the fog. "Come on, let's get down to the courtyard. We shouldn't waste any more time. Every second counts now."

* * *

Y'ra tii'raten! Fe'lo kee'raten!
Yii'ko ta'reh ka!
Hiina tae nasu! Filir naga'than!
Yevor'both nha hauh!
Yevor'both nha hauh!

Tohkah fiisk na'eroh! Tauri sul mar'ehm!
Folh ki rau hak'ara deh!
Folh ki rau hak'ara deh!
Hul! Rah!
Hul rah ul a'karam tii'loh!

Leon had summoned his trusted inner circle as soon as he had been notified of the chanting. He was now surrounded by his myriad advisors and generals.

To his immediate left were the leaders of the three military orders in service to the Crown. First was, Rupreckt vohn Yeshtaburg the Lord Commander of the Royal Guard, followed by High Lord Garrydd Glynddwyr of the Bluehelms, and Imiisah Ifelen Lady of the Royal Hunt.

On his right stood Junior Major-domo Iskren Ithell, Senior Major-domo Imuhlair Vaust, Knight-Commanders Kyeit and Cecil as well as Kinokaze and Valence, Menalaea, and finally Thrae, who attended on behalf of her father Aurichalcum.

Aurichalcum had elected to remain at the palace and ensure that life continued as normal there—though it was likely his motives were much deeper than that, no one pressed him on the true nature of his request.

Hau'farh, though not technically a member of the inner circle, was also summoned as the leader of the Lau'thso and political ally of the Crown. His input was to be considered, and the choice of whether his small, limited band of Lau'thso would join this fight lay upon his shoulders.

Additionally, Ilana remained at the palace and kept watch over the Khaleeshir until they were required.

Leon could not decide what to do until he had assessed the situation and knew what he was dealing with. He didn't have control over his army either, which added further complications to the possibility of any kind of plans for warfare. Leon had only the Bluehelms, the Royal Guard and a few hundred Huntsmen, but the barons would need to

383

raise any additional forces. That had been one of the unfortunate outcomes of his father's revolt. Leon's only tools right now were defence and diplomacy, and he was hoping the latter would be all that would be needed.

By the time they had all reached the wall, the fog had cleared, and the chanting had only grown louder and louder as time passed so that it now echoed across the entire city, end to end. Now anyone could hear it. The chant was likely being amplified with magic. With the fog parted, the city could see where the chanting was coming from, and the tidings were not good.

It had been Qul'den who had told them what the threat was before the fog had even cleared, but with the fog gone, it confirmed he spoke true: an entire army of Qiri'aran soldiers had surrounded the city and were here for war and blood.

Leon did not need to guess who had sent them.

"Tenebrae," Leon had declared. "He's sent his armies to our doorstep. Has he abandoned secrecy so soon? This shall only serve as proof of what the Darond has been saying. The other nations—"

Thrae cut him off. "I wouldn't be so sure.."

"Who else would have sent the Qiri'ar after us? We all know they serve him."

"*We* know they serve him, but to those sceptical of Tenebrae's return it's just the Qiri'ar attacking us of their own free will," Aurichalcum reasoned.

"But Altimara is responsible for their actions. Even if they don't believe in Tenebrae's return, clearly they'll see Altimara's clear aggression—"

It was Cecil who cut Leon off this time. "In Altimara, the Qiri'ar are not counted as citizens. They are considered an autonomous, sovereign people. In exchange for a semi-annual tribute to the Crown, they're given their freedom. It was likely a way for Tenebrae to reward the Qiri'ar for their loyalty without raising suspicion amongst the Altimaran populace. It looks like they're being exploited and excluded, but in truth, they're being left alone for a payment that Tenebrae has never bothered collecting. Whether Tenebrae collects the tithe or not, the important thing is legally, the Qiri'ar are an independent people who can make their own decisions and foreign relations, with no liability on behalf of the Crown. It's why they're able to come and go from Altimara so easily when her own people require permits upon permits."

"So, you're saying there's no way to prove that Tenebrae or Altimara sent them?" Leon demanded, clearly frustrated.

Kyeit replied. "At the moment, no. Short of an Altimaran soldier being in that army, there is no way to prove who sent them beyond a shadow of a doubt—even if we know the truth. If we can find written orders, or perhaps capture one of their commanders, we might be able to torture some information out of them. But Qiri'ar are known for their tolerance to pain, and I doubt we'd be able to capture one so easily."

Menalaea quickly added. "Besides, Tenebrae is not someone that leaves such an easy-to-find paper trial. I've spent years locked in a battle of spy craft and subterfuge with him. Think about how long his return remained a secret. If our spies hadn't entered the palace looking for other secrets, they'd never have discovered the truth that was being obfuscated."

Leon paced the battlements.

Imuhlair stepped forward. "Your Majesty, I suggest we call the banners. We have enough soldiers in the city to hold them off for now, but we'll need the army to route them and lift the siege. We're surrounded."

"As much as I hate having to ask him for help, you're right. Baron Felidrun is our best solution," Leon replied.

"By your leave then, I shall—"

Leon did not let Imuhlair finish. "No. Stay with me. Iskren, you send out the call to arms. Be sure to send one to each of the Barons, especially the Baroness Pelchar. Lady vohn Veishaupt's navy will be instrumental in keeping the Acturn free. We cannot lose control of the Acturn."

Iskren bowed. "Your Majesty." He soon disappeared from the battlements to follow through on his orders.

Hau'farh spoke next. He approached Leon and placed a closed fist over his heart. "Your Majesty, I know there are few of us, but I would like to pledge myself and the lives of my warriors for the cause. We would stay with you and defend this city and her people if you'll allow us."

Leon's face softened. "That's not necessary. As you say, there are so few of you—you owe me nothing."

Hau'farh puffed out his chest. "You have pledged yourselves to save my people. It is only fair that we do the same for yours. Please, let us fight."

Leon let out a short sigh. "Very well. It is appreciated, Hau'farh. You are a man of honour and bravery. The acts of the Lau'thso will not be forgotten in this country. High Lord Garrydd, take Hau'farh and his people to the armoury and see they're properly outfitted for battle. Tell the quartermasters to begin opening the weapons vaults, we'll require them soon for the rest of our forces."

The High Lord saluted his monarch, then disappeared with Hau'farh to prepare for the fight.

Leon then turned to the Lord Commander of the Royal Guard. "Lord Commander vohn Yeshtaburg, I charge you with rallying the defending forces—no citizen levies to start. Bluehelms, Huntsmen, and Royal Guards only for now. If things get dire, we'll only take those who would volunteer themselves, otherwise the people should not be made to suffer for the madness of our enemy. Also, ensure that the people do not panic; they must be kept calm. Panic will not serve us in the days to come."

If the Commander disagreed with his king's decision, he did not let it show. It was not in his list of duties to question the orders given to him, only to carry them out. He disappeared to follow those orders as quickly as they were issued.

Next, Leon turned to Cecil, Kyeit and their dragons in mortal form. "I think you know what I'm about to ask of you."

Cecil smiled. "We'll bring them."

"Make sure they're armoured—if they aren't already. They have a habit of knowing things they shouldn't."

Kyeit rolled her eyes. "Always. Every time."

"The dragons as well," Leon added. "We must be prepared for battle at any moment. Bring Hana and Aurichalcum back here with you."

The foursome bowed and quickly departed to get the Khaleeshir as commanded.

Finally, Leon turned to Menalaea.

"The usual I presume. Murder, poison, spy craft?" she asked.

Leon shook his head. "Not quite. Menalaea, you have contacts in most of the taverns and pubs across Enayra don't you?"

Menalaea's confusion was visible. "Just about. Why?"

"How many bards do you know?"

Her confusion deepened, but she pressed forward. "Quite a few."

"Get me every bard in this city. Can you manage that?"

Menalaea was now speechless.

Leon elaborated. "If they want an orchestra, we'll give them one. This chant is meant to unnerve us, to make us break before they even fire a single shot. I don't intend to make it easy. On the contrary, I intend to return fire in like kind."

Menalaea nodded but did not complain or question Leon's judgment. She departed with a swish of her cape, stalking off into the city to see Leon's commands carried out to perfection.

Leon knew Menalaea well enough to trust that she would understand the importance of his plan. She too was a woman of unorthodox methods and appreciated the element of surprise and shock. The best way to defeat your enemy was to surprise them—that was a lesson Leon had learned from her after all.

For now, Leon was left alone, staring out across the wide-open field from atop the parapet. Before him lay the massive sea of Qiri'aran warriors who were here for blood and victory, and they would not leave until they'd had it. Enayra was changing, and so was the war. Whether victory or defeat be at hand for Ethon, whatever happened here today would change the continent forever, and things would never be the same again.

* * *

Kanaahn and the other Khaleeshir had finally been called to the front. The dragons remained at the castle, to be dressed in their armour and would arrive at the walls when the battle began—there wasn't enough room there for all of them.

Kyeit and Cecil had come to summon them, as expected, and neither of them was surprised to find the Khaleeshir waiting patiently, if a bit anxious, in full armour, and prepared to fight the first battle in a war that hadn't even truly begun yet.

Valence and Kinokaze had gone off to be strapped into their own armour before the siege truly started.

Unlike on the trip to Filiddyn Castle, where the group had been brought to the castle using the main roads and thoroughfares, the Khaleeshir were escorted down to the outermost wall by using the walls themselves. The group criss-crossed and traversed the long and weaving spider web of walls and fortifications to reach their destination.

From atop the grey-stone battlements, Kanaahn could understand the value of this kind of fortification, even more so when he looked down over the parapet to see the people in the city down below.

The streets were crowded with panicked people. Kanaahn could hear the wail of children, the worried muttering of a scared populace. People jammed the streets to gather,

386

to find family, to hunker down, to maybe try and escape before the siege, to gossip in the markets, or to buy as many goods and supplies as possible to prepare for the long siege. Guards were trying to keep order, but the Bluehelms were preoccupied with manning the walls and preparing for the siege, so there were too few guards to keep the people calm.

Kanaahn could hear more sounds coming from where the harbour was. He could see the crowds amassing by the water, looking for a way to get out of the city before the worst came to pass. He could hear the cries of anger and fear as the people realized that the massive harbour chains had been raised, and all traffic in and out of the city had been halted until the siege was lifted.

There would be no escape for these people. They would share the fate of the defenders.

"Leon must be agonizing over that," Arial muttered. She had noticed where Kanaahn's attention had gone.

"What do you mean?"

"He cares for his people. He doesn't want to trap them here, but it's safer for them behind these walls than it is out there. They risk being killed or caught up in the siege in a worse way."

"I'm sure they'll understand," Kanaahn replied, trying to abate his own worries as much as Arial's.

Arial gave a non-verbal response, but her concern, for the people and Leon was clear on her face. Arial couldn't hide her thoughts from Kanaahn, they had known each other for too long. He placed a hand on her shoulder and gave her a comforting look.

Arial gave a weak, but silent, smile. They did not discuss the matter further.

Eventually, the Khaleeshir arrived on the battlements and were greeted by a concentrated orchestra of pandemonium. Runners and pages ran up and down the entire length of the wall, transporting notes between commanders. Quartermasters dispatched wagonloads of supplies, ensuring that the defenders were evenly stocked across the entire wall. Commanders barked orders and shored up formations to ensure that the defenders were evenly distributed across the fortifications all around the city. An even distribution of soldiers would be necessary to avoid a breakthrough if the enemy climbed the parapet and attempted to breach the walls.

It was official, war had come to Ethon. The sights and sounds of Xiar were returned, and everything started to grow eerily familiar. In fact, were it not for the large number of musicians and bards tuning their instruments and spacing themselves out evenly between the crenelations, Kanaahn might have thought they had found and been transported to the now-lost city.

The group found Leon in a command tent half a kilometre down the wall. Soldiers parted the tent flaps to allow them to file in at the behest of Kyeit and Cecil.

Leon greeted the Khaleeshir immediately. "I do apologize. We don't have the time to put you in charge of the defences like Hunter did at Xiar. Not to mention I have less power over my armies than he did."

"We don't need to command anything," Kanaahn replied. "Just let us fight, that's enough for us."

"We're not blind to the effect our presences have on armies," Arial added.

Leon nodded. "I appreciate it. I'll ensure my commanders and captains know that you are there as their equals, even if you have no official title or role in the army. They should follow if you ask them, should you require a force behind you. But, failing that, they won't be barking orders at you, at the very least."

Shooter shrugged. "We should hope."

Arkas turned back towards the parapet. He could see it from the small gaps in the tent fold. "Is there any way we could pick them off before they even reach the walls?"

Leon shook his head. "We don't have the manpower. The only soldiers we have that could do that would be the Royal Hunt, and I can't risk them. We don't know what the Qiri'ar are capable of."

"They've fought with Tenebrae before. Surely someone must know something." Shooter questioned.

It was Thrae who responded. "That's the problem. No one has fought the Qiri'ar in a thousand years. We don't know anything of their current battle tactics, strategies, or what their Blood Witches are capable of. We can be certain blood magic will be involved, and we know they're able to fight beyond the limits of a normal human, but we can't confirm much more than that."

Aurichalcum stepped forward. He had arrived at the front after the Khaleeshir had been summoned, nominally in Hana's place, as he had refused to allow her near the walls for the battle to come. "Even I have not battled the Qiri'ar before. I can be of no help, unfortunately."

"What about Qul'den? Surely he'd know something," Shooter suggested.

"He was unable to be of much help. Qul'den has never lived amongst the Qiri'ar of Altimara. He and his people have lived separately from the Qiri'ar for many generations, and they don't practice blood magic." Leon explained. "He was able to confirm that, at the very least, the Qiri'aran army should refrain from attacking civilians and innocents. They'll limit their rampage to soldiers, warriors, and defenders—anyone with a weapon in hand and armour on their body is fair game."

"I already like them more than the Altimaran army," noted Kanaahn.

Leon nodded. "Qul'den explained that the Qiri'ar of Altimara is steeped in their ancient warrior culture, but they do have rules of honour when at war. Death in battle is a glorious end, especially at the hands of a worthy enemy, and while the defeat of foes is honoured, the murder of innocents is not honourable. We have that much to be thankful for, at least."

Arkas's brow furrowed. "So, you suggest we just sit here until they attack?"

"I cannot risk my soldiers so early in this siege. We're limited until the barons' armies arrive, and I'd rather not call up citizen levies if necessary. It could be weeks before we're reinforced. This city *must* hold out until then. A significant loss of forces in that time could mean the end."

"Do we have an idea of when they'll start attacking?" asked Cecil.

"Presumably when they stop singing," replied Leon.

"Who knows when that will be," added Thrae.

"Is that what the bards out there are for?" Shooter asked. "I couldn't help but notice. They seemed out of place."

Leon smiled. "On a normal battlefield, they would be. But as I told Menalaea: if the Qiri'ar want to use music to demoralize us, I intend to return fire in like kind. Words can be more powerful than any weapon if used correctly. Music even more so, I believe."

"Maybe if we play them a lullaby they'll fall asleep," joked Shooter.

Leon ignored the jest.

Menalaea suddenly entered the tent, silent as a leaf falling from a tree. "Leon. They're ready." She disappeared just as quickly as she had arrived.

Everyone exchanged a quick, but tense glance. Now would be the moment of truth, and either the doubters or Leon would be correct. There was only one way to find out who it would be.

They filed from the tent, Leon at the head of the column, and out onto the parapet. Menalaea waited, next to an old and wizened-looking musician.

Kanaahn's stomach turned a bit. He would be lying if he said he had no doubts about Leon's plan. But Kanaahn's experience with battle was limited, and the only war he had experienced was the Siege of Xiar. Altimara did not play psychological games like the Qiri'ar were trying. Their methods were more direct and far more destructive.

Menalaea introduced the old man next her to, gesturing to him and Leon as she made introductions. "Your Majesty, this is Faulen. He's head of the Minstrel's Guild in Ethon."

The old man bowed. "Highness. It has been a long time."

Leon smiled at the man like he was an old friend. "I do remember you. My coming-of-age party. It was you who played that day; the lute I believe."

Faulen beamed. "You remembered?"

"Your music was beautiful; I could never forget it. To my knowledge, I've been told you played at my parents' wedding as well?"

Faulen's smile only grew. "It was, indeed, Highness. Thank you for remembering me."

Leon's cheeks went pink with embarrassment, but he managed to keep his composure otherwise. "Please, there's no need for formality—nor any time. I have summoned you here, as you can see, for the most urgent of matters."

Faulen nodded. He looked out over the battlement to see the chanting army massed at the city's doorstep.

Y'ra tii'raten! Fe'lo kee'raten!
Yii'ko ta'reh ka!
Hiina tae nasu! Filir naga'than!
Yevor'both nha hauh!
Yevor'both nha hauh!

Tohkah fiisk na'eroh! Tauri sul mar'ehm!
Folh ki rau hak'ara deh!
Folh ki rau hak'ara deh!
Hul! Rah!
Hul rah ul a'karam tii'loh!

"The most urgent indeed," he noted. "What would you have us do? Not fight I hope." Faulen chuckled as if he had said the funniest thing he had ever heard.

Leon smiled kindly. "As a musician, you know the power of music. You know what they're trying to do with their chant."

Faulen nodded. "Oh aye. You'd like us to do the same to them?"

"Exactly!"

Faulen scratched his bearded chin, thinking over what was being asked of him. "What did you have in mind?"

Leon grinned from ear to ear. "Do you know the Song of Defiance?"

Faulen laughed.

Many of the Estian soldiers and bards within earshot began to grin with similar mirth.

"I'd say there isn't an Estian who doesn't know that song, and certainly no bard worth their salt in this country would ever exclude that from their repertoire. Consider it done, Highness."

"If you need me to transmit the message, I can. Magic could make that possible faster than any runner," Leon offered.

"It would be appreciated."

Arial stepped forward. "Let me help. I can broaden the range and ease your burden. If we split the spell between us, we won't use as much mana. We'll need as much mana as we can muster for the fight to come."

Leon hesitated. Whatever his doubts were, they were unclear to Kanaahn. If he had to guess, some mixture of concern and pride. But whatever reservations Leon might have had, he knew Arial was right, and in the end, he nodded his assent.

Arial stepped forward and placed a hand on his shoulder. Leon in turn placed a hand on Faulen's shoulder and extended his mind outwards until it brushed against the old bard's, and Arial followed suit. Then, together, they pushed their minds outward, extending the reach of their consciousness until it enveloped most of the city. Arial was able to use Adalinda to help her broaden her range and extend the spell even further. Once all the bards and musicians upon the walls had been connected by their minds to the telepathic spell, Faulen began to speak.

"Bards and musicians of Ethon. Most of you know me. I am Faulen. We have been called here today, to use our skills and aid our city and our people. You may wonder, how can we, humble musicians, be used against such a massive army at our gates?"

Faulen paused for effect.

Honestly, Faulen was correct, even Kanaahn had his doubts.

"But we know the power of music. We know how songs can stir the hardest hearts to feel and move even the coldest of creatures to compassion. Song has long since been used to bolster and demoralize, to lead armies and keep time in battle. Even now, our mighty Qiri'aran foes seek to defeat us with the power of song. They want us to despair and fear, they wish to weaken us before the fighting even starts. But we shall not surrender! We shall not falter! We may be but humble bards and minstrels, but we have been called upon by our king, to sing and play for our nation! Just as our ancestors before us did during the Great Siege when they composed this song. We shall honour their memory and sing the Song of Defiance once more! We must not allow our people to falter, and we shall not let this city fall!"

A cheer rose from the battlements amongst the bards and musicians. The soldiers, and others who had not been privy to the speech, seemed as confused or concerned as Kanaahn and the Khaleeshir. But Leon looked even more determined to see this through. It did not take long for the musicians to begin playing their instruments, and within moments, the harmonized sound of lutes, flutes, drums, pipes, and hurdy-gurdies echoed from across the wall top in a single sonorous note.

And then the music began.

It started with just the instrumentals; the musicians played a bouncy plucky tune that repeated the same few bars over and over again. No one sang at first, and Leon explained that it was traditional to open this particular song with just the instrumental. But after the instrumental opening had been completed, the singing began, led by Faulen.

Nedda fäyr tí çişe, gotul ab tae thrút.
Nedda fäyr yí fydden, ur húth pír tae başi.
Nedda. Nedda, nedda, nedda.
Nedda fäyr yí gotul.
Nedda, nedda.
Nedda fäyr tí ãym.

Kanaahn did not recognize the language they were singing in, and even Leon seemed momentarily thrown off by the choice of language. The Khaleeshir exchanged glances before Thrae explained.

"It's Old Gerovian. This Song was composed in a similar situation during the War of the Grand Coalition when all the nations of Enayra combined their strength to defeat the Gerovian Empire and her growing dominance of the continent. Towards the end of the war, this city came under siege by the coalition armies, and in defiance in the face of their imminent defeat, the emperor had this song composed and sung from the wall tops. It's said the city held out for thirty-seven days, and the musicians didn't stop playing the entire time. Legends say the music finally stopped when the emperor finally lay dead, and the last member of the Royal Guard had fallen. It was then the city fell."

"Legends and lies. The music only lasted a week," Aurichalcum replied grimly. "But it worked as intended. The city *did* hold out for thirty-seven days, and the coalition armies were forced to fight for every inch of ground they gained even after they breached the walls."

"I had expected Common," admitted Leon. "But this may work better."

The singing continued, repeating the same chorus, without end.

For the first little while, it was only the bards and musicians who sang. Their voices rose over the battlements, but they did not match the might of the Qiri'aran army across the field, who still mostly drowned out the Fatian players. But soon enough, the soldiers on the walls joined in. At first, one soldier at a time, then a small squad, or a commander with the hopes of inspiring his men. Soon, a few captains here or there joined the chorus. But quickly the choir began to grow, and before long every defender atop the walls was singing.

Every soldier came out onto the battlements and sang the Song of Defiance alongside the bards. Some brought out their own instruments, pulling out flutes, lyres, and lutes. Most simply added to the orchestra by banging their weapons against their shields to keep time with the rhythm or slamming their spear butts against the ground.

Kanaahn could feel the walls themselves quiver and shake as a few thousand spears slammed against their walkways.

391

The singing soon grew ever louder as Kanaahn could hear the panic in the streets below stop. Silence filled the streets...and then the people started to sing.

All kinds of voices rang up from across the city; young old, male, female, melodic, disjointed, uneven, and even out of tune and tone-deaf voices joined the chant. Some sang in Old Gerovian, most sang in Common, but the effect was the same, and the chorus grew louder, drowning out the Qiri'aran army, who had even seemed to stop for a moment to hear the response.

Leon smiled wide. It was working. His plan was working. Then he too joined the chorus, singing in Old Gerovian.

Thrae followed suit shortly after, then Cecil, Kyeit and their dragons. Next came Menalaea, who sang in Common. Leon's commanders, realizing they were the only ones not singing, added their voices to the music. Even Imuhlair joined in.

Though confused, and unsure of the lyrics, the Khaleeshir finally joined in as well, carefully following Menalaea's lead in Common.

Never shall this city, grovel at your feet.
Never shall we falter or beg for your mercy.
Never. Never, never, never.
Never shall we grovel.
Never, never.
Never shall we die.

The sounds of singing echoed across the entire city. From east to west, tens of thousands of people had come out from their homes, stopped in their tracks, and raised their voices to the sky to oppose the army that sought the destruction of this city and the disruption of their peaceful, happy lives.

Every word carried weight; every note played was a reminder that whatever the Qiri'ar wanted from this city would not be so easily won. The people would not simply roll over and die. They would not capitulate or negotiate. They would not give in; they would not surrender. If the Qiri'ar wanted this city, if they wanted a victory here today, they would need to bleed, deeply and severely, and they would need to kill every last person in this city to do it.

No one, from the lowliest stable boy to the soldiers on the walls, would let this city fall without a fight if it came to it.

Ethon would not fall.

Chapter XLIV

Drakhart had heard the city sing back to the Qiri'ar. Though the Qiri'ar faltered momentarily, stunned into silence by the resolve of the people and defending army, they quickly redoubled their efforts and started up a new chant. They upped the tempo of their chanting and chose a more repetitive war prayer than they had previously. This one was an exaltation of Tenebrae's mighty power, while also beseeching the great dragon for assistance in attaining victory.

Their words reverberated across the open plains before the city.

Vihl'ku'lehg, Vihl'ku'lehg
Vihl'ku'lehg gahl bo'sha yigru.
Vihl'ku'lehg, Vihl'ku'lehg
Vihl'ku'lehg vel'thru fa'helyia.

Vihl'ku'lehg, Vihl'ku'lehg
Vihl'ku'lehg gahl bo'sha yigru.
Vihl'ku'lehg, Vihl'ku'lehg
Vihl'ku'lehg vel'thru fa'helyia.

Vihl'ku'lehg, Vihl'ku'lehg
Vihl'ku'lehg gahl bo'sha yigru.
Vihl'ku'lehg, Vihl'ku'lehg
Vihl'ku'lehg vel'thru fa'helyia.

Despite the retaliation of the city, Drakhart was not worried. A few hours of resistance would not win them this battle. The Qiri'ar were tireless and could chant for days on end on devotion alone—it was a normal part of their religious devotions. But now, by combining that religious fervour with blood magic, and a lust for battle; it only amplified their abilities. It had only been a single day, but the Qiri'ar were ready to chant for weeks if need be, until Baron Felidrun arrived.

For now, Drakhart concerned himself with watching over the siege from his command tent, as well as working on his studies left to him by Elandyr'ni. He had read through the reading Elandyr'ni had left him for the day and had practised the spells she had told him to practice...but now he wished to work on his own independent study.

Drakhart sat himself at the table and began to draw the rune for "osprey" upon its surface. A rat would not serve him here; Drakhart needed a view from above, and a bird like an osprey would aid him well in that regard.

With the rune drawn, Drakhart encircled the rune with a runic circle, binding his spell with intentions and limitations, and more important, specifics. Specifics were very important with blood magic. The parameters of your spell needed to be exact. Finally, Drakhart cut open his palm and dripped his blood atop the table.

He began to chant the incantation as Elandyr'ni had taught him, and the single candle that sat atop the table flickered and sputtered but would not die. Drakhart continued his incantation, his words growing more and more intense, and his voice gaining volume the more he repeated the enchantment. Blood trickled from the wound on his hand and down his wrist. Somehow it was both cold and warm simultaneously, and Drakhart watched as the blood, like lines of red ants, was drawn towards the spell written on the table.

The blood that had been dripped on the spell bubbled, frothed, and wriggled like some globular maggot—and then the shadows reached out from all around Drakhart. The tendrils of darkness reached out like a hungry kraken, seeking to envelop and swallow its prey. The shadow wriggled and wreathed itself around the blood until the entire shadow and blood mass began to morph and change into a bird.

He stopped the spell and stared in amazement as an osprey of shadow and blood sat staring at him from the middle of the table. The small creature blinked its ruby-red eyes and cocked its head to the side. The creature clacked its beak, chirped, and bobbed its head. It was a perfect facsimile.

Drakhart closed his eyes...and saw himself, but through the eyes of the familiar. The world had a tinted red appearance, likely from the blood, but that did not harm the clarity of the vision.

His eyes shot open, and it took him a moment to realize that his sight was connected to that of his familiar. He could see what the creature did, and feel what the creature did. Their minds were separate but the same.

Drakhart gathered his composure, stood up, and held out his arm. The osprey let out a small chirping cry and landed on Drakhart's forearm. Drakhart expected the claws to dig into his flesh, but instead, the creature's talons seemed to melt away where they met resistance.

This would do well.

Drakhart walked over to the tent flap and carefully pulled back the opening, then let the osprey fly off into the darkening night sky above. Now he would have his eyes on everything. He would be able to watch the battle as it unfolded and would be able to direct his soldiers more efficiently and watch them in real-time.

When the bird disappeared into the dark sky, Drakhart closed the tent flap and sat himself down in a chair. He pulled out a small kerchief and dabbed at the sweat on his forehead. Then he drew a rune on his bleeding hand and muttered a quick spell that sealed the cut.

Drakhart felt his palm, on the spot where he had just been bleeding moments ago. He wondered how many of those cuts he had made since becoming a warlock. How much blood he had spilt. How much of his life force had been dripped away in the pursuit of power? Somewhere, in the darkest corner of his mind, Drakhart asked himself...was it worth it?

He clenched his fist and closed his eyes. He was the shadow bird once more.

Drakhart felt a cool breeze caress his face. It blew through the shadowy feathers on his wings. He looked down to see the Qiri'aran armies cheering and chanting. They raised torches, waiving them about in the darkness. Ahead of him, the city, bright as ever, continued to sing their response to the Qiri'ar, as loud and powerful as ever. The bell towers rang out across the city—they had been added to the cacophony of the rebellious rabble sometime around midday. He circled the battlefield, riding the winds, watching both the city and his army. There was nothing beyond his sight now; nothing beyond his knowledge...nothing beyond his power or control.

Drakhart opened his eyes a few moments later and smiled. The first thing he felt was an odd numbness and tingling in the back of his head, something that seemed to blur his vision. It was both confusing and oddly euphoric.

Drakhart took a deep breath and felt the euphoria surge through his veins. It was like a concentrated shot of power that ran through him as if the adrenaline in his body was being released all at once. If this is how good he felt with such a simple spell, Drakhart could only imagine how much better he would feel when he cast more powerful spells.

As his knowledge grew, so would the euphoria, but more importantly, so would his power. He would be unstoppable. No one would be able to defeat him. Not Arial, not Kanaahn, perhaps not even Elandyr'ni. He would be beyond them all, between his natural power and his status as Khaleeshir.

Yes. The power was *definitely* worth it.

* * *

Per'eth and several Qiri'ar stalked silently through the tall grasses at the edge of the massive dike. The large earthwork, shored up by dirt, and stones, and reinforced with timbers, kept the waters of the Acturn and Lake Ardona from sweeping across the flood plains and inculcating the fields around Ethon with water. But more important, the raised earthwork dikes were defensible points in the landscape that allowed the Baroness Pelchar to defend and guard the river from any threat.

At one point, many of the fields had been underwater as part of Lake Ardona, and the Acturn River had been at least twice as wide as it was now.

For as long as any Estian could remember, every spring and fall—when the rains fell heaviest and most frequently—the river Acturn would flood and swell, as would Lake Ardona. To protect the settlements and farmland that sat in these floodplains, a series of levees were built to hold back the engorged waterways. They were imperfect measures and were prone to leaking, or breaking outright if the waters went particularly high. They crumbled easily under neglect, which occurred often when the realm was in chaos—which was often.

But that way of life changed several centuries ago, when the vohn Veishaupt family, who had made their fortune monopolizing much of the trade that travelled up and down the Acturn and across the lake, as well as overseeing the largest goods importer in Estion, sought to increase their wealth and ease their troubles with the tumultuous and ever-flooding river and lake system. They were granted a mandate by the reigning monarch—some say in exchange for a large sum of money—and spent much of their own personal wealth to push back the waterline with a series of dikes, dams, berms, and levees.

Remnants of the ancient earthworks, used for centuries before the new systems were built, still existed in the fields—the Qiri'ar had crossed over the odd and out-of-place bumps and ridges that now served as boundary markers between farmer's fields and the borders of settlements—but they had fallen into disrepair and disuse under the vohn Veishaupt infrastructure.

For their service to the Crown and their country, the vohn Veishaupt family were granted a lordship; originally, it had been a simple viscounty, but over time they spun their fortunes into a dukedom, several counties, a handful of viscounties, and eventually, their current barony.

Because they had poured their own money into the infrastructure project, they were given complete control and hegemony over all waterways in Estion, and Lake Ardona—they'd even had a ministry created for this purpose on the king's council. While their main river of concern was the Acturn, they also held sway over the Terthon in the south, up until the Danaen border and the Viilas until it disappeared into the mountains separating Estion from Asardaea. With their command over the rivers, and of course, Lake Ardona, the vohn Veishaupts expanded their trade empire, solidified their hold on Estian trade, and eventually were put in charge of the Estian navy.

While the vohn Veishaupts were now staunch defenders of the Crown under their current leader, the Baroness Pelchar, they had spent centuries previously building up their military fortifications along the entire length of the river and around the shores of Lake Ardona to protect their investment, and their trade from both the Crown and their fellow nobles.

It was the mission of Per'eth and the Qiri'ar that served under him to infiltrate these fortifications and take control of them. The Baroness could not be allowed to use the river to reinforce, supply, support, or otherwise evacuate the city. The Acturn would be taken by the attackers and held at any cost. Victory at Ethon had to be absolute and unquestionable. And it was Per'eth's job to ensure this mission ran smoothly.

To that end, he had taken his force granted by Lord Ghast—a little over a thousand warriors and Blood Witches—and divided them up into smaller attack forces. They would not need to hold the entire river, but just enough of it that they could maintain control and blockade it. It wouldn't be that hard to do. Most of the canal was drained in several sections down its length while maintenance crews and builders cleaned and repaired the canals.

This work was done under the watchful eye of the Baroness Pelchar's soldiers. The garrisons were pitiful, and once the Qiri'ar swept through the fortresses along the canal, they would be able to take and hold them easily. As long as they kept the canals drained, and the fortresses manned, nothing could go wrong.

Per'eth was pressed flat against the side of the slope that led to the canal. He scanned the immediate area, making sure that no one was near enough to see him. There wasn't a soul in sight, save for a shadowy shape circling above. It was hard to tell what it was, being dark, but it looked like some kind of large bird. Whatever it was, it wasn't about to tell the Baroness Pelchar's soldiers that a Qiri'aran attack force was here to kill them and take control of the river.

Per'eth poked his head above the edge of the slope that led up to the canal once more. He and his attack group were just outside one of the checkpoints positioned along the canal. Men were working down at the bottom of the canal, and though Per'eth couldn't see them, he could hear them moving and talking.

Carefully scanning the checkpoint, Per'eth could see that despite serving a mainly administrative function—checking papers, conducting searches, loading, and off-loading cargo as needed being among some of the duties—it was fortified like a military installation.

Chains could be dragged across the canal, as well as a large portcullis and a studded gate. According to Lord Ghast's intel, a barracks for soldiers was located inside the walled checkpoint. The walls had walkways atop them, and encircled the entire checkpoint, with covered, fortified bridges and towers flanking the gates on each side. Small ballistae were mounted along the walls at regular interviews as well. Once they took this checkpoint, and his other forces took theirs, they could bar themselves inside and use it against the very armies that sought to benefit from this defences.

Luckily for Per'eth, while the soldiers from the barracks were patrolling along the edges of the canal, and even along the bottom of the canal, they were more relaxed now that maintenance was ongoing than they would normally be. Less traffic meant fewer people, and it meant lighter duties—babysitting, as Per'eth heard one guard put it.

Per'eth could smell the alcohol on him as he passed. The soldier hadn't even noticed Per'eth pressed against the side of the slope. Luckier for Per'eth, the gates were currently wide open, the portcullis was up, the chains coiled safely in their gatehouses, and the ballistae unmanned and unloaded. It would make the attack easier.

The Qiri'aran captain spied a little longer. All and all, he counted forty soldiers, double the civilians. The civilians would be spared and locked in the barracks, the soldiers killed by his warriors. Their blood would be harvested, as was customary. Per'eth grimaced. This attack couldn't even be classified as a warm-up before a training exercise for the Qiri'ar.

His scouting complete, Per'eth crawled, stealthily and quietly, back down the slope of the canal, towards his soldiers waiting in the shadows below. He smiled like a child, the night before Idu'nayah. "No more than two score," he relayed in Qiri'ar to his group of sixty strong. "We can take them easily."

"Should we rush them?" asked Vol'ulm, his second in command.

"It doesn't matter at those numbers." El'ugae spat somewhere to her left. She tilted her head left and right and popped the bones in her neck, then hefted her twin axes to her shoulders.

"We must not abandon caution," warned the Blood Witch Vae'lah. "Just because we have the advantage in numbers, and our powers, does not mean we can afford to run in blindly, without thinking. Lord Ghast would not approve—Great Yishunar would not approve."

Per'eth was inclined to agree. "We must keep causalities low now and reserve our numbers to stave off potential attacks to reclaim the river later. Eventually, the Baroness will know she has lost the canal, and she will send her forces to retake it. That is when numbers will matter." Per'eth turned slightly, seemingly addressing nothing. "What does the guard schedule look like, Huol'daoh?"

A figure seemed to materialize out of the shadows. Their voice was barely a whisper and came from all directions, and no direction simultaneously. Huol'daoh was exemplary of a Qiri'aran Scout. "The soldiers will change shifts within the hour. Their guard is down, and so there is always a ten-to-fifteen-minute period during the shift change where there is no one on duty because of this oversight. They'll be in the barracks, exchanging flasks and banter as the two shifts meet. We can catch them unawares."

Per'eth grinned. "If we can trap them in the barracks, we can get inside, and take them down while they're still in there. If we're quick enough, the workers may not notice. They won't notice a few extra shouts and screams when the soldiers normally get rowdy. How many entrances into the barracks?"

"The main door," whispered the scout, "And a wall gate around the back. The gate is normally double-barred and locked from the inside. It's guarded by a portcullis as well. Meant for escape or for times of emergency. They are present in each of the compounds along the river."

"We'll break in through the wall gate and slaughter the soldiers in the barracks. With them down, we'll just need to take control of the compound and round up the civilians," Per'eth commanded. He turned back towards the Blood Witch Vae'lah. "Let the other groups know what the plan is. We'll strike simultaneously."

Vae'lah closed her eyes and stood there, silently communing with the other Blood Witches spread out across the length of the river. When she was finished, she turned back towards Per'eth. "Will you be needing access to the Uhun?"

Per'eth nodded. "To break through the door, it will be necessary, but close the lock after that has been accomplished."

Vae'lah nodded, and Per'eth turned back towards the outpost. "Let's get into position. Once they start the shift change, we'll strike. We cannot allow the enemy to see us coming. Surprise is imperative."

Per'eth led his attack force up the sloping edge of the canal, sneaking ever so quietly up to the edge of the wall. Once he had received the signal from Huol'daoh that the guards had begun the shift change and were congregating in the barracks, Per'eth started the attack.

Vae'lah communicated with the other strike forces that the attack was to begin immediately. When the message had been passed on, Vae'lah began to focus on her next task.

She pulled a small vial from a chain around her neck and uncorked it. The copper smell of blood filled the air as the seal was broken. Vae'lah dipped her index finger into the top of the vial and withdrew out a small smear of the crimson liquid. Then she carefully recapped the vial, and with the most delicate of movements, Vae'lah ran her bloody finger down a series of tattoos that wrapped around her left arm. The blood instantly changed from red to gold as it touched her golden tattoos, and Vae'lah began to chant her incantation just under her breath.

Her lips moved, and she swayed back and forth as she chanted, but few could hear the words she spoke. The detail and enunciation of the words were lost to the ambient noise of her jewellery clattering while she swayed and shook and rocked back and forth.

Vae'lah threw her head back, still chanting in a whisper, but mouthing each word perfectly, as she had learned since she was a child. The words were intentionally kept secret, for none but a fully trained and capable Blood Witch should have the knowledge and power to unlock the power within their tattoos—their Uhun.

The longer she chanted, the brighter her tattoos glowed, as did the blood she had streaked across them. They shone with a warm light like a smouldering fire.

All the while, Per'eth began to undergo the usual transformations. He doubled over to start and could feel his muscles bulge, nearly tearing, under the strain and effort. His veins grew engorged across his skin. His mouth hung open in a silent scream, and he could feel the blood and adrenaline rush through his body, making his head swim. Per'eth's mind slowly went blank, as every thought and memory was temporarily replaced with the single-minded objective: "Destroy the gate, kill the soldiers." The one thought Vae'lah had kept in his head, and it was now his sole purpose.

Per'eth felt himself recede to the place within his mind where he became a passenger within his own body. He could see his arms and legs move and could feel the world around him, but he had no recollection of performing these actions. He moved as if by instinct and inhibition, not by choice. Like a waking, lucid dream, he pressed on towards his goal.

Somewhere in the back of his head, all the mental noise that normally went through his head—stray thoughts, and the like—had been replaced by the low humming and beating of a drum. Rhythmic, disembodied singing and chanting echoed through his mind. It was not unlike the songs of prayer and thanks that the Qiri'ar offered up to Tenebrae...but there was something different about this. It made every hair on Per'eth's body stand on end, and chills ran down his spine.

The Blood Fugue had taken hold.

Like some mindless golem, Per'eth could do nothing but obey the commands placed upon him by the tattoos and the Blood Witch. Without a Blood Witch to control the opening of the proverbial flood gates, Blood Warriors would merely rampage until they died from their wounds, or their bodies finally broke down and collapsed from exhaustion or the excessive wear the tattoos and their power put on the body. Using this form shaved time off your life, after all. All power came at a cost. Overuse and abuse could kill just as easily as an enemy sword or arrow.

In this state, Per'eth cut a terrifying figure. No doubt, if anyone who was not Qiri'ar could see him now, he would be the most terrifying image they could have ever conjured.

Per'eth rushed to the door and felt his hands close around the cool steel of the portcullis that protected it. He could feel the rust against his pores, could feel it flaking off as he grabbed the trellis with his bare hands. This gate had barely been used, he noted, as he attempted to lift it. It had rusted down to its mechanisms.

There would be only one way forward now.

Per'eth began to tug at the small iron portcullis, grabbing the iron as hard as he could, and pulling as an ox would pull a wagon. He could hear the iron protest in response, the metal roared and squealed as it attempted to resist Per'eth's newfound strength and maintain its tenuous resting place within the stone wall.

But it wasn't enough. The gate shuddered, then started to move.

* * *

Yaegr sighed, took a swig from his wineskin, and sighed again. "I hate maintenance. Worst time of the year."

His comrade, Elius, who was about to head off for his shift, concurred. "Most boring job in Enayra. Sit around while these bricklayers and stone masons mess around in the muck and filth."

Vesthenna shrugged. "There's something to be said about the ease of it, though. We're being paid to stand around and watch these poor souls work. So long as nothing goes wrong, we can do whatever we want out here in the sticks. Not like guard duty at the Baroness's castle, or watching the docks, or even keeping the peace in Pelchar. We don't have to chase people. No one's shouting at us for something we can't control. We don't have to break up fights, or stand around in the hot sun or blistering cold. We just sit around an empty fortress and drink while someone else does all the hard work."

Yaegr took another swill of the warm wine. "I don't know about you, but I didn't join the Pelchar Brigade to sit on my ass all day and get paid for it."

"Yeah you did it so you could flirt with the baker's daughter and get paid for it," joked Elius.

"Well, I married her in the end, didn't I? Besides, it's not like you're one to talk. If I joined to flirt with his daughter, you joined for the charity of her father, the way you nearly ate him out of house and home every time we passed through."

"He kept offering free samples. Baker's dozen and all," Elius replied defensively.

Yaegr smirked. "That's not why they make the extra. Captain Toltun had to ban you from the bakery after a while because you were starting to outgrow your armour."

Elius opened his mouth to reply, his face indignant and offended, when something shook the entire building. A loud boom and the screech and whine of tearing metal echoed from the rear gatehouse.

"What in the Nine Hells?" Elius muttered.

The guards all looked at each other.

With another boom, the building shook, dust and bits of stone fell from the ceiling, the large bits clattering as they hit the ground.

The soldiers felt their pulses quicken. Each of them drew their weapons and approached the rear guardhouse. The sound continued at regular intervals, though it seemed to be getting louder and quicker each time.

"Someone's coming through the back door," Yaegr said in disbelief.

"How? The portcullis is down, the door is barred. They'd have to be half mad, or half-crazed to break through that," Elius replied.

More soldiers made their way towards the rear guardhouse.

Just as Yaegr reached the gatehouse door he heard the terrible sound of the chandelier come crashing down in the middle of the main room. Soldiers screamed, scrambling to get out of the way of the heavy, flaming wheel. The sound that accompanied the destruction of the chandelier was the loudest yet. The sound mixed the splintering of wood, the cracking of stone, and the sounds of debris clattering down a hillside.

Yaegr swore and reached for the door handle. Just then, the sound stopped. He cocked his head, waiting a moment before he turned the handle to look inside.

Silence.

His pulse pounded in his ears and his heart attempted to leap from his chest, up his throat and out his mouth—as did his dinner—but Yaegr steeled himself and opened the door.

The door had barely swung open on its hinges when a large battle axe came swinging down and cleaved through his head, spraying blood and brain matter across the door frame. It took a few seconds for Yaegr to drop, but drop he did, hitting the floor with a heavy, metallic thud, his body twitching as the enemy ripped his axe from where it had embedded itself in Yaegr's skull.

The guards were in shock. But before they could react, the room was filling with Qiri'aran attackers. Witches, warriors, all of them spilling forth from the rear guardhouse like blood from a gaping wound. Somehow they had ripped through the iron portcullis that protected the small single door, tearing the grating free from the stone, and then broke down the door in a single blow.

Elius and the others had barely snapped free from their stupor and disbelief when they noticed that they were already losing. Several guards were already dead, lying slaughtered in pools of their own blood, or lying as crumpled broken piles of twisted metal and flesh where some witches had simply compressed these once living humans in on themselves, armour and all, like some giant hand had reached out and crushed them.

Elius roared a battle cry, trying to rouse himself and his friends to action. The battle was not lost yet, they could still fight back. But a blade through his exposed throat ended his defiant roar, and Elius went down like the rest of his fellow soldiers.

All around him, he could see, as his life slowly faded and the world grew cold, his friends falling, one by one, hitting the floor. Some whole, some in pieces. Some exploded, some were ripped apart, with a horrible tearing sound, a wet splash and the clattering of metal. What had once been a barracks of eighty living soldiers was now a tomb for countless bloody smears and fleshy piles.

The fight was over before it had ever started.

Chapter XLV

The night passed slowly, even arduously for the defenders of Ethon. The Qiri'aran army was still chanting away, and while the singing from the defenders had died down somewhat as civilians went to sleep for the evening and continued about their days—even going instrumental at times—the bards continued to sing and play, organizing their musical retaliation in shifts now. The soldiers chimed in here and there, but the attitude had become much more subdued since the glorious act of defiance that had broken out earlier that day.

Leon and his advisors had come up with a more concrete plan for defending the city in that time. Music would not stay the siege forever. With their limited numbers, Leon could not afford to spread his lines too thin across the walls, and it was agreed that larger units would be formed and stationed evenly across the wall top, concentrating around gatehouses and towers. If need be, they could be spread out to fill gaps in the defences. If at any point a portion of the defences became hopelessly overrun, an immediate retreat would be made to the next section of walls. Keeping defensive lines moving and mobile played to the city's strength and helped them make up for the deficiency in numbers.

The dragons were to be kept at the palace for the time being but would remain in their armour, in case the attack started. There was simply not enough room for them down on the walls.

Djall had made it very clear that he was not pleased with this decision, considering he had been rushed into his armour, and would now be forced to keep it on.

Imuhlair and Iskren were to oversee goings on at the palace, since being on the front was not necessary, and outright dangerous for the two non-combatants.

Hana continued to remain at the palace at the behest of Aurichalcum, who, after the meeting with Leon, returned to keep an eye on the young Tsuru and declared he would not participate in the battle to come.

Only the commanders, King Leon, Menalaea, the Khaleeshir, Kyeit and Cecil remained on the front lines. They were spread out across various tents and encampments.

Leon had considered sending the Khaleeshir back to the castle to continue their training until the true siege began, but ultimately decided against it—their presence was good for morale and might help ease the troops as they anticipated the charge of their enemy.

Instead, the king had asked them for advice and input on the defence plans. At one point, he had even suggested asking the green dragons for help defending the city and dispersing the enemy army. Surely, with the dragons on their side, the siege could be ended without any loss of life on the part of the defenders. But the Khaleeshir had made the green dragon's position clear. They had been reluctant enough to allow the Khaleeshir safe passage through their territory, it was almost certain that any request for military assistance from the Green Dragon Clan would be met with immediate refusal, if not outright hostility.

"How can they hope to remain out of this fight? We cannot hope to defeat Tenebrae alone. We need the dragons by our side as much as the armies of Enayra. We cannot do this alone," Leon protested.

Right as he may have been, that did not change the reality of the situation. The green dragons would not be miraculously coming to their aid, nothing short of an attack on their sanctuary or the final battle would rouse them to fight.

Aside from providing input and advice to Leon, the Khaleeshir spent their time watching the enemy from the walls, taking turns standing guard and keeping an eye on the movements of the Qiri'aran host across the field.

Late in the evening of the fifth day after the siege started, it was Kanaahn and Shooter's turn on watch at the section where they were posted.

They leaned against the crenulations of the parapet, watching the enemy army chant away into the night. Even with their eyesight, in the darkness of the hour, and the moonless, overcast night, they could not make out much more than a dark mass of bodies, cloaked in shadow, and the dots of bright lights where fires and torches had been lit across the camp.

"I know you've only been studying the language for a month and a half, but can you understand any of what they're saying?" Kanaahn asked.

Shooter shook his head. "Kind of. My understanding isn't perfect and Qul'den's methods are...unorthodox. It sounds like a prayer or exaltation to a higher power. Probably Tenebrae, but that last part is speculation based on context. Can you understand anything Cecil says in Asardaean?"

"Only the swear words," Kanaahn joked. "Asardaean isn't easy, and she speaks so fast. There are so many rules and idiosyncrasies to the language—and I'm learning three versions of it at once. I almost wish I had chosen Espian to start with. I have an easier time with Draconic. Don't even get me started on declensions."

"What are declensions?"

"Declensions are what happens when you read words but make up the pronunciation like you've never spoken any language in your life."

Shooter laughed. "I think I made the better choice in language."

Kanaahn nodded. In truth, it wasn't what he *really* wanted to talk about. What he wanted to bring up was a topic he had trying to avoid for months after he had accidentally learned about it.

Arial had warned Kanaahn against saying anything, that Shooter hated that even Arial knew, and was incredibly embarrassed and ashamed about it. But Kanaahn couldn't keep going, pretending that he didn't know about what Shooter's parents had subjected him to.

At first, Kanaahn had agreed. Even knowing made him uncomfortable. But as time passed, Kanaahn felt it was important to be honest with Shooter—partly for the sake of their friendship, but also because the knowing was eating away at Kanaahn.

Now was the time Kanaahn had decided he was going to tell Shooter that he knew. And yet, when presented with the perfect moment—for the most part—Kanaahn couldn't bring himself to conjure the words and draw them from his throat. They caught in his tracheae, refusing to leave, like a rabbit caught in a snare. They struggled, as did Kanaahn, but the words would not come out.

Shooter, ever aware of the people around him, seemed to notice Kanaahn's mood grow tense and nervous. He said nothing but made a note of it.

"Hey, Shooter..." Kanaahn started, finally managing to wrestle the words free from the death grip in which his nerves had held them.

Shooter gave a non-verbal response.

"I..." Kanaahn started. He had not liberated as many words as he thought. He felt his stomach tighten. It felt as if he had just eaten fire.

Again, Shooter gave a non-verbal acknowledgement of Kanaahn's words.

"Look, there's something I want to talk to you about."

Shooter said nothing but could feel his pulse quicken. He wished Kanaahn would just rip off the poultice.

Kanaahn was determined to just say the words and get them out. "Shooter I know."

Shooter went from anxious to confused.

Kanaahn lowered his voice to a whisper that only the two could hear. "I know about your parents. What they did to you."

And with that, the anxiety returned. Shooter's emotions went between betrayed, hurt, defensive, anxious, scared, and even angry. How did Kanaahn know? Had he spied on something he shouldn't have? Did he always know and never say anything? Did Arial say something, or someone else perhaps?

"No one told me," Kanaahn said, pre-empting the confusion within Shooter. "I heard it, by accident. When you were recovering after Drakhart turned on us. It wasn't intentional—with our new abilities, I could hear a butterfly breathing from a mile off, and we hadn't yet learned how to cope with it."

That was an exaggeration, but it helped to ease Shooter's nerves.

Kanaahn continued. "You were talking with Arial, and you mentioned...what they did to you. Your reaction to the news of their deaths was confirmation that it was true—not that I doubted you...I...I'm sorry, Shooter. I'm sorry I never knew."

Shooter smirked, trying to hide his complex feelings—for the first time in his life, unsuccessfully. "What's there to apologize for? I never *wanted* you to know. But I can't change what's happened, and now you're aware."

"If I had known I'd have done something," Kanaahn replied.

Shooter shook his head. "And that's why I didn't want anyone knowing. I can fight my own fights. I don't need people stepping in and making a fuss over it. It would've been more of a hassle than it's worth. Besides, as bad as they were, I could handle it. I handled it this long, right?"

"That's not an excuse Shooter..."

Shooter quickly changed the subject. "Well, they're dead now. So, it doesn't matter. Hey, Kanaahn, since we're being honest, can I confide something in you?"

Kanaahn wasn't going to argue the subject change. "What is it?"

"...Something's not right here. I have a bad gut feeling that we're all being taken for a ride."

"How do you mean?"

"This whole siege. I can't explain it, but something isn't right. We're surrounded by superior numbers, and above that, they're Qiri'ar."

"And?"

"Kanaahn, we know what they're capable of. We've heard the stories growing up, and even now that we're Khaleeshir. We saw that woman at Xiar use her tattoos to lift Drakhart *and* Ölüm's body at the same time, and then teleport the entire army away. The tales I've heard from Qul'den only add credence to the power of their blood magic and tattoos."

"What are you trying to get at?"

Shooter inhaled sharply. "Kanaahn, come on. Don't act naïve. Why don't they just attack? They're just standing there, singing, trying to psyche us out. It feels like they're waiting for something, and whatever it is, they're hoping that it's too late by the time we figure it out. We should tell Leon."

"I understand your concern, Shooter. But I think that's just the nerves talking. It's natural to have doubts—"

"It's not doubts, Kanaahn!" Shooter pleaded. "I need you to listen to me. I know we're new to warfare, but one thing we learned in Xiar was that siege warfare is as much a game of time and resources as it was a game of skill and strategy. The supplies of both sides are limited, and so you need to ultimately look to exhaust your enemy's supplies faster than you exhaust your own. An attacker has two ways to do that. You either press the attack and get your enemy to spend defenders and resources, a little at a time trying to fight you off. Each time whittling away at them until nothing remains. Or, failing that, you play with your enemy's mind. Prolong the siege; stall them out of their walls, either by starvation or exhaustion. Bring enough supplies for a prolonged siege and seize your enemy's resources from outside their walls."

"You think they plan to starve us out?"

"I don't know, but I think they planned to play the long game from the beginning. They're looking to stall us for a reason, and whatever the reason, it's building to an endgame that's going to catch us unawares."

Kanaahn mulled over Shooter's words. "I admit that it's possible, but I don't know if we should be devolving into a panic over it."

Shooter pressed his argument further. "Kanaahn, the Qiri'ar have laid siege to the capital of Estion, but no one saw them coming? No one saw an army of thousands march across the border? Either someone let them in, and is colluding with them, or they magically sprang out of the ground, and I know which one I'm more likely to believe right now."

"Are you blaming Baron Felidrun?"

"I don't know if it's him, but it was definitely someone."

"So, what? We're just supposed to waltz up to Leon and tell him one of his own countrymen betrayed him and every other Estian?"

"It's not as far-fetched a reality as you might think. Drakhart betrayed us, and how long did we know him?"

Kanaahn didn't answer.

"Tell me you feel it too?"

Kanaahn still said nothing. He puzzled over what Shooter had been saying. There was some merit to his words. Maybe even some nuggets of truth, but regardless of what *might* be true, there was currently only one truth: this city was under siege, with a full population of innocent people inside its walls. Neither surrender nor escape was possible anymore. They would have to stand and fight.

"Please?" Shooter nearly begged.

"Shooter...I'm not saying I don't believe you. But I don't know what difference it would make. The city is under siege either way, and we're surrounded. We can't surrender, and we can't escape. We have no choice anymore but to wait out the siege and fight back when the time comes."

"Why can't we live to fight another day? What good is fighting if we're just going to die?" Shooter argued, his temper rising.

"You don't know that. That's the fear talking."

"Of course, it's fear talking! You'd have to be an idiot not to be afraid. The Qiri'ar are not to be taken lightly, even if the stories may be exaggerated. I think we're all being foolish about this because we're letting our pride get in the way. I think Xiar was a lucky win, and I don't think lightning's going to strike twice. And yeah, I'm afraid that we're outpowered, outmanned, and outclassed. I don't think we're strong enough to fight an army of blood-crazed Qiri'aran soldiers. I think if we keep going down this path, something bad is going to happen."

Kanaahn's temper flared up in return. "Then you go in that command tent and tell that to Leon, and his commanders. You tell the King of Estion and his people that the Khaleeshir are too afraid of losing to fight. That we're going to lose, all is hopeless before it begins, and we might as well give up now."

"Kanaahn that's not what I meant—" Shooter started.

"Shift's up boys!" A captain sauntered up to the two Khaleeshir.

It was Captain Onwyn, who headed the group of soldiers positioned on this portion of the wall. He made no indication that he had heard Shooter and Kanaahn's heated conversation.

Either way, it was now his turn to take the watch. "You can head back to the tent and get some shut-eye. I don't know how much longer we'll be able to get decent sleep. They're liable to attack any minute."

Shooter shot Kanaahn a look, which Kanaahn quietly returned.

Though they said nothing else to each other for the remainder of the night, the memory of their argument burned brightly in both of their minds, and hearts long after dawn had come, and though the worst of it was behind them, the feeling of enmity had yet to dissipate.

* * *

By morning the heavens had opened and begun drowning the defenders and attackers alike in an endless torrent of rainfall. Within hours the fields between the Qiri'aran army and the city had been turned into a half-flooded mire of muck and misery.

But still, the rain did not let up.

By the end of the tenth day of the siege, the water level of the lake had risen so high that it was beginning to swallow up the harbour in the city and was even threatening to breach the dikes that kept the waters normally at bay. If that happened, the fields surrounding the city would flood. It might help the city, but the lower quarters would flood as well, and while it would keep the attackers at bay, it would cause other problems.

According to Leon, the waters had not risen this high in nearly a generation, and it was very inopportune for it to do so now of all times. The morale of the defenders was already starting to wane. The cold, hard rain chilled them to the bone and made watching the walls an unpleasant and difficult job. The singing and playing bards were sent indoors, for they could not play and sing in this rain.

But the Qiri'ar did not stop, and despite the loud rain, they could be faintly heard still chanting from across the fields.

Moreover, it had been two weeks since the siege had started, and there was no sign of the barons, nor of the Baroness Pelchar, who was supposed to be coming up the river to alleviate the city with her navy. She should have arrived by now, and it was incredibly distressing that she had not even sent word of her arrival.

Imuhlair watched from a window at the palace as rain obscured the world outside as far as the eye could see. He could not see the attackers or even the city below. Heavy droplets splattered against the stones of Filiddyn Castle with such force they seemed to shake the castle down to its very core.

The old major-domo's face was as ever taught and grim, his lips pursed in a perpetual frown. He folded his hands behind his back, grasping a ring of keys that clattered while he walked, and stalked through the halls like some tall and grandiose stork, ensuring that everything still ran as normal.

He would not have a single toe out of line. Just because the city was under siege did not mean that the day-to-day operations needed to crumble. Once the barons arrived with their armies, and the siege was lifted, life would return to normal, and Imuhlair would not have it said that he allowed standards to slip.

After doing his rounds for the morning, Imuhlair returned to the south-eastern tower, where the offices of state were. Iskren's, the King's, and each of the offices of the ministers, and their aides, were all located on various floors of this tower. In fact, Imuhlair's own study was just down the hall. But it was not his study that Imuhlair was returning to. As he drew the keyring closer to his face, and sifted through the many keys, his long, narrow, skeleton-like fingers grasped the key that would unlock the door to his true destination: Iskren's study.

Imuhlair checked the hallway, making sure no one would see him. When he was sufficiently pleased that the coast was clear, he gently slid the key into the lock, turned it, and slipped into a crack in the door like a formless wraith. He closed the door behind him ever so quietly and proceeded to lock the door from the inside.

He needed to be quick. Time was of the essence. The longer he took to find what he was looking for, the greater the chance that Iskren would return from his current duties and discover Imuhlair in a place he was not meant to be, and worst of all, uninvited. The two major-domos had their own separate offices for a reason, and both doors were kept locked when they were not in. Imuhlair could not feign ignorance if he was discovered.

The old Major-domo immediately focused on the desk. Where else would someone keep their most valuable and closely guarded secrets, after all?

The previous search of Iskren's quarters had proved fruitless. Imuhlair could understand, Iskren could not risk a chambermaid happening upon anything secret while cleaning. But Iskren's study was the one place where he and he alone had the right to enter. Even King Leon did not enter his major-domos' studies uninvited.

Imuhlair rifled through the many drawers of the desk, sifting between papers and through notebooks. He was careful to return items as they had been after moving them, so as not to arouse suspicion in his junior.

He was frustrated that after minutes of searching, what he was looking for had still eluded him.

Then, while shuffling through the lowest, deepest drawer on the bottom left side of the heavy desk, Imuhlair noticed something strange. The drawer sat recessed within the desk, enclosed on all sides, but as Imuhlair pulled the drawer completely forward, it seemed to stop short of how long it had appeared. Imuhlair closed the drawer, rolling it back in slowly until he felt it hit the front side of the desk, and was resting comfortably within its framing.

There was a false back to the drawer.

A smile crept across Imuhlair's face as he slowly puzzled out the mechanism that kept the false back locked. He adjusted the position of the drawer very slowly, as one would a safe dial. Gently, he pushed it back and forth several times until he finally heard three concurrent, distinct clicks. On the third click, the false back loosened and fell forward into the drawer.

Imuhlair's fingers snaked behind the false back and pulled it forward. Inside this secret compartment, Imuhlair found exactly what he was looking for. The small metal stamp that was the royal seal, a folded and sealed letter, and several sheets of paper that had been emblazoned with the gilded seal of the monarch.

Imuhlair was satisfied with the results of his search. He had found exactly what he was looking for. This would be exactly what he needed to remove Iskren. Having found what he came for, Imuhlair wasted not a second more. He closed the false back of the desk drawer and put everything in the drawer as he had found it, then closed the drawer again.

He gave the room a final visual sweep, his mouth curling into a triumphant smile. He had won. With that, Imuhlair slipped the sheets of paper and the stamp into his robes, securing them in a small pocket he had sewn into his lapel and departed the room as quickly and quietly as he had entered it.

Imuhlair kept his face as still as stone; unmoving and unemotional. He did not let his pleasure show on the outside. With these slips of paper, the letter, and the royal seal, Imuhlair would finally be vindicated. For with a few things, he would regain his position of most trusted advisor. Iskren was finished, and no one would ever be the wiser that he had been his own undoing. After all, no one had witnessed Imuhlair's deceitful actions that day. No one would be privy to his burglary of Iskren's study.

None of course, except for Iskren himself, who had been hiding behind the curtain the entire time, watching as Imuhlair perused through his desk. Looking like a man at the market, sampling the latest wares from Espias.

Having heard the commotion at the door as Imuhlair fiddled with the keys, Iskren had doused the candle he was working by and slipped behind a heavy curtain by the window. He remained completely still and silent. His deception had worked, and Imuhlair was none the wiser of his failure.

But one thing was certain to Iskren, King Leon would need to be informed. Now he had the evidence he needed.

Chapter XLVI

It was the dawn of the fifteenth day—the end of the third week—when the rain finally subsided. It was far from bright and sunny, and the weather remained grey and miserable, with a cold wind blowing in off the lake. Anything was better than the bone-chilling torrential downpour that had preceded the lull in the weather.

Everyone's nerves were frayed and on edge. The chanting of the Qiri'ar hadn't stopped, and now it was beginning to affect everyone's sleep. Soldiers lay awake at night, fearing that at any moment, a wave of Qiri'aran attackers would pour over the parapet and slaughter them all in their sleep.

The only thing keeping the defenders calm was the fact that the fields between the attackers and the walls were a swampy, muddy mess with deep and deadly pools of water. Ditches and dips in the landscape suddenly became muddy ponds. It was the kind of mud that could swallow up a heavy cart and wagon, never to be seen again.

The lower levels of the city, especially those nearest to the harbour, were mostly submerged in half a metre of cold water. Despite this, the rain *had* helped the city. It would keep the attackers at bay, at least that was the hope, and would help stave off the worst until the barons arrived.

Word of their whereabouts finally came around noon on the sixteenth day, when a messenger bird arrived from Lord Gruffydd, notifying Leon that he had gathered his group of eastern barons and their armies, and together they were marching on the capital. They were not far from the capital and were about a day's march from the outskirts of the city.

The plan was to attack the Qiri'ar from behind using the woods. The enemy army had seized and closed all roads leading to the city, so this was the only avenue available for attack. The forces in the city were to remain on alert but were not to open the gates and engage the enemy while Lord Gruffydd's forces engaged the Qiri'ar, in case the Qiri'ar were trying to lure the defenders into a trap.

Leon, only an amateur at warfare, decided that seemed the sensible option. If the Qiri'ar suddenly turned towards the city and turned the siege into an assault, it would not do to have his entire army outside of the safety of the walls. Leon had no doubt the Qiri'ar could manoeuvre their forces in such a way that they could assault the city and hold off the barons simultaneously, if even for a time.

Word of Baron Felidrun's arrival with the Cabal faction of barons had spread across the ranks like wildfire, and some morale had been restored by the news. Murmurs went around that the siege would soon be broken, and the relief of the defenders was palpable.

Some wondered if perhaps this would allow the king and the baron to reconcile their differences and begin working together more amicably. Captains didn't even bother trying to silence the rumours, for they too hoped that this meant a wonderful new future for Estion and her people. If the barons and the king could be reconciled, it would be better for everyone.

Iskren had barged into the tent shortly after Leon had received the missive. "Leon, we need to talk."

Leon looked up from his desk, clearly waiting for Iskren to speak.

"Privately," Iskren clarified.

Leon frowned but looked to his advisors and attendants. Without a word, they shuffled from the command tent. "What is it, Iskren?"

Iskren's concern was plain on his face. "Leon…you asked me to gather proof."

Leon massaged the bridge of his nose. He grew ever weary of this. "This again?"

"You told me to gather proof," Iskren insisted. "I have done so."

Leon sighed. "Very well, where is the proof?" He held out his hand, expecting Iskren to have it ready.

Iskren did not hand Leon anything, however, and instead, smiled. "Summon Imuhlair, and ask him to turn out his pockets, including the one hidden in his lapel."

Leon gave a stern look. "Iskren I don't have time for games."

"Trust me. Please? We are friends, are we not? Have I ever lied to you, or led you astray?"

Leon paused for a moment, then assented. "If this goes nowhere, you *will* answer for it. Do you understand?"

"Perfectly."

Leon poked his head out of the tent and told someone to summon Imuhlair from the palace.

The wait was only a half hour, but it felt like days. Leon sat, staring at Iskren with a combination of disbelief and frustration.

Iskren stood, a smug look etched into his face like a knight errant that had just won the biggest tournament in the land.

Eventually, the scowling Major-domo soon arrived, as had a small crowd of commanders, captains and soldiers, who milled about in front of the tent, pretending not to be spying on the proceedings.

Even Shooter, who had heard whispers about Iskren's accusations from further down the line, had crept towards the tent to spy on what was happening.

Leon had his back to Imuhlair when the man entered the tent. But his voice sounded serious, even angry. "Imuhlair. Turn out your pockets."

Imuhlair kept his cool and emptied the contents of his pockets onto a makeshift table in the corner. There was nothing but a kerchief.

Imuhlair stifled a smug smile meant for Iskren.

Leon glanced at Iskren, who urged Leon to proceed. "Now the pocket in your lapel."

Imuhlair's mask broke, and for the first time in a long time, Imuhlair's face finally showed his inner emotions. Shock, betrayal, hurt, but most of all, surprise, and embarrassment. "Your Majesty?"

"Please, just do as I ask."

Imuhlair slowly reached into his secret pocket. "But if I may ask what this is about?"

"Some serious allegations have been levelled against you, and I've been told that the proof could be found in your lapel pocket," Leon explained. "It is my prerogative to investigate."

Imuhlair's face paled, but he did as he was bid. Slowly, with shaking hands, he produced a few sheets of Leon's royal stationary, the iron stamp bearing the royal seal, and the letter—still unopened—that had been found in Iskren's desk.

Leon was not pleased. He grabbed the papers from Imuhlair's hands. Imuhlair had never seen the king upset, but the stress of all the recent circumstances combined had pushed Leon to the edge. "Why do you have this?"

"Your Majesty, I found them in Iskren's desk—"

"What were you doing in Iskren's desk?!" demanded Leon, his voice and temper rising.

Imuhlair slowly regained his composure. "What were *these* doing in Iskren's desk? That was my question. I don't trust him, Your Majesty. He oversaw sending word to all the barons so they could call the banners to war, but only those who are against you seem to have answered the call. Something didn't seem right, so I decided to investigate a few weeks back, and discovered those in Iskren's desk."

Only the reigning monarch could possess the seal or stationary. To break that law was treason. Stationary could be granted to diplomats and advisors for the sake of diplomatic and political missives, but anyone caught with stationary in their possession that had not been authorized by the monarch was guilty of treason.

"And what of the letter?"

"I don't know its contents, Your Majesty. I wanted to tell you before opening it, but I highly suspect it's the letter that was meant to go to the Baroness Pelchar. I doubt it was ever sent."

Leon's temper cooled slightly. "If you found this in his desk, as you say—for you have no proof that this is true—why did you not bring it to my attention sooner?"

"I felt I would need more proof if I was to convince you of Iskren's misdeeds, Your Majesty. I am aware he is your friend, and you feel he has served your interests well, but I do not trust him. I believe him to be a traitor."

"How rich. The traitor is caught, and he tries to turn the tables back on his accuser—"

Leon did not need to speak to silence Iskren. His glare was enough to immediately force the young Major-domo to shut his mouth. Leon's eyes were daggers, his gaze was poison. The king wheeled back on Imuhlair and stared hard at him with an exacting gaze. "These are serious accusations, Imuhlair."

Imuhlair did not relent. "As are the ones levelled against me, Your Majesty."

Determined to get to the bottom of this mystery, Leon turned to Iskren. "Iskren, why do you have this?"

"I admit, I stole the royal stationery. But I did so only to bait Imuhlair into acting. I knew he was duplicitous, but I needed proof."

"Your intentions may have been noble, if obsessive, but your theft of the royal stationery and the royal seal still amounts to a serious crime. I could try you for treason, especially with your admission of guilt."

Iskren knelt and bowed his head. "I understand the seriousness of my crimes, and I accept any punishment that may come. But I will say before a court, and before you here, that I am only guilty of loyalty: to my country, to my king, and to my friend."

Imuhlair scowled. "You will not weasel your way out of this!"

"You've always been jealous of me Imuhlair! You thought that I was coming for your job, and you never liked that Leon wanted to replace you. But I never thought you'd sink so far as treason to be rid of me," Iskren spat.

"What treason have I committed? I did not steal the stationary."

"No, but you have betrayed your king all the same." Iskren stood, his face twisting into a wicked smile.

Imuhlair cocked his head in confusion.

"What are you talking about, Iskren?" Leon was just as confused.

"The contents of the letter," Iskren answered. "Imuhlair assumed the worst of me. He believed that the letter was the one meant for the baroness. That perhaps, I had not sent it in a deliberate attempt to sabotage the defence of the city. I assure you I have done nothing of the sort. The message was sent, though I cannot explain why no reply was ever returned. Even the bird did not return. I've sent two follow-up letters, and still, no response has come, nor bird returned. Perhaps Imuhlair knows something about that."

Imuhlair stood there, mouth flapping open and closed like a dying fish. "I-I would never! How could I possibly? How could...what would make you thin—"

Iskren's smile grew. "What I do know, is that if our dear Senior Major-domo here had taken the time to actually open and read the letter, as perhaps he should have, he would have realized what it was, and would have done what should have been done in the first place: burn it."

"What do you mean, Iskren?" Leon asked.

Imuhlair was stunned into silence.

"Open the letter," Iskren urged.

Leon did ask Iskren asked. He broke the wax seal on the letter and unfolded it. He read through the contents and his eyes widened as he saw what was written on the letter. Leon's face went from shock to anger, and he wheeled on Imuhlair with a speed and ferocity the two major-domos did not know was possible from Leon.

"Traitor!" Leon spat.

"I beg your pardon, Your Majesty?"

"You are a traitor. This letter is proof of your treason."

Leon thrust the letter into Imuhlair's chest. The bird-like man staggered at the force.

He grabbed the letter and began to read it himself, and his confusion turned to surprise.

Imuhlair glowered at Iskren. "Where did you get this?" His voice was a low growl.

"It was delivered to me by mistake, shortly after I took my role as Junior Major-domo. It was addressed only to 'The Major-domo' and was brought to me when you were unavailable. I read the contents and have kept it close by ever since, in case I ever required it. It was the reason I never trusted you."

Leon grabbed Imuhlair by the front of his robes. "How long have you been spying on me for my father?"

"Your Majesty. I...this was over a year ago. I haven't—"

"How long?!" Leon demanded. He shook Imuhlair.

Imuhlair grew quiet. He had been defeated. He had played a dangerous game and lost. Realizing it was over, he came clean. "Your father, the former king, asked that I keep an eye on you, and report on your actions as king. He was worried you might act contrary to his advice and wishes. He was concerned—"

"—That I would bring the Crown and kingdom to ruin in six months. Yes, he always made sure I knew how he felt—in those exact words, mind you! So, you spied on me, and advised me how my father asked you to, is that correct? You acted against my wishes at times because they went against the wishes of my father."

"I only acted in the best interest of this kingdom and the Crown. I sought what was best for everyone. I am loyal to you; I would not call my actions treasonous."

Leon released Imuhlair with as much force as he had grabbed the old man. "You were loyal to my father. I always knew you were his man, but I never thought you'd act against me like this."

"But Your Majesty. Your father only—"

"Who is King of Estion, my father or me?" Leon boomed.

At this moment, his calm and casual demeanour was gone, and once more, dressed in full armour, sword at his hip, and the crowned helm atop his head, he became the image of a great and mighty king. He was almost the spitting image of his tyrannical forebearers, mighty and bearing terrible wrath.

"WHO. IS. KING?" Leon bellowed again when no answer came.

Imuhlair's response was meek, barely a whisper. "You are, Majesty."

Leon stepped menacingly towards Imuhlair. "On whose head does the crown sit?"

"Yours, Majesty."

Again, Leon stepped closer to the old man, forcing him to step back. "Who sits upon the throne, viper?"

Imuhlair was afraid now, and his responses grew quieter. "You do, Majesty."

Leon was now in Imuhlair's face, inches from his hooked nose. "Whose face is on the coinage, worm?"

"Your face, Highness."

"In whose name are the parliaments formed?"

Imuhlair bowed his head in disgrace, he was too ashamed to respond.

"Was it you who intercepted the missives to the Baroness Pelchar as well? Perhaps seeking to undermine Iskren? I always knew you were jealous of him, but I did not think you'd go as far as to sabotage this kingdom to get back at him."

"Your Majesty I would never do that!" Imuhlair pleaded.

"How can I trust you? You've lied to me since I took the throne. You broke into Iskren's office, you stole from him. You accused him of the very treason you are guilty of. Instead of bringing to me any proof of his guilt, you unknowingly brought me proof of yours."

Imuhlair was silent. He stood there, head bent, like a scolded child.

Iskren swore he saw tears in the old man's eyes. It was glorious.

"Have you nothing to say, you wicked man? Does the snake no longer have the wherewithal to his sweet words in my ear? Perhaps the worm wishes to crawl back into the muck and filth where it belongs?"

Imuhlair found his voice. "Majesty, please understand. Your father—"

Leon snapped. But instead of rage and terror and yelling, his voice was icy cold. His words were the dead mid-winter, but they cut like a knife to the bone. "Speak no more of my father, wretch. And no more shall you call me Majesty or Highness. I am no longer your king; now I am become your judge, your jury, and once this siege is over, your executioner. You will be tried and executed for treason; I swear it. And I shall deal with my father later."

Leon called for the Bluehelms, who arrived immediately. "Take this man away. He is to be stripped of all titles and positions, and is to be jailed, awaiting trial for treason."

The Bluehelms saluted and wasted no time in slapping manacles on Imuhlair before dragging him away to be imprisoned.

The major-domo did not even attempt to beg for mercy, he simply cooperated and went along quietly.

Leon remained with his back to Imuhlair and Iskren. He could not even look at the traitorous major-domo.

Iskren waited until the Bluehelms were gone to break the silence. "I'm sorry for the deceit, but I'm glad we could weed out the traitor in our midst."

Leon still had not turned to face Iskren.

"Leon?" Iskren asked. He approached his friend but was stopped when Leon wheeled around, still trembling with anger.

"Have we?" Leon asked.

"Pardon?"

"Have we actually removed the traitor in our midst?"

Iskren was speechless.

"You knew what Imuhlair was doing this whole time, but you insisted on waiting to tell me. You claimed you had no evidence, but if you had brought that note to me before I would have listened sooner. You lied to me, Iskren. And there is still the matter of your theft of royal stationary and seal. You didn't need to steal it; the note would have sufficed."

"I...I wanted to be certain. I couldn't risk being wrong. It would only harm my reputation at court," Iskren argued.

"Because you have done me a service, and because of our past friendship, I will not charge you with treason for the theft of my possessions, but you still lied to me. Begone from my sight."

"...Am I being dismissed?"

"You are being dismissed from my presence. Until such a time I can look upon you once more without feeling pain in my heart." Tears welled in Leon's eyes. The betrayal of Imuhlair had hurt him more than he had expected. Though the two did not always see eye to eye, Leon had at least thought Imuhlair an honourable and loyal man. But the lies and secrecy perpetrated by Iskren, a friend of his since youth and a close confidant, had cut the already wounded Leon even deeper.

Iskren opened his mouth as if to say something, but no words came out. He bowed his head and left the tent without another word, ignoring the obvious crowd of onlookers that had gathered outside the tent.

$$* \quad * \quad *$$

Shooter's assessment of the situation had been grim.

He had spent much of the affair hiding behind a crate around the rear of the command tent, blending in with the shadows—just as Menalaea had taught him. Shooter would need to thank her for her tutelage later; he hadn't realized how useful it could be outside of spycraft.

But Shooter's mind was now in overdrive. He was convinced, now more than ever, that something was wrong, and nothing made sense. Despite Shooter's doubts and his doubts about his doubts, Shooter couldn't let go of the fact that something was bothering him about what Iskren did. Anyone else might have written off the entire interaction between the major-domos and the king as perfectly normal. A tale of political intrigue, an old and bitter major-domo desperately trying to cling to his power and influence after a change of monarchs by seeking to undo his younger replacement and rival.

But something about that seemed far too perfect for Shooter to pass over.

Shooter's instincts, learned from a lifetime of growing up in what many called the armpit of the world, had been honed, sharpened and combined with his many teachings from Menalaea.

Kula had taught Shooter that if something seemed too good to be true, it certainly was. Menalaea had taught him to examine everyone's motives in another light. No one in life acted without just a little self-interest. While their greater intent may be to help others, and while the outcome of their actions may do just that, nothing was ever done wholly for free and without thought of personal gain of some kind.

Iskren had definitive proof of Imuhlair's betrayal but had insisted on breaking the law and committing treason to further prove his point—a point that would not have needed further proving if he had simply shown Leon the letter sooner.

Shooter ran through the questions he felt burned brightest in his mind. Why did Iskren wait so long, and why did he bait Imuhlair into stealing the items from his desk? What was the purpose of delaying the downfall of a traitor, unless Iskren was covering for something or someone? Or perhaps the goal was blackmail, and Imuhlair was looking to free himself from the shackles Iskren had placed upon him. How did Iskren even know Imuhlair would try to steal these items from him? Moreover, why did Iskren wait so long for Imuhlair to become his own undoing? Why did he not report the theft when it happened?

On that same point, why did Imuhlair wait, once he had definitive proof that Iskren had committed treason, and why did Imuhlair not read the note sooner? Was the old man so certain of Iskren's guilt that he hadn't bothered to check the letter?

Furthermore, why had Iskren gone so far as to reseal the letter after reading it? What purpose did that serve?

In the end, Shooter could do nothing but accept that, for now at least, he would be left with more questions than answers. Only time would provide more information, and Shooter would keep an eye out for it.

"Did you hear about Imuhlair?" Kanaahn asked as Shooter slipped back into the small tent they shared with four other soldiers.

"No, what happened?" Shooter lied.

"Imuhlair has been accused of treason against the Crown. He's been stripped of his titles and powers and has been jailed. They'll put him on trial once the siege is over."

Shooter pretended to be shocked. "How did this happen?"

"Iskren seems to have been the one to bring this all to light. But in doing so, he broke a few laws himself and earned the ire of Leon. It's been said he'll be tried too, but other soldiers seem to think Leon will spare his friend. Either way, Leon is not happy with either of his major-domos right now."

Shooter shrugged and feigned irreverence. "I can't say I'm surprised. Never liked the old man—reminded me too much of a bird. He was always stalking about, scowling at everything that breathed. How did we not see this coming, really?"

Kanaahn rolled his eyes.

The two had been at odds not too long ago. He and Kanaahn had not fully made up, but they were at least talking again. There was an unspoken agreement between them—Shooter wouldn't talk about his doubts, and Kanaahn would apologize and admit he was wrong when Shooter turned out to be right. In the meantime, the siege and morale of their fellow soldiers were more important than who was right or wrong.

The same unspoken agreement as always.

What Shooter hadn't admitted to Kanaahn was that Shooter had come to realize that Kanaahn *had* been right—partly. If Shooter made his doubts public, it would only serve to further demoralize the already flagging army. After today, Shooter knew a few too many incidents like what had happened in the command tent and this army would crumble before the assault even started.

But Shooter couldn't—nor wouldn't—relinquish his doubts, and so he remained vigilant, ever watchful for signs of trickery and deceit, which only made him double his examination of the situation between Iskren and Imuhlair.

It seemed too well timed, too well planned. What were the chances it would unfold like this, hours before the barons were set to arrive? The same barons who had openly opposed the current king.

There was still the matter of the Lady vohn Veishaupt's silence, and whether a message was ever actually sent or received.

There were simply too many coincidences, and Shooter did not believe in coincidence.

* * *

Arial, who was positioned on the western walls of the city with Arkas, had heard about the ordeal between Iskren and Imuhlair within an hour of the event happening. Immediately upon hearing the news, she abandoned her duties atop the wall and rushed off to see if Leon was all right. Arial had immediately been worried for Leon's state. He had been betrayed by both of his trusted advisors—one a life-long friend—and was no doubt in great turmoil. The Khaleeshir and her teacher had grown close throughout her training, and while Arial would not presume to call herself as close to Leon as Iskren might have, she still cared enough for him to make sure he was okay.

Rather than protest, Arkas had offered to cover for Arial—not that he'd need to do much. The soldiers the two served with were rather deferential to the two teens on the virtue of their status as Dragonkin. If Arial had gone missing—and to see the king no less—they weren't likely to complain too much. At most, the two Khaleeshir would need to regale them with more stories in repayment for turning a blind eye. So long as the captain or commanding officers didn't find out, they'd be fine.

She had arrived at Leon's tent as quickly as she could. Arial did not even bother to wait and see if Leon was willing to accept guests. She approached the tent, pushed past the bewildered guards—who tried and failed to stop her—and entered the tent.

Arial found Leon sitting in an uncomfortable-looking armchair, his head resting on his left hand, staring off pensively into space.

"Leon?"

Leon turned to look at her. He did not respond.

"I heard what happened."

Leon closed his eyes. "Gossip gets around fast it seems. I have been a fool. I deserve this."

Arial frowned. "No, you don't. You were not wrong to trust the two people you were supposed to trust more than anyone."

Leon shook his head. "I could have accepted if Imuhlair was acting against me because of personal dislike. I could have accepted if he was colluding with Baron Felidrun or even the Qiri'ar outside our walls. But the fact that he was working against me with my own father hurts the most."

"You and your father don't have the greatest relationship, I gather?"

"Not in the slightest. We've always disagreed—about everything. He believes I should have spent more time devoting myself to my military studies. That I should have been a warrior king like our ancestors like he was at my age. I should have been currying favour with the nobility and the armies they control in his opinion. But I've never liked that. I never liked how he let the nobles run roughshod over the people. It was only sparking rebellion amongst the already critical republican and partisan groups. A king is here for all his people, not the benefit of the powerful. I've done everything I could to curtail the power of the nobility and increase the power of the people. I sought to find a compromise between the two groups by tipping the scales back towards the other side again. But my father has tried to stop me at every turn, and it seems Imuhlair was helping him do it. I can't believe I've been so foolish."

Arial knelt beside Leon. "You're not foolish. You can't be so hard on yourself. This isn't the teacher I know. You put your faith in someone, and they took advantage of it, but you can't entirely blame yourself. What else were you supposed to do, mistrust your major-domo?"

Leon sighed. "And what of Iskren? I trusted him, and he too betrayed my trust and broke the law. For what?"

"Did you ever give him any indication you might not fully believe he was telling the truth about Imuhlair?"

Leon paused. "Well—"

"This is a yes or no question."

"I didn't believe him when he first brought these accusations to my attention. But he also provided no proof and did not indicate that he had any."

"Would you have believed him if he had shown you the letter at the time?"

Leon remained silent. He thought for a moment, but in his heart, he knew the answer.

"I'm going to take that as a no," Arial replied. She gave a small smile. "Iskren broke the law, and perhaps you two have some things to talk about. But he's your friend, and he did what he did for the greater good. In the end, he exposed a traitor in your midst, and while he may have gone about it in the wrong way, the intention was there to help. He only ever had your best interests at heart."

The king sighed. He leaned forward, his face in his hands. "I think the worst part was how upset I got. I said horrible, terrible, vile things to Imuhlair. He's a traitor, but he's still a human. I was just so incensed at the time—but I acted in anger, and that's not right. It's no way for a king to act.

"Perhaps not. But you can't be expected to be perfect all the time."

"Yes I can, I am king after all."

"You were a human before you were king." Arial grabbed Leon's hands and pulled them away from his face. "And being human is far more complicated than being king. But you can't change the past; only seek to repair the damage. Apologize to Imuhlair before his trial, and to Iskren as well."

Leon couldn't help but smile. "I might disagree with your point about the difficulties of kingship," He stood up and began to pace back and forth around the tent. "But perhaps you have a point. I still feel a damn fool, though."

"We all need to act foolish sometimes, so we can remember what's important to us."

Leon crinkled his eyebrows. "That makes no sense."

Arial's face went red with embarrassment. "I was trying to be clever...but it seems I'm not at my mother's level just yet."

"The attempt was appreciated. Thank you for coming to check on me, Arial."

Arial shrugged and turned away. "I was worried. You've become a good friend in the time we've known each other—and you literally saved my life a few weeks ago. I was just returning the favour."

Leon chuckled. "I would invite you to stay and have some lunch, but I have a meeting with the commanders soon about the impending arrival of the barons—and I believe Arkas can only cover for you for so long before people start asking questions. I have a feeling you did not get permission to be here."

"I was off duty?" Arial lied.

"Uh-huh." Leon pretended to believe her. "Well, perhaps you should return before your watch duty starts, then. I wouldn't want you to get in trouble on my account."

"I'm a Khaleeshir; technically a foreign volunteer. What are they going to do, court martial me? Put me to death? Put me in the stocks?"

Leon laughed. "Perhaps you'll be dragged before the king in chains for your treasonous abandonment of the front."

They shared one last laugh before Arial turned to depart.

She stopped, just on the other side of the tent flap, and gave one final look back before rushing back off to her post on the western walls.

Chapter XLVII

Lord Gruffydd's army marched at a leisurely pace. He had already mustered the soldiers, called the banners, and stockpiled the supplies long before the king had called for his aide—but the king didn't need to know that. Now he just needed to march from the encampment outside of Felidrun to meet the attacking Qiri'aran army at Ethon.

By now, Lord Gruffydd had reached his destination. Part of him had hoped that the march would have taken longer and allowed the defenders of the city to wallow in their helplessness a little longer—especially the boy king.

Nothing could be changed now, however. If he delayed his arrival for the sake of his ego would only risk drawing the ire of Baron Felidrun's true ally. He had sent word to them, using one of his messengers, to let the Qiri'ar know they would be arriving shortly. The plan was to form battle lines behind the Qiri'ar and pretend to attack them from the rear. In full view of the city, the baron's forces would engage with the foe. At the last second, however, both the Qiri'ar and the baron's army would turn the tables on Ethon and turn to attack the capital in unison.

Drakhart had assured Baron Felidrun that the Qiri'ar were whittling away at the defenders' morale as planned. They were flagging and would be ripe for the slaughter when the assault began.

To the king's credit, he had organized an attempt to boost morale and fight back against the demoralizing chants of the Qiri'ar, but the chilling rain and the tireless music of the Qiri'ar had quickly whittled that away again.

The Qiri'ar had also seized the river-turned-canal that was the Acturn. With the canal already drained of water, and now under the control of the attackers, the city was completely isolated, and unaware that that was the case. There would be no Baroness Pelchar come to save the boy king. Not that she had even received the call to arms from the king in the first place. Drakhart's tampering had blocked those messages from leaving the palace. Not the baroness, nor any of her Reformists, would be able to save the city now.

Part of Lord Gruffydd still felt guilty, not for his betrayal of his countrymen or king— not really—but because his betrayal meant betraying his old friend, Khomandar. The two had been friends since their youth, and when Lord Gruffydd had heard whispers of rebellion by the nobility against Khomandar's father, he went immediately to the young Crown Prince to explain the situation.

To Gruffydd's surprise, Khomandar did not rally the armies of his father against the nobility, but instead joined the nobility against his corrupt and power-hungry father and brought an end to the rule of absolute monarchy in Estion.

The Princeling's Revolt put a powerful group of nobles in charge of the affairs of state with the express blessing of their new monarch. The oligarchical structure of the new government kept the nobles happy, and the king on the throne, with some semblance of power. It wasn't a perfect relationship, but it worked, and it kept the wheels of government turning for a long time and it kept the kingdom stable.

But King Anducaerleonis had ruined it. His attempts to diminish the powers of the nobility and put those same powers in the hands of the masses did not sit well with most of the nobility, Lord Gruffydd included.

The people could not be trusted with the governance of the nation; they were prone to panic, uneducated, and quick to act in their own self-interest. Sure, Lord Gruffydd and the nobility acted in *their* self-interest at times too, but that was their due for the stress and hard work that was ruling. Nine people acting in self-interest occasionally was much better than hundreds of uncouth, uneducated commoners acting selfishly.

There was only so much wealth to go around, and as far as Lord Gruffydd was concerned, the nobility had earned it. The people had not.

"Your Lordship, a report from the outrunners." Lord Gruffydd's lieutenant had interrupted his thoughts, breaking the monotony of the march with his words.

The Baron waved his hand and indicated that the man should continue the report.

"The rains have turned the fields around the city to mud. They've yet to dry. We'll be unable to deploy the siege towers. It will also mean approaching the walls will be all the harder, and the men are likely to get stuck in the mud."

Lord Gruffydd had to admit, part of him was disappointed. Much time and care had been put into ensuring the efficiency and durability of the siege towers. But they could always be saved for later. But more concerning was the effect the mud would have on the mobility of the soldiers.

He did not betray his worries and instead replied in a mocking tone. "Then I suppose the Qiri'ar will have to earn their reputation. A little mud should not be much trouble for them."

The captains that travelled in the baron's company laughed as if on cue.

"Let them pave the way for us," one captain suggested. "We'll follow along in their footsteps. If they're so unstoppable, it shouldn't be a problem."

"We're just normal men!" jeered another captain. "We can't be expected to trudge through the muck like we're frolicking in a field."

Lord Gruffydd allowed the jeering and teasing to proceed for a little longer before quieting down his men. What had started as a joke had gotten the lord thinking? His normal soldiers would be nearly immobilized by the thick mud and large pools of water. It *would* be safer if the Qiri'ar cut the path to the city first, allowing the soldiers to follow.

He looked down at the outrunner. "Send a message to Lord Ghast and let him know that we'll expect the Qiri'ar to clear us a path to the city. If they need to throw down planks, or simply stamp the land flat, so be it. I don't care how they do it, but those are my new demands."

The outrunner bowed and departed, taking the message with haste to Lord Gruffydd's new allies.

* * *

Drakhart had not been pleased with the messenger that arrived from Lord Gruffydd. It would make approaching the city more difficult, and slower. He had not hidden his displeasure at the Baron's new demands. On the contrary, he had been certain to tip his hand and put his frustration on display for the messenger.

Drakhart grimaced. "The Crown hasn't even touched his head yet, the city's still in enemy hands, and he's already making demands like he's king around here."

The messenger said nothing, but his look was troubled, and Drakhart could tell he would be reporting this to his master.

Drakhart dismissed the messenger shortly after that, and once he was certain that the messenger was gone and out of earshot, he let a smile spread across his face. "Do you think he believed it?"

"Definitely," replied O'lomec, Kinu'watan of the Qiri'ar.

"We must make the Baron believe he has us inconvenienced. He's already unnerved that we managed to get an army across the border and to the city gates unnoticed. He does not trust us, and so we must not give him reason to suspect what we are truly capable of," Elandyr'ni added.

Drakhart already knew that he would have to deal with the problem of the mud eventually. The fields were no longer that, they were swamps of sorrow, and mires of misery, where deep puddles of muck and water stretched like a thick, vile soup across the once grassy landscape. The weeks of rain had not been kind to the dry fields, and even the Qiri'ar would struggle to make the trip to the wall in that mess.

Realizing the problem, Drakhart had had it dealt with quietly and in secrecy. Several Qiri'ar had been sent to the treeline to fell several of the ancient trees that stood there and saw them into planks.

Drakhart's forces used the rain, night, and fog to obfuscate their movements—from both the sight of the city's defenders and from Baron Felidrun's spies—and once logged, the trees were carried to the tunnels that they had used to arrive at the city. The trees were old, and wide, and so the planks themselves would be wide enough to drive a wagon over. They would not support the weight of siege towers, but they could get the combined Estian and Qiri'aran forces across the muddy no-man's land to the city walls.

"Won't His Future Majesty—" O'lomec spoke the title mockingly. "—be suspicious, with how quickly we'll have the solution together?"

Drakhart shrugged. "You would be surprised what people are willing to believe about the Qiri'ar. You are certainly fearsome and respected warriors, but all sorts of myths, legends and lies have wound up amongst the truths. Let him believe what he wants, we'll use the lies to our advantage."

"Just remember that we cannot lose the alliance with Estion. It's too vital to the war effort," warned Elandyr'ni.

Drakhart knew this well, it had been the entire reason behind Drakhart's assignment, and the whole crux of his plan. In previous Enayran struggles since the end of the War of the Grand Coalition, Estion had done its best to remain neutral. They made too much money selling to both sides during times of war to risk picking a side. The looting, sacking, and chaos after their loss during the War of the Grand Coalition, combined with memories of the Anarchy, and years of internal instability kept Estion too worried to enter the war and risk being on the losing side.

So Estion bet on the importance of their lumber resources, and they knew it was the right call. Estian lumber kept the warring navies repaired and kept the shipyards churning out new ship, and Estian charcoal was needed in every forge across the land—it was simply the best.

With a Darond-friendly king on the throne of Estion, there would be no chance Estion would remain neutral in the war to come.

Espias and Asardaea could not produce their own charcoal, or lumber, for their resources in that regard were sparse in comparison to Estion. Altimaran intelligence had noted that both nations had enough lumber stockpiled to last six months, if war were declared tomorrow, and enough charcoal stockpiled to last nine if usage remained at the expected highs.

This was why Drakhart needed a king friendly to Altimara and hostile to the Darond on the throne, and Lord Gruffydd provided that opportunity. Gaining Estion as an ally meant nothing, since their military strength was negligible, and would be a harder sell than guaranteed neutrality. Keeping Estion neutral would still allow them to sell to both sides— if at differing rates, hopefully in favour of Altimara—and it would keep Asardaea from invading from the north to depose a hostile monarchy. Neutrality was not a crime, after all.

In the end, Drakhart knew, it didn't really matter *who* sat on the throne, so long as they remained out of the war, and friendly enough with Asardaea. But Lord Gruffydd had the trust of the nobility, and most of the army. A monarchy under his rule would be the most stable and save Altimara from having to field an occupation force to maintain peace and control under a weaker puppet.

Drakhart looked at Elandyr'ni and the Kinu'watan. "Lord Gruffydd should be arriving soon. Get the planks prepared for deployment. We won't want to delay our attack too long once the ruse is lifted."

Not a second was wasted.

Chapter XLVIII

Olivia Helga Tatiana Brunhild vohn Siebold-Kettler unt vohn Veishaupt, Baroness of Pelchar, Viscountess of Sieberg, Friedund and Ittyn, Duchess of Isya, and Countess of Belegra, Chancellor of the Navy, High Admiral, Minister of Waterways, and captain of the *Sea Emerald* stood at the bow of one of her lesser barges. It was not a fancy seafaring warship, but a barge meant for transporting goods up and down the Acturn. This ship transported everything from livestock to luxury goods, but today, it would be used to carry the people of Ethon to safety, just like every vessel she had recruited into her armada.

"How long until we reach Ethon?" the Baroness asked.

The navigator checked his charts and instruments. "At this speed, we should be there by the end of the day today."

"And not a moment too soon," the Baroness scoffed.

She had received a letter about a month and a half prior from a Darond contact known as Ruoth. He had tipped the Baroness off to a potential plot by her nemesis, Lord Gruffydd, though he was scant on proof, or details.

The Lady vohn Veishaupt, not one to point fingers without evidence, had done her own plotting, for she had never trusted the loyalty of the Baron of Felidrun. Rather than accuse the Baron Felidrun without proof to substantiate her claim, she assumed and planned for the worst-case scenario.

All commercial traffic up and down the Acturn came under the control of the vohn Veishaupt family, and they had exclusive commercial use of the canal, only public and non-commercial private traffic was out of her purview. But when that canal went under service and maintenance, her ships used this secret tunnel system. It was how she kept her commercial shipments punctual during the maintenance periods.

Now, it would be Ethon's only hope for assistance.

Three weeks prior, word had come through the Lady vohn Veishaupt's spies in the palace that the city had been surrounded by a hostile army of Qiri'ar and that the king was calling the banners to save Ethon. The Lady vohn Veishaupt had not waited for her letter to arrive and immediately prepared to sail up the secret tunnel to protect the city. She had commissioned every commercial, public, and privately owned vessel in Pelchar, and amassed an armada that she would sail down the secondary canal tunnel to alleviate the siege on the city. She doubted she would arrive in time to save the day, but she might arrive in time to evacuate the civilians and government loyal to His Majesty.

The Baroness did not trust the Baron Felidrun, and she did not trust him not to be in league with the attacking army. She had an idea that he was behind this—more reason to hurry.

But they still needed to hurry. Sadly, the going was slower than she had anticipated. The tunnel was not meant to handle a fleet as large as what the baroness was forcing upon it.

The plan was to evacuate the citizenry to safety using the boats and combine her forces with those of the King to prepare for a fighting retreat. With their forces combined, they would give up the capital and drawback across the Acturn, and then withdraw to Pelchar.

In the end, the Baroness's fears had been well-founded, and she found herself glad that she had departed when she did. Just that morning a messenger hawk from Pelchar had caught up with her fleet. It warned that Lord Gruffydd was not only set to arrive earlier than expected but that the call to arms had never arrived for any of the western barons. If Ruoth had not warned her in advance, she would have been caught unawares and would still be in Pelchar right now while Estion lay besieged. By the time she had rallied the same forces she now commanded, it would have been far too late.

With that new information, the Lady vohn Veishaupt had no illusions that she had been correct in her assessment of the situation, and the plans she had made. It was clearer, now more than ever, that the defenders would be unable to hold the city. Especially when faced with the combined might of the Estian barons and the Qiri'ar.

The city would need to be strategically sacrificed so that rebellion against the Cabal and Lord Gruffydd could continue in earnest through other means, and from another base—be it Pelchar, another city, or even the wilds and forests of Estion.

The Baroness, a seasoned warrior who had spent her youth fighting across Enayra as a mercenary, was not above fighting a guerrilla war against a usurper for the sake of her monarch, friend, and country.

With the possibility of that outcome in mind, she had made her biggest preparation before sailing from Pelchar and sent a messenger to the Estian Republican Army, seeking a temporary truce and alliance—the ERA were masters of guerrilla tactics in Estion, after all.

While the Reformists never had as much of an issue with the Republicans as the Cabal had, nor were they openly at war with one another, the Reformists and ERA had engaged in several skirmishes by nature of principle.

The ERA fought against both Reformist and Cabal forces with an equal dislike, as both represented a monarchy that they wanted abolished in favour of a representative, republican democracy.

But the Lady vohn Veishaupt knew that no matter how much the ERA hated all monarchs, they would likely be willing to broker a truce with a constitutional monarch, rather than the absolutist, oligarchical monarch that Lord Gruffydd would be if he took the throne.

It would not end the conflict between the two groups forever, but for the time being, they would work together to deal with a larger, worse threat.

In another stroke of brilliance and foresight, the Lady vohn Veishaupt had anticipated an invading army would take the Acturn Canal. It would be the first target she would take had she been in their shoes, and any commander worth their weight in gold would do the same. 'Whoever controls the Acturn, controls Estion,' as the saying went.

So, she intentionally left the Acturn lightly guarded.

When the Qiri'ar had attacked and taken control of the canal, the Baroness had used the retaking of the canal as bait for the ERA. Under the pretext that she had not the forces to save the city *and* retake the canal, she had begrudgingly—or so she let the ERA believe—agreed to allow the Republicans to retake it for her as a "concession" in their treaty.

They were to retake it and hold it at all costs. The Baroness and Leon would regroup their forces with the ERA once they had withdrawn across the Acturn, and together the three armies would retreat as one.

The Lady vohn Veishaupt knew there would be dues to pay for the alliance. The Baroness had never met the mysterious leader of the ERA in person. All communication and negotiations had been done via go-betweens and messengers. This leader styled himself as both General Koltaris and the "Big Boss."

To make negotiations easier, he had waived all promises and concessions from the Crown for the time being, aside from the reclaiming of the Pelchar. The General claimed that deposing the tyrannical usurper was of greater importance than the thought of gain for the moment—but only for the moment.

General Koltaris appreciated that the Lady vohn Veishaupt had thought him a worthy ally to combat the wickedness of Baron Felidrun. He had thought himself an honourable man, and so was willing to work through the details of concessions *after* Lord Gruffydd was defeated.

By then, hopefully, Lady vohn Veishaupt and King Leon could come up with a sufficient list of concessions that could be made and allow both sides to meet in the middle.

Hopefully, it would be enough. Fighting two consecutive wars would be costly.

But those would be problems for later. None of this meant anything if the Baroness Pelchar did not reach Ethon as soon as possible.

Chapter XLIX

The Qiri'ar Camp grew eerily quiet around midday.

Soldiers all along the walls let out audible cheers, jeers, and sighs of relief when the chanting and singing finally stopped. But they soon found the dead silence that replaced it to be even more unnerving.

It didn't take everyone long to realize that the silence was not because the Qiri'ar had given up. It was quite the opposite because there was now no doubt that the main assault would start soon.

Everyone could feel the tension in the air. Stomachs tightened, the hair on the back of people's necks and arms stood on end, and some younger soldiers were already throwing up over the side of the wall as they lost their nerve.

Kanaahn and Shooter looked at each other, then at the massive army pooled just outside of the city.

They had been here once before. The odds had been a little more even, and the soldiers had just been normal Altimarans. The Qiri'ar were a whole different beast; stronger, faster, and mightier than any Altimaran soldier. The stories were famous, and they only worked in favour of the attackers.

Kanaahn didn't want to admit that Shooter was right, but the longer the siege drew on, the more fear slowly gripped Kanaahn's heart like an icy hand. He knew that fighting off an army of Qiri'aran attackers would be harder than anything he had encountered at Xiar. At least there would be a second army positioned outside the Qiri'aran encirclement that would allow the defenders to take the enemy from both sides. Attacking from two fronts would be their saving grace.

Kanaahn cleared his throat. "You know, whatever happens…"

"Yeah," replied Shooter. "I know. Me too."

Kanaahn nodded.

Xiar had been a victory. But whenever Kanaahn remembered that day, now with the benefit had hindsight, and without the taint of adrenaline or excitement, he couldn't help but feel he had lost something in that battle; a part of himself. He couldn't describe it, nor exactly how he felt about it, but Kanaahn knew for certain that the scars of war had left their mark on Kanaahn and the other Khaleeshir, and he could the shadow of it all closing in again. He knew that the feelings would disappear in the rush of battle, when the only thing that existed was the desire to survive, by any means necessary. But once this fight was over too, it would no doubt return, this time greater.

Kanaahn could only imagine, and what he envisioned filled him with dread.

The two friends silently looked back at the Qiri'aran Army. This time, they squinted their eyes towards the tree line, trying to better see what was coming out of the forest.

"Do you see that?" asked Shooter.

"Yeah. It's faint, but I can see them," Kanaahn replied.

"What's that?" asked the nearby captain.

"Look at the treeline, can you see the movement?" asked Shooter. "I think Lord Gruffydd's armies are here."

The captain looked confused. "I don't know how many of you can see that."

Shooter blushed. "Apologies. Must be a Dragonkin thing."

The captain shook his head and pulled out a spyglass. He scanned the treeline using the instrument, only to find that Shooter and Kanaahn spoke true. The captain let out a whoop. "I think you're right; the baron is here!" He turned back to the soldiers, lounging about on the wall. "Someone send word to His Majesty! Lord Gruffydd's army has arrived at last—" he turned to his remaining soldiers "—Keep your eyes on the field, boys. You'll see a battle unfold like any other."

"What if the baron needs us?" asked a young soldier, barely older than Kanaahn.

"Then we'll throw open the gates and join them on the battlefield. Hit the enemy from behind," the captain answered matter-of-factly.

Shooter and Kanaahn exchanged glances. The city guard had heart, and their tenacity was commendable, but their experience in warfare was lacking—and it showed. Even ignoring the fact that Leon under Lord Gruffydd's instructions expressly forbade his forces from joining the fray, it was a terrible strategic risk, and it could cost countless lives and the city itself if they tried it.

Regardless, the Khaleeshir were in no position to change that, and they would have to make do with the hand they'd been dealt.

By the time word had gotten around the entire city that Lord Gruffydd had arrived, his armies had already left the treeline and had begun assembling into battle formations just beyond the reach of the forest.

The Qiri'aran army had turned to face their new threat, hurling chants, curses, and jeers at the barons' armies assembling around them.

Defenders crowded around their captains, nearly hanging off the crenulation, to get a glimpse of the action to come. Their captains kept them abreast of the finer details, watching every movement unfold their spyglasses.

Kanaahn and Shooter didn't need a spyglass to see what was happening.

"Why don't the Qiri'ar attack the baron while his army is assembling?" asked one soldier.

A captain laughed. "They must be shocked. They're probably shaking in their boots now that they realize this conquest won't be as easy as they thought."

Shooter and Kanaahn exchanged a worried look.

"What about the baron? Why didn't he form up his ranks in the treeline and attack with the element of surprise?" an older Bluehelm asked.

"Nah the trees are so thick, it's hard to do that properly. They wouldn't be able to hold proper formations in that forest, and their lines would come out too thin and uneven. They'd be ripped apart in seconds."

Another glance was exchanged between Shooter and Kanaahn. These soldiers brought up good points, and the more they saw, the more worried the two Khaleeshir grew.

"Shooter…" Kanaahn said, his apprehension clear.

"I won't say it. But thank you for finally coming to your senses," Shooter replied.

"Something's not right."

"I know, Kanaahn."

"We need to tell Leon and the others."

"I know."

"See if you can reach Kyeit and Cecil. They were posted closest to the command tent."

"Already on it."

Kanaahn smiled and placed a hand on his sword. "You think they'll listen if we told them?" He gestured to the soldiers around him.

Shooter shrugged. "Probably not, but if you could try to get them to realize it would help us. Now let me focus."

Kanaahn turned to the captain who was narrating the goings on out in the field. He took the captain by the arm and pulled him aside, away from the crowd to avoid causing a panic. "Captain, get these men under control and into formation. We need to be ready."

"What are you talking about?" the captain scoffed. "The Baron Felidrun is here. He'll handle the Qiri'ar."

Kanaahn lowered his voice to barely a whisper. "Captain, something is wrong. I can't explain it, but I don't think Baron Felidrun is here to save us."

"Are you saying the baron betrayed us?" The captain did not attempt to lower his voice. The Dragonkin and the captain soon began to draw a crowd. The captain was not amused with Kanaahn's warning.

Kanaahn's patience was wearing thin. Time was running out. He no longer cared if he caused a scene. "Captain. You've been with the Bluehelms for a while, I assume?"

The captain puffed up his chest. "Fifteen years."

"Did they ever teach you the basics of warfare?" asked Kanaahn.

"Why would they?"

Kanaahn rubbed his temples. While a fair point, it was not helpful. "I've been on a battlefield. I've studied warfare, however briefly. I was at Xiar. The first thing they taught us was never to give up the element of surprise or ignore any chance at gaining the advantage over your enemy. Lord Gruffydd has done just that by taking the time to put his troops in formation within range of the enemy, in full view of the entire Qiri'aran force no less. The Qiri'arans gave up the advantage by not attacking Lord Gruffydd while they were getting into formation. Wouldn't you want to take advantage of those odds?"

The wheels in the captain's head were slowly turning, Kanaahn could see that reflected in his face. The realization of what Kanaahn was trying to tell him was washing over the man as he puzzled through the facts and logic. But it wasn't fast enough for Kanaahn's liking.

A yell rose from across the fields, as the two armies roared and charged at each other in full force.

The hair on Kanaahn's neck stood on end. They were already out of time. Whatever happened next, Kanaahn could only pray the mud would slow them down.

"The battle's begun!" cried a soldier from the rampart.

Everyone ran to the walls to see the two sides clash. The captain was lost in the crowd—whatever conclusions he had been coming to were now lost amongst this distraction.

Kanaahn looked desperately at Shooter.

Shooter's face was grim. "I reached Kyeit and Cecil. They came to the same realization too just now. The dragons have been made aware and are warning Hana and Aurichalcum, the others are in the loop."

"And Leon?"

"I couldn't reach him, but Arial is closest to the command tent. She's going to find and warn him if she can. She'll let me know how that goes."

"Shit," Kanaahn hissed through clenched teeth. "Are Cecil and Kyeit not near the command tent?"

"They went to reinforce an area of the wall that was light on commanding officers. They're not stationed anywhere close to the command tent anyway, and they don't want to leave their forces without leadership if we're about to be attacked."

Kanaahn turned back to the captain. He struggled to keep his frustration and anxiety in check. "Get these men to their positions and ready for battle, *now!*"

"Listen, Dragonkin. While I respect what you're doing for Enayra, I don't take orders from you."

Kanaahn's fists clenched so tightly he could feel his armour creak a little.

Suddenly, from the field, the yelling stopped. The two sides froze. The expected clash never happened.

Kanaahn's gut lurched. He could sense what was to come.

The Qiri'ar turned around. The supposed relief force, meant to drive away the attackers lined up behind their former enemies, and together, they looked up at the city. War horns blared from both armies. The Qiri'ar shouted out in Qir'to'ah.

For but a few minutes the whole world seemed to slow down. Kanaahn was seeing time pass at a quarter of the speed. He could feel the wind start blowing, tousling his hair and blowing across the battlements. Kanaahn caught the faintest whiff of blood on the wind. He didn't need the gift of prophecy to guess what was about to happen next.

A sudden and gut-wrenching roar erupted from the Qiri'aran army. It was a primal sound, like the first scream of a newborn baby mixed with the feral roars of a rampaging bear. Their fabled tattoos had been activated. Now they would be an unstoppable force unleashed upon the city and her defenders.

The Qiri'ar, and Baron Felidrun's armies behind them, rushed towards Ethon, ladders, and weapons at the ready, calling war cries as they went.

Kanaahn wheeled on the stunned soldiers surrounding him. Captains and soldiers alike stared bewildered by the betrayal they had just witnessed. They gawked dumbly at the massive host coming to take their city. Hopelessness was taking over, working its way into their hearts and minds. If Kanaahn didn't do something soon, they'd surrender before the battle even began. There was no time for grand, flowery speeches or words of noble encouragement.

"Captains!" roared Kanaahn. "Get your soldiers in position NOW! No matter what comes over the top of that wall, we must defend this city. Get a hold of yourselves or I'll throw you over the top myself!"

It took a few moments for the soldiers to come to their senses. Their doubts were not fully assuaged, and their morale was permanently dented by the betrayal and the idea that they'd have to fight Qiri'ar. But they were no longer stunned into inaction, and that would be enough.

The soldiers immediately bustled around like a busy colony of ants.

Crates of arrows and sling stones were dragged towards the parapets. Weapons were drawn, and captains called for the fires to be lit to begin heating the cauldrons of grease that had been stockpiled.

Arial had managed to get through to somebody at the command tent because the scene was being repeated across most sections of the wall by now. In areas where it lacked, the soldiers soon followed suit with their comrades.

"A little harsh, but effective," Shooter mentioned.

Kanaahn shrugged. "We didn't have time for anything else. Hopefully, the mud will slow them down."

No sooner had Kanaahn spoken than did he notice the Qiri'ar throwing down large planks of wood. It did not take him long to figure out where they got the wood.

Shooter smirked. "So much for that hope."

"Then they better get into defensive positions faster," muttered Kanaahn, "Or this will be a short siege."

* * *

Arkas watched the enemies charge the wall with a mix of disbelief and chagrin. He could hear the attackers' wooden plank walkways rattling under the weight of countless warriors.

The Qiri'ar made up the bulk of the main force, and many in the front carried tall, heavy ladders of thick wood and iron barding. Whatever hope there was that the mud would slow down the attackers had evaporated.

The only blessing was that the planks were too small to carry the weight of siege towers. Structures that were that tall, heavy, and filled with hundreds of men would only push the planks deeper into the muck. Siege towers had nearly overwhelmed the Xiaran defenders in his last battle. Arkas remembered soldiers flooding the wall tops in an endless deluge, like endless waves against the shoreline.

It was a small blessing, but it might be enough—or Arkas hoped.

Though he knew better than to be too complacent, any hesitation or weakness along the defensive lines, and they would buckle. If they buckled, the Qiri'ar would overwhelm them just as easily.

Arkas peered over the wall.

The attackers had already reached the base of the fortifications. Arrows rained down on them like a deluge of hail. Stones and pots of oil were being flung over the side as well, but unlike at Xiar, the Qiri'ar didn't seem affected by the pain.

The Estian attackers screamed and cried out when they were hit by enemy arrows or bolts of magic. But the Qiri'ar were silent. They bore their wounds and injuries as if under some sort of trance. Arrows stuck out of their bodies at odd angles. Their skin had quickly blistered where the oil had burned them; some had even lost entire layers of skin, and flesh, and were now showing patches of bone beneath.

But still, they kept moving. They kept coming.

Arkas fired a flurry of arrows at several attacking Qiri'ar and instructed archers and slingers near him to follow his lead. They would aim for the head, and bring down as many of the enemy as possible.

Some Qiri'ar who had been struck in the head with arrows or large rocks slowed, some fell, but only after their heads had been turned into pin cushions.

Arkas frowned.

The shots had been well placed and fired by competent archers. It didn't matter. The Qiri'ar were moving like inhuman monsters. Their Blood Fugue, as he had learned it was called, made them stronger, more powerful, and near impervious to pain. They still bled, they still hurt, and they could still be killed, but it was harder.

Much harder.

Arkas froze and watched as several Qiri'ar marched to the walls with ladders. The ladders were massive, made of sturdy Estian lumber and girded with iron. Iron spikes protruded from the base of the ladder, likely to anchor them into the ground, and more spikes protruded from the side that would face the wall.

It didn't take Arkas long to guess why that was, nor did it take the Qiri'ar long to demonstrate their practicality. The massive ladders were placed flush against the walls, and immediately the defenders tried to force them back. The ladders didn't have hooks at the top of their side rails, as most siege ladders did, but the defenders found themselves unable to force them back. Something held the ladders in place.

Arkas spotted several Qiri'ar at the base of the ladders, muscles straining as they held the ladders against the wall. As they held the ladders steady, other Qiri'ar hammered away at the lower rungs—made of iron by the sound of it—to anchor the ladders into the ground.

"Open fire! Don't let them get those ladders anchored!" Arkas commanded.

Arrows whistled down towards the swaths of enemies below. Stones banged against the wall and cracked off the skulls of the attackers. Slings twanged as the leather stretched and shot lead projectiles over the parapet.

But it wasn't enough. It did not stop the Qiri'ar. Even riddled with arrows, bruised, broken and bleeding, they kept moving, kept positioning the ladders. Even when they were felled, another Qiri'ar would emerge from the throng to keep their place.

Trying to stem the flow of soldiers was like trying to hold back the tide or stop leaves from falling from a tree. But still, Arkas refused to give up, he and his soldiers kept firing, kept throwing rocks, kept pouring pots of boiling grease and oil over the top of the parapet.

With the bottoms of the ladder firmly submerged in the muck, the Qiri'ar turned their hammers towards the metal joints where the rungs met the stiles. With each strike, the spikes along the length of the ladder were driven further into the mortar and stone.

It only took five blows for most Qiri'ar to drive the spikes home, and firmly secure the ladders in place. The iron spikes were now firmly embedded in the stone walls, and it would take nothing short of a team of oxen to pull them back out.

And then the enemy began to climb.

Arkas grit his teeth and kept up his onslaught. He fired arrows at the Qiri'ar as they climbed. They would not reach the top without paying a price. It took two to three arrows to the skull to bring down these blood-crazed fiends.

At one point, Arkas watched in amazement as a Blood Warrior fell from the ladder, his head impaled by four arrows through the eyes and temple. When he fell, he caused several warriors below him to lose their footing, and they fell with him. The warriors fell, tumbling down the ladder, bouncing off each other, bringing even more with them.

Sixteen bodies hit the ground, and fifteen bodies stood back up. Limbs were broken and bent at odd angles, they were covered in blood and rent with cuts, bone stuck out of gaping wounds where arms and legs had snapped like a branch in a storm. But the monstrous Qiri'ar simply popped their dislocated limbs back in, ignored their other wounds, and returned to climbing the ladders.

Arkas was horrified. His fellow soldiers were horrified. How did one fight *this*?

They could only be thankful that the Estian traitors under Lord Gruffydd had pulled back once the Qiri'ar started climbing the walls. It seemed they would not be joining the assault of the battlements to start. It was a small blessing, though if the Qiri'ar kept climbing at this rate, it wouldn't matter much.

Arkas slung his bow across his body and drew his short sword. The time of arrows was done. "Draw weapons! Fight back! Don't let them get a foothold!"

But it didn't make a difference. The Qiri'ar came over the top like waves breaking against a sea wall. They splashed over the battlements and started to cut their way through the defenders.

Blood splattered across the stone wall top, pouring from the bodies of the fallen, and making the ground slick. Warriors on both sides fell, some were felled by blades in combat, others by slipping on the blood and hitting their heads, and others still were attacked as they fell. Qiri'ar and Estians alike pounced upon downed enemies like a pack of hungry wolves and stabbed at the fallen warrior until they no longer moved.

"Hold! Hold, damn you! Ethon must not fall!" Arkas cried.

But the screams of battle overwhelmed Arkas. The soldiers around him could no longer hear his voice amidst the chaos. The cries of the mangled and the dying filled his ears, but Arkas hardened himself, shut out the fear, and plunged himself into the fray.

* * *

Back-to-back. Surrounded. Steel weapons glinting in the sunlight. Sweat coated their bodies beneath their armour. The smell of blood. The crackle of magic. Ozone and sweat and copper on their tongues.

This was how Kyeit and Cecil found themselves once again. For the second time in six months, they were in the thick of a siege.

They had taken command of a swath of soldiers who had been light on commanders and captains, and their rule was absolute after many of the highest-ranking captains were cut down when the Qiri'ar had come over the walls.

The defence of the wall was going better than they had hoped, but worse than they would have liked.

Many of their own lay dead, killed by the initial wave of Qiri'ar that came over the top. But thanks to Cecil's quick thinking and Kyeit's ability to take charge without hesitation, they had arranged their soldiers into shield walls on either side of the battlements, walling in the Qiri'ar that were coming over the rampart. Soldiers were instructed to spears and shields to keep the attackers at bay. The strongest and bravest of the soldiers would remain outside the shield wall, under the command of Kyeit and Cecil, to help fight off the enemy and keep them from breaking through the shield walls.

At first, this strategy had worked wonders, but as the battle raged on and enemies precipitated against the battlements like rain, the defenders were beginning to flag. Sure, the Qiri'ar were paying in blood for every inch they took, but they were gaining ground nonetheless, and their numbers seemed endless.

Kyeit and Cecil had found it harder to rotate soldiers between the shield wall and the enclosed battlefield. Wounded soldiers could not be replaced as easily, and more and more of their skirmishers were going down under the onslaught of the Qiri'aran attackers.

The two Knight-Commanders had been taught Qiri'aran battle strategies during their schooling with the Darond, in preparation for a final war with Tenebrae. At the time, the two had always thought the Qiri'aran siege methods to be a bit overconfident, even foolhardy.

Typically, the Qiri'aran strategy demanded that they only send enough soldiers over the top as they deemed necessary. Never more than at a one-to-one ratio with the number of defenders. But for every Blood Warrior that fell, two more would go over the top to take their place, slowly wearing away at the enemy's strength and numbers, and slowly overwhelming them.

It seemed, to the inexperienced Knight-Commanders, that this kind of slow deployment could be easily beaten back. But now, in the thick of battle, Kyeit and Cecil saw the merit in that method, especially when combined with weeks of psychological warfare and the Qiri'aran Blood Fugue.

Using this tactic, the Qiri'ar were slowly becoming unstoppable.

Kyeit dodged left. She narrowly avoided her enemy's axe.

The axe had lodged itself in the stone, and Kyeit took advantage of the moment. With a quick stab to the female warrior's head, Kyeit cut her foe down.

Behind Kyeit, Cecil was locked in combat with two Qiri'aran spearmen. They stabbed at her, thrusting their spears at her head and midsection.

Cecil nimbly dodged. With quick footwork, she danced around them. She could not get in at an opening like Kyeit had. The spears kept Cecil at bay, and while Cecil had landed many strikes on her opponents, it was like a bee repeatedly stinging a dog. She had caused her foes to bleed, but she could not strike them with any lethality. If she struck one, the other spearman would come at her. All Cecil could do was dodge and strike, slowly whittling down her foes. Eventually, the blood loss would take effect.

Kyeit had lunged forward towards the next opponent. She now fought a Blood Warrior deep in the fugue who was attempting to barrel through a brigade of ten soldiers that were trying to stop his rampage.

She had cut deep into the warrior's knee, and while this slowed him, it did not stop him. He hobbled around, swinging his blade and cleaving through soldiers with ease. Kyeit needed to stop him before his allies came to his aid.

Meanwhile, Cecil had come up with a clever, if desperate, plan.

The woman to her left thrust her spear towards Cecil's stomach, while the man on her left aimed for her head.

Cecil stepped back and repositioned herself.

Her enemies closed the gap as anticipated. They continued to jab their spears at her, aiming to drive her over the edge of the parapet and into the waiting jaws of the attacking army below.

But Cecil did not give them the satisfaction. She grabbed a sword from a fallen comrade and went on the attack. She charged the two spear fighters.

Strike after strike, Cecil did not let up. She constantly pressed upon the spear fighters, forcing them back and always keeping them on the defensive.

They kept deflecting and blocking her strikes. But that was fine. The point was never to harm them, it was simply to manoeuvre them right where she wanted them.

Finally, Cecil had pushed the spear fighters towards a pool of blood that had formed at a crux between the bodies of fallen Bluehelms. Between Cecil pressing the attack, and the slickness of the blood, the soldiers lost their balance. A single misstep was all it took, and the woman slipped and fell, cracking her head on the stone. She flailed and took out the knee of her companion, and he quickly joined her on the ground.

Cecil didn't waste a second, and jabbed her two swords into their faces, and then again through their throats—just to ensure that they were dead and stayed that way.

Her enemies gurgled out a few final words. Cecil couldn't understand what they said, but it was probably some form of curse or commendation. It always was, regardless of the language.

Either way, Cecil did not linger. She returned to the fray. She had to stem the flow of soldiers and hold the battlements at all costs.

On her side of the battlements, Kyeit still struggled with the large warrior she had wounded earlier.

The enemy's knee had been sliced partway through. Kyeit's blade had parted skin and flesh and made easy work of the ligaments and the meniscus but had stopped after hitting the bones of the joint. Partly because the man's leg was like an Estian oak, and partly because Kyeit had nearly lost her head cutting as far as she had. It had been a calculated risk.

She had managed to avoid the worst of the blow, but the backswing of the Warrior's axe had caught Kyeit in the side with the dull side of the axe head and winded her. Kyeit could feel the wound already start to bruise over, just above her right hip. Unfortunately for her, the pain was affecting her movement.

The massive man, no longer interested in playing with his food, limped away from Kyeit and towards the shield wall.

Kyeit refused to let him go. She was determined. He would not break through. She let out a roar and charged after the Blood Warrior, ignoring the pain in her hip.

The tip of her blade guided her path and she aimed for the warrior's spine and was surprised when her blade met its mark. Kyeit could feel her blade sink into his muscled flesh. There was resistance, but it sunk in, deeper, between the ribs, scraped against bone, bit through organs, and finally stopped at the hilt. The tip of the blade now protruded from the other side of the warrior's abdomen.

But even this did not stop this monster of a man. He did not die. He did not fall. He did not even stagger. But he did turn, slowly, like a lumbering giant.

Kyeit's blood ran cold.

The Blood Warrior roared in her face. She could smell his breath, and spittle issued from his mouth. The back of his hand collided with her face, and spots of light clouded her vision. Kyeit's eyes watered, and she felt herself float through the air before hitting the ground. The back of her skull slammed into hard stones and made her skull explode with pain.

From the ground, Kyeit could make out the vague shape of her attacker. His blurred form raised his axe above his head. He was going to kill her.

Shit.

This was the end.

She couldn't react in time. She ached everywhere, and she was still dazed. Kyeit opened her hand and realized she had lost her sword. She was unarmed and defenceless. Cecil was busy with her own fight, as were the other soldiers. She was alone, and no one was coming to save her.

Kyeit shut her eyes, and for the first time in a very long time, she prayed for a quick death.

But it never came.

In a matter of seconds, Kyeit heard thunder. Then screams erupted all around her; screams of genuine terror. There were cries of awe. Then the sound of a very panicked Blood Warrior. Something massive roared from well above where Kyeit lay.

She could feel a rush of wind above her, followed by the smell of burning flesh and hair, and the sounds of a man screaming as he burned alive. Kyeit could feel an intense heat from not far above her.

Kyeit sat up, her vision slowly returning, and saw the greatest sight she could have asked for at that moment: Valence.

"I'm sorry we're late, Kyeit."

"Not a moment too soon." Kyeit stood. She rubbed the back of her head. She winced and could feel blood where the back of her head had split open on the cobbles. Her skull didn't feel broken, but she was bleeding and bruised. Kyeit would have to heal it later.

After a moment, Kyeit noticed that the battle had come to a halt on her section of the wall. The sight of Valence and her massacre of the Blood Warrior had awed both sides into stunned silence.

The charred corpse of the warrior was held firmly in Valence's grasp. Valence only smiled in response.

Kyeit looked up and saw that it wasn't just Valence that had come to her aid. The other dragons had come too, and the massive shadow of a brass dragon confirmed that Thrae had joined the fight. Her massive bulk nearly blocked out the sun, and cast large shadows beneath her.

Then, Kyeit noticed that Valence had been armoured at some point. *"You rarely wear armour anymore."*

"Thrae need not worry about most weapons at her size and age, but the Qiri'ar are stronger than most average humans. Kinokaze and I thought it prudent to be safe. We

had Aurichalcum reinforce our armour—and that of the Khaleeshir—with some enchantments. They're not completely impervious to damage and magic or magically assisted attacks such as enchanted weapons may still pose a problem. But at the very least, weapons like this—" Valence motioned with her head to the smouldering and warped remains of the enemy's axe. *"—won't do much to us at least."*

Kyeit frowned. *"You ruined my sword."* Indeed, Kyeit's sword had been caught in the blast of dragon fire and had been melted and fused to the stone walls.

"Better than dying," Valence offered.

Kyeit wasn't going to argue with that.

The lull in the battle had begun to wear off around her. Kyeit managed to slip between several soldiers who made an opening for her in the shield wall. "I need a new weapon," she called to the soldiers around her.

Someone immediately pressed a longsword into her hand. It wasn't her blade, but it would have to do for now.

Kyeit looked back beyond the shield wall and watched as several Qiri'ar came over the top of the battlements. Four more Blood Warriors and two Blood Witches in all.

She needed to get back in the fight.

Kyeit called out to the soldiers around her. "Anyone who's able, come with me back into the fight. We need to hold them off—take out the witches first!"

Several brave men and women formed up around her, ready to defend their city from these attackers.

"Shall I stay and help?" Valence asked.

"Go where you're needed. We'll be okay. If we get overrun, I'll call. But other sections of this wall don't have a Knight-Commander like me in charge and could use a dragon like you."

Valence hesitated. *"If you insist. I will come if you need me."*

With that, the dragon flew off. As she passed over the wall, she loosed small bursts of flame down on the most overrun parts of the wall. She flew south, following the shape of the wall closely.

Kyeit's mind went back into the fight the instant Valence left. She raised her blade above her head and cried out. "Soldiers, to me!"

Together, she and the eleven others charged back through the shield wall and into the fray once more.

* * *

Magic seemed to slow the Blood Warriors down. That was something Arial and Leon had learned quickly, and together they managed to hold the area nearest the command tent.

Leon favoured flames, while Arial swapped between lightning and ice. Together, the two had put up a formidable and deadly defence. With the walls above the eastern gate secured by the Mage King and the Khaleeshir, the various commanders that had been gathered at the command tent were free to take some soldiers and lead the charge in fortifying other parts of the defence that were noticeably beleaguered.

While fighting off the Blood Warriors, Arial had to resist the urge to heal soldiers as they fell around her. She knew that healing them on the front would only be a waste. They'd only get injured again, and Arial would have wasted mana she could have conserved for other spells. It was a harsh reality, but the least she could do was defend the wounded soldiers while medics attempted to extricate them from the walls.

Arial raised her hand and shot a bolt of lightning at a Blood Warrior. The spell caught him in the face and sent him spiralling back over the parapet, back to the ground below. They might be able be able to push back the attackers at this rate, Arial thought.

And then the first Blood Witches started to come over the top. Suddenly magic wasn't as effective anymore.

Six came over the wall at once, and immediately the Blood Warriors diverted their attention from Leon and Arial to the soldiers that surrounded them.

Arial bit her lip. She knew without her and Leon's help, they'd soon be overrun by the unstoppable force that was Blood Fugue. But she could not risk ignoring the Blood Witches, or she and Leon would pay the price for it.

The Blood Witches, covered head to toe in tattoos and golden jewellery, stepped forward and split into two groups of three. They surrounded Leon and Arial. Their hands crackled with red static energy. The metallic stench of blood hung heavy in the air around them; it was so prevalent that Arial could almost taste it.

It would not be the first time Arial had fought a blood magic user. She had battled Drakhart at Xiar, and though he had been a novitiate warlock at the time, it had still left her exhausted. To Arial's credit, she too had been new to magic herself, and she had had much training under Leon since then.

But Arial knew that even with fledgling skill, Drakhart wielded blood magic with brutal efficiency and to terrible effect. Arial feared how she would fair against well-trained, life-long Blood Witches. For all her training, she had relatively little practice defending against and combatting warlocks and witches.

For all her doubt, Arial could not give up now. Too many lives counted on her. She was Khaleeshir. She didn't get to be afraid.

To start, Arial remembered her training and for now, stuck to basics—she would need her energy to last. She weaved a spell in as few words as possible, casting a protective ward over her body to protect her from the worst of the damage to come. Not a moment too soon, as the Blood Witches unleashed waves of red lightning at her.

Arial felt her hair stand on end, and she could taste the static in the air, mixing with the taste of blood. The attack nearly pushed her off balance, but she was otherwise unharmed.

Leon, with a little more experience and knowledge under his belt, had managed to cast a similar ward but wove in a few words that would allow him to absorb the spells and convert them back into mana. Using the energy of the attack against the Blood Witches, Leon lashed out with spears of ice.

Despite his youth, Leon was an accomplished mage, and the speed and cleverness of his casting caught even the experienced Blood Witches off guard.

An ice spear caught one in the hip, while the other two managed to deftly dodge out of the way—but just barely.

Arial made sure to memorize the words Leon had used for his shield and made a note to ask him for instruction later. Now was not the time to experiment with new magic.

She turned her focus to the two Blood Witches directly in front of her. Arial was at a skill disadvantage and an experience disadvantage. She had never fought more than a single mage at a time before. Even when she fought on the battlements of Xiar, the mages had never thought to team up and overwhelm their opponents, and most fights ended up being magical duels fought in single combat.

Perhaps it was an unwritten rule amongst mages, but the Blood Witches held no such traditions or qualms. Arial was thankful she still had a few tricks up her sleeve.

Trusting the strength of her wards a little longer, Arial began an incantation, doing her best to shrug off the repeated blasts of crimson lightning that the Blood Witches inundated her with.

She drew a talisman from within her robes, and her chanting grew louder. Power thrummed through the air, into the talisman, and up through Arial's staff. Even the Blood Witches could feel the power Arial was drawing on.

They watched in awe as Arial materialized a large, ferocious bear from within the talisman. The familiar surprised the Blood Witches, who had not prepared for a bear familiar to rampage across the battlements.

The spirit creature was massive. It was taller and wider than a horse carriage. The bear's somewhat luminescent fur was the colour of a stagnant pond. The flesh on its head was completely peeled back to reveal an exposed skull. Set within the hollow sockets were two glowing blue flames that served as the creature's eyes.

The spirit bear let out a roar that shook the walls to their foundations. In a flash, it leapt across the battlements, pounced upon the nearest Blood Witch and began to maul her.

The Blood Witch screamed. Though the creature was a spirit, it was corporeal, and its massive claws rent her flesh. The witch loosed waves of her crimson lightning to force the bear off her, but the creature would not relent.

The witch drew a dagger and then sunk it deep into the bear's shoulder. Once more, the bear shrugged off the attack.

The spirit bear opened its mouth wide, nearly unhinging the bone, and snapped its jaws shut around the Blood Witch's head. Her life came to an end with a wet crunch and a snap.

With the Blood Witch dispatched, the familiar charged off to fight the other Blood Warriors that were rampaging across the wall unchecked.

Arial slammed the butt of her staff against the stone floor just behind her. Without turning, she drew again upon her reserves of mana and raised a magical wall to block a wave of flame from the Blood Witch behind her. No wards would've stopped that.

With her rear protected, Arial used her free hand to attack the Blood Witch in front of her. Blue-white lightning shot from her fingertip, creeping and spider-webbing across the space between her and her enemy in an instant. Arial caught the Blood Witch in the side of her face.

The woman wailed and grabbed her burning face.

Arial could smell burned flesh and hair and was reminded of Xiar; she ground her teeth and maintained composure.

This was not Xiar. These were Qiri'ar. They would not think twice to do the same or worse to her. This was war, they would have burned her alive if they had the opportunity.

This was not some nameless soldier who had been lied to and sent to war to die for a cause they'd never know. The Qiri'ar knew what they were fighting for, and for whom.

Arial raised her hand, and without thinking twice, shot a spear of ice through the screaming witch's chest. Blood sprayed across the ramparts and the woman fell to the ground dead.

Arial turned her attention back to the final Blood Witch who still struggled to break through Arial's magical wall. She hoped to end this one before more came over the battlements.

The Blood Witch had resorted to desperate measures to cut through the magical wall. The witch had drawn her blade and augmented it with her blood magic. The blade was engulfed in shadow and wine-red flames. It was deadlier than any other, for it could easily cut through her magical wards just as Drakhart's blade had made short work of Kanaahn's enchanted armour at Xiar.

The wounds received by these wicked blades would be harder to heal and would certainly leave lasting scars. Even after healing, wounds from these blades could leave phantom echoes of their pain behind for years.

Arial needed to be careful.

She swallowed her fear and prepared to go on the offence. There would be no defending against this Blood Witch and her blade. Arial would simply need to be as nimble as possible to avoid the blade and ensure that she kept her opponent at bay. Distance was her friend.

Arial started with lightning.

The Blood Witch dodged the attack deftly.

Next, she tried an ice spear, but her opponent split the spear down the middle with her blade. The two halves melted under the heat of the enchanted flames.

Every time the Blood Witch dodged, she moved forward and drew nearer to Arial.

Arial felt panic grip her. She shot a torrent of flame from the palm of her hand. But the attack was too disorganized and reactive, and the Blood Witch was able to jump aside in time.

When the flames ceased, Arial noticed that the Blood Witch was only a metre from her, and Arial felt her blood run cold.

The Blood Witch charged. She moved faster than Arial had anticipated. Arial could barely move out of the way in time and tripped over herself in the scramble to avoid the attack.

From the ground where she lay, Arial stared up at her attacker. The Blood Witch bore down upon her, her face contorted into a terrible, wicked smile. She raised her enchanted blade, point facing downward, and prepared to finish Arial off.

Arial closed her eyes instinctively...but her death never came.

There was no pain, no burning flames, no wicked laughter as her enemy drained the blood from her cooling corpse. There was only the enraged roar of a wild beast. Someone groaned, and then Arial heard the distinctive, but faint sound of bones cracking.

When she opened her eyes, Arial could see her familiar standing over her where the Blood Witch had been. The Blood Witch lay sprawled out, leaning against the side of the ramparts.

The massive spirit bear had side-swiped the witch with enough force that she had been sent sprawling into the crenulation. The impact had cracked her skull and severed several vertebrae in her spine. It was a horrific injury, especially as it had not killed her completely. Indeed, the Blood Witch lay there, her eyes darting back and forth. Fear was clearly etched in her face.

A fireball suddenly erupted from somewhere behind Arial. It raced for the broken Blood Witch and engulfed her in a torrent of flames. She didn't even scream as she burned. Her hair and clothes had burned away. Her features were only vaguely human anymore. The wall top now reeked of burning hair and flesh.

Arial turned and saw that it had been Leon who had cast the spell.

He ran over and immediately threw a magical barrier up around them to give the two a reprieve from the fighting. "Are you okay?"

"I'm fine," Arial replied. She managed to stand under her own power. In truth, she felt a little light-headed. The familiar was drawing more energy from her than she realized.

Leon had noticed. "You might want to recall him. He's not worth your life."

"I'm okay," Arial argued. She tried to walk back towards the fighting, but stumbled, nearly tripping again as she went.

Leon pressed a canteen of water into her hands. "Drink this and recall the familiar. He's drawing too much mana from you."

Arial knew that Leon was right. She wanted to protest, but the world was spinning, and words were hard. In the end, Arial could only concede.

She pulled the pendant from around her neck and held it up. The familiar let out a low grunt and disappeared back inside the anchor.

"I didn't even know you'd learned to do that. I only taught you about familiars in passing. You weren't supposed to actually *learn* how to summon one for a few months yet," Leon said. His tone was a mixture of admiration and concern.

"I thought it might come in handy, so I read ahead and figured the rest out myself. It seems to have paid off." Arial took a deep drink from the canteen. The water, though warm, was still just as refreshing as it would have been coming from a spring. Slowly, the world stopped spinning, and the dizziness and tingling went away.

Leon wanted to frown. He wanted to scold Arial for her recklessness. But he was far too impressed and far too worried. "Your natural skill is admirable, but you should be more careful with new magic. I would hate it if anything happened to you. New magic should always be practised in the presence of another mage, in case of accidents. As your teacher, if you'd like to read ahead as you put it, come speak with me next time, and I'll gladly guide you through the basics."

Arial took another sip from the canteen before she handed it back to Leon. "I was outnumbered and outclassed. The familiar was my only hope to combat them. I find myself lacking..."

"You were thrown into a situation you weren't prepared for. There's no shame in admitting that. You still fought off three Blood Witches who were far more advanced in their studies than you. That's an achievement. You've recognized your weaknesses and shortcomings, now as your teacher, I'll help you work on them."

"If we make it out of this fight alive, I'll take you up on that offer." Arial gestured to the blood and carnage that surrounded them, just outside of the safety of the barrier.

Leon smiled. It was a gesture that felt out of place on the battlefield, but a welcomed one, nonetheless. "Let's stick together for this fight. I'll be your familiar, and you'll be mine, or so to speak. We'll cover each other's backs and fight together. Maybe you'll even learn something along the way."

Arial couldn't help but feel some of her fear melt away. "I'll try not to read ahead this time."

A panic set in amongst the defenders as six more Blood Witches, flanked by twelve Blood Warriors in full Blood Fugue came over the top.

"Shall we?" Leon asked. He dissolved the magical barrier. Lightning danced across his fingertips.

Arial produced a fireball in her left hand. "Lead the way."

* * *

Shooter and Kanaahn had seen their portion of the wall overrun immediately. A large portion of the soldiers they served with them had died within a few minutes after the first wave of Blood Warriors crested the walls.

Despite Kanaahn's harsh warnings, and Shooter's attempt at maintaining calm and composure, the lack of discipline amongst the ranks and the sheer shock of the betrayal by the Baron Felidrun's forces was too much for the soldiers.

Some ran, fleeing their duty and the battle post haste. Some begged for their lives but found no mercy but a quick death. Some stood there dumbfounded before a weapon of some sort cleaved through their flesh. In the end, all of them died.

The ground was slick with blood and gore. there were fewer defenders than attackers. The defenders were at serious risk of losing that portion of the wall.

They needed to get a message to Leon. The plans they had decided on dictated that the lines would pull back if their positions became untenable. They had to pull back to the next line of defence. But the forces at the southern-eastern portion of the wall were spread too thin against opponents that vastly outnumbered and overpowered them. They would not survive a tactical retreat if they did so alone. They needed to link up with another force and defend the next set of lines, but no other portion of the wall was in as bad a shape as this one. Leon would need to call for a general retreat, which would also mean evacuating civilians from the city below.

But Kanaahn and Shooter were unable to get word to Leon. They couldn't spare a single man or woman to act as a messenger, and it was hard to communicate telepathically from halfway across the city while they were also fighting for their lives.

The two Khaleeshir were currently bogged down in a battle with a particularly large Blood Warrior.

She had to have been two metres tall, and she had more muscles on her than Kanaahn knew was possible. The warrior swung a massive hammer around, cracking the stone ramparts apart with powerful successive blows. Ruin and devastation were all that remained after the massive iron hammer collided with anything unfortunate enough to get in its way.

Soldiers were knocked from the ramparts. Some were simply crushed by the impact as their armour imploded under the force of the blow. Bodies and crates of supplies were sent flying along with chips of stone. Nothing was safe from the wild swings of the crazed warrior. Even her own allies were not safe from the collateral damage of her wide swing.

Shooter and Kanaahn could only dodge. They were separated, positioned on either side of her. They couldn't get close enough to attack because of the hammer, and they couldn't block, or the hammer would shatter their weapons.

Worse, Shooter was out of throwing daggers, having used them up early in the battle to take down several Blood Warriors while they climbed the ladders in a vain attempt at preventing them from topping the walls. Most of Shooter's personal collection of knives was back in his room at the castle. He kept a few of the more sentimental and less expensive ones with him, in the end. Shooter had wanted to avoid losing or damaging his knives in the heat of battle; he had lost two and damaged one at Xiar, and he wanted to avoid it happening again. They were precious to him.

This fight could not go on much longer, however. It would only end poorly. Someone needed to at least distract the Blood Warrior if the two were going to take her down.

Then, an idea came into Shooter's mind. It was desperate, foolish even—some might say stupid—but it was all he had.

Shooter tore the helmet from his head. He screamed at the Blood Warrior to get her attention. The woman wheeled around; a glare fixed on her face. Once he had her attention, Shooter threw his helmet at her with all the strength he could muster.

The Blood Warrior roared her battle cry and met the challenge head on. Using the flat of her hammer, she swung with both arms and struck the helmet in mid-air. There was a loud clang, and the helmet went flying out over the parapet and out into the fields below the walls. With their hearing, Shooter and Kanaahn heard the helmet hit one of the Baron's soldiers with a resounding, metallic bang, and a loud cry.

The Blood Warrior smirked. She saw the desperation in Shooter's tactics and took the time to gloat.

What she hadn't seen was Kanaahn taking that opportunity to strike, just as Shooter had intended. It wasn't until she felt the warm liquid spill onto her feet that the Blood Warrior noticed Kanaahn had pierced her through the back with his sword.

The blade had been driven in up to the hilt. But it didn't kill the Blood Warrior. The shock wore off, and the rage took over. With a roar, she turned to face Kanaahn, and her fist collided with his chest. His breastplate was dented, and the wind was driven from his lungs. Kanaahn collapsed, gasping for air and dry heaving.

Shooter sprang into action at that moment. He would not lose the opportunity he had created. He drew two long daggers he'd been gifted by the Royal Hunt and leapt onto the Blood Warrior's back. He buried his blades into her shoulder and spine.

The warrior cried out and swung herself back and forth, but Shooter clung on for dear life. He used his left blade, sunk deep into her flesh, as a handhold, and repeatedly stabbed at the warrior's back and shoulder with the other.

Blood sprayed into Shooter's face, and he could taste some in his mouth, but he didn't let up. He stabbed again, and again, and again. He stabbed until his arm ached and he finally drove the last stroke of his blade through the Blood Warrior's neck. She cried out, gurgled her last, and collapsed on the ground. Blood spilt from her mouth and neck wound as Shooter withdrew his blades and returned them to their sheaths.

He pulled Kanaahn's katana from the warrior's body and wiped the blood off. From there, Shooter didn't waste a second and ran to Kanaahn. "Are you okay?"

Kanaahn had just managed to get back his ability to speak. "It'll bruise, but I'll live."

Shooter pulled Kanaahn to his feet and handed him his blade. "Are you sure?"

"Yeah. Thank you," He motioned to the cooling body of the Blood Warrior. "Now if we can do that a few thousand more times we might win."

Shooter's face was grim. "I need to get to Leon and warn him. I'm the fastest, and I can get there with the least issue. Besides, you can lead these soldiers better than me."

Kanaahn nodded and rolled his shoulder. He could feel it pop with every movement, but it would hold. "I agree. Get going; we'll hold the wall. Get him to pull back to the secondary defensive lines. We're not going to hold here much longer at this rate."

Shooter was caught off guard. "You sure you don't want to argue back?"

"I didn't believe you when you suggested something was wrong weeks ago. If I had listened earlier, maybe we could have avoided all this. I'm not arguing back this time. Go before more people die."

A Blood Warrior roared from behind the Khaleeshir. He brandished his massive axe and charged at them like an angry bull.

"Go!" Kanaahn yelled. He shoved Shooter out of the way and ran to meet the Blood Warrior head-on. "Hurry!"

Shooter turned and did as he was told.

* * *

Hana and Aurichalcum watched the fighting unfold from atop Aurichalcum's tower. Despite Aurichalcum's insistence that Hana lay down and rest, lest the pain of what she was feeling overwhelmed her, the young girl insisted that she watch the battle below.

Hana had declared that she was young, and so the opportunity to watch history unfold before her was a rare chance. She also declared that those whose deaths she would inevitably feel deserved the dignity to at least have their final moments witnessed, if even from a distance.

She would not listen to Aurichalcum's protests, nor would she listen to Menalaea, who had been there in Aurichalcum's quarters atop the highest tower in the caste until recently. Menalaea, both a mother and a kind and caring soul, had tried to get Hana to lay down and rest, but even she could not sway the determined young girl from her vigil.

Menalaea could not stay long, as she had been sent back to the palace shortly before the fighting began to oversee a small detachment of soldiers that had been left behind to defend—and in the worst-case scenario evacuate—the castle and the people that remained there. She left the girl in Aurichalcum's care and returned to the soldiers she oversaw to ensure their morale would not waver as the betrayal of Baron Felidrun became clear.

For much of the opening stages of the battle, Hana had worn a brave face and stood strong. But now her bravery was wavering. Her vigil was becoming painful, and the pain was all-consuming. From the grimace on her face, it was clear to anyone that it had started to take its toll on her mind and body. Tears rolled down Hana's face and she gripped the stone railing with all her strength.

"Has the pain not eased?" Aurichalcum asked in an incredibly gentle and soft voice. In truth, he knew the answer.

Hana retched and threw up over the side. She stumbled and nearly collapsed. *"I feel it all. Every life as it ebbs away. Every soul snuffed out. Make it stop. Make it stop."* She trembled and shivered as if she was lost in the frozen wastes of Anglum.

Aurichalcum supported Hana's weight. Her skin was ice cold and slick with sweat. Every muscle in her body tensed at once and he could hear her grinding her teeth from the effort.

"Come, lie down. Let's not push yourself." He picked Hana up in his arms and carried her over to a plush divan he kept in the corner of his room *"Rest. Standing will not ease the pain."*

Hana reached for the ceramic cup filled with water, but she could barely make out the vessel in her state. Everything was blurred, and tears clouded what the nausea and brain fog didn't. In the end, Aurichalcum handed her the cup.

Hana gingerly sipped on the water. She found it hard to swallow; she feared she would throw it up almost immediately, but Hana managed to keep it down. *"Do you feel it too?"*

"I do."

"Why...why doesn't it affect you the same?"

Aurichalcum gave a sad smile but kept his gaze averted. He paused briefly before responding. *"I have felt it for much longer, so I have grown accustomed."*

"Be honest. Was it ever like this with you?"

Aurichalcum looked down at his feet. He could not lie. Not to her. *"...No. Never. But I am also a dragon; a dragon almost as old as the very land of Enayra itself, and I have endured worse pain in my years."*

Hana sipped more water. *"Say what it is you're holding back."*

"...Humans were never meant to experience that. There was only ever one who was supposed to feel it, and she died long before most of us were born."

Hana frowned. *"It's never been this bad. Normally, it's someone passing peacefully in their sleep. At worst, it's someone who's very sick; maybe they died in childbirth, sometimes a little more violently, but it's over quickly. But this...this is just suffering. This is hellish...and there's so much of it."*

Aurichalcum took the empty vessel from Hana and placed it down on the table nearby. He refilled it from the jug of water kept nearby. *"War has never come to the capital before—not in your lifetime anyway. No one expected it would return."*

"Perhaps someone should have read the possibilities," Hana joked weakly. Her sunken, tired eyes attempted to betray the exhaustion she felt and the pain she endured. She was covered in a fevered sweat. The girl looked as if she was suffering from blue fever.

Aurichalcum chuckled softly, more to ease Hana than anything. He needed to keep her calm and comfortable, for the pain would surely only grow worse as the fighting continued—and who knew how long a siege could last?

The dragon was old enough that he could remember the longest siege on record in Enayran history. It was the Siege of Malatrion during the Fourth Asardaean-Espian War late in the Age of Conflict. It had been the only time in Enayran history that enemies of Asardaea had successfully landed an invasion force on Asardaean soil. The Espian armies landed, disembarked, and lasted long enough to besiege the Fortress City of Malatrion despite attempts from the many Asardaean legions to expunge them.

In the end, realizing that the legions could not halt the advance, Queen Amelia Despina recalled her armies to the capital to prepare for the siege. The bridges were burned, and the island that Malatrion sat on was isolated. If they could not defeat their enemies, Queen Amelia would outlast them.

The siege lasted sixteen months, and only ended after the Espian army—losing patience and running low on supplies after such a prolonged siege—revolted against their general. The Espian general, Tanahashi Tsunetomo, was forced to sue for temporary peace to allow his forces to withdraw back to Espias.

Upon his return to Espias, General Tanahashi was sentenced to death by the Espian emperor for his inability to take the city, and for his calling for a retreat.

The Asardaeans responded to Espian aggression by amassing the largest invasion force in Enayran history. Three hundred thousand soldiers, comprised of a combination of citizen levies, foreign volunteers, and professional legionaries.

The invasion force never made it to Espias. By some sick twist of fate, they were wrecked at sea in a massive storm off the southern coast of Danaen. A full three-quarters of the invasion force was lost at sea, including most of Asardaea's senior military officers and Queen Amelia Despina herself.

Both countries had been completely depleted of funds, resources, and soldiers, and were forced to agree to ceasefire and eventually negotiate a lasting peace.

Petty humans and their petty squabbles. That was all Aurichalcum saw it as at the time. He and his kind had refused to get involved to end the fighting throughout most of the Age of Conflict. If the humans wiped themselves out fighting one another, what did the dragons care? The humans were so short-lived they might as well have been temporary. But dragons? Dragons were forever. The drazhani would outlast humanity, and once more would Enayra be theirs and theirs alone—as was intended.

How wrong they had all been.

Hana opened her mouth as if to cry out, but no sound came forth. Instead, her mouth formed a silent scream, reflecting a silent facsimile of the agony inside. The pain had returned even stronger than ever in a new wave of trauma. It was worse now than before. Her whole body felt like it was on fire, and she continued to writhe in anguish.

A spear to the leg. A hammer to the skull. Flames crawled up her body. Lightning consumed the left side of her face. Something crushed her skull with its powerful jaws. More flames burned her. Ice pierced her. She felt her body crumple after hitting the ground. She felt blades cut her. Axes shattered bone and parted flesh. Her innards spilt from her body. Her eyes were pierced with arrows. Each time, the pain grew, adding to a symphony of agony and death, and the chorus of suffering and anguish grew in crescendo as she finally gave voice to the torture she was enduring. Hana screamed as she had never screamed before.

Aside from the aghast worry on his face for Hana's wellbeing, Aurichalcum showed no greater pain or discomfort than a slight bit of indigestion. He barely noticed it, the dying. It did not come close to the pain he had felt on the Kahnair Plains a thousand years ago, nor the pain he lived with since.

Aurichalcum knelt beside Hana. He took her hand and did not let go.

She squeezed his hand in response. She struggled to bear the pain as she squirmed around on the divan.

Aurichalcum said nothing, but he held her hand. He held her hand through it all. Through the screaming. Through the squirming. Through the vomiting. Through the sobbing tears. Even after she had finally passed out, finally driven into unconsciousness from it all, still Aurichalcum held her hand.

Who would have thought, Aurichalcum thought to himself, that the Great Brass Dragon, Aurichalcum, Lord of the West, would find himself in such a state over a human—a child no less.

Perhaps there is a reason for that. Perhaps you are more alike than you care to admit.

Aurichalcum grimaced as the female voice cut through his head. *"Not now, mother."*

Neither of you chose this path, yet you walk it bravely. You both owe your lives to a decision made for you. One that greatly changed you in many ways. You both face pain head-on, though your suffering comes from different sources. Need I continue, my poor misanthropic son?

Aurichalcum did not respond. He was indignant at his mother's proselytizing.

Ignore me all you like my child. But one day, you will have to accept that I love them too—as much as I love you all. They are here now, and they will not simply disappear. One day, perhaps you will see in them what I do, and I know this girl will help you with that.

Aurichalcum remained silent and shut his mother from his mind for the time being. He did not need to listen to another lecture. He was not some hatchling to be scolded. He was a Great Metallic Dragon, a leader of his people. He would not be talked down to.

Hana stirred, though she was still out cold.

Still, Aurichalcum held her hand.

* * *

Shooter had somehow managed to make it to the central command above the eastern wall gate.

He had dodged constant attacks by enemy Qiri'ar, both Blood Warriors and Blood Witches. In some areas, the battlements were so crowded that Shooter had to hop from merlon to merlon to get around the mass of bodies throwing themselves at each other. They hacked and slashed at each other with weapons; bled and died with one another.

Shooter witnessed Blood Witches glide across the ramparts with glowing crystals and hunger in their eyes. They absorbed the pools of blood he had grown accustomed to early in the fighting.

He didn't have to guess what the purpose of this grim harvest was. Blood magic needed blood to fuel it, and blood could often be in short supply. Shooter couldn't stop to end this bloody harvest; any second he wasted was a second the defenders lost and brought them all one step closer to defeat.

The cries of his fellow defenders spurred him on, and every fallen comrade and bleeding corpse pushed Shooter to run faster and harder towards his final goal.

Shooter finally made it in almost record time. He wasted not a second more to locate Leon.

"LEON!" Shooter called out vocally and mentally across the battlefield with enough force to stagger some of the combatants.

A Blood Warrior reared on him, looking to cut him down with a broadsword. Shooter dodged the blade deftly and took off the warrior's arm with his short sword. The Blood Warrior barely flinched. Not that it mattered; a few moments later, the warrior's head parted ways with his shoulders when the opponent he had been fighting attacked him from behind.

Leon's response came not long after the warrior's body hit the ground with a thud.
"Over here. Little busy."

Shooter scanned the battlefield. He looked for any sign that would tell him where he might find Arial and Leon.

He saw them. They were engaged in battle with two Blood Witches. The fighting looked intense, and even at a distance, Shooter could tell they were beginning to tire, and from the fighting, it looked like the Blood Witches knew it too.

Shooter ran towards his friends, blade brandished. As he approached the Blood Witches, he slashed through the side of the one nearest to him. He knew that without the Blood Fugue, the Blood Witches were as susceptible to pain as anyone else, and the Blood Witches, the key to unlocking the Blood Fugue, were not able to enter such a state themselves. The witches needed to be alert and present to support their wild, rampaging allies. It was the Blood Witches who started and ended the Blood Fugue. This much, Qul'den had taught him.

The witch screamed and grabbed her side. Her concentration and spellcasting had been broken. Now she was defenceless.

It was enough of an opening for Leon.

He unleashed a torrent of flame upon the Blood Witch. She screamed her last, and after one final horrific shriek, her burned husk fell to the ground amidst a whirlwind of smoke and ash.

With Leon's attention now freed of the Blood Witch, he was able to turn and assist Arial in finishing off her opponent. Together, Leon and Arial launched alternating strikes of ice and lightning that knocked the Blood Witch off her feet before a nearby soldier finished her off by taking off her head.

Leon turned to Shooter. "Thank you. Now, what is it? Is something wrong? Did the defences at your station fall?"

"No, but they will if we don't pull back to secondary defence lines. The numbers in our sector are too thin to withdraw and fight simultaneously. Even *if* we reach our secondary defence lines, we'll be wiped out in seconds. I don't know how many other sectors are in the same predicament. I think it would be best if you called for a general retreat to secondary defensive positions."

Leon's face looked pained. He'd been mulling over this decision himself. He wanted to make the call but feared judgment or backlash if he did. Shooter could see it plainly in his face.

"Please, Leon. Do it for your people, if not for us."

Leon did not respond.

"Leon," Arial tried to intervene. "We're being overrun here too. We can hold out for now but for how much longer? Shooter is right; it's for the best."

"I know," Leon admitted. "I know…"

"Then what's stopping you?" asked Shooter.

"I'm afraid to make the wrong call. I'm afraid to fail my people and lose the city. I'm afraid if we pull back, we'll project weakness. It could harm our morale and strengthen our enemy. But I'm also afraid that if I don't make the call more people will die because of my inability to act."

Leon turned and looked out at the fields below, where the forces of Lord Gruffydd milled about as the Qiri'ar rushed the walls.

"I thought it would be enough to boost our morale through song, as the Qiri'ar did, and defy our enemy against all odds. I thought once Lord Gruffydd arrived we'd have the Qiri'ar trapped between a hammer and anvil, and we'd break the siege quickly and continue with our lives. But now we're betrayed, the barons on our side are nowhere to be seen, and no one is coming to save us."

The betrayal of Lord Gruffydd had shaken and surprised Leon as much as anyone else. The two had never seen eye on to eye on anything. More often they not, they spent more time fighting and squabbling in government than anything else, but no one would have expected that Lord Gruffydd would have betrayed his king and countrymen and sold them all out for a chance to usurp the throne.

Shooter also suspected there was more to Leon's fear than he was saying. There was someone else Leon was afraid of failing, though Shooter didn't dare guess who that could be out loud.

"Only we can save ourselves, Leon." Arial placed a hand on Leon's arm. She took his hand in her own and pleaded with him. "Shooter's right. We need to pull back."

"I won't abandon my people in the city below," Leon warned.

"We're not asking you to, but if you don't utilize the city's elastic defences like they were meant to be, you'll be condemning all of us to die here," Shooter answered. "That was the plan, wasn't it?"

Leon set his jaw. "I'll send word to the bell towers and get the watchmen to blow the signal horns. I'll personally lead the evacuation efforts and get the people to the harbour. If the worst comes to pass, we'll evacuate as many as we can by boat, but in the meantime, at least they'll be safe. I'll have to split our forces, but the Bluehelms and I will focus on the evacuation, sector by sector. We'll keep the people behind our forces, and we'll make a fighting retreat towards secondary defences. Once we're behind the wall top gates of the secondary defence lines we'll barricade the gates and hold for as long as possible. If the secondary defences fall, we withdraw to the third position, and so forth. As a last resort, the people will evacuate before we do. There are tunnels under the city we can use to escape to Pelchar once the people are out safely. I'll ensure that the castle is evacuated as well."

"We should use the dragons to help slow down the enemy forces during our retreat. It'll be easy for them to overwhelm us if they wanted but slowing them down with dragon fire from above may work to our advantage," Arial added.

Up until now, the dragons had used flames sparingly on the wall tops. In part, it was because flame could be unruly, and easy to go wild. If they weren't careful, they risked setting their own allies ablaze along with the attackers. The wall tops were too narrow and packed full for accuracy. But once they separated the two sides again during a retreat, the dragons could easily bathe the attackers in hellfire. However, they would still have to be careful not to be shot from the sky by a warrior deep in the Blood Fugue, or a Blood Witch's spells.

Shooter grinned. "Dragon fire, the great equalizer."

"Let the dragons know," Leon added. "But make sure they're careful about it. They're still young and vulnerable. Even Thrae has had to be careful against the Qiri'ar unless she's flying at full size, which is unwise in such proximity to the city."

"I did notice her flying higher," Shooter said. "I'll tell Risasi to pass it along. I'm going to get back to Kanaahn and help him pull our forces back to the second position."

"I'll lead the soldiers here while you take the Bluehelms to the city to evacuate the civilians," Arial declared to Leon.

Leon nodded. "Be careful."

Shooter put a hand on Leon's shoulder. "You too." He looked over at Arial, then gave her a quick hug. "And you also."

The trio went their separate ways. None of them wasted a second longer than necessary.

Shooter turned and ran back towards Kanaahn's position as ordered. As he ran, he reached out across the constant connection he had with his partner. "*Risasi?*"

There was a delay before the dragon replied.

"*What is it?*" He sounded haggard and upset.

Shooter relayed Leon's plans to Risasi as quickly as possible. He was thankful the communication was mental, or he would have stumbled and stuttered to get that out as fast as he did.

"*It's the correct decision. The situation looks dire from up here. If we wait any longer the whole front would become unsalvageable. I will let Thrae and my siblings know the plan.*"

"*Thank you Risasi.*"

Shooter hesitated for a moment.

Risasi didn't wait for the question to respond. "*Kanaahn's overwhelmed, but he's holding as best he can. He's brave if nothing else—perhaps foolishly so. You should hurry though.*"

"*At least he hasn't leapt over the wall yet to take on the Qiri'ar at the source.*"

"*If he loses any more soldiers he may just,*" Risasi joked.

Horns blared out across the city from different guard towers. Their deep, dulcet tones cut through the sounds of death and battle. They were soon joined by the harmonious clanging of every bell tower in the city.

The signal had been given for retreat.

Within seconds of the first horn, the Estian defenders were crying out for retreat. Soldiers were looking to their captains and commanders for orders. Shooter could hear the shouts erupting around him.

"Pull back to the second line!"

"Retreat! Retreat!"

"The king has called for us to fall back!"

"Thank the Mother, we may yet live!"

The defending army had been awaiting the call, and it came not a moment too soon for them.

"Be safe," Risasi warned Shooter.

Shooter didn't respond, but his emotions bled out across their mental connection and made it very clear to Risasi how he felt.

Shooter had gone back to running from merlon to merlon. He would not waste a second, and he ran so fast his legs ached. He knew even a second's delay could be deadly to more than just himself.

A few Blood Warriors attempted to attack him from below. They swung their weapons at him. The merlons would crack and shatter into shards under the weight of the hammers and axes. But Shooter would deftly fly and leap over the blades as they swiped at him.

Then Shooter soon saw something that gave him pause and upended his entire purpose.

From the corner of his eye, Shooter saw movement in the city streets below. The streets had long been abandoned, as people sought to barricade themselves within their homes and root cellars—some going to stay with relatives in higher parts of the city as they sought to put more distance between themselves and the fighting.

Shooter looked down into the city where he witnessed, with his keen eyesight, a shape he made out to be Iskren walking down the main road towards the wall. Based on the road he took, and the direction he faced, Iskren had come from the castle. But why he had even left the castle to head for the wall to begin with troubled Shooter.

Iskren had been ordered to wait in the castle after Imuhlair's betrayal. Despite Leon's disappointment with him, someone needed to ensure the Major-domo's work was being done in the castle while Leon was overseeing the defence of the city, and Imuhlair was in prison.

On top of that, he was not a soldier, and so he would be useless on the overrun battlements—especially now that the word had been given to pull back the secondary defensive positions. Even the most important missives and updates from the castle would have been sent by messenger, or via carrier bird.

Something wasn't right, and it nagged at Shooter until he could not ignore it. He froze, perched atop the merlon like some large predatory bird, and watched Iskren continue the city streets, unguarded and alone.

From what Shooter could make out, he was headed towards the east wall gate. Iskren's destination combined with Shooter's distrust of him, and when Iskren checked over his shoulder four times in half as many minutes, the trifecta of coincidences birthed an incredibly terrible feeling in Shooter's gut.

He had made up his mind at that moment that he needed to do something, and he would do so—consequences be damned. Nothing could be worse than if he ignored this, in Shooter's mind.

Shooter jumped from the merlon, landing with cat-like agility on the nearest rooftop. He inched his way closer to Iskren. He stalked across the rooftops quietly and silently, just as Menalaea had taught him. Shooter wondered why Menalaea hadn't noticed Iskren disappear from the palace; nothing escaped her gaze. He supposed that Iskren had used the chaos of the evacuation to slip away unseen.

The streets would soon be filled with Bluehelms and fleeing civilians. This was a fact Shooter could hear ring true across different neighbours not far away, as Bluehelms shouted out to the citizens to leave their houses, rally in the streets in an orderly manner, and begin making their way towards the harbour immediately.

Iskren's window had to have been narrow and deliberate, Shooter reasoned, but the Major-domo had not expected to be seen by a Khaleeshir—no one else would have noticed in the middle of battle, and at that distance. Shooter would find out what the man wanted to hide.

There was no such thing as coincidence. That was merely a fact. It was a fact Shooter lived by, and a fact that had saved his life more than once.

Chapter L

If anyone had come walking through the forest near the Acturn canal that day, they would not have noticed the army of freedom fighters assembled in the branches of the massive trees, or inside the depths of bushes scattered across the forest floor.

They would not have noticed that these men and women were armed to the teeth if armoured quite poorly. Nor would they have seen them, lying in wait, daubed in paint and mud to blend in with their surroundings.

Any passer-by would simply not have seen these armed fighters watch the Acturn canal fortresses with such a dogged intent that the whole forest could have caught fire around them, and not a single one of them would have noticed.

But what these ill-fated hikers *would* have noticed was the wave of explosions that erupted along the entire Acturn canal, spewing stone and dirt and people high into the air before gravity brought them crashing back down in a broken heap.

They would have seen the broken bleeding bodies of Qiri'aran warriors lying in the rubble of the fortresses they once held.

They would have seen the water of the Acturn come flooding down the ruined canal like a tidal wave and burst through the dikes and levees that once held them back.

They would have watched as, slowly, the fields around Ethon flooded and sunk beneath the ever-growing surface of Lake Ardona again for the first time in nearly sixteen hundred years; flooded—even temporarily—for the first time in six hundred.

They would have heard the cries of broken Qiri'ar, no longer in their Blood Fugue, cry out for help or healing.

They would have seen the rain of incendiary arrows arc through the sky and put an end to the lives of those broken victims.

They would have heard the cheering of a thousand freedom fighters ring out in celebration of their success, and the cries of tens of thousands of birds and beasts flee in terror at the sudden explosion. The sound of the battle at Ethon would have ceased for a time, as everyone tried to figure out what had just happened, for the very ground had shaken in that explosion.

These unfortunate people who so foolishly picked today of all days to walk through the woods near the Acturn canal, would not have seen much else, for they would have quickly caught a blade through their ribs, and it would all have been over for them.

Ogdyn Veers, captain of the Felidrun chapter of the Estian Republican Army rallied his squad of soldiers to pick through the wreckage of the once proud canal fortress.

Bodies were dragged out of the wreckage and stacked in a pile to be burned. Any unlucky enough to still be alive were quickly put out of their misery. All along the ruined parts of the canal, similar scenes took place.

"What should we do with these woodcutters, boss?" asked a tall, bearded man daubed with green and brown paint and dressed in similarly dyed clothes.

Ogdyn shrugged. "Throw 'em in the pile with the rest, I guess," he replied indifferently. "Shouldn't have been snooping around where they didn't need to be."

"Did they really deserve that boss?" a slender, older woman with greying dark hair asked.

"Maybe not, but they would have just gotten in the way of phase two," Ogdyn answered.

"And what's phase two?" the woman asked.

Ogdyn turned and put his hands on his hips. "Everyone in the capital heard and saw that explosion. It won't be long before they send soldiers over here to investigate, which is exactly the point, and what the Baroness asked of us. We'll keep them busy until the city can be evacuated."

"So, we're supposed to die for those noble bastards?" a young, wiry boy asked. He couldn't have been older than seventeen.

Others murmured agreement.

Ogdyn stepped up to calm potential dissent. "They'll be along as soon as the people are evacuated. Together we'll fight a retreat to Pelchar, at which point the guerrilla war begins."

"You expect those royalists to keep their word?" a voice called from the gathering crowd.

Ogdyn's answer was swift, and his voice boomed out across the immediate area. "I know you must be feeling some apprehension, allying with the enemy and all. But I trust the Baroness's and the King's word a lot more than that bastard Gruffydd. At least with the Baroness you know where you stand with one another. And I hate to admit it, but as far as royalists go, they're not as tyrannical as the rest."

"And what about after this is done? What then, we wait for them to crush us?"

"We'll deal with that when we get there," Ogdyn replied. He grinned wide, and his eyes grew wild. "Now no more questions until we're done here. If you question this arrangement, you question the Big Boss. You know what happens when you question the Big Boss."

The crowd immediately grew silent. They dispersed to carry out their assigned duties. No one wished to cross the famed "Big Boss", leader of the ERA.

There were many legends told about him amongst the republican freedom fighters. The stories had been passed around so long by so many that myth and fact had blended and become indistinguishable.

Some stories said he was an old man who had suffered under the tyranny of King Aethalmenis III and had since sworn revenge against the royal family and the nobility that propped them up. Others claimed that the Big Boss had been the young, devilish heir to the republican destiny of Carolus Vingrus. A ne'er-do-well who had descended from the first republican, and who came from a long line of freedom fighters. Some said he wore an eyepatch, having lost an eye in battle with the king's forces. Others that he was covered in head to toe in the scars of his many battles. Some stories claimed he was bald, others that he had long flowing hair. Even more stories claimed that the man had two hooks where his hands should be after he lost them in a fight with Baron Gruffydd.

What was the truth? Even Ogdyn didn't know.

No one ever really saw the Big Boss. He communicated mostly by messengers, go-betweens, and written orders. He rarely ever came out of his hiding hole—he was the most wanted man in the entire kingdom after all. If anyone recognized the Big Boss he'd be in jail, tried, and executed faster than anyone could blink.

Regardless of what the truth was, the Big Boss was a dedicated republican and a worthy leader. Though he hid himself and lived his life constantly on the run, he had never led his men falsely.

Ogdyn would follow the Big Boss into the depths of the Nine Hells and back.

"Hey Ogdyn." It was the older woman from earlier.

"What's the matter now Vinella?" Ogdyn asked.

"I thought we were already planning to hit the canal before we made this deal with the baroness?"

Ogdyn grinned from ear to ear. "She didn't need to know that. We spent too much time and effort getting our men inside those forts as workers. She almost ruined the whole plan by moving up the annual maintenance."

Vinella chuckled. "Never one to waste a good barrel of naphtha jelly, eh Oggy?"

Ogdyn frowned. "I told you not to call me that in front of the others."

Vinella only winked, then walked away without another word.

Ogdyn turned back to examine the damage the explosives had done. It had been the Big Boss's plan. He had gained insider knowledge of when the Baroness Pelchar was starting the annual canal maintenance and had planned to strike at that moment.

The Big Boss had instructed his chapter leaders to send their soldiers into the fortresses disguised as maintenance workers. From there, the Big Boss had contacts that could smuggle in barrels of naphtha jelly that could be primed, charged, and set off using magic.

The barrels were buried from halfway up the Acturn to well down the beaches along Lake Ardona. Once they went up, they would blow the dikes that held back the river and lake from overtaking the floodplains that had been drained for farming centuries long past. The constant rain over the last few weeks only acted to swell the river and the lake and made the devastation and flooding even worse.

Soon enough, most of the area surrounding the capital would be underwater. The fields would be wrecked, and it would be months before the dikes were fixed and the water drained. An act like that would have crippled the Kingdom of Estion, and driven up the price of grain. The Boy King would have had to have released grain from the grain stores; though Lord Gruffydd and his greed would never have allowed that to happen. The House of Lords needed to give the final say on that.

The people would have paid the price for the shortage and the Baron's greed, and the plan was to use that anger and resentment to incite revolt against the monarchy and the greedy barons of Estion. The ERA would turn the suffering of the people against the oppressors to start a fire that would cleanse the land.

If the people were angry enough, it would matter little whether the ERA had been responsible for the explosions in the first place or not. In the end, the people would only care that they were suffering and that the king was doing nothing to help them. Logic mattered little to the hungry, desperate masses. All they'd want was someone to blame, and that someone would be right at the top of it all, whether it was their fault or not.

Hunger, starvation, desperation, poverty; all of these would be turned into fuel and weaponized to feed the outrage, and once the anger had been fuelled and let loose, like wildfire, it would not be stopped.

The plan had been genius, if perhaps quite devious and duplicitous. But in the end, it mattered little to the ERA *how* they won their fight. The end goal was supreme to all other concerns, and how they got there mattered little. If the price for freedom from the oppressive tyranny of monarchy were a few lies and a few dead innocents, so be it.

Even if half the country had to burn as recompense, it mattered not. Homes could be rebuilt. Towns resettled. Populations would be reborn. Livestock replaced. Crops resown. Trees replanted.

In the end, all that mattered was that the people of Estion were free of the yoke of the Crown, and got what they so rightly deserved, after years of civil war, civil unrest, and endless suffering: a representative democracy of elected officials.

Ogdyn turned back towards the massive pyre of burning bodies behind it. The smell of burning hair had shaken him from his thoughts. There was nothing quite as vile as the smell of burning hair—except maybe wet feathers. Ogdyn could live with the flesh; it wasn't much different from roasting a pig, but the hair...he never got used to the hair.

"Once all the bodies are burned, and you're done stripping the valuables from the wreckage, get back into those woods and get into position. We need to hold the northern bank until the Baroness arrives. We can't do that standing around with our heads up our asses, milling about like the town gossips."

Ogdyn's voice was like a bullwhip. It boomed and cracked, cutting through the air with a snap. It was so loud it reached even the farthest edges of where his group worked. It spurred his soldiers on faster, brave men and women all.

They'd need to be brave to face what was coming. The Blood Warriors were formidable, and in a state of Blood Fugue, near unstoppable. Guerrilla tactics would slow them down, but the losses would be considerable still. But it was better than meeting them head-on. At least this way they stood a chance.

Ogdyn looked out over the waters of the distant lake. The lake shone like a sea of sapphires in the late afternoon sun. "You better show up, Baroness, or there'll be Hells to pay. Mark my words. We don't make deals like this lightly."

Chapter LI

Dragon fire had indeed been a great equalizer; at the very least it had slowed the Qiri'ar enough to allow the remaining soldiers to reach the secondary defensive positions.

Though those in the Blood Fugue could not feel pain, they were still subject to mortality, and bathing them in gouts of hot flame, torrents of lava, clouds of toxic gas, bursts of lightning, and bolts of freezing ice certainly had an effect.

It helped further that the Qiri'ar had seemingly begun swapping out their exhausted first wave of warriors. This created a small gap in the intense fighting that allowed the defenders to withdraw without the immediate threat of pursuit, however briefly.

But soon the fresh and ready second wave arrived. Fresh to the fight and full of vigour, they continued cleaving through defenders as if there had been no pause.

Furthermore, the presence of dragons and their various elemental attacks had caused the Qiri'ar to re-evaluate their methods, and now Blood Witches flanked entire attack groups and were seen in greater numbers. They raised shields and shot magical attacks at the dragons to keep them from getting too close.

As if that wasn't enough, Blood Warriors had brought bundles of wooden javelins and iron-tipped spears to throw at the dragons, adding to the barrage of attacks that the dragons risked every time they would swoop in for an attack.

Thrae had been hit several times, but her size allowed her to shrug off most of the damage. But at a most inopportune time, she was forced to return to the castle and assist in the evacuation efforts there. This left only the four Khaleeshir, Valence, and Kinokaze to sweep over the entire city to protect the defenders as they retreated.

Unlike Thrae, who could easily ignore the projectiles and magical attacks, the younger dragons were not so fortunate, and though their armour would protect them from the worst of it, the enchantments could only do so much.

In the end, the dragons were forced to retreat as well. There were too many projectiles flying at them, and Valence and Fyete had been wounded too severely to continue fighting without seeking immediate medical attention.

Whatever slowing effect the dragons had on the attacking forces was lost.

Adalinda departed, insisting that if she could no longer harry the attackers, she would accompany Leon and the civilians to safety, and help the Bluehelms keep the walled harbour protected. If any enemy warriors got through the defensive lines and reached the harbour before the defenders she would be there and help.

Kinokaze, while reluctant to stop her sweeping attacks on the Qiri'aran lines, had chosen to assist Adalinda in that endeavour. Adalinda was the smallest of the dragons by nature of her clan's physiology, and while she was still a formidable foe, even against a Blood Warrior, a larger companion was always welcomed by a white dragon.

Risasi remained on the battlefield, despite being ordered to pull back, as had Djall. Together the two watched the battle unfold from above. Instead of engaging in combat, they chose to utilize their positions from the sky to alert the defenders of the ground of enemy troop movements. Any time the Qiri'ar moved or sent new units into battle, they would send word to their partners or other commanders below. Since they flew too high for the Qiri'ar to attack them, and the attackers had no dragons themselves, the two dragons kept a detailed record of all troop movements they saw.

Leon had gotten the civilians past the third defensive positions, and almost two-thirds of the city had made it to the safety of the harbour. Those who remained were well behind the front lines of the fighting, and the soldiers fought tooth and nail to buy the civilians— their families—as much time as possible to get to safety.

There was hope of a reprieve when, from nowhere, the city was shaken to its core by a massive explosion from somewhere off to the northwest. Attacker and defender alike watched in disbelief as dirt and water from both the Acturn and the shores of Lake Ardona closest to the city were thrown into the air like a child had just thrown a tantrum.

What had once been a well-constructed and cleanly kept canal was now a gaping wound that ran from the lake towards the sea. The blood that poured from it was the very waters it once kept back. Water was pouring from the overflowing lake into the lowlands around Estion. The fields were flooding, and the attackers would soon be standing waist-deep in freezing water if they did not act quickly.

No one knew how or why the dikes had suddenly exploded, and at any other time this would have been another devastating event, but for once it seemed, the defender's terrible luck would work in their favour.

The defenders were hopeful that Qiri'ar would now need to split their forces to begin repairing the dikes and minimize the massive flood that was to come. The aggressors could not ignore the torrent for too long, or it would hamper their siege. Already they stood ankle-deep in the rushing waters of Lake Ardona as the lake sought to reclaim its ancient territory from the people of Estion.

But rather than send the Qiri'ar, as hoped, it was the Baron's soldiers that broke off from the main army to assess and repair the damage. A large amount of them had been sent to the canal.

"This tells me that the Qiri'ar had seized the canal as well," Leon had said across a mental link, using Thrae as an anchor point to reach across the city with ease. *"If they're sending that big a force to the canal, then they had soldiers stationed there."*

"It also means they knew about the annual maintenance. They attacked and took the canal at the most opportune of times. It was not a coincidence" added Kanaahn.

"Not even Leon knows when the maintenance happens. How could they have found out?" asked Arial.

"It means we have a spy," Arkas answered.

"Has anyone heard from Shooter?" Kanaahn asked. *"Is he anywhere on the walls, Risasi?"*

"I haven't heard from him. I can feel his presence in the city below, but he refuses to answer my calls, and he has dimmed our connection. I do not know why."

"Keep trying," Kanaahn replied. There was a strain in his voice as if he was pushing against something heavy. Then he went silent.

"Less talk, more fighting!" Arkas called. *"Just keep us updated on the enemy's movements."*

Risasi and Djall dipped down and surveyed the fighting below. They were horrified to see that the Qiri'aran solution to being flooded out of their camp was to charge the walls at once and end the fight faster. It was a heavy-handed and obtuse approach to warfare, but when you were a Blood Warrior caught in the throes of Blood Fugue, you had few other options—and the results usually spoke for themselves.

"They're coming! All of them are coming. They're rushing the walls. Brace yourselves!" Djall called out to his friends below.

No response came.

The defenders had done their best to hold out against the overwhelming strength of the Qiri'ar, but they could not hold out forever, and not against such devastating numbers.

Djall and Risasi watched in helpless horror as the secondary defences were breached, one by one. The gated defence towers built at the intersection of the criss-crossing web of walls had been used to hold back the enemy, but one by one, the doors were broken.

Djall and Risasi could hear wood splinter, hinges scream, and stone split. The tower situated at the crux of the Western Markets, the Weaver's Enclave, and the Woodworker's Enclave was the first to fall.

The doors had been hacked to pieces, and finally unable to bear the relentless hammering of the Qiri'ar, they gave way to a tidal wave of blood-thirsty, senseless warriors who sought only to spill blood and cleave flesh. Victory was their only goal.

The dragons watched them pour into the tower like an army of ants. This scene was repeated across the whole secondary defence line, and once more the city was a chorus composed of the sounds of battle and slaughter, sung in harmony with the screams of the dying.

The soldiers were now in a state of panic. The dragons could hear them scream; cursing, calling out to whatever higher power would listen. Some begged for mercy, but they did not find it at the other end of a Qiri'aran blade. There was a call to retreat to the tertiary defence line. Others called to flee the battle entirely. Others tried to surrender. Some still charged screaming towards the harbour, looking for sanctuary amongst the populace.

The defenders' will had been broken, and their army routed. The city was surely lost now.

Djall looked to Risasi. "There's nothing we can do to aid them?"

"We cannot give them back their spines," Risasi grumbled. "We'll head for the harbour; it seems everyone else is. Kanaahn and the others will likely head there with what remains of their soldiers. We'll regroup and begin evacuating the civilians to safety."

"What of Shooter?"

Risasi's face was resolute. "Shooter will be fine. I can do nothing to aid him at this juncture. He will find us when he is ready. I know him, whatever he is doing, it must be urgent."

The two dragons tucked in their wings and pulled into a dive. As they neared the city, they could smell the blood and sweat in the air. They made haste for the harbour, though they made time to blast fire, lava, and noxious gas at pockets of attackers. It wasn't much, but every enemy dead could serve to tip the scales back in their favour.

"Leon, we'll be arriving shortly. We'll help you defend the harbour. The front lines are breaking down," Risasi warned.

"I've noticed. We would appreciate the help. We should start evacuating the people. I'll get the Bluehelms to assist me. Once you're here, you can help Adalinda and Kinokaze protect the gate."

"How are Fyete and Valence?" wondered Djall.

"They're still being worked on, but they will heal," answered Leon.

Fyete had been pierced through the side by a barbed iron-tipped spear. The enemy had managed to throw it with enough force that it had just barely grazed her heart. If Fyete had moved in the wrong way, or driven it in any deeper, she would be dead.

It was Valence that had insisted she go seek help immediately. It was also that distraction that had allowed the enemy to strike at Valence. Two javelins had gashed her neck open. One had embedded itself in her clavicle, and the second had managed to cut through the tendon of her front left leg at the knee joint. Between the blood loss and the pain, Valence barely made it to the harbour. But, aided by Kinokaze and Adalinda, the silver dragon had managed to get there just before she collapsed.

Djall and Risasi cut the connection with Leon. The king needed to go about his duties, and the dragons had incoming projectiles to avoid.

They beat their wings, gathered speed and altitude, and flew high above the city at top speeds. It was from up here that Djall finally noticed something on the lake that he had not noticed before.

"Risasi, are those boats?"

Risasi scanned Lake Ardona. "I supposed. There have been boats there all day. Most are trying to watch the battle from a safe distance. Others are just going about their day unbothered."

It was true that boats and barges had travelled across the lake for the entire length of the siege, going between the small lakeside towns and villages as normal.

As far as these small-town people were concerned, the siege was a city problem, far removed from their daily lives. Civil wars had been common enough in Estian history that even after so long, to see the capital besieged once more was just a normal fact of life to the people. As Leon had put it when he quoted an old Estian saying: 'It mattered not who sat upon the throne that day, for tomorrow it might change, and taxes would still be due.'

Even after word had spread that it was the Qiri'ar attacking the capital, the people still went about their daily lives, though more and more boats would slow down and stop to watch the siege from far away. It was the presence of these commoner crafts that had initially caused Djall to miss the large flotilla that was now headed straight for the city.

"No, Risasi. Look—" Djall pointed with his snout. "—They're coming for the city; the harbour."

Risasi's lips curled back into a snarl. "Another attack? How many fronts did they plan for? Come, we shall burn their pathetic wooden vessels to ash before they even reach the docks."

"No, Risasi wait!" Djall cried. To his astonishment, Risasi did not charge off and burn the flotilla to flotsam anyway.

"What?" growled Risasi.

"I agree we should investigate together but…what if it's the baroness that His Majesty was expecting to arrive?"

A guttural rumble echoed from deep within Risasi's chest. "Then she's bloody late, or she's a traitor too."

"Didn't you say Shooter suspected foul play was afoot, and that someone had interfered with sending the word to the baroness?"

Risasi mulled it over. "It was a possibility he was considering, yes."

"Well then, why don't we go there and figure it out? See what this flotilla wants with a besieged city, dear brother?"

Risasi looked to the harbour below. "What about Leon? Won't he need our help?"

"Look at you, thinking through the consequences for once," Djall snarked. "Fine. Which one of us will help our sister, and which will go to the flotilla?"

For once, Risasi did the opposite of what Djall expected. "You go to the flotilla; I'll help defend the harbour. We're better suited for those tasks."

"Are you…feeling all right, Risasi?" Djall asked with genuine concern.

Risasi snorted. "Yes. Why?"

"Because you're being oddly mature and level-headed for a change."

Risasi's lip curled. "You're better with words, and I'm larger than all of you. Besides, I am eager to rend the flesh of my foes and burn them to an ashen crisp. It doesn't take a genius to figure out who should do what task."

"Ah, there's my brother. I was beginning to miss you."

Risasi snapped his jaws at Djall, but the green dragon had already taken flight towards the mass of ships that were headed for the harbour. He doubted anyone down below could see them yet, as they were still aways off. Besides, they were too preoccupied with the attackers on the walls than the lake behind them.

Djall bee-lined for the boats as fast as his wings and the winds would carry him. The closer he drew, the more he noticed that boats were not warships, but cargo ships and large passenger barges with wide builds and fat bottoms. This was not an armada meant to attack the city, that much was for certain.

He made sure to fly low to the surface so those aboard could see him coming. Djall knew surprise would not be his friend in this situation.

Djall levelled out before the bow of the lead ship, righted himself, and flapped his wings to keep himself level and aloft with the woman who stood on the prow. His wings billowed the sails of the cargo ships and disturbed the surface of the water with a myriad of ripples and small waves.

The crew stared in disbelief—most had likely never seen a dragon before—and some looked ready to fight off Djall if he proved hostile. Hair and beards were tousled in the gust caused by Djall, but the lady on the bow, grizzled, wounded, and missing her arm, seemed nonplussed by it all.

Something told Djall it could be no one else.

"Baroness?" Djall asked.

The woman's face remained unchanged. "Yes?"

Djall felt relief wash over him. "I am Djall, one of the Khaleeshir, partner of Kanaahn. I noticed your ships from above the city and came to investigate. We were not expecting you."

The Baroness cracked a smile. "I was...delayed. I do apologize. How is the situation in the city, Djall?"

"Not well. The morale of the defenders is completely shattered. They're on the retreat, and the Qiri'ar have claimed most of the city. The defenders were supposed to be pulling back to the tertiary defensive lines, but most just made a break for the harbour."

The Baroness remained calm, despite the grim news. "How is His Majesty?"

"He has used the Bluehelms to evacuate the civilians from their homes, and he's currently with them at the harbour. They're preparing to evacuate as many of the civilians as possible right now, but the attackers will soon have them boxed in and our defences have worn thin. We don't have long."

"And Baron Felidrun's forces?"

"They've not joined the fight. They seem to be letting the Qiri'ar do all the work. Though recently the dikes were blown along the lakeside and up the Acturn. The fields have started flooding already, and the Baron seems to have sent a large portion of his forces to staunch the flood waters and repair some of the damage. A large portion of his forces were sent to the canals—we believe they had a force there that they are going to either reinforce or check on."

The Baroness replied with calm and poise. Every word was well-measured and carefully chosen. Nothing shook the confidence of the Baroness Pelchar. "I had no idea the situation had so deteriorated. Tell King Leon I shall make haste. Don't worry about the canal, it's been covered. I'll double our speed, and we shall be to Ethon as soon as possible to assist in the evacuation efforts. My soldiers will disembark and join His Majesty's remaining forces to buy the people time to escape, and then we shall flee the city, and make our way across the Acturn, and back towards Pelchar on foot."

"Why on foot?" Djall asked. "Would it not be faster to join the civilians on board the boats?"

"We cannot risk the enemy attacking Pelchar in retaliation while we're on the boats with the civilians. If we march back to Pelchar on foot it will take longer, yes, but we'll put ourselves between the enemy and our destination and ensure that Pelchar is safe."

"Very well. Is there anything else I should pass on?"

The Baroness pondered for a moment. "Reassure His Majesty he did all he could. We may have lost the battle, but the war has just begun. You cannot win a campaign in a single day."

For the first time, the Baroness seemed to show a hint of genuine emotion. Her calm, calculated demeanour and carefully chosen, methodical word-craft melted away into genuine concern for King Leon and the kingdom. It was clear that the two were close, and that a genuine friendship had formed between Baroness and King.

"It shall be done, Baroness. We shall look for your arrival. Please hurry."

"Would that these ships could fly. We will have to make do until that becomes possible."

Shooter hated it when he was right. It usually meant that something terrible was about to happen. This day's terrible occurrence confirmed that Shooter had been right to be suspicious of Iskren ever since he had revealed Imuhlair to be a "traitor."

Shooter followed Iskren from the rooftops. He stayed just far enough behind his target so as not to be noticed.

At one point, Iskren ducked into an alleyway and waited. For a while, neither of them moved while the Bluehelms ran door to door, and down the streets, yelling and screaming to evacuate and follow them. People ran screaming from their homes. They carried nothing but their children and a few days' worth of food hastily thrown together in their efforts to flee the danger that was to come.

No one seemed to notice Iskren crouched in the shaded alley; why would they? They were too busy fleeing for their lives. The entire time, Shooter alone watched Iskren from behind a baker's chimney, still warm from that morning's fire.

After what felt like an eternity the people had finally been evacuated from that neighbour, and from the sounds on the wall above, it sounded as if the defenders had already begun moving towards the secondary defences.

The sound of battle was quickly moving further north and only when Iskren started moving again did Shooter follow suit.

Iskren weaved through the once-more abandoned streets towards his goal. Though soon enough, another delay had stalled both Shooter and his prey.

A large, distant explosion had shaken the city to its core. Shooter had been unable to determine the origin of the explosion, only that it had not been—thankfully—the Qiri'ar breaching the outer walls of the city to pour into the streets like a flood.

Shooter would soon realize how prophetic that moment of thanks would be.

He got his confirmation about Iskren when the Junior Major-domo had reached his goal. It took Shooter a few seconds to realize that Iskren had led him to the eastern gate of the city.

Iskren made his way post-haste towards the gatehouse door.

Shooter almost rolled his eyes when he realized that Imuhlair's tour of the city was starting to come in handy. Because of the old Major-domo, he knew the east gate was the largest and grandest of the gates heading into the city of Ethun. It was known by many names. Some of the names it had had over the years were the King's Gate, the Campaign Gate, or the Gate of Conquest.

Whatever the name used, the gate's original and most important purpose had always remained the same. It was the gate by which the monarch would enter and leave the city with the army when Estion was at war. During peacetime, the monarch would favour the smaller western gate, or the harbour if he travelled by boat. The incredible size of the eastern gate was made clear whenever Estlon went to war. The gate and tunnel entrance through the wall had been built tall and wide, to accommodate large armies, siege weapons, the monarch's retinue, and their personal guard.

Up close, Shooter saw that the gates were even larger than the city gates at Ottogard, which had been kept intentionally narrow to stave off attackers during a siege. A dragon the size of Glay'ak could walk down the gate tunnel comfortably. Shooter could only imagine what it would look like if they were opened.

The massive eastern gates were kept closed during peacetime, but the smaller—though still large—wicket doors would be opened to normal traffic, such as traders with their carriages, farmers and their livestock, and everyday foot traffic.

Right now, both were closed and barred and the portcullis on either side had been lowered to keep out the attackers.

Shooter's stomach lurched as he realized why Iskren had come here to the gatehouse. The Junior Major-domo was seeking to betray the city and his monarch by opening the King's Gate for the attackers.

The Khaleeshir was resolved to stop Iskren before he succeeded. The Qiri'ar were so formidable they had already overwhelmed the defenders by attacking over the tops of the walls and flooding the battlements with incensed Blood Warriors and Blood Witches. But if they also entered through the gate and made their way through the streets, the defenders would truly be helpless to stop them.

Shooter didn't know how far or how much of the city Leon and the Bluehelms had yet evacuated, or how close to the harbour they were, but the evacuation would only end in disaster if the gates were opened. The Qiri'ar would not touch the civilians; Qul'den had explained to Shooter that no honour came to a Blood Warrior who slaughtered an innocent, but the same could not be said for the traitorous soldiers that served Baron Felidrun.

He leapt from the rooftop and followed Iskren into the gatehouse. Once at the door, Shooter lifted the latch as quietly as possible and gently opened the door inward.

With some hesitation, Shooter poked his head inside the door. He scanned the gatehouse, making certain that Iskren was not waiting there for him. Certain it was safe; Shooter entered the gatehouse.

He closed the door behind him as gently as he had opened it, then scanned the room. It was just a normal—if abandoned—gatehouse. There were desks with stacks of paperwork. Keys hung from hooks along the wall. There was a door along the right side of the room that led into the gate tunnel, and Shooter could see that it had been double-barred and pad-locked several times over.

In the far back of the room was a barracks for the guards, and a small holding cell to the left of the barracks. Beside the holding cell was a separate, double-barred cell for contraband items confiscated at the gate checkpoint. The weapons racks beneath the stairs on the left side of the room had been emptied, no doubt to arm the defenders before the siege.

But for all Shooter saw, Iskren was nowhere in this room. Shooter turned to the stairs. That was the only place that remained. It was also where the mechanisms were that operated the gates and portcullises.

Shooter swallowed some bile and ascended the stairs. He took each step carefully to ensure that they did not creak and alert Iskren to his presence. He kept his short sword drawn just in case.

As he climbed the stairs, Shooter could hear the loud but slow sound of gears turning and clicking. It wasn't the gates being opened, Shooter realized, but the mechanisms that controlled the clocks on either side of the wall gate. He looked up to see that the massive gears high above his head turned and spun at varying speeds, and a massive pendulum swung back and forth. It was impossibly large.

Further scanning the mechanisms above his head, Shooter could make out various sets of chains, pulleys, cogs, and gears that were not moving. These were no doubt part of the gate mechanisms.

Shooter scanned the simple mechanism room for the cranks and winches that controlled the gates. During the tour Imuhlair had given the Khaleeshir when they arrived, he had explained that Leon himself had constructed new gate mechanisms that made the act of opening the gate as fast and simple as one person turning the appropriate crank handle. Using varying sizes of gears and other types of mechanisms, Leon had put the entire weight and strain of the gate and portcullis on the mechanism rather than the person turning the crank directly.

Sure enough, Shooter found four sets of winches on the far back wall from where he now stood. But to Shooter's surprise, Iskren was not there.

But how? Unless...

Shooter wheeled around; blade raised. He flicked his sword effortlessly and parried aside the blade that had been aimed at his back. "Iskren. I wondered where you'd got to."

"How long have you been following me?" Iskren had been as surprised to see Shooter as Shooter had been by Iskren's sudden attack. The only difference was the fear in Iskren's eyes.

"Since you crossed down into the lower city."

"So, then you've figured out why I'm here?"

Shooter rolled his eyes. "It doesn't take a genius to figure out why you're here at the gatehouse to the city's largest gate, while everyone else has been ordered to evacuate."

Iskren jabbed his blade towards Shooter.

Shooter sidestepped the blade and returned an attack. He caught Iskren's hip, but the damage was minor.

"You may have fooled King Leon when you framed Imuhlair, but you didn't fool me. I'm willing to bet you're the reason the Baroness Pelchar never arrived to defend the city before Baron Felidrun did."

"You should have minded your own business, Khaleeshir," Iskren snarled.

Shooter sunk into a stance and grinned. "You should have kept your cards closer to your chest and been smarter about which ones you played."

Iskren lunged.

Shooter parried.

Their blades clashed and the sound echoed against the stone walls of the room, adding to the music of the turning gears, and swinging pendulum.

Iskren pressed the attack again. He aimed high, then low. Each time Shooter was able to block or deflect the attack, but Iskren kept the offence up and prevented Shooter from returning attacks of his own.

Shooter side-stepped Iskren's next swipe at his midsection. He knew if he kept stepping back, Iskren would have him backed up against a wall, and that was a recipe for disaster in a fight.

Shooter side-stepped Iskren's next attack. Iskren had thrown himself too deeply into the attack and ended up perfectly placed in front of Shooter and open to attack.

The Khaleeshir slashed at the Major-domo, but Iskren turned at the last second and blocked the attack.

Shooter's sword grated against the edge of Iskren's. Iskren manoeuvred the blade away from his body, but Shooter pressed hard against Iskren's blade. He summoned every ounce of strength his Khaleeshir body could muster and managed to graze Iskren's shoulder before being thrown off again.

Iskren grabbed his shoulder. He pulled his hand away to examine the red blood that trickled from his flesh wound.

But Shooter would not let up the attack. He seized the initiative and attacked Iskren with a flurry of blows.

Shooter struck high.

Then to the left.

At Iskren's already wounded hip.

Shooter went for Iskren's head again.

Then to the neck.

At the shoulder again.

But time and again, Iskren blocked deftly.

Shooter gnashed his teeth, and he could feel his frustration getting the better of him. It was as if Iskren could see through each of Shooter's attacks. The Major-domo had rarely failed to block a single strike. To Shooter's credit though, it looked as if Iskren was tiring, and Shooter knew he needed to continue to press that advantage. Iskren, not a habitual fighter, did not have the endurance that Shooter had developed through his recent training.

Shooter charged again at Iskren, closing the gap in two paces before launching into an even faster set of strikes, slashes, and lunges. He threw everything he had into his attacks. There was no room for doubt or hesitation.

He thrust his blade at Iskren's mid-section.

Iskren blocked that with a sideswipe of his sword.

Shooter spun and used the momentum of his turn to slash at Iskren's neck.

Iskren ducked.

Shooter kept his cool and aimed a thrust at Iskren. He feinted a strike to the gut and switched to the knee at the last second. This time the blade connected. Iskren cried out. Shooter could feel his blade tear through, flesh, muscle, ligaments, cartilage, and the meniscus of the knee before catching on the bone with a jarring thwack.

But instead of the relief or triumph, Shooter was left puzzled. Something felt wrong. His blade was narrow and short. It wasn't a flesh cleaver designed to cut through flesh and bone like butter. Moreover, he hadn't swung his blade hard enough to cut to the bone. The flesh had parted too willingly. Something felt off—

Pain.

Horrible pain.

He felt a warm feeling spread across his chest. Shooting pain spider-webbed across his back from the spine. Shooter tried to cry out, but blood spilt from his open mouth instead. He looked down to see Iskren's blade poking through his chest. Tears and pain blurred Shooter's vision and he could feel his strength start to waver.

How?

Shooter could hear Iskren's voice behind him. "Did you know that my late brother was an incredibly skilled mage? He so excelled at his craft that at the age of twenty-seven he was made Grand Enchanter of Altimara. He was particularly skilled with illusory magic. I was never as good at it as he had been, but he taught me some of what he knew, and it seems it's come in handy finally."

The Iskren that Shooter had stabbed dissolved, as did the rest of the room. Suddenly, the sounds of a veritable screaming horde joined the sounds of the pendulum and gears, muffled by the thick stone between the mechanism room and the gate tunnel below.

Shooter felt as if he had just taken a serious blow to the head. The room spun, his lucidity waned, and he couldn't tell if this was all a dream and he was already dead, or if he was slowly going insane. He felt like a passenger in his own body.

He stumbled and fell to his knees, clutching at the blood that soaked across his chest and sped from the hole in his leather armour. Iskren's blade remained buried deep in his body.

"Unfortunately for my brother, his ambition seems to have finally caught up with him. My uncle Calandor told me that he had passed after contracting the blue plague, but I know how things are in royal courts. It's a very cutthroat environment and it's only a matter of time before the people on top become targets for those below them. I suppose my brother and I were alike in that way—overly ambitious. I became a target for Imuhlair because I leveraged my friendship with Leon to get this position, and my brother became a target for whoever replaced him."

Shooter looked around. He realized that the entire fight with Iskren had been an illusion. From the very first strike. Iskren had used that guise to open the portcullises and the eastern gates. By the time Shooter realized, it had already been too late. The enemy armies had already rushed into the city. There would be no closing these floodgates.

Shooter reached a hand out towards Iskren and managed to summon a single word. "Fucker..."

Iskren smirked. "How petulant. I admire your tenacity, but you'll die here."

"Why...?" Shooter asked. He struggled to remain on his knees. His whole body wanted to go lifeless and collapse, but Shooter would not give in to the pain or death.

"Because my uncle asked me to and because, as I said, the royal court is a cutthroat place. I stood to gain greatly by a change in power. My uncle would have put a good word in for me, either here or in the Altimaran Court. Leon... was friendly, but he was a blind idealist who would have squandered away his wealth and power for a people who neither cared for him or nor deserved the kindness he showed them. The people are weak by nature, and any power he would have handed over to them would simply have been abused by those at the highest places in society. It would be no different from the monarchy he sought to diminish. It is the nature of people to throw themselves subserviently at the feet of those in power, whether they chose to put them there or had those leaders forced upon them."

"How...cynical..." Shooter's vision was going; he didn't have much longer. He reached up for the railing just out of the corner of his eye but missed and his hand landed at his side, buried beneath his cloak.

"Perhaps, but that doesn't mean I'm wrong. Now, if you excuse me, I must be going. I do hope whatever happens to you is quick, though I suppose it's too late to be painless. Oh well." Iskren turned on his heel and walked towards the stairs.

Now was Shooter's chance.

He gathered the last of his strength and pounced on Iskren while his back was turned. From within the folds of his cloak, Shooter produced his favourite blade, one from his personal collection that he had always kept on him: a six-inch knife with a hilt shaped like a dragon with inlaid ruby eyes. Truthfully, the rubies were fake, but that didn't stop Shooter from favouring the blade on the day-to-day, just as he favoured the use of his left hand.

Shooter clutched the knife in that same left hand and jammed it deep into Iskren's neck. This time, the motion felt right, and the blade sunk into flesh as it should. The tip of the knife shot out the other side of Iskren's neck and blood sprayed across Shooter's face.

Iskren gasped and gurgled, he tried in vain to grasp at the knife, but it was too late.

Shooter grinned to reveal his teeth and mouth had been stained by Iskren's blood. He looked the very picture of a vengeful spirit—pale, haggard, and bloodied. He could feel his anger get the best of him, but at this point, rage—and adrenaline—were the only things that kept him alive and moving.

"You're not the first person to stab me. But you are the only one stupid enough to get it wrong. Word of advice, motherfucker: pull the blade out after you've stabbed someone, otherwise they don't bleed out fast enough."

Shooter grabbed the hilt of his knife and a handful of Iskren's hair.

The man choked out what might have been a scream, but the knife had punctured his voice box. Instead, Iskren spat mouthfuls of blood as Shooter, flexing every muscle in his arms, twisted his knife and Iskren's head.

The blade tore through the remaining bone, muscle, and flesh and Shooter ripped Iskren's head from its body. The Major-domo's neck erupted in a fountain of blood that painted Shooter's face like a canvas.

Shooter's rage boiled over and he roared his triumph to the world.

Iskren's body hit the floor with a dull thud, and Shooter tossed the man's head to the side with disgust. He did not deserve a proper burial.

It was the screaming of the hordes outside the gatehouse and the shattering of glass that drew Shooter from his rage and back to reality. The adrenaline left his blood, the anger passed from his system. Shooter felt dizzy, and the pain of his wound returned.

He needed to leave the sword in until he reached a medic, but every time he moved the sword grated against his spine and caused him excruciating pain. Shooter would not be able to walk back to the harbour in this state—especially not when he was surrounded by an army in the midst of looting and ransacking the emptied city.

Shooter stumbled down the stairs, taking care not to trip and fall the rest of the way. He grabbed the railing tighter than he had grabbed the knife. He could feel his feet drag with every step, but Shooter had vowed he would not die here. He would make it back to his friends.

After a slow and cautious trudge down the stairs to the main floor of the gatehouse, Shooter opened his mind up once more and reached out to the only person who could get here fast enough to rescue him.

"Risasi...help..."

That was the last thing Shooter remembered before he collapsed on the guardroom floor.

* * *

There were maybe one hundred and fifty soldiers left under Arkas's command when he met Imiisah Ifelen. Most of them had melted away when the second defensive lines gave way.

Arkas had thought they'd at least make it to the third line.

After the second line collapsed, he had about four hundred and fifty soldiers who remained to fight alongside him. Arkas led them in a brave fighting retreat with his short sword drawn, cutting down any enemy that got too close.

Arkas had emptied his quivers of arrows long ago, but he refused to stop fighting just yet.

The arrival of Lady Imiisah had served to galvanize the remaining soldiers under Arkas's command, and her own two hundred soldiers bolstered the confidence of both forces.

The two agreed to retreat towards the harbour together, and they would make the Qiri'ar fight for every inch along the way. They had hoped to buy Leon and the civilians as much time as possible.

Arkas and Imiisah arranged their spear-wielding forces at the rear guard of the column while willing and capable soldiers, including Imiisah and Arkas, joined them to fight off the oncoming horde. The soldiers used their spears like a swarm of angry hornets to keep the Qiri'ar at a distance, while the remainder of the melee rear-guard focused on cutting down the enemy to stop the whole column from being overwhelmed.

The column of soldiers had managed to make it almost to the harbour in this formation, but it all fell apart a few hundred metres from the harbour doors. Most of the column of soldiers nearest the harbour doors broke formation and fled towards the harbour. They banged against the thick doors, begging to be let into the safety of the walled compound. Their morale had completely crumbled.

When the vanguard dissolved, it caused the middle of the column to follow suit, and soon enough Imiisah and Arkas were left alone with an ever-diminishing rear-guard.

Arkas called out to the soldiers as they fled. He beseeched their better nature, and their soldierly duty and honour. But it was all in vain. They did not stop.

In some ways, Arkas couldn't blame them. In the same circumstances, with the same lot in life, with less responsibility on his shoulders, he might have done the same. But now there was nothing for it but to stand and fight. It was all he and Imiisah could do. Fight and inch ever closer to the harbour.

Every second they bought for Leon was another civilian saved, and that was, in itself, a small victory. These loyal few would keep to the plan as agreed upon. Once they reached the stairs, they would break and join the other soldiers in the harbour.

Ironically, Arkas, Imiisah, and all who remained upon the walls despite the overwhelming odds also fought for the safety of the soldiers who banged upon the harbour gates to be let into the harbour.

Ladders were thrown over the top of the impossibly high harbour walls for the soldiers to climb. With the evacuees safely inside and withdrawing, the doors would not be opened again lest the safety of the harbour be compromised.

Soldiers pushed and shoved one another to be the first up the swaying rope ladders. Seeing this, the defenders atop the harbour walls threw down more ladders. The squabbling ceased, and desperation turned to determination.

By now there were only a score and a half of the rear-guard left, including Arkas and Imiisah. With grit and determination, they had managed to almost reach their goal. The stairs to the city below were just in sight, and most of the soldiers had gotten over the top of the wall.

"We should get ourselves to the walls as well. We don't have far to go, and we won't last much longer," Arkas called to Imiisah.

"Just a few moments more," Imiisah replied. "Just a little more. They need more time."

"I think it would be unwise! Let me call the dragons for cover. Their fire will hold back the enemy long enough for all of us to get to the ladders."

Fate soon proved Arkas correct.

Imiisah did not respond. Instead, she preoccupied herself with a Blood Warrior that had charged at the wall of spears without a care in the world. The warrior swung her massive two-handed sword and sliced through spear shafts like a scythe through wheat. Soldiers fell, spraying blood from stumps where limbs once were.

Imiisah's twin swords were knocked from her grasp and sent flying into the streets below. Uncowed by her predicament, Imiisah grabbed an unbroken spear from a fallen comrade. She thrust the spear-tip at the Blood Warrior and caught her in the side of the neck.

But the Blood Warrior did not go down.

Fuelled by magic, rage, and instinct, the female warrior grabbed the spear in Imiisah's hands and snapped it as easily as a child could snap a twig. Now defenceless, Imiisah could not stop the sword blow that cleaved her head from her shoulders.

Arkas cried out, his hand outstretched. He did not notice the Blood Warrior that had crept around to his right, but he felt the warrior's axe slice through his forearm. He felt the blood spray from his now gaping wound.

Arkas screamed from the pain and grabbed his bleeding stump. He held it as close to his body as he could. White lights twinkled in the edges of his vision, and Arkas almost wanted to vomit from the pain. Arkas struggled as he tried to wrap his bleeding stump in his cloak to staunch the bleeding.

He was too dazed and preoccupied to block the knee to the side of the head. Arkas felt his head snap to the side. His world seemed to turn upside down and Arkas's entire body was aflame with mind-numbing pain. He lay prone on the ground, his face pressed into the stone ramparts.

The soldiers around him screamed and panicked. Both of their commanders—one a Khaleeshir—had just fallen. As far as they knew, Arkas had died like Imiisah.

Arkas could only listen helplessly as the remaining soldiers were butchered like pigs at the slaughter, squealing just as loud while their lives were snuffed out in horrific ways.

He croaked, trying to call for help, dazed and confused.

The warrior that had parted Arkas from his right arm seemed to notice and returned to finish the job. The Blood Warrior kicked him once, twice, three times in the ribs, driving what little air Arkas had out of his lungs.

Then the warrior picked Arkas up by the back of his neck. He snarled at the Khaleeshir and punched him in the face. With a hearty laugh, he tossed Arkas off the side of the battlements into the city below.

Everything went black before Arkas even hit the ground below.

Chapter LII

It was not supposed to go this way. Though Aurichalcum could not say he was surprised.

The Qiri'ar were formidable, and the betrayal of Lord Gruffydd had harmed morale. The defenders had looked upon Lord Gruffydd and his allies as saviours. They had spent weeks expecting Lord Gruffydd's arrival to be the end of this siege, but instead, he and his armies had turned against the Crown and joined the Qiri'ar in attacking the city.

Even if they did not send their soldiers over the walls, the actions of the traitor barons had dealt a massive blow to the defenders. It was a blow that had been exploited by the Qiri'ar.

Looking back on the weeks that led up to the siege, Aurichalcum supposed that things had been doomed from the start, and in truth, the defenders had been defeated before the battle even began.

He suspected someone had betrayed them internally; that someone Leon had deemed to be Imuhlair, though Aurichalcum was not convinced. It was too convenient an answer. The true culprit was likely still at large, having framed Imuhlair for his actions. The betrayal, the siege, and the defeat of His Majesty was likely a plan set in motion long ago—far longer than anyone truly realized.

But it was far too late now for regrets.

Hana stirred in Aurichalcum's arms. She had grown weaker, and her condition had not improved. Nor was it likely to improve as the defenders' morale was shattered and the dying only grew more frequent and brutal.

The palace had been evacuated completely not long ago. Aurichalcum had planned to leave last. He did not want the staff or anyone else to see Hana like this. It was undignified, and furthermore, it would raise too many questions. None but a select few knew the truth of Hana's predicament, and Aurichalcum was intended to keep it that way.

"There you are!"

Aurichalcum turned to see Thrae and Menalaea.

"Why didn't you evacuate with everyone else?" Thrae demanded. "The castle could be overrun at any moment."

Aurichalcum shrugged. "I do not fear these humans. Besides, we must keep Hana's condition a secret. How would I explain her current state to the gawking masses?"

"You once told me that a dragon as old as yourself did not have to explain himself to anyone," teased Menalaea.

Aurichalcum did not find it as amusing as she did.

Thrae changed the subject. "Well, nonetheless we should move quickly. Everyone's already at the harbour, and Leon is in the middle of evacuating civilians."

Hana stirred again. She was barely lucid, and her eyes remained closed, but she raised her head as if to speak. *"What...what of...the Khaleeshir?"* She barely managed to get the words out before she collapsed again.

Thrae and Menalaea frowned.

Hana was getting worse.

Menalaea did not need to check Hana's forehead to see if she was now running a fever. Her body was unable to handle the stress it was being forced through.

It was Menalaea who replied. "We've lost contact with them. When the lines collapsed, half of the forces fled back to the harbour in a disorganized deluge. From what we can tell, those who remained to fight are slowly being overrun, but under the Khaleeshir's leadership they are doing their best to buy His Majesty and the evacuees as much time as possible."

"Will it really matter?" Aurichalcum asked. "Why not do that from behind the safety of the harbour wall?"

Aurichalcum had a point. The harbour had been built to serve as one of the city's last two resorts during a siege, the other being Filiddyn Castle. The walls were double thick and tall—taller than the city walls—and while they were connected to the outer city wall, the ramparts ended at the harbour wall. There was only one door in and out of the harbour, and the entrance had three portcullises and reinforced ironwood doors clad in iron so that no one could burn or smash their way through.

No doubt, the Qiri'ar would find a way, but it would not be easy, or quick.

"Djall has just let King Leon know that the Baroness is on her way," Menalaea explained. "She's brought boats to evacuate the people. With her help, there will be enough boats to get all the civilians out by water. We don't know why she's late, how she managed to show up just in time, or how she got here without the Acturn canal, but I'm not about to question a miracle."

Aurichalcum handed Hana over to Thrae. He handled her as one would handle a priceless glass heirloom. "Take her for me. There is one more thing I must do for His Majesty before I join you. I will be along as soon I am finished."

"What could possibly " started Menalaea.

"It is important. His Majesty asked me, should the city ever fall, to do what I am about to do. I can say no more, but he will understand."

No one questioned Aurichalcum further.

"Lord...Aurichalcum..." Hana had come to once more.

"What's the matter, Hana?" Aurichalcum asked.

"Don't...don't let them...don't let them...they are..." Her words were incoherent and her sentences were incomplete. Aurichalcum could not make head nor tail of what she was trying to tell him.

"Rest now, Hana. We'll get to safety soon enough," Aurichalcum said.

"No…" Hana reached her trembling hand across her body and touched Aurichalcum's arm. Despite her fever, her hands were ice cold to the touch, and it sent a shiver up Aurichalcum's spine.

Immediately, Aurichalcum had experienced something he never had before. He witnessed the visions Hana had seen. He saw the Possibilities. Aurichalcum soon came to understand what Hana was trying to show him. While she trained the Khaleeshir, she had read their possibilities, and now, in her weakened state, she showed Aurichalcum what she had seen.

Aurichalcum was not particularly skilled at divination and possibility—Aurum was far more skilled than any of his siblings at the skill—but he tried his best to understand. He saw many things, much of it was blurry, and even more of it confused him, but he saw the visions as the Khaleeshir and Hana would have.

Aurichalcum saw Arkas standing in a river, flanked by an orchard on one bank and a pile of half-dead, moaning bodies.

He saw Arial upon a crumbling bridge. Before her was a winding mountain path; lonely, cold, and empty. Fraught with dangers and peril. Behind her, was a cottage built upon the innocent dead, who cried out for revenge upon the Khaleeshir.

Then he saw Shooter stand at the edge of a massive fissure in the ground. He stood before a faceless woman with hair the colour of saffron. But the pit called to him, sending dark tendrils of shadow out from below to envelope him in its all-consuming embrace.

Aurichalcum saw Kanaahn at a diverging path in a desolate woodland. Ravens croaked and cajoled to take the right path, but the path on the left seemed so much more comfortable and inviting.

The scenes dissolved and replayed, again and again, and for once in his life, Aurichalcum felt alone and overwhelmed. The visions confused him, but the emotion of what he was seeing was clear. He could not understand what truly lay before the Khaleeshir, only that the decisions would be difficult, and not all their scars would be visible on the outside.

Suddenly, the visions ceased, and Aurichalcum heard words echoing through his head. He recognized them as a memory he and Hana had shared after she had read the possibilities of all the human Khaleeshir.

"Do you believe they'll make the right choices, Hana?"

"I cannot say. Nothing is definite. But I have hope that they will. We have to believe they will, or we have nothing. Destiny is a lie, but hope is very real."

Even after Aurichalcum's consciousness returned to reality he felt haunted by all he had seen.

"What's the matter?" Thrae asked.

It occurred to Aurichalcum he had spent the better part of a very long, awkward pause standing there with a vacant look on his face, lost in thought.

"Nothing," Aurichalcum lied. "I had a thought. Get going, you have no time to waste. I'll be along shortly."

"Promise me, Lord Aurichalcum." Aurichalcum heard Hana's voice in his head. *"Promise me."*

Aurichalcum felt his heart grow heavy. *"I promise, little one. I shall ensure that no harm comes to the Khaleeshir. It is as you said."*

Aurichalcum did not wait. He turned on his heel and without so much as a goodbye to Menalaea or his daughter, stalked off to uphold his promise to King Leon.

He would see to it his promise to Hana kept, but for now, his goal was the throne room.

* * *

The arrival of the Baroness Pelchar brought a wave of cheers and elation across crowd of the defenders and evacuees.

It was no wonder why, there was little else to be thankful for on this day. Three hundred thousand people were being forced to evacuate the only homes they'd ever known. They had lost friends, family, and loved ones in this siege. Even soldiers who hadn't lost their lives had still lost limbs, digits, and litres of blood.

Kyeit, Cecil, Kanaahn, and Arial aided in getting the civilians and the most wounded of the soldiers onto the boats in as orderly a manner as possible. It wasn't easy, and the people had begun to push each other in the rush to get to safety. They arrived in throngs, and panic had set in. Time was running out, and the people knew it.

The Qiri'aran attackers battered at the reinforced doors of the harbour wall with all their might. With each strike, the doors gave way just a little more. Cracks and splinters had already appeared in the reinforced wood and steel.

It was like thunder from hell. It sounded as if the attackers were attempting to beat their way through the defensive doors and walls with their bare hands. For everything the defenders had seen that day, none of them would put it outside the realm of possibility. The power granted by the Blood Fugue was as horrific as it was awe-inspiring.

The sound of looting and rioting by Baron Felidrun's forces in the city beyond added to the tone of the evacuation. The dragons circled above the harbour walls, raining down fire from above to keep the Qiri'ar at bay and buy everyone more time. All except Risasi who had left his post and flown off into the city without a second word.

Fyete and Valence had been healed of their wounds, and while they circled the defences from a little higher up than others, they were back in the fight as soon as the healers had finished.

There weren't many of the captains and commanders left. Lady Imiisah had reportedly fallen according to a few soldiers who had served with her. Others mentioned that Arkas had fought and fallen alongside her. Last they knew he was still out there. From atop the walls, none of the soldiers could see any defenders remaining outside the harbour walls.

Lord Commander vohn Yeshtaburg had fallen early in the battle. He had gone down fighting no less than three Blood Warriors.

Commander Glyndwyr of the Bluehelms had fallen during the retreat to the secondary defences. He had been reduced to a desiccated husk by a Blood Witch.

Hau'tarh had been gravely wounded in the fighting and had been carried to the harbour by four of his remaining Lau'thso warriors. Of the thirty Lau'thso that had escaped captivity, only eight remained including Hau'farh.

Shooter was still missing as well. No one had been able to account for him since he had warned Leon to make the call to retreat.

Things were looking grim.

The Baroness Pelchar disembarked her craft by leaping from the forward bow to the dock below. She kept her hammer resting in the crook of her neck as she approached the small make-shift command centre Leon had set up by a wooden fishmonger's stall.

She bowed to the king. "Your Majesty. I came as fast as I could."

Leon returned the bow with a hug. "How did you get here if the canal was under repair?"

"That is a longer story than we have the time for," the Baroness replied.

"And the other barons that sided with you?" asked Leon.

"At Pelchar with a portion of our forces. They're there to ensure that Pelchar is not entirely defenceless while we make our retreat. How are we escaping this harbour? Do you intend to fight your way out of the city?"

Leon shook his head. "My grandfather spent a good portion of his reign building tunnels across the entire city. He was prepared to flee at any moment. We should be able to use the one at the harbour here to reach the northern shores of the Acturn."

The Baroness smirked. "The bastard. That works perfectly, I promised our allies that we'd join up with them and make the retreat to Pelchar together. I'd hate to come across a liar."

"Allies?"

"I'll explain in detail later, but I've made a deal with the ERA."

Leon's eyes widened. "So, the dikes...?"

"I had no idea that's how they'd do what they do best, but I can't say I'm surprised. Don't look a friendly dragon in the mouth."

"I'll look it in the mouth the second we have the time to do so," Leon argued.

Kyeit approached Leon. "We're trying to get the people boarded as quickly as possible, but we still need more time yet."

"How long?" asked Leon.

"I don't know. We're trying to evacuate three hundred thousand panicked civilians. However long you can buy us," Kyeit replied in earnest.

The Baroness brandished her hammer. "My soldiers will buy you as much time as you need—or we shall die here trying."

"There's not many of us left, but my soldiers and I will do our best to help. Keep getting the people on the boats as quickly as you can, and once they're out of the harbour we'll start getting the remaining soldiers into the tunnel. It's just below the statue of my grandfather there—" Leon pointed to the one spouting water from the tip of his upraised hand in the centre of the square. "—I know what magic is needed to open the path."

"There's another problem..." Kyeit continued. "Arkas is still missing, as is Shooter. Risasi disappeared into the city, but Djall seems to think that may be related to wherever Shooter is. Fyete's unable to sense her partner. I fear the worst."

Leon's mood darkened. "What do you propose we do then? We can't leave without them."

Kanaahn and Arial approached the group before Kyeit could respond.

Arial spoke first. "We just heard from Risasi. He's found Shooter, but he's wounded. He was over by the east wall gate, and the gate was wide open. The Baron's forces not trying to stem the flow of the water seem to have entered the city from there."

"Who opened the wall gate?" Leon demanded.

"Unknown, but Risasi is returning with Shooter right now," replied Kanaahn. "Arkas is still missing though."

"We should send out a search party," the Baroness suggested.

Kanaahn shook his head. "There's way too many Qiri'ar out there. If we send anyone over that wall, they'll be overwhelmed and killed in an instant."

"What's your suggestion then?" Leon asked.

"Let us go look for Arkas at the very least," Arial pleaded. "We'll search from above with our dragons and once we find him, we'll bring him back."

"We can't, in good conscience, let you go out there alone," Kyeit argued. Though she spoke to everyone present, her eyes were fixated on Kanaahn.

"We can't in good conscience allow anyone else to die today. We're not your average soldier. We're Khaleeshir. Arkas is our friend, and we're going out to find him," Kanaahn argued.

The Baroness stepped between the two parties. "Give them a chance. We'll keep enough soldiers here to hold the harbour, and anyone we can spare we'll start evacuating into the tunnels. If you don't return in a reasonable amount of time, we'll send out a search party." Lady vohn Veishaupt turned to Kyeit. "Which of these ships has the least number of civilians on it?"

Confused, Kyeit motioned to a smaller passenger barge on the eastern end of the harbour. "That ship is entirely wounded soldiers."

"I'll hold that ship here. Shooter, was it? He already requires medical attention, and my gut tells me Arkas will as well. If any of you should be wounded in your rescue attempt, the boat will be here for you."

Leon knew better than to argue against Lady vohn Veishaupt. The Baroness Pelchar was a formidable woman with a knack for charming others to her side. Whether it was confidence or natural charisma, few could disagree with her plans, no matter how foolhardy or desperate.

Kyeit admitted defeat. "Very well. But allow Cecil and I to remain here to hold the harbour. The Khaleeshir are our charges, and I'd see them back here alive."

Kyeit looked at Kanaahn once more.

The Baroness nodded. "Very well. Your Majesty, can you lead your soldiers to safety through the tunnels? I'll remain here with my forces to hold the harbour and await the return of the Dragonkin."

"Yes ma'am," Leon replied. He scurried off to his grandfather's statute to begin the progress of opening the hidden entrance.

Djall and Adalinda landed in the harbour area shortly after the group dispersed, and Kanaahn and Arial mounted their dragons with haste.

Kyeit ran up to Djall's side and took Kanaahn's arm before he could depart. "Be careful," she pleaded.

Kanaahn placed his other hand over top of Kyeit's. "I will, I promise. I'll be back before you know it."

There was a pause as the two looked each other in the eye.

Djall cleared his throat and adjusted his wings.

"I should go..." Kanaahn said.

Kyeit only nodded in response. Her cheeks turned a lighter shade of red.

"I love you." The words left Kanaahn's mouth before he even knew what he was saying. He could hear Djall snicker across their mental connection, but he didn't care.

Kyeit smiled and called back. "I know."

Kanaahn's face was as red as Risasi. He didn't even care that Djall continued to mock him inside his own head, or that Arial, who had been party to the whole conversation by virtue of her improved hearing, attempted to hide her excitement.

Besides, none of that mattered after the four Khaleeshir crested the top of the harbour wall. They looked out upon the city and came face to face with the destruction. At that moment, any talk of love vanished.

Parts of the city had been set ablaze during the looting. The Khaleeshir could see the smoking as it rose and curled up into the sunset sky to join the dark clouds and deep hues of the evening sky. They could hear the shouts and hollers of soldiers celebrating their purloined treasures. They could smell the burning wood as it mixed with the burned hair and flesh that wafted off of large piles of burning bodies.

"They've already begun burning the dead," Arial mentioned.

"I don't smell as much blood as I should," added Adalinda.

"The Blood Witches likely saw to that cleanup. No doubt the burning bodies have been emptied as well," Kanaahn replied.

"No time to worry about that. We should look for Arkas," warned Djall.

Djall and Adalinda spread out over the city. They flew out of range of any projectiles the Qiri'ar could throw at them, but with their eyesight, they could still see the street level clearly enough.

From the testimony of several soldiers, Arkas and Imiisah were last seen near the harbour gates, though they were still atop the walls trying to hold off onslaughts of Blood Warriors.

Djall chose to sweep towards the west, while Adalinda curved east. Arial and Kanaahn helped scan the ground as well, using their keen eyesight to do so.

Everywhere they flew they saw destruction. Most of it was perpetrated by the soldiers of the traitorous barons. They cared not for breaking into the harbour or even participating in the siege. It seemed Lord Gruffydd left most of the actual fighting and dying up to the Qiri'ar.

The sounds of the harbour door being beaten with heavy weapons could still be heard even a half kilometre from the harbour area. The Khaleeshir needed to hurry to find their friend. The gates would not hold forever, and neither would the Baroness and her forces. They were far too outnumbered.

Arial suddenly cried out across the mental link. *"Down there!"*

"What is it?" asked Kanaahn.

"We can smell blood...and burning," Arial answered.

The burning wasn't too significant—there was burning everywhere across the city. Flesh, hair, timbers, homes, the remains of lives once lived happily and peacefully. But the smell of blood was unique. Everywhere else the blood that had spilled across the battlefield and from fallen warriors had been claimed by the Blood Witches...but not below.

Kanaahn knew it was worth it to investigate. *"We'll come over to you. Wait for me before you descend. We'll go investigate together."*

"I'm already on my way down. If it's Arkas, he's wounded. I need to get to him before anything bad happens."

"Take Adalinda with you at least!" Kanaahn protested.

"The streets are too narrow for her down here, and the rooftops won't support her weight. I had her bring me as close to the ground as she could get. You'll see her circling above. That's where I am—hurry!"

Kanaahn swore at no one in particular. *"When did Arial get so reckless?"*

"Do you really have any room to speak?" Djall asked.

"Silence you big green lizard."

* * *

Adalinda had dropped Arial on the rooftop of a nearby building. It looked to be a tavern, though whatever it was mattered not any longer. Flames had engulfed half the building.

Just across the burning building, on the other side of a narrow laneway, was a bakery. The chimney smoked as if the baker had left his fire burning, though the place had likely been abandoned for hours.

Someone had relit the baker's oven.

Arial scanned the laneway below and saw a trail of blood leading down the steps. From what little she knew of tracking—all of it learned from Arkas over the years—whoever had been through here was severely wounded and had gone into the bakery. It had to be the same person who relit the fire.

But why relight a fire? From Arial's point of view, it was likely to cauterize a serious wound.

It had to be Arkas.

Arial made her way down from the roof into the street below. She used a bit of her remaining mana to cast a warding spell around herself just in case she was caught by surprise. It would stop all but the worst of physical and magical attacks, and at the very least keep her safe until Kanaahn arrived.

She abandoned caution as she reached the laneway and ran into the bakery.

"Arkas!"

Arial burst through the front door and scanned the room. She could not see him. Perhaps he was in the back, where the ovens were?

Arial hopped the counter and ran into the back room of the bakery. When she entered the backroom she found Arkas, and the state she found him in horrified her. Arial covered her mouth with her hands and stifled a scream. Tears welled in her eyes.

Arkas lay there unconscious. His right arm had been severed halfway up his forearm. By how clean the cut appeared, it had clearly been done by a bladed weapon. The end of the arm stump had been burned, and recently. The smell of burned flesh was still fragrant in the bakery.

479

He was lying there, propped up against the base of the ovens. A smouldering fire crackled away inside the stone oven. Arkas's cloak lay tattered and bloodied across his lap. It was clear he had used it to staunch the bleeding until he could burn the wound closed. He must have passed out from the pain after he cauterized it.

Arial ran to her friend and knelt behind him. She immediately checked for a pulse and was relieved to find that he was alive, however weak he now was.

"Kanaahn. I've found Arkas, please hurry he's—"

The floor creaked behind Arial. She turned in time to see a Blood Warrior grinning at her from the corner of the back room.

Shit.

"I knew if I waited here someone would come for him. You can't help yourselves, can you?" the Blood Warrior asked. "Always leaping to the aid of those who need it, even at the cost of your own safety."

Arial stood up. She was not afraid, quite the opposite. Her desire to help and protect Arkas above all else galvanized her will. Arial would not be felled here. "You've made a grave mistake."

Arial raised her hands and gathered all her power into her fingertips. Her ward flickered and faded as whatever power sustained it was redirected towards Arial's next spell. Bright blue-white lightning shot from Arial's fingers and spread across the room before her. The lightning struck the walls, carving out chips of the heavy plaster. Cups and flatware cracked and shattered when hit by the stray bolts. Pots and other utensils that hung from hooks in the ceiling rattled and clanged as bolts bounced off them.

The Blood Warrior raised his wooden shield to protect himself from the lightning, but in vain. The edge of his shield splintered from a lightning strike and a bolt caught him in the face. He roared and grabbed at his eyes. A few extra bolts caught in him the chest and neck, but soon Arial was forced to stop the lightning barrage as her mana slowly petered out. If she pushed herself any further, she would die.

Arial stumbled and tried to keep her balance. Her head swam, her knees felt wobbly, and she could feel vertigo kick in. She was experiencing mana exhaustion. She had used too much of her mana and now she paid the price. Arial wanted to vomit but somehow managed to hold herself together.

Despite taking several searing blows from the magical lightning, the Blood Warrior did not fall or die. Instead, he only seemed to grow more violent. Enraged, the Blood Warrior threw himself at Arial and knocked her back with his shield.

Arial flew across the room and stopped only when her head and spine collided with the stone exterior of one of the ovens. Sprawled out on the ground, Arial gnashed her teeth and struggled to stand up.

Once on her feet, Arial stared down the Blood Warrior and raised her hand to cast another spell.

She never got the chance.

The Blood Warrior closed the gap between them and swept Arial's legs out from underneath her. She landed hard on her side.

Arial rolled over and pushed herself up on all fours in the struggle to get back on her feet.

The Blood Warrior roared. He would not let Arial leave here alive, and to that end, brought the edge of his shield down on the back of Arial's skull.

Arial could feel her head snap back as she was driven to the floor. Her skull made an audible crack. Her vision swam worse. She felt dizzier than before, and when Arial tried to utter words to cast a minor protective shield she found she could not summon the words to do so.

Her voice seemed to catch in her throat, and the words jumbled in her head. Arial tried to force the words out, but they came out slurred and backward. Repeated attempts to speak only led Arial to projectile vomit on herself and the floor.

The Blood Warrior sneered at her. "I think I'll leave you to your suffering for now, and deal with your friend first. I'll return to you later. I promise you it will be a quick death." Then he turned his hulking frame towards Arkas and raised his blade high.

From the little Arial could make out in her concussed state, she could see the blade was aimed at Arkas's head—or maybe it was his midsection. Whichever was the case, it would be a fatal blow. Arial tried to call out, to do something, anything, to save Arkas.

It was then as if in answer to her prayer, Kanaahn arrived. He rushed through the doorway into the kitchen and slammed into the back of the Blood Warrior.

Arial could hear the shouts and grunts as Kanaahn, and the Blood Warriors grappled each other on the ground.

It was the last thing she remembered before she fell unconscious.

Chapter LIII

The throne room had an empty and sombre atmosphere about it now that it had been abandoned. Not long ago it was full of life when Leon would hold court here. The House of Lords would meet, there would be arguments, and Aurichalcum would hate it all.

Now this place was as desolate as a ruin.

Aurichalcum moved a wall banner to the left of the throne to reveal a hand-shaped imprint on the wall. With a wave of his hand and a few whispered spells, the handprint lit up with a matrix of runes and carvings. Aurichalcum could feel the hum of power from the enchantment.

He had once known the woman who had created this specific spell.

"I never did agree with all this. But if anyone was going to muck about with the leylines...I suppose I'd rather it be you and your offspring. He's young and naïve, but he's wise beyond his years. He'll make a great ruler with the right guidance. You would be proud."

Are you feeling sentimental?

Aurichalcum's face soured. *"Must you plague me even now, mother?"*

Always, my son. It was the promise I made to all our kind. I will always be here.

A pause.

Until the very end...

"...It's appreciated."

Will it destroy the Nexus?

"No. Only the chamber where the experiments were conducted. We cannot allow this information to fall into the wrong hands. If my br...if he were to get a hold of this knowledge it would doom us all."

My poor Ten'ebraex...

"For once could you not be a mother?"

Aurichalcum reached up and cut open the tip of his finger with his sharp teeth. He drew symbols into where the palm of his hand would fit in the indentation, then placed his hand inside the groove.

Immediately he felt stone and earth churn and shift deep beneath the palace. The ground rumbled beneath the castle ever so faintly. It grew in intensity slowly but surely until it reached its crescendo...then ceased. Once more the castle grew quiet.

The rune matrix around the indent grew dim, then ceased glowing, never to awaken. The spell had been triggered and its purpose was served.

There was only one thing left to do, and yet Aurichalcum found himself hesitant to do it. He found himself reminiscing on the past. Aurichalcum remembered how incensed he was when he learned that Xiar had been experimenting with their Mana Core, and how the High Mage had been looking to use that research to create weaponry. To pervert the very lifeblood of the leylines and the planet towards wicked means was unthinkable, unconscionable. It was all Aurum and his siblings could do to keep him from burning the city of Xiar to the ground, lack of wings be damned.

Aurum had argued that it was a good thing that one of the humans had seen the folly in the High Mage's actions. While Aurum did not condone the act of murder, Idora—Leon's mother—had prevented the worst possible scenario. Aurum gave Idora his blessing to continue her research on the condition she kept true to her word and used it only to improve the lives of people. The use of her research to create instruments of war and destruction was strictly prohibited and would result in censure and punishment by the Metallic Dragons.

Aurichalcum, already an advisor to the Estian Crown, was left to monitor and oversee Idora's research.

And then Idora died, and her son, Leon, had picked up where she had left off.

Aurichalcum believed him to be a fool, at first. The old dragon thought it would be Leon who finally broke the pact, but as the boy grew and matured, Aurichalcum grew ever surprised—even proud—of the kind of man and king Leon had grown up to be.

He was unconventional, but he was a man of his word—a man of honour. Leon cared for his people, and he sought to make their lives better. He sought to relax the iron grip of the monarchy and nobility. Moreso, when Leon learned that the secret to finishing his mother's research was to use blood magic, he elected to find another way.

He had earned Aurichalcum's begrudging respect that day. Too often had Aurichalcum seen humanity trade their convictions for power. For the easy path. They wanted to achieve such lofty goals but would often sacrifice their morality in pursuit of it.

Humans had never been meant to wield blood magic, and Leon understood this—better than most.

Aurichalcum remembered meeting Hana as a child and helping her when her parents were bereft of any way to cure their sick and dying infant. The blue plague had nearly ended her life long before it began. Aurichalcum, uncharacteristically moved by the fate of a small, insignificant child, offered the parents a choice. He always thought he would live to regret it, and yet the girl consistently surprised him.

Then there were the Khaleeshir. They were so young; perhaps a bit misguided and naïve at times...but their hearts were in the right place. There was a genuine earnestness about them. Perhaps his mother had not made a mistake, as he had initially thought. With a lot more training, and the right guidance, maybe these Khaleeshir could finally defeat

Tenebrae for good, and bring some semblance of balance back to Enayra; all Enayra, both humans and dragons, as it was meant to be.

"No. Which is why this is necessary. I will buy them time, and I will smash this army of the traitor's sycophantic heretics. Then I shall return to aid in the training of the Khaleeshir."

"Though we indeed grow weary, and our strength is diminished, I have no less vigour in me now than I did a thousand years ago. I will fight, no matter the cost. Besides, it's not as if we have much longer in this world...you know better than most. As Enayra weakens, so do we. Our fate is tied to this world."

No response.

It was time anyway. He would do what he felt was necessary to buy everyone the time they needed to flee.

For the first time in a thousand years, Aurichalcum felt his bones and muscles shift. His hands grew, changed size, and became claws. His skin morphed from soft and pale flesh to bright metallic scales the colour of the most brilliant, polished brass.

Aurichalcum felt himself grow, beyond the confines of his mortal form, beyond the confines of the throne room, of even the confines of Filiddyn Castle. Stone and mortar parted as the massive dragon took shape within the halls of the ancient fortress.

For the first time in a millennium, Aurichalcum *felt* like a dragon.

When he finally stopped growing, the entirety of Filiddyn Castle had been levelled, as had most of the grounds and surrounding walls and buildings.

Aurichalcum, The Great Brass Dragon, towered tall over the city. Scars covered the entirety of his body, leaving horrible disfigurements and bare patches where his scales would no longer grow back. His tail ended in a rounded stump; it was merely half as long as it should have been. His wings were completely missing, and only scared, disfigured flesh marked the spot where they had once been connected to his back.

Aurichalcum was quite unlike any other dragons anyone in this day and age would have seen. His body bore the same shape and resemblance as his daughter Thrae. They shared the same dorsal spikes along the length of their back, and their general profile was similar. But the differences lay mostly in the head and neck area.

Whereas Thrae had four horns, two on either side of her head, that curved backwards like two thick, ivory longbows, and a thick mane of shaggy white hair that started at the base of her skull, Aurichalcum had neither of those features. Instead of four horns, Aurichalcum had a large bony frill that flared upwards from the top of the skull.

Two horns erupted from the twin apexes of the frill and curved outwards like a set of bull's horns. Instead of being white like ivory, Aurichalcum's horns were the same colour as his scales. Two more horns erupted from his forehead, just above his eyes—though the left horn had been snapped off about halfway down its length.

Rather than a flesh snout with lips that most dragons had, Aurichalcum's muzzle more resembled a sharp, parrot-like beak.

Aurichalcum roared so loud he visibly shook the nearby forests. The waters of the Acturn and Lake Ardona rippled and churned from the vibration.

A dragon as large as this had not walked the surface of the world, nor been seen by humans since days long forgotten—and Aurichalcum was not even at his full size.

He would not need it to smash these pitiful insects before him. Not even the Blood Fugue could stand against the might of a Metallic Dragon.

* * *

Boom.

"We'll never get the people out in time!" Kyeit called.

Boom.

The sound of hammering against the door echoed with a rhythm as the Qiri'ar beat their fists and weapons against the door to the harbour.

Boom.

The doors had begun to bulge inward. Iron and wood were twisted and warped like a giant had attempted to punch through the doors. Though reinforced with hardened iron, the doors had been battered so badly that the question of the Qiri'ar breaking through was a matter of "when" and not "if." They had already ripped through multiple iron portcullises with their hands and weaponry.

Boom.

Scores of soldiers pressed their bodies against the door, hoping to stem the tide of the attackers. Some had grabbed massive timbers from the shipyards. These massive timbers would be cut down to repair any ships in the dry dock. Now they helped brace the door against the might of the Qiri'ar attack.

Shouts erupted from captains and soldiers alike.

"Push you sorry bastards! Puuuuush!"

"Do not let these mongrels take the harbour before the civilians are gone!"

"PUUUUUUUUUSH!"

Boom.

Thirteen boats remained docked as the last couple hundred people were evacuated. They had to board and set sail before the wall was breached. If that happened, they would be slaughtered along with the remaining soldiers who had not yet departed through the tunnels.

Boom.

"Just keep evacuating as fast as you can. Evacuate until that door is breached, and then get those boats out of here. If anyone is left, tell them to get into that tunnel and start running," Leon called.

Boom.

People cried out in fear, and a child started sobbing in his mother's arms.

Somewhere across the harbour, an infant wailed.

Kyeit could hear someone calling for his loved ones, a woman calling for her son, a child calling for her grandmother.

It was pandemonium.

Boom.

The shield wall that had formed in front of the Baroness and King Leon braced for the worst.

Boom.

Then silence.

The pounding stopped, and all eyes turned towards the top of the hill where Filiddyn Castle was built. The sound of cracking stones and falling debris echoed across the city. It sounded like an avalanche. As everyone looked up at the crumbling ruin of a castle, they realized why.

"What the Hells is that?" the Baroness demanded.

"Lord Aurichalcum..." Leon replied, bewildered.

The dragon's roar tore through the air with such force it shattered ear drums. Everyone clutched their heads and covered their ears from the pain.

Then more silence.

The entire harbour froze. The entire city froze. To bear witness to the majesty of The Great Brass Wyrm was a rare sight indeed. Some in the harbour bowed down and remained prostrate before such a sight. Others offered up silent prayers. But most people stood and stared dumbly as they saw a Great Metallic Dragon tower over their city.

Even Kyeit, who had spent time with Kanothir, was bonded to Valence, knew Kinokaze, and had even beheld the majesty of the Great Argentum, was impressed. "In days long past, many of the first humans thought the early Altimarans fools to worship dragons. But how could you not encounter something like that, and believe it was anything but a god?"

Cecil only nodded in response.

The Baroness cleared her throat. "I may recommend we take this opportunity to retreat."

"But—" Kyeit started.

The Baroness did not allow her to finish. "Lord Aurichalcum is doing this to give us the time to escape. If you listen, you will hear the pounding against the gate has stopped. The attacks are stunned at the sight. I suggest we use the opportunity presented to us."

Sure enough, everyone in the harbour could hear the armies of the Baron Felidrun and the Qiri'ar move away from the harbour walls. The Estian traitors seemed to be in full retreat, while the Qiri'ar charged up the hillside towards where Aurichalcum now perched upon the remains of Filiddyn Castle. The Blood Fugue was not to be underestimated. Aurichalcum's fortuitous decision to take on his true form had saved everyone in the harbour a horrible fate, or at the very least, delayed it.

"What about the Khaleeshir?" asked Cecil.

"I will remain with my personal guard to await the return of the Khaleeshir. Once all but the last of the ships are out of the harbour, everyone else is to evacuate. I will be along with the Khaleeshir as soon as I can."

"Do you want us to have the dragons stay with you?" asked Leon.

"No, I'd rather they escort the flotilla. Most of our armed forces are here and will be on the march to Pelchar. The people will need protecting until they reach the safety of the tunnel."

Leon still had no idea what she was talking about. The Baroness had never once mentioned a tunnel before now, but he trusted the Lady vohn Veishaupt and knew better than to ask questions at such a pressing time.

He turned and called out to his remaining soldiers. "You heard her. Get the people onto the ships, and then get out of here! Anyone not part of her guard, you're with me."

"*Valence. Did you hear any of that?*" Kyeit asked.

Valence paused before she responded. "*Bits and pieces. Forgive me, it is an honour even for myself to witness the true glory of one of the Ancients.*"

"I understand," Kyeit replied. "*Go with Fyete, Thrae, and Kinokaze to escort the flotilla.*"

"*Understood.*"

Kyeit hesitated.

"*Yes?*" asked Valence.

"*How is Thrae?*"

"*She will leave her father willingly. He already reached out to us and told us that we must protect the people. Aurichalcum will find us and join us once he's bought us enough time to escape. He will not fall here this day.*"

Kyeit was relieved.

"Kyeit!" Cecil called.

Kyeit realized she had been standing there aimlessly as she spoke with Valence.

"*Go. We'll speak another time,*" was all Valence said.

The silver dragon circled the harbour from above, then took off over Lake Ardona to catch up with the rest of the flotilla. Thrae was close on her tail, and Fyete and Kinokaze took up the rear to protect the boats that lagged.

"Coming!" Kyeit called back to Cecil.

Chapter LIV

Ogdyn and his forces held the northern shore of the Acturn as if the very fate of Enayra depended on it.

As doubtful as his forces were about their new alliance with the Lady vohn Veishaupt and the Crown, they would not give up the perfectly good opportunity to kill royalist forces—especially those that served Lord Gruffydd, the worst of his kind.

Even better, the Big Boss's plan to blow the dikes had paid off in spades. The Baron Felidrun's forces, who had come to stem the tide of the flood and repair as much damage as possible, could not get close to the Acturn without being caught in a deluge of arrows. And by now the flooding in the fields had gotten so bad that movement on the southern side of the Acturn was almost impossible to do with any haste.

Most soldiers stood in water up to their waists, and those who were lucky enough to be on the high ground were still submerged up to their knees in cold, rushing, river water. The Baron's forces stood shivering in their metal armour. Many tripped over the harsh terrain, others from the arrows that rained down from the northern bank. Those that fell never got back up. Their armour quickly filled with water and kept them beneath the surface of the water. Only bubbles marked their final resting places, counting out the precious few minutes of air they had left until they succumbed and drowned.

Ogdyn shouted a war cry from the tree branch where he was stationed. His soldiers whooped and shouted in response. Someone blew a harmonica, and another started belting out the words to *'Death to the Tyrants, Long Live the People'* the unofficial battle hymn of the ERA.

Personally, Ogdyn preferred *'My Young Lass from Pelchar'*; he always was more partial to a good revenge story. But Ogdyn knew if you couldn't beat them, join them, and began singing along with the chorus:

And we swear to you,
This very day you'll rue!
We'll leave you broken on the battlefield!

"I hope they heard us from the capital!" jeered Vinella.

"I hope not," Ogdyn replied.

"And why not?"

"Because I'd hate to make an enemy of the Baroness so quickly," explained Ogdyn.

Vinella scowled. "You fool Oggy. She'll be our enemy once we've dealt with Baron Felidrun. What difference does it make whether it's now or then?"

Ogdyn shrugged. "Call me what you will, but I'd much rather fight alongside the Baroness to deal with our shared enemy than fight both Felidrun and Pelchar. Besides, the Big Boss won't be too pleased if we muck up his deal."

The fighting suddenly stopped with the appearance of a massive dragon amidst the crumbling ruins of Filiddyn Castle.

Ogdyn couldn't believe it until he heard the roar. The sound raced across the open plains, rippled the waters of the floodplains and lake, and slapped him and his soldiers in the face. Some were even knocked from their perches in the treetops.

The creature was massive, and it inspired both awe and fear in all who bore witness. It didn't take long for the Baron's forces to begin making their retreat through the waist-high water. They had completely abandoned their efforts to staunch the bleeding flow of the river Acturn.

Perhaps Baron Felidrun had recalled them, or perhaps they sought the chance to witness a battle against a massive, ancient dragon. Whatever the reason, the river no longer seemed important to them.

Ogdyn wasn't going to question the cause of their reprieve. Nor was he going to waste a chance presented to him so readily. "Take stock of our losses and get people down in that water to start fishing out bodies. Take anything of value and pile it up on the riverbank. Once we've taken record, we'll get it loaded up and sent off to HQ for redistribution."

"Not gonna take your pick of the best gear, Oggy?" teased Vinella.

Ogdyn jerked his thumb at the ancient dragon on a rampage in the city. "Something tells me I've exceeded my luck for today."

One of the scouts shouted from off in the woods. "Commander! We have more soldiers here!"

Ogdyn, Vinella, and most of their soldiers raised their weapons and hopped down from the trees where they were perched.

Ogdyn called his forces into formation with their backs against the river. "I knew it was too good to be true. Bastard Felidrun must've outflanked us somewhere. Keep an eye on our asses in case they come back and hit us from behind!"

"Wait!" cried a young man's voice. "Don't shoot! We're friendly!"

"And how do we know you're not just lying to trick us!" called Ogdyn.

"Because I'm not with the Baron," replied the voice. The men drew closer as he talked. He was unarmed and his hands were raised, though he looked as if he had just been through the Hells. He was dressed in fine armour, though his scabbard was empty, and his sword was missing. The tattered remains of a cape clung to his shoulders. The boy was covered in dried blood and filth. In the end, it was his long platinum hair that gave him away to Ogdyn.

"You're the boy king," Ogdyn realized.

"Leon. Just Leon, don't even have to add the king," Leon replied. "I just escaped the city with my men, and those the Baroness brought with her."

"And where is she?" demanded Ogdyn.

"Holding up the rear guard. The Dragonkin got...delayed. She's holding the harbour until they return safely, and she'll be along shortly."

The boy who claimed to be king seemed honest enough. But Vinella wasn't convinced, and judging by the disgruntled looks of his men, they were none too pleased either.

"How do we know he's really the king, Oggy? He could be some fake stand-in here to trick us!" Vinella whispered.

"Maybe Vee's right, commander. How can we trust him? He's one of them!"

Ogdyn swallowed hard, trying to parch his quickly drying mouth and throat. "How do we know you are who you say you are?"

Leon smirked. "Does anyone have a gold piece?"

Vinella sneered. "How can I when your Barons keep robbing us with their taxes!"

One of Ogdyn's soldiers spat on the ground. There was an angry murmur across the line. Tensions were rising quickly, and if Ogdyn and Leon didn't act fast it would erupt into a brawl. Ogdyn had been entrusted to keep this fruitful if temporary, alliance intact, and if his fighters caused it to fall apart, the Big Boss would have him flayed and strung up at the busiest crossroads in the kingdom.

Leon acted before Ogdyn could. "Look, I know you hate me. You hate the nobility. I know why you fight, how you fight, and what you fight against. I am your prime target, I get that. Any other day, you'd be rushing over yourselves to stab me, and I'd likely be ordering my men to take you in peacefully to stand trial for your crimes."

There came another, louder, angrier murmur from the crowd.

"But for now, we are allies. Your boss made these arrangements with the baroness—I'll admit without my knowledge. But if this is what we must do to ensure we both survive—that our country and our families survive—then I am willing to put aside my differences with you and work together. You can stab me when this is over, I promise. But there is something we have in common, and it needs us to work together to protect it."

"Oh yeah, and what do *we* have in common, your highn-ass?" spat Vinella. She looked proud of her vicious pun.

Leon remained calm and collected. "We both love Estion. We love our friends, our families; the very people that make up this country. You fight for them, and so do I. We may have different ideas about how to fight for them, and what to fight for, and even what a future for them looks like, but our goals are the same. Right now, Baron Felidrun and his new Qiri'aran allies are the biggest threat against those people and both of our goals. It would behove us to work together and stop them, and if we can do that, I'd gladly lay down my life to fight alongside you. There would be no greater cause to die for than for Estion and our people."

There was dead silence in response. For a moment Ogdyn expected the entire thing to collapse and blow up in Leon's face. He expected bloodshed, prepared for the worst, and was even ready to stab a few of his allies and friends to preserve this fragile alliance.

Then Vinella spoke. Her voice was still filled with contempt and dislike, but it was gentler than it had been earlier, and the mockery had disappeared. "I don't like monarchs. I can't say I was a big fan of your father or your grandfather. I can't say I'm really a big fan of you either..."

Vinella looked back at Ogdyn.

"But Oggy and the Big Boss says we gotta play nice. And I'll give you this: you're a genuine son of a bitch at the least. I almost believe you care about Estion and the people. Maybe I'll live to regret those words, but so long as you don't prove yourself false, and keep me believing in you...I'll be willing to stay my blade and work together—if for Oggy's sake more than anything else."

"I'll take that as the highest compliment I'm worthy of," Leon replied. He gave a quick bow to Vinella.

"But you watch out once this is over. Don't expect any of us to go soft on ya!" Vinella quickly added.

Leon smiled. "I expect no less."

To say Ogdyn was relieved was a gross understatement, but lacking a better word, relieved would have to do. He hadn't realized he had held his breath for the entire exchange and quickly went about trying to make up for each lost second.

After a few more barked orders from Ogdyn, his soldiers returned to their given task of stripping down the dead soldiers in the water.

Leon approached Ogdyn after the last order was given. "Most of my own soldiers are tired, and the Baroness's forces don't directly answer to me under normal circumstances. But I think I can convince them to help with your efforts here—if you'll have the help?"

Ogdyn raised a brow. "Why would you help us loot those bodies?"

"Call it a sign of good faith?" Leon replied. "Besides, I'd rather see those resources go to you than back into the hands of Lord Gruffydd."

A wry smile crept across Ogdyn's face. He held out his hand for Leon to shake. "I won't be bowing to you, mind, but I think you and I will get along just fine—for now at least. Name's Ogdyn. Commander of the Felidrun Chapter."

Leon took Ogdyn's hand and grasped it firmly with his own. "Leon, king of...well, you know."

Chapter LV

Kanaahn had rushed into the bakery with a fury he had never known.

He didn't know what was wrong, but he could sense, deep in his heart, that something was very amiss, and that Arkas and Arial were in danger. He found his premonition to be correct when he finally found them at the mercy of a Blood Warrior. Upon seeing the state of Arial and Arkas, Kanaahn let his rage take over.

He charged into the back of the Blood Warrior and threw him to the ground. The Blood Warrior grabbed Kanaahn's leg when he fell and brought the Khaleeshir down with him.

The two rolled and grappled with one another. Fists were exchanged, and both men aimed for the head and body.

Kanaahn could feel his helmet crumple under the repeated blows, and at one point bits of sharp metal cut parts of his face. After another punch to the head, Kanaahn could feel a sharp pain in his nose, and blood began to pour through the neck of his helmet, and he knew his nose had been broken. He was only thankful that this warrior did not seem to be in the midst of the Blood Fugue.

Kanaahn slammed his fist into the Blood Warrior's side. He felt the man's ribs crack and heard the air being driven from his lungs. With the Blood Warrior incapacitated, Kanaahn disengaged from the floor grapple and stood up.

He tore his warped helmet from his head.

Blood smeared the lower part of his face, leaking from his nose. He could taste it on his lips, in his mouth, and in the back of his throat as it poured from his sinuses. His whole head ached, but the rage kept Kanaahn fighting.

"Get up!" Kanaahn yelled at the warrior.

When the Blood Warrior struggled to move, Kanaahn slammed his heel into the man's chest. Bones cracked under the force of the blow.

"I said get the fuck up!" Kanaahn's voice echoed through the empty building. "You want to pick on my friends, and attack them while they're defenceless, but can't even stand up and face me one on one in a fair fight? You're a coward, and I'll make sure everyone knows you died like a coward!"

The Blood Warrior grew enraged. He leapt to his feet and picked up his fallen blade.

Both fighters charged in. Their swords met in the middle.

Kanaahn managed to block each of the Blood Warrior's vicious blows with his sword. He could see chips fly from the edge of his now-notched blade.

The Qiri'ar continued to press the attack. He swung violently and wildly in any attempt to cleave flesh from Kanaahn's body.

Without warning, Kanaahn heard his blade snap. Half of his sword flew across the room with a metallic clang before coming to a rest in a corner. He just managed to dodge the rest of the strike as the Blood Warrior's blade buried itself in the wooden floor.

Kanaahn looked at his sword in bewilderment. Loss, grief, and heartache immediately overcame him as he realized the only connection he had to his father had been literally sheared in two.

Then rage swallowed him and took control of Kanaahn's rational thought. It didn't matter if the sword could be reforged or repaired, or even if the damage had been his fault in the first place, Kanaahn would see this Blood Warrior pay.

Kanaahn threw aside half of the sword in his hand and swung his armoured fists at the Blood Warrior's head and body. But his hesitation a moment before had allowed the Qiri'ar to read his movements and dodge his attacks.

The warrior grabbed Kanaahn by the arms and pulled him into his knee. Kanaahn was winded and his breastplate collapsed inward under the force of the blow.

The Blood Warrior continued his onslaught.

He put Kanaahn down and charged at him, driving his shoulder into the Khaleeshir's chest. The Blood Warrior shoved Kanaahn across the room and through the wall of the bakery.

Kanaahn's limp body flew through the wattle, daub, and timbers of the outer wall and collapsed like a ragdoll atop the pile of rubble. He wondered if he had yet crossed the threshold of death. He couldn't move, his body felt broken and none of his limbs would move as directed. Kanaahn could only lay there, watching the sky while the Blood Warrior mocked him from the other side of the hole in the wall.

Kanaahn could hear the warrior's lumbering gait as he walked back to his sword and withdrew it from the timber floor.

"I thought I'd let your little friend die last. But I think now, it'll be you. It won't be quick like hers," the warrior spat.

Kanaahn felt so small and helpless. Failure began to consume him, and he wanted to shrink away and disappear forever. If anyone heard how he had failed here today...perhaps he was better this way. If he were to die...perhaps this was the best way.

"*Djall...*"

The dragon did not respond at first. When his voice finally replied, it sounded frantic. "*Risasi has Shooter, but he came under attack trying to save him. He's been wounded. We're escorting him back to the harbour, he needs us to help keep him up. We'll be there as soon as we can. Hang in there!*"

Kanaahn closed his eyes and accepted his fate.

Then, he saw it, deep in his mind, like a small flame in the darkness. The faintest flicker of hope within him. Something that kept him alive and hanging on. The part of him that refused to roll over and die.

A voice entered his head.

I wondered how long it would be before we spoke again, Kanaahn. Though I suppose our previous communication has been non-verbal.

"Who are you?"

I am the very reason that you are what you are. I go by many names.

"Could you tell me some of them? That doesn't help."

You may know me best as the Earth Mother.

"Why are you here? Am I dead?"

Not yet. But you must hurry.

"What can I do? My body is broken, my sword as well. I have no weapons, and my armour has been destroyed."

If I am here speaking to you, it is because you are ready to accept my power.

"Don't I already use your power?"

The Khaleeshir have my blessing and my protection. But they are not the only ones in Enayra capable of calling upon my power.

Rise, Kanaahn.

Rise.

Kanaahn opened his eyes.

He gasped for air like he had been held underwater. A sudden heat overcame his body, and he felt full of new vigour and life. Kanaahn could feel his bones snap back into place. His wounds healed themselves as his body began to pull itself back together. Kanaahn's limbs moved, and he stood up.

He could see a blue-green aura surround his body. Kanaahn felt stronger than he ever had since taking the Covenant. He looked up to see the scene he had walked in on repeated. The Qiri'ar, his sword raised above Arkas, ready to end the Khaleeshir's life. Arial lay unconscious on the floor not far away.

Kanaahn went to move and felt his breastplate constrict his movement. No wonder, it had been crushed against his body. It no longer served a purpose for him. Kanaahn reached across his body and grabbed the edge of his breastplate. Then, with as much ease as he would have uprooted a flower, he tore at it. He could feel the leather straps that held his armour together snap, and Kanaahn tossed his breastplate aside with a loud clang.

Now finally unrestricted, Kanaahn's body began to shift and change. He watched as his skin went from soft, human flesh to hardened green scales the colour of emeralds. He could feel his face flatten. His nose disappeared, replaced by two narrow slits.

Fangs replaced his teeth, and his tongue grew long, skinny, and forked. It flicked between his teeth and tasted the air.

Kanaahn's eyes must have changed as well, because the way he perceived colours changed, and by moving his newly grown second eyelid he could see everything that gave off heat; the oven, his friends, the Blood Warrior, even the rats hiding in the floorboards of the bakery.

His muscles grew, and he could feel a new strength come over him. From the base of his spine sprouted a long, skinny tail with a double spike on the end.

Despite all the reptilian changes, Kanaahn's long hair remained. And he could feel two massive, white-feathered wings erupt from his back. They felt awkward and made his shoulders heavy, but Kanaahn would have been lying if he had said he wasn't somewhat elated by the sudden idea that he could fly.

The new body would take getting used to, but somehow, deep in his soul, Kanaahn knew what to do with it.

The Blood Warrior looked up. His face was confused and shocked to see Kanaahn standing. "How...?" Then he saw Kanaahn transform, and his confusion became utter terror. "Shit! You're a d—"

He never finished his sentence.

In seconds, Kanaahn had closed the gap between them and shoved his hand into the gut of the Blood Warrior. Kanaahn's hand parted muscle, flesh, and organs as if he were smashing a pumpkin. His fingers felt around, then finally, he felt them grasp his target: the spinal cord.

Kanaahn grabbed hold of the man's spine and *squeezed*.

The Blood Warrior cried out, blood erupted from his mouth like a gruesome volcano, and his eyes rolled back into his head, but he was still very much alive—for now.

Kanaahn lifted the Blood Warrior off the ground. He could barely feel the weight of the man.

The warrior screamed in agony. "I'm sorry! I'm sorry! Please spare me!"

Kanaahn remained coldly silent. The anger and base instinct took over once more. He couldn't help himself. It felt too right—too good.

The warrior screamed again, but this time it was not from the pain. He looked as if he had seen a demon. "Help! Help me! He—"

Kanaahn grew tired of the screaming. He wrenched his hand from the Blood Warrior's body and took the man's spine with him. There was a horrible, wet crunch. Bones popped. Ligaments snapped. Flesh tore with a horrible wet squelch.

The man screamed in horrific agony for only a second before the pain was gone, along with the feeling in his body, and his life. The Blood Warrior hit the ground with a wet thud.

Kanaahn threw the man's spine back at him.

He turned towards Arial and Arkas and reached out a bloodied hand. Then the aura around him dissipated.

As soon as it had come upon him, the transformation reverted, and Kanaahn was once more just a wounded, sixteen-year-old boy. The strength and power that had filled him only moments ago disappeared, and Kanaahn's entire body ached again.

He realized at that moment he had not been healed. Kanaahn's body had only managed to use whatever power he had possessed—even if temporarily—to cobble itself back together long enough to defeat his foe. Once the power left him, so did the temporary triage.

Kanaahn's legs gave way to the pain, exhaustion, and the damage. He folded before he could take another step.

He hit the ground with a hard thud and the world began to spin. Once more his body was unresponsive and uncooperative, and Kanaahn felt as if he was at death's door.

But this time the voice did not come to save him or comfort him, this time he was truly alone.

Then his consciousness faded, and Kanaahn was out before he could blink again.

Chapter LVI

When word reached Drakhart that the defenders were evacuating via the harbour, his mood had soured, but he did not give up hope. He had vowed to capture the king, and he would do just that. Drakhart would not allow his quarry to leave so easily.

He pivoted the Qiri'aran forces and sent them against the harbour. To Drakhart's delight, the morale of the defenders crumbled rather quickly after their secondary defensive lines fell, and Drakhart could almost taste their defeat.

But it was a short-lived victory.

The Acturn canal had been lost after an attack by partisan forces. Explosives had blown the dikes and flooded the fields around the city.

Drakhart and the rest of those at the Qiri'ar camp were forced to break camp and flee towards the nearest high ground they could find. A small tent had been erected so Drakhart could conceal himself, but most of the old camp was now underwater.

Things then got worse yet when the Baroness Pelchar arrived. Drakhart swore loudly when he had been informed. Somehow, the Baroness, who had been intentionally excluded from the initial calling of the banners had made it to the city—and just in time to help evacuate the people.

Lord Gruffydd and his forces—while on paper were thousands strong—were as useless as a fire at the bottom of the lake. They had, expectedly, refused to lift a finger to help in the siege or fight on the battlements. They only entered the city when Calandor's nephew opened the gate, and even then, it was not to join the fighting but instead to burn and loot the city while the Qiri'ar died and bled for them.

Drakhart had foreseen this, but it did not make the situation any less infuriating.

Then Drakhart's hopes crumbled further when Filiddyn Castle collapsed from within and revealed Aurichalcum in his true form.

Drakhart could not ignore this new threat.

He would not be capturing the king this day, but not all was lost. In an ironic twist of fate, Drakhart's secondary objective bestowed by Tenebrae, the more impossible of the two he had been given, seemed ever more likely. This siege would not be a total success, but a partial success was better than complete failure.

A Qiri'aran scout burst into Drakhart's tent. The boy looked terrified. "Lord Ghast! The Great Dragon has appeared, what do we do?"

Drakhart grinned. "It's not why I came, but it will have to suffice. Notify the Kinu'watan, and prepare a horse for him, myself, and the Grand Enchantress—immediately!"

Elandyr'ni waited for the scout to leave before she spoke. "What do you think we can do against a Great Wyrm?"

"Before, during our travels, I mentioned that Lord Tenebrae had tasked me with several secret objectives before we left. One of them was the capture of the boy king."

Elandyr'ni nodded. "But he's escaped."

"Yes but it seems it's not a complete loss," Drakhart explained.

"What does Lord Tenebrae want with the king?" Elandyr'ni asked.

Drakhart scanned the open tent flaps to ensure that no one was listening in. He drew close to Elandyr'ni and whispered. "We've been hearing distressing reports from our spies in Asardaea and Espias that they have been working on developing new weapons. When we dug a little deeper into these rumours, we could not find any evidence of what they were working on, only that the research on which their efforts are being built came directly from Estion, and from research being conducted by His Majesty. It seems King Anducaerleonis has been researching and studying the Mana Core beneath the city. He has found a way to utilize mana shards as a power source for new kinds of machines and contraptions. This research, if combined with the research the Qiri'ar have done over the years, could have serious military applications that could work to our advantage, and Lord Tenebrae would like to have access to it, especially if our enemies have already begun to exploit it for their own use. Now, no doubt the king destroyed his research before he left, so we'll likely hit a dead end there...but there was one other task Lord Tenebrae left in my hands."

Again, Drakhart checked through the tent flaps for anyone who might be listening too closely. He stepped ever closer to Elandyr'ni and whispered at a volume just slightly louder than breathing. "I was tasked with finding and killing Aurichalcum. I had assumed the old dragon had escaped with the rest of the defenders. But it seems he stayed behind to buy them more time. He doesn't realize what we have, and it will be the end of him."

Elandyr'ni thought for a moment. Her mind worked quickly to put together the bits of history and lore she knew, the plans of her master, and the context clues provided by Drakhart to finally reach the realization of what was to come. "The Spear of First Father. Lord Tenebrae found it?"

Drakhart smiled. "All thanks to you; you brought him the dagger, and with it, he was able to retrieve the spear. I'm sorry I could not tell you sooner. I was forbidden from saying anything—even the Kinu'watan does not know what is in the bound package I entrusted him with. Spies are everywhere, on both sides, and Lord Tenebrae could not risk anyone knowing the power we now wield—nor what our true objectives were here."

Elandyr'ni nodded. "You were right to keep it a secret. The lengths our enemies would go to get the spear back and bury the research we seek. After all, it is one of the few weapons that can kill a Great Wyrm. I never thought I would live to see the spear returned. I had heard the legends, and how Eshgalon the Great wielded it in the war long ago. It was the weapon he used to bring down the mighty Nulgo'riaz."

Drakhart had only recently heard the stories, but from what little he knew, he was aware of the power the spear wielded, and how it would be a boon for Tenebrae in the war to come. Many of the Great Wyrms would be allied against him. The ancient Great Progenitors, and the Metallic Dragons. They would not be so bold once they realized this weapon was in the hands of Tenebrae and his allies.

"My lord!" It was the scout again. He stood just outside the tent flap flanked by O'lomec and three horses in full tack.

"Send the Kinu'watan in and wait for us at the edge of the camp," Drakhart called back.

The Kinu'watan did not wait a second longer. He barged into the tent, a long, thin package wrapped in furs tucked under his arm. "What is this about?"

"Put the package on that crate and open it," Drakhart ordered. "All will be made clear shortly."

O'lomec, still caked in the blood and gore of the enemies he had slain in battle, did as Drakhart asked. He fiddled with the leather cord that bound the furs tightly. When he finally unwrapped the worn-out furs and peered inside the package, his jaw dropped and O'lomec's eyes went wide.

"Impossible...The Spear of the First Father?"

"The very one," Drakhart confirmed.

O'lomec picked up the weapon in his hands and tested the weight. It was about two metres long and was carved from a single, long piece of alabaster white material. No one had ever been able to determine what the material was when Drakhart had held it, he thought it felt like a cross between wood and stone. It was light and smooth to the touch, but it was solid like it was carved from the finest marble.

There were no ornate patterns or ornamentation carved into the spear, but runes had been carved all along its length and on the spear tip.

O'lomec put two and two together. "You would give me the honour of wielding the blade of my forebearer? You would allow me the chance to achieve a feat that only one mortal before me has ever achieved?"

Drakhart put a hand on O'lomec's shoulder. "Lord O'lomec, the honour comes not from me, but from Lord Tenebrae himself. You would be doing him a great service to accept."

O'lomec closed his fist and folded his arm over his chest. "I will not fail our Lord. I ask, only that I be allowed to thank him when we return."

"I will arrange it," Elandyr'ni chimed in.

"Know that he would trust no one else with this task, but yourself," Drakhart added.

O'lomec held the spear proudly at his side. The runes glowed and hummed, seemingly coming to life in the hands of their new wielder. Despite how long the spear was, it looked like no more than a toy next to him. He and the spear almost competed to see who was taller.

"Come, we should hurry," said Elandyr'ni.

Drakhart agreed. Aurichalcum would level the city if left unchecked for much longer.

* * *

The once proud city of Ethon lay in ruin.

Aurichalcum's emergence had destroyed Filiddyn Castle, and he had proceeded to rampage through the city to expunge the attackers from its walls. His massive claws swiped at walls and crushed buildings. He could not breathe fire—none of the Ancients could—but at his size, Aurichalcum didn't need to.

Waves of Qiri'aran soldiers, Blood Witches and Warriors alike, swarmed around him to attack. Lightning bounced off his hide. Flame barely tickled him. Ice was no more effective than a snowball. Axes, swords, arrows, spears, and javelins were thrown at him from a variety of angles. They were like mosquitoes to him. Barely a nuisance.

By the time Aurichalcum reached the mid-city, entire squadrons of Qiri'ar had been literally stomped out of existence like the insects they were. The armies of attackers no longer sought to attack him, instead it was all they could do to run away. There was no way to defeat a Great Wyrm. Retreat was the only option.

"WHO DARES TO STAND AGAINST ME?!" Aurichalcum's voice tore through the air like a whirlwind. Several buildings that had already partially collapsed from the previous battle crumbled the rest of the way as his voice shook them to their foundations.

Qiri'ar screamed as they ran from his wrath.

From the corner of his eye, Aurichalcum saw three figures on horseback ride up the main road towards him. If he had lips, they would have curled into a smile.

These heathens didn't know when to quit.

Aurichalcum turned—slowly, due to his massive bulk. His steps shook the city, and he crushed more buildings with his claws. His partial tail knocked over part of a nearby wall and levelled a neighbourhood.

"DO YOU THINK I CANNOT SEE YOU? HERETICS! RATS! I SHALL EXTINGUISH YOUR LIVES LIKE THE VERMIN YOU ARE—AS I SHALL ALL WHO SERVE MY TRAITOROUS BROTHER!"

Aurichalcum reared up onto his back legs, then slammed his front claws back into the ground. The cobbled streets cracked, leaving two indents in the ground. The resulting blow sent rippling shockwaves tearing across the city as if an earthquake had just occurred.

Buildings toppled. Statues in a nearby square were destroyed. The destruction was total and thorough. Like a child flattening a sandcastle, Aurichalcum laid waste to Ethon.

Clouds of dust erupted around Aurichalcum's front legs and obscured the destruction he had wrought, but the incessant pound of hooves against the cobbles had ceased, and nothing stirred within the rubble and destruction.

Then came the sound of rock shifting, rubble moving. Something had survived that onslaught.

Aurichalcum could not say he was surprised. Vermin were notoriously hard to kill, and those cockroach-like humans were the hardest of all vermin to kill. This had been a lesson he learned during the Great Purge, and in the early days of dragon-human relations. Unlike Aurum, he had known that the humans would not simply die out or move on. They had a habit of being vile, expansionist, fecund vermin, and to this day he was surprised at how tenacious they could be.

Something moved within the rubble and Aurichalcum swung his head to try and get a better look.

As the dust cleared, he could see a large, burly Qiri'ar standing atop the remains of a ruined building. He carried a spear in his hand.

The dragon would not even bother to block the attack. He puffed out his chest and jeered at the warrior.

"GO AHEAD LITTLE VERMIN! TAKE YOUR BEST SHOT AND SEE HOW FUTILE YOUR ATTEMPTS ARE!"

The warrior drew back his spear and threw it with all his might.

Aurichalcum was surprised at the speed of the spear as it darted through the air. It was as if the weapon was seeking out its target. He felt a slight prick as the blade pierced his chest and sank into his flesh.

It was not more than the bite of a fly to him.

Aurichalcum chuckled mirthlessly. **_"YOU'LL HAVE TO DO BETTER THAN THAT, VERMIN! I AM A GREAT WYRM; YOU CAN NOT KILL ME WITH YOUR—"_**

There was a tugging in his chest, and Aurichalcum suddenly felt his entire being shift for a moment.

The spear that was lodged into his breast was now no longer like the bite of a fly, but a heavy anchor that drew him towards it. The spear seemed to tug Aurichalcum's centre of balance down towards the ground. He tried to resist, but he was powerless against it.

His strength was leaving him, and he felt weaker by the moment. Aurichalcum craned his neck to see the spear and was horrified by what he had missed at first glance. The bright, bone-white shaft of the spear, carved with glowing runes, was none other than the Spear of the First Father.

Aurichalcum's folly finally became clear, and he realized, now, that he had been a fool to underestimate Tenebrae's ability to plan.

The spear drew Aurichalcum's blood from his body as a mosquito would from its prey. Aurichalcum knew that the spear absorbed the life force of those it pierced and would incorporate that power into itself. That power could then be used by the wielder, or even redistributed at will.

That was something that Aurichalcum had experienced first-hand once when he had wielded the blade long ago.

Long, long...ago...

Aurichalcum swayed. He could feel his very essence being pulled from him, and the spear drank of it eagerly. It had been hungry. No wonder, it had been hidden so long.

His strength was almost gone, and soon Aurichalcum would collapse. Dead. He had overplayed his hand and aided in his own destruction. What a fool he had been.

How cruel was fate, Aurichalcum thought, that the weapon that had been used to kill his father—the very blade that had started all of this in the first place—would be the cause of his death.

"Ten'ebraex...even now?"

Aurichalcum spoke to no one in particular. He did not expect a response. But to his extreme horror, his brother's voice answered. It echoed through his head like a phantom, coming from the past to haunt him once more.

No more was Tenebrae a distant being, whispered about in the halls of state or amongst the Darond. No, now he was real and tangible, and Aurichalcum could hear him, feel him, in his mind, like the looming spectre of a coming storm at the end of a beautiful summer's day.

Thus ended the life of The Great Brass Wyrm, Aurichalcum.

Not with a glorious death in battle. Not in a triumphant fanfare and celebration. Not surrounded by loved ones. Not even peacefully in his sleep.

It ended, with a crashing thud that levelled half the city of Ethon, and a pitiful gasp as the last of his life essence had been drained from his body.

* * *

Aurichalcum's claws had caused a shockwave that overturned several city blocks. Houses were toppled, parts of a wall crumbled, and entire neighbourhoods were flattened. Ancient, cobbled streets were now indistinguishable in the destruction.

Drakhart and Elandyr'ni had been thrown from their horses during the violent upheaval of earth and masonry. Their horses died when they were thrown several metres into the air.

Elandyr'ni immediately began casting spells to protect her and Drakhart. Even though they were buried under the rubble, they lived, surviving under the protection of a magical bubble that created a small alcove for them to hide in.

The weight of buildings, roads, walls, and neighbourhoods weighed down on Elandyr'ni, and it took every bit of her strength and focus to maintain the bubble. She gritted her teeth, straining against the weight of it all, but she did not give in. Her tattoos glowed, and blood flowed from several cuts across her body, blood she used to fuel her spells further.

O'lomec had disappeared in the confusion, but his horse's legs could be seen sticking out from underneath a large chunk of a house inside the alcove where Elandyr'ni and Drakhart had been buried.

When the sound of destruction finally died down from outside the alcove, Elandyr'ni knew it was time to extract herself and Drakhart from their foxhole. Whether the Kinu'watan had succeeded or failed, she did not know, and she wasn't sure which would be harder to face.

Elandyr'ni waited a moment for the rubble to settle. Without the constant shockwaves from the great dragon's footsteps, they were less likely to shift. One Elandyr'ni was confident that the rubble that buried her and Drakhart would not shift further, she made a fist and punched the mass of rubble directly in front of her.

Once.

Twice

Three times.

And the rubble crumbled away, freeing her and Drakhart from the small cavern where they had been trapped. The light of the moon and stars poured into the small alcove between the broken walls and fallen masonry.

Elandyr'ni ended her spell and the golden glow of her tattoos faded away.

All the while, Drakhart had watched in dumb astonishment at the feats of strength and magic Elandyr'ni was capable of. Every time he thought he knew the limits of her power, she proved him wrong—and it scared him. But he respected her for it.

"How are you able to use your tattoos without entering the Blood Fugue?" asked Drakhart.

"A Blood Witch can access the same powers as a Blood Warrior, but not at the same depth. We cannot be allowed to succumb to Blood Fugue, for we are the only thing that can control a rampaging Blood Warrior, and we could not do that if we joined them in the depths of madness."

Elandyr'ni did not wait for more questions and indicated that they should get going.

Drakhart followed Elandyr'ni from the alcove. Together the two looked out and surveyed the ruined city. Smoke curled up from neighbourhoods at the fringes of the once-proud city, and flames burned bright against the darkened night sky. The stench of death and gore was everywhere. Large swathes of the city were destroyed by Aurichalcum's rampage, and the Great Brass Dragon himself lay dead, sprawled out atop most of it.

"I would assume, by the corpse, that Lord O'lomec succeeded," Drakhart stated.

The Kinu'watan jumped down from a ruined building nearby. He landed with a heavy thud. "I'd say so. Are you two all right?"

The Khaleeshir and the Grand Enchantress were tired, dusty, and covered in cuts and scrapes, but they were otherwise unharmed.

The Kinu'watan had fared much better. He had leapt from his horse just in time and managed to get to a vantage point atop a nearby building. Aurichalcum's arrogance, and his ignorance as to the nature of O'lomec's weapon, had allowed the Kinu'watan to strike the killing blow.

Elandyr'ni looked up at the massive dragon's cooling, desiccated corpse. "Should I drain the blood?"

Drakhart shook his head. "No need. The spear's done all that already."

"I'll go get it," O'lomec volunteered.

"No!" warned Drakhart. "Lord Tenebrae was clear that once Aurichalcum had been killed, only a Blood Witch—preferably Elandyr'ni—should retrieve it. Use your magic, don't touch it, and wrap it back inside the furs. It must be returned to Tenebrae immediately."

O'lomec was taken aback, but he wasn't about to question a direct order from Tenebrae. "Very well. It was an honour to wield it even as quickly as I did. Such power in such a simple weapon..."

Elandyr'ni pulled a pair of leather gloves from a pouch at her hip. Though they looked plain and well-worn, runes burned into the leather marked the gloves as enchanted.

Drakhart had expected no less of her.

Elandyr'ni pulled the gloves over her hands and flexed her fingers. "I'll handle this. You should go inform His Majesty that his town has been conquered and the crown is now his."

Drakhart sneered. "What's left of it, anyway—at least the city's still above water." Not by much though. Since the Baron's forces had retreated from the Acturn, and the battle ended, they had given up holding back the flood waters, and most of the lower parts of the city were now thoroughly submerged.

O'lomec laughed. "He won't like that."

Drakhart shrugged. "I promised I would hand him the city and the crown. I never said what state they would be in. If he wanted it done better, perhaps he should have joined the fray."

"I'm sure he'll make us pay for this, somehow," Elandyr'ni warned.

"I'm not concerned. I'll go send word to Calandor to begin the trip; the Baron—sorry, the new King—will want the Regency Council present to recognize him as the rightful monarch, as promised. In the meantime, I'll meet with Lord Gruffydd. O'lomec, would you care to accompany me while Elandyr'ni works here?"

O'lomec nodded. "It would be my pleasure. I would love to see the look on his face."

Chapter LVII

The Baron Felidrun—now the self-styled King of Estion—held his make-shift court inside of an estate once owned by the Baroness Pelchar. It had been relatively untouched by the battle, and Lord Gruffydd had seen fit to seize it as some form of poetic justice.

It rested atop a high hill a few kilometres from the city walls and overlooked the city and the surrounding landscape. Normally, the estate was surrounded by endless acres of farmland; fields of golden wheat, orchards extending to the horizon, and even livestock enclosures. But all of that was underwater now, and the estate looked like an island in the middle of a still ocean.

To reach the estate, Drakhart, O'lomec, and their Qiri'aran guards had to commandeer several fishing punts that had been left abandoned in the harbour.

"I cannot help but feel the irony of this situation," O'lomec mentioned as he rowed the boat closer to the estate.

Drakhart understood the reference well enough. Once the Qiri'ar would travel and fish on their culturally sacred Lake Gishan'belor, using similar means. But the lake had been dried up for centuries. It was now just an empty bowl of desolation and dust that could no longer support life.

"Perhaps His Majesty would prefer we redirect the water to Gishan'belor to save his drowned kingdom?" Drakhart suggested.

O'lomec belted out a hearty laugh. It echoed across the water in all directions.

The remainder of the boat trip moved along silently. No one spoke, but the world made plenty of sound around them. There were crickets, despite all the flooding. And the sound of water rushing through gaps in the dikes. This was joined by the consistent sound of the oars as they dipped into the water and pushed the boat forward. Finally came the sound of carrion crying out, as vultures, crows, ravens, and rooks flocked to the city of Estion to feast upon the dead.

A group of Gruffydd's soldiers met Drakhart and his companions at the water's edge. They looked cold and wet—they looked as if they'd been submerged in the water recently—and they were less than happy that they had been posted to stand guard outside of the estate during this cold night.

The soldiers ordered Drakhart and his group to disarm and leave their weapons before they entered the estate. Though O'lomec and his warriors were reluctant, Drakhart assuaged their fears. They would not be here long, and they were among allies. There would be no need for weapons here, surely.

While the group disarmed, the guards tossed dice to see who would be the lucky one to escort the visitors inside. In the end, one of the older guards of the group earned the pleasure of entering the warm estate. Perhaps he could even manage to find a quiet corner to get some sleep and sneak some food and wine from the kitchen.

As he was escorted through the villa, Drakhart made note that the estate itself was not overly ornate or fancily decorated as Drakhart had expected of someone as wealthy as the Lady vohn Veishaupt.

The building itself was well built, an example of fine craftsmanship and made of the best materials one could buy; Asardaean marble of various colours and white basalt imported from Danaen. But the walls were bare and unadorned with art or tapestries. There were no overt signs of wealth put on display anywhere in the building.

Drakhart felt as if he was walking through a very expensive fortress rather than a luxurious villa. No doubt the new king would change that soon enough.

Drakhart and his party were led through the narrow hallways into the main dining hall of the mansion. The former Baron Felidrun sat at the centre of the head table. Atop his brow rested a crudely made crown. His new royal standard was mounted upon crudely cut timber behind him. His loyal clique of nobles each sat feasting and laughing at the head table, stretched out at either side of him. Their families, retainers and other minor nobility in their service were arranged at the four long tables that ran the length of the massive hall.

"Welcome, Lord Ghast," the former baron spoke tersely.

"We come to wish you congratulations, Your Majesty. Long live the new king! I wish to also inform you that the rest of the Regency Council has officially signed paperwork and made a decree to the other nations that acknowledge your rule as legitimate by right of conquest. Danaen is already willing to give their assent to your rule. The Regency Council will soon depart the capital to visit you in person as part of an Altimaran political delegation to officially begin negotiations towards a new trade agreement between our nations."

King Llewyth's lips were so thin they almost disappeared. "I don't see how I have much to be thankful for. Though I have a crown upon my head, and the capital is within my grasp, it may as well be a ruin. The city is devoid of citizens, it's half demolished, the castle has been destroyed, and a dead dragon is lying in my streets. Not to mention that a good portion of my kingdom is underwater, the Acturn canal is ruined, and the dikes have been destroyed."

The music and revelry stopped. Everyone froze and turned towards the head table. They watched the scene unfold with trepidation. Even the loyal nobles nearest the former baron looked uncomfortable at what was to come.

Drakhart bowed his head. Though no one could see it, his fist was tightly clenched. "I do apologize for the destruction caused, Your Majesty, but we had no way of knowing what tricks our enemies would employ—"

"And more so, you have failed to deliver on your promise. I was promised the boy king, that I would execute him myself. Not only did he escape, but he's out there with the Baroness Pelchar and her soldiers, who somehow arrived just in time to save him, despite your assurances that they would not be made aware of the siege until it was too late to intervene. My crown means nothing if the boy king lives. I am viewed as a pretender, a usurper. I am not undisputed!"

The former baron's voice reached a crescendo as he monologued. By the end of his tirade, he screamed so loud that his voice bounced off the walls, echoing across the entirety of the great hall.

He snarled at Drakhart. "Rest assured, whelp. I will resume the timber trade with Altimara, and I will remain neutral in the conflict to come, as I have promised, for *I* know how to keep my word. But I hope your kingdom is prepared to pay double, perhaps triple what they were paying before, and I *will* be increasing tariffs on Altimaran imports. I have a country that needs rebuilding, and now, thanks to the failure of your desert heathens, a civil war to fight. We'll need to come up with that money somehow."

O'lomec scowled at King Llewyth.

Drakhart placed a hand on his ally's bicep. "Calm, O'lomec. Your Majesty if we could talk—"

"Talk? You want to talk?" yelled the former baron, incredulous. "Very well. Everyone, leave us!"

No one moved. Not the nobility. Not the guests in attendance, either.

King Llewyth's face turned red and contorted with rage. "I SAID GET OUT!"

He threw his golden chalice across the hall. The cup clattered and splashed wine across the stone floor as it landed.

Suddenly, benches scraped against the floor. Cutlery was thrown down in haste. Plates were abandoned. Cups were dropped in the scurry to leave. Within moments, the room had been vacated.

Aside from Gruffydd and Drakhart, only O'lomec and the Qiri'ar remained.

Drakhart gave O'lomec a silent look, and though the Kinu'watan was hesitant to leave Drakhart behind, O'lomec did what was asked of him.

Now alone with the new king, Drakhart spoke. "Your Majesty. We did the best we could with the circumstances provided. I assure you; it was not our intention to—"

"Save it," spat King Llewyth. "I knew you couldn't be trusted. I knew from the moment I met you that it was too good to be true."

He stood up and stalked from behind the head table.

Drakhart noticed that beneath his rather regal cloak, Gruffydd still wore his full set of plate armour. He held his great sword by the scabbard. It had been cleverly hidden by the table, laying across his lap while he ate.

"Your Majesty—" Drakhart sputtered.

"I suppose you really should have seen this coming, boy." King Llewyth lumbered towards Drakhart. Each step he took was slow and deliberate. "You're new to nobility, so I'll tell you something that would have saved your life: never trust another noble during a power struggle. Only one can stand above the rest, and the top of the hill is never shared."

King Llewyth drew his blade and tossed aside his scabbard.

Drakhart tried to back away, but it was too late. The king closed the gap between them with speed that betrayed his age. Drakhart felt a pain shoot through his stomach. The former baron had impaled him on his massive blade.

King Llewyth bared his teeth in a wicked grin. "You know boy, if you had been born noble, you might have lived. But you're just an up-jumped peasant. You should have learned your place."

"W-why?" Blood welled from Drakhart's mouth and dribbled down his chin.

"This way I can say you attacked me. When your delegation arrives, they'll be so embarrassed by your actions that they'll agree to whatever terms I give them. I know Altimara needs our lumber and our neutrality. On top of that, I know the truth about your nation's involvement in this regime change. You broke rules to help me, and I intend to squeeze that need for whatever it's worth."

"O'lomec and the others know the truth…" Drakhart was growing weaker, he could feel it.

King Llewyth gently twisted the blade in Drakhart's gut. "How can they when my men are currently murdering them as we speak? An unarmed Qiri'ar without the Blood Fugue is just as weak as any other man. Who is this delegation going to believe, me or a bunch of dead bodies?"

Drakhart heard a commotion from the hallway. Shouts and screams and the sounds of battle echoed from behind the closed doors. His allies were under attack.

But instead of succumbing to the pain and the helplessness…Drakhart laughed. He laughed so heartily and mirthlessly that King Llewyth looked genuinely concerned.

"What are you laughing about boy?" King Llewyth demanded.

"You know, my lord Baron—"

"—I am a king! And if you yet draw breath, you will address me as such!"

"My lord Baron, I think you fail to see the irony of our situation."

Gruffydd roared. He moved to twist his blade further, but Drakhart reached up and clenched his hands around Gruffydd's grip. He held Lord Gruffydd's hands tightly in place.

"Did you of all people truly not realize what was happening? You think it was you who played me, but I played you. I trusted in nothing but the falsity of your words since the beginning, and my visit to your encampment with the Grand Enchantress only confirmed my suspicions. You didn't seem surprised that we had arrived unannounced, which would only be the case if you had been spying on us. I had always planned to discard you once you served your purpose, but I was stuck on the how—now your attack has aided in those plans. I have bodily proof of your treachery…and you? You'll be dead by the time anyone comes back to check on me."

"What are you—"

Drakhart wrenched on Gruffydd's hands and pulled the sword, and Lord Gruffydd, closer to him, driving the blade even further through his gut. "You see Baron—" Drakhart spat blood into Gruffydd's face as he spoke. The usurper's face had gone from triumphant to fearful. "—I am one of the Dragonkin. I can withstand a few more cuts than your average human, and I intend to use that to my advantage. You on the other hand? I bet you'll bleed like a pig at slaughter."

Gruffydd tried to cry out for help, but Drakhart struck fast.

With lightning speed, he released his grip on Gruffydd's hand and slammed both fists into the man's breastplate. Two deep dents were carved into the metalwork, and the usurper was sent flying back into the table and chair he had previously been sitting at. He rolled and toppled onto the floor, winded and stunned.

Drakhart pulled the blade from his gut and stalked towards Gruffydd. "You're the strongest of your clique, Your Majesty." Drakhart used the title mockingly. Every syllable dripped with venom as they left his mouth. "You're a leader...but your allies? They're followers; they're sheep. They joined you against the monarchy because you were the strongest amongst them, but with you dead, I will be the strongest...and no doubt they'll follow me instead. If they don't, they will be killed and replaced. Your kingdom will become *our* kingdom. Estion will be disgraced when its new monarch, who has officially been recognized by Altimara, is known the world over as a traitor and a liar. You attacked a political representative of a friendly nation, and that will mean war. Our armies will sweep in to restore order, since civil war has engulfed the nation, and the monarch has died without issue. We shall place an acceptable regent upon the throne, and force Estion to become a protectorate. Estion will have no choice but to accept whatever terms we dictate to it, or the people will be made to suffer the consequences of any disobedience."

Gruffydd, his ribs crushed, attempted to crawl away from Drakhart. He ducked under the table to protect himself.

A wicked grin spread across Drakhart's face. With savage strength, he grabbed the heavy oak table and tossed it aside with ease. Cutlery clattered as it hit the floor. Plates and glasses shattered against the stonework. Wine jugs broke and spilt their contents everywhere like blood. Food was smeared across the marble.

And there, on the floor, cowering beneath where the table had once been lay Gruffydd. He blubbered, begging for his life, as he realized the tables had been turned on him.

Drakhart cocked his head. "Perhaps I was wrong about you? Perhaps you were not the strongest, but merely the loudest."

Drakhart pounced. He steadied Gruffydd by the shoulder with one hand and impaled him on his own blade with the other.

Gruffydd cried out.

"Before you die, my lord Baron." Drakhart's face twisted into a wicked grin. "I think you deserve to know the truth about your son. It was not King Anducaerleonis who had him killed. It was I. I must admit his death was unintentional—we had no idea who he was when he was killed. Though I suppose it ended up working out for us in the end. Funny, how the death of some nameless, unknown bard gave Altimara its greatest advantage in the war to come."

Gruffydd's face contorted, though whether it was from the pain of having a blade through his gut, or his horror at the realization that he had betrayed king and country because of a lie, Drakhart could not tell. Nor did he particularly care. Lord Gruffydd's feelings would not matter at all in short order.

Drakhart gripped the hilt of the blade with both hands and tugged upwards. What would have been a feat of strength for a normal human was easy enough for Drakhart. With his great Khaleeshir strength, he manoeuvred the blade upwards. He sliced vertically through Gruffydd, splitting his armour, torso, and skull in half from the gut upwards.

The two halves sagged and flopped outwards like a macabre flower in bloom before the whole corpse toppled backwards in a wet, sloppy mess.

Drakhart stood there. His strength ebbed from him. His breath came in short heaves. The blood loss slowly caught up to him. But he wasn't done yet. One thing remained.

With the last of his strength, Drakhart slammed Gruffydd's blade against a nearby stone pillar. The blade broke in two with a crisp, metallic sound. With the half still in his hand, Drakhart impaled himself four times in the gut and chest with such vigorous fury that O'lomec—who had just barged through the door, bloodied, and covered in gore, with a bent sword in his hand—was stupefied.

When Drakhart pulled the blade from his body one final time, he could feel a rush of euphoria take over. He stretched his arms outwards. Gruffydd's blade fell from his fingers and clattered against the ground.

Drakhart threw back his head and stood there, silently, staring up at the decorated ceiling of the great hall. He stood and stared, and dared not utter a word until finally, he could stand no longer.

His strength finally left him, his face—now pale from the blood loss—went slack, and with two final words, Drakhart collapsed into the pool of his own blood that had gathered at his feet.

"I win…"

The Story Will Continue
In

The Chronicles of Enayra
Book 3

Coming Soon!

Drazhanii to Common Dictionary

Unthyr – Lit. "Moon Four", though more often translated as "Fourth Moon." Unthyr is the name of the fourth of thirteen months of Enayra. A popular festival, known as the Last of Unthyr, is celebrated on the last few days of the month to celebrate the coming of spring and the end of winter.

Vit wiluthyr vat ja thanir – A spell that summons a ball of light. Poetically translated, it means "Come forth to me, Little Sun." Though Vit wiluthyr means "small ball of bright light", wiluthyr is the word used by dragons for the Sun, and thus, Little Sun is the Common translation for this spell.

Bizhak Harzok – Translates to "Bloodless Mountain." It is the name of the horrific experiment created by Tenebrae during his previous attempt to control Enayra and usurp the Metallics. This creature was created by grafting the heads of several different coloured dragons to the body of Nulgo'riaz, the Great K'nir of the Orange Dragon Clan.

Tulkaz – Abomination. Though it can be used in plural form. It is most often used to refer to the created humanoid monsters created by Tenebrae. Though no one has ever seen these creatures' faces, rumours state they are half dragon, half human. Other stories claim that they are living shadows bound to a humanoid form. Whatever the truth is, their ferocity, skill, and lack of empathy for those they murder, as well as their efficiency are not rumours.

Khin'shala – The Draconic name for Rishi beasts. The original meaning of the Draconic name has been lost to time, as it predates human arrival in Enayra.

Drazhan nit kidarr drazhan – One of the Primal Laws. It means "Dragon shall not kill dragon." However, there are exceptions to this law, such as the legality of killing those deemed "harzok" or who have betrayed their race (such as Tenebrae and those who joined him). Generally, though, it is considered a grievous crime amongst dragons to kill one another.

Kha'n'kha'lash – Blood for Blood Spell. The name of the ritual used to bind dragon and human, thus creating true Khaleeshir; often described as one soul in two bodies.

Vizka'in'lash – Spell of Bestowment. It is the name for the innate magical process performed by dragons when they pass their memories and knowledge down to their unhatched offspring.

Hrutha Kavahn – Sacred Magic. Another name for some of the earliest magic performed by the First Mother and First Father, before the draconic race even came to be.

Ha'k'nir-ad-Eru-in'fuor-Elthir – The proper, if condensed, title for the Clan Patriarch of a Dragon Clan. The most frequent translations into Common are either Great Patriarch or Clan Father, but the proper translation is Great Father, First of Their Colour.

Ha'k'dir-ad-Erya-in'fuor-Elthir – The proper, if condensed, title for the Clan Matriarch of a Dragon Clan. The most frequent translations into Common are either Great Matriarch or Clan Mother, but the proper translation is Great Mother, First of Their Colour.

Ha'k'nir – Roughly translates to High Father. It is a shortened version of the fuller title above, only to be used by close relations or those closely familiar to the Clan Patriarch.

Ha'k'dir – Roughly translates to High Mother. It is a shortened version of the fuller title above, only to be used by close relations or those closely familiar to the Clan Matriarch.

Dol'viinaeszoth – A common greeting between dragons; also used by humans when speaking to a wild dragon. It translates to "the blessings of Viinaeszoth be with you", or more simply "Viinaeszoth be with you." Viinaeszoth is the dragons' spiritual embodiment of the wind.

Jal k'zir. Vit ul weniri. – "My son. You have returned."

Ha'drazh'ghar Vikwul – The Draconic term for the Blue Dragon Clan. When translated literally, it means "Great Blue Dragon Clan".

Ha'drazh'ghar – Ha'drazh'ghar is the term for one of the Five Great Clans (Blue, Black, White, Green, and Red), and literally means "Great Dragon Clan".

Drazh'ghar – Drazh'ghar is the general word for a dragon clan but is used most often to refer to the so-called "lesser clans" (Orange, Pink, Grey, Purple, Yellow, and Brown).

K'iir – Lit. "Flesh Sister." Used to describe a sister that is blood-related amongst dragons.

K'tir – Lit. "Flesh Brother." Used to describe a brother that is blood-related amongst dragons.

K'vir – Lit. "Flesh Daughter." Used to describe a daughter that is blood-related amongst dragons.

Ulzar'khimal – Another name for Bizhak Harzok. It's translation roughly equates to "Hope Devourer." It was the name primarily used by Tenebrae and his allies for this creature.

Tuir'Delohmeyh – The name of the Darond's headquarters in the mountains of Anglum. It means "Deep Fortress."

Nes'kitroth – Translates to "Second Sight" and is the Draconic name for their second set of eyelids, and the powers it grants them.

Fohl'Diniitor – The Draconic name for the original home of their race, before humans arrived in Enayra, and before the dragons grew numerous enough to populate the continent. It translates to "Great Nest." Today these series of tunnels and holes have been reworked as the Darond Headquarters, under the name "Tuir'Delohmeyh."

Ves'Hurundahl – Meaning "First Sanctuary", is another archaic name for Fohl'Diniitor, now known as "Tuir'Delohmeyh."

Y'thair – Translates to "Master" or "Teacher", though can also translate to "Elder." As dragons are raised communally, it is a common term used by younger dragons to refer to their elders who are not directly related to them but still share a clan. There is a separate term for elder dragons of a different clan.

Y'wiihr – Though this word has come to mean "Student" or "Pupil" in Draconic, it can also translate to something akin to "Youngling" or "Hatchling". In its original context, it was used by older dragons when referring to younger dragons they were not directly related to. In traditional Draconic culture, younger dragons are often raised communally.

Kha'diniitor – Lit. "Blood of the Nest." Translates to nest mate, though despite the reference to blood, it does not always need to apply to a dragon that shares blood. Merely being raised in the same nest is enough.

From Book 1

Drazhani-ad-Khaleesh – Of the Blood of Dragons (lit.) or Blood of Dragons, or occasionally Dragonkin amongst non-Draconic speaking human populations. It is used to specifically refer to the five chosen humans and dragons who are bonded together in a blood covenant to protect Enayra.

Ad – Lit. Of, or of the, concerning possession and belonging.

Khaleeshir – Of the Blood (lit., plural), also kin. The plural form of Khaleesh. It is used as a shortened title for the Drazhani-ad-Khaleesh, specifically when referring to more than one at a time.

Khaleesh – Of the Blood (lit., singular), also kin. The singular form of Khaleeshir. It is used as a shortened title for the Drazhani-ad-Khaleesh, specifically when referring to only one.

Izkari – Freeze (lit. to Freeze), also Frost.

Drazhan – Dragon

Drazhani – Dragons. Also used to describe the draconic race as a whole.

Drazhanii – Draconic. For example, Drazhanii kavahn lit. Draconic magic. Is often used to describe the Draconic race as a whole and is the name of the Draconic language.

Drazhanii Kavahn – Lit. Dragonspeak Magic. The draconic term for the Arcane magic of Enayra.

Kruvir – White. Is used more specifically to refer to white dragons and the White Dragon Clan.

Noram – Red. Is used more specifically to refer to red dragons and the Red Dragon Clan.

Vikwul – Blue. Is used more specifically to refer to blue dragons and the Blue Dragon Clan.

Kuzum – Black. Is used more specifically to refer to black dragons and the Black Dragon Clan.

Benavor – Green. Is used more specifically to refer to the green dragons and the Green Dragon Clan.

Ezar Kanik – The Earth Mother. The first female dragon who birthed all other dragons in Enayra. Alongside her mate, the Earth Father, she gave life to Enayra and the world. Upon her death, her spirit merged with that of the earth's, and she became the planet itself.

Ezar Myna – The Earth Father. The first male dragon who sired all other dragons in Enayra. Alongside his mate, the Earth Mother, he gave life to all the world, especially Enayra. He is said to have removed his finger bone and fashioned the oldest knife in Enayra, with which he and his mate gave life to the land. This knife is now used in the Blood Covenant that creates Dragonkin.

Denthanus – Technically a corruption of the actual word: **den'thanuriil**. Terror, or terrorizer.

Harzok – Lit. bloodless, or without kin. Harzok is a title of great shame among dragons. They place great importance on the bonds of family, unity, and blood—be they chosen or by blood. For a dragon to be considered harzok, they are considered beyond redemption and are shunned by Draconic society as a whole. They are ignored and treated as if they do not exist. Some harzok are so shameful that they are to be killed on sight if they return to dragon society. Once you are harzok, it cannot be undone.

K'inar – Lit. Flesh Spine. Also, spine, or spineless depending on usage.

Vorunda – Coward

K'inar vorunda – Spineless coward. A general insult, but one that carries great weight amongst the ever-prideful dragons.

K'thirqi – Lit. Flesh Kidney. Usually just translated as kidney.

Hu'tar – Fireball, or fire.

K'dir – Lit. Flesh Mother. Also, mother, or matriarch.

K'nir – Lit. Flesh Father. Also, father, or patriarch.

Ja – Me

Thanir – Follow or come with.

Ja thanir – Follow me or come with me.

K'a-thashivir – Lit. See with your eyes. Also, behold.

K'a – Lit. Flesh Eyes. Usually just eye, or eyes.

Na – With, or together.

Shi – See or look.

Vir – Your.

Jar – I, or occasionally, I am.

Wenir – Return or come back.

K'zir – Lit. Flesh Son. Usually just son.

A Guide to Pronouncing Enayran Languages

Enayra is a land that abounds with multiple languages, both current and ancient. Languages have arrived, evolved, and even been created anew across the continent's history. Sometimes, pronunciation or certain language rules can be hard to grasp when written on a page instead of spoken, and so this guide seeks to remedy that by assisting in pronouncing the more difficult aspects of the many languages you'll encounter in this text.

Draconic

Draconic is the language of the race of dragons in Enayra. It is known to have evolved from an archaic form of the language, known by scholars as Ancient Draconic, though very little of this language is understood. It is known that the names of the first dragons—the Patriarchs, Matriarchs, and the Great Metallics—are of Ancient Draconic origin. No dragons remain today who speak this version of the language.

It should be noted that Draconic was *not* a written language before humans arrived. In the wild, dragons "speak" Draconic as a combination of words, flashes of memory, senses (such as sounds, smell, etc.), and even emotion.

The Draconic language that most people are familiar with in Enayra is the written form created by and spoken amongst humans, originally for magical study.

For such an ancient language, there are relatively few rules for this language. Most pertain to the pronunciation of vowels, which remain consistent across most, if not all words, and the usage of punctuation in the middle of words and sentences.

    A – The vowel sound for "a" is always pronounced as "ah", as in "father."

    E – The vowel sound for "e" is always pronounced as "eh", as in "bed."

    EE – The double E vowel pair indicates the long E sound, as seen in "mean" or "feel" and is pronounced as such.

    I – The vowel sound for "I" is always pronounced the same as the double E sound. As Draconic was not a written language before humans arrived and created a written version of the language, it is believed that "I" was used in certain words because it was either more visually appealing or made more grammatical sense to the humans looking to learn Draconic. If dragons had created the written language, words like "Wenir" or "Vikwul" may well be spelled as "Weneer" and "Veekwul."

II – The double II is pronounced as "ai", like in "sky." For example, Drazhanii is phonetically pronounced "Drah-zah-nai."

O – The vowel sound for "o" is always pronounced "oh", as in "go."

U – The vowel sound for U is always pronounced as "oo", as in "music."

Y – The vowel sound for Y is pronounced in the same way as the double I sound. Like the use of I to represent some of the EE vowel sounds, it is likely a human addition when creating a written form of Draconic, meant to aid human learners. It should be noted that the letter "y" appears very infrequently in the Draconic language.

' – Apostrophes are often littered throughout Draconic words. These apostrophes denote a compound word. Apostrophes are not to be pronounced, only to signal that the word is made up of two other words or phrases. It is another human concept meant to aid in reading comprehension and speed translation for students learning Draconic. Compound words with apostrophes should be pronounced as a single word.

- – Hyphens in Draconic are often used to string together words that comprise a single phrase, or title, such as in "Drazhani-ad-Khaleeshir."

High Altimaran

Originally descending from a common root language that also birthed Qir'to'ah, High Altimaran is the language of Altimara that stems from the latter days of the Age of Heroes. It is not spoken frequently outside of the Altimaran Court and royal family and is mainly a language of ceremony, tradition, and scholarly pursuits. Few outside the nobility can speak this language.

While High Altimaran does not appear frequently in this text, it does have a few pronunciation rules to keep in mind.

Ah – When the phoneme "ah" appears in a word, it is pronounced as "ah." However, it is not a simple "ah" like father, but more guttural, coming from the back of the throat, as if one is yawning while speaking. This phoneme appears in the words "Kul'zabahg" and "Haurfahng."

' – Apostrophes also appear in High Altimaran, though very infrequently. They serve a similar purpose and pronunciation It should be noted that Altimaran shares a root language with Qir'to'ah, and it was the ancestors of both people groups that first wrote Draconic down as a written language, adding their concept of apostrophes to that language. The development of the Altimaran language groups was heavily influenced by contact with Draconic, as it was these peoples who were the first to adopt modern Dragomancy, and worship and live in harmony with dragons.

Old Gerovian

Old Gerovian is the language of the people of Estion from when it was still known as Gerovia. It was spoken since the first Gerovians settled in the region, until the fall of the Gerovian Empire in 407 Conflict.

Old Gerovian appears only in a single instance in this text but has many accents and odd sounds some readers may be unfamiliar with. Below is a guide to pronouncing these sounds.

DD – The double D consonant pair is a voiced dental fricative, pronounced, like in Welsh, as "th", such as in "this" or "the."

Ä – The ä character in Old Gerovian is pronounced phonetically. Like the a in "blade", or "made."

Í – The í character in Old Gerovian is pronounced as "ee", such as in "feel" or "wheel."

Ç – The ç character in Old Gerovian is pronounced as "ch", like in "chirp" or "char."

Ã – The ã character in Old Gerovian is pronounced as "ah", but denotes a nasalized, open-mouth vowel pronunciation.

Estian
Eastlands Dialect

After the collapse of the empire, and during the Anarchy, the Gerovian language slowly began to morph into its modern form: Estian. Modern Estian can easily be classified into at least five regional dialects, the most common being the Eastlands dialect, which originated in Felidrun and the surrounding area. It is even the dialect spoken at the royal court.

The Eastlands dialect of modern Estian borrows some elements from Old Gerovian. A pronunciation guide follows.

DD – The double D consonant pair is a voiced dental fricative, pronounced, like in Welsh, as "th", such as in "this" or "the."

LL – The double L digraph is a tricky one to pronounce. It is pronounced like how it is in Welsh. The sound to pronounce this digraph is made by placing one's tongue behind your front, and top teeth, and blowing air around the sides of your tongue.

FF – The double F sound is pronounced as if it were a single f. Like the f in "first" or "fowl."

F – The single F in Eastlands Estian—and only in Eastlands Estian—is pronounced like V, hence the distinction between single and double F sounds. That would mean that Felidrun, in the Eastlands dialect, is pronounced as Velidrun. In Common, and other dialects of Estian, it is still pronounced as Felidrun.

Xiani'ul
The Language of the Xiani

The Xiani are an enigmatic, non-human people group living at the very tip of the northernmost peninsula of Enayra, in Anglum, in their sole city of K'xhk'xan. The peninsula is known as Ch'aak Xiani'bul, or Origin of the Xiani, in the Xiani'ul language. Most humans call it Point Desolate.

The Xiani do not involve themselves in the politics and goings-on of the outside world and prefer to remain isolated in their large, frozen city. They are not human, being something more along the lines of humanoids with some animalistic features.

They are enormous, standing about two and a half to three metres tall, with short, curving tusks that erupt from where the jaw's hinge, as well as snort, trunk-like snouts, like a tapir or an elephant seal. Xiani have two heads, and each head has two tongues, and two sets of ear holes. Their skin is leathery in texture, and of similar thickness to elephant hide, and varies in colour, ranging from ash grey to greyish blue, to mottled yellow.

No one knows where the Xiani originate from, but they are believed to be one of the only two sentient races native to Enayra, alongside dragons. The dragons believe—but are not certain—that the Xiani were created by the Earth Mother in her attempt to create other sentient life in Enayra, but the process was left incomplete with her untimely death.

The Xiani live on peaceful terms with the White Dragon Clan, whose ancestral lands are their settlement, and while the Xiani do not worship the dragons as the humans do, they do respect them and their destructive powers. Xiani will leave regular offerings to the dragons, and even invite them to their settlement to celebrate important religious and cultural festivals together, though few white dragons make the trip nowadays.

Much like with dragons, the Xiani'ul language cannot truly be spoken by humans in its purest form. It is spoken by both heads—and all four tongues working in conjunction—simultaneously, harmonizing their speech so that they resonate together. The Xiani'ul language also requires the ability to mix in specialized grunts and some sounds not audible to human ears—hence why Xiani have two sets of earholes and a trunk. The version of Xiani written down and used by humans to communicate with the isolated civilization is a heavily modified version from the original, which is not originally a written language.

The pronunciation guide is simple, as the language was made to be as simple to learn by humans and Xiani.

> **X** – The X sound in Xiani'ul is pounced like "sh", like in "shore" or "shovel."

> ' – Apostrophes in the Xiani'ul language were not added by humans for the ease of translating compound words but are native part of the language. The apostrophes denote a place in the word where a short half-second breath, or pause, is taken while speaking.

Bonus Content

The Story of Zosime and Volesus

An Excerpt from *"The History of Asardaea and the Enayran Empire"* by Vigrindius the Elder

Zosime and Volesus lived in the early days of the Age of Conflict and were among the first generation of humans born in Enayra. They were born in the northern parts of the realm, in the lands that are now the Kingdom of Asardaea. In those days, Asardaea was inhabited by a loose collection of human tribes. Sometimes they warred with one another, sometimes they traded and allied together to form a coalition against other tribes. For the most part though, life went on with a certain stability lost to the annals of history.

It was in these early days that Volesus, of Gens Tarquinia and Zosime of Romontya met and fell in love with one another. Each was the child of their respective chieftain, and many expected the two to marry. Both Gens had long been allies and a marriage pact between both Gens would elevate their power to contend as one of the strongest in the region. But Zosime's father, Acamas, was a shrewd and cunning man. He had submitted to an alliance with Volesus's father, Quintus because he knew that he could not match the Tarquinians in military might. By exploiting an alliance with Gens Tarquinia, the Romontians were able to secure its borders and build up a larger army, uninterrupted by war or conflict, and when there was conflict, the Romontians ensured they would not bleed alone.

Acamas had watched Quintus age and wither away, and his son soon came to replace him in the twenty-second year of his life—the thirty-second year of the peace between the two tribes. Acamas expected Volesus to be a weak leader, and so when Volesus approached the king and asked for his daughter's hand in marriage—for he had already achieved her required consent—the king refused to acknowledge a pairing between his daughter and the young chief. Volesus was angered but Zosime had long assured her love that her father would not object to such a union if Volesus could but prove himself to her father.

But Zosime did not know of her father's duplicity. Unbeknownst to all, Acamas had planned to marry his daughter off to the chief of the Gens Plaetoria, Vintius, who had promised a large sum of gold and a bequeathment of lands in exchange for Zosime's hand.

Acamas lacked the bride's consent to the marriage but was willing to override that rule as head of his Gens and get his way.

Volesus demanded to see his bride-to-be, but Acamas would not allow the two lovers an audience. Acamas, true to Zosime's warning, stated that he would acquiesce to Volesus's request if he could go out and prove himself. All Volesus had to do would be to conquer a neighbouring Gens—one who had been enemy to both the Septicia and Tarquinia—and gift half the land to Acamas as a bride price, and in exchange, Volesus would have Zosime's hand in marriage. Volesus disliked the deal, but for his love, he would have done anything, and so he agreed.

Volesus went forth and conquered the lands of the once proud Gens Vibia. He declared half the conquered lands, people, and resources as subjects of the Septicia and returned to Acamas with proof of his achievements. Acamas was pleased but would still not allow Volesus to see his beloved, nor would he agree to the union. Volesus held his rage in check. He could not strike down Acamas in his kingdom and expect to get out alive, nor would Volesus risk the wrath of his bride-to-be if he struck down her beloved father. Instead, Volesus offered to prove himself further, and conquer another Gens, if only Acamas would reconsider.

Acamas agreed.

So Volesus went forth with his armies and conquered the lands of another Gens whose name is lost to history. Once more he divided the spoils and lands between himself and Acamas, and again, he came to proclaim his victory before his would-be father-in-law. But again, Volesus's request was refused.

Acamas, finally pleased with his clan's newfound wealth and power, spoke freely with Volesus, and told him of Zosime's marriage offer from the chief of the Gens Plaetoria.

Frustrated, but heartbroken, Volesus threw himself before Acamas and appealed to his mercy, offering any price in exchange for Zosime's hand in marriage. Acamas thought for but a moment for asking, once more, for Volesus to conquer yet another enemy of the Romontians. Volesus was tired of the warfare but would do anything to marry his love, and so he agreed one last time. Three years would pass, and Volesus and Acamas continued the cycle of conquest and petition until only three Gens remained in Asardaea: the Gens Plaetoria, the Romontians, and the Gens Tarquinia. Volesus had built the great city of Malatrion at this time and made this place the capital of his new Tarquinian Kingdom. Acamas too had grown fat off the hard work of Volesus, but still had not given his ascent for Zosime to marry Volesus.

With no enemies left to either the Romontians or Gens Tarquinia, Volesus went once more to petition Acamas, but this time he had come prepared. Chief Vintius Plaetoria had secretly approached Volesus and declared he had been so moved by the love between Volesus and Zosime that he had declared himself an ally of Volesus against the greedy Acamas. When Volesus appeared before the now King Acamas, the king once more refused Volesus's request for marriage and had Volesus escorted from the palace.

Acamas revelled in his wicked trickery. He had gained a third of Asardaean lands by putting in none of his effort or manpower. His armies were strong, well fed, well supplied, and well deployed, while Volesus's was war-weary and still had to fear an attack from the Gens Plaetoria—or so he thought.

With Gen Plaetoria's promised support, Volesus returned with a large army to lay siege to Romontya, the capital of Acamas's kingdom. He was joined by the armies of

Vintius of Gens Plaetoria. Acamas was aghast, but optimistic that he could withstand the siege. Acamas shut himself inside his castle and left his soldiers to defend the city while he partied and feasted. His overconfidence, however, was misplaced. Acamas had not calculated that his well-fed, large army was ineffective in battle. They had never seen war and were poorly trained, overly fat from the spoils, and vastly unprepared. By comparison, Volesus's army was battle-hardened, and full of veterans who had seen their leader bleed alongside them on the battlefield. They were fiercely loyal, and even though Acamas had used Volesus for his selfish desires, Volesus had raised his Gens to a level of prestige and power in the region that went unmatched. With his Plaetorian allies, it did not take long for Volesus to crush Acamas and his forces.

Volesus had his armies pull down the city's walls and allowed them to plunder the palace of its valuables, and he had Acamas captured, bound, and brought before him. But neither Acamas nor Volesus could have prepared for what came next.

After Volesus had Acamas committed to the darkest dungeons of Malatrion for his treachery, he ran to the highest tower to find Zosime, his one true love, only to discover the horrible truth. Before the siege had started, Zosime had fled the palace and the city and escaped the imprisonment that her father had imposed upon her. Since her father saw her as nothing but a bargaining piece to bring him greater power, he cared not to check in on her, and her jailers merely slid food into a slot beneath her door and left her bedroom door locked and heavily guarded. Zosime fled with a few possessions and four loyal guardsmen who would not betray her to her father.

Volesus rallied his forces and set them to scour the land for signs of Zosime. In particular, he had them expect her at Malatrion, expecting her to have tried to reach him at his capital. It was Vintius and his forces that first found evidence of Zosime's whereabouts. Vintius had managed to learn that marauding bandits had attacked Zosime and her small group, and she had gone missing after the attack. Though, he noted, no ransom had been made. But despite the trail running cold, Volesus did not give up hope and chased all signs and whispers of his lover to the ends of Enayra. As he swept across the lands, looking for his lost love, his armies would conquer and claim, and in doing so he became the first to conquer the entire continent and ruled over it as a single unified Enayran Empire.

It should be noted that while Volesus conquered much of the land settled by humans, he did not conquer the lands that lay within the dragons' many territories, and indeed added to their territories to ensure good relationships between humans and dragons. The dragons were given undisputed reign over the lands they claimed and were not made subject to the laws and rules of man. Likewise, humans were banned from encroaching upon the lands of the dragons, upon pain of death. The dragons could come and go throughout the realm as they pleased, and chase whatever prey they wished, even if it be outside of their ancient clan-specific enclaves—though this would later be restricted after the fall of the Enayra Empire.

But the story does not end here, for Zosime was not one to simply sit by and accept her fate. She had indeed been kidnapped by a roving band of Gerovian deserters, who had abandoned the Gerovian Army after a protracted civil war in the city-state had led to its collapse. They had taken to raiding the prosperous lands of Asardaea. These raiders kept their incursions from gaining too much attention, for the most part, by leading small, quick strikes into Asardaean land, raiding only from the smallest settlements and villages, taking only what they could carry, and in this way, their identities and goals were masked and went unnoticed by Volesus's armies. In one such raid, these deserters came across Zosime and her loyal guards. It had been a coincidence but seeing that this woman was someone of great importance, and captivated by her beauty, the raiders took her as a supposed easy prize, hoping to ransom her for a great amount of money.

But soon these raiders came to find that Zosime was not so easily made captive. When she learned that they intended to ransom her, and the amount that the raiders sought for her return, Zosime insisted that the ransom they were demanding for her was too low, and repeatedly insisted they raise it. Eventually, through her guile and honeyed words, Zosime convinced the marauders to abandon the idea of ransom altogether and allow her and her guards to join the raiders. The raiders, impressed and amused by Zosime's ability to command such a presence amongst her once captors, eventually allowed Zosime to take control of the group. It should not be entirely surprising that Zosime could command such respect, for she had been a princess of Romontya. Nor was she some helpless damsel beguiling soldiers to follow her orders. Zosime had, in her youth, received nominal training with basic weaponry under the guidance of her father's war masters, so she was not entirely defenceless. She also received further education in the ways of battle and warfare from them, until Zosime had become fierce with a blade.

Armed and armoured by her new allies, Zosime went forth to find her love. Together they travelled to Malatrion, the capital of Volesus's new empire in search of the emperor. It was here that Zosime wished to reunite with her love, but found he was out across Enayra, conquering lands in a mad scramble to find her. Zosime was very amused by Volesus's commitment to her. She knew she could recall Volesus with a single word to any soldier in the capital, but she also knew that he would be so starved of her presence after all this time that she would not have a moment to leave the palace, all while Volesus may very well continue to conquer the rest of Enayra. And so Zosime decided that she would not reveal herself to anyone in Malatrion, and instead, altered her appearance with magic, and enlisted herself and her new company into Volesus's imperial army. She and her band of warriors became known as the Arbitarii (Old Western Asardaean, translated often as Judges or Judgement Bringers). It was said that the wrath of Zosime and her Arbitarii were like that of divine judgment. And they fought against would be shattered by the hammer of her forces.

As they battled across Enayra in the vanguard of Volesus's conquering forces, the Arbitarii grew in fame and soon swelled in number. To join the Arbitarii became the ultimate end goal of every soldier of great merit and skill, and they became the stuff of legend across the continent. Shortly after Volesus's conquest of Danaen, the Arbitarii were officially elevated as the advanced shock troops of the empire and were renamed the Palatinii (Old Western Asardaean, often translated as Paladins).

Through all this time, by an odd twist of fate, Zosime and Volesus never came face to face for many years. Volesus was often rushing off toward the next place Zosime had been supposedly sighted, while Zosime was posted to different places in the Empire, both to conquer and to maintain order. It was during this time that the Palatinii also took on the duties of enforcing Volesus's laws and meted out both judgment and justice alike. It was not until the final campaign launched by Volesus, where he laid siege to the great city of Kasaadua, that the two lovers finally reunited on the battlefield. Volesus at first did not recognize his love and saw only a mighty and brave soldier who fought bravely alongside him. Side-by-side the two charged into the throng of Altimaran defenders once the siege engines had breached the mighty obsidian walls. But it was not long after they had breached the walls that Volesus came to suspect that the woman beneath the helm, may have been more than just a soldier loyal to his cause. Something in the way she fought, the way she spoke, seemed hauntingly familiar to him. But before Volesus could verify his suspicions Zosime was pierced by an enemy spear, thrown from the rooftop of a nearby building. Zosime cried out and cast her helm off before she fell, and the magic that changed her appearance disappeared and revealed her identity to her love. Volesus regarded Zosime with even greater love and respect than ever he had held for her before. He came to realize that all these years Zosime had fought as one of his brave soldiers, aiding his vision and his empire in the best way she knew how. Indeed, rather than being angered that she had hidden from him, Volesus was full of pride, and more so, an undying love that burned ever brighter for his would-be bride. But saw too, did he, that Zosime's life now ebbed from her veins, and that the wound was fatal, if not grievous, and would surely be the end of her if she was not cared for soon.

Volesus's eyes welled with tears and ordered one of his honour guards to return fire at the man who had struck down Zosime, the would-be Empress of Enayra. The guard, a mage, lashed out and struck the Kasaaduan soldier with a bolt of lightning, catching the man in the face and killing him where he stood.

Volesus had Zosime taken into a nearby alley, where they would be safe from the fighting. He knelt and cradled his love in his arms. Volesus cried out for a mage or a doctor; he declared a fantastic reward for someone, anyone who could heal his beloved before she died. But it was too late. The spear had struck true and pierced her heart. She was dead before she hit the ground, and no amount of magic could save Zosime now.

Not long after the city had been conquered, and Enayra had been fully unified under the banner of Volesus. But he, whose empire now reached from sea to sea. He, who had stretched out his arm and sought to conquer all for his love—to find her, and to be powerful enough to provide for her the greatest life she could ever want—had lost the purpose for which he had acted.

The Palatinii took up Zosime's body and carried it back to Malatrion, where she was laid to rest beneath the Imperial palace. A statue was erected in her honour at the main square in each ring of the city, and she was honoured with two feast days per year, one on the anniversary of her birth, and one on the anniversary of her death. These holidays are still honoured in the modern Kingdom of Asardaea, even in these latter days.

But Emperor Volesus, as the story tells, the greatest ruler Enayra would ever know, sunk into a deep sadness for the remainder of his days. He would not marry and would father no heirs. It would be Volesus's brother, Gaius who would inherit the Empire. Gaius, who had married Zosime's sister Elara, declared upon his ascension to the throne, that only those with the blood of both Gens Tarquinia and the Romontian dynasty could inherit the throne. Though, sadly, and perhaps ironically, Gaius would prove to be a weak and rather ineffectual emperor. While—at least at first—he was respected by the army, he was not respected by his people outside of Asardaea. Many had been taken in by Volesus's natural charm and charisma, and the fairness and compassion he showed to even his most vehement of foes. But Gaius had not been so fair or so kind. Gaius, in an effort not to appear weak, exhausted his goodwill with his brother's generals and people. Gaius cracked down severely on any protest or dissent with regular brutality. Even the slightest whisper of disagreement would often lead to bloodshed.

Things did not improve when boats appeared off the coast of Espias. These large wooden ships, like wooden crates made for the sea, their coloured banners that bore strange, curved writing and foreign symbols flapped in the wind as they approached the shores of Enayra. These people spoke a language that was not Common—a language that Volesus had ordered be created in the halls of learning in Xiar and spread across Volesus's vast empire as the main language of all the peoples of Enayra. These new people, who would eventually come to be known as Espians, landed on the shores of the land that would become their namesake, and war erupted in Enayra once more.

No one is sure who started the conflict between the Enayra Empire and the fledging Espian Empire. Some say the Espians came in peace, seeking only enough land to settle on after fleeing their dying home, and that the Enayran Empire attacked them rather than negotiate. Others say that the bloodthirsty Espians appeared and began to conquer all they could see. It was all Gaius, and his armies could do to hold them back, and Enayra was lucky to lose only Espias to them. Whatever the truth is, the result was the same: a long and bloody war that would see the collapse of the Enayra Empire.

Gaius's generals would not serve him as they served his brother, and many of his best generals had died before or shortly after their first emperor. Their sons and heirs had never tasted war like their predecessors. Even Gaius had not known war as his brother had.

The Province of Espias crumbled under the might of these hardened warriors from across the sea, and the land of Espias was forever lost to the empire. Peace was signed after three short months, and Gaius was disgraced across the empire by his defeat. To this day, the enmity still burns between the Espians and Asardaeans for perceived wrongs of ages long passed.

Things finally reached a boiling point in the Enayran Empire. Between his heavy repression and his defeat at the hands of the new Espian Empire, Gaius's generals deserted him. Many saw their oath of loyalty to Volesus as expired now that he was dead, and that loyalty was unearned by the cruel and weak Emperor Gaius. Others no longer respected a monarch who could not even protect his borders against an outside threat, even with far superior numbers on his side. These generals rebelled against their emperor and murdered him in his palace. Thus, the empire crumbled. The nations of Enayra regained their independence in the conflict, now under the leadership of the generals that had betrayed Gaius, or under their previous rulers.

Asardaea was at the risk of delving back into a series of inter-tribal city-states that had existed before Volesus's rise. Not to mention the very real dangers of a massive Gerovian invasion force massed at Asardaea's borders, that sought to conquer the land for their own and take up Volesus's claims to the empire. It was only due to the quick thinking and strong leadership of Gaius's daughter, the Hero Queen Maude, that Asardaea was kept united under Gens Tarquinia, and able to repel Gerovia's invasion attempt. At the Battle of the Tolrun Pass, Queen Maude turned back a vastly superior force of Gerovia's finest and secured Asardaean independence permanently. Gerovia recognized the Kingdom of Asardaea as an independent nation and successor state the Enayran Empire of Volesus, though Maude herself did not claim the title of empress and did not seek to rebuild the massive pan-continental empire of her uncle. She sought only stability in her homeland and enlisted the Palatinii to help her do so.

The Palatinii were thus divided into the Vindicarii, the Arbitarii, and the Justicarii. The Vindicarii were tasked with policing the kingdom and ensuring peace and stability among the populace. They were responsible for capturing and hunting down fugitives and keeping the peace. The Arbitarii were the judges of the kingdom. They were tasked with mediating compromises between quarrelling citizens, deescalating situations before they spiralled into lawlessness, or settling disputes before they became worse. They would also serve as judges in legal proceedings across the kingdom. Finally, the Justicarii would act as the kingdom's elite soldiers, both on the frontline and the home front. They would also act as executioners in the legal system, for those who were unfortunate enough to be sentenced to death, though they do also have the right to enforce non-lethal sentences as well.

With the Palatinii, the Hero Queen Maude brought peace and security to her new kingdom, and her descendants continue to rule the kingdom to this day, with the Palatinii at their beck and call.

The legacy of Volesus and Zosime continues today in Asardaea, and their greatness is never forgotten.

Dragomancy
The Dragon-Based Religion of Enayra

Dragomancy was founded in the year 10 Conflict (the 10th year of the Age of Conflict) in what is, ironically, now known as Altimara, by a small group of human tribes that had recently settled in the area known as the Mirror Sands, home of the Blue Dragons.

Unlike humans in other parts of Enayra, these humans did not quarrel with their dragon neighbours. The shamans and religious leaders of the humans likened the dragons to their deities, known as Aspects[1]. These early humans decreed that humans who attacked dragons were tantamount to non-believers and blasphemers who had turned on their Aspects and made war with the heavens and the order of nature. This tribe of humans was excommunicated from the greater religion of the other early humans of Asardaea, with whom they shared a common origin. Regardless of their ex-communication, these humans worked with the dragons and instead grafted the Great Dragons into their religion. This tribe of humans decreed that the Great Progenitors and the Great Metallic Dragons were the physical embodiment of their Aspects.

The parallels were as follows:

-   The Great Creator, Inor, was embodied in Aurum, the gold dragon.

-   The Aspect of Life, Ventamir, was embodied in Argentum, the silver dragon.

-   The Aspect of Death, Astalos, was embodied in Aes, the bronze dragon.

-   The Aspect of the Order, Kenivard, was embodied in Aeris, the copper dragon.

-   The Aspect of the Chaos, Vaetaloth, was embodied in Aurichalcum, the brass dragon.

-   The Aspects of the Night and Day, Isunath and Kistharoth, were embodied in the black dragon Ten'ebraex and his mate, Kyna'braxa.

-   The Aspects of Fire and Summer, Caustagird and Waelgarid, were embodied in the red dragon Venu'shael and his mate, Kara'imla.

-   The Aspects of the Plants and Nature were embodied in the green dragon, Sha'janor and his mate, Kina'atael.

-   The Aspects of the Ice and Winter were embodied in the white dragon, Vercith'ae and her mate, Yjosta'gar.

-   The Aspects of the Wind and Spring were embodied in the blue dragon, Keshal'anda and her mate, Vernix'iol.

- The Aspects of the Hunt and Victory were embodied in the pink dragon, Ben'gudiad and his mate Iolor'ondii.

- The Aspects of the Earth and Autumn were embodied in the brown dragon, Kingur'omyno and his mate Beler'iadra.

- The Aspects of the Soul and Rebirth were embodied in the purple dragon, Utgor'olrz and her mate, Ving'ator.

- The Aspects of the Sun and Moon were embodied in the orange dragon, Nulgo'riaz and his mate, Zank'aerdi.

- The Aspects of the Wood and Metal were embodied in the grey dragon, Mangra'tliazj and her mate, Lorgr'adiz.

- The Aspects of Emotion and Knowledge were embodied in the yellow dragon, Junorth'ghahaz and his mate Wenthtyz'volozoth.

These early Altimaran tribes worshiped all the Aspects, but each tribe proclaimed a different pair of Aspects as their patron protectors; one pair for each of the eleven tribes. However, it was decreed that no tribe could claim the Five Great Aspects, for they favoured no one. They were the greatest of the Aspects and could not be understood or influenced by humanity in any capacity.

It would be several centuries before Dragomancy became popular outside of the peoples of Altimara, though within a few decades, the eleven tribes had become three distinct peoples: those of Xiar, those of the Qiri'ar Confederacy, and the first Altimarans. Each group centred itself around Xiar, the Mirror Sands and Kasaadua respectively.

Xiar quickly shuffled the priority of their pantheon worship to give more prominence to Aurum and the Metallics, as it was Aurum who had shown their hero king, Agarthus, where to settle their people.[2]

As time passed in Enayra, Dragomancy eventually became the dominant religion on the continent and finally reached its peak during the Age of Heroes, an age of peace and stability ushered in by the first of the Drazhani-ad-Khaleeshir. This period roughly spans their creation to their death at the Battle of the Kahnair Plains.

Nowadays, Dragomancy is practiced in various forms in all nations of Enayra except for Altimara, Lau'than, and among the Qiri'ar, ironically. The last of the founders of Dragomancy who still believe are the Xiarans. The Altimarans abandoned Dragomancy and went back to an imperfect reconstruction of the Old Religion under the decrees of King Rego. Using old documents and accounts from the earliest days of Enayra, Altimara attempted to rebuild the Old Religion as it had been in the days of the First Arrivals, removing all references to dragons.

The Qiri'arans however, practice a modified form of Dragomancy, though they do not use this name for it. Few outsiders know what the name of this religion is. During the Dragon War against Tenebrae a thousand years ago, the Qiri'aran Kinu'watan, or High Chief as it is often translated into Common, Eshgalon the Mad (or the Wise, depending on your allegiance), proclaimed his tribe's Aspect, The Aspect of the Night and Day, who were coupled with Tenebrae and his mate, as the One True Aspect duality. Eshgalon forced all Qiri'ar to abandon the worship of any Aspect that was not Tenebrae by the sword and by axe, by fire and force, until all Qiri'ar worshiped Tenebrae alone. To this day, the Qiri'ar have not gone back to the old ways and have remained unyielding and loyal to their One True Aspect.

FOOTNOTES

1. It should be noted that Aspects are not the same as gods. Aspects are the powerful manifestations of the spiritual and natural forces of the earth and nature. Each Aspect is considered a duality often seen as two sides of the same coin or two halves of the full whole. The only exception is the Five Great Aspects, the Great Creator, and the aspects of Life, Death, Chaos, and Order, which are each a separate aspect, a whole of a whole, and are paired only with each other. It is unknown why the Sun and Moon were seen as above the other Aspects before the fusing of dragons into the original religion (whose name has been lost to history), nor is it understood why any of the Five Great Aspects are not depicted as dualities like the rest.

2. Agarthus, leader of his clan, came to power when the Qiri'ar Confederacy was being formed out of the disparate tribes of modern Altimara. He did not wish to join the Confederacy and knew if he remained, he and his tribe would be brought into the fold by force. Not wishing to subject his people to slaughter, he led his people out across the desert until he came across Aurum, entirely by chance. However, the Xiarans continued to maintain that it was an act of providence. Aurum felt pity for these lost and wandering peoples and showed them the way to the plentiful Antigorus Valley, where the people, known as the Xiar, founded their new city, and named it for themselves. Grateful to Aurum for his help, the Xiarans erected grand shrines to him, and the other Metallic Dragons. While they continued to worship the other Aspects-as-dragons as well, they no longer claimed to be the main patrons of their previous Aspect, the Matriarch and Patriarch of the Purple Dragon Clan.

The War of the Grand Coalition & Aftermath

Gerovian Empire, 376 Conflict

The Peace of Gerovia is a treaty signed in 407 Conflict. It ended the War of the Grand Coalition after the Sack of Gerovia, which occurred in the same year. The Peace of Gerovia outlines and establishes rules of war, a code of conduct in battle and rules of engagement on the battlefield. It created an observable list of war crimes, a method of trying those who violate these precepts and commit atrocities during war. War since the creation of the Peace of Gerovia has been less violent and less brutal, though it has not stopped atrocities entirely.

Background

The Enayran Empire had fallen. It collapsed in the aftermath of the assassination of Emperor Gaius Tarquinius in the year 94 Conflict. Forty-one years after its founding, and fifty-six years after Emperor Volesus Tarquinius began his conquest of Enayra in the name of his love Zosime.

The Hero-Queen Maude Tarquinia, daughter of Emperor Gaius, raised an army under the banner of her family, Gens Tarquinia. Using the remaining Asardaean soldiers who had been loyal to her uncle and family, she staved off an invasion of Asardaea by the newly formed Kingdom of Ethon (now known as the Kingdom of Estion, and formerly known as Gerovia).

Despite having lost the Battle of the Tolrun Pass, and losing most of their army, Ethonian Kings refused to give up their desire to claim the title of Imperator and become Emperors of Enayra.

After the fall of the Empire, Queen Maude I refused to take up her father and uncle's Imperial trappings. She focused only on her homeland of Asardaea, and the rest of Enayra fractured into several other kingdoms and nations.

The Region of Altimara fractured into the Kingdom of Altimara in the north. In the south, the Kingdom of Xiar declared its independence from the empire. The Qiri'ar Confederation burst forth from the Enayran Empire's corpse in the southeast of Altimara, as did the Lau'thso off the eastern shores.

Espias had secured its borders and had remained independent since the conquest of the region.

In what is now Danaen, the Danaesh had split into separate city-states that centred around the mightiest of the nation's tribes. These tribes, led by powerful and wealthy warlords, would spend several centuries vying for control of Danaen.

The Kingdom of Ethon, as it had been known under Volesus and in the early days of the break-up of the empire, had reformed itself and dissolved the Kingdom of Ethon, and became the Kingdom of Gerovia again in 97 Conflict. This change was brought about after the deposition of the ruling of the Helgeven Dynasty. After their defeat at the Battle of the Tolrun Pass, the dynasty was deposed after a short tenure of two rulers upon the throne. In the year 95 Conflict, several nobles revolted against the Helgevens, led by the Baron of Dorial, who claimed the throne for himself and founded the Dorial dynasty. But ever unstable, Gerovia would see six dynasties sit upon the throne before the War of the Grand Coalition almost two and a half centuries later. The Kingdom of Gerovia was eventually renamed during the ascendancy of the sixth dynasty, the Bergden dynasty. The dynasty reformed its kingdom into the Gerovian Empire in 204 Conflict after it had conquered much of northern Danaen and parts of eastern Altimara, as well as putting the Lau'thso under its suzerainty.

Four centuries of bloody and brutal warfare enveloped Enayra after the collapse of the empire. Each new nation attempted to claim the legacy of Volesus for themselves and conquer all. Only six great nations, not including the Qiri'ar and Lau'thso, remained by the Peace of Gerovia.

The War of the Grand Coalition

In the year 376 Conflict, the Gerovian Empire declared war on Asardaea for the fourth time since the collapse of the Enayran Empire. It had lured Danaen to its side by promising the return of Northern Danaen in exchange for military support. Gerovia also recruited Espias to its alliance against Asardaea, as Espias sought the destruction of Asardaea.

Altimara, seeing an opportunity to gain back its western territories from Gerovia met with Asardaea, Xiar, Lau'than and the Qiri'ar and proposed an alliance against Gerovia. Asardaea welcomed the assistance in defending its nation. Xiar offered the use of their soldiers, arms, and armour, and provided generous loans for participating nations for the financing of this war. The Qiri'ar, who had entered into an informal agreement with the Altimaran kings, entered the war by joining the Altimaran Foreign Legion to battle the Gerovians. Lau'than promised ships to the alliance and raided Gerovian, Espian, and Danaesh shipping across Enayra. Together, Altimara and Asardaea launched savaging attacks into enemy territory.

Altimara battled Espias in the south and Gerovia in the east, while Danaen landed an army on the southwestern shores of Asardaea to divert Asardaea's attention from its front with Gerovia.

Halfway through the war, in the year 394 Conflict, the King of Danaen was killed, and they withdrew from the war to settle their succession rites. As per Danaesh tradition, a king and queen-mother are elected as a diarchy, chosen from one of the many tribes after a series of votes from the public, the nobility, and several competitions meant to test the candidates physically and intellectually. When a king is elected, his mother—or aunt, if his mother has passed, or sister if there are no aunts, or wife if there are no sisters—as the queen-mother. The queen-mother acts as the king's second, his highest advisor, and a check on royal power.

However, in 395 Conflict, when the new King of Danaen, Tsem'bashwa I, and the Queen-Mother Koru'wiya were elected to the two thrones, they re-entered the war on the side of Asardaea, turning on Gerovia. King Tsem'bashwa and his mother recognized that Gerovia had no intention of returning northern Danaen and would likely turn on Danaen once they had taken Malatrion and brought Asardaea low. Gerovia sought to control all Enayra, and the previous king had been too naive to realize this. With Danaen now firmly a part of the anti-Gerovian alliance, the union of nations became known as the Grand Coalition.

This Grand Coalition turned the tide of the war from a stalemate to favouring the Grand Coalition. The war turned against Espias and Gerovia, and by 407 Conflict, the armies of the alliance had marched to the gates of Gerovia City and sacked the city for the eighth time in its history. During the Great Chase, as the series of battles came to be called, three hundred and eighty-seven members of the Gerovian Royal Guard gave their lives for their king and country. Markers can be seen today at the spot where every member of the Royal Guard fell. The markers start five kilometres from the city and lead up in a jagged, zigzag to the steps of the palace and the heart of the throne room.

It was after this war that Gerovia City became known as the Sacked City, for it has been sacked, ruined, burned, and conquered several times by armies both foreign and local more than any other Enayran city—a testament to the country's instability over the centuries, even to this day.

When finally, the Gerovian Emperor had been captured, his armies were forced to surrender to the Grand Coalition. Espias had recognized a lost cause, and had surrendered several weeks before, and so were given clemency for their early penance. The country suffered less damage, and its capital and villages remained untouched and intact. Betrayed by its allies, alone, and utterly defeated and laid to ruin, Gerovia accepted defeat and the war was finally ended after thirty-one, bloody, hard-fought years.

During the peace conference in Gerovia, the Gerovian Empire was dismantled, and the kingdom that replaced it was reduced to much the same borders it retains today. It was agreed that the emperor and his dynasty would be dethroned and replaced by a young Gerovian nobleman who had turned on his empire. The nobleman had declared that it was a sense of justice that had caused the change of heart, for he saw the wrongness of his emperor's ways, but the truth may lie more in self-preservation and expediency.

The war had been one of the bloodiest in Enayran history, killing about forty-two percent of the population of the continent in thirty-one years. Atrocities had been committed, and people—both innocents and soldiers—were brutalized in the most horrible of ways. One account by a Gerovian general denotes that during the Siege and subsequent Massacre of Belisar (a large town in western Altimara), the slaughter of the townspeople had lasted three days, and only ended after he saw several of his men hacking a pregnant woman to death, while she was in the process of giving birth. It was because of these atrocities, and the chaotic, violent nature of the world since the Enayran Empire had collapsed, that the Peace of Gerovia was meant to end war, or at least brutal war, across Enayra. War crimes were codified, defined, and outlined, and tribunals were established for the restitution of those who had suffered. Criminals were tried and executed, fines were paid, and it was ensured that crimes like these would never happen again, and any who broke these laws would be summarily punished by the law. The Peace of Gerovia also established the rules for declaring war, the rules of engagement for warfare, and other such laws that dictated proper decorum and chivalry on the battlefield. It outlines some of the earliest laws for the taking of prisoners and their upkeep. Furthermore, the treaty would also establish the Enayran principle known as the "Balance of Power." The nations would police themselves and each other to maintain a somewhat equitable balance of power between all nations. No one nation would rise above another as Gerovia had attempted, and no great and mighty empires would be tolerated on Enayran soil ever again.

The Aftermath – The Estian Anarchy

With Gerovia in ruins and the capital near razed to the ground, the victors went about rebuilding the country in an image they felt was best suited for the Enayra they wished to see.

The irony of the Peace of Gerovia was that the Sack of Gerovia was so thorough that the city's population of one hundred thousand was reduced to less than ten thousand after the war, and anything of any kind of cultural or monetary value was looted by the Coalition armies.

The Viscount of Yeshtaburg, Vedir dae Ulvethas who had gone against his Gerovian Emperor and aided the Grand Coalition at great personal risk to himself, was installed as the new king, and the Gerovian Empire was reduced to the Kingdom of Estion, centred at the newly rebuilt capital of Ethon—as Gerovia had been renamed. The borders of this new kingdom are much the same as their current borders. King Vedir I, of the House of Ulvethas, worked with the Allied nations to rebuild Ethon and greater Estion. He attempted to turn the once power-hungry, unstable Gerovia into a stable and peaceful nation.

His dream was not to be.

In 415 Conflict, the Grand Coalition withdrew their soldiers and returned home. Ethon had been rebuilt sufficiently enough to stand on its own, and they felt the country stable enough to support itself and stand strong, despite internal divisions between the Crown and nobility. It was not a week after the Grand Coalition withdrew their soldiers that King Vedir I was slain by an assassin while using the garderobe. His body was thrown down the chute of the garderobe, and he was presumed kidnapped. It was not until about two weeks after his murder that his body was discovered (by the smell, of course), stuck halfway down the chute, horribly decomposed, covered in weeks of excrement, flies, and maggots.

The confirmed death of King Vedir I caused the central authority of the Crown to collapse, and the conspirators raised their soldiers against the Crown to take it for themselves. This set off a chain of events known as the Estian Anarchy.

Three sides fought in this chaotic time, each seeking to dominate the other. There were the True Gerovians, who sought to restore the rightful line of Gerovian Emperors to the throne and rise from the ashes to reclaim their imperial birthright. They opposed the Peace of Gerovia and the new Kingdom of Estion. This faction had been the mastermind behind the assassination of the king. Opposed to them on one side were the Royalists, who upheld the Peace of Gerovia, and championed King Vedir I's son, Mendir, as the one true king, and the rightful heir to the throne.

A third faction erupted about halfway through the war. The common folk armed themselves and revolted against both factions. Centuries before Xiar overthrew their monarchs, the Common Cause, as they called themselves--also known as Republicans, Anti-Royalists, and called Rebels by their enemies—rose against both other factions to install an elected, representative republic in place of a hereditary monarchy. The leader of the cause was the former headman of a small town known as Vestillus, Carolus Vingrus. Moderately educated at Gerovia University in the capital, he was the first to propose a rule for the people, by the people, made up of elected officials—like the headman position he held—where the government would be beholden to those they represented.

The Royalists begged the Grand Coalition for their help, but the Alliance refused. The former Grand Coalition feebly cited the Sovereign Independence Clause of the Peace of Gerovia that declared no foreign nation shall impugn on the sovereignty of another nation without invitation. They could not, they claimed, be drawn into a civil war without stepping on Estion's sovereignty. When the Royalists argued that the alliance *had* been invited, the Alliance meekly replied that while the country was in a state of civil war, there was no official government, and so the invitation did not count.

In truth, the once mighty Grand Coalition could not afford to field armies in another Gerovian conflict, as the previous war had left their people weary and near impoverished. The taxes that had been levied had stagnated the economic growth of their nations, and the citizen levies for the war had thinned the working professionals and peasant farmers that remained at home, causing shortages of goods and food. On top of that, the fragile peace was already beginning to fracture, and while the war was still a generation—largely due to financial concerns rather than a desire for peace—Asardaea and Espias were already beginning to circle one another like hungry wolves as they were wont to do.

Rumours of unknown origin circled across the continent, stirring Altimara and Danaen to action. Each nation feared the worst of these rumours: that Asardaea was looking to abandon the Peace of Gerovia and the Balance of Power to take advantage of the chaos in Gerovia to conquer their enemies to the south.

Altimara, their diplomats having been the ones that suggested and drafted the Peace of Gerovia, stood by their Balance of Power ideology, and sought to stem what they viewed as the coming Asardaean claim for continental dominance. They feared that Asardaea would easily restore the Enayran Empire in a bloody wave of slaughter and death if left unchecked.

Danaen too shared these fears. They had faced a hostile northern neighbour under the Gerovian Empire. They had been dragged into an unnecessary war by an ineffectual and weak leader under false promises. They were lucky to have switched sides and gained their promised land back, but they certainly did not want a strong Asardaea bearing down on their northern borders like the Gerovia of the past. They would not trade one imperial conqueror for another.

Meanwhile, Asardaea had lured in the allegiance of Xiar, Lau'than, and the Qiri'ar Confederacy. Asardaea played on these smaller nations' ever-souring relationships with Altimara. While Asardaea had no plans to invade Gerovia, they certainly wished to stamp out the flame of Espias and lay their enemies low.

But that war is another tale for another day.

Back in Estion, the Anarchy raged on for twenty-seven years. During the bloody and violent conflict, Estion lost a further fifteen percent of its total population to the conflict. Entire noble families were wiped from existence. Families turned on themselves and collapsed into discord and infighting. By the end of the war, none of the original leadership had survived. Some were survived by children and grandchildren, but more often new powerful families had quickly climbed to power and dominance in their factions.

The new Royalist leader, no longer a descendant of Vedir I but of an entirely different noble family, brought an end to the fighting by calling a summit of all leaders of the conflict. Estion had nearly bled itself to death. Between the True Gerovians and Royalists, there remained nothing left of their original goals. For the True Gerovians, there was no Gerovian Might to reclaim, for it had withered in the Anarchy. Whoever became emperor would inherit a weakened nation with a strong Asardaea to the north, and a vengeful Danaen to the south. Altimara would not help them, for they were preoccupied with the tensions brewing between Asardaea and Espias. For the Royalists, there was no Ulvethas monarch to restore to the throne, for the entire house had perished on the field of battle, and those who had survived the devastating Battle of the Burning Lake (mere children) had had their skulls dashed against the stones of the shoreline by the True Gerovian army. Only the Republicans still had a cause worth fighting for, and they were slowly gaining ground by picking at the rotting flesh of their two dying enemies.

So, the future king, Baron Belchor dae Graftenhoft, called the True Gerovians and Royalists together. He promised to settle the score between both sides in single combat, but first, they had to unite against the Republicans who stood against everything both sides stood for, and who would upset the careful order of the world with their ideology. Both sides, weary, exhausted, and fearful that all they had fought and bled for would be lost to a republic, joined forces to wipe out the fledgling republicans.

Baron Belchor led his new united faction on an unbent warpath, but he kept to the Peace of Gerovia and did not rape, burn, or pillage. He forbade his soldiers and commanders from further committing the atrocities that had pervaded the previous war and had sunk into this current conflict. Instead of slaughtering Republicans and all their families, he bade all commanders capture only those who fought for the Republicans and arrest only the families who refused to renounce their captured relatives. All threats were held captive until they could be put on trial for treason against the sovereign—whoever would come to wear the Crown. It was in this way that the Republicans were diminished and pushed from the war by their sheer losses.

But the final deciding combat between the remaining two sides would never come. As the two sides feasted and celebrated their victory over the Republicans, Baron Belchor had all the True Gerovian leadership drugged and slaughtered as they slept upon their dinner plates. With their leadership dead, and their families held captive by Belchor's armies, the remaining True Gerovians surrendered to Belchor's hegemony.

They and their families did not last the week.

There was no room for True Gerovians in Belchor's new kingdom. Anyone who had ever been, known, or spoken to a True Gerovian was purged. Baron Belchor took the throne as King Belchor I, of the House of Graftenhoft. He and his descendants would bring stability to the Kingdom of Estion, replant the towering forests, and forge friendships with the Green Dragons of the Emerald Vale. But their peace would forever be cursed. Estion would be more stable than it had ever been, and yet not stable enough.

Peace is not forever in Enayra.

It's said at the time of their death, those True Gerovians who surrendered to Baron Belchor placed a curse upon him and his descendants, known as the Curse of Gerovia. They cursed Belchor with the instability that had plagued Gerovia in its early days as a city-state.

The instability that had carried over into the post-Imperial world, and eventually brought low the Gerovian Empire. The curse that had caused the great city of Gerovia to be sacked repeatedly throughout history. No one knows if this curse is real, but it certainly hasn't helped Estion. Republicanism never truly died, and so the people have always sought more power for themselves and less for the absolutist monarchs. Their zeal ebbs and flows with every monarch, as some are kinder and more benevolent than others, but the kings have slowly lost more and more of their power to their nobles and their people. Absolute monarchs no longer rule in Estion. Every few centuries the people rise, and a new king is chosen, either by the might of the nobility or the people. Nobility rebels and overthrows the king with a new one. New king, new line, new descendant of Belchor, but still the same cycle of peace and chaos.

The eternal cycle of Gerovia and Estion.

The War of the Demitasse Spoon
Kingdom of Estion, 417-420 Conflict

The War of the Demitasse Spoon (417-420 Conflict) occurred during the Estian Anarchy (415-442 Conflict).

The events leading up to the "war" are quite pathetic when compared to the violence and bloodshed it caused and considering the violence and bloodshed of the Estian Anarchy as a whole.

It all started in the summer home of Count Rufus Quintus, of House Quintus, Count of Vuul–the town no longer exists. In 417 Conflict, Count Rufus celebrated a minor victory for the True Gerovians by inviting some of his friends and allies over to his summer home by the shores of Lake Ardona. Among the guests was Count Verim van der Graaff, of House van der Graaff, Count of Mulgrydd–this town, also, no longer exists.

After a party that was said to have lasted three days and three nights, Count Rufus awoke on the fourth morning to find one of his jewel-encrusted, golden demitasse spoons had gone missing. After thorough investigations–involving time and resources that should have, realistically, gone to the civil war–it was determined that Count Verim had stolen the spoon, and absconded with several serving plates as well. Count Rufus, enraged, turned his armies on Count Verim and his family. What ensued is often considered by many anti-royalists to be an example of the foolish decadence of nobility and royalty and serves as an example of how disconnected from reality they can be. It has been specifically referred to by many pro-Republican writers of the day, including the Father of Republicanism, Carolus Vingrus.

The "War of the Demitasse Spoon" as it came to be known, lasted three years, and caused the death of three thousand people, most of them soldiers and innocent townsfolk. It was also responsible for the eradication of two towns, four villages, a logging camp, and finally the deaths of both Count Verim and Count Rufus, and the complete extinction of their noble houses.

And what became of the demitasse spoon for which so much blood was spilled?

Supposedly it had been found within six months, at the bottom of the fountain in Count Rufus's garden. It was later determined it had been misplaced during the debauchery, and Count Verim was falsely accused. But by that point, Count Rufus had held two of Count Verim's children hostage, had assassinated his mother, and had lost several members of his close family to the war. They had gone too far to apologize and risk losing face, and neither wished to show weakness in the face of their perceived "enemy." Instead, they destroyed themselves and each other and caused the deaths of countless innocents.

For a spoon.

Estian Republicanism
Kingdom of Estion, 419 Conflict-Present Day

Carolus Vingrus was the leader of the Republican Rebels during the Estian Anarchy. He was born circa 382-385 Conflict in the small town of Vestillus, south of Yeshtaburg, on the border with Danaen. The son of a landowner, he was educated in the capital in his youth and returned to his village in his mid-twenties. His goal in life was to become an educated beacon for his small, poor town of craftsmen and farmers, and seek their betterment by involving himself in politics.

In 415 Conflict, just before the start of the Estian Anarchy, Carolus was elected headman of Vestillus. He left his town to petition the king for several boons that would ease the financial burdens on his people and allow them to prosper, so that they may be of more value to the Crown. But before Carolus could reach the capital, news reached him that King Vedir I had been assassinated, and civil war broke out between the Royalists and the True Gerovians. Carolus fled back home to ensure his people were safe.

Luckily, the war did not reach Vestillus for four years, but when it did, people were slaughtered, homes were burned, and supplies were "requisitioned" for the war effort by both sides. To protect themselves, the survivors of the Sack of Vestillus (419 Conflict) fled into the woods, under Carolus's leadership, and hid from both armies.

While originally a staunch Royalist, the destruction of his town, the slaughter of his villagers, and the cruelties inflicted by both sides of the conflict embittered Carolus to both causes. It was over the next decade that Carolus grew more disillusioned with the ideas of monarchies and empires and instead began to muse on the thoughts and writings of him and his colleagues at the university. Carolus began to write his thoughts down in a book known only as "The Republican", of which no original copies are known to exist. This book outlined his thoughts for the perfect government: a government of elected officials that sit in government for limited, pre-set terms of no longer than half a decade. These officials can be petitioned by the people and are elected and assembled by the people for the people. These ideas were not new to Enayra, but many of them had been stamped out by strong, authoritarian monarchs who feared their loss of power. Ironically, Carolus's Republicanism found its inspiration in the Danaesh monarchy and its electoral structure.

In 429 Conflict, Carolus, fed up with the ongoing civil war, gathered an army of like minded commoners as his army and entered the fray as a third faction, the Republicans, or Rebels, who sought to do away with the other two factions and with monarchies all together.

But Carolus and his faction would not win the war and instead were defeated and slaughtered by a united True Gerovian-Royalist front. Yet Republicanism would never truly die in Estion, or in Enayra as a whole. Eventually, copies of Carolus's book were found in all corners of the continent. Still, they rooted themselves most deeply in Xiar, who, in 251 Ruin, a little over eight hundred years after Carolus first rose for the cause, finally took up arms against their tyrannical King Antipausus III and deposed him in favour of an elected republic. And in Estion to this day, the peace between the people, the nobility and the Crown is ever fragile, and always ready to crack, and each side seeks to gain more power for themselves.

The Princeling's Revolt

Kingdom of Estion, 998 Ruin

The Princeling's Revolt is a name given to the revolt by the former King of Estion, King Khomandar II against Khomandar's father, King Aethalmenis III, the last reigning absolute monarch of Estion.

The power of Aethalmenis III lies within the machinations of his predecessor King Aethalmenis II (Khomandar's great-uncle). Aethalmenis II had managed to wrest power from the barons and parliament early in his reign. With this power, he purged the nobility and parliament, creating a puppet parliament that existed only to pass his laws and decrees. Both kings were widely unpopular across their whole realm, and they used their wealth and the tax revenue of the state to maintain their iron grip on the realm to hire several mercenary companies that could rival even the armies of the barons. In the eyes of both monarchs, it was fear that kept the people in line. The constant threat and fear of the king's mercenaries breaking into your home at night to kidnap, murder, torture, or disappear you and your entire family and anyone who'd ever sold you a pint. Meanwhile, heavy taxation on the barons limited their ability to maintain large standing armies capable of raising rebellion against the kings and their mercenaries. Wealth poured into the royal coffers, and out of the hands of the barons for the first time in three centuries.

But as King Aethalmenis III aged, his sanity waned. In his later years, he became known as King Aethalmenis the Mad, or King Goatfucker, for he had developed an unfortunate proclivity for non-consenting ungulates. The crown's wealth slowly dried up, as years of heavy taxation on the barons, and the people, coupled with several consecutive years of drought and famine had taken its toll. The people were starving, and could not afford food, let alone the taxes they were required to pay semi-annually, or on all their purchases. The barons were angry, impoverished, and disenfranchised. Everyone had had enough of being forced to dance at the whim of a mad king. So, it was decided in the year 998 Ruin, that on the fifth day of the eighth month, nobles and commoners alike would rise in armed rebellion.

Many had expected the Crown Prince to raise the mercenary bands from their glutinous feasting and drinking and lead them in battle against the rebellion. Though still young, the Crown Prince had proven to be a capable and charismatic commander, with all the cunning and fortitude of a great military leader in the making. But to the surprise of the entire realm, when faced with the choice to protect his father and the Crown or join the barons, Crown Prince Khomandar joined the rebellion. To this day, no one is certain why, but it has been credited by several historians to have been what saved the Crown at all in Estion.

Khomandar was put at the head of the rebellion against his father, and within six months he had shattered the backs of the mercenary hordes, cut them off from their supply of food and finance, and killed his father in cold blood to take the throne for himself.

Khomandar's first act as king was to round up any of his father's advisors, allies, and the remaining mercenaries who had not been killed in the rebellion or were smart enough to flee after the death of their patron. By royal decree, King Khomandar had his forces nail these captives to the trees along the Kingsroad to the capital. It was said five thousand trees were used to make an example of King Aethalmenis III's supporters. Their bones still lay scattered at the roots of these trees to this day and the nails are still embedded deep in the bark.

Most surprisingly, though not unexpectedly, Khomandar did not rule as an absolute monarch as his father and great-uncle had but instead ruled as the head of an oligarchy. He ceded a large portion of the king's ruling power to the barons, whom he kept close at his side. He would help them, and they him. The king carried out a symbiotic, if corrupt, relationship between himself and the nobility.

The people, unfortunately, were lost in the shuffle.

When parliament was finally reconvened in 999 Ruin for the first time in fifty-two years, all the elected commoner positions that had previously existed had been cut from the proceedings, and only nobility were allowed to participate. Taxes were reduced, though, in actuality, Khomandar found other ways to maintain the same tax income for the Crown by implementing dues and fees in other places. Barons were given their fair share of the tax money, but Khomandar ensured the Crown grew equally wealthy.

To this day, King Khomandar II is a controversial figure in recent Estian history. Despised by the people as a despot and an oligarch, the common man will claim he is no better than his father, the same cruel king with a slightly different government. Despite this, the king is loved and worshipped by the military and the barons that control them.

When King Khomandar II stepped down as king in 1028 Ruin and passed the throne to his son, he left his son with an uneasy kingdom that was peaceful on the surface, but near to boiling beneath. Life was lavish and decadent for the wealthiest of society, but those at the bottom suffered and languished through a brutish and short life. It did not help that his son, the now King Anducaerleonis I, was only thirteen at the time he ascended to the throne and was surrounded by eager barons who sought the chance to control a boy king and maintain the status quo and increase their prestige.

Yet despite the odds being stacked against him, Anducaerleonis has shown himself to be a strong leader, unyielding and uncompromising in his beliefs. He has staved off the control of his father's advisors and the control of a faction of overly greedy barons. King Anducaerleonis reinstated elected positions for commoners and even created a separate House of Commons to juxtapose the House of Lords in his government. But while he is beloved by his people, the king is disliked by the military and barons both, who see him as a bleeding heart, eager to drain their power for himself completely. The most vocal of His Majesty's opponents, Baron Felidrun, has openly declared His Majesty a tyrant in the vein of Aethalmenis III during sitting sessions of parliament.

In truth, Anducaerleonis rules with less direct power than even his father before him, as all laws he drafts must now pass both houses before he can declare them binding law. He is also a peace-loving king, who seeks to reduce Estian military might and thus, has passed several laws that reduced the size of the barons' armies in pursuit of peace in Enayra, and to distance himself from the Imperial Gerovian past of his people. But as to whether his actions will jeopardize or harm the Crown and the stability of Estion remains to be seen. Only time will tell.

How Dragons Get Their Names

An Excerpt from the tome: "Tel-ka'tah" or The Naming Ceremony of the Dragons of Enayra, by Amiphorus the Long-winded, written 203 Heroes

Tel-ka'tah is the word used by the dragons of Enayra to describe their naming ceremony; the way in which young hatchlings are named.

Like much of Drazhanii, it is hard to translate directly. Astute students of the language will notice the inclusion of the word "ka" or "kha", the word for "blood." You see it most often used in the words for organs and flesh, parts of the body, as well as abstract concepts of the soul, interpersonal and social relations, and inter-clan bonds and relationships. Blood is clearly an important physical and metaphysical concept for dragon kind–which can be read in my treatise *"The Importance and Concepts of Blood, or "Kha", in Drazhani Culture, Society, and Language, a Treatise of Utmost Importance to the Relationships between the Races of Enayra by Amiphorus the Wise"*.

But I digress.

Many humans wonder where dragons come up with these wondrous and creative names, and how, as soon as a dragon is hatched, they know their name immediately, before even being able to speak one of the two languages of Enayra. I had wondered, perhaps, if the parents of the hatchling can communicate across a mental link with their egg, or perhaps come up with a name and implant the memory of that name inside the egg and the hatchling after they've been laid, but after much research and discussion, and more than a few close calls with angry mother dragons, I've come to learn that this is not the case. It is not those that produce the egg that name the dragon, but the hatchling themselves. As they develop within their chitinous shells, the unborn hatchling cannot communicate with the outside world, but all things that live are always connected to the World herself.

I speak of course about the Earth Mother. It is said among the dragons, there is an ancient covenant with the Earth Mother. She gave them free rein over her lands of Enayra and access to her great fonts of power, and in exchange, she would be mother to them all, including naming their children.

It's unknown–or not remembered–by most dragons whether they discuss their name with the Earth Mother while in the egg, or if she simply bestows the name upon them once they hatch. Some say one, some say they remember the other, and some say it was some combination of the two. If I find more information on this detail, I shall publish an addendum to my great and magnanimous work. However, what **is** known is that dragons hatch knowing their name. But how do they communicate this name? Just because hatchlings cannot speak does not mean they cannot communicate.

In my well-beloved book: *On Dragons, the Lives, Growth, Development and Culture of the Dragons of Enayra as told by the Dragons Themselves for the Human Use of Understanding These Rare and Wonderful Creatures by Amiphorus the Magnanimous.*

The Drazhanii language is more than just words. It's the conveyance of feelings, emotions, memories, images, smells, and sights. Humans cannot truly "speak" Drazhanii until they master all the nuances and subtexts of the language and the way they communicate mentally. Beyond words. Likewise, these hatchlings cannot communicate with words but can force ideas, thoughts, feelings into their parents and siblings and fellow dragons. Being such a small presence, of course, most cannot sense the moment a small hatchling places its name in the minds of those around them.

What a truly wonderful world in which we live. Such beautiful creatures. Almost human in some ways, and more human in other.

The Utovan Rebellion

874-882 Ruin, Kingdom of Altimara

In 874 Ruin (Prosperity by Altimaran reckoning), the Duchess Illirya Vigothren, Duchess of Verthoro, of the illustrious and ancient House of Vigothren (one of the Altimaran Sacred Twelve noble bloodlines), revolted against the Crown of Altimara and King Veldran'ath III Thraendaron. While the exact reason for her revolt has long since been shrouded in mystery, official Utovan records cite the Duchess's frustration with high taxes, increasing absolutism by the Crown, and its subsequent tyranny. Some also suggest that the House of Vigothren never truly believed in Altimara's anti-dragon propaganda and use evidence such as House Vigothren's historically low participation rate in the Glorious Hunt as evidence of long-held discontent with the policies against dragons. Others, usually pro-Altimaran detractors, claim Duchess Illirya was a scorned lover of the king. When he refused to divorce his wife, Queen El'thella, and proclaim marriage to the Duchess, and thus make her queen, and her children the heirs to the throne, she took her anger and funnelled it into a rebellion.

Whatever the cause may be, she and her people rose. The Duchess had also managed to convince several thousand Altimaran soldiers who had grown disillusioned with the Crown and their oath to it, to join her in rebellion.

Being in Kisara, in the desolate and mountainous province of Verthoro, she had a well-placed headquarters for rebellion. The mountains made moving armies and their supplies hard in large numbers, and the cold and snow made it harder to campaign for extended periods as attrition and supply issues would soon set in during any prolonged campaign.

Realizing these challenges, the Duchess relied on guerrilla warfare. She struck hard and fast, each time returning to her mountain fortress in the northwest of Altimara. Each time the Altimaran army would miss her by days and give up chase at the foot of the mountains. For eight years the Crown was unable to crush the rebels, and after losing not a small number of soldiers and supplies, the Crown had had enough.

King Veldran'ath III had finally managed to rally an army large enough to sweep across the mountains, with enough supplies to last two campaigning seasons without the need for resupply. The King chased the Duchess and her fighters into the mountains, seeking to conquer villages and towns as he went. But each time the King's army reached a settlement to claim and conquer, they found it abandoned. Empty. Everyone who had lived there had simply vanished without a trace, leaving many of their belongings behind. Even the city of Kisara was conquered in a manner of hours, as the gates were left wide open, and the city abandoned.

It was later discovered that Duchess Illirya had been biding her time with the raids. She had been moving her people across the border from Altimara to Anglum, setting up a new city at the edge of a frozen lake she named Lake Utova, after the newly founded city-state.

The king had supplies to conquer Verthoro but could not risk a protracted invasion of the frozen, lifeless wastes of Anglum. The cost of that campaign would be too great.

Duchess Illirya had succeeded in seceding from Altimara, and for the past one hundred and fifty-two years, she and her descendants have ruled the new Grand Duchy of Utova, in a constant state of vigilant defence against Altimaran incursions.

While Altimaran armies have never reached the city of Utova, nor travelled very far past the borders, each strike cuts deeper into the heart of the duchy. However, the Grand Dukes and Duchesses have never stopped their guerrilla raids into Verthoro either. Only time will tell who will come out on top in what has been dubbed by some as the War That Isn't.

Gerovia and the War of the Grand Coalition

One might ask themselves: why did Danaen join Gerovia against the Grand Coalition for the first part of the War of the Grand Coalition? Danaen had no loyalties to Gerovia, no shared culture or history. Indeed, they had wanted the large swaths of northern Danaen, specifically the provinces of Huttushu, Gulee and Heligo, back from Gerovia for many generations now. They had more to gain from joining against Gerovia than for it.

Yet, Gerovia was run by cunning, if insidious emperors, who sought nothing less than the complete domination of Enayra in the style of Volesus's Enayran Empire. They could not pierce through the Danaesh wilds with a military due to their need for reekweed, which even in those days was still heavily controlled by the Danaesh Crown. So Gerovia instead began its "soft invasion" of Danaen by intermarrying their princesses into the Danaesh ruling class, seeking to abuse the diarchy to their favour. They bribed chieftains and local leaders in attempts to sway the kingship in their favour. As hoped, these princesses eventually became Queen-Mothers, holding sway over their kingly sons. With their hands deep in the heart of Danaesh politics, Gerovia could begin influencing policy in their favour.

In this way, Gerovia manipulated Danaesh foreign and domestic policy for about two centuries, and at the height of their influence, they were able to negotiate the "exchange" of the northern provinces into Gerovian control. It was not so much an exchange as it was conquest through negotiation, as the Danaesh received, truthfully, very little in return. With northern Danaen under their control, Gerovia now controlled a large portion of the reekweed production, and thus, could easily dictate its will to Danaen even further. And so, Danaen, whether they believed in Gerovia's promise of returning the northern provinces after the war, joined the war on Gerovia's side.

But this war became Gerovia's undoing.

War is expensive, and fighting a war against a majority of the continent is surprisingly time-consuming. The Gerovians believed their control over the Danaesh kingdom was unbreakable. In truth, they may have been right, but they did not account for the sitting monarch to die so soon. The death of the king gave cause for Danaen to temporarily withdraw from the war, and without Gerovian money and political influence funnelling into their royal palace during the election process, a king without ties to Gerovia was elected, and he returned to the war, proclaiming himself on the side of the Grand Coalition. Danaen took their northern provinces back by military force, and the armies of the Coalition pushed towards the Gerovian capital, sacking it, and imposing their terms upon the former empire.

How Ancient Dragons Eat

This might not seem like a very important question, but when you consider how large and how old some of the dragons in Enayra are–and the fact that dragons never stop growing, even if growth slows significantly after about five years–this presents a conundrum.

How does a massive dragon eat without depopulating all the animals in Enayra?

The answer is they don't. The Earth Mother provides for her children. Most dragons will cease consuming food regularly at about five years of age when their growth begins to slow. Dragons, being inherently magical, can sustain themselves entirely on the mana energy provided by their Mother and progenitor. It's unknown if dragon growth slows after five years *because* they stop eating, or if they stop eating *because* they stop growing. Dragons themselves aren't certain–it's just an instinct for them to start drawing sustenance from elsewhere.

Now that doesn't mean that dragons older than five **can't** eat, just that they don't need to eat regularly, or sometimes at all, because calories cease to mean anything for them.

This adaptation has allowed some of the oldest, largest dragons safe from the Altimaran hunting parties, and the White Dragon Clan from dying out in the nearly barren, ice lands of northern Anglum.

The Revenge of Kalis Owynn

The Revenge of Kalis Owynn is a semi-historical folk tale known widely across the Kingdom of Estion, dating from the last days of the Estian Anarchy.

According to the tale, Kalis Owynn was a man from a minor noble family that supported the True Gerovian forces during the Anarchy. His family was ennobled in title only, being raised to the station of Viscounts, but possessed very little in the way of money, presiding over only a small town whose name has been lost to time, and was wiped from the map during this tale. Despite their lack of wealth, the Owynns were well-loved among the people of their small town. They were kind to the working folk and often worked in the fields with the farmers that they had but recently been one of. Every hand was needed while the country was in flames.

It became clear, however, that even in the flower of his youth Kalis was a skilled magic user, and had the potential to become a great mage, though he was formally untrained. He had a rare talent for manipulating magic with song, specifically, he was gifted in the art of pyromancy and was able to use a fiddle to control magical flames, or so the legend says, and he sought to practice his pyromancy at one of the magical colleges in Xiar. But his family could not afford the cost; not alone. As a show of gratitude for the kindness shown by the Owynn family, the townsfolk gathered up as much money as they could scrape together, selling belongings and heirlooms as needed, to be able to pay for Kalis's education.

Kalis went off to Xiar for four years, and mastered the art of pyromancy, controlling the flames like a puppet master with his music. He could make fire dance from a brazier and twirl around the room as if it had been possessed and come to life. Once he graduated, he vowed to return home and show his family how much he'd learned, how powerful he'd grown, and how he wished to use his powers to bring peace to Gerovia and protect his home and family.

But when Kalis returned to his town, he found that the buildings were gone. Only bodies remained, hanging from gibbets in what was once the town square. Kalis tried to determine the identities of these unfortunate corpses, but they were so badly burned, rotted, and mutilated that it was impossible to tell. The fields had been left unmarred, but they were now worked by new people from a new village down the road. Confused, scared even, Kalis went to the town, known as Buracus, to inquire about what happened to his village. He learned from the headman of this town that the old village had been destroyed toward the end of the Anarchy. The headman explained that one day, a Royalist war band led by Marquis Velsan Gryffydd, who served the now King Belchor, descended upon the Owynns' village as they had been known to support the True Gerovian faction during the war. They slaughtered the townsfolk, killed the Viscount and his family, and burned the settlement to the ground so that no trace would remain. The land had since been given to the same Marquis, who had since risen to the title of Baron, and it was he who founded the town, and built his estate upon some lands that had once belonged to the Owynns.

It was at that moment that Kalis swore—privately, for fear his plot may get back to the Baron—his revenge for the kind folk and family he had lost. He spent six months in the town, posing as a musician and building a rapport with the townsfolk. Each night he played at the tavern until word of his skills as a fiddler spread to all corners of Baracus, and indeed to the rest of the province. No one noticed the flames jump and twist in the hearth as he fiddled his jigs and folk songs away into the night.

Using his disguise as a humble bard, Kalis gathered information about the Baron from the common folk that served him, and eventually, earned an invite to meet the man that had killed his family. The Baron had summoned the young bard he had heard so much about—for tales of his playing had by now reached even as far as the royal court at Filiddyn Castle. The Lord Gryffydd's daughter was soon to be married on the last day of summer, to the fourth son of King Belchor. The Baron heard the beautiful tones of Kalis's fiddle and knew his music would be perfect for the event, so his mind was set Kalis was hired.

As payment for his services, the Baron offered Kalis two choices: either he could have a large sum of gold, the amount would be Kalis's choosing or the granting of any boon that Kalis could ask for. Kalis barely suppressed a grin when he chose the boon. So, Kalis plotted his revenge. All the nobility that supported King Belchor and the king himself would be there to witness the marriage of a royal prince.

Three weeks later, the wedding was held at the castle of the Baron, and Kalis played his beautiful song that echoed through the halls of the castle, from the ballroom where he played, right down into the kitchens and cellars...the very cellars where he had planted a magical trap, one set to catch fire to the wooden furniture and alcohol stored there. Stoked by his magical music, Kalis commanded the flames to burn down the entire castle and everyone in it, including himself. The young mage played for the better part of fifteen minutes before anyone noticed the smoke rising out of the cellars–the kitchen staff hadn't noticed as smoke in the kitchen was not abnormal during a day of heavy feasting and much roasting.

Before he began playing, Kalis had used his magic to bar the doors so that no one could escape. People screamed, yet still Kalis's played, and his song grew faster and wilder. The flames roared and scorched the stone, almost melting the thick walls of rock with their intensity and power—enough to match the sorrow and rage that burned in the heart of Kalis Owynn.

The Baron cried out for his wife and daughter, who by now–like many of the guests– were slowly succumbing to the smoke that now filled the ballroom and had begun to choke out the last of the breathable air.

Kalis played faster still; faster and faster with the fury of a thousand infernos. It soon became clear to the Baron that this was no normal flame, and though he could not ascertain its source, he knew very well that the source of these flames was magical. The fire continued to burn its way through the halls, enveloping the ballroom and eventually burst forth from the locked doors and engulfed the entire room.

People coughed, screamed, collapsed, or were crushed by the mobs attempting to escape. People threw themselves from the windows to their deaths in the courtyard below.

Yet still, Kalis Owynn played on.

Finally, after playing almost twenty-seven minutes—one minute for every household of his town murdered by the Baron–Kalis, caked in sweat, grime, and soot, walked over to the Baron. Kalis stood over the dying lord and said: "I have come to collect my boon; your death is the boon I ask. For my family, and my people. Your lives for theirs."

Then, Kalis was said to have disappeared into the flames of the ballroom, never to be seen again, engulfed by the very flames he had stoked. It is believed here he died; his body reduced to ashes, like all the others who perished that day.

When the soldiers encamped in the fields surrounding the castle—having come with their royal and noble lords as part of their retinue—finally put out the flames, the castle had been reduced to a pile of warped, charred, and unrecognizable rubble. Glass and metal had melted to form wicked and twisted shapes, the stone had warped and cracked, and was now charred black with soot. It was not a castle any longer, but a grave. Hundreds, perhaps thousands, lay dead in the carnage. Burned beyond any form of recognition, or reduced only to piles of ash and fractured bones. The king and most of his family were killed. Many of the guests as well. Any who survived the flames were dashed against the cobbles from the fall as they jumped to what they hoped was safety in the courtyard below. Those who survived the fall, often using the bodies of those below to break their fall, were often permanently crippled.

Such was the fate of the heir to King Belchor, who took the throne as Belchor II when he recovered. He became known as Belchor II the Broken, and because of his injuries that day, he could not father any more children, not that he was even willing to remarry, having lost his wife to the flames. His eventual and early death triggered a succession crisis that led to yet another civil war between two of his paternal uncles and his mother's father.

Some say this is proof of the Curse of Gerovia, cast upon King Belchor I who murdered the Gerovian loyalists. Others say this is nothing but a story of revenge against a tyrannical lord. Republicans call it an injustice against the common folk, who also died in that blaze because of the feuding between Imperialist and Royalist factions.

Whatever the meaning one takes from this story, one thing *is* certain: every so often, on the last day of summer, if you go out at dusk to the spot where the castle once stood—still charred, dead and barren to this day—and you call out Kalis Owynn's name, you will be greeted with the faint sound of fiddle music, and a warm breeze will start to blow.

Dragons and the Enayran Empire

In the early days of humanity, Emperor Volesus marched his armies across most of Enayra in search of his lost love. In the process, he united all the disparate, far-flung human settlements, city-states, and kingdoms under a single banner, and formed the first and only Enayran Empire. While the Empire did not last long after Volesus passed, its legacy has enthralled and inspired many copy-cats throughout Enayra's history, most notably the Gerovian Empire before the War of the Grand Coalition.

But what about the dragons? The dragons had been here for millennia before humans arrived, and while their numbers have dwindled since the war against Tenebrae—known by the dragons as the Ulaar ad Kha id Vellu Botahr, or the War of Blood and Many Tears, and by humans as the Dragon War—they will likely outlive humanity on the continent.

Even Volesus and his vast wealth of military experience, tactical cunning, and his sprawling armies could not hope to conquer the dragons at the zenith of their power, and Volesus himself knew as much. It was early on in his campaigns that Volesus understood the roles dragons played in Enayra, their sheer size and power, and that even against small numbers of dragons, humanity had no chance of matching their raw power—not even with newly learned magic, which had itself been a boon granted by the dragons.

Shortly after conquering the city-state of Gerovia, Volesus published the Gerovian Declaration. In this document, still enshrined in Malatrion's Royal Library, Volesus declared many things. Primarily he gave the nations, kingdoms, city-states, and settlements of Enayra a chance to reveal to him any information regarding Zosime, his love who had been stolen away to parts unknown. But he also presented them with a choice, join him willingly, and become part of a great age of humanity, and contribute to a greater future for Enayra, or resist, and be conquered as so many before. Volesus also announced the creation of a single common tongue, known today as Common, that would unite all humans in Enayra under a single language that would allow for easier trade and diplomacy.

But more importantly, to the topic at hand, Volesus dedicated several sections to affirming his respect for the dragons of Enayra, and that he would uphold and honour the ancient borders of the dragon clans across the continent. Volesus declared that no humans should suffer entry into these borders and lands claimed by dragons. The dragons appreciated the gesture, for while they had come to accept that humanity could not be simply turned back to the seas they had first emerged from, neither should humanity's unchecked expansion of Enayra force the dragons from their lands. Indeed, early on many dragons and humans attempted to co-exist peacefully with one another, but despite their attempts to cohabitate in Enayra, humans mistrusted and feared dragons, and dragons found humans short-lived, barbaric, and lacking in respect for the natural world. Some humans actively hunted the dragons, some chose to embrace and worship them, and some treated them with ambiguity and ambivalence.

Volesus could not move the settlements and cities that had already been built and founded, and he could not turn back the wheel of time, but he could prevent things from getting worse, and that was what he sought to do in his declaration. He could not protect and safeguard his empire from dragons, and he could not fight dragons and all Enayra at the same time.

By the end of Volesus's conquest of Enayra, he had conquered most of modern Enayra, except for Anglum—which he saw as a vast frozen expanse that would cost nothing but time, money, and precious lives for very little reward—and the enclaves of the eleven dragon clans. Over time, Volesus was able to prove his words as truth, and he upheld his enforcement of the declaration, protecting dragons and their territories from humans who would do them ill. The emperor even converted from the Old Way Aspectism to Dragomancy—causing many in his empire to follow suit.

For his proven kindness and friendship towards dragons, the Metallic Dragons themselves went to Xiar—a respected place of learning—to assist in the establishment of the first magical college in Enayra. While some humans had been able to befriend and learn magic from dragons, magic was new and unknown to most humans at the time, and the most advanced magic was kept secret from all humans.

Yet for all the progress made towards dragon-human relations, Volesus's declaration would die with him and his empire, and relations would continue to suffer setbacks and issues until the creation of the first Khaleeshir six hundred years later.

However, even today, it is believed by many human scholars, and even many dragons who were alive to remember the Enayran Empire, that the Gerovian Declaration did much to better relations between the two races of Enayra. Volesus and his Gerovian Declaration laid the groundwork for much of the human-dragon relations to this day, and while relations aren't perfect, the borders of the draconic enclaves have not changed—for the clans that remain—even long after the collapse of the empire.

Sizing the Oldest Dragons

The oldest dragons in Enayra are the surviving Clan Leaders of each of the remaining Dragon Clans, and the Great Metallic Dragons themselves. These dragons are, by most estimates, a little over five-thousand years old, and were ancient before humans ever arrived in Enayra.

These ancient behemoths are also some of the largest creatures in Enayra. Known measurements for these oldest beings are as follows. Please note that all measurements are from head to tail.

- Aurum, the Great Gold Dragon is about fourteen kilometres in length.

- Argentum, the Great Silver Dragon is about fifteen kilometres in length.

- Æs (pronounced Ees), the Great Bronze Dragon is about eleven kilometres in length.

- Æris (pronounced Eeris), the Great Copper Dragon is about seven and a half kilometres in length.

- Aurichalcum, the Great Brass Dragon is about thirteen kilometres in length.

- Tenebrae, at the time of his defeat, approximately one thousand and thirty-four years ago, measured about eleven kilometres from head to tail. It is unknown what exactly his late mate, Kyna'braxa, measured, but it can be assumed she was of similar size.

- Venu'shael, Father of the Red Dragon Clan, at the time of his death, measured twelve kilometres, as does his mate Kara'imla.

- Nulgo'riaz, Father of the Orange Dragon Clan, died about ten kilometres from head to tail.

- Both Sha'janor and his mate, Kina'atael measure about eight kilometres from head to tail.

- The late Vercith'ae and her widowed mate, Yjosta'gar of the White Dragon Clan measure about six and a half kilometres long.

- Keshal'anda and her late mate, Vernix'iol, of the Blue Dragon Clan each measure about nine kilometres long.

Pre-Enayran Religions and the Waves of Human Migration

In Enayra, the predominant religion is Dragomancy. It is practised everywhere, evolving out of the Old World Aspectism that the earliest human settlers brought with them. There are a few modern variations and attempts at reconstructing the Old Religion before dragons became involved, practised in parts of Enayra, but a majority of Enayrans practice Dragomancy as their main religion.

However, before Emperor Volesus converted to Dragomancy, and Dragomancy slowly gained traction as the dominant religion in Enayra, many other religions dominated the continent. The religions are best divided and explained through the framework of the four waves of human migration to Enayra—as their origins lie beyond the seas, coming with the first people to settle the regions of Enayra, and eventually (in most cases, anyway) giving way to the Dragomancy dominant world of today.

The First Wave of Humans

The first wave of humans came to Enayra from the northwestern seas. These were the humans that first arrived in the year that's now known as 1 Conflict, or sometimes 3000 Dragons—dates vary based on differing records. These humans brought Old World Aspectism to Enayra and laid the groundwork for modern Dragomancy.

A majority of these first humans settled in what is now Asardaea and became the ancestors of the modern Asardaeans. Two ethno-linguistic groups settled there, known as the Western and Eastern Asardaeans. These Western and Eastern Asardaeans believed in the Old World Aspectism. Their religion was like today's Dragomancy in concept, though recent scholarly investigation has shown that there were originally fewer Aspects than there are now—originally only the main five Great Aspects were worshipped. There was the belief in an afterlife, and it was said those who were good in life would be taken up to the Realm of the Aspects, an unearthly, ethereal realm of perfection and paradise that was your reward for being good. It is from the Asardaean Old World Aspectism that the modern concept of the Nine Hells comes from—for it is not a draconic concept.

Early Old World Aspectism was structured under a strict hierarchy of power within the clergy. These clergymen and women held great sway over the politics and people of the region. Nowadays, the hierarchy is much less strict, but it is still present in Asardaea. Their reach is less controlling, and they no longer seek to steep themselves in politics or strictly dictate the day-to-day lives of the people. Instead, their role is more as a moral and spiritual guide for any who asks.

Another group of these first humans, unhappy with Asardaea as a choice of home, and seeking a deeper connection with the dragons they saw as divine, settled in modern-day Altimara, around the shores of Lake Gishan'belor. These people groups formed smaller tribes and family groups. Some would eventually break off to establish a settlement at

Kasaadua and become the ancestors of the Altimarans. Others left to settle in the Antigorus valley, founding the city of Xiar. Those who remained at Gishan'belor eventually formed a single, unified clan and became the Qiri'ar.

It was in Altimara, under these early peoples that the modern form of Dragomancy began. The Altimarans, Xiarans, and Qiri'arans became the earliest adopters of the new religion and chose to live in harmony with their deified dragons. They did away with the original after-life concept of the Old-World religion and instead came to believe as the dragons do, that when all life dies, it returned to the Earth Mother, to the source of life in Enayra, and would return to support her in renewing and restoring the continent and nature. The ancestors and those who came before us should be venerated for their noble duty in assisting the renewal of nature and the continent. These humans, however, did not do away with the concepts of the Nine Hells. Whereas dragons believe that all spirits go to the Earth Mother, regardless of good or bad, humans believe that the wicked spend their afterlives in different realms of punishment. It should be noted that dragons do not believe in the concept of eternal punishment after death for wicked deeds in life, and instead believe that comeuppance comes in life, from those you've wronged. For they believe, what good is punishment when those you've wronged are not around to see you pay?

Nowadays, Altimara has abandoned Dragomancy for Reconstructed Aspectism, or the Old Religion, as they called it. Since the end of the Dragon War that devastated much of the kingdom, Dragomancy, and dragons, have been banned. While they call their religion the "Old Religion" and claim it to be a return to the original religion of the first humans, the religion itself is vastly different from the original Old World Aspectism. It is merely a rebranded Dragomancy that removes any mentions of dragons and replaces the Earth Mother with "the World", a generic term for the same concept. Altimara executes most scholars who point this out, citing "treason and sedition."

The Qiri'ar, whose original clans and tribes did much of the leg work for early Dragomancy, have also abandoned Dragomancy for a religion that revolves entirely around Tenebrae, or as he's known by his original name, Ten'ebraex and his late mate, Kyna'braxa. During the time of the previous war with Tenebrae, known as the Dragon War, Eshgalon the Mad (or the Great if you're Qiri'ar), was tired of his people being pushed around and abused by the kings of Altimara. Countless Altimaran settlers began to take the land around Gishan'belor, originally the ancestral homeland of the Qiri'ar, and Altimaran fishing boats continued to steal the lion's share of fishing from the sacred lake. Seeking the power to protect his people, Eshgalon made a deal with Tenebrae that saw the Qiri'ar abandon all other gods for Tenebrae. The ancient dragon promised power beyond their wildest dreams, magic the likes of which no other humans had seen or could wield, and respect the boundaries of the Qiri'ar's ancestral lands. The Qiri'ar have never faltered from this deal since—regardless of whether the masses agreed with Eshgalon or not.

The Xiarans are the only people group in the region of Altimara today that still practice mainstream Dragomancy. They claim Aurum as their patron god, for it was he who led King Agarthus to the valley where they settled and built their civilization.

The Second Wave of Humans

The second wave of human settlement in Enayra occurred between the years 2 and 3 Conflict and saw the arrival of two different, unrelated people groups to Enayra. These people settled in two different regions and came from entirely separate origins. Despite being two different people groups, because of their concurrent arrival, their arrivals are grouped as a single wave because they arrived at the same time.

In what is now Estion, though what was then called Gerovia, the first Gerovians arrived from the southern sea. While they had initially thought about settling in what is now Danaen, after initially disembarking in the southern lands, they found the place dangerous and overgrown with flora and megafauna and decided it would be best to settle further north in the more temperate Gerovian region. Here the people settled and founded multiple cities that eventually came under the control of the city-state of Gerovia. These people came without religion and were some of the last people of Enayra to convert to Dragomancy.

The second group of peoples came from the eastern seas and settled on a large reef and an encircling sandbar off the coast of Altimara. This sea-faring group of people is known today as they were known then: the Lau'thso. The people of Lau'than are famed sailors and boat-builders and are just as famous for their sailing songs as they are for their music-based water religion. It's said you can hear a ship of Lau'thso arriving before you see their boat on the horizon.

The Lau'thso believe in only two gods—the Father Sky and the Mother Ocean. According to the Lau'thso religion, all life comes from the water. But Mother Ocean, who is present in all bodies of water, came to love her mortal children more than her husband, and so the sky grew jealous. This is why it storms; it is the Sky Father's attempt to destroy the children that took his wife from him. The seas grow violent in a storm because Mother Ocean fights back against her violent husband. It is why the Lau'thso offer songs of prayer and adoration when sailing, both in times of calm and during storms, to offer support and thanks to Mother Ocean for life and their safety. Because their livelihood, and their source of food, comes from the sea, they are eternally grateful for the Mother's bounty and will sing in praise and worship of their Mother Ocean, often in unison, or a call-and-response style prayer song, and accompanied always by at least one drum and a steady rhythm.

The Third Wave of Humans

The third wave of humans came between 5 and 6 Conflict, from the south-western seas. Their boats landed in what is now Danaen, and these people soon came to be known as the Danaesh. They brought with them their odd religion. Its name is lost to history, but its beliefs have been heavily studied by scholars across Enayra.

Unlike most religions, that give thanks to gods for all things—life, death, creation, destruction, salvation, and more—the Danaesh did not believe in gods above. They believe that all Danaesh, and by extension, all life—both man and beast—were but gods trapped in mortal flesh. They were luminous beings that would one day pass on, leave behind their fleshy prison, and ascend to godhood in The World on the Other Side. This world exists on the other side of every reflection, and any surface that reflects can act as a portal between the worlds.

The Danaesh thus placed heavy importance on ancestor worship, for all their ancestors had passed on to become deities that would protect their descendants. They became familial deities and the patron gods of certain family lines and noble or royal houses. Some were worshipped by many families, and some were only known to a few remaining descendants. Some were forgotten entirely when a family line died out—or because their names were forgotten.

While Danaesh now practices Dragomancy, they kept many of their older customs regarding death and ancestor worship—and the belief in a world beyond reflective surfaces. The Danaesh have syncretized Dragomancy with their original religion to create something new and wonderful. The deaths of family members are still celebrated and lavish affairs. Tears are not shed, and sadness is forbidden. It is customary for family and friends to gather and remember their dead with joy and happiness. It is said in Danaen that it is always best to remember the person as they were in life, and so the attendees share stories and experiences with the deceased. They celebrate their lives and passing, and while their dead no longer die to become gods, they pass on to join the Earth Mother and assist her in renewing the planet, which is a venerable and noble pursuit in death. Death celebrations can last days or weeks, depending on the wealth, fame, and station of the deceased and their families.

Mirrors and other reflective surfaces near settlements are blessed and purified annually at the start of the new year, to avoid wicked spirits and evil beings from dragging people into The World on the Other Side. Reflective surfaces that are not blessed are not to be peered into, for they could still act as a bridge between the worlds, for no one knows what lies on the other side of unconsecrated reflections.

The Fourth Wave of Humans

The fourth and final wave of human migration to Enayra occurred in 90 Conflict when the people now known as Espians arrived off the coast of the region of Espias. It should be noted that their original names for themselves are not written, recorded, or remembered anywhere, and they have simply taken—or been given—the name of the land they conquered for themselves.

No one is sure how the conflict started, or who was at fault, but the result of their arrival was a war between the Enayran Empire and the new Espian people. Unfortunately, Emperor Gaius was not the military genius his brother, Emperor Volesus, had been and he quickly found his armies overrun, and the war was lost. By the time of his assassination in 94 Conflict and the collapse of the Enayran Empire, Espias now ruled the south-eastern province undisputed, as the Empire could no longer raise an army large enough to reclaim it. The Espians have controlled the region as the Empire of Espias ever since. Their rivalry with Asardaea continues to this day. Sometimes antagonistically, and sometimes as a friendly–if highly, almost dangerously, competitive–political alliance.

When they arrived in Enayra, they brought with them a religion that revolved around heavenly beings, that, while still heavenly and powerful, more resembled mighty and omnipotent nature spirits rather than all-powerful, immortal gods. These heavenly beings take on the form of divine animals when on this human plane of existence and use animals to watch over their believers. This religion is known as seishinism in Common, though its Espian name is seishinto, roughly translating to "the way of the spirit."

Unlike Danaen, who syncretized their religion to Dragomancy to create a hybrid of the two faiths, Espias upholds both religions as co-equal within their realm, though parts of both religions had syncretized to the other to some degree.

Many of the heavenly beings brought from across the seas have been forgotten or lost to time and memory. Only the five main heavenly beings of the original Espian religion remain: Suzaku the Vermilion Phoenix, Seiryu the Azure Sea Dragon, Byakko the White Tiger, Genbu the Black Tortoise, and Tenryu the Great Golden Dragon–nowadays Tenryu is often seen as another aspect or familiar of Aurum, the Great Golden Wyrm, who had long made his home near the Espian capital. These five deities are worshipped in both their animal and humanoid forms and are commonly depicted in Espian art and architecture.

If asked why they adhere to two religions, many Espians will explain that they use their ancient religion to guide how they live their lives from day to day. But they adhere to Dragomancy to become one with the new lands they call home and guide themselves towards what they call "The Enayran Afterlife", where they will eventually expire and become one with the Earth Mother. Indeed, the new Espian view of the afterlife is vastly different from the afterlife of Seishinism, where the wicked would be punished, but the good would be allowed to walk between both worlds as an unseen, unheard spirit, quietly watching over the mortal realm, and living a comfortable, if boring and monotonous life in the underworld.

Dragomancy: A Brief History

Here's a question I've gotten many times:

"Doesn't -mancy mean a study of something? Why is the religion called Dragomancy? Does that make it a type of magic?"

Well, in the world of Enayra, its usage for the religion comes from early opposition to religion. Before Dragomancy became the main religion of Enayra, it was originally known as Old World Aspectism, brought by the first two waves of humans to Enayra that eventually landed in what is now Asardaea and Altimara. Aspectism involves the worship of the Aspects of the natural world, dualistic beings that represent two halves of a natural dichotomy. For example, the Aspect of Night and Day, the Aspect of Earth and Autumn, etc. All but the Five Great Aspects are dualistic.

When the humans came to Enayra, many encountered the dragons, and thus, the ancient Progenitors of the Dragon Clans, and the Metallic Dragons. Many, especially in the more traditional Asardaea, proclaimed the dragons to be wicked and false gods. But in the east, the people that would eventually become the Xiarans, Qiri'arans, and Altimarans, saw the dragons as the living embodiment of the Aspects. With this perspective, they began to venerate and worship the ancient dragons as holy beings with some control over the natural world. These humans decided to try and live in harmony with the dragons.

Over time, they restructured their religion to shift worship from the Aspects to the Great Dragons themselves. Since, according to their belief, the Aspects were dualistic, they believed it was reasonable that they could also be two physical beings at once. During this period of religious restructuring, the dragons shared the truth of life and death in Enayra: the Earth Mother. The dragons explained how the Earth Mother and Earth Father had created Enayra together, but by the end of creation, the Earth Mother had diminished and had been buried deep within the cave they called their home and eventually became part of the world itself. The dragons revealed that it was the Earth Mother who was the source of all life and magic on Enayra. Humans were told that all who died in Enayra returned to the Earth Mother via a series of underground mana currents, which are now known as leylines, and these souls replenish the power of the Earth Mother, and the earth itself.

Back in Asardaea, however, word of this new form of Aspectism began to spread. The more traditional clergy of Asardaea had already been beside themselves when they heard about the veneration of dragons as the Aspects, but hearing of this flow of energy, and how all who died returned to the soul of an ancient dragon was simply too much for them. They proclaimed the new religion as heresy. Active measures were taken to try and discredit and squash it. To discredit this new branch of Aspectism and to link it to the new, feared, and mysterious "magic" that humanity had become aware of once arriving in Enayra, the Asardaean clergy proclaimed the new branch of Aspectism *not* to be at all related to True Aspectism, but to instead be a heretic form of magic that used dragons to cast powerful magic spells for evil. They named this "wicked magic" Dragomancy.

Those in the east, who practiced this newly dubbed Dragomancy, knowing the importance of mana to the cycle of life, rebirth, and nature throughout all Enayra, knew that there was truth in the word Dragomancy. Dragons were inherently magical creatures, Enayra was a land permeated and steeped in deep and ancient magics. Mana was the lifeblood of all creation and the world itself, and the fuel for magic. But to these new believers, magic was not evil, magic was the natural way of things in Enayra. They were visitors to this land, and magic was as natural as the basest elements here. So it was that these New Believers took up the title of Dragomancy willing and with reverence. It was a religion with beliefs centred around magic, inherently magical creatures, and mana. It was their old religion married to their new reality. It did not stop these New Believers from being labelled as heretics, but neither did it crush or discredit their belief as the Old Believers would hope. Quite the opposite was true. The practice of Dragomancy began to grow and spread in the East, and before long, the East was a predominant bastion of Dragomancy, while the West still held to beliefs of True Aspectism, though missionaries of the Dragomantic faith were far-reaching enough to secretly begin proselytizing in the west—often at great personal risk, and the cost of their own lives.

The true turning point for Dragomancy in Enayra was its adoption by a young man named Volesus of Gens Tarquinia. As Volesus conquered more and more of Enayra, he realized the truth that Dragomancy spoke and the power of the dragons. Knowing no human army could ever destroy the dragons—at least in his time—Volesus chose to live peacefully alongside the dragons. He respected their territorial boundaries and enshrined their enclaves in law. He even converted to Dragomancy during his wars of conquest in the east. The conversion of the First Enayran Emperor did much to aid in the spread of Dragomancy across Enayra. Many of the old True Aspectism believers soon converted to this new form of Aspectism as political support all but disappeared for their archaic belief system, and by the end of the Enayran Empire, most of Enayra was practicing Dragomancy. Volesus's creation of the first pan-Enayran language, nowadays known as Common, also helped to spread the beliefs, teachings, and writings of Dragomantic scholars.

It should be noted that Dragomancy itself has several branch religions, especially in Danaen, where the Danaesh pre-Enayran religion merged with Dragomancy to create new syncretized religions. These branches are not considered heretical to the mainstream Dragomantic believers, but complimentary to the teaching of Dragomancy. Dragomancy also has no central religious authority, unlike the religion did in the days of True Aspectism in the East. It was Volesus who decreed that the religion belonged to the people of Enayra, and not to the whims of a single societal caste or group. Decisions on the religion are made in large ecumenical gatherings of career and voluntary lay priests, and priesthood, though few of these gatherings have been called in Enayra history. In Dragomancy, a member of the clergy who volunteered from the community is as valid as a priest or priestess who has dedicated their entire life to the cause. The community plays an active part in maintaining the faith and worship practices.

Altimara, since the turn of the era and the days of King Rego, has attempted to revive True Aspectism, as part of their Great Hunt and the purging of draconic influences on Altimaran culture. However, most scholars agree that the reconstructed Altimaran Aspectism is more of a facsimile of the original religion than a perfect restoration. Altimara does not acknowledge these criticisms and continues to uphold its religion as authentic and absolute. Any who disagree in Altimara are put to death for treason and sedition.

The Enayran Calendars

The Enayran Calendar is a complicated beast. While months and days are calculated very much the same across all the many nations and peoples of the continent, the counting of years and the names of ages are different.

For example, the current age of the world is known as the Age of Ruin. The current year, as of Dragonkin, is commonly known as 1034 Ruin. This is the standard in four of the six nations in Enayra. However, in Altimara, the Age of Ruin is known as the Age of Prosperity. So, the year would be 1034 Prosperity. Similarly, in the Grand Duchy of Utova, the city-state located in the frozen lands of Anglum, this age is known as the Age of Freedom, and the current year is 152 Freedom. Utova began a new age upon the foundation of their nation when the House of Vigothren, formerly Dukes of Verthoro, led a revolt against the Altimaran Crown. By the end of their guerilla war against the Crown, Duchess Illirya Vigothren and her people escaped capture when she led her loyalists into the frozen heart of Anglum, establishing a city on the shores of the frozen Lake Erna, which she renamed Lake Utova. Since then, the Utovans have counted the years since the founding of their new land as a new age and named said age for their newfound freedom.

The smaller nations, city-states, and tribes of Enayra have similar divergences for the counting of years and eras.

The Qiri'ar count the years since their foundation as an independent and unified people. It has been two thousand and two years since the foundation of the Qiri'ar Confederacy. They forgo the naming of eras to divide up their history. Therefore, the current Qiri'aran year is 2002.

For Xiar, they mark their calendars since the foundation of the city-state. The city, being founded the roughly the same time as the Qiri'ar Confederacy by an off-shoot people, is also two thousand and two years old, and so the current Xiaran year is 2002.

As stated above, when it comes to days and months, there is little difference among the Enayran people. All humans in Enayra have adopted the Draconic Lunar calendar. Their months are divided by the lunar cycles within the year. One Enayran Lunar Year lasts thirteen lunar cycles or thirteen months. One lunar cycle/month lasts forty days. Each month is comprised of eight weeks of five days each, and every week corresponds with one of the eight stages in the lunar phase. Therefore, a full Enayran year is five hundred and twenty days, or one-hundred and four weeks, or thirteen months.

A Lunar cycle, or month, goes as follows: it begins with the New Moon, then into the Waxing Crescent, the First Quarter, the Waxing Gibbous, the Full Moon, the Waning Gibbous, the Third Quarter, then the Waning Crescent, and finally back to the New Moon. The return to the New Moon is the start of a new month.

The five days of the Enayra week are named as follows: Vindrdas, Thrundas, Villordas, Osendas, and Ygdas. No one quite knows the meaning or origins of these names. Though it is most likely a very archaic and forgotten form of Ancient Draconic that existed in the earliest days of Enayra, long before humans, and indeed even most dragons, had come to be. Even the Metallics the Great Progenitors barely remember how to speak this dialect, though they still retain the accent.

The Enayran months, however, are listed by their modern Draconic names, even in Altimara. The names are as follows, along with their Common translations:

- Vesthyr (First Moon; lit. Moon One)
- Nesthyr (Second Moon; lit. Moon Two)
- Thaethyr (Third Moon; lit. Moon Three)
- Unthyr (Fourth Moon; lit. Moon Four)
- Yaeythyr (Fifth Moon; lit. Moon Five)
- Igrthyr (Sixth Moon; lit. Moon Six)
- Authyr (Seventh Moon; lit. Moon Seven)
- Venthyr (Eighth Moon; lit. Moon Eight)
- Jguthyr (Ninth Moon; lit. Moon Nine)
- Zjethyr (Tenth Moon; lit. Moon Ten)
- Zjevesthyr (Eleventh Moon; lit. Moon Eleven)
- Zjenesthyr (Twelfth Moon; lit. Moon Twelve)
- Zjethaethyr (Thirteen Moon; lit. Moon Thirteen)

In a typical Enayran year, there are four recognizable seasons: spring, summer, fall, and winter. While each season lasts on average three months, summer lasts for an extra month. The start of an Enayran year, and thus the New Year Celebrations, known as the First of Vesthyr or Vestri'vesthyr by the dragons, tends to align with the first lunar cycle of spring.

The Fauna of Enayra: Part I

Denizens of the Altimaran Desert

The fauna in Enayra is as diverse as it can be dangerous.

Despite being a vast desert, Altimara has a large amount of diversity when it comes to the creatures living in its wilds. Some of the more prominent creatures are as follows:

Mhokshi Lizard-beasts

One of the most common animals in Altimara is the Mhokshi lizard-beast.

These creatures are large, reaching a length of 2 metres from head to tail when fully grown and a height of one and a half metres at the shoulder.

They resemble a cross between a Komodo dragon and an iguana with a snout like a crocodile. They are recognizable by their protruding bottom fangs. Their bite is devastating, and they can spit corrosive acid up about the length of their body when threatened.

Ironically, despite their ability to kill, the Mhokshi lizards are surprisingly docile beasts by nature and tend not to attack unless otherwise first threatened.

They are also incredibly well adapted to the deserts of Altimara, and the desertification of the country has only led to a boom in their population. They have special adaptations that allow Mhokshi lizard-beasts to absorb moisture from the air through their skin when water sources are scarce.

Because of their docility, size, and relative hardiness in harsh environments, many Altimaran farmers raise Mhokshi lizard-beasts as a source of food, and their meat is a staple in most Altimaran homes and recipes.

Mhokshi lizard-beasts were introduced to greater Altimara from their original home in the Mirror Sands. They were introduced as a mainstay of agriculture in 232 Prosperity (232 Ruin outside Altimara) by King Hgru'ian I Belator, on the recommendation of Duke Inghur Davenpourte of K'nar Province. Mhokshi lizard-beasts had become a necessary staple after Altimara's desertification had spread to about seventy percent of the kingdom and wiped out most of the viable croplands and grazing fields.

Winged-wolves

Winged-wolves, to those who have never seen one, may sound like some large, winged canine. In truth, they are terrifyingly large, incredibly aggressive bat-like creatures, not unlike a flying fox.

With a wingspan of about two-and-three-quarter metres, a venomous bite that acts as an anti-coagulant and a tranquilizer, and an incredibly keen sense of sight and smell, winged-wolves are feared hunters of the Altimaran sands.

They tend to hunt medium-to-large prey, and some braver winged-wolves have been known to go after Mhokshi lizard-beasts when they have substantial numbers on their side.

Colonies make their homes in abandoned mine shafts and tunnels in mountains and desert mesas. Being incredibly territorial, winged-wolves will very often attack any who enter their territory or get too close to their colony's nesting place.

Winged-wolves will start their attacks by raking their prey with their claws to draw blood and open the skin. Once their prey is bleeding, the winged-wolves will proceed to bite their quarry. The anti-coagulant in the venom prevents the wound from healing, and the tranquillizing qualities of the venom cause the prey to fall into a lucid state of disorientation. The winged-wolves will then proceed to carry their prey high up into the air and drop them from great heights, usually onto sharp rocks or mountainsides, until they're dead. Afterwards, the prey is carried back to the colony and devoured until nothing remains.

They have the appearance of a massive bat with a face like a wolf's. The fur covering their body is short and dark, except for the mane around their neck and shoulders, where their fur is long and shaggy with a deep amber or rust colour. Their wings are leathery, with long hooked claws protruding from their thumb joints. Unless most bats, winged-wolves possess long, thin tails with barbed tips. These barbs are used to attack enemies and prey alike in a manner not unlike a whip.

Males with the largest barbs and shaggiest manes tend to be preferred mates for female winged-wolves.

Gnars

Gnars are odd creatures. Though rarely seen, they feature heavily in Altimaran folklore and fairy tales.

No one is quite certain where they came from; even the dragons do not recognize them as a creation of the Earth Mother and Earth Father. The dragons cannot remember, or even agree, as to whether gnars came from across the sea with humans, came from humans, or were native to Enayra, to begin with.

They live in the deep places of the earth, far from the sun and the eyes of the surface dwellers.

Gnars resemble diminished humans, though they lack the same sentience and ingenuity. Their language is unintelligible, and scholars disagree whether they are speaking a unique language or merely chattering like animals.

They are about the size of a small child, gangly and skinny, and wear nothing but scraps of skins and fur they take from their prey—though some prefer to run about naked. They have long, black nails on their fingers and toes that are sharp as any knife, and sharp fangs and teeth that protrude from their mouths at odd angles. They are completely bald and have sharp, pointed ears. Their skin is sickly and gray, like a decaying whale, and they are said to smell of rotting flesh. The eyes of a Gnar are nearly blind and incredibly sensitive to light, and gnars will only leave their caves for the surface during the night and even then, only for short periods to hunt and scavenge, though it should be noted they are not nocturnal. Gnars will work throughout the day, taking small naps when they tire, and returning to work once they've regained their strength.

Gnars live in colonies beneath the ground and will always hunt in packs. Despite their diminutive size, they are not foes to be taken lightly, and they do not discriminate in their choice of food. They've been known to be omnivorous, and eat everything from bugs, to cacti, to livestock, and even humans. While gnars favour young children due to their inability to defend themselves, particularly brave and hungry gnars have been known to kill and eat adults.

Because they are known to eat children, many parents in Altimara use gnars as a sort of boogeyman and warn their children to behave or they'll be left out at night for the gnars.

One episode in Altimara's history relates that in the year 576 Prosperity (576 Ruin outside of Altimara), the famous Altimaran scientist and eccentric nobleman, Mourin Beriun, Baron of Gaol, theorized that gnars could be domesticated and put to work in Altimaran society to help excavate and work mines, and for pest control on farms. Mourin had been able to gather a dozen gnars from the wild and settled them in special underground chambers on his large estate.

After three years he found himself caring for a small colony of about three hundred gnars settled in and had managed to get them to respond to a combination of whistles and verbal commands, reinforced with scraps of food and shiny objects. However, Mourin's overconfidence got the better of him, and he underestimated the craftiness of his gnars. One night, when he slept, the gnars had managed to break free of their underground pens. They tore Mourin and his servants apart, then attacked the town in the middle of the night.

When King Veu'sur III Kondorin arrived a week later, responding to Baron Mourin's invitation to view the progress of his pet project, he found that half the town had been reduced to a ruin, and its people lived in fear of the gnars' night attacks. After learning what had happened, he had Gaol put to the torch, its people moved, and the lands abandoned. A garrison was stationed nearby at a temporary camp, and the Great Gnar Hunt began, marking a period of gnar bounties that offered large sums for dead gnars.

While the hunt ended after four years, it is said in local legends that the descendants of Mourin's gnars still live beneath the ruins of Old Gaol, and occasionally, they stalk the streets of New Gaol, looking for fresh meat. This part of the story is considered apocryphal by most scholars, who claim that most of the gnars were eradicated in the Great Gnar Hunts; though very few will travel to the Old Gaol to confirm this.

Rishi beasts

Rishi beasts are large, winged serpents. They have feathered wings, a venomous bite, large fangs, and a tail with an odd axe-head-shaped bone at the end used for attacking enemies.

These beasts are aggressive and make their homes in the high places of the world, often near dragons, so they can poach off their prey. Because of this, dragons and Rishi beasts have a contentious relationship. Dragons tend to kill Rishi beast swarms on sight, while Rishi beasts often rely on dragons to scavenge their meals. It is not that they can't hunt, but that they tend to prefer the easiest meal possible, and another larger creature's leftovers are the easiest, largest alternative.

Rishi beasts are known by many names. In Common, they are also known as Rishi beasts, false dragons, or flying snakes. In Draconic, they are known as harzok vitur. While no exact translation exists for either word in Common, the closest translations are usually listed as "bloodless counterfeit" or "bloodless forgery." It does not help that vitur is also the Draconic word used to describe an illusion, which causes contention among human scholars over the true meaning of the word.

Many humans believe that Rishi beasts are closely related to dragons. Dragons do not share this sentiment, nor do they appreciate it. If one speaks with a dragon, it is probably best not to suggest any relationship between the harzok vitur and the great drazhani,

They take the name Rishi from the Rishi Mountains, a chain of mountains that stretches along the shared borders of Asardaea, Anglum, and Altimara. The mountains begin where Asardaea and Anglum meet the northern Virdrid Sea, and spread down the breadth of Enayra, wrapping around behind Kasaadua and finally ending at the Bergit Ocean in north-eastern Altimara. It is in these mountains that Rishi beasts are most plentiful and make their homes, though they are not exclusive to the Rishi Mountains, and will make their homes in any mountain or high, rocky place where the game is easy and plentiful. Some make their homes in the mesas of the Mirror Sands, where the Blue Dragons once carved their caves and homes into the rocks.

One swarm of Rishi beasts was known to have made its home in Kula during the time of the second generation of Khaleeshir in 1032 Ruin.

On Drazhanii
The Draconic Language

It should be noted now that Draconic is not an exact language, and translations are rough, as true Draconic is spoken with a combination of words, flashes of memory, senses, images, and emotions across a mental link. It should also be noted that Draconic was not a written language originally and is still a mostly oral language amongst the dragons—though dragons did carve a few runes of power to represent certain concepts, ideas, and symbols of the Dragon Clans. A properly written alphabet was only created by humans for the sake of their dragon-based religion and the purpose of magical study.

In Drazhanii, as the Draconic language is called, the apostrophe is used to signify that two separate words are being brought together to form a new word with a new or combined meaning—there are a couple of exceptions to the rule.

Combined words employing the apostrophe should be pronounced as if they are a single word, with no pause between the words. The apostrophe was only added by human translators and linguists to ease translation and readability. If you could figure out the two root words, it would help infer the meaning of the new, combined word.

One example is K'thirqi. K'thirqi is the Drazhanii word for kidney. It translates literally into Common as "flesh kidney." It comes from the words thirqi, and kha which means blood, flesh, or lifeblood. Normally, thirqi on its own is only used when describing a kidney separate from the body of a living being. Hence the distinction between thirqi and k'thirqi. It's important to specify—especially if you're healing using magic. But, when you put the two words together, their meaning combines and changes both worlds into a new, or altered word, entirely.

The Dance of the Camel Bride

Every Kulan knows the famed Dance of the Camel Bride. Both the story and the associated song have long since become ingrained in the local folklore. It has grown in popularity across Altimara, thanks in no small part to travelling Kulan merchants and curious Qiri'aran traders. Taverns and bars as far as Felidrun and Romontya can at least play the song, even if they don't fully understand the story behind it.

The song itself is a shorter retelling of the old folktale and consists of a repeating tune that grows incrementally faster upon each refrain. Eventually, the tune is meant to grow into an almost impossible fast crescendo where it suddenly stops, a single note is played and sustained, and the refrain starts again, very slowly, and gathering speed once more to a final crashing stop. No words accompany this second half of the story, meant to recreate the famed dance that is the namesake of this song.

The intended dance for this song is a flurry of whirling and spinning, until the dancer collapses from exhaustion or dizziness, much like the eponymous camel bride.

The song is played with at least two bagpipes, a hurdy-gurdy, and a drum.

The story itself is a much more fascinating tale. Below is an excerpt from Tumulgan's Tales: A Collection of Folktales from Altimara, written by Tumulgan the Bard, circa 884 Ruin.

Many centuries ago, in the early days of the Age of Ruin, a woman lived in Kula and though her name is lost to time, her story will forever live on. She lived alone, for her parents had passed on, and she worked her craft in camel rearing. This woman raised some of the best camels in Altimara, and everyone from travelling merchants to the Altimaran Camelry, and even Qiri'aran nomads would come to her for their camel needs. Truly, she was the most beautiful woman in Kulu at the time, but she much preferred her camels to people.

During her youth, every boy in Kula tried to win her heart, but each was sent off swiftly. The woman's camels sent them running with what remained of their tails between their legs. The woman had no time for men or marriage, for she was married only to her profession.

After a year of trying to win her heart, the local Kulan boys came to respect her wishes and instead banded together to protect her and her camels from outsiders who had not taken the hint. In return the woman, who had slowly begun to grow wealthy off her camel trade, would put her money back into the village and its people, to help them in times of need, and ensure the townsfolk were cared for. While she preferred camels to people, she still could not bear to see her fellow Kulans suffer and always did her best to help them when they were in need.

As her skill grew in camel husbandry, she and her camels became known across many lands. The word of a beautiful maiden who could raise the best camels and chose to be married to her craft was whispered in every tavern and lordly hall, and people travelled far and wide to meet her. Many bought camels from her, while others merely wished to set eyes upon this fabled maiden. Some thought her odd, others admired her, but very few could not respect her and her craft.

Until, one day, the greedy son of the Duke of Qintarth came from Ottogard to seek this beautiful woman out. He did not seek her out for her camels, for he did not need a dirty, desert beast. He came instead, for her hand in marriage, and he would not take no for an answer. At first, the local boys were able to stave off his advances. He would go to the woman's place and be driven off by the local people who defended her. Eventually, the duke's son returned with his soldiers and forced the villagers to back down in the face of such might.

Every day for a week, the duke's son would march over to the Kulan woman's camel farm and make a play for her love, and each time she sent him home with nothing but a no and a sore groin. As he soothed his injuries and his ego, the duke's son recognized: that the woman cared about her fellow Kulans as much as she cared for her camels, and any injury to either would surely make her more pliable.

So, on the eighth day, the duke's son returned once more, but this time with an ultimatum: marry him, or he would harm the villagers. But still, the woman refused to marry him. She was married to her craft, and she would rather marry one of her camels than marry the duke's son. She would not allow the man to bully her, or her friends, or her camels. The duke's son was offended, spat at the woman, and called her Camel Bride. If she did not marry him willingly, she would be married to him by force, and he would make good on his promise to harm the villagers. But the woman was not afraid and warned the duke's son that if he returned, he would regret it.

He did not listen.

The young noble returned the next day with his mercenaries dragging behind them several village children in chains. The children were beaten and bruised, and after much goading and taunting, the duke's son killed the children, one by one, tossing their heads to the Camel Bride.

It was the last thing he did.

For the Camel Bride was secretly a powerful mage. She kept her powers hidden, but they aided her in raising some of the best camels in Enayra. Magic made all things stronger, as her mother had taught her.

The duke's son died screaming, and his retinue could only watch in fear. Only one was left alive, and he was left to return to the duke the heart, hands, and manhood of his son.

The Camel Bride then turned to the dead children and wept. She called to the sky, to all creation, to beseech the Great Aspect and his familiar Aurum to revive these young innocents from their untimely demise. These children did not deserve their death and had done nothing to deserve it. The woman then began to dance. She spun and whirled, crying out to the world, to whoever would listen. It was said she danced for a full day and full night, until her feet were cracked and bleeding, and she collapsed from exhaustion. When finally, she fell to the sand unconscious, Aurum arrived and granted her wish while she slept.

When she awoke, the Camel Bride rose to find the children alive and well, tending to her camels while the Camel Bride was being cared for by the villagers.

As for the duke's son, the Camel Bride kept the man's head. She dried it, pickled it, so that all his skin and flesh remained, and removed the crown of his skull so that she could use the man's head as a pot for her desert verbena plants.

The following pages were found in the personal study of Tumulgan the Bard after his death. They were buried in a pile of myriad notes and drafts from early editions of Tumulgan's Tales. The pages appeared ancient, if not verified as authentic and were written in a hand that was clearly not Tumulgan's. These pages have not been verified as fact and should be read with a healthy dose of skepticism by academics.

The Camel Bride was not a nameless woman. She was real, and she lived in Kula as the tales say. This tale happened in 205 Ruin, in what is now Kula. Her name was Tisay'lah Uluk'gan. She was the daughter of a Qiri'ar trader and a Kulan merchant who raised camels—their names are lost to time. She was not a mage, but a Qiri'aran blood witch.

Tisay'lah was raised by her parents until her thirteenth year. It was then that her mother disappeared into the wastes to return to Gishan'belor—as all Qiri'ar do each year at the onset of winter—to seek permission from the Great Mother to live her life with her husband and child, never having to return to the capital each year.

When her mother did not return by the summer of her fourteenth year, her father left Tisay'lah in charge of the camel farm and ventured to Gishan'belor to seek his wife. Outsiders were not allowed to set foot within the ancient borders of the Qiri'ar, and even half-bloods required permission from the High Chief and Great Mother.

Tisay'lah knew in her heart she would likely never see either of her parents again. But she had been bequeathed from them two great gifts: the love and art of camel husbandry from her father, and blood magic and herbalism from her mother. She excelled at both, but kept the skills passed down from her mother hidden. Stigma was against her there.

The town knew and liked Tisay'lah's father, and so they helped care for her after her parents disappeared. In return she acted as their healer in times of need, doing what she could to help ease the suffering of the village folk. This part is true. She loved them, and while they were wary of her, they did love her too.

Much of the rest of the story goes the same as most people know. She gained fame and fortune, refused to marry, and devoted herself to her craft. Her suitors in the village eventually became her friends and protectors, and she redistributed her fortune back to Kula. It all happened the same as legends say, right up until the most famous part: her pleading with the Great Aspect Aurum to bring the children back to life.

Tisay'lah was an incredibly skilled blood witch and did not need the Great Wyrm to save these children. She did so herself, using blood magic. She revived the children, wiped their memories, and told them instead it was Aurum who saved them so that no one would suspect she was a blood witch. In truth, she had sacrificed three of her greatest camel studs for their blood price. The woman who had loved her camels more than all, even herself, had found something she had loved even more.

Tisay'lah then sent the children into a slumber for one day with her herbs, wounded her feet to corroborate her story, and proceeded to drag herself with her herbs so the villagers found her unconscious when they came to look.

Until now, no one knew the true story of Tisay'lah Uluk'gan. But there was one child whose mind she could not truly wipe, for I too was of Qiri'aran lineage, and a blood witch in training, through my grandmother and mother before me. I faked my ignorance, for her sake. The world is not kind to witches like us.

But she has passed on, and now it is safe. The truth must be told, for we of Kula loved her, and she truly loved us.

The world must know the truth.

The Fauna of Enayra: Part II
The Deadly Creatures of Danaen

The longitudinal border between the Kingdoms of Estion and Danaen is the longest undefended border in all of Enayra. But it is not because of any mutual trust between the two nations. No, the history of Estion and Danaen had been, until the days of the original Dragonkin, quite antagonistic.

Until the Dragonkin arrived to pacify the nations of the world, there were nearly six centuries of endless warfare and bloodshed in Enayra after the collapse of the Enayran Empire.

The Gerovian Empire, as Estion had once been known, had once held deep, and brutal hegemonic control over the northern provinces of Danaen during the middle of the Age of Conflict, not unlike the rule modern Altimara imposed upon Xiar, and this tyrannical rule was not quickly forgotten by the Danaesh people.

So why leave such an important border undefended? Surely it would be a haven for smugglers, illicit activity, or clandestine raids and invasions into each nation.

In that case, you are wrong.

The creatures of Danaen are large, hardy beasts that are more dangerous than any army could ever be. Yet, aside from four, well-reinforced, and jointly run border checkpoints along each of the major roads between both nations, no other guards are posted along the border, and any who seek to cross at any other point along the borders do so at their peril.

The beasts of Danaen eat humans for sport and work hard to include humankind as part of their daily diet. Only a fool would enter the untamed jungles of Danaen without reason, and even then, that reason had better be damned good.

Only the stench of reekweed, also called stinkweed, shitweed, or corpse grass (ibu'temba in the Danaesh language), keeps these creatures away from humans, or their settlements. The reekweed plant is a naturally occurring plant that grows along the riverbeds in Danaen, and when plucked and dried, it produces a smell not unlike a mountain of rotting corpses. It's unknown why this smell wards off scavengers, predators, and other creatures, but no one's going to argue with the results when they could get eaten just trying to visit their family the next town over. Knowing the importance of reekweed, the Danaesh Crown holds a tight and jealous monopoly over the cultivation, processing, and distribution of this commodity.

Anyone entering the country **must** pass through one of the four border checkpoints run jointly by the Estian and Danaesh governments. Estion supplies half of the soldiers and supplies, while Danaesh provides the remaining soldiers, the funding and the reekweed. Travellers who wish to travel along the road must purchase, at their own expense, as much reekweed as is required to reach the next fortified position along the major roads. Those travelling for business, such as trade, are sold reekweed at a discounted price, compared to those travelling for pleasure. Being that the Danaen government holds a monopoly on the reekweed, prices change like the weather. Some more cynical historians can always tell when something big is about to happen in Danaen; the building of a new fleet, recruiting more soldiers, a coronation, a declaration of war, or even the funeral of an old king, all of it could be predicted by the sudden and overnight rise in the price of reekweed.

Because of the dangerous creatures in Danaen, people will never plan to camp by the roadside when travelling through the country, and so are always forced to buy small amounts of reekweed at a time to get them from trading post to trading post along the road. Travelling merchants and traders will travel between the trading posts along the road, as well as towns and settlements, to sell their wares, and buy more reekweed to keep travelling.

It is a joke among commerce guilds that when one is travelling by land to Danaen to peddle their wares, they are "going out to buy reekweed" or "going to feed their reekweed habit." It is a well-known fact that any profits made at the trading posts and towns of Danaen are always cut into by the high cost of the reekweed needed to keep moving. It doesn't help that the Danaen government demands their fair share in taxes on all foreign merchants peddling foreign wares in their lands as well.

But I digress; below are some of the more dangerous, and more famous, fauna that call the Danaen jungles their home:

Death Birds
Kuku Nemba

The death bird, known in Danaesh as the kuku'nemba, is one of the more famous, and dangerous denizens of the Danaesh jungles.

This large, flightless bird stands at about 2.15 metres from their clawed talons to the top of their head.

These creatures are normally solitary, and hunt alone, but should never be taken lightly. Their large, hooked claws have been known to tear through chainmail. and their serrated beaks are known to bite through almost anything.

Death birds attack by charging out of the thick, dense jungle, and jump-kicking their opponents, raking them open, and sometimes apart, with their deadly talons before finishing them off with their beaks—often by snapping their necks. These birds kill on average four hundred people a year and are even a challenge for most of the large predators of the region to take down.

Terror Birds
Betu Nemba

These creatures are not as large as their death bird cousins, but terror birds—betu'nemba in Danaesh—are just as vicious. What they lack in raw strength and size, they make up for by hunting in packs as small as fifteen, and as large as forty.

These creatures are about the size of a swan. With long, toothed beaks, short-but-sharp talons, and hooked claws protruding from their pinion joints, these creatures resemble something between a medium-sized bird and a bipedal lizard. They work together to pick off their prey and pick them clean.

Terror birds are covered in bright emerald, green feathers, with beautiful tail feathers that resemble a cross between a peacock and a pheasant tail. The tail feathers of these creatures are prized among the kings and chieftains of Danaen and are often seen gracing their most formal and expensive outfits.

It was often said that King Yoru IV the Great had a collection of betu'nemba feather quills, and even kept a breeding pair as pets. Some of his detractors say he kept this breeding pair to feed his political rivals to.

Bifurcated Leopard
Biqu Shubaa

The bifurcated leopard, bi-qu shubaa in Danaesh, is a two-headed megafauna that lives in the deep jungles of Danaen.

These two-headed, sabre-toothed leopards are 1.25 metres at the shoulder and can grow as heavy as eight hundred pounds.

These two-headed creatures are vicious and will not hesitate to make humans a part of their daily meal. They are one of the few creatures that can even attempt to take down a death bird, though it is a rare sight.

The bifurcated leopard is said to have two separate brains and two separate hearts, though the two heads share a stomach and don't normally compete for resources against one another like other two-headed creatures in Enayra. The two heads work in perfect harmony to keep the body alive. They take turns sleeping, eating, and watching for potential enemies. They're incredibly cunning creatures and seem to take pleasure in making their meals suffer before they devour them.

The bifurcated leopard is the official animal of the kingdom and can be seen on the Danaen flag.

Sabre-toothed Jaguar
Kitu Bakku

The sabre-toothed jaguar, known in Danaesh as kitu'bakku, "sword teeth", is a large—1.5m at the shoulder—a predatory cat that stalks through the jungles of Danaen, picking off prey animals and unfortunate travels alike.

Using its black-as-pitch fur to blend into the unending darkness of the thick jungle, the creature is lithe, quiet, and able to sneak up on most prey. They have half-metre long fangs, and three-to-four-inch claws that have been seen to slice through even the finest armours—not to mention their bite force. It is one of the few creatures that can somewhat resist the effects of reekweed. While normally, a sabre-toothed jaguar will stay far away from any processed reekweed, a hungry sabre-toothed jaguar will force itself to ignore the offensive stench to attack caravans for food. Few other animals in Danaen, hungry or otherwise, will do this.

The mounted forces of the Danaen cavalry have managed to domestic several of these creatures for use as war mounts and as mounted cavalry. Well-bred sabre-toothed jaguars go for high prices as both military mounts and private mounts and pets for the wealth of Danaen.

Titanocobra
Bishagwa

The titanocobra, in Danaesh, called bishagwa ("shadow" or "spectre") is a massive cobra, as its name would suggest. Not much is known about the creature except how large it is, how deadly its venom is, and how rare a sighting one is.

It's said that the titanocobra can inject a variety of venom that affects different parts of the body and can also spit a corrosive acid up to 10 metres that can dissolve anything. These claims are based on several centuries of—admittedly few—encounters between humans and creatures, though it's unknown if these are embellishments or the truth. Enayran scientists believe the answer lies somewhere between fact and fantasy.

The largest specimen known to exist was killed for the safety of the people of Danaen by King Imbadwa II in 882 Ruin and was approximately twenty metres long from head to tail. Its bones are on display within the royal palace, and its skin was used to gird the scabbards of the King of Danaen and his royal guards.

Danaesh Great Ape
Kimbuwa

The great Danaen ape, known in Danaesh as kimbuwa, means something roughly along the lines of "human-like."

They are large, orange, or brown-furred great apes that stand at about two metres tall, with a similar arm span. These creatures are incredibly strong and well-muscled. They've been known to uproot trees when enraged or threatened and swing them about as weapons.

Despite this, the Great Apes tend to have a more ambivalent relationship with humans and will stay away from them, so long as the boundaries of their territories are respected. Some scientists believe these creatures can speak and have similar intelligence to humans. Others believe they do not and are only as intelligent as a toddler. No one has been able to get close enough and converse with one to find out, of course.

Despite their incredible strength and propensity for aggressive defence, they are illegal to hunt and kill in Danaen, by anyone, and to poach one is punishable by death. This has been law since the early fifth century of the Age of Conflict. The law was first drawn up by Tsem'bashwa I the Liberator. This is in part due to their near-human nature, their purported intelligence, and because of a tale of unknown veracity.

This tale states when Tsem'bashwa I declared war on the traitorous Gerovian Empire in the War of the Grand Alliance and pushed Gerovia from northern Danaen to reclaim their territory, several hundred kimbuwa charged from the forests and fought alongside the Danaesh people, murdering hundreds of Gerovian soldiers and settlers, and sending the survivors running back to Gerovia. Whatever the truth of this tale is, the fact remains that these creatures are respected by all levels of Danaen society, and when one is found dead in the jungles, they are given an honoured burial. To see one is considered an auspicious sign.

Great Tapirs
Agu Dasha

The great tapirs, in Danaesh agu dasha ("four tusks"), are larger than normal tapirs, about half the size of a Great Asardaean Elephant. They stand at 1.75m at the shoulder. They also have four tusks protruding from their face—a feature lacking in other tapirs of Danaen.

Great Tapirs are normally docile creatures and are often hunted for their meat and their ivory for traditional and ceremonial use, as ivory is very important to the Danaesh people. Every Danaesh wears at least one piece of ivory jewellery or accessory. Despite their usual docility, when pressed, these beasts can gore a human with their four large tusks.

Some Danaesh have taken up the domestication and farming of these creatures for food, though domesticated Great Tapirs don't grow as large as their wild counterparts.

Land Alligator
Semu Semu Tai

The land alligator, in Danaesh semu'semu tai ("the running one"), is not quite your average alligator. At about fifteen to twenty metres long, with lifespans of about two centuries, and four-inch fangs, these creatures can be terrifying in the wild. Their prowess is made even worse by their four powerful legs, positioned directly under their body like a mammal, that allows them to run at speeds of fifty kilometres per hour, these creatures are nightmare fuel to herpetophobes.

Unlike normal alligators, these creatures are dangerous on land and in water. They have been known to hunt in both and are incredibly effective hunters. In water, the alligators live in the ponds, rivers, and lakes of Danaen, and will sit just below the surface with their mouths wide open, waiting for an unsuspecting creature to pass by. Once they feel something brush past their muzzles, their jaws snap shut, and they drag their prey deeper into the water to drown and devour them.

On land, they hunt one of two ways. One way, they bury themselves in moss, and grasses, or even burrow into loose dirt and soil. When a creature passes by, it launches up from its hiding spot to attack and maul its prey. If the prey is too fast for them, then they use their second method. The alligators will run after their prey at high speeds and maul their prey to death.

Their teeth and skin are used for ceremonial clothing by royalty and nobility, as well as extremely wealthy people in other nations in Enayra. The current king of Danaen is known to keep a small number of these creatures as pets in the royal palace gardens.

Bog Bears
Futu Pendu

Bog bears, known in Danaesh as futu pendu (moss mountains) live near the ponds and lakes of Danaen where they primarily hunt fish, but have been known to devour other aquatic creatures and unsuspecting prey.

At about 1.75m at the shoulder, these massive beasts live up to their names and are so sedentary that they grow moss and grasses on their backs. They use this as camouflage when hunting. They submerge themselves below the water line, revealing only their humped backs to the world. They appear as no more than some rock in the pond or lakeside. There they wait for prey to happen by, at which point the bears emerge from the water and swat at their prey with their massive paws. The force of the blow is often enough to concussion, daze, and eventually drown their prey. With their prey dead, these beasts will go to the shoreline to eat, before returning to the water for a new hunt.

These bears are opportunistic carnivores and will devour anything, so long as it is smaller than itself, and made of meat and flesh.

The chieftains and kings of Danaen are known to often hunt these bears for sport and drape themselves in the furs of their kills. It's said there are more bog bear pelts on the walls and floors of the royal palace than any other type of décor.